Pete on Ice

B.J. Baker

PublishAmerica
Baltimore

First printing

At the specific preference of the author, PublishAmerica allowed this work to remain exactly as the author intended, verbatim, without editorial input.

ISBN: 1-4241-6508-3 (softcover)
ISBN: 978-1-4489-2829-3 (hardcover)
PUBLISHED BY PUBLISHAMERICA, LLLP
www.publishamerica.com
Baltimore

Printed in the United States of America

This book is dedicated to my husband and our daughters,
with loving memories of all things good.
Thanks to
Lucy, Larry, and Christopher Clabaugh, John Baker,
Susan Strube, Barbara Sydnor, Susan Pallone,
And most of all,
Matthew and Margaret Barnes

Chapter 1

Friday December 12, 1986

Before he opened his eyes, he knew that he was in his own room. There was a familiar cold about the room that permeated the air, seeping inside him, joining the aching coldness already there. He could smell, not feel, the heat from a boiling teakettle in the adjacent kitchen, separated from his bedroom only by a curtain pulled across the open doorway. He assumed that the rustlings and hushed sounds from the kitchen came from his mother and sister.

He dared to open his eyes. Yes, the familiar gray-green walls formed the confines of his bedroom. A slight tilt of his head, which caused the return of a dull headache, brought the single, ice-covered window into view. The ice, too, was gray-green in color, and followed the window halfway up. He was not sure whether the attenuated light dribbling in above the ice on the window signaled morning, afternoon, or evening. His only clue was the hiss and metallic smell of the boiling teakettle. It is morning then, he thought. His mother would not use the precious tea at any other time of the day.

His body ached as he attempted to move over to his side. He was filled with a deep weariness that he had never before experienced in his twenty-two years. The headache that he had had for three days now became sharp with the movement, rather than dull, as before. His eyes were dry and burning, and a brief wave of nausea flooded through him. For a few moments, he struggled to remember what had happened to him. How long have I been like this? Slowly, the memory of his father's final illness, the one that had claimed the shell that his father had become, filled his consciousness. Of course, it was his father's last assault. Ivan, his father, who had never willingly given him anything, had shared with him this last malevolent thing before dying.

He fought to clear his thoughts, and then remembered the funeral for his father. The only people in attendance were Ivan's immediate family, Misha Presloff, and Grigory Serov. It was a pitiful showing for the world-renowned Russian dissident Ivan Sergeiovich Genchenko's funeral.

Yakov Popov, the interpreter employed by the Red Army hockey team for which Ivan's son played, also made an appearance, but not to pay his respects to Ivan. No, Yakov's purpose in coming was far darker. He threatened the son that he, Yakov, would take the revenge he could not take on Ivan, on Ivan's son, instead.

No one from the extended Genchenko family, or of all the people that Ivan had known and helped, had attended the brief service prior to the burial, which would not occur until sometime in the spring when the ground thawed enough to dig into. Until then, Ivan would remain in a holding area in the bleak Russian industrial city of Lyubertsy where they lived. The Moscow mayor had refused to have the turncoat buried there, in spite of the fact that the Genchenkos, Muscovites for centuries, had a rather large area of one Moscow cemetery dedicated to their family. It was sad to see such an end to the famous Ivan Sergeiovich Genchenko, the once successful and flamboyant Communist Party Member who metamorphosed into an outspoken and infamous dissident.

Lying there in his cold room, with damp bedclothes tangled about him, memories of his childhood and early youth began to run through his mind. He remembered the spacious Moscow apartment on fashionable St. Barbara Prospekt, where his father and mother entertained numerous friends, colleagues, relatives, and other hangers-on. The Genchenkos were considered to be elite Party Members who were leading the way into the wonderful future of an all-powerful Russia. His parents, both professors at Moscow University, were influential and well to do, much of their fortune having been inherited from Ivan's maternal grandmother.

Yes, the apartment in winter, the dacha in summer, were the magnets to which were drawn all the enlightened apparatchiks, intelligentsia, and human oddities in his parents' group. To gather and enjoy their opinions, thoughts, good company, food and drink, seemed the only purpose in many of their lives. Often, their rousing discussions centered on criticisms of the Communist Party, its tenets and its tactics. Of course, although a child, he was aware that there were those, pretending to be friends, who reported every topic of discussion at those parties to their favorite government agency. He and his sister, Katya, had often eavesdropped from the balcony above the drawing room when their parents were having a late-night party in their dacha, and the children had been banished to their rooms. He knew that some "friends" or "guests" preferred to tattle to the Militia, while others, with far darker purposes in mind, such as greed or avenging a perceived slight, reported to the KGB.

Thoughts of the dacha on the lake brought fond memories of Uncle Vanya, one of the few true friends to his parents, and one of the few among those friends who had shown kindness to him and his sister. Vanya resembled a badly dressed Russian bear. His ill-fitting clothes, great height, head of thick brown and flowing hair, booming voice, and broad shoulders made him stand out in any gathering.

"Ah, my homely cygnets," he would say to them. "One day you will be beautiful and strong swans, and you will fly away from this nest of vipers!"

He would then roar with laughter and gather both of them up into his huge arms for a Russian Bear hug, and they would squeal and giggle with delight. The more vodka he had consumed, the tighter the hug. Vanya was not really their uncle, but had been far more kind and generous to them than any of their father or mother's relatives had ever been. He always sought them out at parties to bestow small gifts upon them. Vanya never forgot to bring some little trinket or token for them when he visited. And Vanya was the last of the Genchenkos' friends to stop coming to visit them after Ivan's disgrace and removal from the Communist Party. Following an investigation instigated by one of the "friends" who attended the many parties that the Genchenkos held, Ivan was arrested.[1] However, Vanya remained loyal to the very last, until, one day, he stopped coming to visit his friends.

Death was the reason that he would not return. Vanya jumped from the highest floor of his apartment building, the tenth, when the KGB had threatened him with Lefortovo Prison, or worse, Siberia, if he did not spill all of his suspected secrets to them. When Vanya committed suicide, Ivan added to his own already desperate situation by being foolhardy enough to publicly criticize the government and the KGB. Ivan ended up in both of the places that Vanya had so feared, and left his wife and children to fend for themselves as best they could in their strange new life of destitution. The Party confiscated the Genchenkos' Moscow apartment, lakeside dacha, and all other assets they could get their hands on. The Genchenko family was left with only memories of their former well-fed security, warmth, and comfort.

His mother's voice brought him back to the present as she pulled open the dividing curtain to his room, "Peter…Petrosha, you must try to get up now. Misha will be here soon. You know that today is the day you must leave."

Her voice was low and breathless as she spoke to him. She came into his room gracefully balancing on one hand a saucer and cup of hot tea. A burning cigarette, held aloft, seemingly floated through the air in her other hand; a habit and affectation of her former affluent life.

"Are you able to sit up?" she asked softly, concern for her son evident in her voice.

"Da," he responded in a rasping voice.

Yes, well maybe, he thought. Slowly, Peter rolled over to the edge of his bed, lay there for a moment, and then pushed himself to a sitting position. As he did so, his ears began to ring and buzz, and his vision seemed diminished for a brief time, but he was able to maintain the sitting position convincingly enough for his mother's benefit. After a few moments, he was even able to do what he thought was a reasonable imitation of a smile, although his face felt wooden as he stretched his mouth back from his teeth.

"Here, you must drink this tea, Petrosha. It's sweetened with honey just the way you like it." She returned his smile hopefully while carefully studying his appearance as she took a long drag on her cigarette. With the cigarette smoke slowly flowing from her mouth and nose she said, "You haven't had anything to eat or drink these last three days, so please drink this, I know it will help."

Again, his only response was "Da." He sipped at the tea, ignoring the sting of the hot liquid on his lips and tongue, surprised that it tasted good to him.

"I have all your clothing and gear packed, but I want you to check it to make sure that everything is there for you to take." And again, the hopeful, sidelong glance and smile were aimed at him, as her face was enwreathed in another cloud of exhaled smoke.

He nodded his head, a mistake, considering the pain that the slight movement caused. "Thank you," was the only response he could give while the pain had control of him.

"Katya has already left for work. She was hoping to see you off, and to say hello to Misha, but her supervisors told her yesterday to start an hour earlier today. As usual, there was no reason given." she replied ruefully.

"Nothing's new there," he said bitterly. "When have they ever given reasons for what they demand?" He shrugged, which was another mistake. This time, the pain went down the length of his spine instead of up into his head. The tea, rising in his throat, did not taste so good at this point.

"It's just a little past six. If you hurry, you can get into the bath before old Yelena awakens." His mother laughed as she made this pronouncement. His mother's wonderful laughter was a welcome sound. For many weeks there had been no laughter in their apartment during Ivan's last illness.

Ah yes, he thought, old Yelena. It seemed that every morning she waited at the door of her apartment to see him step out of his door to walk down the hall to the communal bath. There was only one bath on each floor of the apartment building, and tenants shared it, sometimes rather ungraciously. Yelena never contested the bath with Katya or his mother, but she seemed to take delight in causing a disturbance when Peter headed that way. Sometimes she would even pound on the door to the bath, causing the flimsy piece of wood to chatter on its frame. He had often wondered what she might do if the door fell open. Perhaps that was her ploy, who knew? Well, she's been disappointed for the last few days, he thought, I haven't been a proper contestant for time in the bath. This made him smile, even though his mouth still felt unaccustomed to the upward curve of his lips.

Peter stood beside his bed awhile before taking a few, tentative, steps. Not so bad, he said to himself, I can at least maintain my balance. He walked slowly, and painfully, into the kitchen. The warmth of the room surrounded him in a comfortable embrace after the chill of his bedroom.

"Pull that curtain before all our warm air escapes!" His mother shivered and pulled her sweater closer around her shoulders. "Here are your towels, Petrosha. Your razor and comb are on the table there," she said, nodding her head in the direction of the table.

"You'd better hurry, I think I heard Yelena's door open once or twice." She blew smoke audibly from her mouth and nose, then turned and put the cigarette out on one of her beautiful Lomonosov porcelain ashtrays; a remnant of a more prosperous time.

The towels had been setting near the stove, and they were warm to the touch. He wrapped one around his shoulders, pulled on his pants and slipped into his untied shoes, then opened the apartment door as quietly as he could. The hallway was clear, and Yelena's door was closed. He was aware that he would probably not be able to outrun Yelena this morning if she contested his right to the bath. Peter took a deep breath, coughed, and lunged out the door, committed to making an attempt to reach the bath. The door across from his, Yelena's, was nearly pulled off its hinges as the very large woman bolted out of her apartment. Peter caught a glimpse of what appeared to be a mammoth wrapped in dark red brocade. The race was on! Peter was certain that she would overtake him, and squash him against the wall like an insect in the race to the bath.

Yelena was never silent in these contests. She would shout in a hoarse, vodka-roughened voice, to all within earshot that a young hoodlum was accosting her. Peter, pushed by his need to prepare for his journey, mustered the strength to stay just enough ahead of Yelena to win the right to the bath by slamming the door in her face, and locking the rusted bolt. He sank to the floor, his back against the door, breathing in short, burning gasps. Every time Yelena kicked the door, his body would move forward and back with the action of her kick. Forward, back, forward, back. Peter held his throbbing head in his hands, feeling each kick upon the door in his temples.

Finally, satisfied with her performance, Yelena went back to her apartment, muttering obscenities all the while, until, reaching her apartment, she slammed the door so hard that it bounced off the frame without catching the latch. At that point, a deep male voice shouted up from the stairwell that all those on the third floor responsible for this terrible noise at such an early hour would be dealt with severely if quiet was not restored.

Peter listened from behind the door for a few moments before starting his bath. Slowly, he pulled himself from the floor. He unwrapped his soap, razor, toothbrush and comb from the towel, and started to run some water into the sink. He didn't even attempt to fill the bathtub with water, knowing that there would not be enough hot water to fill the sink, let alone the bathtub. Besides, the drain plug on the tub had never, in the ten years that he had lived in this apartment building, held the water back. Why try, now? The sink was quicker.

He thought longingly of the hot showers in the athletes' quarters of various places that he had traveled to as a hockey player. He loved the long, hot showers, plentiful food, comfortable beds, and most of all, *privacy.* It meant a door to close upon the world, and the freedom to choose whether or not to open that door to those who sought entry. He liked that life very much, but in spite of all the wonderful things that he had seen and done, distant places that he probably would never have been able to see without his one small talent, he always returned home to his mother and sister. They were the hostages for whom he would always pay with the loss of his freedom.

As he dried himself after his bath, Peter heard the familiar, rapid ascent of Misha's running footsteps on the creaking old stairway down the hall. He quickly put on his underwear, shirt, slacks, and socks. Shoeless, he threw open the door to the bath in time to see Misha Presloff reach the third floor landing.

"Petrosha, you are upright! You are dressed! You're going to make the journey after all." All this was said as he strode toward Peter with arms wide, ready to embrace him.

"Wait, Misha. Perhaps I am not completely well." Peter cautioned him by holding up his hands to ward off the embrace that Misha would surely have given him.

Misha's face sobered, "Well, you may be right about that one. I can store my greeting away until a better time. Are you well enough to travel?"

My friend, Peter thought, you always see the truth in a person's face. Peter immediately brightened and smiled at Misha. "I am willing to try. How difficult can it be, sitting in an airplane seat for forty-eight hours?" Peter tried to make light of his impending journey.

"On Aeroflot," Misha laughed, "many things are difficult. Staying in the air for the prescribed amount of time to reach your destination seems to be a problem sometimes!" He grimaced as he made this pronouncement.

"Enough, you two." Peter's mother leaned out the door to beckon them inside the apartment. "Misha, don't frighten my son before his long journey. You know how he hates to fly. You should be ashamed!" All this was said with mock severity, and then Eda Genchenkova laughed.

"Where is Katya?" Misha asked, looking around the apartment, noting the made-up daybed that was Katya's bed at night.

Breathlessly, Eda explained in her characteristic rapid commentary, "Katya's supervisor somehow found out that Peter is journeying today to be with his hockey team, and wanted to spoil their goodbyes. You know his team left yesterday for the International Winter Games in America. Today is the last day that Peter can travel to join them, or he forfeits his entire season's earnings. If he misses one game, that's it." With this pronouncement, she snapped her fingers.

Eda continued to lecture them, her hands up in front of her as if teaching a student. "His coach told him that he could play if he could rendezvous with the team before the opening game. They'd be crazy if they didn't let him play, even though he is late because of Ivan's funeral and his Influenza."

"Who wins the games for them, anyway? Bastards!" spat Misha. Then, blushing as he realized his impolite behavior in front of his friend's mother, he said, "Sorry, I didn't mean to say that."

"No need to apologize, Misha. But I'm curious; was it Katya's supervisor, or the hockey coach you were calling a bastard?" Eda said, giving Misha a penetrating look.

"Both, of course! What else?" Red-faced still, Misha looked at the floor.

Peter turned slowly toward Misha, holding himself tightly because of the pain he experienced with even the slightest movement of his head. "We should leave soon. The airline tickets are still with Valeria, and she's going to be a problem, as usual." Peter was beginning to feel pressured about his journey, and action was his way of easing the pressure.

He reached for a second cup of his mother's hot tea. "Misha, would you like some tea?" he asked, holding the cup aloft.

"No thanks. Look, we're all set..." Misha was animated and rubbing his hands together, "Yevgeny loaned me his car for today, Petrosha. I told him that Katya needed to be driven to Moscow for a job interview, and, since he couldn't tell his criminal of a boss that he needed time off, I offered to take Katya in *his* car. I neglected to tell him the part about driving you to Sheremetyevo, by way of the Red Army Hockey Team office. He even put petrol in the tank!"

Misha's lean, tall frame doubled over with laughter. Standing up again, he pushed his thick, white- blond hair back from his face with one hand, while exhaling audibly, "Whew!"

He enjoyed putting one over on Yevgeny, because the man was in love with Katya, and would do anything to get into her good graces, among other things. It didn't matter that Katya was Misha's girl, Yevgeny still plied her with gifts, bought with stolen rubles, and made himself available for any little thing, trying in vain to take her away from Misha. Even loaning his car to Misha was a gift to Katya in Yevgeny's mind.

As Misha told his story, Peter pictured Yevgeny, a big, soft young man, balding before his time, unpressed clothes hanging about his person. How could such a man even think that Katya would glance his way? He chuckled to himself about the incongruity and absurdity of love. He was certain that he would never behave so irrationally. What was the point of love, after all? From the example set by his parents, it seemed a painful, fruitless experience. Why bother?

Standing upright, bathed, dressed, and with two honeyed cups of his mother's hot tea in his belly, Peter began to feel that he would be able to make the journey to the mysterious city in America called Indianapolis. Indian City, he thought, how must such a place look? He had read books on the subject of the American Indians, and their relationship to the Aleuts of Alaska. They were actually one and the same race he had found during his studies. Migration and a nomadic way of life were, at least in part, the reasons why the Indians had populated such a wide and diverse landscape as that found in North America.

Peter slowly put on his father's heavy coat and cap. They now belonged to him, and fitted him much better than his own threadbare winter garb. He had not realized it until just now, but he was as large as his father had ever been. In fact, Ivan's coat was somewhat tight across his shoulders, and short at the hip. Peter remembered always having to look up at his father, cowed, believing then that he would never grow as tall, or be as strong. He had been wrong to have such thoughts. Here he was, wearing his father's rather tight coat, and his father was now only a memory. He felt no sorrow or loss at his father's passing; only relief. Life's irony, he thought.

Although his head still ached, and he felt lightheaded and queasy, he decided that it was time to start out on his journey. Misha was standing ready at the doorway to the little apartment that Peter, his mother, and sister called home.

Peter looked around briefly, grabbed his travel bag, kissed his mother, said, "Dos vedanya, tell Katya her big brother loves her," and strode out of the door.

Misha scrambled down the three flights of stairs before him, sounding as if he might be falling, rather than descending on foot. Peter, the lighter of the two, and more graceful, followed quietly and quickly after him. As Peter went out into the cold air, his throat and eyes burned with his first inhalation. Closing his eyes, and swallowing quickly, he managed to recover from the dizzying descent of the stairs and the initial onslaught of the cold.

"I parked over here," Misha called and waved from the alley next to the apartment building. "Someone must have been ambitious, digging out the snow in this alleyway so well. They must have known that I was coming." He smiled widely, still in a good humor over the change of scenery that taking Peter to Moscow would bring.

When both were in Yevgeny's car, Misha turned to Peter and said, "You look like cold shit."

"...as opposed to the warm variety?" Peter made a wrinkled-nose face of distaste at Misha.

Misha waved a dismissive hand at Peter, "I didn't want to worry your mother by saying anything before, but you look like you've just come off of a bad vodka binge. Are you sure you can make this trip?" Misha started the car, forced it into gear, and moved out into the street.

Peter, smarter now, said, "Da," instead of nodding and stirring the pain in his head.

"What happens when you get there and can't play hockey?"

"I'll think of something."

"Well, you'd better do some serious thinking. Will they leave you stranded in that Indian City?" The Russian words for Indianapolis literally translated into Indian City.

Peter laughed shortly at the absurdity of Misha's statement. "Of course they won't. Think about it. Yakov, our self-important team interpreter, would never do something that might be of help to me. Stranded in America? Oh no. Instead, he'd see that I was shipped back to Russia and put in the army. Then he'd see to it that I'd be sent off to Afghanistan. It's goodbye from then on. He's told me as much when he's threatened me before."

"Why does he hate you so much?"

Peter's reply was one word, "Ivan."

"Yakov knew your father?"

"You might say that. Of course, their acquaintance was made in Lefortovo Prison, so the association was never based on friendship. It was prisoner and interrogator; that was their association. Yakov could not match wits with my father. He was never able to get any useful information on anyone else from Ivan, and so was demoted because of his failure. Ivan was a very stubborn man."

"But I saw him at your father's funeral. Why would he come if not to pay his respects?"

Peter laughed derisively, "He was there only to assure himself that Ivan was actually dead, and to deliver a message to me. He had the gall to speak to me at the funeral about transferring his hunger for revenge from my father to me. Apparently, he didn't believe that Ivan had suffered enough during his years of imprisonment. Ivan's smuggled writings made him world-famous in a world eager to hear the voice of a Russian dissident, while Yakov languished in obscurity.

"Have you read any of my father's other books? He's especially renowned in the West, where anything bad written about the Soviet Union becomes a best-seller. His books are available on the underground here, if you can afford to buy them. I have been told that he was actually a very good writer."

"Your family hasn't seemed to prosper with your father's fame, so where's the good in that?"

"None, as usual. My father didn't do a thing to help us after he was arrested. He never wrote to my mother, my sister, or me in all the years of his imprisonment. I'm also certain that he didn't ask his relatives to help us, either. The truth is that they disliked Ivan's little Jews. We never heard from any of them in all the time that he was in prison. None of them attended Ivan's funeral, either. They were probably afraid of contamination. By us, or by Ivan, I couldn't say."

Misha shook his head in surprise. "Katya has never said anything to me about any of this."

"She wouldn't. Why speak ill of the dead, after all? What's the purpose in that? My mother is the same way. I didn't know until after Ivan died that my mother had to pay off his gambling debts in addition to having to make a life for Katya and me."

With this statement, Misha turned to look at Peter, eyes wide, questioning. He gave a low whistle and shook his head. "Your lives have been more difficult than I realized."

"You'd better just look at the road. I don't have anything more to say about Ivan." Peter put his chin on his chest and closed his eyes.

"But how did you survive? You once told me you were only twelve when Ivan went away to Siberia."

Peter opened his eyes and stared out the windshield at the winter landscape. "We were hungry a lot of the time."

"That makes me so angry for the way Katya has been treated most of her life. I want to give her a better life, and I will."

"I took care of my family, Misha. Sometimes it wasn't so easy, but I took care of them."

Peter, wanting to end the conversation, started on a new subject, "How many more kilometers to Moscow?"

He didn't want to think about things he could not change. He felt the stirrings of a familiar sadness. Why dwell on the past? The cold, aching place in his chest began to spread.

"We should reach the outer ring in about thirty minutes, maybe a little longer. What's your flight time?"

"I don't know. Grigory said late afternoon when he spoke to me at Ivan's funeral, but I'm not sure." Actually, Peter had been very surprised to see his coach at the funeral. It took a certain amount of courage to attend Ivan Genchenko's funeral, and Peter had not known that Grigory possessed such courage. Grigory always bowed to Yakov's directives regarding all team matters. Perhaps Yakov was not aware of Grigory's lapse. After all, Yakov had come early to insult and threaten Peter, and then slunk away like a hyena, yipping and barking of revenge.

Misha's eyes again widened as he looked over at Peter. "You don't know what time the plane is leaving?" Then, upon reflection, said, "It doesn't matter, anyway. Aeroflot never flies on schedule."

Peter agreed, "That's my opinion, too, but the biggest problem is Valeria. She has my airline tickets. You know that she's Yakov's Moscow mistress, and so has no liking for me? Apparently, she's gullible enough to believe Yakov's promises of marriage when he dumps his wife, so who knows what she believes about me?"

"You know this for a fact?" Misha grinned at Peter.

"Everyone knows that Valeria must be treated like delicate porcelain, or Yakov's wrath will be raised. What other evidence is needed?"

The road they traveled was poorly maintained, and very slippery in spots. It was too cold for more precipitation, however, and that was a good thing because Yevgeny's tires had little tread on them.

Misha frowned in concentration as he drove. "Why don't you try to get some rest?"

Without replying, Peter closed his eyes. Rest. Hadn't he been in bed for three days? Well, there was rest, and then there was stupor. Most of his three days in bed had been the latter. He could not recall ever having been so ill. Well, there was the time that he had been shot.

Chapter 2

The street was deserted at 6:30 in the evening. A mid-January snow was falling heavily in the darkness, and there was more than twenty-five centimeters of it on the ground. The wind had picked up, and it was hard for fifteen-year-old Peter, weighed down with a sack full of food, to make his way from the main street, with its ghostly-glowing street lamps, to the unlit side street heading toward his apartment. Lyubertsy in warm weather was inhospitable. In winter, it was a continual misery.

Peter's family, driven from Moscow after his father's disgrace and arrest, had been banished to Lyubertsy, a factory town southeast of Moscow, where his mother had gotten work as a language and piano tutor. She earned barely enough to pay the rent on their tiny, one bedroom apartment. Earning enough money for food was Peter's responsibility, and he and Katya worked hard at odd jobs to earn what little money they could. At fifteen, Peter did clean-up work on weekends in one of the numerous factories of Lyubertsy. Katya waited tables and washed dishes at a small restaurant near their apartment. Eda insisted that her children attend school during the week. Education, she often told them, was the first key to finding a rewarding life.

Ivan had been released from prison early that cold Monday morning, and had arrived home in an ill temper, cold and hungry. Only Katya and Peter had been at home when Ivan arrived. He had been dumped from a militia car unceremoniously onto the street in front of the apartment.

Because her job started at 6:30 every morning, Eda had gone to work before Peter or Katya had awakened for school. This was now the custom in their home.

Peter and Katya were preparing to go to school when Ivan pounded on the apartment door, demanding entry. Peter opened the door, and both of the children gasped as Ivan pushed past them into the apartment. Not knowing what to say, they silently stared at him. After all, he had been gone for more than three years and they had not heard a word about, or from, him during that time.

"Where is your mother?" Ivan had demanded.

He had not offered to embrace them, and did not appear happy to see them. "I asked you a question," he growled, glaring at Peter.

Katya gave a stricken look at Peter and began to tremble. Peter stood silently, not moving, but in readiness for the blow that would surely come from his father's hand no matter if Peter answered him or not. This was how their relationship had always been from Peter's earliest years on.

"Answer me!" Ivan moved a step toward Peter, and Katya winced, waiting for the blow to fall.

Peter stepped in front of Katya protectively. Finally, in a controlled and quiet voice, he replied, "My mother is working. She works from early morning until late at night for very little money, thanks to you."

Ivan's eyes narrowed at this perceived insult, and he raised his hand to slap his son. Peter did not back away from him as the blow fell across his cheek, leaving an angry red mark there. Katya began crying softly, afraid to give louder voice to her sorrow for fear of reprisal from her father. Peter continued to stand protectively in front of her.

"Do you think you can stop me if I wish to strike Katya, too?" Ivan laughed harshly, a hateful sound, as he reached around Peter to grab Katya's arm.

Peter struck his father squarely in the face, stunning Ivan enough to make him let go of Katya and stagger backward a few steps. Blood ran from Ivan's nose, and the disbelief in his eyes showed that Peter had hurt him.

"You are never to touch Katya again, do you understand?" Peter's voice had a controlled fury about it. His green-gold lionesque eyes were fierce as he stared directly into Ivan's. Ivan, still in shock from Peter's punch, reeled back onto a chair, shattering one leg of the chair as he fell onto it, and then rolled onto the floor. He looked up at Peter from the floor, waiting for derisive laughter at his predicament, but saw only the icily controlled fury on his son's face.

Peter stated slowly and quietly, "I am now the man in this home, and I will not allow you to hurt my sister or my mother ever again. If you wish to stay here, you cannot raise your hand again to any of us. If you do, I will surely kill you."

Peter's eyes, still full of fury, held his father's. Ivan looked away, unable to endure the hatred that he saw in his son's eyes.

Behind him, Peter could hear Katya's audible gasp of dismay at his words, "Don't be afraid, Katya, he won't hurt you again, I promise you."

"But Peter, I am afraid, now, for you." Katya sobbed aloud.

Peter turned and hugged her to him, looking back over his shoulder at Ivan. "Please Katya; don't be afraid, he's not going to cause us anymore trouble." Peter's eyes again pierced Ivan's, with the silent message conveyed that Peter had meant what he said.

Peter walked Katya to school. Neither was dressed warmly enough for the palpable cold of the Russian January. It grabbed at their faces, their hands, and their feet, causing pain wherever bare skin might be exposed. They walked quickly, not speaking, as the intake of air for speech was chillingly painful. When they had finally walked the two and one-half kilometers to the school, Peter stepped inside the comparatively warm school building to tell Katya that he had to go to their mother's workplace and warn her of Ivan's return. Tears welled up in Katya's beautiful green-gold eyes, the mirror of his own, but she controlled herself because there were other students nearby. She nodded and attempted a smile. Peter smiled back reassuringly.

"You agree that I should let our mother know that he's back?"

Again Katya nodded. "Da," *yes* she said quietly. Her mother might be very frightened otherwise, she thought.

"Will you come to school when you have told her? I would feel so much better having you here. Please don't go back to the apartment without me." Her eyes were begging him not to do anything foolish.

"I promise you that I will come back here as soon as I can." He patted her shoulder, then turned quickly and went out the door into the cold.

By the time he reached the Sharansky School, an old brick mansion where the wealthy of Lyubertsy, a very small and elite group, sent their children, Peter's feet had become numb with cold. He went directly to the small business office where he thought his mother might be. Eda taught English and piano to the students, but she also worked in the office. That was the reason her hours were often so late. She finished her teaching duties at 5:00 p.m., but often had typing and filing duties that kept her past 9:00 p.m. Eda would often work during lunchtime so that she could get home earlier. The administrator would have kept her later, but he was kind enough to realize that she would miss the last public transport, and have to walk home alone late at night in the bitter cold.

"Is Eda Genchenko with students right now?" Peter inquired.

A round, dark-haired woman looked up and stared at him for a moment. Then, seeming to gather her wits about her, she said, "I believe that is true. Do you need to speak with her at this time?"

The woman's stilted manner and language irritated Peter, but he remained polite. "Da, I would like to speak to her briefly, if I can. Will you contact her for me?" He smiled at the woman.

When he smiled, the pain in his left cheek reminded him of his father's slap. Now he understood, perhaps, why this woman had stared at him.

"Is the issue of great importance, or could you wait to see her if she is presently unavailable?"

Peter, tiring of the game said, "I am her son, and I have a message of great importance to her."

"Very well, I will see if I can find her. Please wait there," she said, indicating a nearby chair with an emphatic nod of her head.

The woman, who had been seated, stood up, and she was scarcely taller standing than when she had been sitting. Gnome-like, she waddled through the doorway and looked back at him as if to say, *sit.* She then disappeared into the dimly lit hallway.

Within a few minutes Peter's mother appeared with the gnome. His mother's clothes, though outdated and old, looked somehow elegant on her tall, erect body. He had not really thought of his mother as being tall or beautiful, but the contrast between the two women was very great, and he realized that she was both. There was apprehension on his mother's face, and he saw that she moved her eyes over him, and then looked around the room. Immediately he saw that she was fearful that something had happened to Katya.

"Mother, Katya's fine. She's at school." He watched as relief flooded his mother's face.

"What is it, then, Peter?"

"Let's go where we can speak privately," he replied, looking over at the other woman who watched them both intently. Had her ears, which stuck out of her hair, actually swiveled, catlike, to catch even the softest word? He blinked his eyes. Of course not, it was just his imagination.

Peter and his mother went out into the hall, and walked a few paces toward the outer door. His mother turned expectantly toward him. Then she saw his face fully.

"Peter, your cheek, what has happened? Was there an accident?"

He took both of her hands in his, "Mother, Ivan has returned." He did not use the word father, because he had long ago given up on the concept of Ivan as his father.

Eda's face fell, "Oh, no, Peter, it cannot be. They said he could not return this time. Their evidence of dissidence and corruption was too strong."

"He came this morning before Katya and I left for school."

Eda took her son's face in her hands, turning his head to look at the bruise on his cheek, "Now I see very clearly what has happened to you. Is Katya also marked? He always liked to make both of you cry at the same time. He always told me, "If one twin cries, the other should, also." I knew then that I should run away with you and Katya to someplace where he couldn't hurt you anymore." Just as Katya's had earlier, his mother's eyes filled with tears.

"I told him that he could not hurt any of us again. I threatened him, and when he hit me, I hit him back. It shocked him, and his nose bled. Cowards don't want to see their own blood. He won't hurt us again."

As he spoke, Eda kept shaking her head, "Peter, he will only wait until you are unaware, and then he will hurt all of us. You are only a fifteen-year-old boy. You cannot stop him." Her eyes were very sad as she said these things to him.

"Mother, I promise that I will not let him hurt you or Katya. Please believe me; he won't ever touch you again."

His mother nodded, dismissing him, "I can't argue with you now, Peter, I have to return to my class. Today they are speaking sentences in English, so it is an important day for them. There are many parents in attendance, so I must go." Eda smiled and kissed her son on his wounded cheek.

"I will be home before you arrive, mother. All will be quiet, wait and see." Peter smiled back at his mother and turned to go.

"I suppose he was hungry, as always. Can you find something for him to eat?" Eda asked as Peter was leaving.

"Da," he said. And he walked out of the school entrance into the cold wind and snow.

Peter remembered on the cold walk back to his school that he and Katya had not eaten their breakfast that morning because of Ivan's arrival. Hunger gnawed at him, and he could feel himself tire as he rounded the last corner on the street where his school was located. To his surprise, Katya was waiting at the door for him.

"Why aren't you in class?" he asked.

"Peter, it is lunchtime, and I forgot to bring something to eat. I didn't want to just sit there while everyone else was eating, so I came out here to wait for you." Her usually pale skin was even paler as she chided him for being gone so long.

"I talked to mother about Ivan," he said. "She didn't like what she was hearing, but we can work it out, I think."

Peter glanced around the empty hallway, "Come on, Katya let's go find something to eat."

Her eyes widened, "We shouldn't leave school, Peter, they're not happy with us as it is."

"You're ready to faint from hunger; I can see it in your face. Let's go."

They walked out into the cold again, straining against the wind as they headed for the Lyubertsy downtown area where there were a few restaurants that might have something edible to serve. It was still too cold to carry on a conversation, and walking against the wind was sapping what little energy they had left. Upon reaching the center of the city, they chose the closest building with a food sign in the window in order to get out of the terrible cold.

A rather large, red-faced woman watched them as they entered. Eyeing their well-worn coats, she said, "You must buy something to stay in here. I can't afford to have people just soak up my heat. Who will help me pay for it?" She scowled at them, as if to scare them away.

When this failed to intimidate them, she narrowed her eyes and asked, "Why aren't you in school? Maybe I should call the Militia."

Peter, undaunted by the woman's manner, went over to the display case to look over the potentially edible things that might be housed therein. He looked down into the woman's eyes, and she averted her face, mumbling that Russia's youth were a useless lot.

Peter removed some coins from his pocket, counted them, and pointed to the meat pies in the display case, holding up two fingers to indicate the number he wanted to buy. "I'd also like two glasses of hot tea sweetened with sugar cubes."

The woman's face became an even darker shade of red as she eyed the coins in Peter's hand. Business had been very slow for her today. "Only two sugar cubes per cup," she said abruptly.

Two meat pies were clumsily flopped onto worn and cracked plates, and cups of hot tea, steaming in the chilly air of the shop, were placed on the counter in front of Peter.

"How much?" he asked.

"Seven rubles…" the woman stated flatly.

"What about the sugar cubes?"

Exasperated, she waddled away, returning with exactly four sugar cubes, no more, no less. "There!" she said with a spiteful snap, slapping the sugar cubes down onto the counter and then grabbing the rubles off the counter with a sweep of her hand.

"Thank you," Peter nodded and smiled. It was important to always be polite to one's elders, he thought ruefully.

Peter and Katya huddled together as they ate, talking quietly about what they should do now that Ivan had returned.

"Mother told me to get him something to eat." Peter told her.

Katya asked, "We don't have much money, how will we buy anything?"

"I have some ideas, but we have to go home before I can do anything." he replied.

"I am afraid to go back there." Katya looked at Peter, her eyes wide and fearful.

Peter shrugged, "We have to go back. What do you think he will do to our mother if we don't?"

Katya cast her eyes downward, and her lower lip began to tremble, "I hate to think about it."

"I won't let anything happen to you, or mother, believe me." Peter placed a hand on her arm gently.

As Peter and Katya walked back to their apartment, the skies opened up to unleash a heavy snow with huge flakes that stuck to their clothes, hair, brows, and lashes. The wind also picked up, swirling the snow in small whirlwinds around them. Why is the wind always in my face, he wondered? Couldn't it sometimes be at my back?

Peter was outwardly calm. He knew that his sister was terrified of returning to the apartment where their father was waiting, and he didn't want her to know that he, too, was afraid. He attempted to distract Katya by scooping up enough snow for a snowball, then throwing the snowball at some target. This could have proven to be disastrous, but he picked his targets carefully. He didn't throw at any of the pedestrians, no matter how tempting, or wide, a target they might be, but did strike many of the statues that they passed along the way. Marx and Lenin, after all, did have some usefulness.

As they approached their building, Peter looked up at the windows of their third floor apartment. His father's gaunt face stared down at him from the sitting room window. Brace yourself, Peter thought, it's going to be a very long day. There was no doubt in his mind that his father would retaliate for Peter's having hit him. Only the timeframe was unknown. Ivan had always proven to be an expert at revenge.

Peter and Katya hurried up the narrow stairs of the old building to the third floor, but then slowed considerably the last few steps, in dread of the next encounter with their father. Peter entered the apartment first, with Katya behind him. He wasn't sure what to expect from Ivan, so he told Katya to stay back for a moment or two. His father was sitting on the daybed facing the door. Ivan's eyes, cold and angry, were fixed upon Peter. There was a dark bruise across the bridge of Ivan's nose.

"You've been gone far too long. Where have you been?"

"I wanted to make sure that mother knew of your return, so she wouldn't be surprised to see you," Peter answered coolly.

Katya slowly entered the apartment, keeping Peter between herself and Ivan. She quietly closed the door, and stood in front of it.

"Well, where is my food? I haven't eaten for two days. There's very little in the kitchen." Ivan jerked his head in the direction of the tiny room. "I ate what was there, but my gut is still empty!"

Ivan's voice had a hysterical ring to it. The all too familiar sound that Peter remembered so well from his childhood, just before Ivan lost control and started hitting him, his sister, his mother, or destroying the furniture.

There were quick steps on the stairs, and then Eda flung open the apartment door. Her gaze quickly flew from her children to her husband. He hadn't harmed them, as far as she could see. Her eyes then stared unflinchingly into Ivan's.

"Why are you here? Haven't you caused us enough pain?" There was a fierce brightness in her eyes from anger and unshed tears.

"It was not my choice. None of my relatives came forward to escort me from Lefortovo. There was no limousine, no fancy conveyance. Even cousin Leo stayed away," he said sarcastically. Ivan's eyes narrowed. "I don't blame them, actually. Who, after all, wants to be associated with, or contaminated by, me? The risk was too great for any of them to take."

"So you visit this misfortune on us, then? Your little Jews, as you like to call us. I tell you, things have changed. Your little Jews are afraid of you no longer." Eda stood with her children, putting an arm around each.

"There is nowhere else for me to go..." Ivan replied in a subdued voice, as he looked out the window behind the daybed.

"Well, at least there is finally a valid reason for choosing us." Eda shook her head in resignation.

Eda turned to Peter and whispered, "Take some of our emergency fund to buy some things to eat. There are beets, cabbage, and some rice available today on the square. Just go to the square. The lines aren't very long."

"My coat's wet and the snow isn't showing any signs of stopping soon." Peter did not relish another long walk in the cold and snow.

Eda said, looking at Ivan as she answered Peter, "Take your father's coat and hat. He won't be going out into this weather any time soon."

She turned to go into the kitchen, and, watching to make sure that Ivan didn't follow her, took some money from beneath the tablecloth. A good hiding place, after all, she thought. She heard Ivan's reply to her suggestion.

Ivan shrugged, still holding Peter in his angry stare, "Yes, just be on your way. It's getting late, and the kiosks could close before you get there."

Returning to the dayroom, Eda hugged her son. "Peter, please be careful," then handed the precious, hard-earned money to Peter.

Peter quickly put on his father's coat and hat, searched for, and found, a scarf to tie around his face and neck, and placed newspaper between his stockings and shoes as a moisture barrier. He then turned to wave goodbye. Bounding out the door and down the stairs, he knew that he must hurry because he couldn't trust his father to be alone with his mother and sister.

Peter ran, as best he could, through the deepening snow toward the square at the heart of Lyubertsy. Eleven blocks did not seem much of a run on an ordinary day, but the snow was deep, wet and slippery, slowing his progress to a jog. By the fourth block, his lungs were burning.

The snow put a new face on Lyubertsy. It hid the dark ugliness of pollution-stained buildings, and almost obliterated the grime and debris in the streets. Street lamps, at least those that were lit or had bulbs, barely gave enough light for him to accurately measure his progress as he ran from well to well of sickly gray light. There were very few passersby. Who would come out into such a snowstorm unless they were pressed to do so, or were just plain foolish? Peter decided that he was probably the latter.

During his lonely run, Peter tried to think of how he was going to protect his mother and sister from his father. Ideas tumbled through his head. It wouldn't be a problem while he was there to protect them, but what about the time he must spend working, or going to school? A familiar coldness began to settle deep inside Peter. It was not the coldness of the air through which he was running, but the bleak coldness of being without hope. Where or to whom could he turn for help? The answer as always: nowhere and to no one. Peter had never indulged in self-pity. Survival had taken all of his strength and internal resources. How could he feel sorry for himself when almost every action he took required him to do battle? There was no energy for that kind of indulgence.

Peter skidded around a corner and onto the square. With relief, he saw that the lines of shoppers, foreshortened because of the weather, were still there. He quickly assessed which kiosks held the food items he needed, and he planned how to go from one to the other without much time lost.

Within an hour and a half, Peter's knapsack was full, and he turned back toward his apartment. His feet were now thoroughly chilled in spite of the newspaper lining his shoes. Paper was not as good as an extra pair of warm stockings. His hands and fingers stung from the cold. He couldn't run as well now that he had the extra burden of the foodstuffs in the knapsack slung over his shoulder that hung down past his hip. A feeling of panic was building within Peter. He was frantic to get home to his mother and sister. What had his father been doing while he was gone?

Peter turned another corner, and was surprised to see a car stopped in the middle of the street in front of what appeared to be some sort of shop. He wondered briefly about how the car had been able to make forward progress in the snow. Well, he thought, maybe it's stuck there and can't go on. Peter thought about helping the driver of the car, but then decided that he did not have the luxury of time. After all, there were Katya and his mother in the apartment with his violent and unpredictable father. Family first, he thought, and hurried past the car.

As he did so, the passenger side door of the car opened and a man shouted, "Ivan!" in a deep voice.

Peter, enshrouded in his father's clothing, and obscured by the scarf around his face and neck, turned toward the voice.

"You're dead now!" the voice shouted, and Peter heard a strange, sharp sound; *crack*, then felt a sharp, burning pain in his right side.

Peter pulled the knapsack aside, and saw a bright red stain on the bag and his father's coat. He heard a woman scream, then another sharp *crack*, and blackness closed in around him. The last thing he heard was the slamming of a car door, and the sound of an engine revving up.

"Mother, mother, they're gone," the young woman called to another woman standing fearfully in a doorway directly in front of where Peter had been shot.

"They will come back to finish their business. Come away from there!" With her words, the woman depersonalized the man bleeding in the gutter. "You can do nothing, Natalia, come away, come away!"

Natalia lifted the scarf from the face of the fallen man. "Mother, it is Peter," she cried. "Remember Peter Genchenko, the boy who defended me? We can't leave him like this!"

"Come away, or I will close the door and lock you out, foolish girl!" the woman shouted.

"There is food in this bag, mother…enough for us for the rest of the week. Please, help me to help Peter."

The woman hesitated, and then moved out of the doorway and onto the sidewalk. She looked fearfully up and down the street to check for a return of the car.

"Give me the bag!" she shouted at her daughter.

Natalia threw the bag into the middle of the street. "Not until you help me with Peter. Please mother, help me."

Natalia's mother swore as she grabbed Peter under his shoulders. "Take his feet, won't you? I can't lift him unless you help!"

The two women half-carried, half-dragged Peter through the doorway and into their apartment. "Go back and get the food!" Natalia's mother pushed the girl back toward the door.

"Will he be all right?" Natalia bent over to look into Peter's face. "Oh!" she cried. "His head is bleeding." Turning toward her mother, she said, "Can't you stop the bleeding? You're a physician! Can't you save Peter?"

"It is only superficial, see?" The woman turned Peter's face so that Natalia could see the wound more clearly.

"It's his other wound that I'm worried about." She began stripping Peter's coat from his body.

"They may come back. I've got to cover the blood." Running back into the street, Natalia retrieved the bag, took it into the apartment, and returned to the street. Her mother, again coming to the doorway, called to her. "What are you doing now?"

Natalia, using her mother's hallway broom, cleared the telltale drag marks from the street, scooped up the bloody snow and placed it in a paper bag, then again brushed more snow into the street to cover where Peter had lain. The last thing that she did was to use the broom handle to break the bulb on the streetlamp.

"Why did you do that? Now our place will be dark…perfect for criminals to prey on us!"

"Hush, mother, I've got to hurry. Please, just help Peter. He needs your help, can't you see?"

Natalia ran down the street until she reached the next block of apartments. When she found a working streetlight, she dumped the bloody snow from the paper bag onto the snow in the street and used her feet to make what appeared to be drag marks into the doorway of the building. She dropped the remaining bloody snow in the hallway of the apartment building and ran outside.

Running to the end of the block, Natalia crossed the street, and then doubled back toward her own apartment. As she cautiously worked her way back, she ducked into doorways, and used the falling snow and poor light to stay hidden. She crept forward slowly, and then saw a black car turn into the street two blocks ahead. She quickly ducked into another doorway. Breathing rapidly and shaking with fear, she watched the approach of the car. It stopped in front of her apartment, and a figure emerged slowly from the passenger side of the car. Even from this distance, she could see that the figure was very large, and was probably a man. She saw him stop, then look around near the entrance to her apartment. Time seemed to stand still as the figure walked back and forth in front of her building. Finally, he raised his arms in the air, as if to indicate that he could not find what he was looking for, and returned to the car. The sound of the closing of the car door, muffled by the falling snow, sounded oddly more distant than it actually was.

Natalia used the time before the car started moving again to open the door of the building where she had been hiding, and step inside. The hallway smelled of ancient cabbage dinners and human waste, but she felt safer inside than out. The hallway was poorly lit, and she was surprised that there was any illumination, given the talent of most apartment dwellers for pilfering even the dimmest of light bulbs for their own use. Looking up, she could see the reason that the bulb was unmolested. It hung a great distance above the hallway, and couldn't be reached from the stairs. Only someone with a ladder could ever hope to reach it. Ladders were even scarcer than light bulbs.

Natalia ventured a peek through the dirty window of the outside door. What she saw caused her to jump back from the window, nearly faint with fear. The car had stopped in front of the building in which she was hiding! Heart pounding, and knees weakened with fear, Natalia turned and knocked on the nearest apartment door. After what seemed like minutes, but was probably only fifteen seconds or so, an elderly gentleman with long, curling earlocks of hair, the sign of a Hasidic Jew, answered the door.

"You wanted something?" he asked with a small bow to her, keeping his eyes fixed upon hers.

"Uh, yes, yes, I wondered if you might give me a drink of water, I am feeling faint, and I have a long way to walk to get home." she lied.

The old man raised his thick white eyebrows until they shaped a large, inverted "U" above his questioning eyes. "You are merely thirsty, or are you hiding from someone, something?"

Natalia opened her mouth to speak, but was unable to make a sound. Tears filled her pleading eyes.

"Come in, child." the old man took her by the arm, and closed his door just as the building entry door banged open.

The old man placed a finger to his lips, and listened at the door. His body was straight and erect. He appeared to be holding his breath, as if the sound of his breathing might bring whoever was in the hallway to his door. Then he shook his head and grimaced.

"They are coming this way." he whispered to her.

Natalia shivered in fear, and the old man recognized her terror. He turned his head and said, "Jezebel, please come here."

A low growl came from an adjacent room, and the scraping of claws on linoleum could be heard. The largest dog that Natalia had ever seen emerged through a darkened doorway, and stood looking at her.

"Jezebel, it is time for you to speak," said the old man, lifting his arms as if to conduct a symphony orchestra.

Jezebel, playing a part that she had long become accustomed to, began barking in a deep, ravenous- sounding bass. The old man continued to wave his arms, and the dog barked on. When he dropped his arms to his sides, he turned to listen at the door. Jezebel had obediently stopped barking as he did so. This lull gave the massive animal the opportunity to turn and gaze at Natalia. Jezebel's head turned to the side as if to ask a question of Natalia…friend or foe?

Natalia reached to touch the old man on his shoulder in order to get his attention. Jezebel immediately let her know that this was not the thing to do by opening her jaws to show Natalia her teeth. However, not a sound came from her throat. Jezebel's master, after all, had bidden her to be silent. Natalia could hear footsteps outside the door that paused for a moment, and then went on. The outside door groaned as it was opened, and then slammed shut. The old man continued to hold a finger to his lips for silence. At that point, a ticking clock in the next room became audible, heightening Natalia's feeling of unreality.

Finally, the old man turned back toward Natalia and Jezebel. "Our potential guests have decided not to call upon us. I cannot say that I am sorry for their lack of manners." His Russian was impeccable, as if he might be a university professor, or some other sort of academic.

"You are still thirsty, perhaps?" he inquired of Natalia.

"Uh, yes, I'm still thirsty," she managed to answer in a small voice, "and I must thank you for helping me."

"Well," said the old man, "you seemed quite frightened, and the only threat that I could perceive was our would-be visitors." Again, his eyebrows formed a questioning "U" above his intelligent eyes.

Avoiding his implicit question, Natalia replied, "I must get back to my apartment. My mother is waiting for me."

"Indeed," he replied. "May I accompany you home? Jezebel and I always take a walk at this time of the evening."

"Oh, there's no need for that. You've been too kind already."

The old man lifted his hand and said, "*I* may not be much protection for you, but I can assure you that Jezebel strikes fear into the heart of anyone considering foul play."

Natalia smiled at this, and then agreed to an escort. "I'd be happy to have your company and Jezebel's too."

The old man went to a hall tree standing near the door. "Here, put this shawl around you, and wrap some of it over your head. You will be transformed from a *shiksa* to a Jew. Also, remember to walk three paces behind me and to the right. This is how you would walk with me if you were my granddaughter."

He smiled at her for the first time. "By the way, why are you walking here in the ghetto? Do you live nearby?"

Natalia nodded, "My father was Jewish, and that's why my mother and I live here."

"You said your father *was* a Jew?"

"He died many years ago."

"Ah," he answered, nodding his head. "But they would not allow you to live anywhere else?"

"Nyet," she replied.

Wrapped warmly in his great coat, his wide-brimmed black hat squarely on top of his head, the old man, his dog, and Natalia, went out into the snow. Jezebel walked ahead of them on her leash. She did not strain or pull at the leash as Natalia had expected. It was evident that Jezebel looked after her master very well.

By now, the snow was very deep, and quite difficult to walk through. When they reached her apartment building, Natalia thanked her benefactors and turned to enter her door. The old man watched as she stopped at the door and unwrapped the shawl from her person. She folded it nicely, and returned it to him. Jezebel was otherwise occupied, and did not wish to acknowledge Natalia's departure.

The old man nodded and smiled. "Take care in this dangerous world in which we live," he said, and then walked on.

Natalia opened the door to her apartment, afraid of what she might find there. "Mother?" There was no answer. The apartment was very quiet.

"Mother, where are you?" Natalia was beginning to fear the worst. Has Peter died?

She took off her wet outer garments, hung them on the back of a chair and went in search of her mother and Peter. The apartment was much larger than Peter's because Natalia's mother was a physician, and her father's family had once been wealthy.

As Natalia approached the kitchen she heard a stifled groan and then a loud gasp. She began reciting aloud a prayer that she had heard her father say many times.

"Hear our voice, O Lord our God; have compassion upon us, and accept our prayer with favor and mercy, for You are a God who hears prayer and supplication."

Upon entering the kitchen, Natalia saw that her mother had used the table for her operatory. Peter lay upon his left side on the table. There was the hiss of boiling water from a teakettle on the stove, and as Natalia looked at her mother, she could see a frown of deep concentration on her face. It was her mother's "physician's face" and she had seen it many times when her mother was treating the sick.

"Get over here and help me! He's strong as a young bear. You will have to hold him down; I've given him something for his pain, but it isn't holding him very well."

Natalia rushed over to the table, and in a quavering voice she asked, "What can I do?"

There was blood spattered everywhere, on the floor, the wall, the table. Natalia felt sick at her stomach.

"Talk to him and tell him what I'm doing. If he doesn't cooperate soon, I don't think I can save him. He's going to bleed out if I can't get these wounds closed."

Her eyes filling with tears, Natalia went to Peter's head and started talking to him, her voice shaking with emotion, "Peter, Peter...it's Natalia

Mihaleva. You remember…from school? I'm going to help my mother while she's treating you. Please listen Peter. You've *got* to lie still. I know it hurts, but mother's a physician, and she can help if you will only lie still." At this, her voice broke, and she began to cry.

Peter, his eyes tightly shut against the pain, grimaced, then said, "I hear you." It was all he was able to say to her between his clenched teeth.

"Natalia, the towel, *now*!" her mother shouted, holding aloft a bloody object in her forceps to get a better look at it. "There! It's the bullet! Now I can pack this wound and start on his head. Wash the wound area first, and wipe the blood from his back. You can help me roll him over then."

The blood was bright red and Natalia could feel what little she had eaten earlier in the day rise in her throat as she washed Peter's wound and back. Again, tears filled her eyes.

"This is no time for emotion, Natalia, so wipe your eyes and get on with what you are doing." Natalia's mother, still in the persona of *the physician,* wanted to finish quickly.

Peter felt himself being half-lifted, half-rolled to his back. He cried out when the weight of his body pressed against his wound. The pain was searing, burning its way into his brain.

"Take care, girl, take care." The physician admonished her daughter.

Looking directly into Peter's face for the first time, the physician let out a long sigh of relief. The head wound *was* only superficial, but, characteristic of a head wound, had bled profusely even though she had packed a pressure dressing against it before she started on the abdominal wound that went through to his back.

"Natalia, use a fresh towel, dip the end of it in the boiling water, let it cool a bit, and wipe off this wound."

Still the demanding physician, she looked around at her daughter, commanding her as if she were one of her nurses.

Peter tried to open his eyes but found that the lids were stuck in place. He began to struggle, but then felt strong hands holding him on either side of his head.

"Listen to me young man. Don't move. Don't thrash around. Do you know that you have been shot? Well, you have, and I'm only trying to help you, so be still until I can repair the wound on your head. Your eyes will open once we wipe away the dried blood."

Peter nodded his head in acquiescence, a painful action that he immediately regretted. Natalia Mihaleva, who is Natalia Mihaleva, he wondered? Then, as his thinking cleared somewhat, he remembered Natalia. She and Katya had been attacked by several of their particularly vicious schoolmates last year. Natalia was Katya's friend from school. He hadn't seen her since then.

Peter spoke, "Natalia, I remember you. You're Katya's friend, aren't you?"

"Yes."

Natalia began wiping the blood from Peter's eyes. She tried to be as gentle as she could, but she realized that he was wincing from pain.

"I'm sorry to hurt you, but mother said that I have to wipe the blood from your face and eyes. I'll try to be as careful as I can."

Peter smelled tobacco smoke, the familiar Bellomore, a cheap Russian-made cigarette. The odor seemed to be a combination of burning tobacco and old rubber tires.

"Are you smoking, Natalia?" Peter asked.

"Oh no, that is my mother. She is resting in the sitting room while I prepare your wound for her to suture. Smoking is her only means of relaxation. Mother knows it isn't good for her, but the hours that she works in hospital are extremely stressful."

"I don't know very much about hospitals. I've never even seen the inside of one."

"You have missed very little, then." Natalia's mother returned to the kitchen to complete her work.

Peter's eyes were now open, and he gazed about the room, taking in windows, doors, and any other means of escape. His eyes came to rest on the very pretty face of Natalia Mihaleva. She returned his gaze, and he could see by the redness of her eyes that she had been crying. She wiped away any remaining tears with the back of one hand and then smiled at him. Natalia's mother, the physician, was putting the last few sutures in the wound above his left temple.

"What happened to me?" He asked, looking up at the physician.

"You've got some very serious enemies. They almost succeeded in killing you not more than an hour ago," she replied.

"Why...?" Peter started to ask.

"Instead of *why*, you should ask *who*, young man. Two men in a large black car, probably a Lada, shot you. They came back, you know, to see if they had finished the job. Natalia covered your tracks and led them elsewhere."

Peter felt the pain returning with an increased intensity as the wound near his left temple was being sutured. He closed his eyes briefly to rest, intending to ask more questions of his rescuers. The suturing completed, the physician lifted a hypodermic needle to look at the measurement of drug that she had drawn up. Satisfied with her calculations, she injected the drug into Peter's upper arm. He hardly moved when the needle entered his flesh.

"This should help him to rest for awhile, and it will also keep him pain free." Natalia's mother sighed aloud.

"Can we put him in bed now?" Natalia looked down into Peter's sleeping face.

"We can try. Can you believe it? He was conscious enough to get up on the table himself. I don't think getting him down will be as easy. He must weigh at least 75 kilos."

Peter awoke to strange kitchen smells and an unfamiliar room. The bedclothes wrapped around him were clean and sweet smelling, almost perfumed, he thought. Bright sunlight streamed in through a high, narrow window above the bed. Looking around the room, he decided that it must be the room of a young girl. Multi-colored ribbons were tied and hanging around a mirror attached to a dresser. On the dresser were displayed several porcelain dolls in beautiful gowns. He remembered having fine furniture such as this dresser when his family lived in Moscow, before his father's disgrace.

Continuing his visual tour of the room, he saw that there were bookshelves with books. Someone actually still owns books! How interesting, he thought. As he looked at some of the titles, he recognized books that he had read, and some that he had not. He remembered how easy and seemingly stress-free his life had been in his younger years, in spite of his father's evil temper. Then, he had loved nothing better than to find a quiet place to read a good book. Now, that pastime was lost to him. Other, more pressing matters such as providing food and shelter for his mother and sister had taken over his life. Survival, he thought, takes precedence over everything.

He touched his left temple, and found a thick bandage there. Gingerly, he reached down to his abdomen, and lightly pressed the area that was tender and painful. He vaguely remembered a woman who said he had been shot. Who was the woman who had repaired his wounds?

Slowly, as if a painting was being revealed panel by panel, he recalled standing on a snow-covered street corner, and seeing a black Lada stopped in the road near him. He then recalled being shouted at by a man who called him Ivan. There was an odd sound, and he had looked down when he felt a sting in his side. There was a second odd sound, and his head felt as if he had been hit by something, causing him to reel backward. Now it all fit together, someone in the car had shot him!

When full recall returned, he felt a surge of panic. Where was he? How long had he been here in this bed? What had happened to his mother and sister? He must get up; go home.

Peter pushed himself into a sitting position, ignoring the immediate fiery pain in his right side, back, and head that this movement ignited. He frantically looked around the room, searching for his clothing. In bed, he was clad only in a large man's shirt. He swung his legs over the side of the bed and stood upright, just as a young woman came into the room.

Startled, she gasped, "Peter! You shouldn't be standing up! Your wounds…" her words trailed off, and she seemed rooted to a spot just inside the door.

"Who are…" he began to speak, then, his legs giving out, fell back onto the bed.

The young woman quickly came over to him, helped him back under the covers, and said, "You should *not* be moving about! My mother will be angry when she finds out that you have been out of bed."

He felt dizzy and nauseated; too weak to respond. Panic seized him again as he looked wildly about the room. He threw back the covers and tried to sit up a second time. Natalia gently pushed him back.

"Please, Peter, you've been hurt very badly. If you struggle, your wounds may open again. *Please* don't hurt yourself! My mother will be home soon, and she can help you."

"Where am I?" he asked weakly, realizing that he had no strength to fight, or to do anything but cooperate with this young woman.

"Don't you recognize me, Peter? Last night you said you knew me. I'm Katya's friend, Natalia, remember?"

Peter closed his eyes. Wearily he said, "I wasn't at my best last night but, yes, now I remember. You're the one that Katya helped when some of the students attacked you last spring."

"*You* saved us both, Peter. Katya and I were very frightened. They called us names; dirty little Jew girls, among others. We knew we weren't welcome at school, you know, but until the others chased us, we didn't realize how much they hated us. When I told my mother what had happened, she was *so angry,* and wanted to complain, but I talked her out of it. That would have only made things worse for me, and Katya, too."

Focusing on the memory, Peter said, "There must have been six or more students running after you."

"Cowards find safety in numbers," Natalia replied.

Turning to look at her, and ignoring the pain that this movement caused, he asked, "They never bothered you again, did they?"

"No, you were *wonderful.* I think you scared them all nearly to death when you caught Dmitri. He was much larger than you, but he literally flew through the air when you pushed him aside!"

Tiring of the subject, Peter again asked, "Where am I? Is this your apartment?"

Peter urgently needed to know where he was. His fear grew in direct proportion to his lack of understanding of his present circumstances.

"This is where my mother and I live, Peter. You're not far from your place…less than a kilometer, I think."

"Good, then I can make it home." He again tried to rise from the bed.

"No, no, don't do that, Peter. Please, wait for my mother. She can help you. All I can do is give you water and food, but mother will know whether you are fit to go."

Peter could see the concern on her face. Natalia looked as if she were about to cry.

"Where are my clothes?" Peter asked through clenched teeth.

"I won't tell you that until my mother gets home. Then, if you are still so foolish as to want to try to leave, she can tell you what might happen to you."

Even though she was upset, Natalia's voice was firm. Peter knew that she was serious in her intent to keep him there until her mother returned.

"Please try to understand, Natalia, I think my mother and sister are in danger, and I don't want anything to happen to them." He was not above begging for his freedom for their sake.

Natalia came over and sat down on the edge of the bed. She was so light that the bed hardly moved when she sat down.

Taking his hand in hers, she said quietly, "I know that you are worried about your mother and sister. When you were out of your head, you called out to them, and it sounded as if you were afraid for them. If you wish, I can walk to your apartment to let them know where you are, and that you're all right. Would that help you?"

Peter shook his head, and, closing his eyes tightly against the pain, he began, "No, you see, my father has returned, and I don't know what he might do to Katya and my mother. He has a terrible temper. You have no idea what it is like to have someone who is violent in your life. If you went there, he might try to hurt you, too. He's unpredictable, irrational, and mean. You can't reason with him."

"You've got to calm down, Peter." Natalia tried to smile at him.

In spite of all that was running through his mind, he thought of how pretty and kind she was. In a normal, less complicated life, wouldn't it be wonderful to have someone like this lovely girl for a friend...perhaps more?

They continued to talk, and Natalia, after bringing him some broth and tea, told him what had happened on the evening that he had been shot by the men in the black Lada. As she described what had occurred, his eyelids became heavy and his mind began to wander aimlessly. Her quiet presence soothed the intensity of his need to leave until at last, he fell asleep.

When Peter again awakened, the room was in twilight. The sunlight was no longer coming in through the window above the bed. He could hear voices indistinctly coming through the closed door of the bedroom. They were women's voices, and they seemed to be arguing.

"Natalia, I have told you we cannot keep this young man here. If he wants to go home, well, let him go. Don't you think the men who shot him are still looking for him? Use your powers of reasoning! It's very dangerous for us to have him here."

"Certainly you don't think he can get to his apartment by himself in his condition?" Natalia was angry at her mother's lack of concern for Peter.

"You still think like a child, Natalia. Surely you are aware of the danger. Can't you see why we can't keep him here?"

"Just one more night mother, please. You can give him something to make him sleep, and then I will help him to get home tomorrow morning."

Shaking her head in disgust, Natalia's mother said, "You haven't heard a word that I have told you! If those men are still lurking about, do you think that you could possibly save this boy if they wanted to finish him off? Then what would they do to such a foolish one as you?" Throwing her hands in the air, she went into the kitchen.

"Mother," Natalia began again, following her into the kitchen. "I can take him home after dark. It would be difficult to identify him then."

"Tomorrow night he goes then, Natalia, and not a day more."

Natalia's mother continued to shake her head, mumbling angry words under her breath about all those she considered her oppressors: the Communist Party, the Chief Surgeon of her hospital, shopkeepers, attempted murderers of all stripes who filled her hospital with patients who could not pay for their care, and finally, her daughter, who had become the continuous daily voice of her conscience.

When Natalia went into the bedroom to check on Peter, she found him sitting up in bed waiting for her, "Are you hungry, Peter?"

Ignoring her question, Peter said quietly, "Your mother is right, you know."

Natalia averted her eyes, "You heard us?"

"She must think that I can travel. I didn't hear any concern in her voice about that."

"She is very afraid for me, Peter. I am all the family that she has now. My father died, and my grandparents have long since passed away, too. She has no brothers or sisters; no one, and I don't think she wants me to do anything that might put me in danger."

"Da, I understand what you are trying to tell me. But what I don't understand is who did this to me? Why would anyone want to shoot me?"

"Lyubertsy is not a safe place, especially for a Jew. You know that, Peter."

"Tomorrow night, then, I'll go home?"

"I promise," Natalia smiled at him. "And I asked if you might be hungry. Are you?"

"Nyet." Any hunger he may have had, disappeared with his growing apprehension of what he might find when he returned home.

"All right then, go back to sleep. I'll waken you in the morning."

The following morning, Natalia came into the bedroom with towels, soap, and a basin of hot water, "Bathing is required for your trip. It also looks like you could use a bit of a shave. You can't go home in the condition that you're in without scaring your mother and sister to death!"

Eyes wide with apprehension, Peter said, "You don't intend to bathe me, do you?"

For the first time, Peter heard Natalia laugh aloud. It was a beautiful sound. "Of course not…you aren't really an invalid, you know."

When he was alone, Peter shaved and bathed quickly. The water became cool much too fast, and he hated the feeling of the chill when the water evaporated from his skin. But the smell of the soap was fresh, and reminded him of his earlier years when fine soaps were commonplace.

They're able to afford some luxuries, he thought. And then he considered that Natalia's mother was a physician, and her wages could buy some things his mother's, sister's, and his, combined could not. Well, it was best not to dwell too long on such thoughts. Better to just get bathed, get custody of his clothing, and head back to his home. Finished with his bath, he wrapped the woman's robe around him that Natalia had given him.

An undercurrent of fear ran through his thoughts of returning home. What if the men who had shot him were still waiting somewhere to complete their work? What then, and why? What possible reason could anyone have for shooting him?"

Natalia knocked on the bedroom door, "Peter, are you presentable?"

"Da, come in," he said.

"Oh, you look much better. Are you hungry now? I have some bagels, lox and sweet tea for you. If you don't mind, I'll join you. Do you think that you can make it to the kitchen?" Natalia's words tumbled one over another, and her cheeks reddened.

He thought to himself, she's shy, and for some reason, I embarrass her. Why do I embarrass her?

"Lead the way," he replied.

Natalia took his hand gently, and started for the kitchen with him in tow. "It's really only a few steps, Peter, but take it slowly."

Peter decided that Natalia's admonition to take it slowly wasn't needed, as he had no intention of awakening the pain in his head and side again. Gingerly, he followed her through a sitting room filled with floral pillows, overstuffed furniture from a bygone era, and glass figurines. Photographs hung on the wall and there were thick rugs on the floor. He couldn't feel the cold floor on his feet the way he did in his own apartment. Apparently, Natalia's mother favored the color blue, as everything in the room was some shade of that color.

Upon entering the kitchen, Peter saw that it was three times the size of his own, and nicely warm. He looked around, remembering his first time in this room. He decided that Natalia and her mother had done a thorough job of cleaning up after him. He remembered blood on the wall, the table and floor. But now, the room was spotlessly clean.

The table was set as if for guests. There were bagels, lox, sliced onion, pickles, and various jams put out on a pristine white cloth. There were napkins beside each of two porcelain plates, and silverware that actually matched. Peter smiled. Natalia was very kind to have gone to this much trouble just to feed him.

"Sit down, Peter," Natalia invited. "Do you like honey with your tea?"

"Oh yes, always," he replied, sitting down on a very comfortable wooden chair with a floral and lace pillow on its seat.

Natalia poured the tea, and for a time they ate in silence. Peter looked about, and noted with approval all of the little touches, chintz curtains, brightly painted cabinets, handmade rugs on the floor, that, when put together, made the room cozy and inviting.

Finally, after there was an awkward period of silence, he asked, "How long have you lived here, Natalia?"

He liked saying her name; the way it rolled off his tongue. She's so pretty, too, he thought.

"I don't remember ever living anywhere else, but my mother tells me that once we lived very well in Moscow, when my father was still alive." Natalia unconsciously brushed back her heavy, long, dark hair, and looked directly into Peter's eyes with her own large and lovely dark eyes.

Momentarily disconcerted, Peter hastily said, "Moscow. My family once lived in Moscow, too. But then my father disagreed with the Party over a friend's 'suicide', among other things, and my mother, sister, and I ended up here. Perhaps you may have heard of Ivan Genchenko's imprisonment? The Party made an example of him."

"When I told my mother who you are, she said that your father wrote books about democracy, capitalism, and freedom while he was in prison, and the manuscripts were smuggled out of the country. She said they were published outside of the Soviet Union and sold all over the world. Is that true?"

Peter shrugged, "It could be propaganda or it could be fact. If it is fact, my family hasn't seen any of the profits, and if it's propaganda...well, who knows? The Party is not above telling lies."

"You must not speak those sentiments aloud to anyone, Peter. Otherwise, you might end up where your father did." Natalia looked concerned, and even a little frightened by Peter's candor.

"Well, I am steeped in obscurity, and no doubt considered a nonentity by the Party. How could I possibly be a threat to anyone?" Well, of course, there were those men who tried to kill me, he thought.

Peter realized that he was beginning to tire, and told Natalia that he needed to go back and lie down for a while. Was he going to have the strength tonight to return home? He felt less sure than he had when he bathed and shaved earlier.

Natalia sensed that Peter was in need of rest, even before he voiced his need, and so assisted him gently back to the bedroom, helped him into bed, wrapped in her mother's robe. She managed to help him roll backward onto the pillows. After covering him, she crept toward the door, but turned back when she heard a muffled, "Thank you," from Peter.

"Rest well," she answered, and closed the door.

When Peter awakened again, it was to the aroma of something that smelled delicious. Natalia came into the bedroom with a tray of food, and a steaming cup of tea.

"Are you ready for your supper?" She smiled at him as he sat up in bed.

"Oh, yes." he replied.

"I made a stew of lamb and vegetables for you. It will give you strength for your journey home."

"It's tonight, then?"

"Yes, but only if you are up to it; I won't let my mother push you out if you're not able to get home safely."

After Peter had literally cleaned his plate down to the china, Natalia returned his clothing to him, freshly washed, repaired, and ironed. Even his father's coat had been mended. He wondered how she had been able to clean the blood from his things, given the amount that had been spilled. She added a pair of thick woolen stockings that she told him had been her father's.

"Won't your mother be angry about these stockings?"

"No," replied Natalia. "My mother never looks at my father's things. She has them all packed into a large trunk that she keeps under the bed in her room. She dusts it off from time to time, but I have never seen her open it. Besides, your stockings were so full of holes that I couldn't repair them."

Embarrassed by his lack of even the most basic articles of clothing, Peter changed the subject. "I've been looking out of your bedroom window today, and I think that I know exactly where your apartment is in relationship to mine. It's less than a kilometer, isn't it?"

Natalia nodded, "Yes, but if you're not up to the walk there, we can postpone this trip until you feel ready to go. I have already told my mother that I won't do anything to harm you, and she knows that I mean what I say."

"I *have to* get back to my mother and sister, Natalia. I can't wait any longer. Even now, I'm afraid of what I might find when I get there."

"We will go, then. Just let me get my things." Natalia hurried out of the room to dress for the cold and difficult walk to Peter's apartment.

Outside, the two stopped momentarily to adjust to the cold and blowing snow, and then set out for Peter's apartment. They walked slowly, arm in arm, as if they were lovers. Passers-by gave them little notice, but when cars approached, Natalia would turn and wrap her arms around Peter's neck, as if they were about to kiss. When the cars drove away, she would whisper encouragement to him, knowing that the trek, difficult for her, must be exhausting and painful for him. Finally, they turned the corner onto his street, and trudged the last few steps to the door of his apartment building.

"You live on the third floor, Katya once told me. I'll help you up the stairs and into your apartment so that I am sure that you will be all right, Peter."

"Natalia, you have been wonderful to me, but I can't ask you to face what I am afraid might be a very difficult, if not dangerous, situation with my father. He's very unpredictable, and I don't want him to hurt you if he loses his temper, which is what I think will happen when he sees me. After all, I've been gone more than three days after what should have been a short trip to buy some food for him."

Natalia stepped in front of Peter and without a car in sight, stood on tiptoe, wrapped her arms around his neck and kissed him gently on the lips. It was only a brief kiss, but it surprised him.

"If your assessment of your father is accurate, I don't want him to undo what my mother and I have done for you. Be still…I'm not afraid of your father. He may not get into a temper if I am there to explain to him what happened to you. Besides, you told me that the coat you are wearing, and *were wearing* on the night that you were shot, is your father's coat. Perhaps you were not the target at all. Have you ever thought of that?"

Peter opened the door to his apartment building where the familiar smells of cabbage and dust lay waiting to assail his nose. Dazed by Natalia's kiss, and her words of doubt as to whether his father, rather than he, had been the target of the men in the black Lada, Peter agreed to let Natalia help him up the three flights of stairs to his apartment. He was grateful to her for her insistence on helping him, because he knew that he might not be able to climb the stairs on his own.

Peter tapped out the coded knock that should let his mother and sister know that he was the one tapping on the door, and no one else. He heard a rush of footsteps, and the door was thrown open by both his mother and sister.

"Peter, *Petrosha,*" they cried in unison, tears filling their eyes.

They stood in the hallway, one on either side of him, and hugged him very hard. He didn't protest, even when the pain in his side became almost unbearable.

However, Natalia, who had up to that point been unnoticed, intervened on his behalf, "Please take care, Peter has been hurt, and you are squeezing him in the very place where he was wounded."

Again in unison, mother and daughter said, *"Wounded?"* and looked with astonishment at Peter.

Taking the lead, Natalia said, "Shouldn't we go inside?"

Once inside his apartment, Peter dropped into the nearest chair, completely spent by the walk from Natalia's apartment. The three, almost insurmountable, flights of stairs to his own apartment almost finished him. He looked around, expecting at any moment that his father would appear in an angry rush to grab him and beat him. Instead, all he heard were his mother's and sister's questions, words tumbling one upon the other.

Finally, he gathered enough strength to ask, "Where is Ivan?"

Katya spoke first, "Two men came on the same night that you disappeared, and forced him to go with them. He recognized them as two of his inquisitors from Lefortovo Prison."

"He begged them not to take him again, but they dragged him out into the foul weather without even a coat," his mother added.

Peter looked at Natalia in surprise, "You were right."

Chapter 3

"Petrosha…wake up, we're here." Misha shook Peter by the shoulder; then shook him again.

Peter sat forward with a start, then immediately regretted the quick movement. His head continued to throb, and the long-since swallowed tea threatened to reappear. He looked around, and realized that they had arrived in front of the arena where his team practiced, the Red Army Arena. The building was old, with a dull gray façade that was beginning to crumble for lack of attention and repair. Windows of the building that faced the street were cracked and taped in several places. A small pile of shingles from the awning at the front door was stacked next to the door. No one had bothered to pick them up when they fell, although most of the recent snow had been swept away from the entry door.

"It's time to do battle with Valeria." Peter did not feel up to the task.

"Yakov's girl?" asked Misha.

"One and the same."

Peter got out of the car slowly. The door of the Zhiguli groaned as an old man might if he were slapped. Peter grimaced at the sound, "Yevgeny could do with some lubrication for these doors."

Misha laughed and said, "Do you want me to go in with you, Petrosha?"

"Only if you like to be irritated, frustrated, and insulted. Valeria is very good at what she does. You might say it is her calling. She is a perfect fit for her job of protecting the team's assets, and does so as if they were her own."

"I'll watch the car, then." Misha gave Peter a wide grin.

Peter went to the door of the arena, pushed it open, and found that Valeria was in the process of shutting off the lights.

"Too late! You are too late. I told Grigory that I would wait for you only until eleven this morning, and here you are at eleven-oh-five." Her long, narrow face was twisted into a deep scowl that caused her chin to deviate slightly to the left.

Yakov must be blind, Peter thought, and then said, "The roads were treacherous this morning, and I got here as quickly as I could."

"Eleven a.m. is what Grigory told me. After that, I'm not responsible for you." Valeria was behind a counter with folded-back metal doors that she began to close.

"Wait, I have to get the airline tickets and the cash allowance for my trip!" Peter ran over to the counter, and vaulted over it to the other side.

Valeria's eyes bulged in fear, and her jaw became slack, "The Militia, I'll call the Militia, and you will have to leave!"

"Yes, call the Militia. That will allow them to come in and go over your books and loot the building. Oh yes, call the Militia. I welcome the chance to tell them about Yakov's little set-up with you. You're the source for his spending money, aren't you? What other possible reason could he have for even looking your way?"

Peter began to approach Valeria, and she cringed like a cornered animal. Tears flew out of her eyes as Peter came toward her.

"Please don't hurt me. I'll give you the tickets and the money, but then you have to go away. You will go away, and you won't hurt me, will you?"

Peter stopped his forward progress, "I'll go away when you give me the tickets and travel money. Otherwise, I'm going to sit right here," he said, pulling up a chair.

Valeria quickly scooted her thin body sideways past Peter's chair, unlocked a drawer in the desk, grabbed an envelope, and tossed it to Peter. She then attempted to make herself even smaller by pressing herself against the wall behind the desk.

"Please, you said you'd go if I gave you the tickets and money."

Peter opened the envelope, checked the tickets and counted the travel allowance. Scowling, he turned toward Valeria.

"This isn't the amount that Grigory said he would leave for my expenses. Where is the rest of the money?"

Visibly shaking now, Valeria attempted to speak, swallowed, and made a second attempt, "Yakov made me give him some of the money. He said that you weren't going to be able to join the team, and that the money wouldn't be missed. I just did what he told me to do. *Please don't hurt me.*"

Puzzled by her loss of control and evident fear, Peter rose from the chair. Using his forearm for balance, he again vaulted over the counter, and went over to the front door. As he opened the door, he looked back at Valeria, who, still shaking and crying, had not left the wall behind the desk.

Outside, Peter went quickly to the Zhiguli and got in. "Let's go."

"You got the tickets and your money then?" Misha's eyebrows lifted as he questioned Peter.

"Most, but not all of the money, and the tickets are there. Can you get me to Sheremetyevo in two hours? Aeroflot will take off at two this afternoon."

"No problem. I can get you there in plenty of time."

"So, let's get going."

Peter turned to look at the window in the door of the ice rink. Valeria was not looking out at him as he had expected. He wondered why she wasn't glaring out at him as she usually might do.

"How did things go with Valeria?"

"I'm not sure. At first she acted infuriatingly normal, but then she went into a crying fit, and acted as if she was scared to death of me."

"What did you do to scare the poor woman?"

"Nothing, really," Peter shrugged. "She was in the process of turning off the lights and locking the doors, and was acting nastily normal with insults and threats. But then, she sort of had a meltdown and began blubbering and shaking, begging me not to hurt her."

"Just a spontaneous meltdown? You didn't do anything to cause the change?" Misha began to grin.

"What are you getting at, Misha?"

"Well, did you lose your temper? Did you chase her around the desk? What did you do?"

"I had to stop her from locking the metal doors over the counter. Otherwise, I wouldn't have been able to get the tickets and money. All I did, really, was jump over the counter, and tell her that she had better give me the things that Grigory had left for me to pick up."

"Peter, you have no idea how you look when you get angry. You'd scare the devil himself. I have seen the way you look during a hockey game, or a brawl with the Lyubertsy thugs, and believe me, you can be very scary. It's a wonder that Valeria didn't fall over and die on the spot when you lost your temper."

Peter shook his head, "It wasn't like that. I didn't threaten her at all."

"You didn't need to make threats. All you had to do was scowl at her the way that you are now beginning to scowl at me. You can be very, very scary!" Misha laughed aloud.

The rest of the drive to the airport was mostly quiet, with some conversation about Misha's intentions toward Katya. He and Katya had been seeing each other for two years.

"I've been saving for two years now. By next August, Katya and I will be able to marry, that is, if she will have me, and you don't get angry with me and cancel the wedding. Of course, I plan to talk with your mother about it, too, but Katya and I have made some very good decisions, and we are truly made for one another." Misha looked over at Peter for his reaction.

Calm now, after the battle with Valeria, Peter smiled at Misha. "Katya has made a very good choice, and I know that you will take good care of her. She needs someone who is kind, decent, and committed to her, and you are that man."

"You really mean that, don't you?" Misha was touched.

"Da," replied Peter, realizing how important his approval was to Misha.

Sheremetyevo was, as usual, in a mess. The weather contributed its own impediment, while cars, trucks, buses, and other conveyances pulled up in front of arrival entrances to the terminal in a hodgepodge mass of confusion and noise. The Militia stood by and mostly watched the action without intervening until serious bodily harm was imminent. There were black market hawkers of various and sundry items, who were unmolested by the Militia, thanks to generous donations of goods, dollars, and even nearly- worthless rubles, among other things, to Militia members.

Peter wearily took all of this in as he thanked Misha for helping him to get to the airport. He grabbed his duffel bag that contained nearly all of his worldly possessions, gave Misha money for petrol for the return trip, waved, and entered the airport. He saw Misha looking at him through the now dirty windshield of Yevgeny's Zhiguli. Misha smiled and waved, and Peter again waved goodbye to him.

Inside, Peter looked around the terminal, located his flight on an electronic board, and checked to see whether it might actually run on time. There was only a small, one-hour delay listed, so he hefted his duffel bag and went over to the international boarding area. Looking out of the filthy windows, Peter saw that the airplane was already there. He wondered how long it would take the crew to clean and change the plane over for boarding. Then he laughed to himself. Cleaning was probably not going to be something that was routinely done on Aeroflot.

Peter found that he was beginning to be very hungry. But, his main concern was that he would not become ill on the airplane. He hated to fly, especially on Aeroflot. Maintenance on the airplanes was haphazard, and depended on which piece of equipment needed parts the most. He knew, however, that he had no choice if he was to join his team and actually play hockey. He would only earn his salary if he played. That was the way the Soviet Union took care of its athletes. Play for pay. No play, no pay, quite simple, really. Without this extra bit of earnings, he wasn't sure how his little family would survive for another year.

Finally, the boarding call came, and Peter stepped onto the airplane. Upholstery and painted surfaces were dingy from cigarette smoke, and the cabin reeked of the same. The air inside was visible: a dull blue-gray from exhaled smoke. Peter calculated the hours of the first leg of his journey, about twelve, he thought. Well, perhaps he could sleep through most of it. His throat became dry and sore almost immediately in the befouled air in the cabin of the airplane, adding to his misery. He had forgotten to buy anything to eat or drink, and he was sure that there would be no foodservice or drinks offered on the long flight to his next connection.

The engines on the jet coughed into life, and stewards called for a fastening of seatbelts. That is, if your particular seat has functioning seatbelts, thought Peter. His did not. Peter looked around the cabin of the old airplane, wondering if it would actually be able to fly for twelve hours. He was a pragmatist, and also a fatalist, and so decided to lie back in his seat and try to rest. The weariness he felt was bone-deep.

Peter awakened at approximately the point of no return, the midpoint of the flight. He did not feel refreshed, but was thankful that his nausea had not returned. The elderly lady sitting in the seat beside him introduced herself, and told him that she was going to visit her relatives in the United Kingdom. Peter congratulated her on such a nice opportunity. Mrs.Petrovna, he found, was generous. She shared her water and large teacakes that she had baked, with the nice young man sitting next to her who shared her name. Peter drank the water thirstily, but ate only one teacake, afraid that he might not be able to keep it down in his still unpredictable stomach. Mrs. Petrovna showed him photographs of her children and grandchildren, and he was astounded to find that she had twelve children, four boys and eight girls. Presently, her grandchildren numbered twenty-three, but she was hopeful of her last two children producing at least two each of their own. He was certain that Mrs. Petrovna's good fortune was at least in part due to Party connections, but he did not envy her seeming good fortune. There is a price for everything, he thought. Some of us are unwilling, perhaps unable, to pay the price the Party would extract eventually.

Fortified with the teacake and a little water, Peter again slept. This time, his rest was more comfortable. When he finally awoke, he found that Aeroflot was circling for a landing at Heathrow, his connection for the second leg of his flight. Great Britain was a very interesting place. He had played hockey here, in an exhibition game, for the Royal Family, no less. The Royals, however, had remained distant, ensconced in a private viewing room, high above the ice. Peter's sight was much better than most, and he could make out details of articles of clothing worn by the

Queen. Why would she wear such a ridiculous hat, or *any hat*, for that matter, to a hockey game? His team thrashed the Brits, winning six to one. He smiled at the recollection. He loved playing, and winning in hockey. On the ice, there was no sadness, unhappiness, or inequality. All were equal in the game. Only talent and strength counted. Nothing else mattered.

Peter's trek through Heathrow for his connecting flight was wearisome, and he was glad that he could immediately board his airplane on arrival at the gate. The cabin was clean, smokeless, and the bathrooms one of which he visited, were spotless. Briefly, he wondered why the Soviet Union could not arrange the same type of service on Aeroflot. Was capitalism, after all, the only answer? He recalled that German airplanes were as spotless and clean as the Brits'. For some time, he had thought that Germans were possibly more demanding than other cultures, but he decided that he was wrong. No, it seemed that the only culture that was out of step with the mainstream was the Russian culture. Why is that, he wondered?

British Airways prided itself on following departure times to the minute. The takeoff was smooth and uneventful. It was less noisy, rumbling, and less interior vibration of cabin walls than Aeroflot, he decided.

When the seatbelt lights were extinguished, stewardesses served beverages and sandwiches to passengers in an orderly and efficient way. Peter was impressed by the speed with which the stewardesses covered the large cabin filled with hundreds of passengers, until all were served. Peter asked for, and received, bottled water, only. He was still unsure of his ability to eat anything solid, and so drank the water instead of something with sugar or other nutrients.

Peter dreaded the overseas flight. Somehow, flying over the ground still left a little hope of survival if something went wrong. He believed that his chances for survival, in the event of a mishap while flying over the ocean, would greatly decrease above the water. For most of his life, he had lived in a landlocked world, with the exception of the time that he and his family had spent in the dacha by a beautiful lake near Tver, northeast of Moscow. He had enjoyed water sports such as swimming and diving when he was a child, but those times were merely dim memories. An ocean full of endless water held no appeal to him at all.

Try as he might on this flight, he could not sleep. He was certain that the cause of his restlessness was a mounting tension related to the reality of his predicament. Peter knew that he was physically not ready to play hockey. Whatever the illness was that he had contracted from his father, it had wrought havoc on his usual good health. In order to play his best he had to get back into playing form as soon as possible. He did not, however, have the luxury of time to do so. He would have to be fit and ready to play when his plane touched ground in the Indian City. There would be no 'second chances' because Yakov would see to that. Yakov would love to send him back to Russia without a penny of his salary paid to him. Grigory, helpless to defend Peter, would have to let him go. And *that* is my reality, he thought.

Peter was in the second, aisle, seat halfway back on the left side of the huge airplane. His tossing and turning, in attempts to get comfortable, caught the attention of a stewardess.

She approached him to ask in a clipped, very British accent. "Is there a problem?"

He understood and spoke English quite well. His mother, in addition to her professorial duties at Moscow University, had also taught both of her children to speak English. Eda believed that it was very important for them to do so in an ever-changing world where English was fast becoming the universal language.

"I am well, thank you." His reply was formal, and reflected the way in which he had been taught.

The stewardess smiled at him and said, "May I get a cup of coffee or tea for you? It would be no problem at all. A hot drink often relaxes a passenger enough so that he can rest a bit. What do you say?"

Peter followed what she had said, and told her, "A cup of hot tea with some honey would be most appreciated."

"Very good then, I'll be right back with your tea."

True to her word, the stewardess brought Peter a large, steaming cup of decaffeinated Earl Grey, "I thought it best to bring the decaffeinated kind so you wouldn't be further stimulated."

"Thank you for being so kind."

Peter made a conscious attempt to slow his anxious thoughts in order to relax. He sipped at the large cup of tea until he had downed it all. Then, leaning back in his seat, he turned his head to the side and quickly fell asleep.

A half-hour later, the stewardess came by with a blanket and carefully covered Peter up so as not to disturb his sleep. Poor fellow, she thought, his clothes are almost threadbare. With looks like his, he should be smiling from a clothing or toothpaste ad. Hearing another summons via the stewardess call bell, she went on her way.

The pilot's strong British accent was Peter's wake up call. "We have started a holding pattern over Kennedy which, we are told, should last for thirty minutes or less. There is the threat of a weather front moving in from the west that could cause some delays in connections. As always, British Airways will do its utmost to see that you make your connecting flights. Thank you for flying British Airways."

The overhead speaker crackled and then fell silent. Peter was very surprised to be awakened by the announcement from the pilot, and sat up in time to see an interesting sight, indeed. New York City, viewed from the air, was impressive by any standards, but was overshadowed by a huge black cloud behind it to the west that showed occasional flashes of lightning. Spectacular, thought Peter. Then, a sobering thought struck him. Was something he could not control going to defeat his attempt to join his team? He wondered, too, why there was a *thunderstorm* in December? He had never seen a December warm enough in Russia to allow a thunderstorm to occur. Apparently, this was not so in the United States.

After more than thirty-five minutes the holding pattern of flight began to wear on the passengers, and Peter could hear murmured complaints that were beginning to become louder. With the onset of the thunderstorm, the air became more turbulent, and the 'bumps' upward and downward were starting to cause squeals of fright from some passengers. Peter sat back in his seat and began to concentrate on maintaining his calm state. After all, how could he do otherwise? As always, when confronted by some overwhelming event, Peter retreated inside himself to gather his strength for whatever battle he might face.

The pilot's voice returned to the loudspeaker, "It looks like we are going to divert to BWI, since the storm is not so heavy there. I apologize for any inconvenience this might cause our passengers, but the tower has just given us the order for this diversion. Please report to the International Desk there, and ask for other continuing flights to your destinations. On board, the stewardesses will assist you as best they can. On the ground, there will be other assistance available through British Airways and the International desk. Again, thank you for flying British Airways."

BWI...what, or more to the point, *where* is BWI, wondered Peter? He felt the big plane accelerate from its holding pattern speed, and then begin to make a wide turn southward. Peter knew that if his new flight arrangements cost more than the original tickets, he might be stranded in a strange city. Briefly, he wondered how he had even been allowed to fly by himself out of the Soviet Union to rendezvous with his team. Certainly those who controlled his, and every other Soviet citizens' movements, should have considered what would happen if, for reasons beyond anyone's control, a flight might be diverted. What then? Peter began to perspire as his imagination flashed different situations with which he might be faced in a strange place called BWI.

Within ten minutes, the pilot returned to the loudspeaker: "It looks as though we might reach Baltimore/Washington International Airport ahead of the storm. The tower has told us that all flights into and out of the airport will be canceled after 12:00 noon Eastern Standard Time for at least the next four to five hours until the storm goes out to sea. In the meantime, British Airways will do its best to make acceptable arrangements for your continued journey."

This time, there was no, "Thank -you -for -flying—British—Airways" from the pilot. Peter guessed that the pilot might just have his hands full at the present time with the winds leading the storm, given the way the airplane bobbed up and down and then sideways like a cork on the open sea.

They touched down within twenty minutes of their diversion from Kennedy. As the passengers left the plane, stewardesses, pale with fatigue, pored over flight schedules in order to field questions of those who had missed their Kennedy connections. Peter did not bother to ask any questions. He decided that his best opportunity was to present himself to the International Desk as quickly as possible. To this end, he gathered his strength, threw his duffel bag over his shoulder and, following the signs, began to run through the terminal to the International desk. When he located the desk, he was winded, and verging on collapse. By this time, he was sure that he could not play for his team this evening. He looked at the clock above the desk. The time was 10:25 a.m. Eastern Standard Time. He knew that his destination maintained Eastern Standard Time year 'round because, out of curiosity, he had checked the time zone. Therefore, if he could not get a flight to Indianapolis within two hours, he would not be able to play this evening, and would forfeit his salary for the game.

There were two people ahead of him at the International Desk, and at first, he didn't see any progress. Then, he heard a woman's voice call, "Next," and he moved forward. He saw a very attractive black woman behind the counter. The woman looked bored, but was efficient as he told her of his situation. She immediately began searching her computer for an open seat on a flight to Indianapolis.

"You speak English very well, yet you are Russian," she said, looking at his passport.

Peter nodded. "My mother was a linguistics professor at Moscow University."

"Genchenko, Genchenko," she said, still looking at his passport, "I seem to remember a few years back some excellent treatises on democracy versus totalitarianism written by a Russian of the same name; a relative, perhaps?"

Peter, dumbfounded by this turn of events, nodded an assent. Though ashamed, he would not lie.

"My father," he said simply.

"I'm enrolled in a Russian studies program at George Washington University, and your father's work is excellent. Have you read his books?"

"No, they are banned in Russia." Peter looked down as he replied.

"Yes, you're right. I hadn't thought of that." The ticket agent now saw that she was embarrassing him.

"Well, you are one lucky young man. I will take you through our customs inspection here, because I can put you on a Delta flight to Indianapolis routed through Atlanta in thirty minutes. You won't have to change planes in Atlanta, and you will arrive in Indianapolis at 1:45 p.m. EST. You'll have to hurry though, because the gate is in terminal A."

Beaming, the ticket agent stamped Peter's new tickets, opened his duffel bag to inspect its contents, stamped the customs inspection in the appropriate spot on his documents, and sent him on his way, "Tell your father he has a fan in Baltimore!"

Peter, hurrying away from the International Desk, could not believe his good fortune, brought about by his father's fame, no less! His dash back through the terminal cost him dearly, and by the time he reached his gate, the nausea, headache, and dizziness had returned with a vengeance. The first boarding call had already been made. Peter stepped up to the ticket taker at the gate, boarded the plane, found his seat, stuffed his duffel bag in the overhead storage area, and then fell into his seat, spent. Rivulets of sweat made their way down his spine, and his hair was damp at the nape of his neck from his exertion. He put his head down between his knees briefly to keep from fainting, but lifted it again as someone touched him on the shoulder.

"I'm in the middle seat…sorry," a young girl of about twelve looked at him closely, "You okay?"

Peter nodded, feeling the thump, thump in his head become stronger with the motion, "Yes, I am oh kay." Peter put a very Russian emphasis on his English reply.

"Here, drink this. My mom gave it to me and told me to use it if I started to feel sick. I think you look worse than I feel."

The girl smiled a steely grin. She had a mouthful of hardware that Peter recognized as some kind of correction for misaligned teeth, connected by what appeared to be crisscrossing rubber bands. The pale skin of her face was sprinkled with freckles. Her large blue eyes, probably beautiful, he thought, were hidden behind huge glasses.

"What is it?" The contents of the bottle looked a vile, frog-like shade of green.

"My mom's a nurse, and she mixes this up for me every time I go to Atlanta to see my dad. They're divorced, so I travel a lot on airplanes. It used to be awful when I would get sick, so my mom invented this stuff. It's great for when you feel like you're gonna puke." The girl made a decidedly unladylike face, and acted as if she was vomiting.

Peter's stomach churned with the girl's pantomime, "Perhaps I will drink some of it later."

The girl leaned forward in her seat to more easily look into Peter's face, "You talk funny."

Peter agreed. "I do."

"You sound like that guy from James Bond who was an evil Russian. Is that what you are?"

"You are a bit young to be a fan of James Bond aren't you?"

"My mom loves Sean Connery. She says there's no one else who can play James Bond better. We always play videos of his James Bond movies. She also says there's no one in the world as sexy as he is, but I wonder what she'd say about you?"

Peter put his hand out, "Give me the bottle. I am sure that it can't make me feel any worse. It might just put me completely out of my misery."

"Yeah, sometimes my mom gets carried away with this stuff, but she said this batch was light."

"What is 'batch'?" Peter had not heard such an English word before.

"Boy, you really *must* be a foreigner! A 'batch' is something that you mix up. It could be something to drink, or even something like cookies. Haven't you ever heard of a 'batch' of cookies? It's like, a *bunch* of something, a whole bunch, only it's a batch!"

Peter, only catching every other word of the girl's rapid patter, decided that she would continue her explanation if he didn't indicate that he understood what she was trying to tell him, so he told her, "Oh, now I see. Thank you for your excellent illustration."

She laughed out loud, opening her mouth widely to show all the hardware therein, "We 'illustrate' in art class, but we 'explain' when we want to tell someone how to do something." She gave him a sidelong glance.

The pilot interrupted the girl's interrogation of Peter, "We've been cleared for takeoff. However, we're going to have to fly a bit of a different flight pattern to fly around the storm front. In case you might be wondering, thunderstorms *do* sometimes occur in winter if the temperature's right. It's the old warm front cold front thing. Anyway, we should be touching down in Atlanta by 11:30 a.m., Eastern Daylight Time. If our schedule works well, we should have those of you who are going on to Indianapolis there by 1:45 p.m., Eastern Standard Time, and then we will take our Chicago passengers west with us. Everything depends on our turnaround time on the ground in Atlanta. Keep your seat belts fastened, please. We may have a bit of turbulence after takeoff until we fly around this front. Delta thanks you for your business."

"Oooh, it's going to be *bumpy*!" The girl grimaced, showing only half of the hardware in her mouth this time.

Peter decided that he would try a tactic to calm the girl, "You know," he said, "airplane rides are much smoother when you read a magazine and remain completely quiet."

"Y'think?" the girl asked.

"Absolutely."

"Before I quit talking, tell me your name."

"Peter."

"Well, Pete, my name is Lindsey, and you are about to witness the *most* quiet that I've ever been." She made a motion as if to zip her mouth closed.

Peter put a finger to his lips to assure her that he would be quiet, too.

Actually, the flight wasn't at all bad. The only turbulence the entire time was a few minutes after takeoff when they encountered some headwinds that had spun off from the towering storm front that glowered at them from the north, making menacing dark faces in its swirling clouds.

Peter noticed with relief that Lindsey had fallen asleep. He opened her green brew and sniffed, then closed it quickly. He was certain that he would not be able to fool his nose long enough to drink any of it. To get comfortable, he stuck his long legs out into the aisle, but instead of resting, he used the time to review the playing schedule for his tour. There were five games playing the U.S., Sweden, Canada, Norway, and Finland.

He hoped that he would be up to the task. He knew that if his team played well, there would probably be a reward from the Soviet Games Authority for winning the games. He counted on winning, because he knew that the additional earnings would be helpful to his family.

Self-doubts crept into his thinking, but he wisely brushed them aside. If ever he needed to be positive in thought and deed, now was the time. Still, he knew that he was not physically one hundred percent ready to play, and he *needed* to be. Grigory would only tolerate a little problem, not a big one. If he showed up unable to play, Yakov might see to it that Grigory put him on the next plane back to Russia.

Yakov loved to scare Peter with one word: Afghanistan, which he repeated often in Peter's presence. Sometimes Yakov would look at him and just mouth the word and smile an evil smile. Peter knew that if Yakov had his way, Peter would most certainly end up as a lowly foot soldier in Afghanistan. This isn't doing me any good, I must think of something else, he decided, and then involuntarily shuddered at the prospect of being shipped off to the barbaric place that had ruined the lives of so many young Russian men.

Peter cherished the quiet aboard the airplane. It seemed that everyone had used the flight from BWI to Atlanta to relax and count their blessings over finding a flight that wasn't canceled due to the weather. The towering storm was still visible when he looked back out of the window toward the north. It reminded him of some of the storms that had swept over the family dacha on the lake near Tver when he was a child. A thunderstorm with jagged forks of lightning over flat, open Russian countryside was spectacular, indeed.

To his surprise, Peter even began to feel a little hungry. He noticed that the flight attendants had finally started some type of service, probably beverage only, after the turbulence had died down. When the attendant got to him, all Peter could think of to drink that would not upset his already queasy stomach was water, so he asked for a bottle of Perrier. Lindsey continued to snooze next to him, and he asked for a soft drink for her, as well, so that she would not feel left out when she awakened. He recalled how he had felt at her age when his father had caused him to feel left out of things, most things, he thought to himself. He couldn't really remember any warmth or kindness directed toward him from his father. There had only been conflict between them.

The pilot was as good as his word, and the airplane rolled into Atlanta's Hartsfield Airport, International Terminal, gate 6, at 11:28 a.m. The stewardess announced connecting flights with gate numbers, and told those passengers who were going on to Indianapolis to please stay put. Ordinarily, all passengers would have to disembark. The flight crew was going to make every effort to maintain their scheduled arrival in Indianapolis, she assured them.

Lindsey, who had awakened a few minutes earlier, and renewed by her nap, began talking non-stop again to Peter. "Thanks for getting the Coca-Cola for me, Pete. Did you know that a lot of Atlanta was built with Coca-Cola money? My dad says if it weren't for Coke money, Atlanta wouldn't have so many tall buildings. Well, I gotta go. This is where I meet my dad." She got up to retrieve her bags from the overhead compartment.

"Let me help you," Peter said, as he stood up to open the overhead compartment for Lindsey.

"You're even taller than Sean! I can't *wait* to tell my mom about you." Lindsey gave Peter her most toothsome, and therefore metallic, grin.

"Sean?" he asked, looking puzzled.

"Connery, Sean Connery. *You* know, like we were talking about James Bond before. You're taller than he is, I can just tell."

"Well," Peter shrugged, "Height is not so important."

"My mom's six feet tall, so *she* thinks height is very important. She hates it when one of her dates is shorter than she is."

"Dates?" Peter was again puzzled, thinking of the fruit of the date tree.

"Yeah, when she goes out with somebody, like to a movie or dinner, y'know?"

"Uh, yes. Now I see what you mean." He did not have a clue as to what Lindsey was talking about, but he smiled down at her.

"Oh, wow! You even *smile* better than Sean." Lindsey hugged herself and rocked back and forth.

Peter reached into the overhead compartment and brought out two bags that seemed to match. They were covered with brightly colored stickers and pictures of what he supposed were celebrities. He recognized one of the pictures as the actor Sean Connery in his best James Bond tuxedo, complete with a rather large handgun. Peter smiled, thinking to himself that he had just overshadowed Sean's appeal to the twelve-year-old girl beside him.

A stewardess hurried over to them, "Is this young lady departing the plane?"

"Uh-huh," Lindsey nodded.

"You need to hurry up a bit. We're trying to get all departing passengers cleared from the airplane so that we can prepare for the next flight." The stewardess looked up and smiled at Peter, tilting her head to the side as she did so.

"I'm ready to go, just back up a little." Lindsey nudged the stewardess with her elbow then turned to Peter, and used a stage whisper to tell him that the stewardess was flirting with him.

"Goodbye Lindsey." Peter took her hand in his for a moment, and bowed slightly toward her.

"Bye, Pete. I hope I see you again sometime." Lindsey blushed, then turned and hurried down the aisle.

"Lindsey, just one moment," Peter called out to her. "Here is your green potion. I did not need it, after all."

She turned around and grinned, "Keep it for the next time you fly. I don't think it ever spoils. Besides, if you smelled it, how could you tell? 'Bye Pete." She waved, and then hurried off the airplane.

Delta Flight 1212 touched down at 1:42 p.m. at the Weir-Cook Airport in Indianapolis, just as it started to snow huge, wet flakes that clung to the wings of the airplane. The pilot gave his robotic announcement that he was glad that the flight had been comfortable, uneventful, and on time.

"Thank you for flying Delta," the pilot said.

Peter jumped up from his seat when the seatbelt light went off. Grabbing his coat and duffel bag, he turned toward the front of the airplane, impatient to get off, and get to the place called Market Square Arena. Slowly, the airplane emptied, and Peter made his way down the aisle. As he entered the terminal, he recognized Yakov Popov standing in the waiting area.

Peter approached him, "How did you know of my arrival?"

"Valeria contacted me and told me how you threatened and scared her. You will pay for your actions." Yakov's face was twisted with hatred.

"My airplane connections were all changed around because of a storm. How did you know I'd be here at this time?" Peter was persistent with the ugly little man.

"Grigory checked all the flights. Of course you know how worried he would be to think that his team would have to play hockey without you. He leaves nothing to chance, so he asked the American who is heading up the sports medicine team if he would trace your itinerary. The fool did so, and now you are here. You must be suited up and ready to play by 7:00 p.m. tonight. You don't look as if you are able to play. Still have your virus?" Yakov gave Peter a wicked smile.

"I will be ready when the time comes." Peter was terse, and did not wish to give Yakov any more information than he had to.

Outside the terminal, Yakov hailed a cab. "I told Grigory that I did not think you would be able to play tonight. By the looks of you, I know that I am correct." For emphasis Yakov laughed a short, harsh laugh.

In the cab, Peter closed his eyes. His headache had returned. What if I can't play tonight? Fear ran through him like an electric current. The nausea had returned, as well. Every time he opened his eyes, Yakov was staring at him with hatred evident in his gaze.

After a swift ride around what seemed to be a circular three-lane racetrack completely choked with cars whose drivers competed for supremacy, they arrived in the downtown area of the large city. Peter was impressed by the cleanliness of the streets and building fronts. Obviously, the Americans liked cleanliness. Of course, his most recent measures were the familiar, very dirty streets of Lyubertsy and the clutter of Moscow in the winter. This city called Indianapolis looked sanitized compared to Lyubertsy. Prosperity was evident in every window, doorway, and building. Not so in Lyubertsy; prosperity bypassed it quickly, afraid to tarry for fear that some mayhem might ensue.

"Go around to the athlete's entrance of Market Square Arena." Yakov told the cabdriver.

Peter was puzzled by the strange name of the arena. Market Square sounded more like a farm market than a place where athletic competition took place. Then he saw the huge domed edifice before him. Is this the place, he wondered? The cabdriver had swiftly brought them around a large circle in what seemed to be the center of the city. He looked at the monument standing in the middle of the circle from several angles as the cab sped around it. He read to himself the English phrases written on the monument. Americans also liked war memorials he decided. Peter had always been impressed with the monuments of Red Square. Of course this monument was not on so grand a scale as those in Red Square, and not nearly so colorful. As Peter looked upward, he also took notice of the snowfall. The ground was covered with several inches now. Just like Russia, he decided. Will I ever be able to escape the cold and snow?

Chapter 4

Sunday December 14, 1986

"Damn, damn, *damn it,* Myron, you stuck me with the Neanderthals!"

She pounded the steering wheel with one hand to punctuate her displeasure, while loosely holding onto it with the other. The odd-shaped Mercury Cougar sped quickly on the snow-covered passing lane of I- 465, the beltway around Indianapolis, before catching I-65 to head toward the downtown area. But her little silver bullet, as she called it, was not going as fast as she needed to go. Late as usual, she was trying to make up for lost time, but making very little progress due to the snow and heavy traffic on the main artery loop around the city.

"Now wait a minute, Nik, *you* volunteered to help with the International Winter Games. I didn't promise you anything, except that I would try to get one of the women's volleyball teams for you. It's Garibaldi's fault, not mine. He changed everything around, including the assignments. The reason that he gave me for the switch was that you speak Russian and that would help in working with the Russian hockey team."

Finally reaching her exit, Nikola Kellman turned to her passenger and asked, "But did you protest at all? Of course not! It wouldn't be politically correct to argue with that greasy, bald-headed, womanizing idiot, now would it?"

"Nik, you know that he can make or break my senior year residency. He's not above giving me all the shit-work cases he can find so that he can make my already miserable life unbearable. Besides, why do you only call me Myron when you're mad at me? It's Ron, Nik, *Ron*. No one else calls me Myron...well, just your mother." Red-faced, he folded his arms across his chest, turned his head toward the side window, and fell silent.

Speaking to the back of his head, the thick dark hair curling at the nape of his neck, Nik said, "Yesterday was a nightmare. Grigory, the coach, was okay, and his shadow, Vladimir, was too, but that little weasel, Yakov Popov, the Team Interpreter, was in my face every five minutes trying to tell me what to do. I finally asked him if he had a medical degree, and he backed off, but he watched me like a hawk the whole day. He kept telling me about the 'star' of the team who hasn't arrived yet. For some reason, I think the bastard was being sarcastic, because every time Grigory was within earshot, Yakov would start in about the 'star' of the team being absent. Also, I heard some pretty heavy give-and-take in Russian between the two of them about the 'star'. I think Yakov hates the guy's guts, but I couldn't pick up on any reason. Finally, Grigory turns around to the weasel and shouts at him about whether or not he wants to win these games, and says he knows the consequences if they don't. The weasel shut up then."

"I love your colorful language, Nik, but sometimes I think that I'm engaged to a longshoreman masquerading as a beautiful and talented young woman. How can I ever take you home to the folks?" Ron turned back to his fiancee and smiled.

"Bullshit."

"See what I mean?" He shrugged in resignation.

Nik pulled her silky, straight, sable-brown hair behind one ear. Ron found the gesture rather endearing. He liked her hair just at shoulder length, the way she wore it. He had always favored tall women who were very, very, blond. How had he ended up engaged to a dark-haired, dark-eyed spitfire of a woman just a shade over five-feet-four inches tall? He thought about the first time that he had seen her. She had been having a heated discussion with another med student about a rehab approach for an athlete after knee surgery. As she warmed to her subject, he watched her eyes light up. He couldn't help himself; he entered the discussion with questions of his own that he posed to her. Immediately, the bright eyes turned toward him, lighting him up inside. He had been struck by lightning, and had pursued her for months before she would even agree to have lunch with him.

"I'm sorry, Ron. Sometimes I say things that I shouldn't. But GariBALDi *is* an idiot, *and* a womanizer, and you know it. You know why, too. Remember how I told you he summoned me to his office for a special project, kept me waiting, then breezed in loosening his tie, and unbuttoning his shirt to show off his hairy chest? What a moron! He pitched some deal where he wanted me to do research with him, but I had already heard how he'd moved on some of the other female med students, so I told him that I didn't have time, and wasn't interested in his special project. He was livid! I could tell by the squint of his eyes that he would cause me problems if he could. Well, the bastard succeeded; the Neanderthals are certainly a problem."

"Look Nik, these games will only last for a little over a week. Can't you just accept your fate, and learn something from the athletes? I would be willing to bet that you'll learn a lot from the Russian athletes. Maybe this will all be worth it in the long run."

Nik looked at Ron with a wry smile, "Mister, you should be a used car salesman."

"No money down, and a dollar a week, because old Ron *needs* the money." Ron parodied a popular local television commercial for used cars.

Nik pulled into her designated parking space at Market Square Arena. There were, after all, a few perks for being the team physician for the Russian hockey team. She quickly jumped out of the car and headed for the medical staff door.

Waving at Ron, who hadn't completely gotten out of the car yet, she called, "Lock it, will you? I've got to get inside and get started. See you at six. The first game is at seven. 'Bye!" The door to the entrance slammed behind her.

Inside the building, Nik made her way to the training room assigned to the Russians. Surprisingly, it was one of the best in the building. She decided that this was a way to show them how nice it is in the good old U.S. of A.

She hit the double doors at a jog, shrugged out of her coat, throwing it down on her desk, put on her lab coat, and she was ready for the Neanderthals. Several athletes were already in the room, preparing for practice by whirl pooling, taping, or stretching. Thank God for Mickey and Tom, the trainers assigned to her. They were professional, helpful, and really knew their stuff. Both had degrees from Anderson University, a college known nationally for its Athletic Trainer's program, in the small city of Anderson just north of Indianapolis.

Nik was behind a curtain examining the knee of Ilya, one of the right wings on the team, who had a painful left knee, when she heard some commotion near the door of the training room.

"Dr. Kellman, Dr. Nik Kellman. Is Dr. Kellman here?" Yakov was shouting, and the sound of his voice immediately irritated Nik.

Nik looked out from behind the curtain, "I'm working on one of the athletes. Have a seat and I'll be right with you." She observed that there was a rather tall and poorly dressed young man standing with Yakov; actually towering over the weasel.

"This cannot wait. I want to introduce you to the star of the team, Peter Ivanovich Genchenko." Yakov's voice was dripping with sarcasm.

Ilya said in Russian, "Petrosha? He's arrived? We are saved!" His smile was broad, and he hadn't a clue that Nik could understand his Russian words.

Other athletes called out in Russian, "Peter! Hey, Peter, you're here!"

Well, Nik thought, at least the *players* are glad to see this guy. "Mickey, can you do a work-up and taping on Ilya's knee? He's a negative drawer sign, and there's no swelling or bruising. I guess I'd better go see what the fuss is all about."

"Sure, Doc, any special tips for the knee taping?"

"No, just the usual serpentine and circle, and make sure it's tight, but not a tourniquet, okay?"

Mickey hung his head in mock shame because the Doc had had to re-tape another athlete's knee when he had taped it too tightly. He raised his head and grinned sheepishly at the doctor.

"You never forget anything, do you?"

Nik smiled back at Mickey, "Nope."

She walked over to Yakov and the young man, "So the star is here, is he? We'll have to do a quick history and physical, a little blood work, and a baseline treadmill. I don't want any surprises when he gets out there to skate." Nik looked around, "Where's Grigory? I thought that he was going to the airport with you."

Yakov shrugged elaborately. "Grigory asked me to escort Genchenko from the airport. After all, the coach cannot be bothered with such a lowly task, and Vladimir was busy as well. They have other, more important things to do."

Somehow, Yakov always seemed to put a verbal sneer into everything that he said to Nik. Perhaps it was just the way he spoke English, but she doubted that.

Nik turned to introduce herself to the new arrival. She looked up into his face, and was puzzled by the look of surprise that she saw there. All of a sudden, he slumped forward, toward her. Yakov, with a look of distaste and contempt, stepped away from them. Vladimir, the assistant coach, approached but did not offer to help. Instead, he moved beside Yakov.

Nik shouted, "Mickey, Tom, over here, quick!" The young man's weight was beginning to push her backward.

"Right here, Doc!" Mickey placed his arms around the fallen man's torso, immediately freeing Nik of the man's full weight.

Skidding to a halt in front of the group, a large young man said, "Doc!" Tom's eyes were wide with concern. "You okay Doc?" He threw his massive bulk into the task of moving the man's remaining weight off of her.

"I'm fine, I'm fine. Let's get this guy over to a cart where I can examine him. Mickey, put a call in for Dr. Ron Michael. Tell him to get over here right now! His pager number is over there on the board." She nodded her head toward her desk area. "Damn it, get moving, *now*!"

Tom threw Peter over one shoulder and carried him to a training table. Nik quickly pulled the privacy curtain as Tom put Peter on the table gently. Several athletes were standing around, trying to see what was happening. Yakov opened the curtain, and came in to have a look at the athlete on the table. He seemed pleased by what he observed, and his smile looked wicked. This cemented Nik's bad opinion of him, and made her certain that, for some reason, Yakov really hated the guy.

"Tom, please escort *Yakov* out of here. Take him over to the cafeteria, or better yet, set him up in the VIP suite. Convince him to stay there." Nik returned Yakov's contemptuous stare with one of her own, something her assistants called her freight train stare because, they said, it would stop a locomotive in its tracks.

Tom smiled widely, "Sure, Doc, be glad to. C'mon Mr. *Yakov*, we're goin' for a walk." Tom took Yakov under one arm, lifting him up on tiptoe, and dragged him toward the door. Yakov was so surprised and intimidated by the big man, he didn't protest at all.

Nik quickly made an initial assessment of the fallen athlete's status. Starting with the head, she found that his pupils were equal and reactive to light, no papilledema, no nicking of vessels, no hemorrhage noted. His ears were clear, tympanic membranes pink, without bulging, exudate, or shininess. His mouth gave no indication of injury or bleeding. His neck was soft, without rigidity, and the lymph nodes were mostly soft and clear. His temperature was 99.4 degrees Fahrenheit, as taken in the ear. Then add a degree for the actual reading of 100.4. Blood pressure was 90 systolic over 60 diastolic. She frowned; that's low. His heart rate was 94, rapid but strong, and without arrhythmia. S1, S2, and S3 cardiac sounds auscultated with the bell of her stethoscope were good.

His lungs were essentially clear, although it sounded as if he might have a resolving pneumonia in the lower left lobe. His respirations were 28, rapid, but in keeping with his elevated heart rate and temperature. She palpated and listened with the diaphragm setting on her stethoscope to his abdomen in all quadrants, stomach tympany, liver dullness, abdomen soft, all within normal limits. The abdomen was essentially negative. What's going on here? She checked the mucous membranes in his mouth, and then pulled down on both lower eyelids to check for color and moisture. She found light pink conjunctivae with little moisture there. Next, she pinched a fold of skin on his forearm; it remained pinched up for more than fifteen seconds, indicating dehydration.

This guy is very dry, and very pale, she thought, as she methodically checked him over for any injury that might have caused him to lose consciousness. Brushing his thick, overlong, dark blond hair away from his face, she checked his pupils, and they were equal and reactive to light. His ears were clear. There was no indication of a brain insult. Her puzzlement increased. She was deep in thought when Mickey returned.

"Mickey, I want to do a blood glucose on this guy, stat. When I touch him, he feels kind of shaky, trembling and slightly diaphoretic. Maybe what we have is a low blood sugar in addition to some dehydration. Let's roll him over. I want to get a good look at his back. Maybe there's a rash or something there. Did you contact Dr. Michael?"

"No such luck, Doc. He didn't answer the page. Nancy's on the desk and said she'd let us know when he calls."

Damn! Where is he? Nik was frustrated. She could really use some help right now. They rolled Peter to one side while Nik checked his back and hips. She had already checked his arms. No needle marks or bruises there. She palpated around his kidneys. Nothing there, either, she decided. His skin was clear, and without rashes or eruptions. There were, however, 'stripes' or marks indicating old injuries low on his back. There was also what appeared to be an old gunshot wound, as evidenced by a round and puckered scar on the right side at about waist level. *Whoa*, she thought, briefly wondering about the origin of those injuries. Very perplexing, she thought, but who really knows what it's like to live in Russia?

Nik said, "Now let's roll him toward me. I want to check his flank on this side."

As they rolled Peter back toward Nik, she looked down into his face, and saw a single tear roll from the corner of one eye. For some unknown reason, this observation brought on a feeling of inexplicable sadness inside her. Why is he so sad? She gently wiped the tear from his cheek. When he moved slightly, she realized that he was awake.

Nik began speaking quietly to him in Russian, "Gdye bolna? *Where does it hurt?* Have you been sick recently? Just nod your head if you have been. We're going to draw some blood in order to determine your blood sugar level and your electrolytes. Will you give your consent for the blood work? Are you diabetic?"

He sighed deeply and opened his eyes to look directly into hers. His eyes were very unusual because of their green-gold color, like that of a lion.

"Minya rvalo. *I have been sick.* The answers are yes and no. Yes to the first question and no to the last. I haven't been able to eat or drink very much for the last few days because I have been sick. I am not a diabetic, and you have my permission to draw blood."

His voice was surprisingly deep, rich, and mellow for someone who appeared to be so young. You have beautiful eyes, she thought. I wonder how many hearts you've broken?

Then, disturbed by her momentary lapse, and very surprised at herself, Nik said abruptly, "Let's get that blood drawn, Mickey."

Mickey stepped around the end of the cart, supplies in hand. He drew several different colored tubes of blood to complete all the testing that the doctor had ordered.

"I'll be right back, Doc. It shouldn't take more'n fifteen minutes, or so for most of these tests."

The laboratory was immediately adjacent to the training room, and technicians were on duty all hours that the athletes were on the premises. The quick turnaround from the lab was crucial to treating the athletes.

"Eemya? *What's your name?* Do you know what day this is?" Nik was testing the athlete for alertness and orientation.

"Minya zavoot Pyotr. *My name is Peter*, and this is Sunday, December 14th, 1986." He didn't tell her his surname.

"Well, Peter, I think you may have low blood sugar and dehydration secondary to whatever your illness of the past week might have been. Coach Grigory told me before you arrived that you had just lost your father. He also said that you have had some type of influenza. You may have a resolving pneumonia in your left lung, too, because there were some rales and ronchi, uh, rumblings there. Here's what I think we should do: First, we'll get a chest X-ray to rule out pneumonia, then I'd like to do some fluid and electrolyte replacement to get your blood sugar and electrolytes where they need to be. I'm sure you'll start feeling better pretty quickly after that. Have you had some nausea, muscle pain and headache along with your dizziness?"

"Yes." Peter nodded his head, bringing on the pain that he had felt earlier. Putting his hand to his head, he wondered if he would ever learn not to do that.

"Still hurts, doesn't it? I think those symptoms are a result of your dehydration and low blood sugar. Ah, here are the stat lab results. Thanks Mickey."

"You're welcome, Doc." Mickey liked being helpful.

Nik looked quickly up and down the reports, "Peter, you're amazing! Your blood sugar is 40, and you are sodium and potassium depleted. Your hemoglobin and hematocrit are elevated, indicating hemoconcentration, and your total protein and albumin are low; you're not eating well. You must be Superman to even be talking to me. Well, let's start an IV for replacement therapy. Do I have your consent?"

Peter cleared his throat, "Yes. Uh, doctor? Will I be able to play tonight?"

Nik started to shake her head no, "Not tonight, but maybe tomorrow if you're feeling better."

Peter's eyes widened as he said, "Please, I've *got* to play tonight. Yakov will cause me a great deal of trouble, may even get me sent home, if it looks like I'm not going to be able to play."

Nik looked intently at Peter and realized that what she saw in his face was fear. "Are you really worried that Yakov could have that much influence with your coach? He's only the team interpreter, isn't he?"

Peter said only one word. "Nyet." *No.*

Again Nik looked intently at Peter, trying to understand what he was telling her. If Peter's last answer meant anything, she thought, Yakov was probably some kind of an agent, accompanying the team in order to keep them all in line. That would answer her questions as to why Grigory, the coach, tolerated Yakov's continual interference in all issues with the team.

After a moment's pause she replied, "There's no guarantee that you'll play tonight, but here's what we can try. Let's run some fluid through you to normalize your electrolytes and rehydrate you, give you some easy-to-digest carbohydrates with a little pre-digested protein and fat, give you a rubdown, let you sleep a couple of hours, then see what we have to work with when you wake up. Are you agreeable?"

Peter managed a smile, "Yes, I'm sure that I'll be ready to play."

"Good, then that's settled."

Switching to English and turning to her assistant, she said, " Mickey, give this athlete a rubdown while his I.V. is going, give him some liquid carbohydrates with light protein and fat orally, maybe a half-liter, let him sleep for about two hours, then we'll reassess his condition. I don't want anyone, and that includes his coach, and *especially Yakov,* in here without my permission, okay?"

"Everything will be fine, Doc." Mickey was always an optimist.

Looking at Peter, but continuing to speak in English to Mickey, Nik said, "Oh, and shave his head, too."

Mickey laughed, "You really mean that Doc?"

Peter's eyes flickered momentarily, and Nik poked him in the chest with her forefinger, "Gotcha!" She grinned playfully.

"What is gotcha?" he asked in Russian.

Nik replied in English, "It means that I've caught you in the act."

She laughed, but it was not a derisive laugh. It just showed that the doctor was a person with a strong sense of humor.

"English?" Peter asked Nik in her own language.

"English. I was pretty sure that you were listening and understanding everything that I was telling Mickey about your condition. Your body language gave you away."

"I see. And you aren't Russian, either, are you?"

"Oh no, *I'm* not Russian, but my mother is. She made sure that my brothers and I learned her native tongue. My father is German, and I can speak his language, too. Given the history between Russia and Germany, you might say that I have an interesting family. Well, let's get going on your treatment. Time's a'wastin'."

Puzzled by the doctor's last comment, Peter asked, "What does awastin mean?"

"It's just vernacular, you know, common usage; slang. It means that time is going fast, so we had better get going."

"Yes, slang, I have heard of that term." Peter's mother had told him that much of the commonly used English language in America included heavy usage of slang.

Mickey came over to the training table with an intravenous set-up, "You want to do the stick, Doc, or should I?"

"I'll do it, but let's take him over to the rub-down room first. We can just wheel him on this cart. That way, if he still feels light-headed, we won't risk a fall." Nik tucked the intravenous set-up under the blanket covering Peter.

Mickey nodded, and began moving the cart out of the curtained area, and into the main training room. All of the athletes who had been there previously, plus others who had come in afterward, were still waiting to see what had happened to Peter.

"Petrosha! Are you playing tonight?" One of the athletes came forward.

"Ilya, I am fine. We'll play together tonight. The doctor has fixed me up as good as new." Peter waved to all of them as Mickey and Nik rolled the cart out of the door.

When they reached the rubdown room, Nik tried the door, "Damn, it's locked. Wait here and I'll run back and get my keys." Nik turned and jogged off at a fast pace.

"Okay, Doc. We aren't goin' anywhere." Mickey called after her.

Peter watched as the doctor quickly ran down the hall, her hair flying back. Her strides were rhythmic and graceful. She must be some kind of athlete, too, he decided. He had never seen a doctor run that way before. Most of the doctors that he had dealt with were in very poor condition in comparison to the athletes they treated. This doctor seemed to be the exception. Peter laid back and closed his eyes for what he thought was a brief interval, and was surprised when he heard Dr. Kellman returning.

Nik came back at a dead run. Skidding to a stop, she said breathlessly, "I hope I picked up the right key."

She had. Inside the room, Nik prepared Peter's arm for the needle and deftly inserted it, hitting the vein on the first try. He was surprised that there was so little pain.

She started the intravenous infusion, and said, "He's all yours, Mickey. Take good care of him. I'll be back to check on him in an hour or so. You've got my pager number, right? Call me if the I.V. infiltrates or you have any problems with it. Keep it going at about one-fifty, or two at the most."

"Yeah, Doc, I'll keep an eye on the arm. No infiltration allowed. Don't worry, he's gonn'a be great. See ya' later."

Nik hurried back to the main training room. Everywhere she looked, there were athletes waiting for her opinion, or treatment, or encouragement. This is overwhelming, she thought.

"Who's first?" Nik turned to see Dimitri as he stepped forward. Another knee, she thought.

When Nik saw Tom return, she was relieved to know that she would have help in getting the athletes ready for the evening game. There were so many things to be done.

Over her shoulder, she said, "Okay, Tom, pick one and let's get started."

In the rubdown room, Mickey briefly left to get the carbohydrate, protein, and fat solution for Peter. He returned with the mixture, ready to drink in a bottle with a straw. He held it out to Peter and told him to drink all of it, but slowly. Peter liked the taste of the solution, but wondered if it would stay down. His headache was less painful in the short time that the intravenous solution had begun to drip into his vein. Perhaps the doctor was right after all.

"Are ya' finished with the drink?" Mickey was across the room, preparing something for the rubdown.

"It's almost gone." Peter decided that the drink had actually tasted very good, and had gone down easily, leaving no feelings of nausea.

"Lie down on your stomach, and I'll start with your back and legs. You're gon'na enjoy this. All the athletes like rubdowns."

Peter turned over onto his stomach and closed his eyes. Mickey started with Peter's neck and shoulders then began to methodically work each muscle down his back. Peter relaxed, and, in a dream-like state, relived his embarrassing entrance into the training room.

Yakov had talked incessantly and hatefully to him during the drive from the airport to the arena, and Peter's head had felt as though it might burst from pressure and pain. When they finally stepped into the training room and Yakov had called out loudly for Dr. Kellman, Peter's ears were buzzing, and his vision had begun to fade. The last thing he remembered was looking into the face of a beautiful young woman. What startled him about the face was that it was a very *Russian* face; high cheekbones, perfectly oval, with dark eyes that slanted slightly upward at the outer corners. When he regained consciousness, the same woman was speaking to him in Russian.

By that time, Peter had lost all hope of being able to play with his team. Everything had been too much of a struggle. Obstacle after obstacle had been thrown in his path, and he had tried to overcome each of them. He knew, however, that he could not overcome his health problems by himself. He felt alone and defeated until the woman started talking to him in his own language. When he opened his eyes, he saw that it was the doctor that Yakov had been calling for, Dr. Kellman.

She had smiled reassuringly at him, and then rapidly questioned him in Russian about recent illnesses or diabetes. Unaccountably, he began to have a return of some small hope that he might be able to recover enough to perform. If only she will help me, he thought, I should be able to do what I need to do.

Reliving the experience filled him with hope, and, feeling warm and comfortable as his massage progressed, Peter fell into a deep sleep. When Mickey realized that the athlete had fallen asleep, he stopped the massage and covered him with a soft blanket from the warmer. Mickey wiped the rubdown oil from his hands, washed them, checked Peter's I.V., and grabbed a timer from the counter before he dimmed the lights in the room. He then stepped outside the door, closing it quietly behind him. He dragged a chair over to the door, set the timer for two hours, and sat back for a little relaxation in his otherwise busy day.

When Nik finished with the last of the athletes, she glanced at her watch, and was surprised to see that more than two hours had elapsed. It was nearly time for the Russian team to do its warm-ups before the beginning of the game they would play against the Swedes. I'd better go see how Pete's doing, she thought. She laughed at herself when she realized that she had called the athlete Pete instead of Peter.

"Well," she said aloud, "he looks more like a Pete to me, with his thick, wildman Viking blond hair and green-gold eyes. There's an impish Pete in there somewhere."

A man, walking in the opposite direction, glanced at her with raised eyebrows as he passed. Nik just smiled, shrugged, and kept going. So I talk to myself, she thought, who cares?

Nik found Mickey and Peter quietly talking together when she returned to the rubdown room. They were standing, and she realized that the athlete was taller than most of the hockey players that she had dealt with during her short stint as 'team physician'. As she approached, both looked at her expectantly.

"Here comes the last word," said Mickey.

"How are you feeling, Pete?" Nik watched him closely to see if he showed any objection to her shortening of his name. Seeing none, she continued, "It looks like you're back on your feet, at least. Do you have any aches, pains or nausea?"

Peter smiled, "It's a miracle. No dizziness or nausea, and the headache is gone I hope, for good. I'm ready to play tonight. All I need now is your permission to play."

Holding up one hand, Nik said, "Whoa, whoa, let's not get carried away. I've got to check you over before I can certify that you're good to go. Sit down on the edge of the table, and I'll see what's what."

Nik listened to Peter's heart, lungs, checked his blood pressure and pulse, and then said to Mickey, "Let's do a stat-lab for blood sugar and the 'lytes. He's pinked up considerably from the way he looked earlier, but I want to at least make sure that our replacement therapy did the trick. Also, I didn't do the chest X-Ray earlier, or the EKG, no time, but I'll get them done tomorrow. Mickey, could you set them up for sometime tomorrow before practice?"

"Will do," replied Mickey. "Is there anything else, Doc?"

"No, that's fine, and, thanks Mickey. Well, there is one thing more. Don't tell anyone that Peter speaks English. It could cause him some problems."

"Yeah, I see what you mean, Doc." Mickey nodded his head and smiled a crooked grin.

Turning back to Peter, Nik told him, "I want to see you in the clinic tomorrow, and Mickey will show you where, around eleven o'clock so that I can give you a thorough examination. Your coach mentioned that you have a right-sided hip pointer that's an old injury. I want to check that out. Mickey, this athlete's okay to play if his stat-labs continue to look good. Give him a hip-wrap on the right, just to prevent any further injury there until we can see what's going on."

Mickey handed Peter his duffel bag and said, "Let's go!"

Peter, his heart filling with unexpected joy at the prospect of being given a chance to play, said solemnly, "Thank you, doctor."

Nik called after him as he ran to catch up with Mickey, "Any sign of pain, weakness, or *anything*, you tell me. Do you hear that?"

Peter turned back toward her, "Yes, YES!" His face was glowing, and he actually smiled at her. He jumped in the air with one fist raised, and then ran after Mickey.

Chapter 5

Sunday Evening

The red-suited Russian team came charging out of the tunnel into the arena, taking the ice as if they owned it. Nik stood up to get a better look at the players as they ran past her on their blades. She searched for number 17, Pete's number. The noise and uproar of the crowd and the loud music blaring from the sound system were disorienting. Some of the local fans were frenzied, jumping up and down, waving their arms, and hissing and booing the Russians as they took the ice. One last player, number 17, hurtled past her, and as *he* took the ice, Nik felt a little burst of electric excitement inside. It's Pete, she thought, *it's Pete.*

The crowd began chanting, 'I-van, I-van, I-van the Ter-ri-ble', over and over again, getting louder and louder with each chant. Nik wondered whom they were shouting for, or at, when she suddenly realized that all the noise and excitement had started when Pete skated onto the ice. He was skating in a pattern with his teammates, looking down and shaking his head as he skated.

The Swedish team skated onto the ice from the opposite side of the arena, and the crowd hit a fever pitch. Gladiators versus Neanderthals, thought Nik. Let the games begin! She was surprised to find that she was clapping her hands and jumping up and down to the beat of the music like the rest of the crowd.

Ron came up to her from behind, laughing, and then shouted so that she could hear him over the din, "Looks like you really hate these Neanderthals that you're stuck with!"

Making a sour face at him, she put her mouth against his ear and said, "Yeah, yeah, yeah, it's really horrible, isn't it? Hey, why didn't you answer your page this afternoon?"

Giving Nik a quick hug, he said, "I didn't get any page this afternoon that I know of. Why?"

"I needed your help with number 17. We had a little trouble with him, but I'll tell you about it later."

"Okay, got'ta go. I'm helping the other side tonight. After the game, the coach wants Garibaldi and me to have dinner with the Swedish team. Is that okay with you? "

Smiling, Nik said, "So what's new? You're always politicking."

With a grin and a wave, Ron bounded up the stairs, two at a time. "Tomorrow!" he called.

Overhead, the loudspeaker blared, the announcer's voice matching the fever pitch of the crowd, "FACE- OFF!"

The face-off was between player number 17 for the Russians and number 12 for the Swedes. The referee threw the puck down and a red blur swept it toward his Russian teammate, Ilya.

"Yeah, PETE!" Nik was into the game.

Nik stayed vigilant throughout the hockey game, watching Peter's every move, hoping that he wouldn't tire, or show signs of illness. When he had bench time she made an effort to ask how he was doing. Even at rest, Peter was in the game. His focus was complete, and he answered her questions sparingly, if at all, depending on the action on the ice.

When he was on the ice, watching him skate was to be enthralled with how easy he made it appear. He had a natural grace, as if he were a dancer, which made some of the other skaters look robotic and clumsy in comparison. He skated around or through the other players' formations effortlessly, plying the puck here or there as he wished. Nik noticed that he shared the limelight, too, and assisted his teammates more than he attempted to score.

In the last thirty seconds of the third period, the Russians and Swedes were tied at one goal apiece. The Swedes had possession of the puck and decided to pull their goalie in order to place another offensive player on the ice, increasing their chances of scoring another goal to win the game. The offensive player they chose was known as a policeman; an intimidating enforcer who had the reputation of roughing the opposing team's players by boarding or body checking players as he saw fit.

Play started in a face-off circle in the Russian attacking zone. The puck was picked up by one of the Russian defensemen. The Swedes' policeman body checked the Russian defenseman who was helping the goalie, sending him flying into the boards headlong. The Russian player bounced back, stunned for a moment, but then got up on his skates and turned to face his tormentor. The Russian player used his stick to butt-end the policeman in the abdomen, doubling him over. Whistles blew, as the linesmen simultaneously called the illegal maneuver, and the Russian defenseman was sent to the penalty box for two minutes for a minor penalty. This effectively sent him out for the remainder of the game and the Russians' man-advantage evaporated with the penalty.

The linesman re-started the play in the face-off circle of the Russian attacking zone. This time, another Russian player took possession of the puck during the face-off. Peter played the left wing position. His forte was offense, and the left wing position was mostly offensive, so he was a natural skating in that position. His agility and ability to skate rings around most of his opponents made him a deadly left wing that could assist another player or attack the goal equally well. Peter's attention immediately focused on the Swedes' policeman after the attack on the Russian defenseman. Because he was an experienced hockey player, Peter knew that the policeman was only just getting a good start, and would do whatever it took, boarding, body checking, cross checking, or hook checking, to gain an advantage over his opponents.

The puck was passed to Peter, and he skated back toward the blue line, with the policeman in hot pursuit. The forward line, which included Peter in his left wing position, the center, and the right wing players, recovered the puck when Peter did a flip pass up off the ice and over the Swede policeman's stick to the right wing player. Peter knew that he now had the policeman's undivided attention, and the two skated around each other, each taking the measure of the other player.

Peter's teammates, the center, a defenseman, and the right wing, had taken the puck across the blue line, passing it back and forth, and were attacking the unmanned Swede goal. Peter swung to the left, coming up the ice toward the empty goal. The Swede defensemen were skating back and forth in the area of the goal, attempting to protect it from the Russian onslaught. There were twelve seconds left on the clock. The policeman playing the left wing position, followed Peter toward the goal. The policeman attempted to charge Peter from behind, but at the last possible second, Peter deked, swung right, and circled around and behind him. Realizing that he had been out-skated, the policeman turned and attempted to high stick Peter, but Peter had again deked, and moved skillfully away from the raised stick.

Again Peter skated after his forward line teammates, giving only one backward glance at the policeman and a quick upward glance at the clock. Seven seconds left in the game. He headed into position for a pass at the crease, the eight by four feet rectangle directly in front of the goal. The Russian right wing gave Peter a drop pass as Peter came up from behind him. Peter deked right, then left quickly, as he maneuvered around the Swede defensemen. He slapped the puck into the Swede's net, and swung around behind the goal.

"Goal, it's a GOAL for the Russians!" Shouted the announcer.

Peter heard the ending buzzer...music to his ears. His teammates skated over to him, grabbed him, and put him up on their shoulders in celebration of his winning goal.

Back in the training room, Nik prepared to administer to various aches, pains, injuries, and assorted complaints from the athletes. Buoyed by the win over the Swedes, everyone seemed to be in a festive mood. Athletes were boisterously calling back and forth to one another, and, not realizing that Nik understood their every word, some were getting rather raunchy regarding what to do after the game. She began to blush, much to her chagrin. Peter came to her rescue by asking his teammates to find other ways of celebrating.

He called out to a few, "Ilya, Misha, Josef, let's be more professional. After all, who knows whether what you are saying might be overheard by Yakov, Grigory, or even Vladimir? You know how they will react, especially Yakov, so let's not give them any reason to come down hard on us."

An undertone of grumbling and mumbling could be heard, but the athletes settled down to pay more attention to their various strains, sprains, and bruises. Nik wanted to examine Peter first, to make sure that he had come through the game without injury, but thought that the right wing player that had been body checked by the Swede policeman was probably her first responsibility.

"Where is Slava? I think he may be in need of some help from Mickey, Tom and me."

One of the players, already lying on a training table, raised one arm into the air when he heard his name. Nik headed toward him, and passing Peter on the way, gave a quiet aside to him in Russian, "Are you all right?"

Peter, in the act of unlacing his skates, did not look up, but simply said, "Da."

Peter headed to the showers after he took off his skates and outer uniform. He was feeling the aches and pains that he usually had after a game, but nothing more.

Slava was badly bruised on one side where the Swede policeman had slammed him into the boards. Nik did a neuro check of his head first, then eyes, reflexes, orientation and alertness. She methodically and systematically checked his ribs, flank, and abdomen for signs of internal bleeding or fracture. The athlete indicated by pointing to the whirlpool equipment that he wanted to sit in a whirlpool to ease his aches and pains.

Nik said one word; "No." She shook her head in the universal gesture for the word, no.

Looking around for Yakov, she called for him to come over to her and translate something to the athlete. She didn't want anyone else on the team to know that she understood and spoke Russian.

Her explanation of why she didn't want to use the warm whirlpool on the athlete tonight caused Slava to sit upright on the table. She explained, as Yakov translated, that there was the potential for bleeding into the soft tissues, which was always a risk after such an encounter. It was best not to use heat the first twenty-four hours. A light rub-down, ice, and a non-aspirin pain reliever would be better until the extent of the injury, and bruising, could be determined. The athlete hung his head in mock misery, hoping that the doctor might feel sorry for him.

No such luck, thought Nik. Yakov translated as Nik told the athlete, "I'll see you tomorrow morning at 11:30 in the clinic. Don't be late. If you have any problems tonight, you can call the service and they'll call me," she said, and then moved on to another athlete.

Nik worked her way through the athletes with Tom and Mickey's help, and then there was only one, number 17. Peter had pushed a training table against a wall, and he was sitting on it with his back supported by the wall. He looked as though he might fall asleep at any moment.

Yakov stood across the room talking to Grigory, but kept his eyes on Peter, and started across the room when he saw that the doctor was going to examine the athlete.

"You are a miracle worker, doctor," said Yakov. "How did you manage to put Genchenko back together for the game, drugs?"

Nik whirled on Yakov, and in a low, angry voice said, "You will not speak to *me*, or will you disparage this athlete in that manner ever again, *do you understand*?"

Glancing back at Grigory and Vladimir, Yakov shrugged, and then said, "I was only joking, doctor. I certainly would not insult you in front of Coach Grigory, now would I?"

"I want you out of this training room *now*, do you hear? You've used up the last of my good manners for one day, so out you go! Tom, Mr. *Yakov* is leaving. Help him to the door, will you? You and Mickey can call it a night, too. I'll see you at seven in the morning."

Smiling, Tom said, "Sure, Doc, see you in the A.M." Turning his gaze toward Yakov, his grin got wider, "Mr. Yakov's gon'na leave right now with Mickey and me."

Tom took only two steps toward Yakov, and the little man bolted from the room. Tom and Mickey followed him out the door, waving and laughing as they left.

Grigory, and his "Ichabod Crane-ish" assistant coach, Vladimir, watched the action from a corner of the room. Seeing Yakov run out of the room was comic relief for Grigory after a long and exhausting day. He, too, laughed, and Vladimir, taking his cue from Grigory, laughed as well.

Grigory addressed Nik in his deep, booming voice, "Yakov is beginning to take you more seriously, doctor, now that your very large assistant has his full attention."

"You could say that, Coach. But tell me again, please, why you need a team interpreter when you speak perfect English yourself?"

Grigory, standing a full 6 feet 10 inches, and more than a head taller than his lanky assistant coach, strode across the room very quickly for a man who probably weighed more than 250 pounds. He was balding, and mostly gray, but his face belied the other outward signs of aging. His ruddy coloring, and great dark, craggy brows over black eyes added an accentuation to his overall physique, making him appear larger than life.

"That *is* a good question, doctor, but I have no credible answer for you. Just consider Yakov as a necessary evil who sometimes gets in the way of what we, the Russian team, actually do. I'd like to say that he is harmless, but he is not. Please remember that I told you that."

Turning toward Peter, Grigory smiled widely, and in Russian told him, "You surprised even me when you skated out on the ice tonight, ready to play. Yakov told me that you were in no condition to skate, and that you should have stayed in Lyubertsy. Who could have imagined that you'd recover so quickly?"

Peter had moved away from the wall and was sitting on the edge of the table, his legs dangling, moving back and forth. Tired from his all-out style of playing hockey, he was in no mood for an interrogation by his coach on the current state of his health. However, he did owe Grigory an answer, because of the man's past kindness to him, and the way in which he had always protected Peter, as best he could, from Yakov.

Starting slowly, Peter replied in Russian, "If it weren't for the doctor," Peter indicated her with a nod of his head, "I wouldn't have been able to play. She seemed to know what was wrong with me right away. Anyway, there were no *drugs* involved in my recovery, as Yakov would have you believe."

Grigory nodded his large head, and Vladimir followed suit. It seemed that Vladimir was trying to be Griogory's mirror image.

Switching to English, Grigory said, "Doctor? How is it that Genchenko has recovered so quickly?" He raised his eyebrows in expectation of an answer.

Nik's reply was professional and in-depth, "By history, this athlete had a flu-like syndrome that left him dehydrated, and electrolyte-depleted. After his long flight to get here, he was dizzy, weak, nauseous, and had a severe headache. That's what usually happens when you've had a viral illness that has left you dehydrated. Do you know what I mean by electrolytes, Coach?"

Grigory pursed his lips, "Yes, I have seen athletes that were so depleted after a strenuous practice or a game that they collapsed. Is that what really happened with Genchenko?"

"Pretty much. I took the liberty of replenishing his fluids and electrolytes intravenously, and I also gave him some pre-digested protein and a carbohydrate boost. That, and a good nap, re-charged his engine, and you saw what he could do tonight. He was not seriously ill, but had I not helped him out with the I.V. fluids and nutrient supplements, which are, of course, all legal to use prior to a game, he wouldn't have been able to play."

"I see. Well doctor, you have saved our team a great deal of difficulty. You have no idea how much, because Yakov reports our every move. Had we lost tonight instead of winning, Yakov would have been lobbying to send Genchenko back to Russia, you can be sure of that. Having seen how he can play hockey, you know that Genchenko really *is* the star of the team."

Out of the corner of her eye, Nik could see that Peter was looking down at the floor and shaking his head. She wondered briefly why he disagreed with his coach, and whether he knew how talented an athlete he truly was?

Nik replied, "Peter is to come to the clinic next door tomorrow at eleven o'clock for a complete history and physical, so that I can be sure that he is healthy and can continue to play."

"There is a question about his readiness?" Grigory was immediately alert to the potential of losing his best player for the rest of the tournament.

"No, Coach, but it is my obligation to make sure that there are no underlying problems that could endanger Peter if he continues to play."

"Good, that is appropriate, and I would expect no less from you, doctor."

Turning to Peter, he boomed in Russian, "Genchenko, you have a clinic appointment with the doctor tomorrow at 11:00 a.m. Do you know where the clinic is located?"

"Da," Peter replied, "I know where it is."

"Do not be late. Doctors should not be kept waiting. Have you been assigned a hotel room? You will need your rest tonight in preparation for our game with the Canadians tomorrow."

"Nyet, Yakov was supposed to help me check into the hotel, but everything changed when I…when I…" Peter was obviously embarrassed by what had happened earlier.

Nik intervened to cover Peter's lapse. She didn't want to tip her hand regarding her grasp of Russian, but she wanted to get Peter away from Grigory's relentless questioning.

In English she said, "Coach, I'm not sure what you have arranged for Peter, because he has arrived late, but I can take Peter to the hotel tonight since Yakov has left. It's on my way home. What time is Peter due at the training table in the morning?"

As the doctor spoke, Vladimir's interest in her grew. Did she know what Coach Grigory had been asking Peter about, he wondered? Perhaps I will have to solve this little mystery. Vladimir was a quietly cunning individual who was always looking for an advantage.

"By seven at the latest. I want the team in the weight room afterward for a light, post-prandial workout."

Switching back to Russian, Grigory told Peter, "Be sure that you show up for meals, Genchenko. There will be none of your forgetfulness about eating this time. Is that clear?"

Peter's reply was one syllable, "Da." *Yes.*

In fact, Peter was ravenously hungry right now, but decided that there was nothing that he could do about it. Overall, he thought, I'm fine, maybe a little tired, but fine. Peter scooted back to his previous position on the table, leaned against the wall and closed his eyes. He could hear Grigory and the doctor talking, but their voices were quiet, and seemed to be fading as they walked toward the door. Images of the day tumbled through his mind, the flight, Yakov, the busy road, his collapse, the game; all swirled around in his head.

Nik came back to Peter's side, only to find him sound asleep. How can he be sleeping when he's sitting up? For a moment, she pondered what to do. She wasn't sure how he might react if she tried to awaken him, but she knew that she had to get him settled in the athletes' hotel so that he could get a good nights' sleep.

"Petrosha," she called softly to him in his own language. "Pete, it's time to go to the hotel."

He didn't move at all. There was no indication that he had heard her. For several moments, Nik puzzled over what to do. Then, remembering how she used to awaken her older brother when they were children, she reached for Peter's hand, and squeezed it gently. His hand was large, yet beautifully shaped, she thought, as she studied it, turning it over.

Aloud, she said, "I wonder what your parents look like, Pete."

"They are not so different from me, I guess." Peter sat up, stretched, and yawned widely, covering his mouth as he did so.

Then he smiled at Nik. "Thank you again for helping me today. I was at the end of my endurance, beyond help, I thought, but there you were to put me back together. I can never thank you enough."

Nik, though startled, deftly covered her momentary lapse, "You need to be settled in the hotel, Pete. A good night's sleep is just what you need right now. My car is close by, and I can take you to the athletes' hotel, go in with you, and make sure the arrangements are okay. I haven't checked you over after the game, but if you don't have any complaints, it can wait until tomorrow."

He looked at her for a long moment, gazing directly into her eyes. Here, I think, is a safe person, not one who wants, or needs anything from me, but one who looks beyond another's exterior to see the soul within.

Those were his mother's words, once upon a time, when he had thought that he was in love. Eda had said, "Can you see her soul in her eyes, Peter? If you cannot, if there is no connection there, then you will not be happy." His mother had been right, but of course, he had had to learn his own hard lesson. He realized now that his mother had probably been talking about herself and his father. No doubt that was from whence her wisdom had come.

Nik looked back into Peter's green-gold eyes. In them, she saw…sadness, aloofness, reticence? Perhaps all of these, but why was that so? What kind of life has this young man had? Judging from her initial examination of him this afternoon, she could see that he had endured physical abuse, but from whom, and why?

Abruptly, she said, "Well, let's get going. I think your duffel bag is over there in the first locker. Your team members saved that one for you. Did you know that they call you Number One?"

Uncomfortable with the off-hand compliment, Peter shrugged and changed the subject, "Doctor? Is it possible that I might get something to eat before you take me to the hotel? The game has made me very hungry. I have my stipend, so it will cost you nothing, but I would really like to eat *something* before I sleep."

Nik laughed, placing a hand against her forehead, "Of course! I haven't eaten anything since breakfast, myself! After all the energy that you've expended, I'd guess that your blood sugar has dropped again."

Pulling Peter's duffel bag from the locker, Nik threw his coat at him and said, "Let's go, I know a little restaurant where you can get the best pizza that you have ever eaten. You do eat pizza, don't you?"

"Oh yes, that would be wonderful."

Walking down the long corridor of the building to the back parking lot, Nik kept an eye on Peter, hoping that he wouldn't show any signs or symptoms of low blood sugar, like dizziness or worse. Dear God, she thought, don't let him conk out on me before I can fill his stomach. Nik quickened her steps, glancing over at Peter to make sure that he was keeping up with her, and finally reached the large exit door, where she bade goodnight to the security guard there, wishing him a good and quiet night.

"This is it; my 'whee' little car." Nik unlocked the passenger side, signaling for Pete to get inside out of the cold. She had named the car 'whee' because she got such a kick out of driving it, and not because of its size.

The snow had stopped, but there seemed to be at least another three or more inches on the ground. She mentally thanked her father for insisting that she get snow tires last month.

Peter looked around as he got inside the car. The parking lot lights glistened off the silver paint of the car, making little starbursts over its surface. Inside, there was a new leather smell, and the car was immaculately clean inside in comparison to Yevgeny's Zhguli, or the cab that had brought him to the arena.

"What is this car?" His curiosity had been piqued by the odd shape of the rear window of the car, and the plethora of electronics within.

"It's called a Mercury Cougar."

Turning toward her passenger, and noticing the puzzled look on Peter's face, Nik smiled and said, "Yes, a cougar is a large, rather mean, cat. That's why the carmakers name their products with such outlandish names. They would have buyers believe that the new car they have chosen is a mean machine.

"What's in a name, anyway? For instance, tonight I think the crowd was shouting Ivan the Terrible at you. What would be the reason for that?" Nik was curious.

Peter, looking straight ahead, said, "For some reason, my father's first name, Ivan, follows me wherever I play. It started in this country when I played three years ago in New York City during a Red Army exhibition game with their professional team. Apparently, the crowd did not expect the Reds to win, and when we started out skating and out scoring their team, the crowd started shouting Ivan the Terrible at us. I guess it must have stuck, because your fans are still using it. It is very insulting to me, to us, because of what Ivan Grosny, *the* Ivan the Terrible, did to the Russian people. Have you read much Russian history?"

Looking at the doctor, he continued, "If so, you might remember that Ivan favored very large frying pans for unusual cooking purposes."

Nik shuddered and made a face, "My mother made certain that I studied *all* Russian history, the good, bad, and the horrible. Let's not dwell on bad old Ivan. But did you make the leap between his last name and the capitol of Chechnya, Grosny? He certainly lived up to his name. The Chechens aren't very easy to deal with either. My mother spent a lot of time teaching my brothers and me about the history between Russia and Chechnya."

Peter was uncharacteristically talkative, "Well, maybe we could discuss something more pleasant, perhaps the weather? Your city seems to have a climate that is similar to Moscow's. It surprised me to see all of this snow, and having a cold wind always blowing at my back. Moscow is farther north, and gets its weather from Europe, mixes it with the foul weather of Siberia, and presents the Russian people with terrible cold, much snow, and a great deal of suffering."

Nodding, Nik replied facetiously, "Ah, I see that you are an optimist! Most Russians are reputed to have this dark-spirited, melancholy outlook, but you must be the exception. Seriously, though, the weather we are having now is unusually harsh. Normally, we have snow and ice, but this year it has been really bad."

Peter actually laughed before he replied, "If *I* am an optimist, how bad can things really be? So...your city doesn't often look like this?"

"Not exactly. Well, here we are. Giuseppe's Primo Pizza Palace has never seen the likes of us."

Nik left her car parked precariously near a snow bank created when the lot had been plowed. It was the only space left, and she skillfully worked her car into it. Giuseppe's, as usual, was packed. Slipping and sliding toward the door, holding onto each other, Nik and Peter went inside.

The first assault on Peter's senses was the noise. It seemed that everyone inside the warm building was talking, shouting, singing, at once. Somewhere, there was a source of an obscure Italian opera, blaring over the rest of the commotion. The last, and best, assault on Peter's senses was the magnificent fragrance of freshly baked pizza. Mamma mia, he thought to himself, why wasn't I born Italian?

Nik grabbed his sleeve and lead him over to a little corner table that was quaintly covered with a red and white-checked tablecloth, and

decked out with a Chianti-bottle candle. They had barely gotten seated, when a voice, loud enough to be heard over the din, called out to them.

"Hey, hey, it's the Doc! Doctor Nikola Kellman in the flesh." A short, round and balding man fairly skipped over to the table.

"Who have we here? Why, it's Doctor Nik, but who is this strange young man with her? Does Doctor Ron know that you've taken up with another man?" Giuseppe's laughter overpowered even the booming opera.

Nik put her finger to her mouth, "Shhh...no one's supposed to know!"

Then, laughing, with mirth dancing in her eyes, Nik introduced Peter to Giuseppe, "This is Peter Ivanovich Genchenko, the star of the visiting Russian hockey team. Pete, this is Giuseppe."

"You guys just beat the Swedes tonight. I heard they were pretty tough, too! So you're the guy they call Ivan the Terrible?"

Peter looked ruefully at Nik, and then answered Giuseppe, "Actually, I am not. Besides, that name is not a good one to be given to anyone. It's rather insulting."

"Oh, no, I wouldn't do that to the Doc's guest for anything in the world! You believe me, Doc? You know we love you around here." Giuseppe had his arms spread wide as a gesture of sincerity.

"Don't listen to him Giuseppe. He asked me to bring him to the best pizza place in town, and you know that this is the only place I'd consider for that honor. Come on, Pete, let's order something good."

They ordered a Great Giuseppe with the works, and finished with a pitcher of root beer. Peter had balked at first upon hearing the word, beer, but Nik had assured him that it wouldn't cause him to break training.

Giuseppe left to fill their order, and Nik, looking across the table at the serious-faced Peter, said, "You need to lighten up Pete. Giuseppe meant no harm. I'd be willing to bet that he's never cracked a Russian history book, so he probably knows very little about the real Ivan the Terrible."

"What is lighten up? Grigory complains that I'm underweight for my height as it is now, if that's what you mean."

Nik couldn't help herself. She had to laugh. When she stopped to catch her breath, she told him, "Well, that one lost something in the

translation! Lighten up means to relax, be cool, hang loose. Don't take everything that is said to you in a serious way, that's all. You just mortified that old man, and Giuseppe is the sweetest man I know."

When Peter asked, "What is mortified?" Nik was saying the same words with him.

"We are going to have to get you an English/Russian dictionary for sure. Um, mortify, let's see…it means to hurt or humiliate someone. I don't think that you'd intentionally do that, would you?"

"No, but perhaps I am more my father's son than I realized."

What a strange answer, thought Nik. You approach and withdraw, approach and withdraw, Pete, and she wondered why that was so? Something in this young man's life had wounded him so deeply that he did not seem able to enjoy the simple pleasures of life. In their short acquaintance, she had seen him helpless, the way he was when he first arrived, fearless, the way he was on the ice, warm, when he had looked pleased that they would share a meal, and cold, the way he had behaved toward Giuseppe. It's very strange, she thought, and very sad, too, for him.

The food arrived. Giuseppe had placed a rush on the order as an act of contrition for insulting Nik's guest. Giuseppe served the pizza himself, deftly placing a large slice on each plate, telling them to eat heartily and enjoy while pressing a thumb and forefinger to his lips, the universal sign for enjoyment. After Giuseppe left the table, Nik poured Peter a large glass of root beer, and watched him drink it down quickly.

"You're really thirsty, Pete, I should have known to give you something to drink after the game."

"Don't worry, I am fine. It's just that when my appetite and thirst returned, it was overpowering. Your choice in pizza was perfect. This is *wonderful*."

"Good." Nik watched, bemused by the man with the ravenous appetite.

Unbelievably, and very quickly, they had eaten most of the large pizza, and had finished the large pitcher of root beer. Giuseppe's was beginning to empty. Tomorrow was, after all, a working day. Unknown to Peter, Nik

had signaled to Giuseppe to put their meal on her tab that she paid weekly. Nik pulled on her coat, indicating to Peter to do the same.

"We need to get you into your hotel room for the night, Pete. I'm bushed too." Holding up her hand as she realized that Peter would want to know what bushed meant, she told him, "Tomorrow, I'll tell you tomorrow."

"We must pay first," said Peter.

"Nope, it's on my tab, and I'll explain that tomorrow, too." Nik smiled at Peter

Peter decided that he liked the way that this woman smiled at him. There seemed to be no pretense, no concealed issues, with her. He liked that about her.

The doctor's appetite for pizza had surprised him. She didn't push the food around on her plate the way Natalia had always done. This woman seemed more real than any he had known before.

Weariness began to overtake him, and he was ready for a hot shower and warm bed. It didn't matter where the shower and bed were located. He just needed sleep. His eyes felt gritty and dry, and his muscles were beginning to let him know how much he had abused them during the game.

Nik took him to the athletes' hotel, the Westin, in downtown Indianapolis, and she was astounded to find that all the Russian reserved rooms had been taken. The desk clerk told her that the Russian rooms were under the purview of Yakov Popov, and that he had turned the last room back to the hotel that day. It had already been filled, the clerk told them. Nik turned to look at Peter, who, in turn, looked resigned to Yakov's meanness.

That weasel bastard…I'll fix his little red Russian wagon, Nik decided, "What types of suites do you have available?"

The desk clerk, raising an eyebrow, told them of the choices, being particularly emphatic when he discussed prices. Nik chose the most expensive suite for Peter.

"Concierge level will be fine. My guest will require a jacuzzi, and a king-sized bed, too. Add the cost to Mr. Popov's account for the Russian team."

"I'll have to get pre-authorization for that." The desk clerk was all business.

Nik took out her games identification that showed she was the Russian Team Doctor. "This is all the authorization that you'll need."

Nodding, the desk clerk completed the sign-in, and handed Peter a special pass-key to the concierge level, "You will need this key to activate the elevator to open at the concierge level, and it will also open your room. I hope that you have a good stay with Westin. If there is anything that we can do for you, please do not hesitate to let us know." He signaled to the nearest bellhop for assistance.

Nik wanted to see Peter's luxurious suite, and so followed the bellhop, who was carrying Peter's duffel bag as though it might be filled with soiled laundry, to the elevator.

Inside the elevator, the bellhop, observing that Nik had no luggage, asked, "Is this your first time in Indy?" He looked directly at her.

Feeling a little ornery and aggravated by the bellhop's snooty attitude, Nik replied, "Oh no, I'm in and out of Indy hotels all the time." She then gave him a wide smile.

When they arrived at the concierge level, Nik took Peter's arm as they walked out of the elevator, "Here we are, sugar."

She beamed up at Peter who closed his eyes and shook his head because he understood that the doctor was getting even with the bellhop for his judgmental attitude.

The bellhop quickly opened the door to the suite, turned on the lights, showed them the various amenities in the room, and headed toward the door. Nik smiled at him as she handed him a ten dollar bill.

"Thanks," she said, winking at him.

The bellhop bolted out the door, and didn't look back.

Looking around the room, Nik said to Peter, "This should meet your needs quite well, I think. Yakov will pop a blood vessel when he sees this. Serves him right…he shouldn't have been so mean as to cancel your room. Believe me, Grigory will hear about this."

"You enjoy a good joke, don't you doctor?" Peter leaned against a wall near the full-sized bar, his eyes half-closed, too tired to even look around the room.

"Sometimes, but this is no joke. Yakov will have to pay for this suite out of his Russian account. The mouse will roar for sure. As soon as I get home, I'll call Grigory to let him know what happened. You're going to have to tell me about Yakov's animosity toward you, because, for some reason, I think he's more dangerous than he looks." Nik stifled a yawn. She was feeling rather sleepy herself.

"Well, good night Pete, I'll see you at eleven sharp tomorrow morning in the clinic."

"Good night to you, doctor. I will be there"

Nik walked over to the door, turned, and said, "I apologize if I embarrassed you in the elevator. The devil made me do it."

Peter decided on some mischief of his own. "I wasn't embarrassed, Dr. Kellman. I was flattered. Would you care to stay?"

Briefly startled, and with cheeks reddening in embarrassment, Nik stuttered, "Oh…uh, no, that was just a way of getting that smug little bellhop's goat. What I mean to say is…uh, I'll see you tomorrow."

As Nik opened the door, Peter said one word, "Gotcha." His laugh was warm and mellow.

For a moment Nik stood motionless. Finally, she replied, "I guess so!" She was laughing too as she went out the door, swinging it closed behind her.

Peter looked around the spacious suite and gave a low whistle. Yes, Yakov *would* probably pop a blood vessel as Dr. Kellman had speculated. The thought gave Peter a moment's pleasure.

And then he thought about Dr. Kellman. He couldn't give voice to his feelings about her. They were jumbled and all mixed up, and, given the day that he had had, he was too tired to think about feelings. All he knew was that she had been extremely kind to him, and that she had gone well out of her way to help him.

Walking slowly, and a bit stiffly now, Peter went over to the huge bathroom, saw a large walk-in shower with thick towels stacked on an ornate table, disrobed, dropping his clothes on the spot, and stepped into the shower. At first, he had the water turned up to the point that his shoulders stung, but as he finished his shower, he lowered the temperature until it was almost tepid. He had learned that it was best not to step out of a hot shower into the colder air of a room after a game, because his muscles could cramp. He didn't want anything to interrupt or prevent his sleep. He really needed to sleep. The soft and thick towel that he used absorbed all of the water from his skin. He quickly brushed his teeth. Peter had no pajamas to put on, so he would sleep as he usually did, naked. He was too tired, even, to pick up his clothing from the floor. Tomorrow, he thought, I'll do it tomorrow.

Peter turned off all of the lights in the suite, and opened the draperies that covered one entire wall to look outside. The city lights twinkled with Christmas colors before him. Hearing an airplane above, he looked up, surprised that he could easily read the Federal Express logo on a jet flying low over the city toward what he thought was the direction of the airport.

The sky had cleared after the daytime snowfall, and he could make out several celestial formations, even though the city lights were bright enough to obscure most of the nighttime sky. This is a beautiful city, he thought. It would be a very nice thing to bring his mother and sister here for a visit, or even to live. They would be so very excited to explore such a city as this. Turning back toward the room, he didn't bother with the television set, but went directly to the bed, pulled the thick comforter and blanket aside, and slipped between the soft, clean sheets.

Chapter 6

Monday December 15, 1986

When Peter awakened, he glanced at the bedside clock radio, and was surprised to see that morning had come so quickly. Peter pulled the covers aside to sit on the edge of the bed. He stretched, yawned, and then leaned forward, elbows on knees, resting his face in his hands.

He remembered his restless, dream-filled night. One person, he recalled, had been most prominent in his dreams; the woman he had met only yesterday, Dr. Kellman. She was easy to dream about. For some reason, with only the slightest of acquaintanceships, she had impressed him. Had the usual feeling of aching cold emptiness inside him diminished a bit?

Peter washed his face, brushed his teeth, and picked up the clothes he had left on the bathroom floor the night before. He dressed quickly in a T-shirt, athletic shorts, sweat suit, thick socks, and his well-worn athletic shoes, looked in the hotel directory for the exercise area, grabbed his room key, and headed out the door.

He was impressed by the cleanliness and orderliness of the hotel. The carpet was clean, without a dotting of cigarette butts, and the walls were not damaged, marred, or written upon. This is probably the way most of the people in this country live, he decided. He couldn't even detect the slightest odor of tobacco in the hall, or the elevator as he entered. Privaskhodny! *Wonderful!*

The elevator stopped at the fifth floor, where the directory had indicated the exercise area would be located. Looking left to right, he saw double glass doors close by on the right. As Peter pushed through the doors, he saw only one other person there, a middle-aged, balding man walking on a treadmill at slow speed. Peter observed that America had early birds, too, but this bird was rather slow.

He chose a treadmill, checked out the controls, and set about his workout. His resting heart rate was 60 beats per minute, according to the monitor on the treadmill. After five minutes his warm-up, moderate speed, caused him to break a sweat, and then he raised the incline and speed on the treadmill to the next level. Peter began running slowly at first, in rhythm with the hum of the machine. Within fifteen minutes, he was running flat out, the incline as steep as it would go, and kept that speed up for ten minutes. His heart rate reached 150 and stayed there during this peak performance. Peter began to reverse the process, slowing gradually, until he was in his cool down walk. At that point he noticed that the other man, who had been exercising when he came in, was watching him on the treadmill. After five minutes of cool down, Peter stopped the treadmill, toweled off with a towel he had pulled from the rack, and walked over to the weights.

Peter looked over at the man, who was still standing on his treadmill, watching him, "Hello." Peter nodded his head in greeting.

"I've never seen anyone hit the treadmill that hard. You must be a professional athlete, or in the military." The man was owl-eyed, and gave a long whistle.

Looking back at the man, Peter shook his head, "No, I'm not a professional athlete, and I'm *definitely* not in the military. I'm just an amateur hockey player here for the International Winter Games."

"Okay, okay, now I *really* feel bad! You're not a professional? Geez, you looked like Superman on that thing. My name's Shelly, Sheldon Levin, what's yours?"

"Peter Genchenko"

"What country?"

"Russia."

"A Russian, huh? Hey, you speak English very well."

Peter nodded and smiled, "Thanks. I'd better get back to my workout before I cool off."

"Oh, yeah, by all means, I didn't mean to keep you from your workout. I just wanted you to know how impressed I was to see what you could do on the treadmill. When's your next game?"

"Tonight at 7:00 o'clock, Market Square Arena."

"I'm definitely gon'na be there. Who's the opposition?"

"We are skating against Canada." Peter began setting up the weights for his workout.

"*That* ought'a be some game. Those Canucks can really skate. Hey, I know somebody who scouts for pro hockey. He does business with our marketing firm sometimes, and he's in town tonight. If you're as good on the ice as you are in here, you'll really be somethin'. Maybe I'll bring him along."

Peter smiled at Sheldon Levin, "It seemed like the arena was full last night when we played the Swedes. Good luck getting tickets."

"Oh, don't worry about that. My company always has tickets available for whatever is playing in town; off-Broadway plays, rock concerts, sporting events, whatever is going on, we can get you in to see it. We have a block of two hundred tickets every year for the Indy 500. People really love that, believe me. I come into Indianapolis every two months or so to check on our local office on my way to New York. We're affiliated with the Chamber here, y'know, the Chamber of Commerce. They want us to be happy, get it? We scratch their back, and they scratch ours."

"I think so."

Peter understood. America was not so different from Russia, after all. Only, in Russia, it was the Party that could arrange anything for anyone, as long as they were in a position to pay, or to help the Party. There was always a debt that came due when the Party wanted something from the debtor.

"Look, uh, here's my card. Do you have one? I'd like to get in touch with you sometime, especially if my friend the scout likes your style on the ice." Sheldon Levin held out a nicely engraved and very important-looking business card to Peter.

Finally, Peter had to laugh. "I haven't brought any with me," he said, patting the pocket of his shirt. "Besides, I'm returning to Russia at the end of next week, when the games are over."

It was funny, really, that this man thought that Peter would have a business card. Things like that cost money, and in Lyubertsy, a roof over one's head, and something to eat were more important.

"Hey, that's okay. I have connections with the Winter Games promoter, so I'll be able to find you. It doesn't matter if you go back to Russia, either. I've got some business interests there, too." Sheldon Levin was full of surprises.

Looking down at the card in his hand, and then looking back at Sheldon Levin, Peter replied, "Thank you." He placed the card in his shirt pocket, and turned back to the weights.

"See you on the ice!" Sheldon smiled and waved as he started for the exit door of the exercise room.

Peter waved back at him, and started his weight workout. He worked on his neck, chest, arms, back and shoulders, then went right into his abdominals, buttocks, and ended with his legs, upper and lower. Peter was methodical as he worked, doing twenty repetitions, in sets of three for all his muscle groups. He decided that he'd better stop before he pushed himself too far, but he knew that he needed to feel the burn in his muscles before he quit. Otherwise, the workout would do him no good. But the last thing he wanted to do was injure himself on the weights before a game.

Sitting up on the bench, he gingerly placed his hand alongside the area in his right groin that gave him chronic pain. Sometimes, the pain was almost unbearable, but he had found that if he hung upside down from the back of a sofa, or lay head down on an incline for a few minutes, the pain would ease. He had convinced his coach that he had a chronic hip pointer, a condition where the abdominal muscle attachment to the hip was strained or pulled. Usually, Peter's unorthodox hanging treatment would temporarily take care of the problem. There were even times when he would place a rolled up sock and tape it against the painful area prior to skating if his other treatment didn't fully alleviate the pain. Peter had learned to cope with his problem. How could he do otherwise? It wasn't as though he could actually have it taken care of. Yakov would be all over Grigory trying to convince him that Peter was a liability, not an asset, to the team, if it appeared that Peter actually had a medical problem.

Again toweling off, Peter put his sweat suit on and headed back to his room to shower and dress. Briefly, he wondered how he might get something to eat without having to go to the athlete's training table for breakfast. Yakov would be there, and Peter didn't need his venom and vitriol this morning. Peter called the elevator with his concierge level key, and stepped on the elevator when the doors opened. Immediately, he wished that he had not. There was Yakov, his face red and eyes bulging at the sight of Peter.

"You!" he shouted.

"Who else could be so fortunate?" asked Peter, turning his back on the furious man.

"The hotel registrar just told me that *you* are staying on the concierge level. He also told me that *Dr.Kellman* authorized the room. *How dare that stupid bitch cow...*"

Peter turned quickly to face Yakov, his voice hoarse as he shouted in anger, "Enough! Don't say another word if you value your life. I swear that I will wring your pitiful neck if you say another word!"

At that moment, the elevator doors opened, and a young couple got onto the elevator. Apparently, both had heard Peter shouting at Yakov through the elevator doors before the elevator had stopped, because they both stared at him. Although they probably did not understand Russian, they nonetheless seemed acutely aware that there had been an argument between the two men.

Peter's heart pounded, and he was certain that his face was red with anger, but he could not calm himself down. When the elevator reached the concierge level, he keyed the door, shot a parting angry scowl in Yakov's direction, and strode out into the hallway.

Yakov shouted at Peter as the elevator doors closed, "Bastard!"

Peter reached his room, had trouble with the lock because his hands were still trembling with anger, but finally managed to unlock the door. At first, he tried walking off his anger, striding back and forth across the room until he could calm down enough to sit on the edge of the bed. He had long since lost any sense of an expectation of fairness in the world. There was no fairness, no justice for anyone. The strong ruled; the weak suffered. It was as simple as that.

Peter and Katya had been treated very badly by anyone who knew the identity of their father, from the time that Ivan had been banished from the Party and jailed. No, of course there was no fairness in the world. Everyone was pushing for an advantage. No one, except his mother and sister, even cared whether Peter took his next breath. I'm feeling sorry for myself, he thought. That's no way for a man to behave. He knew, however that it was not *all* self-pity, but helplessness and hopelessness in his situation that he could do nothing about. Yakov had the power, and he, Peter, did not. There was no advantage for himself that Peter could see. Yakov could harm him, even see that he was sent back to Russia, and then to the war in Afghanistan, if he so chose. Hadn't he often told Peter that he would do so? Peter knew that Yakov fully intended to take out his revenge on him, because he could not take it out on Ivan.

Finally, Peter stood, stripped his exercise clothing from his body, and went into the shower. He held his head under the hot, strong stream of water until his thoughts began to clear. What was the purpose of anger, anyway? It did nothing to change his situation.

The best that he could hope to do was to continue to play hockey for as long as his body would allow. He knew that there was no way that he would, or could, ever get ahead. No way to provide anything for his mother and sister beyond what they now had. And, after the few years that he had to play hockey, he would be discarded in favor of some younger, healthier player. He had seen just such a thing happen in the three seasons of hockey that he had already played. One older player, surprised that he had been cut, had even cried in front of the other players. Peter had vowed that he would never let that happen to him. Sometimes, all a man had was his pride; if he lost that, what then?

Even as the hot water sprayed down onto his back, Peter felt the return of the familiar aching coldness inside him. He grabbed the shower handle and forcefully turned it off, stepped out of the shower, toweled off roughly, and went into the bedroom area of the suite to dress. Having few choices of wearing apparel, he pulled an ancient, nondescript sweater over his head, stepped into a pair of threadbare jeans, donned patched socks and thin-soled shoes, and was ready to go. Glancing in the mirror over the bar, he realized that he hadn't combed his still-wet hair. Peter held the edge of the bar and took several deep breaths, letting the air out through pursed lips. Finally reaching a more calm state, he went into the bathroom again, dried his hair with the hairdryer provided there, and combed it out. It was overlong about his ears and neck, but he could not afford to have it trimmed. Back in the bedroom, he looked at the threadbare clothed, longhaired reflection of the down-on-his-luck man in the mirror, shrugged, and threw on his coat as he strode out the door.

Rather than chancing another encounter with Yakov in the elevator, Peter keyed the lock on the stairs, and bounded down five floors, taking the stairs two at a time. He grabbed two apples from a large basket on the registration desk in the lobby and headed for the revolving door to the street. So much for breakfast, he thought, taking a large bite out of one of the apples. Peter had earlier studied a map of the downtown area of the city, and knew how to get from the hotel back to the arena. His plan was to get some "ice time" for skating drills, his own drills, not Coach Grigory's.

When Peter reached the outdoors, a Moscow street scene greeted him: snow, snow, and *more* snow. Briefly, he wondered how much snow had fallen since he had turned in last night. He started jogging in the direction of the arena. His thin-soled shoes gave him little traction as he careened around passers-by, but soon he was in sight of the arena. Peter had remembered to bring his athlete's identification tag, and quickly gained entrance to the area nearest his assigned training room.

The locker room was deserted at this hour. Peter opened his locker, grabbed his sports bag, then ran out the tunnel to the ice, where he changed into his own ice skates, figure, not hockey, on a bench close to the ice. He was in luck. The arena lights were half-lit, but no one, as yet, was on the ice. Peter vaulted over a gate, took a deep breath, filling his lungs with the cold air coming off the ice, and began to leisurely skate around the elongated oval of ice. As he skated, he picked up speed until he was literally running with his skates on.

His workout took about thirty minutes, and then he began to skate for his own enjoyment. He imagined that he was back in Moscow, skating with Katya in the Red Army ice arena. When they were small children, his sister and he were paired up and trained as ice dancers. Peter and Katya went every other evening, accompanied by their mother, to skate and to learn routines. A very famous ice dance choreographer had singled them out as potential stars in ice dancing. He had suggested that they stop their formal schooling in favor of full-time training, and told their mother that structurally, "…everything is in the right place if Peter and Katya work hard." The choreographer had said that they were physically perfect for the sport, and they had a wonderful opportunity to become famous, not only in their own country, but also throughout the world.

All of their training and promise had come to an abrupt halt when Ivan and Eda fell from grace in the Communist Party. Suddenly, talent notwithstanding, Peter and Katya were no longer allowed to train in the Red Army arena, and were shunned by the very people who had favored them previously. Katya had cried and cried about their loss, but to no avail. Their mother had told them, truthfully, that nothing could be done to help them. The episode left his sister with a seemingly permanent melancholy, and she became even more shy, quiet, and withdrawn than she had been previously.

Shaking his head to clear the memories, Peter skated in slow circles, working up to more intricate patterns, and then he began to do the compulsory movements that he and Katya had learned so long ago. He heard the music for the dance moves in his head, a romantic ballad of triumphant love that he and Katya had been assigned for one of their early performances, where they had placed first in the competition. Oblivious to his surroundings, Peter didn't realize that he had an audience.

Nik sat at the north end of the arena, high up in the bleachers. She was spellbound by what she saw. He's so much more than just a hockey player, she thought, so very much more. She had come into the arena to look for a piece of equipment, a blood pressure cuff that might have been left in the Russian box after the game last night. She had entered from a lower level, but upon seeing Peter on the ice, Nik climbed up near the top of the seating in order to watch him without being seen. How wonderful. He's truly a talented skater, she decided. Briefly, she puzzled over why he was playing hockey instead of pursuing a professional figure skating career.

Obviously, he must have had some very intense training to do so easily on the ice what she knew to be very difficult. He has a gift, a wonderful gift, but he will probably never be able to use it. The sadness that Nik had detected in him from the very first, she decided, possibly stemmed from his unfulfilled dream.

Peter finished the ice dance, bowing low at the finish, and then skated over to the gate where he had left his gear. As he was taking off his skates, he caught a movement out of the corner of his eye, high up in the arena. Looking up in that direction, he saw Dr. Kellman, and waved at her in greeting. She waved back and stood up to pantomime applause for his performance. Peter turned to finish tying his shoes, and when he looked back to where Dr. Kellman had been, she was gone. He felt a sort of odd disappointment that he had not had a chance to talk with her. He wanted to share his happiness, his buoyancy, with her. But then, he decided that he would soon see her in the clinic, and would have the opportunity to be near her. Again, he felt an odd sense of unreality. Why was he looking forward to seeing and talking with her? Wasn't she just his doctor, and really no more than a friendly stranger? Idiot. I am an idiot, he said to himself.

Peter was actively hungry now. The apples that he had taken from the hotel registration desk had gone down very quickly, but had left him unsatisfied. With his duffel bag over his shoulder, he began walking in the outside corridor of the arena toward the athlete's clinic, following Mickey's directions from the day before. He spied a beverage machine, looked over the menu quickly, and bought two pints of milk that he downed in less than a minute. He started walking toward the clinic again when he heard Yakov's distinctively annoying voice nearby. Ducking into an alcove that was darker than the main corridor, Peter waited for him to pass by. He saw that Yakov was talking to two of Peter's teammates. How odd, he thought, what would those two have to do with Yakov? Peter overheard a remnant of a sentence, "...if all goes as planned, you will both be rewarded handsomely..." The three passed by quickly, as if in a hurry to get somewhere. Peter congratulated himself on having avoided another confrontation with the hateful little man.

Putting thoughts of Yakov and his treacherous meddling aside, Peter again started toward the clinic. He was earlier than the time that the doctor had told him, but he was anxious to get the examination over with. His biggest worry was the so-called, hip pointer that he knew to be something else entirely. A Russian doctor, unattached to the hockey team, had examined him more than a year ago, and had told him that he had a hernia. The doctor didn't seem too concerned about the finding, so Peter put what he had learned aside. If Grigory, or especially Yakov, knew that he had a physical problem, it might cause either of them to take him off the team roster. Also, an injury such as this might hamper his ability to skate and to earn a living for his mother and sister. They were always first and foremost in all of his thoughts and plans. It was an easy decision; he would play hockey as long as he was able to do so. He couldn't, or wouldn't, look beyond that time.

Chapter 7

Monday, Late Morning

Upon his arrival in the clinic, Peter found that there were actually three athletes' clinics, all in a row, with flags of different countries on the doors. That makes it easy, he thought, for anyone who doesn't speak or read English. The third door displayed a Russian flag, among others. Pausing for a moment, Peter pushed the door open, and went inside. There was no one behind the counter, and Peter looked around the waiting area. He was alone in the room. Hearing sounds of papers shuffling, and of someone, a woman, humming a song quietly, Peter followed the sounds past the gate at the counter.

He called out, "Dr. Kellman? Is Dr. Kellman here?"

The paper shuffling stopped, and Dr. Kellman peered around the door nearest to where Peter was standing.

"Peter, you were *great* on the ice this morning. Where did you learn to skate like that?" Nik smiled widely at him.

She was dressed in her uniform of khaki slacks, a blue buttoned-down collar shirt, penny loafers, and a slightly large white lab coat, with tortoise shell reading glasses perched atop her head. She continued to smile at him, and waved him into the office with a sweep of her hand.

Stepping inside the room, Peter said, "I wanted to talk to you before anyone else arrived in the clinic. It's in regard to my hip pointer that Grigory talked with you about."

Nik could see that Peter was ill at ease, and wondered if he had been having a return of his symptoms of yesterday. For some reason, his demeanor tugged at her heart.

"Close the door and sit down, Pete, and make yourself comfortable." Instead of stepping behind her desk, Nik sat in a chair next to Peter.

They were speaking in English, and Peter's grasp of the language was nearly perfect. "Doctor," he began, "I want to tell you that I have a hernia, not a hip pointer, on my right side. I've known about it for more than a year, but I have chosen not to say anything to my coach because it may get back to Yakov. I don't want him to have anything to do with my private affairs. He would only use the information to cause me harm."

Nik paid him her full attention, "Go on, it sounds as though this injury, or whatever it is, is more serious than you led me to believe yesterday."

Looking down, Peter nodded his head. "Yes, it is more serious than I even want to acknowledge, but, as team physician, you have the right to know what my condition really is."

At that moment, a young woman looked inside the room, "Dr. Kellman? Oh, I didn't know that there was a patient with you." She quickly stepped outside the room.

"It's okay, Cheryl, this athlete just came in to talk with me. Have any of my appointments arrived yet?"

"No, not yet, but there are only two scheduled. I just wanted to tell you that Tina's running a little late, as usual. Is that going to be a problem?"

Nik sighed, "Tina's always a little late. She knows that I can't start the physical exams until I have a nurse to assist me. Oh well, just let me know when she arrives. Thanks." Nik shrugged her shoulders and looked up at the ceiling.

Cheryl quietly closed the door, and her retreating footsteps tap-tap-tapped away on the tile floor.

Peter was afraid that he had said too much to Dr. Kellman, but he knew that it was important that she was fully aware of what his problem actually was. He bowed his head, again looking down at the floor, unsure of how to continue.

Nik waited for a moment, allowing Peter to regain his composure. She realized that his admission of less than perfect health had been very difficult for him. "Pete? Look, it's not the end of the world. A hernia repair is almost nothing when you consider that you'd only be hospitalized for a day. Then you'd be off for less than six weeks, and you could return to practice on a limited basis."

Peter blanched, "No, that's impossible. I couldn't stop playing for that long. Grigory wouldn't let me continue to skate with the team."

Nik tried to reason with him, "I understand your concern, but it's *not* that big a deal, Pete. Athletes have surgery all the time. It just takes a little adjustment in their schedules, some rehabilitation, extra practice and so on, to get back in shape."

"No!" Peter raised his voice, "You *don't* understand! I can't have surgery *here*, and no one will touch me at home. My family..." he started to say, and then fell silent.

For a moment, Nik felt a sense of...what? Loss? He has a family, she thought. He's so young, and yet he has a family. The silence in the room was broken by the buzz of the intercom on her desk. Nik stood and leaned over the desk to press the intercom receiver button. Cheryl informed Nik that there was a man by the name of Yakov Popov in the waiting area, and that he wanted to talk with her.

"He's looking at the list of clinic appointments, and is demanding to talk to you about someone by the name of Genchenko. He is *very* impolite, Dr. Kellman."

"Bring the appointment book and come in here, Cheryl. Tell Mr.Yakov Popov that he will have to sit down and wait his turn to talk to me."

"Okay Dr. Kellman."

Before Cheryl turned the intercom off, Nik and Peter heard Cheryl say, "*Sit down Mr. Popov.*" and heard his Russian reply, calling the receptionist a stupid slut.

"That *jackass* will not tell me what to do in my own clinic, and he's not going to abuse my staff, either."

Nik was angry until she looked over at Peter. He had been pale before, but now he looked like a ghost. Cheryl tapped on the door, and then slipped inside Nik's office.

"Here's the book, Dr. Kellman. Mr. Popov wanted to know to whom you were talking, and I told him it was none of his business. He overheard some of *his* yelling at you." Cheryl nodded her head toward Peter.

Suddenly, there was a pounding at the door. "Dr. Kellman, I demand to know who is in there with you!" It was Yakov.

Startled, Nik said, "What the *hell* does he think he's doing?"

She got up from her chair, said, "Stay here!" to Peter and Cheryl, opened the door, went out into the corridor, and slammed the door behind her

Yakov spat invective at her in Russian. He actually tried to intimidate her by getting in her face to spew his insults.

Nik laughed in Yakov's face, "You'll have to speak English, and you'll have to calm down before I will take you seriously."

"Genchenko," he growled, "I want to talk to you about Genchenko. Who is in your office?"

"That is none of your *business*, Yakov. You should know that I must maintain confidentiality in all my dealings with patients."

"I looked in your log book, but there was no name listed. To whom are you talking?" Yakov took what he meant to be a menacing step toward Nik.

Again, Nik laughed in his face. This time, however, she forcefully placed a hand against his chest. "Back off Yakov. What are you, anyway, the KGB?" Nik was beginning to have fun.

Red-faced, Yakov spluttered, "I have reason to believe that Genchenko should not be playing hockey at all. Someone has told me that his injuries are more than he admits to."

"There you go again, interfering in my area of responsibility. I'll give you two choices here. The first one is that I am going to call security to have you removed from the premises. The second choice is that I will put you in one of my patient rooms, and I will see you when I have a moment between patients. The choice is yours."

Yakov swore in Russian, calling Nik, among other things, a stupid bitch cow, his favorite epithet when dealing with a woman he could not control. When he saw no response from her, he decided on choice number two.

"Which room?" he snapped.

"Wa-a-a-y in the back, the last room on the left; number seven. I'll have Cheryl escort you there." Nik opened the intercom, and asked Cheryl to come out with the appointment book.

Cheryl stepped slowly out of Nik's office, taking care not to open the door too widely for fear of revealing the other occupant of the room, "Here's the appointment book, Dr. Kellman, and no one has signed in yet."

"Yes, I know Cheryl, and I have tried to convince Mr. Yakov here that it really is none of his business. Would you please put him in room seven, and close the door? Thanks, Cheryl."

Cheryl walked down the hall as though she might be walking on eggshells, and Yakov followed. When Nik heard the door to room seven closed on its latch, she returned to her office, patient log in hand.

Peter was standing at the window behind the doctor's desk, looking out through the dusty Venetian blinds into the snow-covered street outside. He had been pacing restlessly up and down while Dr. Kellman was talking with Yakov. Cheryl had watched silently as he moved back and forth from the window to the door until the doctor called her.

Several times Peter approached the door, but would then stop and turn away. Coward, he thought, you are hiding behind a woman because you are afraid of what Yakov will do to you. He turned to face the doctor when she came into the room. His face held no glimmer of warmth, no expression at all.

Finally, he spoke. "I'm sorry Dr. Kellman. I was of no help to you at all with Yakov. He is a vengeful, mean little man who usually gets his way. This time, he wants me dropped from the team and sent back to Russia. I won't be able to help my family at all this year, and I don't really know what I am going to do. But Yakov will have his way, I am sure."

Nik shook her head, "No, Pete, Yakov will *not* have his way about you or anyone else here. I can see very clearly that he is a mean little man and I'm also beginning to see that he has a vendetta against you."

Peter's eyebrows went up, quizzically. "Vendetta? What is…?"

"He's out to get you for some reason. *And* he's very serious about it. Let's not go into that just yet. He's waiting to talk to me in one of the back clinic rooms, and I'll get rid of him as soon as I can. Right now, I think I have a quick solution to your immediate problem. Here, sign the book, and put 10:45 a.m. next to your name. Actually, you are one of only two appointments for today, but he doesn't know that."

A soft tap on her office door caught Nik's attention, "Yes?"

"All clear." Cheryl poked her head inside the door, grinning widely now that the danger was over.

The outer clinic door burst open, and was then slammed shut by a robust young woman hurrying into the clinic, cheeks red, long brown hair flying, saying, "I'm sorry, I'm sorry, I'm SORRY! The traffic into town is a real mess! Do we really need more snow?"

She looked upward, arms outstretched, as if beseeching a deity, then quickly shed her coat, boots, and hat to reveal her nurses' uniform underneath the heavy outerwear.

"Tina," Nik beckoned her to come closer, "third time's a charm." Nik cocked an imaginary gun/finger at her assistant.

"I know, Doc, but have you looked outside within the last twenty minutes? It's *awful out there.*"

Glancing down the hall for assurance that Yakov had not come out of his room, Nik told Tina to get room one ready for an athlete's examination.

Tina did a double-take when she saw Peter, "Who's the lucky athlete, this time?"

"This is Peter Genchenko, one of the Russian hockey players. Be nice to him. He's had a bad day, so far."

"The pleasure's all mine, Doc." Tina seemed smitten, and looked up at Peter with a slowly widening grin.

Nik decided that speaking to him in Russian might alleviate some of his apprehension. "Pete, I want to apologize to you for my complete lack of understanding about your situation. I've handled everything rather badly this morning, including the confrontation with Yakov. Let's go ahead and do your physical work-up, if it's all right with you, and then we can discuss where to go from there."

Peter's affect was flat, and he didn't look at Nik when he replied, "There is no need for an apology, Dr. Kellman. Of course you were right about my condition, and you handled Yakov very well, so don't feel badly on either account. I, on the other hand, feel like a coward. *I* should have been the one to confront Yakov, not you, and I am ashamed that I did nothing to help you. "

Nik placed a hand on his shoulder, "Look, Pete, you were in a bad situation for which you had no solution. You were damned if you did help, and apparently, damned in your own mind, if you didn't. Yakov would certainly have taken some negative action against you, if he had known that you were the one talking to me in my office when he came in. I think he must have heard enough of the conversation to put two and two together, and figure out that whoever I was talking to had some kind of physical problem."

Peter was completely deflated from the high that he had been on while skating alone on the ice earlier in the day. The cold ache inside him had returned with a vengeance. He made no reply to the doctor.

"Room one's ready, Doc." Tina poked her head into Nik's office.

"We'll be right there, Tina."

Taking Peter's arm, Nik showed him to room one. Inside, she explained what the examination consisted of. Continuing to speak in Russian, Nik instructed him regarding the patient gown laid out on the examination table.

Nik told him, "First, you have to get a specimen of urine, then come back in here and remove your clothing. The patient gown is for you to wear during the actual exam. Open the door when you are ready and I'll come back in."

Peter went into the tiny bathroom adjacent to room one and provided the asked-for specimen. His brief bout of optimism last evening and early this morning had been shattered by the events of the day thus far. After seeing Yakov in the hotel elevator and arguing with him, then, nearly running into him in the corridor of the arena, and finally here in the doctor's own clinic, where the wretch had tried to frighten and intimidate her, Peter was completely deflated. Still smarting from what he considered to be cowardice on his part, Peter felt cold and numb inside. The ice inside him had returned and was colder than he could ever remember.

His movements were mechanical as he complied with Dr. Kellman's request to strip and put on the patient gown. When he was finished, Peter opened the door and sat on the end of the examination table, head down, feet dangling.

Peter looked up as Dr. Kellman came into the room first, followed closely by the nurse, Tina. Both busied themselves at the counter along one wall of the room. Dr. Kellman turned to him, and began explaining to him in Russian what she would do, and in what sequence. All the while that the doctor spoke to him Peter was aware that the nurse was watching him very closely. He wondered, briefly, if the nurse expected him to jump from the table and run out the door. Well, he thought, that's not a bad idea. He was ashamed for his earlier lack of courage, and was certainly embarrassed at the thought of having Dr. Kellman examine him with this female stranger in the room.

Tina spoke to Nik, "Doc, since I can't ask him any questions for my nursing assessment, I'm going to have to count on you to give me the information I need."

"That's okay, Tina, I'll share with you as I go. Let's get started." Nik turned and gestured to Peter to stand up.

"Gosh, Doc, have you ever seen a man with beautiful feet before? And his hands…look at his hands. The fingers are long and so nicely shaped. Wow, he's beautiful all over." Tina always said exactly what she was thinking.

Nik reddened, "*Tina*, will you at least *try* to be professional?" She looked up at Peter, whose eyes showed some return of expression and warmth.

In Russian, Peter said, "Maybe she has good taste in men."

"Let's just get through this, shall we?" Nik was resigned to her fate.

She ran through a review of systems, maintaining Peter's modesty by keeping his gown in place as best she could. She then handed Peter a towel to lift his private parts away from the area to be examined. She used the left groin area for a baseline normal before examining the right, affected, groin area. All the while, she dictated to Tina as she made observations. Upon examination of the right groin area, she found that the Russian doctor had been correct. There was an inguinal hernia on the right. Because of Peter's size, and the width of his hips, his frame was large; it could even possibly be a femoral hernia, but a hernia, nonetheless. *Damn*, she thought. I was hoping the Russian doctor was wrong. She asked Peter to cough, cough once again, and then cough a third time. Yep, that's what he's got. What can I do to help him? He needs help for his family. This last thought again brought on the feeling of loss that she had experienced earlier. What is the matter with me?

Nik told Peter to sit on the end of the table, and then gently pulled his gown away from his arms and chest. His shoulders were wide, his arms were long and well muscled, and he had a broad chest. There was not an ounce of superfluous flesh anywhere to be seen. There was a large tuft of red-gold hair in the shape of a triangle standing on its pointed end that covered the area between his breasts. His chest narrowed down into a washboard upper and lower abdomen, and again, there was no fat or roll anywhere. Yes, he is beautiful, she thought. Although it surprised her, she agreed wholeheartedly with Tina's earlier comments. What am I doing here, thinking like this? Embarrassed, and with a slight trembling in her hands, Nik began to examine Peter's body for injuries or undiagnosed problems.

Starting with his head, Nik pointed to an elliptical scar above his left eye.

"Hockey," he replied.

She pointed to a mark across his chin.

"Father," was his response.

There was an interesting scar on his right temple. It looked like a gunshot wound.

"KGB," he said.

Nik looked directly into his eyes. Pete was back, and his expressive green-gold eyes told her, "So what?"

Nik lingered a long time over the examination of the puckered scar on Peter's right upper, outer abdomen.

Peter's reply was again, "KGB."

Gesturing for Peter to lie back on the table and roll over onto his stomach, Nik examined some odd scarring in the form of stripes that criss-crossed his lower back.

Leaning down next to his face, Nik asked, "And these?"

Peter replied with one word, "Father."

Nik felt sick to her stomach. Peter seemed stoically unaware that his injuries were anything but the usual wear and tear for a twenty-two year-old.

Cheryl's voice came over the intercom, "Dr. Kellman, your second appointment just called and canceled. Mr. Popov is out here with me again, and he's looking at the appointment book."

"Tina, please go out and tell Mr. Popov that I am not going to have time to see him this morning. Tell him that I will talk with him tonight in the presence of Coach Grigory."

"Will do, Doc." Tina opened the door and let out a mouse-like squeak when she came face to face with Yakov.

Yakov stared venomously at Peter, who was now sitting on the end of the examining table. Peter glared back at him.

In Russian, Peter growled, "You will leave, if you have any sense. Otherwise, I will wring your pitiful neck."

Nik stepped between the two men. Facing Yakov, she said, "I will speak with you later this evening, when Grigory can also hear firsthand what I have to say. Earlier, I gave you two choices, but now you have only one. I will not hesitate to call Security if you do not leave immediately. You have no authority, or business, here."

Yakov turned abruptly on his heel and strode toward the door of the office. He turned and shot another venomous look at Peter, whose examination room was in a direct line with the outer door. He then pushed through the door, causing it to hit the wall with a loud bang.

Nik was almost afraid to turn back to Pete. What must he be feeling? His angry threat against Yakov, delivered in a deep and harsh voice, had frightened her. Was he capable of doing the man harm?

Peter turned his face away from the doctor. He didn't want her to see just how angry he was with Yakov. Peter fought to regain control, wrestling with the demons that he had fought over and over again. When he lost his temper completely, he believed that he could behave like Ivan had always behaved toward his family. He did not want to be like Ivan. He would rather die than be like Ivan. Slowly, he willed his breathing to return to normal. Then he turned to look at Dr. Kellman.

"Again, I apologize for my behavior, doctor, and I am sorry that you had to witness this unfortunate outburst."

Nik looked into his eyes and saw that they were still clouded with anger. His face had taken on a fierce look that worried her very much.

Attempting to calm him, she said, "It's all right, Pete, and it's understandable that you would become angry with such provocation from Yakov. I won't allow him to interfere in whatever decision you and I reach."

Nik then spoke to Tina, "Send the samples to the lab, and finish your written assessment. I'm going to check next door to see if you can help out there the rest of the day. We are all finished here, and there's no reason why you'd have to stay."

"That's okay, Doc, I can run over to Dr. Harmeyer's clinic. I heard he was going to be real busy today with the Canadian hockey team. They have lots of injuries and special needs after their game with our U.S. team yesterday."

"Good. Let me know what Dr. Harmeyer says. If he doesn't need you, you can take a half-day with pay. It'll probably take that long for you to get home anyway, with this rotten weather." Nik was always generous with her employees.

Cheryl asked, "Can I leave early, too? I just heard on the radio that my son's daycare center is closing in the next hour, and my husband's not answering his pager."

"Sure, that's fine with me. Who wants to be out in this weather if they don't have to?"

To Peter, Nik said in Russian, "Go ahead and get dressed, Pete, then come into my office and we will discuss your situation."

Nik returned to her office and started writing up the incident with Yakov Popov. The devious little twit, she thought. How in hell can he get away with his behavior?

Her telephone rang, and she picked it up quickly, with a no-nonsense, "This is Dr. Kellman."

"Hi, Kitten, did you think that I had dropped off the end of the earth?" Ron sounded harried and tired.

"Oh no, I knew that you'd think about me sometime this week or this month, well, certainly by the end of the year, and then call me. How are you doing?"

"Not good, not good. One of our doctors had to drop out of the games, so I've been assigned to his work in addition to all of the other stuff I'm doing, by "guess-who"?"

"Could it possibly be GariBALDi?" Nik liked emphasizing the doctor's name to match his balding pate.

"You got it on the first try. Look, can we get together for dinner or something on Tuesday? The game is early on Tuesday, so I thought we could do something together afterward."

"I can see that you've already forgotten that my mother's going to entertain the Russian hockey team with an open house on Tuesday night. Pay attention, man. Sometimes I wonder what you're thinking when I'm talking to you. Oh well, men never listen very closely to what women have to say, so why should you be the exception?"

Ron sighed audibly into the telephone receiver, "Look, hon', I have to go. I'm due at our team's training table in an hour, and I've got lots to do before then. I'll call you tonight about ten, or maybe eleven, okay?"

Nik exhaled her own sigh. He doesn't remember that today is my birthday. "Fine, I'll talk to you then."

Nik was busily writing when Peter tapped on her door. Now fully dressed, he walked slowly into her office. The expression on his face, more than anything else, showed her that he would rather be somewhere, anywhere, else. The poor guy, she thought, he's had a bad time since he got here.

"Doctor, can we talk later? I'm going to have to find somewhere to get something to eat. I missed the training table this morning."

He looked down at the floor briefly, and then continued, "Actually, I avoided the training table because I knew that Yakov would be there. He's probably waiting outside for me right now, but I know that I need to eat something, or I'm going to end up the way I was yesterday."

Nik thought a moment before answering him. "How would you like to sing Happy Birthday to me over lunch? It's my birthday today, and Mickey and Tom gave me a gift certificate for Churchill's over on Pennsylvania Avenue." Nik took a crumpled piece of paper from her lab coat pocket and held it in her hand.

Peter cleared his throat and attempted a smile, "Happy Birthday, and thank you for the invitation, but I don't think that it would be a good idea for you to be seen with me. It would be in keeping with Yakov's typical behavior to lurk somewhere outside and follow me to wherever I might go. Usually I can outrun or outsmart him, but I wouldn't want to get you involved in any trouble."

Nik said, "Hmmm. Let's see." She drummed her fingers on the desk for a moment, "Follow me."

First, Nik locked the clinic door after placing the closed sign in the window. Next, she beckoned to Peter to follow her out through the back door of her office.

"Let's go down to the security area and borrow some boots and coats. They're always glad to help."

Peter followed Nik down two flights of stairs that brought them to ground level. They then turned left and went through a short tunnel that opened into a large room lined with lockers and security gear.

"Hey, Doc, what can I do for you today?" Terry, the rotund on-duty sergeant called out to Nik from his desk as she and Peter entered the Security Base. There was background radio traffic, and the fluorescent lights were high above the floor, making the area seem shadowy and unreal.

"Hi, Terry. Is it possible to borrow two parkas and two sets of boots for about an hour? This is Pete, one of the athletes that I take care of, and we have an errand to run, but the weather's not cooperating."

Terry looked briefly at Peter, and said to Nik, "That'd be okay with me, Doc. Look's like you'll need an extra small and an extra large for the jackets and the boots, right?"

Nik grinned and also looked up at Peter, "Probably so, Terry. Thanks a bunch."

Terry walked over to a large pile of coats and started rummaging through the stack. "Let's see if I can find some that are dry. The weather's been bad so much lately, that it's hard to stay ahead with dry coats for everybody. Here, try these."

He handed the coats to Peter and Nik. "The boots are over there, and you'll need to trial and error those to see which ones fit. See you later, I got'ta call Nelson and Ivy to check their status." Terry waved, and returned to the radio on his desk.

Nik tried on several boots, found some that fit, and pulled them on first. Good fit. Then she tried on the parka. It was a bit large for her, but who cared? She turned to watch Peter, who was already in his boots, and was zipping up his parka.

"Pull up the hood. We're traveling incognito!" All that was showing from the furry-rimmed hood were her bright eyes.

Nik waved and gave a 'thumbs up' to Terry as she and Peter left the area. They made their way to the front entrance of the arena, and, sure enough, there was Yakov, leaning against a wall, having a cigarette. Peter stopped abruptly at the entry door when he caught sight of Yakov.

Nik took his arm and pulled him through the door. "Don't worry, Pete, he can't see your face, and these parkas have 'Arena Security' in bright yellow five-inch letters across the back. He'll never recognize you, so come on, I'm hungry."

The snow was swirling around street corners, and pouring into the heart of the city. Nik had never seen so much continued snowfall in all her memories of growing up in Indianapolis. There must be a foot-and- a-half on the ground already, she thought. She saw that Pete was keeping his pace slower in order to walk in step with her. The sidewalks were treacherous underfoot, and the streets were just as bad.

Nik pulled at Pete's arm, and pointed to a sign about a block away. "Churchill's," she said.

Peter nodded, "Good." He ached with hunger.

Once inside Churchill's, Peter and Nik felt some warmth, and the wonderful aroma of many different foods cooking. The floors were wet from boots, and damp coats were hung here and there on clothes hooks. The smell of wet wool joined the otherwise tantalizing food smells.

A waiter called out to Nik after she shed her disguise of parka and boots. "Hey, Doc, what're you doin' out in this messy weather?"

"Good question, Phil. I guess it's just because I'm starved, and there's no decent food in the arena. Besides, it's my birthday."

"Well, Happy Birthday, Doc! You probably won't name the year, will you? Find a booth you like, and I'll come over to get your order real soon. The place is really jumping today, and the floors are real slippery, so watch your step." Phil handed Nik two menus as he dashed by her.

Peter indicated a booth next to a window that was fogged up from the inner heat and the outer cold. When they sat down, Nik rubbed a small area clean and peeked out.

Turning to Peter she said, "We haven't been followed," and then smiled at him.

For some reason, Peter's heart turned over when she looked at him and smiled that way. Flustered, he opened the menu and began poring over the offerings therein. Nik tapped him on the arm.

"Are you okay? Are you getting dizzy? I can get some pretzels or something pretty quick. Just a minute…"

Nik jumped up from the table, in search of food for Peter. "Hey Phil, we've got a low-blood-sugar crisis about to happen. Do you have anything that my guest can eat quickly?"

Phil turned from the bar. "Uh, sure Doc, let's give him some orange juice and crackers. Here, take this juice and I'll toss the crackers over to you." Phil dipped his hand into a bowl filled with cellophane- wrapped crackers setting on a serving table. "Incoming!!!" Phil tossed pack after pack at Nik, but it was Peter who caught them all.

"What did you say to him?" Peter was curious about Phil's cracker-tossing skills as he quickly emptied the large glass of orange juice.

"Oh, I just wanted to hurry him up. I know that you're hungry, and I didn't want a repeat of yesterday."

Peter nodded, "I see." He peeled open several packages of crackers and crunched through them very quickly.

As he ate the crackers, Peter realized that this kind young woman had gone out of her way once again to make sure that he was all right. Inside, Peter felt the spread of emotional warmth toward her, displacing the cold ache that was so often there. It had been a very long time since he had experienced such a feeling, and it disconcerted him.

"Here I am Doc, just like I promised. What can I getcha?" Phil's sharp-featured face pointed directly at Nik.

"Have you decided, Pete?"

Peter nodded, "A gentleman always lets a lady order first." He spoke in Russian.

Phil's already pointy ears seemed to perk up at the sound of a foreign tongue, "What's that? Did you want to order something?" Phil looked from Nik to Peter and back expectantly.

"I'll have the French dip. Churchill's French dip is wonderful. Oh, and I'll have a Pepsi with that."

Peter looked at Nik, and then addressed Phil in English, "French dip sounds interesting. I will have the same. However, I'd like to have more orange juice as a beverage. It tasted wonderful."

"Thanks…!" Phil's voice trailed off as he ran for the kitchen with the order.

"Well, say it, Pete." Nik already knew what the question was going to be.

Peter laughed aloud, "I assume that 'getcha' is like 'gotcha', only less so?"

"You'd be quite right, then." Nik rubbed another small area of window clean in order to look out into the street. She wanted to ask Peter about his family, but didn't know how to begin.

Finally, she said, "Pete, tell me about your family. How many children do you have?"

Peter was glancing at the wine list on the table when Nik asked him the question, and his head came up abruptly.

"What?" He was puzzled by Nik's question.

"You said that you were concerned for your family. I just wondered how many children you have."

Peter laughed, "I'm not *married*, and I don't have any children. Where did you get such an idea?"

"Well," Nik began. "You *did* say that you were worried about your family because of your injury."

Peter shook his head. "I was talking about my mother and sister. *They* are my family. I am the only son, and so I must be sure to take very good care of them."

Nik felt an overwhelming sense of relief. He's not married, not a father. Suddenly, she felt that her feelings were transparent, and that Peter could see her relief. Nik could feel her face beginning to turn red. Oh no, he must think that I'm a meddling idiot.

Phil's timing was superb, "Two French dips, with fries and coleslaw. A Pepsi for you, Doc, and an orange juice for you, sir. Need anything else?"

Yeah, thought Nik, a little composure would go well with the French dip. Looking up at Peter through lowered lashes, Nik asked, "Are we all set?"

"Couldn't be better," he replied. Peter liked the way the doctor looked at him through those thick, dark lashes.

Phil scurried off again, trailing his words. "I'll...bring...the...check... in...a...minute."

Although he was ravenously hungry, Peter waited for Nik to start on her sandwich first. His mother had worked very hard to make certain that her children were well mannered. Thinking about his mother brought the doctor's unusual question into perspective. Was she relieved to learn that he was unmarried and *not* a father? He could see that she seemed a bit rattled, or *something*, when he had told her that his only family was his mother and sister. How strange, he thought. Why should she care about such a thing at all?

Finally regaining her composure, Nik began to eat her lunch. Peter followed suit very quickly, and she felt sorry when she realized that he had been waiting for her to start, and that he had been so hungry.

How am I going to fix Pete's training table situation with Yakov? She knew that Yakov would not be open to anything that might make Pete's life easier. Maybe, she thought, I can work something out with Grigory so that Pete could get some breakfast in the training room.

Peter had been watching Nik for some time, wondering what she was thinking. She is unusually quiet, he thought. Could she be upset about something? Ordinarily, Peter was able to gauge or judge someone's attitude or temper, but today he wasn't doing very well with Dr. Kellman.

Nik seemed to be lost in thought, until, looking up, she realized that Peter had finished his lunch, and was looking at her expectantly.

"Oh, gosh, I've been impolite."

"No…no you haven't. I was just trying to see what was troubling you. You seemed to be somewhere else, that's all."

Peter wanted to reach over and touch her hand to reassure her that everything was fine, but stopped himself before he did so. He did not want the doctor to think that he was becoming too familiar with her. He had no right, after all, to touch her for any reason, yet he wanted to do so very much. He knew that their lives were light-years apart, and would always be that way. Peter pulled his hand back from the center of the table.

Nik looked around for their waiter, "Phil must be one of only two waiters in here today. It's the rotten weather that we're having. No one can get around in this stuff. Ordinarily, Indy does fine with bad weather, but we've had snow, upon snow, upon snow. Even the pavement on the streets has been covered for almost two weeks."

It was Peter's turn to rub a clear space on the window to look outside, "You don't like snow? Well then, you should stay far away from Moscow in the winter. Did you know that large groups of women, mostly old enough to be grandmothers, keep Red Square swept clean after every snowfall?"

Nik nodded, "My mother told me that once, and it was mind-boggling to think of such a huge task being carried out by old women. I wonder how many have suffered heart attacks and strokes from the strenuous work of keeping Lenin's Tomb cleared of snow?"

Peter made a rueful face. "The Party would never publish the statistics, even if they were available. They would just extol the strength and virtue of our stalwart Soviet women."

"The Party," Nik said. "That's a real misnomer, isn't it? The thought of a *party* brings to mind happiness and fun. I've heard that the Communist Party is neither."

"Speaking as a former Young Pioneer, I can tell you truthfully that, although I enjoyed some of the other children's friendship and companionship, the Party was all business, and used every conceivable method to indoctrinate Soviet children in the Party's version of history."

Nik watched Peter's face as he talked, and realized that there was a deep bitterness in this young man toward the Communist Party. He did not hide his disillusionment; Peter was a very straightforward kind of man. She liked that in him.

"Your father is Ivan Genchenko. Am I right? My mother asked me whether or not I knew if he is your father."

"Was. Ivan *was* my father. His funeral, and the sickness that I caught from him, are the reasons that I wasn't with the Russian team when they arrived here for the games.

"Ivan was in and out of prison for more than ten years, and brought his last illness home with him. Fortunately, I was the one who became ill. My mother and sister didn't catch whatever it was that Ivan had when he came home. The Party, and its 'arms and legs', the militia and KGB, didn't want to bother with Ivan when they knew that he was dying. They dumped him on us, knowing full well that he would rather go anywhere else than be with us."

"Couldn't he have been taken to a hospital, or some treatment center, where he could get medical attention for whatever was wrong with him?"

Peter wanted to reply, you are very naive, Dr. Kellman, but instead told her, "No, perhaps for some high-level apparatchik, or Party official, but not for Ivan Genchenko. Have you read his trilogy of books on capitalism, democracy, and freedom? Ivan fell from grace in the Party, and their hatred of him, and cruelty toward him and his family, are legendary. My mother, sister, and I were banished from Moscow, and sent to live in a sewer called Lyubertsy after my father was imprisoned in Lefortovo."

"But the books, Pete, didn't the publication of those books help your family?"

Peter's laugh was derisive, "You make an assumption that is inaccurate. Whoever smuggled the books my father wrote while he was in prison received the money and royalties. My father's name, the infamous dissident Ivan Genchenko, was what actually sold the books. Ivan, by anyone's measure, was a talented writer, and was the author of more than ten volumes on Communism before he got kicked out of the Communist Party.

"My mother often told me that his writing ability was what brought them together in the beginning. Ivan went to study in Warsaw as a young man. His father had insisted on it when Ivan had gotten into some kind of bad situation with a woman from a well-to-do family in Moscow. The woman was married, and it caused quite a stir. It was an embarrassment for my father's very prominent family, too. So Ivan was sent to what most of his family considered to be the ends of the earth, Poland, as punishment until the gossip could quiet down."

Nik sat, chin in hands, elbows on table, listening to Peter. "And, had it not been for your father's misbehavior, he might not have ever met your mother. What a story! You could write a novel about that, couldn't you?" Nik was interested in hearing more of Peter's family history.

"Perhaps it started out like a fairytale, but that's not the way it ended. I think that my mother often wished that she had never met Ivan."

"But you talk about your sister, and your mother, too. It's quite evident that you care deeply for them, and protective of, and responsible for, them. If your parents had never met, there would not have been you or your sister. What is your sister's name?"

"My sister's name is Ekaterina. Katya is the diminutive of Ekaterina, a term of endearment. She calls me Petrosha, which is the same thing for my name."

"Who is the older; you or your sister?"

"Katya is older than I am by six minutes."

Nik put a hand to her mouth, "Twins! You mean you're a twin?"

"Yes, twins. Had my mother only carried one child in her first pregnancy, there would not have been a second."

Nik tilted her head to the side and asked, "Why is that?"

"My father often told my sister and me that he had never wanted to have children. Especially, he had not wanted to have children with our mother, a Polish Jew. According to Jewish Law, a child born to a woman who is a Jew is considered to be a Jew as well. Ivan always told us that our heritage was too obvious. He told us that we had Polish Jew eyes, because of their color."

"Your eyes are certainly unusual. I don't think that I have ever seen anyone with your eye color before."

Nik paused, "And I didn't know that the mother determines that the offspring are Jewish. Wouldn't the same be true if it had been your father who had been the Jew?"

"Oh no, a child supposedly fathered by a Jew cannot be considered to be a Jew, because the Jewish man might *not* be the father of the child."

"Are you serious? Isn't that a little paranoid?"

"No, you see, survival is of primary importance to the Jew. Unless the lineage can be traced with certainty, the Jewish race, as they are called, might become extinct. They would disappear from the face of the earth by what is called assimilation. That's why Jewish law is so strict and unbending. The law must be absolute in order to ensure survival."

At that moment, Phil ran over to their table, rolled his eyes and said, "I'm sorry this took so long." He then dropped the check on the table by lifting his little finger from the edge of the tray he was carrying, and hurried away, the tray teetering on one hand, and a handful of soiled glasses in the other.

Nik looked briefly at the check, and then scrawled her signature on the back of her gift certificate. Well Phil, she thought, you're getting a ten-dollar tip this time. She didn't want to wait for change after she glanced at her watch.

"Can you believe that it's already one forty-five? We've been talking a long time! Practice starts at two fifteen." Nik got up and hurriedly tossed on her coat and gloves.

Peter did the same. The doctor is back, he decided, all business again. Peter shrugged into the heavy coat, pulled up the hood, put on his gloves and said, "I am ready for the cold."

They stomped out the door in their heavy boots, and Nik gave a wave to Phil. "See you…"

Phil gave a, thumbs up, sign and grinned at them. "Stay warm, if you can!"

The wind was now in their faces, and even with the heavy coats, boots, gloves, and hoods, the wind had a sting to it. Although the street beneath the snow was level, they found that they had to actually climb moguls and thick patches of snow that snow removal equipment had piled up, and the wind had whipped into little hills and valleys. On one such hill, Peter lost his footing, and went sliding down the other side, coming to rest on his back in the snow.

Standing at the top of the hill, Nik waved an arm in the air and said, "Now you see the great hockey player, Peter Ivanovich Genchenko, has lost his sure footing, and has embarrassed himself before the masses."

Looking up at the doctor from his vantage point, Peter decided to share his misfortune. Reaching up and grabbing her ankle, Peter tugged until she fell screaming down the short incline, landing on top of him. They were both convulsed with laughter, until Peter, quiet now, looked into her eyes. You are a special woman, he thought. How very special you are. He felt that her eyes, dark and framed with thick lashes, spoke volumes, but he was unable to say one word to her.

Nik broke the spell, "Pete, we've got to get back to the arena."

Peter nodded, and lifted her easily into a sitting position, then got up from the snow himself. He reached down, took her hand, and pulled her up beside him. The snow continued to fall, dampening the sounds of the city around them. Peter gently brushed the snow from the doctor's coat, and they started walking toward the arena.

They trudged through the snow as quickly as their heavy boots and the slippery, wet snow would allow. When they finally reached the arena, both of them were breathing hard. The arena was now lit up, even though it was mid-day. They could see that there was a long line of people already waiting to buy tickets for tonight's twin bill: Russia versus Canada, and the U.S versus Sweden.

Peter and Nik ran right past Yakov, who was standing just inside the doors as they entered, without being recognized. Peter was elated. He knew that Yakov wanted nothing more than to get him tossed from the team. I've got to stay away from him, Peter thought, no matter what the cost.

They jogged in an easy lope side by side, until they reached the security area, where Terry was waiting at the door. When he saw them, he made a big production of checking, tapping, and putting his watch to his ear.

"You two can't tell time, can you?" He gave them a lop-sided grin.

"I'm sorry, Terry, I really *did* intend to get these duds back within an hour, but the restaurant service was slow today, and the going was very tough." Nik returned Terry's grin.

"That's okay, Doc, I was just kiddin' you, that's all. No one has needed the coats or other stuff, so it's not a big deal. I just got back from my break, so I didn't really miss you until about five minutes ago. Has the snow let up?"

Nik flipped the hood of her coat back and shook her head. "Not much, but maybe just a little. It's really slippery out there." Nik gave Peter a sidelong glance and smiled.

Peter deftly slipped out of coat and boots, stuffing the gloves into the pockets of the coat. He turned to help Nik out of her heavy garb, and held her by the elbow as she balanced while slipping out of her boots.

"Thanks again, Terry, it would have been a lot colder out there without these coats, and I, we, really appreciate it."

With a wave of her hand, Nik stepped out the door, with Peter close behind. They walked/jogged at a fast pace until they were within sight of the training room, and then their steps slowed considerably.

"Happy Birthday, Doc," Peter smiled down at the doctor.

"Thank you." It was a pleasure, she thought, but didn't give voice to her feelings. She was becoming very comfortable, perhaps too much so, in this young athlete's company.

"I'll be in the training room in ten minutes for my hip wrap." Peter told her.

"Good. Are you feeling better now? You seem to be doing better."

"Don't worry, Dr. Kellman, I'm fine," he replied.

Nik watched as Peter walked toward the athletes' lockers. Was there such a term as macho grace she wondered? If so, Peter Ivanovich Genchenko had more than his share.

Chapter 8

Monday Afternoon

Peter returned to the training room even more quickly than he had told the doctor that he would. It had taken very little time to retrieve his hockey practice gear from his locker, and he had jogged back to the training room so that he would be ready to get out on the ice for practice. As he entered the room, he looked to the right and left to find Dr. Kellman. Two of his teammates, Josef and Nikita, looked at him and then turned away quickly without acknowledging his presence. Briefly, he wondered what their problem might be, but for now, his mind was on hockey. Ah, there she is. He saw that the doctor was working with Ilya's knee.

Peter jumped up and sat on the table beside Ilya, giving the other player a soft jab to his ribs. "How is your knee?" Peter was hopeful that Ilya would not have to sit the bench for the game with the Canadians. The two athletes played very well together, and each depended upon the other when things got rough.

"Petrosha, I tell you, this doctor is *wonderful.* She knows her business, as you can see. When have you ever seen my knee stabilized so well?"

"Perhaps *never*? At least not with some of the trainers we've had." Peter put his arms out wide as he said this.

The two athletes laughed together at this bit of irony. Even though they played with one of the best non- professional Russian hockey teams, they had very little in the way of supplies and assistance. The Party always promised equipment and other necessities, and money to get them, but they seldom came through.

Nik, of course, was listening to Peter's interaction with Ilya, but was trying to remain neutral for Ilya's sake, because she didn't want him to know that she spoke his language. She had discussed her options about the language issue with her mother, who concurred with her decision not to let the cat out of the bag. Both felt that it might cause the athletes to be less spontaneous, and might even make them uncomfortable, so Nik hadn't breached her intent until Peter's mishap upon his arrival.

It delighted Nik that Pete had come over to the table where she was working. This fact slowly dawned on her, and caught her by surprise. How can this be? I've only known him for a little more than twenty-four hours, and here I am, acting like a teen-ager with a new boyfriend. I've got to stop this, she decided, but how am I going to do so if my feelings are spontaneous and without forethought?

Nik indicated in pantomime that she would wrap Peter next. Mickey and Tom had started early in the Doc's absence and had made short work of the other athletes' needs. The team would be taking the ice for practice in fifteen minutes.

"Tom, could you start the other team members toward the ice? I'll have Pete's wrap completed in about five minutes, but I don't want Coach Grigory to have any wasted time on the ice."

"They're on their way, Doc. See you out on the ice." Tom herded the athletes together and moved them toward the door.

The room was empty now, and Nik set out the supplies for Peter's hip wrap. She felt shy because of her earlier reaction, and didn't look at him right away. She was trying to regain her composure.

Finally, in a quiet voice, she said, "Slip out of your thermal underwear, unless you'd rather have me tape your hip over them."

Peter replied, "It would be a more stable wrap if you used underwrap and then tape over my shorts. There would be less slippage of the tape that way, and I can get through practice without having to adjust the wrap. That's how I usually like to have it done."

Nik took a deep breath and then looked up at Peter. There was mirth in his eyes. You're not making this any easier, she thought, but said nothing. Nik's hands trembled ever so slightly as she started Peter's wrap, but she concentrated on the task at hand, and soon his hip wrap was in place.

"How does it feel? Try moving and stretching, that's the test of this particular wrap."

Nik watched as Peter moved about, bending and stretching to see if the wrap would move. Finally, he bent to pull on his insulated underwear, and she knew that he was comfortable.

"It works well, Dr. Kellman. I think you got it right the first time." Peter smiled at her as he quickly put on the rest of his practice gear.

"You'd better get out there on the ice before Grigory misses you, Pete." Calm now, Nik returned his smile.

Peter dashed ahead and Nik followed. Mickey fell into step with Nik as he came out of the supply room with a basket of filled water bottles and the first aid kit. The corridor had an eerie quiet with the exception of Peter's running steps that were now becoming distant. Then Yakov, and two of the athletes that he had seemed to be thick with lately, came out of a side corridor just behind Peter. Yakov was in the middle, and he had a hand on each of the players' shoulders. Although she couldn't hear what he was saying to them, she was aware that something was not quite right about this scenario.

Mickey started to say something to Nik, but she hushed him. She was straining to hear what Yakov was telling the players in Russian. She pointed a finger in their direction, and pantomimed, by cupping one hand behind her ear.

"Listen," she whispered. "They look like they're plotting something. Who is Yakov talking to?"

Mickey frowned for a moment, and then whispered back, "I think it's Josef and Nikita, but I'm not sure."

"Well, I think the three of them are up to something, God knows what, but I wouldn't trust any of them, especially Yakov, to behave like adults."

The trio disappeared around a corner, still unaware of Nik and Mickey behind them. Nik picked up her pace. Then she realized why she had been suspicious when she saw Yakov with the two athletes. The athletes were in full gear, with blade covers over their skates. The odd thing was, they both had hockey sticks already in hand. Usually, the equipment was with the trainers in the practice box. Why would they have their hockey sticks with them now? It puzzled her. Then she realized that the sticks were a different color than the red practice sticks the players ordinarily used. Nik picked up her already fast pace. She was almost running now. Mickey looked over at her, trying to keep pace, realizing that she must be concerned about something, but he wasn't sure what it might be.

By the time that Nik and Mickey entered the Russian box near the ice, they were at a dead run. As they stopped, out of breath, Nik heard Yakov speak to Josef and Nikita in Russian.

"Get him!" Yakov turned to sneer at Nik and Mickey as they entered the box.

Josef and Nikita took the ice, traveling in two directions, but as Nik came up to the box door, she could see that their point of convergence would be Peter, who was standing with his back to them, talking with Coach Grigory, Vladimir, and Ilya. As the two players picked up speed, they began pounding their hockey sticks on the ice. To Nik's horror both sticks broke, leaving jagged edges and sharp points. Nikita and Josef, now armed with potentially lethal weapons, continued to speed toward Peter. Dear God, she thought, oh, dear God, they're after Peter!

In Russian, Nik screamed, "Peter! Peter, za ti! *Look behind you*! Apasnast! *Danger!*"

When Peter heard the doctor scream, he turned to look back at her. As he did so, he saw someone coming at him with a broken stick upraised and he instinctively ducked, narrowly escaping Josef's lunge. The sound of skates digging into the ice on the other side of him caused him to turn in time to see Nikita speeding toward him, broken stick raised to the level of his throat. Peter dodged, but was grazed across his right temple with the sharp end of the broken stick. Immediately, blood spurted, and Peter threw down one of his gloves and held his hand to the wound. Grigory, Vladimir, and Ilya had also jumped out of the way, and were dumbfounded and unmoving, gaping at Peter's blood on the ice.

Again, Peter heard the doctor scream, "He's coming back on the left! Birigees! *Look out*!"

Peter saw motion out of the corner of his left eye, and then ducked before he grabbed Josef at the hips, tossing him backward, over his shoulder. He heard him hit the boards, and then Josef let out a scream of his own. He was impaled through his thigh with the broken stick that he had tried to use on Peter. The other attacker, Nikita, took off across the ice to get away from Peter.

Nik and Mickey ran out onto the ice, slipping, skidding and lurching until they reached Peter and the other injured player. Mickey had had the sense to grab the first aid kit before starting out onto the ice, and he knelt and opened it quickly, pulling out a large sterile pad to staunch the flow of blood from Peter's temple. The ice was red around him with blood. The one eye that Nik could see had a look so fierce with anger that she was frightened.

"Where is he? Where is that pathetic little bastard? I'm going to kill him! *Oobeet yevo!*"

Peter pushed Mickey away as he scanned the area for Yakov. He whirled around and finally saw Yakov hiding behind Grigory. Peter threw the bandage on the ice, and started after him.

Nik saw Tom nearby and shouted, "Stop him...stop Peter! He's got an open wound that's bleeding!"

Tom had his skates on, and if it hadn't been for the angle in his favor, he could not have caught Peter on the ice. When Tom reached Peter, he did a flying tackle in order to bring him down. Peter struggled under Tom's much superior weight, but couldn't get up.

"Hold it, hold it, *damn it*!" Tom tried to calm Peter down, and even though he outweighed Peter by more than eighty pounds, he had his hands full.

Grigory and the rest of the team had been too stunned to react to the mayhem at first. But then, as if awakening from a terrible nightmare, they all erupted at once, shouting and cursing back and forth, until Nik shouted back.

"Off the ice, *now*, GET OFF THE ICE!" Nik's angry voice could be heard above the din.

Grigory put his hands out in front of him in a placating way, "Doctor, what are you saying? We have just had an accident, and you're telling us to get off the ice? We need this practice time before tonight's game. We can't leave without a practice."

Aside, he spoke to Yakov and his team in Russian, "Stay right where you are, we will get this straightened out quickly, and we are *not* leaving the ice."

Filled with cold fury, Nik answered him in Russian. "Oh yes you *are* leaving the ice. I have sent an alarm out, and the security team will be here shortly." Nik looked over to where Mickey was giving first aid to one of the attackers.

Grigory, amazed at the doctor's *instant* Russian, said, "I did not know that you could speak our language, Dr. Kellman. We must have been very entertaining to you."

Ignoring him, Nik called out to Mickey, "How is he doing?"

"He's stabilized Doc. That's about all I can do. I've left the stick in the wound. I don't know what's going to happen when it's removed."

Turning toward Peter and Tom, Nik shouted, "Is Peter okay?"

"I've got the compression bandage back on, but he's sure going to need stitches. He's starting to calm down, too."

Nik called back, "Has security radioed you yet?"

"Affirmative, Doc. In fact, there they are, right now."

Terry was in the lead, with three officers following him. Their boots gave them surer footing on the ice than Nik or Mickey, in shoes, had.

Terry was formal as he addressed Nik, "Dr. Kellman, we received a call from one of your staff that there was trouble out here on the ice. What's going on?"

Nik looked directly at Yakov as she told the officers about what had just happened. She was so angry that her voice was breathless as she described the attack on Peter.

"That man, Yakov Popov," she said, pointing a finger directly at him, "somehow arranged for two players from the Russian hockey team to attack another team member. The player who was attacked was injured, and one of his attackers was injured, as well. The second attacker skated away, but I'm sure that he won't go far. He's a Russian national, and I don't think he's got anywhere to hide."

"Mr. Popov, we will need to talk with you." Terry beckoned to Yakov.

"I want the team off the ice, Terry. I'll call the committee to get their opinion about what just happened, but for now, they're out of here." Nik was emphatic, and pointed to the gate by the Russian box.

"OUT!" Terry also pointed in the direction that Nik had indicated.

The players, still in a daze over what had just happened, started toward their box. Nik saw Ilya skate briefly over to Peter to see if he was going to be all right. Then Ilya skated back with his teammates and, one by one, they filed through the gate. For want of anything better to do, they sat down together on their bench, talking quietly among themselves.

To one of his officers, Terry said, "Go see if you can find the other attacker. He can't have gotten very far in the gear these guys are wearing."

Turning back to Nik, he began, "Dr. Kellman, once the team is off the ice, what do you want my officers to do?"

"For starters, give Mr. Popov the third degree. I'm not sure that you're aware, or not, but I speak and understand Russian very well. Popov's been after Peter Genchenko since he arrived, and today, I heard enough of what Yakov was telling the two players that attacked Peter to know that Yakov's intent was to injure him, at the very least."

Yakov had an officer on either side of him, and his expression was one of extreme disgust. He glared first at Nik, and then at Peter, who returned the glare with one of his own, raising a fist at him, as well.

"Take him down to the holding cell, and I'll be there shortly. The Indy police will be there, too, in a little while. I just got the page, and they gave me a *priority 1*, meaning they're on their way." Terry was still all business.

Grigory approached Nik, trying to smile and make light of what had happened, "Surely, Dr. Kellman, you aren't going to spoil our practice over this misunderstanding?"

Nik shook her head, "It's too late for such a lame excuse, Grigory. You know as well as I do what just happened, and you know perfectly well that if Josef and Nikita had succeeded, we'd be carrying Peter's dead body off the ice right now. Tonight's game is in jeopardy, too. I'm not sure what the committee's decision is going to be, but you and your team may be heading back to Russia tomorrow if the committee wants to do that."

"But this is not that serious. Certainly you can see that? Genchenko got a scratch, and Josef was wounded, but that doesn't mean that we shouldn't be able to play."

"You have let Yakov run your show, Coach, and he's done a bad job. This morning, he barged into my office to interfere with my examination of Peter Genchenko. He was vile and threatening to me, my staff, and to Peter Genchenko. He called me several foul names in Russian, because he had no idea, just as you had no idea until now, that I understand and speak your language."

"What was your purpose in not telling us that very important fact? Perhaps you've had an agenda of your own?" Grigory's face took on a hard look.

Terry intervened, "Dr. Kellman, we have located the other attacker. He injured a police officer during his apprehension, and now he's scared as hell."

"He ought to be! Thanks, Terry, you've been great. Nikita needs to be questioned, too, because I think that he will be able to tell you just exactly what has happened, and who is responsible." Nik looked around for Peter, wishing she could go to him.

Persistent, Grigory came up to Nik, speaking very quietly in Russian, "Listen to me doctor, we *must* play tonight. Genchenko's future, as well as the future of the team, is at stake. If we get sent home because of this situation, Yakov will make all of our lives, but especially Genchenko's, miserable. He has that power, no matter what your police say, or do, to him."

Grigory's words struck a chord with Nik, because of Peter, but she did not want the coach, or Yakov, to get the upper hand in this situation, so she ignored him, and turned away to see about Peter.

When Tom had left his side to help Mickey with the other injured player, Peter sat on the ice near where he had been attacked, his head swimming. He tried to watch Dr. Kellman talk to Grigory, but the effort only made him dizzy. He was out of earshot, but he could see that a battle of words was being waged between them. His heart was beginning to drop back to its normal pace, and his breathing had slowed, but his anger with Yakov was still boiling within him. Peter looked down at the ice, red with blood, all around him. My blood, spilled for what purpose? He knew Yakov would never rest until *all* of his blood was spilled. Peter instinctively knew that this was so.

With some effort, Peter finally wrenched his gaze away from the blood, and tried to clear his thoughts. He realized that his situation had become untenable, and that he was going to have to reach a decision and do something desperate and final in order to keep himself healthy enough to support and protect his mother and sister. A resolve, borne of anguish, heartache, and suffering began to take shape in his mind. How would the world be changed if Yakov ceased to exist? From Peter's perspective, it could only improve. How many others, whose lives had been damaged or destroyed by Yakov, would agree with his own opinion? Grigory would certainly be among those who clamored for justice because of wrongs committed against him by Yakov. Would Grigory rejoice? Yes, his life would definitely be much improved in Yakov's permanent absence.

"Pete…Pete," Nik called to him, taking him by the shoulder. "Let's go back to the training room. I've got to see to your injury."

Startled by this intrusion on his thoughts, Peter instinctively pulled away from her grasp forcefully enough to knock her backward onto the ice, "*Nyet!*" he shouted.

"Hey! Watch out there, Genchenko!" Tom skated quickly toward the Doc, wanting to protect her from harm.

Nik lay still for several moments, and then slowly rolled over onto her side and pushed herself up off of the ice. Her shoulder ached where she had hit the ice, but her first thought was for Peter.

"It's okay, Tom, Peter's still not himself after what's happened. He's probably a little concussed, and I shouldn't have grabbed him."

Tom offered her a hand and Nik stood up gingerly, trying not to show that she had had the wind knocked out of her. She had hit the ice with her left shoulder first, and turning her head to look at her lab coat, she could see that she had picked up some of Peter's blood from the ice. Her stomach contracted, and she felt as though she might be sick right there. Quickly, she put a hand up and squeezed her nose shut. Taking a few deep breaths through her mouth, she felt the nausea and urgency subside. At that moment, she realized that there were tears streaming down her face, and she used the backs of her hands to wipe them away. Tom gaped at her, and looked as though he might be trying to say something.

Nik put her hand up to silence him, "Tom, please help Peter back to the training room. I'm going to have to put some stitches or steri-strips in that head wound."

Nik turned away, embarrassed that she had nearly lost it there in front of Peter, Tom, and Grigory, who was standing close by.

"Wait, doctor, can't you reconsider your ridiculous order to take our team off the ice? We *must* have this practice time to prepare for the Canadians!" Grigory had a desperate look on his face as he trailed after Dr. Kellman.

Nik put her hand out to fend him off. "Get away from me! I don't give a *damn* what you say. You must have known what Yakov was planning, and I don't care if you get sent home to rot in a Russian jail forever!"

Grigory stopped as though he had been shot. Then, recovering somewhat, he hurried after his team, mumbling obscenities about what a 'shit-hole' the U.S.A. was, and how stupid women, in general, could be.

Tom helped Peter to his feet, and was less than gentle with him. Tom was still very angry that Peter had knocked the Doc down.

"C'mon, Genchenko, get a move on. The Doc said she's going to put some stitches in that hard head of yours."

Peter had seen the doctor's tears, and was inwardly cursing himself for knocking her down and hurting her. How could he have taken his anger out on her? She was the only one who had really helped him, had given him a chance to play, and had *fed* him when he was hungry. She had smiled and laughed with him, had seemed to care about him, and he had harmed her enough to make her cry. Suddenly, he was feeling very sick. He pulled Tom to a halt and then vomited on the ice.

"Aw shit, Genchеko, can't you do anything right?" Tom was completely disgusted with Peter.

Nik ran the gauntlet past the Russian team in the box, trying to keep her eyes straight ahead, but seeing the questioning and hurt looks on their faces anyway. Just then, she saw Ron heading toward her from the outside corridor, and she ran the few steps into his arms.

"Good Lord, Nik, what's happened? Garibaldi paged me and said that you'd had some trouble with the team." He held her close against him, and then realized that she was crying.

Her voice was muffled as she told him, "They tried to kill Peter. I couldn't stop them, and they just about got the job done."

"Who tried to kill him? What's this all about?" Looking down at her, he realized that she had blood on her lab coat.

"What the hell…?" He touched the lab coat where the blood saturated the cloth on her shoulder, and she winced.

"Who hurt you?" By now, Ron was angrily looking around to find a guilty face.

Nik, still buried against Ron's chest, shook her head, and then looked up at him. Her tear-stained face caused his heart to turn over.

"It wasn't intentional. I just grabbed Peter when he was still in shock, and he pushed me away, that's all."

Ron looked around the gathered athletes, trying to spot Peter. "The schmuck! He shouldn't have reacted that way to you. Where is he?"

At that moment, Nik saw that Tom was taking Peter out through another gate, and she was glad that he had had the forethought to do so. Peter was looking in her direction, and their eyes met briefly. Then Nik turned back toward Ron, and he tightened his arms around her protectively.

"I've got to get back to the training room, Ron."

Nik knew that Peter would need at least some kind of treatment, and she didn't want him to have to wait for her. What a terrible day *this* has turned out to be, she decided. My twenty-eighth birthday will certainly be a memorable one for all the wrong reasons.

Chapter 9

When Nik arrived in the training room accompanied by Ron, Peter was already there, sitting on one of the training tables. His demeanor was one of defeat. His head was down, and he wasn't even moving his feet. He looked like a condemned man, awaiting an unfair sentence. The bandage over his right eye was saturated with blood, and his jersey and pants were also bloodstained, evidence of a bad day on the ice. Tom stood by his side, looking the part of the executioner. Tom's face was set in a scowl that accentuated his large features, and made him more menacing, even, than his imposing six feet ten-inch frame.

Standing near where Peter and Tom were waiting and out of earshot of other athletes as they came into the room, Ron turned to Nik and asked, "Do you want me to do the stitching on this guy, Nik? He could still give you some trouble."

Nik was looking at Peter as Ron spoke. She could see that Ron's words hurt Peter, because he dropped his head even more, and turned toward the wall.

"Ron, Peter's not in the wrong here. *He was the one who was nearly killed.*"

"He knocked you down, Nik. Maybe he didn't start the whole thing, but he's certainly part of it." Ron put an arm around Nik's shoulders protectively.

Out of the corner of his eye, Peter saw this gesture of affection, and his heart dropped even lower in his chest. He felt completely defeated in every way that a man could be defeated. He had almost lost his life, had been injured, possibly enough to prevent his playing hockey, which would impact his ability to take care of his family, and he had harmed someone that he cared about. Up until that moment, he had not consciously admitted that he actually cared for Dr. Kellman, but there it was, right in front of him. At that point, his self-esteem was at rock bottom.

Nik had been mulling over what Grigory had to say about what would happen to Peter if the Russian team did get sent home because of today's events. Her clarity of thought had returned, and she made a decision.

"Ron, you can talk to Garibaldi and the committee. My first commitment is to the athletes. *You* got me into this whole thing, and now I think that *I* should make the decision as to what to do about this situation. Here's what I want to do. Let the Canadians have the ice for practice immediately, and my Russian team can go one hour prior to game time. Tell the committee that I will write up a thorough report of what has happened, and that it was mostly the work of one man, Yakov Popov, who has been making trouble since he got here. Tell them that I don't want the whole team to be punished because of the work of one idiot. Also, tell them that I checked, and the game is *sold out* tonight. I am sure that they wouldn't want to return all that money, now would they?"

Nik could see that Ron was relieved, and would like to accept her solution. He had a huge responsibility for the success of these games, beyond the medical aspect with the athletes.

"Well," he started, "I can see what Garibaldi says about it."

"Now is the time for a little blackmail, Ron. I have Garibaldi on tape making indecent proposals of a non-medical education nature to me. The bastard actually had the gall to come on to me in his office with a half-baked weekend plan for two last summer on Mackinac Island. Tell him about that up-front, because if he thinks I am protecting my team, he will do just the opposite of what I want. Also, tell him that I have friends at the Indianapolis Star and Channel 6. He'll have a stroke over that." Nik folded her arms across her chest as she finished.

Ron stood there for a moment, mouth open in amazement at what he had just heard. He squinted his eyes half-shut and looked straight into

Nik's eyes.

"Well, you're really full of surprises, now aren't you?" Ron cracked a lop-sided smile and hugged Nik tightly.

Nik wriggled from his embrace and nodded her head, "Go be the messenger, but don't let him kill you. I can assure you that he will be furious about this. Oh well, our program won't lose that big box office tonight, will it?"

Peter, who was close enough to hear their conversation, couldn't believe his ears. Was the doctor saving him once again?

Nik turned toward Grigory and his athletes, who had straggled in one by one, to sit and wait to learn what their fate might be.

Nik spoke to them in Russian. "This is what we are going to do about what has happened today. Dr. Michael will speak with our Medical Director, Dr. Garibaldi, and will then tell the committee how we are going to proceed from here. First, the Canadian team will practice in our place this afternoon, and then our team will practice during the hour before the game with the Canadians. We will then start the game on time with their team. The committee may take some sort of action or censure against our team because of what happened, but *we will play tonight*."

Bedlam ensued. The athletes were vocal and physical in their rejoicing. Grigory could be heard roaring above the din.

"We will win," he shouted, fists raised. "We will win!"

Nik walked over to Peter and said, "Do you think we can tape you back together for the game tonight?"

Peter raised his head, and his eyes met her still tear-reddened eyes. "Da." *yes,* was his only reply. Had he tried to continue to speak, his voice would surely have failed him, as emotion over her speech to the team still had control of his heart.

"Tom, can you get me a prep kit and suture set? I'll need the set with silk suture for the skin."

"Right away, Doc." Tom hurried off to a storage cabinet.

Nik again looked into Peter's very sad eyes. "Don't be sad or sorry about my fall. You'd been attacked, and what you did was just a protective reflex. It was 'textbook', and I shouldn't have made the mistake of startling you. Actually, I owe you and the rest of the team an apology. I over-reacted when I threw the team off the ice. I wasn't thinking straight, and I was still in a panic over what almost happened to you."

"You saved my life," he said simply, looking down at the floor.

Nik could see defeat in every line of his body. "Pete, you and the team are not going to be sent home. You just heard me tell them that news. I realized that, if Yakov didn't succeed in maiming or killing you, his third choice would be that the team would be sent home, and that you would be blamed. I'm not going to let that happen."

His question, delivered as he raised his head again to look at her was, "Why are you doing this?"

"This morning…" Was it just this morning, she thought? She began again, "This morning, when you became angry, and told me that I didn't understand your situation, you were right. I had not the slightest idea of how fragile your existence really is, until this afternoon. I saw what Yakov's true intent was."

Peter saw the doctor's eyes fill with tears, and it was almost more than he could bear. He wanted to console her, to tell her that he hadn't really blamed her for not understanding what his life was all about. How could she understand, when her life was so different from his?

"I'm truly sorry that I didn't comprehend what you have been up against. No one should have to live like that." Nik brushed a tear away from her cheek.

Peter took her hand in his, engulfing it in his own, feeling the dampness of the tear she had brushed from her cheek still fresh there. "Please forgive me for striking you and knocking you down."

He looked at the bloody shoulder of her lab coat, "And I am so very sorry that I hurt you and made you cry."

Nik started to reply, but Tom arrived with the prep and suture kits, eyeing Peter with a malevolent stare as he came into the cubicle.

"Here's the stuff, Doc. What else can I do to help you?"

Nik slipped her hand from Peter's, and took the kits from Tom. "Could you please check to see if anyone on the team needs attention? There may be some loose wraps."

"Okay, Doc. Call me if you need any help with this guy." Giving Peter a parting glare, Tom left the cubicle and pulled the curtain closed.

Nik went to the sink and scrubbed her hands thoroughly, drying them on a paper towel from the dispenser over the sink. Her actions were mechanical and automatic as she opened the prep pack on a Mayo stand, using sterile technique. On a second Mayo stand, Nik opened the suture pack, also using sterile technique.

Turning to Peter, she told him to take off his jersey, and to pull his hair back from the wound. Peter complied, pulling his jersey off quickly. When he tried to free the hair from his wound, he found that it had stuck to his skin, held there with congealed blood. Nik could see that it was painful for Peter to pull the hair away from the area.

"Wait just a minute, Pete. Let me wet the area with some of the prep solution. It should free your hair from around the wound."

Nik donned the prep gloves, wet a sponge in the prep solution, and gently began to rub some of the dried blood away from Peter's wound. She was relieved to find that Nikita's broken hockey stick had not done as much damage as she had feared.

"Well, this doesn't look nearly as bad as the initial bleeding indicated." Nik looked at Peter and smiled.

Peter felt as if he were being hypnotized. The doctor's nearness, and now her gaze, combined to heighten his sense of unreality. He could detect a light fragrance on her person. It was like fresh air and flowers, mixed with a very soft musk. She was close enough to him that he could feel the warmth radiating from her body. Peter was afraid to move for fear that he would break the spell that she was casting over him.

Nik continued to gently rub the blood away from Peter's face and scalp. She, too, felt a sense of unreality at being so close to Peter, touching him. She continued to wash the wound until it was ready for suturing, and then dried it with the sterile towel from the prep kit.

Nik tossed her gloves into the used prep pack, went over and washed her hands again, dried them on the sterile towel from the suture pack and then put on the pair of sterile gloves. She opened the vial of Xylocaine in the pack, and drew up one milliliter of the drug into the small syringe also included in the pack.

"This will sting a bit, but it's much better to numb the suture area because the stitches tend to pull when I tug a little to tie the knots. Is that all right with you?"

Peter nodded, but said nothing. He was afraid to speak for fear that his voice would betray what he was feeling. The sense of unreality continued to cling to him. Rationally, he knew that there could never be anything between them, but his heart was behaving in a particularly irrational way at the moment. He feared the thaw that the doctor had caused to begin within him. It meant that he would feel emotion again, but with the emotion would come pain. He had had enough pain in his life. It would be best to remain frozen, and without emotion. That was the only way to survive.

Nik deftly and quickly sutured Peter's wound, relieved to find that the artery was intact. She could feel the quickening in Peter's temporal pulse, and wondered why it had increased. Was she hurting him more than she realized? And then she thought about this new wound on Peter's face. It made her sad to think that this would be another scar for Peter. How would he describe this one to the next doctor that examined him? He'd probably just say, "hockey" the way he had when she was tracing the various scars and old injuries on his body during his physical exam.

When she finished suturing Peter's wound, Nik gently patted it dry with a sterile four by four, put some triple antibiotic cream on the wound edges, and then pulled steri-strips for extra reinforcement across the wound before putting a sterile dressing on it.

"Done." Suddenly, Nik felt very weary. She wanted this day to be over.

Peter sat motionless. His feelings were at the opposite pole from the doctor's. He did not want this moment to end. He had enjoyed the doctor's touch, had been briefly, if fleetingly, happy in her closeness, in her soft scent, in the wonderful warmth of her body.

Grigory broke the spell when he moved the curtain aside and asked, "How is Genchenko doing?"

"He's almost as good as new. For the game tonight I'll put a hard plastic protector over the wound for safety's sake."

Grigory let out a long sigh of relief, "We are back in business, then?"

"Yes, for now." Nik gave Grigory a long, hard look that implied that he needed to watch his step.

Nik turned when she heard someone calling her name. It was Terry, hurrying over to her, his bulky coat slowing his progress through the gathered athletes.

"Dr. Kellman, the Indy police are going to release Yakov Popov in about an hour. I got a call from the Desk Sergeant, and he said the Russians were pulling diplomatic strings, in spite of what Popov tried to do to Peter Genchenko. They didn't seem too interested in the athletes involved, though, and they are still in custody. Well…one is in the hospital, and the other's waiting to be questioned."

Peter overheard what the security officer was saying to the doctor, and he stiffened with anger. Bastard, he thought, Yakov will probably start plotting again the moment he gets the chance. Anger began to burn inside Peter again.

Nik spoke to Grigory in a crisp tone. "I don't want Yakov anywhere near this team tonight, or for the rest of the games, for that matter. Is that clear?"

Grigory replied, "I have no control whatsoever over Popov. He comes and goes as he pleases, and I cannot tell him to stay away."

Nik spoke to Terry again. "If you see Popov, detain him. I absolutely do not want him anywhere near this team. I'm very certain that he will try to hurt Peter again."

"Yeah, Doc, I understand your concerns. We are going to keep him out of your way even if we have to sit on him. You've got my word on that."

Nik breathed a sigh of relief, "Thanks again, Terry. You and your staff have been great about this whole thing."

Nik looked around the room, taking in the very different demeanors and speech of the athletes. They had gone from despair to good humor rather quickly, she decided. Then her gaze returned to her special charge.

"Peter, try to walk around a little, and see if you have any problems. I don't think that you're going to have any, but be careful. If you get dizzy, or feel nauseous, let me know immediately, okay?"

Nodding assent, Peter slowly stood up from the training table. He wasn't sure how his balance might be. His head ached on the side that he had been struck, and the wound stung. He walked on his skate blades, without blade covers, something he ordinarily would not do, to where Ilya was standing. Peter was glad that he was not dizzy. When Nikita had gouged him with the broken hockey stick, he had hit Peter hard enough that his neck had snapped back, and Peter was afraid that he might have a concussion, even though the doctor assured him that he did not.

Ilya put his arm around Peter's shoulders, and asked, "You're going to be able to play tonight?"

Peter smiled and told him, "Da, no problem."

"It really was Yakov's fault, you know. I don't believe that Josef, or Nikita would have done this on their own. Grigory is really afraid of Yakov, and I don't blame him." Ilya was angry.

"Don't worry, Ilya, Yakov's going to leave me alone from now on." Peter's delivery was stone-faced.

"How can you be sure? You know what a bastard he can be, and you now know what he is capable of doing."

Yes, thought Peter, I certainly do. "I said don't worry, Ilya. All we have to do is win hockey games. We both know that we can do that, so we just have to focus on what we can do, and forget about everything else."

"I know, Peter, but when I saw what was happening to you, I just froze. I couldn't do anything. I'm ashamed, because I failed our friendship."

"You think that *I* didn't freeze? If the doctor hadn't warned me, especially about the second attack, I might not be standing with you now."

"Petrosha…" Ilya swallowed hard. "I can't bear to think…"

It was Peter's turn to place an arm around Ilya's shoulders. "Yakov didn't succeed. *He's* the one who got arrested. Wouldn't it have been interesting to have been there when he was questioned by the police?"

All of a sudden, the training room became quiet as the team realized that Yakov was standing in the doorway. He had a sardonic look on his face as he scanned the room, his eyes coming to rest on Nik.

"So, Dr. Kellman, you thought that you could banish me from my team. Well, I am back, and you can do nothing about it."

Before Nik could reply, she saw Peter lunge at Yakov. He caught Yakov at waist level, and the smaller man flew through the air, coming to rest on the floor of the outside corridor. Peter grabbed Yakov's shoulders and hauled him to a sitting position, shaking him furiously as he did so.

The training room was immediately in an uproar, with athletes shouting and pushing each other to get a better look at Peter and Yakov.

"Peter, no…please stop!" Nik's voice betrayed her fear.

Grigory intervened, his large frame and greater weight giving him the advantage over Peter. Mickey and Tom also jumped into the fray and helped to pull Peter from Yakov. Terry and two of his security officers rounded the bend in the corridor just as Peter was pulled from Yakov, who had begun to bleat like an injured sheep.

Terry was out of breath, red-faced and angry. Gulping air, he shouted, "I gave you fair warning, Popov, but you wouldn't listen to me! *Now* I think you might have some idea of why I tried to keep you away from this team. They don't want you, and it's dangerous to your health to be around them after what you tried to do today."

Peter, fists balled tightly, was ferociously angry at having been stopped in his attack on Yakov. After more than two years of Yakov's viciousness, Peter had had enough. He was beyond reason at this point, and he wanted only to prevent any further abuse. He pulled his breath through bared teeth in quick gulps, and he could feel the bile rise in his throat. His nostrils flared as he breathed, and his face was a mask of cold fury.

Nik could see the ferocity of Peter's anger toward Yakov, and she realized that it could prove to be his downfall. His anger was frightening to see. She felt helpless to do anything, and very afraid for him. Nik wanted very much to go to him, to comfort him, and she knew that she could not. Her heart ached for him.

"Doctor Kellman..." Terry touched Nik on the shoulder to get her attention. He had been trying for a few moments, realizing that she had had a very bad day, and wanting to give her a break.

"Doctor Kellman, I'm going to take this Popov character back to his hotel. How in the hell...uh, sorry...I don't know how he got past us, and I'm really sorry that there was such a ruckus."

Nik wanted to say that it was not his fault, but Terry *had* let Yakov weasel his way back into the training room. Wearily, she said, "Terry, I know that you feel as bad as I do about this whole thing. None of it has been your fault, so you don't have to apologize."

Terry, his coat open, had his hands on his hips and eyes on the floor. "Well, I could have done a whole lot better than I did."

"Please Terry, just take him away. I never want to see that man again." Nik pointed in the direction of Yakov.

Yakov had finally pushed himself up off the floor, and was looking around, owl-eyed and fearful, to see where Peter had gone. He moved closer to the security officer in order to derive some protection.

"Let's go Popov. You're going to have to stay away from here for your own safety. If you aren't smart enough to know that by now, well then, you'll just have to take the consequences."

Terry had run out of patience. He turned and started to walk away, and Yakov didn't have any choice but to follow him.

Grigory had been standing a few feet from Yakov. When Terry and Yakov passed him, Yakov made a gesture, pulling a finger across his throat, and glared at Grigory.

Grigory got the message. He knew that Yakov would carry out his threat. He also knew that this would be the last time that he would ever be allowed to coach a Russian hockey team. Yakov would ruin him. Grigory would be disgraced, and stripped of the one thing that he loved, his hockey. He ground his teeth in impotent rage.

Peter had seen Yakov's gesture to Grigory, and he realized just what it meant to Grigory and the rest of the team, including himself. It served to harden his anger even more.

Mickey came back into the training room to tell the doctor that the Canadians had graciously left the ice a half-hour early so that the Russians could get their practice in before the game. Well, that was a good thing, she thought, but it follows so many other really bad ones. Nik didn't hold out much hope that her team would prevail over the Canadians. Too many bad things had happened in a very short time. It had been like a roller coaster. As she looked around the room, she could see that the team's momentum had been slowed almost to a standstill, and she was at least partly responsible for it. Damn, damn, *damn.* She recited her litany of frustration.

In Russian, Nik told the team, "It's time to get back out on the ice for practice. The Canadians have given us a break, so let's make the best of it."

The athletes seemed sluggish and slow to respond to Dr. Kellman's words. Peter realized that the team was looking at a loss in tonight's game, before the game ever got started. He didn't know, after the events of the day, whether he could muster the strength to be the spark plug for the team tonight. His head ached, and he had hurt his back when he had thrown Josef over his shoulder. He was beginning to feel stiff, and it worried him, because he had been injured at other times when his muscles were cold and stiff.

Tom barked out instructions to the team. "The re-wraps need to stand over there by the tables, and you others can get out on the ice and start your warm-up rounds. *Get going,* we don't have a lot of practice time!"

Even though some of the team didn't understand English, many did, and they began to move. Tom looked over at the Doc and she gave him a thumbs-up, and silently mouthed, *thank you.*

Peter was passing by the doctor when she reached out to touch his sleeve, "Are you going to be able to play tonight?"

"There is no other choice, is there?" Peter, his anger diminished, was low-key to the point of stoicism.

"Are you feeling dizzy or nauseous, any head pain…anything?" Nik could see how tired and deflated Peter's earlier anger had left him.

"No, I am fine," Peter lied.

He turned away to follow his team members, and Nik's heart dropped. She saw the line of his shoulders, and knew that he carried the weight of the world on them.

Chapter 10

The game was sold out in spite of the weather. The stands began filling quickly as soon as the doors to the arena opened. People hurried into the stands as though someone might be overtaking them to vie for their seats. For some reason, there was a boisterous quality to the crowd that differed greatly from the game with the Swedes. As people rushed in, the noise level increased exponentially. An organ, playing pre-game music, added to the decibel level and cacophony via the sound system. The Zamboni scooted along the ice, smoothing it to a frozen glass-like surface.

Large Russian and Canadian flags hung from cables above the ice. Tonight would be a red night. Both teams would be wearing red, and it appeared that the majority of the spectators would be wearing red, too. Set-up crews worked furiously in twos and threes to make sure that all was in readiness for the game regarding the sound system and lighting. Nik looked up to see two men walking on the catwalk high above the ice. Whoa! Just looking up at them made her dizzy. Who has the cajones to do that? Nik had long ago resigned herself to her own acrophobia.

Well, Nik thought, this has been a red letter day thus far, so tonight should be no exception. She had cleaned up by showering in the women's dressing area, and had used her emergency change of clothing and smock to at least present a professional appearance. She pulled her hair back in a ponytail just to get it out of the way. The shower had helped to revive her, somewhat, but she still felt weary and uneasy.

The afternoon practice had not gone well, and Grigory had been disgusted with his team. Dispirited, no one seemed to be able to follow the plays that would be the keys to whether the team would win or lose this game.

Nik's spirits were also low as she watched how badly the team, and especially Peter, fared during practice. Several times, when Peter skated over to the bench for water, Nik asked him if he had any pain or discomfort, but he had been noncommittal, saying that he was all right. The practice ended with Grigory storming off the ice and out the exit. It was a bad moment for everyone.

Nik, with the help of Tom and Mickey, had gotten the team ready for tonight's game. There was very little of the pre-game chatter that had gone on the previous day. Mostly, there was silence in the cavernous training room, but it spoke volumes about how badly the team members were feeling.

Because of the practice switch, there was no time for a meal, and so she gave the athletes the same liquid protein and carbohydrate solution that she had given Peter to give him a boost when he had first arrived. Nik had apologized to all of them, and had told them that tomorrow night she would make it up to them at the open house her parents were hosting in their honor.

Out of the corner of her eye, Nik saw two men walking toward her from the stands. She didn't recognize either of them, and wondered whether they might be connected with the Indy Police Department. Well, she thought, what else can happen?

One of the men offered his hand. "Hi, I'm Sheldon Levin, and this is Marty Pelham. We're here to watch Peter Genchenko skate tonight."

"Was he expecting you?" Nik's affect was flat.

"Uh, I told Genchenko that I'd bring my friend Marty, here, to watch him play tonight. Marty's a scout for a couple of NHL teams and he's always on the lookout for new talent." Sheldon adjusted his glasses by pushing them up on his nose, and grinned an infectious grin at Nik.

"Peter told you to come tonight?" Nik was slow in reacting.

"Well, I saw him working out this morning at the hotel, and if he plays hockey anything like he does his workout, he must really be something on the ice. I talked with him a little while and told him that I'd see him tonight."

Nik realized that this was something important to Peter, and tried to smile as she said, "I'm Dr. Kellman, the team physician. Would you like to sit with me on the bench to watch the game?"

Sheldon and Marty beamed, and said in unison, "Thanks!"

Sheldon handed Nik his card, and Marty did likewise. Nik looked at them and was impressed with their credentials.

"Can you give these to Genchenko? We'd really like to talk to him after the game."

"I'll see that he gets them. But, you've got to wait until the game is finished. He doesn't need any distractions before the game." Nik hoped that she sounded properly firm and professional.

"Thanks, Dr. Kellman, we really appreciate the great seats." Sheldon Levin was about as happy as a man could be.

At that moment, the crowd erupted with shouts, stomping, and applause as the Canadian team took the ice. Nik watched them, and she realized that the team was *big*. They looked more like football players in hockey gear. Oh Lord, she thought, this team looks very tough.

The Russian team, to her surprise, came out into the arena as though they had been catapulted onto the ice. They began to skate furiously in a tight pattern, each man cutting behind another and turning sharply to complete the serpentine pattern, then turning and skating backward through the same formation. The crowd went wild. Nik realized that number 17 was leading the team through their pre-game exercises. His face was set in concentration, and she saw that he was completely focused on what he was doing. For some reason, a bit of hope rose inside her. Peter looked the same way that he had when he took the ice against the Swedes, with the exception of the bandage on his right temple.

Grigory, with his shadow, Vladimir, came out and stood beside Nik. She looked up at Grigory and saw that he did not seem angry anymore. His arms were folded over his large chest much in the same way that he had folded them the night before. Finally, he looked down at Nik and smiled.

"I don't know how, but Genchenko has convinced the team that they have a chance against the Canadians. He actually managed to talk them into believing that they could overcome what happened today." Grigory was shaking his head in disbelief.

"Peter didn't say much when Tom and I were getting his wrap tightened before the game. When did he talk to the team?" Nik was curious.

"I was trying to think of something to say to them before the game, and Genchenko started talking. He told them that they could get rid of the bad things that happened today if they concentrated on transferring their feelings into action on the ice. He said that they shouldn't take out their anger and disappointment on each other, but should use them against the Canadians. It was an interesting speech, and I could see Ilya, Mikhail, and the others starting to get excited." Grigory shrugged his large shoulders, as if he couldn't understand how Peter had turned the team around.

Nik's heart skipped a beat, and when she turned to look out onto the ice at the team, she could see that they were not the same team as the one that she had watched during practice. Peter was definitely leading them, giving them cues and signals, exhorting them verbally, physically interacting with his teammates. Nik had her hands in the pockets of her lab coat, and she fingered the two business cards. Perhaps it would be all right for these two men to watch this game. Perhaps, too, Peter could work a miracle.

The buzzer sounded, and the teams gathered in their boxes. Grigory pointed to those team members who would be in the starting lineup, and Peter was one of them. Each of the players listened carefully to Grigory's plan of attack, then took each other's hands, raised them, and shouted in unison, "Vmyestye! *Together!*"

Nik entered the box. She wanted to check on each player's readiness, and to see whether there had been any problems encountered during the pre-game skate. In particular, she wanted to check Peter's head wound to make sure that the dressing was intact. When she approached him, he looked at her, and she could see that he was calm.

Before she could ask, he said, "I'm fine, Dr. Kellman, so don't worry. There is no pain." He touched the dressing.

Nik felt a lump in her throat. "Good, that's good, Pete. But please let me know if there's a problem." She gently touched his dressing, and then went on to check another player, although she looked back at Peter briefly as she moved away from him.

The buzzer sounded, and the starting six from both teams leapt out onto the ice, the goalies heading for their respective goals. The spectators, no matter their allegiance, erupted into a thunderous roar, with stomping and clapping in rhythm to the loud music from the organ.

At first, there was just a small contingent that started chanting, "I-van, I-van, I-van the Ter-ri-ble." Others took up the chant, until it seemed that most of the crowd was shouting it. Peter didn't need this added thorn in his side, but he couldn't ignore the insistent chant. It was thunderous. He shook his head, then filled his lungs with the cold air off the ice and continued to the face-off circle. He only hoped that he could last for the duration of the three twenty-minute periods in the game.

He didn't say it often, but this time he said aloud, "Bokh pomasch minya pazhalsta." *God help me please.*

Nik knew that the chanting must be hurting Pete. She saw him shake his head, but there was nothing to be done, so she went back to the bench. Sheldon and Marty were standing and shouting, just like the rest of the crowd. Bedlam ruled, and Nik could feel her own excitement build. A chance, she thought, all he needs is a chance. Please God, let him at least have a chance to win. Perhaps Pete, in spite of what had happened to him today, would show these two men that he could play hockey better than they had ever seen it played before.

It was an all-out game. Both teams played strongly, roughly, but it seemed that the larger Canadian players had the advantage. They were the first to score, and had done so quickly, within the first two minutes of the game.

Peter realized that, even though his height gave him an advantage, he did not have the bulk of the Canadians, and it would be foolhardy to get tangled in the boards with them. Instead, Peter, leading his team, played a more cerebral game. He was faster and more agile than the Canadian skaters, and he knew it. He finessed most of his attackers by luring them into the boards as he narrowly escaped contact. It was a new twist on board checking. Most of the time it worked, but he had also been slammed into the boards a couple of times by one player, in particular, who was mucking; scrambling and battling for the puck in the corner with Peter. Peter played left wing, a mostly offensive position, and his nemesis played right wing, but Peter found himself confronted by the Canadian player time and again.

Every time that Peter, with some help from Ilya and Mikhail, decoyed a Canadian skater into the boards, Sheldon and Marty would shout, jump up from their seats, and wave their arms in the air. Nik decided that they must like what they saw as Peter's strategy began to yield results. He had one, then a second, goal very quickly. The Canadian team seemed dazed, and the Russians did not let up.

At the beginning of the third period, the Canadians had gotten a second wind, and had scored two more goals. The score was two to three in favor of the Canadians. Peter had begun to tire by the end of the second period, and Grigory had benched him for some rest.

Nik went to the bench to check Peter's wound to make sure that it had not begun to bleed again. He had taken his helmet off, and Nik saw that his hair was darkened with sweat. She bent down and touched him on the shoulder. When he looked up at her, she could see the strain in his face. He was pale, too, and it scared her.

Nik crouched down next to him and spoke into his ear. "You need something in your stomach, don't you?"

Peter nodded his head, "I am very tired, doctor." Momentarily, he hung his head.

Nik made a quick decision. She waved at Mickey on the bench behind the team, and he came running.

"What d'ya need Doc?"

"Get me some more of the high carb/protein drink as fast as you can. Also, bring some of the electrolyte drink, too. I'm going to mix up a cocktail for Peter."

"It's in the fridge in the training room, isn't it?" Mickey hesitated for only a moment.

"*Yes*, now get going!"

Grigory came over to them, concern wrinkling his forehead, "Is there something wrong with Genchenko? I need to put him back in the game."

"He's okay, Coach, but he's going to need something to replenish his fluids. Give me just a minute, and then you can put him back in the game."

"We don't have many minutes left." Grigory looked long and hard at Peter, then turned and walked away.

Nik saw panic in Peter's eyes. "Doctor, I've got to get back on the ice!"

Mickey ran up to them. "Here you are, Doc, I brought a big cup to mix the stuff in, too."

"Well, open it up and mix it!" Nik had lost all patience.

Startled by her response, Mickey quickly opened the bottles, and began mixing Peter's drink.

"There you go, Peter." Mickey handed him the cup.

Peter took a long drink with his eyes closed. After the fourth deep swallow, he opened his eyes.

"I'm ready to go back in now…tell Grigory." Peter stood up and strapped on his helmet.

By the time that Nik got Grigory's attention, Peter was at the gate. Grigory immediately called for a time-out.

Nik watched from a distance as the Russian team circled around Peter and Grigory. Tom and Mickey quickly passed out water bottles, and Peter grabbed one, too. Turning it up, Peter filled his mouth and swallowed deeply several times, and then splashed some on his face. The players nodded their heads as they listened, and each touched Peter on his shoulders, or patted him on the back.

Twelve minutes were left on the clock. Peter stared for a moment at the scoreboard; two to three in favor of the Canadian team. He didn't believe in miracles, but he felt that he would need one to win this game. His team members' concern for him, expressed in their gentle touching of his shoulders and back, had touched his heart, as well. It surprised Peter, because he didn't usually allow himself the luxury of feelings. There was always the cold place inside him, frozen over from the many years that he had had to battle his father, and others who threatened him and his family.

Face-off was between Peter and a very large Canadian. They eyed each other, sticks raised in readiness for the puck to drop to the ice. The Canadian, not realizing that Peter could understand what he was saying, called him a red son-of-a-bitch.

Peter replied in English. "You're wearing red, too, so maybe *you* are the red son-of-a-bitch." Peter's response surprised the Canadian, leaving him open-mouthed, with nothing to say.

Peter chose Ilya and Mikhail as potential receivers, and had positioned them in areas where he thought that he could place the puck if his stick was the first on the ice when the referee threw the puck down. He *had* to take control of the puck. There was no other choice. A rivulet of sweat ran down his back. He knew that he was not at his best tonight. But he also knew that he couldn't let his teammates down. The greater good, he thought, the greater good. If he couldn't do it for himself, he would do it for them.

The puck went down, and Peter swept it to Mikhail. Ilya was close by and took the puck on a pass from Mikhail. Then Peter took a pass from Ilya, and sped ahead of them, his Canadian shadow chasing him up the ice. Just before he crossed the blue line, Peter deked, spun tightly, and skated back toward Ilya. The Canadian didn't stop, crossed the blue line, and continued into the attacking zone as Peter again turned and brought the puck across the blue line. The linesmens' whistles blew in unison.

"Great!" yelled Sheldon as he stood up to cheer Peter's move.

He elbowed Marty, "Look at that! Did you see what Genchenko did?"

Marty was grinning from ear to ear, "*Oh yeah! Offside!*"

The crowd was standing, shouting, clapping, at a fever pitch. *No one* was shouting 'Ivan the Terrible' now. They were cheering Peter on. Nik didn't understand the reason for the tumult, but she knew that it meant something good for Peter.

Again the Russians and Canadians were brought to the face-off circle. Peter's strategy was to shake the Canadians up, and break their rhythm of play. The linesman tossed the puck down and Peter sent the puck to Ilya. He skated quickly around and behind his Canadian shadow, thus becoming *his* shadow. Peter followed him for a short distance, deked, spun quickly away from him, and went up the left side of the ice as fast as he could go toward the Canadian goal. Ilya and Slava were already there, passing the puck back and forth between them. Mikhail followed Peter. The Canadians were struggling to keep up.

"Marty, look! Look at Genchenko! Have you ever seen anything like him on the ice?" Sheldon was far too excited for a man of his age and girth.

Nik, sitting next to him, hoped that he wouldn't need cardiopulmonary resuscitation. However, Sheldon had a point. Peter's skill was so far above most of the other players, from either team, that it was a joy to see him skate. The crowd loved it, and they were now calling "seventeen, seventeen," and also clapping and stomping.

Peter reached the goal and circled quickly around and behind it. The goalie went from side to side of the goal nervously trying to anticipate whatever Peter was trying to do to him. Mikhail, Ilya, Slava, and Vanya began crossing back and forth in front of the goalie, appearing to rush into the attacking zone toward the goal, passing the puck between them. The Canadians, catching up to the Russians, were furiously trying to get around the linesmen without doing them bodily harm.

Peter split the defense by breaking through two Canadian defenders and catapulting into the attacking zone. Suddenly, Peter was in the crease in front of the goal. Mikhail, in possession of the puck, using Slava for a screen, made a snap pass to Peter, who put the puck into the goal. Immediately, the red light came on, indicating the goal. The goalie had tried to smother the puck with his body, but had not succeeded as he sprawled flat out on the ice in front of the goal.

"SCORE! Genchenko's got a hat trick!" The sportscaster's excited voice boomed over the loudspeakers.

The spectators were on their feet. It was clear that they were applauding Peter's play, but it puzzled him. The only thing that he had done was to play the game to the best of his ability. He believed that all of the other players did the same, so he was surprised when the crowd singled him out. What about Ilya, Slava, Vanya, Mikail, Arkady, and the rest of the Russian team? Without them he would be nothing.

Peter again checked the clock. Three minutes to go. Mikhail was in the face-off circle with Peter's Canadian shadow. The puck went down, and the Canadian sent it to his left wing. Close by, Peter stick checked the left wing and skated away with the puck. The crowd roared as one voice, "Seventeen, Seventeen!" The Canadians called time out.

Grigory was a different man, and therefore, so was Vladimir, who took his cues from him. Grigory now had some reason to believe that his team might be able to win tonight.

Smiling, he told them, "We can finish this one, and in our favor, too. But you have to be vigilant. They are one of the best teams that you have ever played, so take care.

"Now, to strategy; Peter has the puck, and I want him to pass it to Vanya, then hang back until the Canadians show us what their defense positions will be. Mikail, you and Ilya will go right up the center. I'm putting Boris in for Slava, and I want him to rag the puck until Peter comes charging in from the left with Dmitri. Then, Boris will pass to Peter, and *both* will rush the goal. This is the play we tried in practice this afternoon. Hopefully, all of this will result in a goal."

Nik watched from a short distance away. She was intent on trying to detect any changes or problems in the players. She realized with more than a little surprise that she was especially concerned for Peter. The larger Canadians had punished the Russian team at every turn, and Nik's concern was very real.

Mickey and Tom watered the team as Grigory talked strategy. Peter glanced over at the doctor and smiled. Nik felt his smile all through her body in little electric bursts. He's going to be okay, she thought, he's going to make it through this game.

Grigory bent forward, putting his arms around the closest players, "It has been a bad day for our team, but this win could change it all. Tomorrow, we will play the Americans if we win tonight. Otherwise, we might not get a chance to teach them a lesson. Let's not forget what happened in 1980 during the Olympics. Does anyone remember Captain Mike Eruzione and his U.S. hockey team?"

Grigory's words had a profound effect on the team. Tired though they might be, they were energized by the thought that they could face, and defeat, the Americans.

With their arms around one another, they shouted their battle cry, "Vmyestye! *Together!*"

The Russian team had possession of the puck when play resumed. The Canadians were, if possible, even more aggressive than they had been before the time out. Peter's cerebral play turned into a combination of finesse and aggression. He skated a fine line between them, always a skate blade or two from disaster.

The Canadians and Russians traded the puck back and forth many times without success at either goal. There was much mucking, battling in the corners for the puck, and board checking, not to mention a slashing or two, and a spearing, that hadn't been seen or called by the referee or the linesmen. A rough play call had been made against two Canadians, and one Russian, Slava, who spent time in the penalty box for rough play that *had* been called. The Russian goalie, Arkady, had several saves, and had smothered the puck twice. The Canadians were relentless, however. Peter knew that sooner or later they would score, no matter the defense. It was simple mathematics; statistical probability. Something his father had always used in predicting recurring events.

The last time that Peter looked at the clock there was a minute and ten seconds of play remaining in the period. The Canadians were in possession of the puck, and Peter was chasing the Canadian center up the ice. Peter caught him before the Canadian reached the attacking zone and body checked him. Peter quickly took the puck away from him, and deked to the right, passing the puck to Vanya, skating past him, and taking the pass back from Vanya, then sending it to Boris. Peter was literally skating rings around the Canadian players.

Nik was enthralled watching Peter skate. It truly amazed her, all things considered. Where does he get the energy to do this? She saw, too, that Sheldon and Marty were spellbound watching the way Peter and his team controlled the ice.

The spectators had quieted considerably, and seemed to be into the game, raptly watching the action on the ice. Nik looked at the clock. One minute on the nose.

Boris was ragging the puck, wasting time until Peter sped up the left side of the arena and came charging into the attacking zone where Boris hurried to meet him. Vanya was being harassed by a Canadian player, but was managing, nonetheless, to be in position if Peter needed to pass the puck. Two Canadian players attempted to squeeze Peter between them, but ended up slamming into each other. One of the Canadians then fell very hard on the ice. Peter looked back briefly and smiled. Sometimes his strategy worked better than even he could hope.

The arena again erupted into a thunderous roar, "Seventeen! Number Seventeen!"

Nik felt a tap on her shoulder. It was Ron.

He cupped his hand near her ear, "How are you doing, Nik? Are you okay?"

Nik nodded, "I'm much better. Look at how the team is skating; even after what happened today!"

"Yeah, they aren't doing too badly. Who do you think has the edge?"

"*We do!* Just watch Peter. He's amazing!"

"Is he the one?"

"Yes, he's the one who was attacked this afternoon by that idiot, Yakov."

"...*and* the one who knocked you down?" Ron wasn't smiling anymore.

Nik gave him a rueful look, "I explained what happened, Ron. It was as much my fault as his."

A few feet away, Marty and Sheldon jumped out of their seats, arms raised above their heads. "He scored! He scored again!" Marty *really* liked what he saw.

The announcer was shouting over the loudspeakers, "This Genchenko is *phenomenal.* He's got goal number four!"

The crowd was stomping, clapping, and shouting, "SEVENTEEN, SEVENTEEN!"

Nik looked at Ron, and she felt more than a little irritated that he had diverted her attention from the game, and Peter's score. It startled her when she realized what she was feeling.

Ron got close to Nik so that she could hear him over the din, "Nik, I've got to get back to the other side. Can I call you later tonight? We haven't had much time together this week."

Ron had recognized something in Nik's attitude, and it troubled him. She seemed distracted. This was, after all, the woman that he wanted to, no, would, marry. He knew that he hadn't been the model fiance, and he felt badly about it. It wasn't a good thing when a man neglected the woman he loved. He put his arm around Nik's waist briefly and kissed her cheek.

Nik leaned toward Ron, "That would be nice. I'm going to stay overnight at my mom and dad's, so don't call too late." Nik smiled at him, even though she was still a little annoyed.

"Well, I'm off..." Ron returned Nik's smile and started to leave.

"I knew that." Nik replied, but Ron didn't hear her over the noise of the crowd as he walked away.

The buzzer sounded the end of the game. The Russians had won!

Grigory came over to Nik. "Can you believe it? We have won. WE HAVE WON!" He gave Nik a bear hug.

When Grigory let go of her, she immediately looked out onto the ice to see the team's reaction. All the team, bench sitters, and active players, were rejoicing at center ice, hugging and back slapping each other, and circling Peter, who, at that moment, looked toward the bench, and waved at Nik, then gave her a thumbs-up. Nik waved back at him. Someone touched her shoulder, and Nik turned to see who it was.

Sheldon spoke close to her ear so that she could hear him, "Can you get us a few minutes with Genchenko? I have never seen anyone like Peter Genchenko on ice in all my life, and Marty feels the same way!"

Nik laughed and replied, "I'll try! The team will be coming off the ice in a couple of minutes, and I'll let him know then. And your reaction is not surprising, because there is *no one* like Pete on ice!"

"Amen, Dr. Kellman, amen!" Sheldon Levin was in absolute agreement with her.

Mickey was gathering some of the equipment into the carryall. Nik went over to him and offered to help.

"That's okay, Doc, I can get this stuff." Mickey didn't look directly at Nik when he replied.

Nik bent down next to him. "I owe you an apology, Mickey, I lost it when I thought Peter was going to get sick again. I shouldn't have yelled at you, and I'm sorry."

Mickey finally looked at Nik and told her, "It's not a problem Doc. I was just surprised when you snapped at me. That isn't like you."

"No, you're right, I was really out of line. Today has been a very trying day, and I haven't been myself."

Mickey smiled, "You got *that* right, Doc."

The team crowded into the Russian box, and then headed toward the tunnel. Tom was there to direct traffic and to protect them from the spectators. The players included him in their celebration by swatting him on the shoulders, or grabbing his hand to shake it. They were jubilant, enjoying the moment, slapping and pounding on each other. As Peter approached Nik, he reached out and touched her on the arm.

"Spaseeba. *Thank you.*" His eyes held hers, and he smiled at her again.

Nik nodded, smiled back, and told him, "You are very welcome. Oh…Peter, I have two business cards for you. They're from those gentlemen over there." Nik pointed to Sheldon and Marty, standing near the aisle.

Peter looked over at the two men, recognized Sheldon, and waved at him. Sheldon and Marty hurried over to Peter and began congratulating him on his performance during the game. Nik noticed that Grigory was watching this exchange. He was obviously curious as to the nature of the contact. Nik was glad that Yakov wasn't there to make trouble. Until now, she hadn't even thought about the little weasel.

Peter had not taken the business cards, so Nik put them back in her lab coat pocket. Conflicting emotions tumbled inside her as she watched Peter talking to the two men. Nik didn't know whether to laugh or to cry. She was happy for Peter and his team, yet she knew that this triumph would be short-lived, and it left her with an undertone of sadness. When these games were finished, he would leave, and she would never see him again. But, for now, they had won this game. *Against all odds, they had won!.*

The training room was back to bedlam. Joyous noise and celebration reigned. *Very* tired now, Nik wanted to finish out the last of her physician's duties and just go home. Then she remembered that she was going to stay with her parents tonight. She had promised her mother that she'd help her with the preparations for the Tuesday buffet for the team. She couldn't go back on her promise. Marina, her mother, had invited her several times recently to come visit, or to go shopping, or to visit the museum of art, have lunch, or whatever. Nik knew that her mother missed her, and, truth be told, she missed her mother too, but school, work, and now this added responsibility with the Russian hockey team had taken the last bit of personal time that she had.

Grigory and his assistant coach, Vladimir, approached Nik as she entered the training room. "Doctor, you worked wonders with the team today. We are indebted to you."

Grigory spoke and Vladimir nodded in agreement. He hardly ever spoke. Most of the time, Vladimir just nodded his head when Grigory talked.

"From what I saw tonight, they did very well on their own, but thank you for the compliment." Nik realized that she might sound ungracious, but, given the behavior that Grigory had exhibited earlier in the day, she didn't really care.

Peter's eyes tracked the doctor as he sat on the floor, his back against the wall, waiting his turn for her to check him over. His skates were on the floor beside him. He had pulled off his jersey and padding, and put them behind his head as a pillow. His body was sore all over. Any movement brought on a protest from one or another of his muscles. The wound on the right side of his head was stinging, and when he touched the dressing, it felt wet. Would the doctor be able to fix it again so that it wouldn't cause him any trouble during the next game? Her skills had proven helpful so far, and yet he knew that she couldn't work miracles.

He closed his eyes briefly and ran through in his mind the game his team had just won. He was truly amazed that they had prevailed. He had bluffed his way through the first period, unsure of the best strategy to use with the Canadian team. They were intimidating with their size and skill.

Peter had looked for any weaknesses that he and his team members could capitalize upon. Finally, he decided that it was the Canadians' dependence on physicality that could be used against them. As a team, the Canadians wanted to make contact with their opponents. They went out of their way to send anyone who got in their way into the boards. Once Peter saw this weakness, his strategy then became a game of cat and mouse. He lured them, time and again, into the boards, only to disappear at the last moment.

When Nik finally got to him, Peter was sleeping. She hesitated before touching him, afraid that it might startle him. Her shoulder still ached from the results of their earlier contact, and she didn't want to precipitate another potential flare-up from him.

"Pete…Peter, wake up." Nik called in a gentle voice, speaking his native tongue, so as not to startle him.

He smiled and opened his eyes, "Don't worry, doctor, I don't have the energy to do anything stupid again."

Nik indicated a training table and Peter, groaning as he pulled himself up from the floor, crawled onto it. Most, if not all of his muscles made themselves known by sending angry messages to his brain. Work your miracles, if you can, doctor, he thought. He grimaced as he climbed up on the table.

"Well, Pete, you did it. You and your team, in spite of all that happened today, punched the lights out of those Canadians. Do you think you can do the same with the American team tomorrow?" Her eyes shined with unshed tears.

Peter cocked his head, surprised at the doctor's emotion, then gave her a wry smile and said, "Mozhit bit." *Perhaps.*

"Let me look at that wound. It's been oozing and the bandage is saturated with blood and serum."

Nik gently pulled the bandage from the side of Peter's head. She noted that the bleeding had stopped, and there was congealed blood along the line where she had approximated the wound edges. That's good, she thought. She began to carefully pull the limp steri-strips from the wound.

They weren't holding anything, anyway. The stitches, though, had held very well. Not bad, she thought, not bad at all.

"I need a prep kit. I need to clean this wound. Overall, though, it looks very good, Pete." Nik gave Peter a reassuring nod, and then turned to go in search of a prep kit.

He watched her walk away from him. She's graceful, like a dancer, he thought. There was no exaggerated hip movement, only a fluid stride, with straight shoulders and head held high. Her dark hair had shining red glints under the fluorescent lights, and moved softly as she walked. Even in such plain clothing, without adornment of any kind, she's lovely. He swallowed involuntarily. There was a lump in his throat, and his heart turned over in his chest.

Nik returned quickly, with Tom at her side, "Tom offered to help with your dressing change. He needs some practice."

Peter was disappointed, and he saw that Tom was still angry with him. It showed in his eyes. Peter exhaled a long sigh and prepared himself to submit to Tom's ministrations. To his surprise, however, the doctor was the one who washed her hands and opened the prep kit. She put on the gloves, prepared the solution, wet the sponges and began cleansing his wound.

"How are you feeling now, Pete?"

"Much better than I did before," he replied in Russian.

"You scared me during the game. Were your symptoms similar to those that you had when you arrived?"

"Da, *yes* but not nearly so intense. I don't think I'm completely recovered from whatever I had before I came here."

"You're probably right. This is only your second day here, and it's been pretty tough for you." Her hands were gentle as she began to dress his wound.

Peter could again feel the radiant warmth of this lovely woman's body. Her closeness was a heady experience for him, and his breathing was shallow. He didn't want to break the magic of the moment, but Tom intervened.

"Should I clean this stuff up, Doc?"

Nik had completely forgotten that Tom was standing behind her. "Oh…Tom, you startled me."

She placed the palm of her hand against her forehead. "I didn't let you do the dressing change!"

"That's okay, Doc. You did it a lot better than I could've."

Tom grinned at her before he turned a sober face to Peter. There was a silent warning there; don't hurt her again.

"Tom, Peter's ready for the whirlpool and a rubdown. Do you think you can help him with that? I've got Slava and Ilya to look at now."

"Yeah, sure Doc. I'll fix him right up. C'mon Genchenko."

Peter looked at the doctor, stood up from the table, and followed Tom.

He turned to say, "I will see you in the morning."

Nik smiled and nodded at him. "Yup."

Puzzled, Peter started to ask, "What is…?"

Nik burst out laughing. She pointed to the whirlpool. "Go!"

Chapter 11

Marina sat on her comfortable sofa, an open book in her lap. A fire was burning low in the fireplace, most of the lights in the large room were turned off, and the television was dark. Only the lamp beside her was lit. She had decided to wait up for her daughter. All of the preparations for the buffet for the Russian hockey team had been completed earlier in the day, with Marina's friend Alice's help. Marina knew that her Niki was much too busy to actually help her with the buffet, but it had been a nice thought.

Niki's fiancé had called around eleven, and Marina told Myron that Niki wasn't home yet. He sounded somewhat disappointed, but she had assured him that Niki had called at ten, saying that she would be home by eleven or twelve, at the latest. Marina liked Myron, she never called him Ron, and they made small talk for a few minutes. He then said that he'd better turn in; tomorrow was going to be a busy day.

A car door closed outside, and Marina went to the door in anticipation of seeing her child. When she opened the door, a cold wind brought a mist of snow into the foyer.

"Niki, I'll open the garage and you can put your car inside. It's going to snow a few more inches tonight."

Nik stood beside her car looking at her mother, overnight bag in her hand. "Okay, but can you take this? I'll start up the car again."

She ran up on the porch, gave her mother a quick kiss on her cheek, handed her the bag, and ran back to her car. Marina carried the bag over to the stairway, and then hurried over to activate the garage door opener.

Nik pulled her car into the garage, turned off the engine and lights, and got slowly out of the car. Marina could see that her daughter looked tired.

"Niki, come in, come in," Marina beckoned. "I'll make a cup of hot chocolate for you while you get ready for bed."

Nik wasn't surprised that her mother had waited up for her. She would have been surprised if she had not.

"Sounds great. It's been a long day, and tomorrow is going to be more of the same."

Mother and daughter hugged, kissed each other's cheek, and held each other at arm's length. Nik was a younger, slightly taller, version of her Russian mother. From whence had come the perfectly oval face, high cheekbones, and the slight up tilt at the outer corners of her beautiful eyes? Niki looked as much a Russian beauty as her mother.

"Myron called to talk with you around eleven. He sounded as tired as you look. He said you had a really, really bad day, but didn't elaborate. Perhaps you could enlighten me?" Marina looked at her daughter and raised one eyebrow questioningly.

Nik put her hand up. Halt. "It's nothing, mother. I think Ron was exaggerating." Nik did not want to burden or frighten her mother with the events of the day.

Marina laughed a soft laugh, "Okay, Niki. Go get your pajamas on, and we will have our hot chocolate."

"I'm sorry that I didn't get here in time to help at least a little."

It was Marina's turn to put her hand up. Halt. "Go get comfortable, lyoobeemy, *dear*, and we will talk a little while."

Nik grabbed her bag, and headed for the stairs. Duchess, the family dog, waylaid Nik on the second step. Duchess, a gorgeous dun-colored, yellow-eyed Weimaraner, loved Nik. She leapt for joy, and whined her love with each jump.

Marina called softly, "Hush, Duchess, you will wake Papa."

Nik, with Duchess close behind, ran up the familiar curved staircase, hurried across the balcony overlooking the great room, and opened the door to her childhood bedroom. The room remained exactly as it had been when Nik was in high school. She and her mother had collaborated on a re-design of the room when Nik started high school, and Marina had kept it as a shrine to Nik's teenage years ever since.

When she was eighteen, Nik had told her parents that she was going to start Pre-Med at I.U., and would not be attending the School of Music there, as they had expected. Her concert grand piano sat silent, all but forgotten, in the library downstairs. Memories. There were times when she wished fervently that she could wipe out some of those memories. Her life, and that of the rest of her family, had changed irrevocably when Nik was twelve years old. Don't look back, now. Let's keep everything light and sweet, shall we?

Nik came down the stairs in a thick terry robe, a light shade of pink, with matching warm slippers that graced her feet, both from her high school wardrobe. It was heaven. For the first time today, she was comfortable and warm. She could smell the aroma of the hot chocolate. Her mother was waiting on the sofa, cup in hand. Nik's cup was setting next to a plate of her mother's cookies on a table by her father's chair, and there was a small, brightly wrapped package there, too. Nik curled up in the chair, caressing the hot chocolate cup in both hands, and Duchess crawled into the chair beside her. Her mother had put a dollop of whipped cream with shaved chocolate on top of the steaming drink. Ah, the comforts of home.

"Happy Birthday, Nikola. It's after midnight, but as far as I'm concerned, it's still your birthday." Marina smiled at her daughter and blew her a kiss.

Nik picked up the gift and opened it to find a delicate pair of intricately designed pearl and diamond earrings, "Mom, they're beautiful!"

She placed the earrings in her pierced ears, "Thank you, mom."

"You're welcome, dear. Your father wanted you to have them. They were his mother's, you know."

Nik put her fingertips to one ear, "I remember that she wore these for my first recital, didn't she?"

"Yes, she did, Niki, and she always wanted you to have them."

Mother and daughter sipped at their hot chocolate quietly for a while, each looking into the dying embers of the fire on the grate.

Finally, Nik broke the silence. "What time did dad go to sleep?"

"It was after eleven, I think. He finished his newspaper, but said that he couldn't stay awake for the news on TV. I think he's doing too much at work."

Nik nodded and looked her mother in the eye. "I believe that you also have some experience with that."

Nik's mother, like her father, had worked for Eli Lilly for many years. The company had always come first for her parents and for her aunt and uncle, her parents' siblings, who had also worked there.

Marina and Klaus loved working for Eli Lilly, the pharmaceutical giant based in Indianapolis. Marina worked as a chemist, and Klaus as a chemical engineer. First generation Americans, the Russian Marina and the German Klaus, had met during their student years at Purdue University, and had married after graduation. Marina's years with Lilly had been interrupted by the births of her three children, but she had maintained her position at Lilly, sometimes to the detriment of the children, because she was so dedicated to her work, and often got extra work piled on when others did not carry their own weight.

This situation prevailed during the growing up years of her children. Marina regretted the loss of so many of those years when she could have been forging closer relationships with them. Instead, her children had had Nina, a wonderfully kind and warm woman, who had been their nanny, confidant, and caregiver throughout their formative years. Mikhail and Nikola still kept in touch with her, and showered her with cards and gifts as if she were their real mother.

Marina's sister, Irina, and Klaus' brother, Karl, also attended Purdue University. Both two years older than their siblings, their professions were the reverse of Marina and Klaus'; Karl was the chemist, and Irina the chemical engineer. Even though there were two years between them, they had all started college at the same time. The four were inseparable during their college years, and didn't pair off until their senior year. In fact, according to stories told and re-told during many family gatherings over the years, it had looked as if Marina and Karl were going to pair off, but then Klaus suffered a bicycle accident, and Marina had been the one to take care of him during his convalescence. Thus their close and intimate relationship was begun.

Irina and Karl also married soon after their graduation from Purdue, and worked for Eli Lilly, too, until they had moved ten years ago to Western Pennsylvania. Their marriage had produced a son, Hans, whose mathematical genius eventually earned him a scholarship to MIT when he was sixteen, and a Life Magazine cover. A quiet child, and an even more quiet young adult, he committed suicide at age nineteen without leaving a note or a clue as to why he had done so. Brokenhearted, his parents had moved away from the home that they had established when they were a family in Indianapolis, and retired to a small town in Western Pennsylvania called Muse, hoping to put some of their memories behind them.

Marina finished her hot chocolate first. "Niki, what time do you expect your athletes to arrive tomorrow evening?"

Nik thought a moment before replying. "Well, the game will start at three o'clock, so everything should be completed, including the after game repairs to the players' various injuries, by six or so. I think that seven to seven-thirty will be a good time to get started here. It takes thirty to forty minutes in good weather to get from downtown Indy to Geist, so the only real variable is the weather. It may lengthen the travel time, but since the party's buffet rather than formal, I don't think that will be a problem, do you?"

Marina rubbed her eyes and yawned. "Probably not. All I have to do is put out the chafing dishes for the hot food, and some ice under the cold. All the food is prepared. The plates, napkins, silverware and the rest of the table service are already set out in the dining room. Alice helped me. She's such a good friend."

Nik sighed audibly. *Mea culpa*, she thought, *mea maxima culpa*. I guess my bad day was my own fault, and not helping was, too. "I *am* sorry, mom, that I didn't get here in time to do my share of the work."

Marina replied in a quiet voice, "Niki, you volunteered. I didn't ask you to help. Besides, I'm not upset, so why are *you* getting upset with *me*?"

Nik shrugged, "I'm not upset, mom, just tired. It's time for bed."

"Before you go up, would you put Duchess out for a few minutes while I clean up the hot chocolate dishes?"

"Sure." Nik gave a low whistle, and Duchess jumped out of the chair.

This is the strangest winter I have ever seen, thought Nik as she opened the back patio door for Duchess. The snow has been relentless since just after Thanksgiving. There must be more than a foot on the ground, and it's still snowing.

Duchess loved the snow, and didn't need any coaxing. She jumped off the porch, not bothering with the snow-covered steps, and began leaping around in the snow like a giant, ungainly, jackrabbit. Her performance made Nik smile as she remembered how Duchess' mother, Lady Gray, had loved the snow, too, and how she had followed Nik around, even copping rides on Nik's sled, as Nik sped downhill toward the frozen Geist Reservoir in front of her home. Nik's brothers, Mikhail and Josef, or as Nik called them, Mikie and Joey, loved wintertime, and had buried Nik and Lady Gray in the snow more than once.

Being the youngest child, Nik was resourceful and patient, and usually got even one way or another with her brothers. Her best get even strategy had worked time and again. Before school, when her brothers were completely dressed, and having breakfast, Nik would do her Oops routine, and spill a glass of milk or juice on one or both of them. *Gotcha!* Of course, she had to clean up the spill, but she, and her brothers, knew that she had gotten even for some misdeed on their part. It got so bad at times that they chose to sit on the other side of the table, but that didn't always prevent some prank or another by Nik.

Memories. Nik felt a sense of melancholy settle over her as she watched Duchess enjoying the snow. If it was possible, she felt even more tired, just standing there, than she had when she had left the arena.

Earlier, Nik couldn't locate Pete before she left the training room. Mickey, Tom, and she had cleaned up quickly after the athletes, and the last time that she had seen Pete was when he stepped out of the whirlpool, grabbed a towel, waved at her, and went into the dressing area.

When she went through the training room before closing up for the night, she saw that Pete's locker was closed and locked. She felt a sense of disappointment, and then decided that she needed to get over this silliness. *What the hell is wrong with me?*

By the time she had driven to her parent's home, through snow and intermittently heavy traffic, and *more* snow, it was past midnight, and she was worn out. Her shoulder ached, and so did her head.

"Come on Duchess, come on girl." Duchess was having too much fun and didn't want to come in. Nik slipped out of her slippers, and walked barefoot onto the porch in the snow. Her toes were almost immediately numb. She used to do the same thing when she was a child, but she hadn't remembered just how cold deep snow really was on bare feet.

Finally, Duchess got the idea that she was supposed to come inside. She bounded up the stairs, running past Nik and skidding to a stop on the rug by the door.

"Whoa, I said whoa you varmint!" Nik sounded like Yosemite Sam, one of her favorite cartoon characters when she was a child.

Duchess raised one paw at a time to be toweled off. Nik laughed to herself. How many dogs willingly help to get cleaned up after a romp in the snow?

"Okay, Duchess, let's go upstairs. Goodnight, mom. I might not see you in the morning. I have to be downtown by seven, so I'll probably leave here at six fifteen, or so."

Marina nodded and hugged her daughter. "Sleep well Niki."

Chapter 12

Yakov was sitting on his bed smoking and watching television. He had just talked to the Desk Sergeant at the Indianapolis Police Department regarding Nikita. He couldn't understand why the police were still holding Nikita. It infuriated Yakov that he couldn't force them to tell him anything. He was powerless here. It wasn't like Moscow, where he could order underlings around, and could even intimidate some others who thought they were beyond his reach.

His other worry was Josef, who was still in the hospital. The surgery to repair his leg injury had been successful, but beyond that information, no one at the hospital would tell Yakov anything more. They wouldn't even tell him when Josef would be discharged from the hospital. The hospital spokeswoman said that he, Yakov, would have to ask the Russian Hockey Coach if any further information was needed! *Stupid bitch cow that she was*!

Earlier in the day, he had tried to telephone his superior in Moscow, but had been unsuccessful after three attempts. He had wanted to begin telling *his* version of the days' events, so that it would be more damaging to Grigory and Genchenko. Above all, Yakov wanted to destroy Genchenko. If Moscow would only order Genchenko back to Russia, Yakov could take care of the rest. He threw his ashtray across the room, where it shattered against the wall. He was filled with impotent rage, and had no target upon which to vent his anger.

Someone pounded on his door. It startled Yakov, who was easily spooked. Naked to the waist, he grabbed his shirt off the bottom of the bed, put it on, and headed to the door. He looked out the peephole to see who it was, when the caller pounded on the door again. Yakov jumped back, but he had recognized the man outside his door. Uneasy, he was unsure as to whether to open the door.

"Go away! I don't want to talk to you!" Yakov raised his voice, and it came out falsetto, sounding like a frightened woman.

The caller pounded on the door again. He was not going to go away. Yakov paced back and forth nervously behind the door. The caller pounded even harder, and Yakov jumped back once more. Finally, he made a decision.

Gingerly, hands shaking, Yakov released the lock on the door, leaving the chain in place. He should not be afraid of this man. Slowly, he opened the door just a crack. It was what the caller had been waiting for. He put his shoulder to the door, and easily popped the chain from its mooring.

"Astanaveetis!" *Stop!* Screeched Yakov.

Without saying a word, the intruder entered the room, grabbed Yakov by the throat, and broke his neck with one powerful twist. He dropped the little man to the floor, kicked him once, and then walked out the door, closing it behind him. Looking to the right and to the left, he saw that the hall was empty, and walked to a nearby stairway.

The flocked cloth wall covering directly above the full ashtray that Yakov had thrown against the wall had begun to smolder. Yakov's lit cigarette from the ashtray had spread sparks to the wall, and to the nearby draperies. Within minutes, there were flames licking up the wall and draperies.

Peter ate a small supper in the hotel dining room before it closed. He knew that he had to eat something solid, so he ate broiled fish and cooked vegetables. It was the closest kind of meal that he could think of that would taste like something his mother might cook. His thoughts had turned to her and his sister after he had escaped serious injury earlier in the day at the hands of Yakov and his accomplices. He missed his mother and sister very much, and this food made him feel closer to them. He charged the meal to his room. It was easier to do it that way than to try to grapple with money and exchange rates. He was too tired to think about anything that took concentration.

Bone-weary and aching, he headed for the elevators and the quiet of his room. A hot shower, a soft bed; that was all he would need tonight. As Peter walked out of the restaurant, he saw Grigory across the lobby and waved at him. Grigory, who was alone, without Vladimir, stared at Peter, finally waved back, and then turned and walked toward the front entrance.

It didn't take long for Peter to get into bed. He had hurried through his shower, left his clothing where he had dropped it, quickly brushed his teeth and got in bed. He lay on his back, looking up at the ceiling, where there were patterns from the light coming into the room that filtered through the sheer curtains on the windows. He thought about Dr. Kellman, and wished that he could have talked with her after the game, but then decided it was probably better that he had come straight to the hotel. Peter realized that he was monopolizing too much of the doctor's time, but he enjoyed her company and felt good when he was with her. Finally, he rolled to his side and fell asleep quickly.

Peter's dream was of a beautiful summer's day at the dacha by the lake in Tver. He, Katya, and two boy cousins, Sergei and Misha, were playing in the spring fed, cold, pristine water. At one point, all four of them were under the water, trying to see which one would have to come up for air first. A loud, sustained noise invaded his dream, and he tried to swim up out of the water. He was in a deep sleep, and felt that he was moving in slow motion. He came up out of the bedcovers gasping, legs kicking, arms waving, as if he were breaking the surface of the lake in his dream.

Slowly, he realized that the sound he was hearing was some sort of alarm. As was his custom, he had been sleeping naked, so he had to quickly find some clothing to wear, and shoes, then he ran to the door. The lights in the hall were blinking on and off, and the noise level was much higher there.

Peter knew that the elevators would not be running, and followed the signs to a stairway. He could smell smoke as soon as he entered the stairwell, and briefly wondered whether he was doing the right thing by using the stairs. His heart was pounding as he descended the stairs two and three at a time. He heard voices above and below him, and then saw several people in differing stages of dress in front of him. One man, middle-aged and rather portly, had a suit jacket, undershorts, socks without shoes, and a towel thrown over his shoulder, with a small woman, wearing only a thin nightgown, hanging onto his arm. The stairwell became noisier as others joined the downward flight.

When he hit the lobby, Peter continued on toward the front entrance doors where he saw hoses running into the lobby and up another stairway. He saw several fire trucks outside, ice glistening on the trucks and along the hoses on the ground. Firefighters' protective outer gear was encrusted with ice as they scrambled, slip-sliding on the frozen sidewalk. The lights on the trucks made the scene look like daylight, and caused everything that was ice-covered to glitter and flash.

Three different news vans were parked across the street, kept distant because of police and fire barriers, and Peter could see that video cameramen and photographers were moving back and forth, filming and shooting the action, while news anchors, bundled in heavy coats and hats, reported on the event in front of television video cameras with bright lights.

Peter felt a hand on his shoulder and turned to see Ilya, and most of the rest of his teammates. The lobby was full of people, some dressed, but most partially or poorly put together. Ilya was wearing jeans and nothing else.

Peter laughed as he looked at Ilya's bare feet, "You must be cold, my friend."

"Well, yes, but I couldn't find my shirt and shoes right away, and I decided that the fire alarm meant business."

Vanya and Mikhail asked almost simultaneously, "Has anyone seen Grigory?"

"I just came down the stairs, and haven't seen him so far." Peter hadn't really thought about Grigory until now.

Mikhail said, "He's on my floor, the twelfth, and I didn't see him, but the hallway and stairs were very crowded. Do you think he's still in his room?"

Peter replied, "I saw him leaving the hotel about eleven o'clock. He waved at me, but didn't come over to talk. Maybe he isn't back yet."

As Peter and his team members talked, an ambulance and a coroner's van drove up to the entrance of the hotel. The ambulance crew, with radios in hand and gurney rolling, came into the hotel and were pointed toward one of the stairwells by a hotel security guard. Two very official-looking people got out of the coroner's van carrying medical bags, and followed the ambulance crew into the stairwell. Three policemen in uniform came behind them.

Arkady told his teammates that he thought that his floor might be where the fire had started. He was on the seventh floor. When he heard the alarm and came out of his room, there was dense smoke at the far end of the corridor, and he had sought the stairway at the opposite end of what seemed to be the source of the fire.

A voice came over a loudspeaker, "Would a representative of the Russian team please come to the registration desk?"

The Russian athletes looked at one another questioningly. They turned to see who might go to the desk, and saw Vladimir, their assistant coach, making his way there.

"What do you think that's all about?" Boris asked Peter.

Peter shrugged, "I have no idea."

Peter and his teammates talked and milled about with the other hotel guests, watching the firefighters do their job. After more than two hours the loudspeaker activated again.

"We have gotten the all clear signal to return to your rooms. However, those on the seventh floor please report to the registration desk for potential reassignment. The elevators are now available for use. Please accept the management's apology for any inconvenience you may have encountered."

The elevators were immediately mobbed, and Peter decided to take the stairs. He said goodnight to his teammates, and as he was walking toward the stairway closest to his room, he saw the firemen pulling their hoses out of the other stairwell. He would not want that job, of that he was sure. Fire frightened him. It was one of the main reasons that he hated to fly. Every picture that he had ever seen of an airplane crash included a fireball, or the blackened result of a terrible fire. No, a fireman's job would be the last thing that he would want to do.

Peter had gone up three flights when he heard clattering and the sound of voices from above. As he rounded the landing of the fourth floor, he met the ambulance crew and the coroner's staff coming down the stairs with a covered gurney. The ambulance crew was laboring under the weight of the gurney. He stepped aside to let them pass, and detected an extremely unpleasant odor. Although he had never before smelled such an odor, he immediately suspected what it was. His eyes met those of the last person in the group, a tall, sharp-featured man, and Peter's suspicions were confirmed. There was a certain look in the man's piercing gray eyes, and Peter knew that someone had died in the fire.

When Peter got back to his room, he paced the floor for a while and watched the local Channel 6 for news of the fire. The news anchor confirmed what he already knew; someone, a guest in the hotel, had died in the fire. Identification was pending until notification of the next of kin could be made. Peter tried several times to call Grigory, but there was no answer.

Peter got into the shower again. He wanted to wash away the odors that had assailed him, the smoke, and the unknown cargo on the gurney. Remnants of the fire, he thought. Even under the hot shower, he shivered. When he finished, he toweled off briskly, rubbing his skin hard, still working on the smoky smell. He felt queasy and uncomfortable. Peter knew that he needed to at least get *some* sleep, but he couldn't settle down. Well, maybe lying down in bed would help to put him in the mood for sleep. As he pulled the covers up, he wondered where Grigory could have gone? It occurred to Peter that Grigory's disappearance might coincide with the person who had died in the fire, and it gave him a start. No, of course it couldn't be Grigory. Peter's thoughts continued to race for a time, but his weariness finally got the better of him and he fell into an exhausted, dreamless sleep.

Chapter 13

Tuesday, Early Morning

Marina got out of bed as soon as she smelled the aroma from the perking coffeepot in the kitchen. She looked at the clock on her bedside table. It's only five-thirty, and my Niki's up very early. She wrapped a robe around her, put on her slippers, and quietly went out the bedroom door, carefully closing it so as not to disturb Klaus, who was sleeping heavily, snoring and snorting at intervals.

As she walked down the hallway, she could hear her daughter in the kitchen, humming to herself. Marina came through the great room and rounded the corner into the kitchen.

"Kharoshee ootra. *Good morning*." Marina smiled and kissed her daughter.

"Hi, mom." Nik returned her mother's kiss.

"You're all dressed for work. Do you have time for breakfast?" Marina opened the refrigerator and took out the coffee cream.

Nik took two cups down from the cupboard, "Coffee?"

"Oh yes." Marina knew that this would be a busy day and an even busier evening.

"I don't really have time for anything more than an English muffin, mom."

Mother and daughter sat in the breakfast nook looking out over the frozen, snow-covered lake. Each quietly sipped the fresh coffee and enjoyed the scenery. The toaster oven clicked off and Nik got up to get her English muffin.

"Where is Duchess?" Marina looked around the kitchen.

"Oh…my…gosh, she's still outside!"

Nik quickly ran over to the door. She threw it open, and Duchess leapt into the kitchen, tail wagging snow this way and that as she signaled her happiness at being inside again.

"Come here, girl. I'm so-o-o-o sorry! You must be frozen." Nik began wiping Duchess down, one paw at a time, and belly last.

Nik heard a deep masculine laugh behind her, and turned to see her father standing there. He had a huge smile on his face, and he opened his arms, inviting a hug.

"Nikola, it's good to see you…and Happy Birthday a day late." He wrapped his arms around her and kissed her on the top of her head. Nik came barely up to his shoulder.

"I'm glad to see you, too, dad. Thanks for giving me grandma's earrings. They're beautiful!"

Nik had never had ambivalent feelings toward her father the way she did with her mother. She guessed that she was probably a daddy's girl, but that was okay, wasn't it? Nik noticed that her father's hair was almost all silver now, with a few strands of dark blond remaining. She had always thought that her father had a noble face, kind gray eyes and a warm smile, and now it seemed even more so with his silver hair. He looked very distinguished.

Marina sat quietly, excluded as always, watching two of the three most important people in her life. She missed her son, Mikhail, the third of the three, but he would be home for Christmas. There had been a fourth, but Marina had gotten used to the empty space in her heart, even though she thought about Josef every day.

"Coffee, Klaus?" Marina held up the coffee pot.

"Ja." He patted Marina on the shoulder and kissed her on the top of her head, in the same way he had kissed his daughter.

Nik sat down and quickly ate her English muffin, gulped a few more swallows of coffee, dabbed at her mouth with her napkin and said, "I've got to get going. I should be on the road already."

Once Klaus entered the kitchen, Duchess had eyes only for him. She went over to where he sat at the table and flopped down heavily beside him. Nik could swear that Duchess was smiling up at her father.

"Fickle, you're fickle, Duchess." Nik shook a finger at the dog.

Marina said, "Don't waste your time. Duchess is a one-man dog. She only likes me at feeding time, or when your father isn't home."

Nik's coat was on the back of her chair and she put it on, threw a scarf around her neck, dug in her pockets for her gloves, grabbed her purse and said, "See you-all tonight."

She kissed both her parents on the cheek, shook a finger again at Duchess, and then headed toward the garage.

Marina went over to activate the garage door opener for her. "Good-bye Niki. We will see you tonight."

Outside, Nik saw that it had snowed again. Good Lord! Nik was more than a little worried when her tires lost traction at an intersection that had drifted almost closed overnight. *Damn!* She geared down, kept her tires rolling without spinning, and got through the intersection without getting stuck.

Nik decided to use the Fall Creek Parkway to go downtown, but it turned out to be a big mistake. She really didn't have much choice because she knew that I-465 would be a mess, too, and so she avoided it. It was a stressful drive, with cars and trucks slipping and sliding against curbs, and bouncing out of their lanes when they lost control. Nik managed to keep her car on the road and intact and finally made it to the arena, but it was after eight and she had wanted to get to the training room by seven. Well, so much for being prompt. She let her breath out slowly as she pulled into her parking space; at least she thought that this was approximately where her space was. Who could tell with all this snow?

There were only two other cars in the parking area, but Nik didn't recognize them. Where is everyone? She slogged through the snow to the building entrance. You'd think that they would at least try to clean a walkway. Nik was frustrated and aggravated already, and it was just the beginning of a long day. As Nik walked down the corridor toward the training room, she saw Terry and waved him down.

"Have you heard anything from the Indy police regarding the uproar yesterday?"

Terry raised his eyebrows, "Not yet, but have you heard about the fire at the hotel last night?"

Startled, Nik asked, "What fire?"

"Oh geez, Doc, didn't you know? There was a fire last night at the hotel where the Russian team is staying. Yesterday's troublemaker, Yakov Popov, died in the fire."

Nik felt the breath leave her, "Was anyone else hurt?" Her voice was small and breathless as she asked the question.

"Not that I know of…I spoke to Charlie Allen, who's on the job in the Sheriff's Department, and he said he thought Popov was the only casualty."

Nik's heart was beating so hard that she felt faint, "Thanks…thanks, Terry. I appreciate the heads up."

Nik was almost running when she got to the training room. The door was still closed and locked, and she had to unlock it with shaking hands. Twice she dropped the keys, but finally, she managed to open the door.

The room was cold and dark. Nik fumbled for the light switches on the wall and succeeded in lighting at least one bank of overhead fluorescents. Calm down, calm down, I've got to calm down. Nik stood still for a few moments, trying to regain her composure.

Terry said that no one else had been hurt in the fire, but she had immediately been fearful for Peter. Bile rose in Nik's throat, and she felt sick to her stomach. She walked over to one of the training tables, pulled herself up onto the table, and sat there, still wearing her coat.

Peter awoke with a start, the bedclothes twisted around him. When he looked at the bedside clock, it read 6:25 a.m. in large green numerals. He had slept the dreamless sleep of exhaustion when he had gotten back to his hotel room after the fire. The last time that he looked at the clock by the bed, it had showed 2:30 a.m., and he apparently had fallen into a very sound sleep.

Peter had been worried about Grigory before he fell asleep. What happened to him? Peter knew that Grigory's hotel room was on the seventh floor where the fire had been.

His mind was racing as he got out of bed. I've got to get out of this room. All of a sudden, he felt claustrophobic. He quickly bathed, dressed, grabbed his sports bag, hurried out of his room, and headed through the deepening snow to the arena.

When Dr. Kellman arrived, Peter was sitting on the stairs nearby waiting for the training room to be opened. The angle of the stairs in relation to the training room door made it difficult to see him sitting there. He had seen Grigory and Vladimir attempt to get into the training room a few minutes earlier, but they had been unsuccessful, and hadn't seen him. Peter had felt relief at seeing Grigory, and was very glad that he was all right.

Peter watched as the doctor fumbled with her keys. She seemed to be upset. He stood up to go over to help, but she got the door open before he could get to her. He could see that some, but not all, of the lights inside the room were turned on. When he got to the door, Peter saw that the doctor was sitting on one of the training tables. She hadn't taken her coat off and was sitting very still, looking down at the floor.

"Doctor? Are you all right?"

Nik raised her head in surprise when she heard Peter's voice. She was trembling, and couldn't speak immediately.

Finally, she replied, "The question is, are *you* all right?" Nik's voice was shaky and had a hollow sound.

"You heard about the fire." It was a statement, not a question.

"Pete…Peter, did you know that Yakov was killed in the fire?"

The doctor's question took Peter by surprise, "Nyet, *No,* I haven't heard any news since the fire. Who told you that Yakov was killed in the fire?"

"Terry told me when I came in just a few minutes ago."

Peter moved closer to her, and Nik looked up at him. Had he done something to Yakov? After all, he had threatened Yakov twice in her presence, and had even attacked him. What would happen to Peter if he had carried out his threats? She was not afraid of Peter, but she *was* afraid *for* him.

Peter, already heart sore, saw fear in the doctor's eyes, and he interpreted it as fear of him. His throat constricted and his heart ached even more. *No, it can't be.* It hurt him to realize that she might be afraid of him.

"Pazhalsta, *please*, doctor, don't be afraid of me. I haven't done anything wrong." Peter's voice was rough with emotion.

Nik shook her head, "I'm not afraid of you, but I *am* afraid of what might happen to you if you're blamed for Yakov's death. If that happens, what will they do to you when you go home?"

Before Peter could reply, there were loud voices in the hallway outside the training room. Grigory and Vladimir, along with Arkady and Slava, appeared in the doorway and stopped as though they had blundered into something that they shouldn't have.

"Well," Grigory fixed Nik with a dark stare. "We have been waiting for more than an hour to get in here for some treatment for these athletes. We need to start early today because of the three o'clock game with the Americans. Your Security man wouldn't let us come in without you, doctor."

"I apologize, Grigory, the driving was difficult this morning. I expected Tom or Mickey to get here before I did, but they haven't made it yet." Nik's demeanor was withdrawn and quiet.

"Genchenko," Grigory began, turning to Peter. "Where have you been? I tried to call you in the hotel early this morning and got no answer. You weren't at the training table, either, and I told you before that you shouldn't miss your meals anymore."

"My telephone didn't ring this morning, and I slept through the training table. I came down here to sit in the whirlpool for awhile because I'm still aching from…" he paused, "the game last night." Peter looked warily from Grigory to Vladimir and back.

"Yakov's dead. Did you know this?" Grigory's face reddened and the veins bulged in his neck.

"The doctor has just told me." Peter's face was closed and noncommittal.

Vladimir was looking at Nik as Grigory addressed Peter. He had one eyebrow raised, as if he expected her to come to Peter's aid.

"Good riddance, I say! He was a hateful little man, a vindictive little man, too. You should know that better than anyone else, Genchenko. Did you know that he was trying to get you sent back to Russia? Oh yes, he tried to keep you from coming here, and when he couldn't do that, he worked hard at finding a way to get rid of you. Nikita and Josef were caught in his little web." Grigory didn't mince words.

Peter was taken by surprise at Grigory's obvious contempt for the dead man. He agreed with Grigory's opinion, but Peter hadn't realized that Grigory felt that strongly about Yakov. Grigory had never said anything against him, even when Yakov was at his worst, interfering with the team. Perhaps Grigory had been more afraid of Yakov, and what he could do, than Peter had been.

"Doctor, have you heard anything more about what happened during the fire? I don't know what your police investigators do here when someone dies in a fire. Will they do a post mortem examination?" Grigory's curiosity was obvious.

Nik shrugged and slipped down from the table. "Your guess is as good as mine, but if foul play is suspected, they probably will do an autopsy." She turned to Peter, "Come on Pete, I'll help you get set up in the whirlpool. Arkady, Slava, I'll be right back. Grigory, if you need something else, wait here and I'll talk to you when I can get to you."

Peter followed the doctor to the water treatment room. She walked briskly ahead of him, taking off her coat as she walked. Peter hurried to assist her. He put both hands on her shoulders and helped her as she got out of her coat.

Nik turned to look up at Peter, "I'm sorry that I let you see how upset I was. That was very unprofessional of me. But it wasn't because I was afraid of you, Pete."

Peter was relieved to hear her words. It was as though a weight had been lifted from his chest.

"Thank you Dr. Kellman, that means a great deal to me."

"How's your head feeling?"

Nik needed to change the subject. Peter's heartfelt words had caused Nik's heart to skip a beat, and she didn't want to go there.

"It isn't painful any longer, but I think it will leave another scar." Peter reached up to gingerly touch his wound.

Nik stood on tiptoe in front of Peter and lifted the small bandage covering his head injury. "It looks pretty good, Pete. The sutures are holding nicely, but I'm going to have to change the steri-strips."

For a moment, Peter did not reply. He was enjoying the closeness of the doctor as he looked down into her uplifted face. He again detected the light fragrance on her person, and it was a heady experience.

Finally, he said to her, "When I finish in the whirlpool, I'll come back into the training room and you can change them."

Peter went over to a dressing room while Nik started to fill one of the large whirlpools. He came out wrapped in a towel. Nik glanced at him, and then averted her eyes.

"Go ahead and jump in. I'll get the settings for you, and the timer's set for ten minutes."

While the doctor looked away, Peter got into the whirlpool. He tossed his towel over the handrail and eased down into the turbulent water.

"Is the temperature comfortable for you?" Nik focused on Peter's face. I'm losing my mind, she thought. Why am I so embarrassed? *I'm a doctor, and this should be routine.*

Peter was also embarrassed, and was glad that he was immersed to his shoulders in the swirling, bubbling water. Although he could maintain an aloof expression on his face, there was a part of him that betrayed his true feelings.

"Kharoshee," *Good,* was all that he could say.

"I'll send Tom in when he gets here. Do you think you'll be all right in here by yourself? It's probably not a good idea, but there is only one of me."

Nik realized that she was babbling, but couldn't help it. Abruptly, she turned, picked her coat up from the chair where she had dropped it and headed for the door, her face reddening more deeply with each step. When she got to the door, she realized that she hadn't put the emergency call light within Peter's reach, and so she turned and walked back to him. She reached behind him, grabbed the cord, and tied it to the handrail.

"Use this if you have any problems. Oh, and by the way, when you finish your whirlpool, I am personally going to see that you eat some breakfast."

Peter nodded and watched her walk away again. For some reason, the doctor seemed upset or embarrassed. He wasn't sure which. She had a spot of red on each cheek. Actually, the heightened color was an attractive addition to her beauty, he decided. Relaxing, and leaning back into the warm, bubbling water, he let go of his cares and let the water work its magic on his aching muscles.

Nik hurried back to the training room, hoping that she would find Tom or Mickey, or both, there to help her get through the day until game time. She knew that if she stayed on schedule pretty much, she would be able to get the team patched together and ready for the Americans this afternoon. Briefly, she wondered how she was going to feel during the game. Surely she would be rooting for the Americans, but then she thought of Pete. How would she feel if Pete and his team didn't win this afternoon?

It was a noisy place, the training room, with athletes everywhere, waiting to be checked, poked, prodded or wrapped. She saw Tom first. He was almost head and shoulders taller than everyone else in the room except Grigory. *Oh thank God.* Then, when she saw Mickey working with Ilya, she breathed a long sigh of relief.

"Hey, Nik…Nik, over here." Ron waved at her from the main entrance to the training room.

Nik hurried over to him. "Well, hello stranger. Sorry I wasn't at my parents' when you called last night. I got there about an hour after."

Ron shrugged, "It's okay, Nik, and when I thought about it later, there was no way that you could've made it to Geist by eleven and still get everything done here."

"Smart man. Well, what brings you here this morning?" Nik put her hands in the pockets of her lab coat.

Ron hugged Nik, hands in pockets, and gave her a quick kiss on her cheek. "I'm going to be a little late for the buffet at your parents' house tonight."

"So what's the excuse for this one, Myron?"

Ron winced, "Okay, I know you have good reason to be upset with me, but Garibaldi wants me to stick around for some of the evening game between the Swedes and the Canadians."

"The whole game? He's pissed that he didn't get an invitation to the buffet, so he's going to spoil it for both of us."

"No, not the whole game, he just wants to make sure that everything gets started okay, then I can leave."

Nik closed her eyes for a moment. "You know that mom's going to be disappointed. She'll say she isn't, but it will be all over her face. Dad won't say anything. He understands that a man's gotta do what a man's gotta do. Lucky you."

"Come on, Nik, I'll just be a little late, that's all. Besides, your team doesn't know me, anyway, so they won't be insulted or anything."

"Spoken like a true politician. Look, I have to get in there and help the guys." Nik nodded her head in the direction of the bedlam in the training room.

Ron gave Nik another hug, her hands still in her pockets, looked into her eyes and smiled. "I'll make it up to you. You know I will."

Finally, Nik smiled, too. "Yeah, yeah, yeah. Get going."

She walked back into the training room, and went over to Tom first. "I know you must have had as bad a time getting here as I did."

"*Oh* yeah! In a way, it was kinda' exciting. Just tell me what you want me to do, Doc, and I'll get busy."

Nik thought for a moment, and then made her decision. "Tom, take the right side of the room. We'll use the door as the center. You can have the more serious wraps and things, and call me over when you need some direction. By now I think you know all of the athletes pretty well. Any questions? Oh, and check on Peter Genchenko. He's in the water treatment area. You can go after him if he's not out here in ten minutes or so."

"Okay on Genchenko, and I don't have any questions, not a one, Doc. I'll call if I need you." Tom was smiling a wide smile. She had chosen *him* for the hard stuff.

Mickey was already working on Ilya's knee, and looked up as the doctor approached. "Hi, Doc. Thought I'd get started here, then you can put me wherever…"

"Would you work on the left side of the room, starting at the door, and get the routine stuff out of the way? I'll announce the scheme in just a minute, okay?"

"Sounds good to me, Doc." Mickey was always agreeable.

Nik stood in the middle of the room, held up her hand, and spoke in Russian to the team, "Listen up, everyone. Tom is on the right side over here, and he's going to work with the more complicated problems. Mickey is on the left, and he's going to do the routine wraps. I'll be available to help as needed."

Nik went over to her desk and began sorting through the folders there. She looked for Peter's folder, and it was missing. Where…? Out of the corner of her eye, she saw Grigory approaching her. Vladimir was, as usual, his Siamese twin. Turning toward them, she saw that Grigory was holding something under his arm that looked similar to the folders on her desk.

"Why didn't you tell me about Genchenko? He shouldn't be playing hockey with the problem that he has!" Grigory loomed above her menacingly.

"Have you been reading my medical records?" Nik was immediately angry.

"They are my athletes. I need to know what I am dealing with. From what I can see in this file, I need the advice of another doctor!"

"Give me that medical record *now*!" Nik held her hand out for the file.

"I will take this to the committee, and then you will be removed as team doctor. I can't work with someone who hides critical information about my athletes from me."

"Please go right ahead. You and your team have caused nothing but problems for the committee. What do you think their response will be to your complaint?" Nik's hand was still outstretched for the file.

Grigory hesitated, looked at Vladimir and back at Nik. "Is Genchenko certified to play, according to your examination of him?"

"He's been playing, hasn't he? Now give that medical record back to me!" Nik could see that Grigory was struggling with what to do next. He didn't want to give the file to her, but she had called his bluff.

Grigory, trying to save face in Vladimir's presence, said, "I want to sit down with you and Genchenko to discuss this." He slapped the file against his hand for emphasis.

"Tipir. *Now.*" Nik continued to hold her hand out for the file.

He placed the file in her hand, turned on his heel, and walked away. Vladimir missed several steps, and nearly tripped as he attempted to catch up with Grigory.

This is not what we needed now! Nik was almost at the end of her rope. It suddenly occurred to her that she had thought in terms of "we" and not "I." She had automatically put herself and Pete together in this common struggle.

Peter came into the training room with half of his practice gear in place. Grigory immediately approached him, and shook a finger at him, while talking in an animated way. Vladimir stood quietly behind Grigory. Peter looked over to where Nik was standing, his eyes wide and questioning.

Nik hurried over to Peter's side, "That's enough, Grigory. This isn't Peter's fault."

"Tell me then, whose fault is it that I have had an injured athlete, a great liability, playing on this team?"

"I said that's enough, Grigory We can talk about this after practice. Peter, Grigory has been looking at your confidential medical information without my authorization. Again, this is a breach of committee rules. If I certify this athlete for play, then there is no liability on your part."

All of the athletes in the room had quieted to listen to what seemed to be something controversial between Peter and Grigory. This is almost comical, thought Nik. They look like prairie dogs at attention. Nik turned a wide smile on Grigory, while asking Peter to go over to the rubdown room and wait there until Tom could do his wrap. She knew that the team, already overloaded with problem upon problem, did not need another gut wrenching issue to deal with.

Continuing to smile, Nik lowered her voice and got close to Grigory so that only he would hear what she had to say. "Gloopy, *stupid,* you're destroying your team's morale *again.* Drop this now, and go about your business. Don't you want to win this afternoon? Peter won for you last night, but I think you have a very short memory."

Grigory was surprised by what she said, but he looked up to see that his athletes were paying close attention to what was going on. He knew when he had been bested. Looking back at the doctor, he returned her smile for the benefit of his athletes.

"You are a very good chess player, Dr. Kellman."

As Grigory turned away, Vladimir moved in behind him, almost in lock step. In fact, Vladimir got too close to Grigory, and tripped again.

This time, he fell down, and the athletes roared with laughter. The humor of the situation broke the spell, and the training room returned to its usual din.

"How is it going Tom? It looks as if you've got just about all the difficult cases finished." Nik was happy to at least see some progress in the training room.

"Yeah, Doc, things have gone pretty well. Nobody's having much trouble now. I think Boris bears watching, though. He's got a huge bruise on his left outer thigh."

"I'll take a look at him after practice. Would you do Peter's wrap for me? He's out of the whirlpool and waiting in the rubdown room. Don't forget to take his supplies with you."

"Okay, Doc, I'll get right on it." Tom was not happy about the assignment, but he didn't complain to the doctor. After all, she was the boss.

When Nik checked with Mickey, he had completed his assignments, too. She asked him if there were any problems, and he had said that everything had gone well.

"Mickey, would you go down to the physicians' dining room and bring back a big breakfast; you know, eggs, sausage, toast…for one of the athletes who didn't get to eat before coming in for treatment this morning?" Nik pulled several dollars from her pocket and gave them to him.

"Have you had your breakfast today?" Nik knew that this had been a bad morning for everyone because of the weather.

"I'm fine, Doc, my roommate bought some cheese bagels last night, so we chowed down this morning." Mickey smiled a crooked smile and took the money from Nik.

"Just bring the food to the rubdown room, Mickey, and I'll take it from there."

Peter sat in the rubdown room trying to decide what his best options might be. He was in turmoil, his mind racing. Grigory knows about my physical problem. Is there anything that I can do to finish out these games? Peter had to complete the series of games, or he would not be paid. The security of his mother and Katya hung in the balance. If he couldn't continue to play, how would he get his family financially through until next year? How could they survive? His train of thought was interrupted by Tom's arrival.

"The Doc wants me to do your wrap, Genchenko. Is that okay with you?" Tom could see that something was wrong with Peter, but he wasn't sure what to do about it.

He was just finishing Peter's wrap when the doctor arrived, "Hi, Doc, you want to check this wrap? I'm not sure that I got it right."

Nik came over to Peter and asked him to stand, "How does it feel, Pete? Move around a little bit, and see if it's going to work for you."

Peter slowly got down off the table and started bending. He was trying to see if the wrap would give him enough support, yet still be flexible. He was aware that the doctor was watching him closely. He wanted to talk to her, wanted to know how and why Grigory had found out about his problem. Dr. Kellman had been very good to him, had helped him probably as much as she could. He was certain that it had not been her fault that Grigory had gotten hold of his medical record. She had not betrayed him, but what had really happened?

Tom busied himself with gathering the supplies left from Peter's hip wrap, "Doc, I'm gon'na get back to the training room, unless you need me for something else."

Nik shook her head, "Thanks a bunch, Tom. You did a great job."

Nik continued to watch Peter, and she could see in Peter's movements and demeanor that he was preoccupied. He's worried about what happened with Grigory earlier, she thought. How could he not be?

"Pete, I don't think Grigory's discovery will be a problem for you. I think it's going to be okay."

Before Peter could respond, Mickey arrived with the breakfast that Nik had requested.

"I hurried so that this wouldn't get cold, Doc." Mickey was out of breath.

"Mickey, that's great. I really appreciate this favor."

He replied, "Glad to do it, Doc. Now I'd better get going back to the training room and help Tom clean up the place. I think that Grigory has everyone out on the ice, well, everyone except Peter."

"When you get back there, let Grigory know that Peter will be there ASAP."

"Okay, Doc. See you in a few minutes."

Mickey gathered some supplies from a cabinet and, arms full, left the room to Peter and the doctor.

"I have some breakfast for you, Pete. Do you think that you could eat some of it?"

Peter turned to face her, and Nik was surprised by his apparent calm. Has he reached a decision, she wondered? If so, what might it be?

Peter nodded in answer to the doctor's question about eating his breakfast, "Da, *yes,* and thank you, doctor, I am very hungry."

Peter didn't lie very well. Nik could see that he was forcing himself to eat, but she knew that he had to eat something if he was going to play later this afternoon.

Several times Peter looked as if he might be about to speak to Nik, but then seemed to think better of the effort. Finally, he finished his breakfast, swallowed the last of the milk, and stood up.

"I'd better get back with the team, doctor. I don't know what Grigory will do, but I at least have to try to do the best that I can."

Peter and the doctor didn't speak as they walked quickly back to the training room together. Peter finished putting on his gear in silence, and left the training room, heading for the ice. Nik watched him go, thinking again that she wanted to help him but didn't know how.

Chapter 14

Tuesday Morning

It was becoming a trend. The practice had not gone well. Peter had been made to sit the bench when he had arrived late. Nonetheless, he paid strict attention to everything that Grigory said and did during the practice. Peter knew that Grigory was an excellent hockey coach, and he also knew that he needed to learn the strategy for the game this afternoon. Throughout the practice, Grigory did not look at him even once. Ilya and Slava spoke to Peter quietly when Grigory and Vladimir weren't looking, but most of the players, although puzzled by Grigory's treatment of Peter, didn't tempt fate.

Nik stayed in the background, coming forward only to check an athlete if there was a problem. Mickey and Tom seemed subdued, as well, and Nik realized that, even though they might not outwardly show their admiration for Pete, they nonetheless liked him. How odd, she thought, even Tom, who seemed to dislike Pete, actually admired him.

The practice ended, and all the athletes, with the exception of Peter, started the trek back to the training room with Grigory and Vladimir in the lead. Peter remained alone on the bench, head high and shoulders straight. Nik watched from a distance, unsure about approaching him. He seemed to be concentrating very hard on something. Tom and Mickey had followed behind the team, leaving Nik and Peter alone.

Nik called to him tentatively, "Pete…are you coming back to the training room?"

At first, it didn't seem as if he had heard her. But then, as though returning from a distant place, Peter looked at her.

"Don't worry doctor, I am fine. I just need some time to think things through." He looked down for a moment, and then, looking straight into her eyes, he continued. "Grigory isn't going to let me skate today. He's angry, and he has a right to be. I wasn't truthful with him, or you, for that matter, about the true state of my health."

"You had good reason to keep the problem to yourself. I didn't really understand why, at first, but now I do."

Nik did not approach Peter. She remained several feet away, wanting to come nearer, yet accepting that he probably wouldn't welcome her intrusion.

"Please go ahead without me, doctor, I'll be there in a few moments." Peter was staring out at the ice as he spoke.

Nik turned and walked into the tunnel. She walked slowly. Filled with helplessness, she really didn't know what to do. She couldn't *force* Grigory to let Pete skate. It's up to Pete now, she thought, and wished that there was something, anything, that she could do to make it easier for him. When she reached the training room, most of the athletes had headed to the showers. She checked her watch, and was surprised to find that it was already ten-thirty. The morning had gone quickly.

"Where is Genchenko?" Grigory had come up from behind her, his silent partner, Vladimir, approaching from the other side.

"He will be here in a few minutes. Why wasn't he allowed to participate in practice?" Nik's eyes bored into Grigory's, and her freight train look was in place.

"He knows the rules. If he's late, he doesn't practice, and if he doesn't practice, he doesn't start. It's a very simple rule that few of the players break. Genchenko cannot be an exception to this rule."

Nik shook her head in amazement. "You *dumb ass*, don't you know what you have done?"

Grigory's craggy brows went up in amazement, "What business is this of yours? *I* am the coach, and *I* will decide who plays and who doesn't play."

"Doc, could you come here for a minute?" Tom's voice held a strong note of concern.

Nik turned her back on Grigory without responding to him, and went over to where Tom was working with Ilya. She saw a look on Tom's face that she had not seen before. It was as though something had frightened him.

"What's up Tom?" Nik tried to smile reassuringly at Ilya, who was sitting on the training table in front of Tom.

"Watch this"

Tom grasped Ilya's left lower leg and pulled it gently toward him, while stabilizing the knee with his other hand. The lower leg came forward; a positive drawer sign, indicating an unstable anterior cruciate ligament in the knee.

Oh…my…*God*, thought Nik. He's blown his knee. She closed her eyes for a moment to regain her composure.

"Let me check that Tom." Nik sat down in front of Ilya.

She, too, elicited the drawer sign on Ilya's knee. Outwardly calm, she looked up at Tom and nodded her head.

Nik talked to the athlete in Russian. "Ilya, we're going to need an X-Ray of your knee. I'm concerned about some lack of stabilization there that Tom showed me. It could be serious, but we won't know until we look at the films. I didn't see anything happen during practice. Was there something that I didn't see?"

Ilya, his face pale, asked, "Is it very bad, doctor? It can't be too bad, because it doesn't hurt very much. I was just pulling off my skates, and then my knee felt funny."

"Let's get the X-Ray first, Ilya, and then we'll know more about what to do."

Nik didn't give Ilya any false assurances. It wouldn't be fair to him to do so.

Ilya called out to Peter, who had just come into the training room, "Petrosha, please…" He waved at Peter to come over.

"What is it, Ilya?" Peter's affect was subdued as he came slowly over to where Ilya sat on the training table.

"My knee…it's my knee. I think that something is very wrong with it." Ilya's face betrayed his fear.

"Come on Ilya. Let's get the X-Ray the Doc ordered." Tom rolled a wheelchair over in front of Ilya, and lifted him, by himself, from the table to the chair.

Peter looked at the doctor, a question in his eyes. She did not respond verbally, but shook her head and shrugged. *I don't know.* Peter understood, and rubbed the back of his head.

"If it is all right with you, doctor, I would like to go with Ilya for his X-Ray."

"I think that would be very helpful, Pete. Tom, let me know when you get back."

Nik watched the three go out the door, her heart sinking. Just when you think things can't get worse, they go straight to hell, she thought.

It was time now for the first shift training table mid-day meal. Coach Grigory wanted an early meal for his athletes because of the three o'clock start of their afternoon game. Feeding athletes was a precise and complicated process. They needed calories, and plenty of them, but they didn't need an overfilled stomach, or undigested food to get in the way of their game. Nik called the kitchen to check on the readiness of the meal, and was told to send her team down.

"Listen up everyone, the training table for our team is ready now, and I've been told that it will be open for the next forty-five minutes. You'd better get going in that direction if you want something to eat before the game."

Most of the athletes were still subdued from their less-than-positive practice session and Coach Grigory's ill temper. However, when Nik made her announcement, they started milling toward the training room exit.

Mickey called Nik to the telephone, "Hey, Doc, X-Ray's on the line."

The news was not good. Ken Brockman, the Radiologist on duty, called Nik with his preliminary findings regarding Ilya's knee.

"Nik, it looks like he's blown an ACL. The X-Rays are textbook. I wish I had better news for you."

Nik sighed, "Thanks for giving me the news so quickly, Ken. Who's on ortho today?"

"Bill Reynolds is on today and he's good with ACL repair. What does the coach say?"

"I didn't want to jump the gun with Coach Grigory. He has a bad temper, and things aren't going very well today so far. Let me talk with him and I'll call you right back."

"Just have me paged. I'm going to be pretty busy this morning. Everyone's got some kind of ortho problem today so I'm not sure where I'll be at any given time."

"Okay Ken. Thanks again for being quick about the reading."

Nik hung up the telephone, and sat staring at the wall for a moment. She dreaded breaking the news to Grigory. Finally, she got up from the chair and went looking for him, hoping to find him without Vladimir at his side. She hated the way that Vladimir looked at her while she was talking to Grigory. He gave her the creeps.

"Grigory, I need a word with you." This time, Nik was the one who startled Grigory.

"What is it now, Dr. Kellman? I don't want to hear any more pleas on Genchenko's behalf." Grigory's face was set in a scowl, his brows low over his eyes.

"That's enough, Grigory. You're out of line, and you know it. Do you want to hear what I have to tell you?"

"Well?" Grigory wanted to be as difficult as possible for the doctor, and he glowered down at her.

Nik let him have it straight, "Ilya has a torn anterior cruciate ligament. Most doctors call it a ruptured ACL. The ACL is part of the internal stabilization of the knee. I sent him for X-Rays, and the Radiologist just called to confirm my diagnosis. My advice is to send him to the hospital for an ACL repair as soon as possible."

For once, Grigory was dumbfounded. "How did this happen? He wasn't having any trouble during practice."

Nik fixed Grigory with an angry stare. "Since your team arrived, I have been taping Ilya's knee. You refused initial diagnostic X-Rays for Ilya when he got here. The records you presented me with were misleading and incomplete. This could have been prevented Grigory, but you wouldn't let me do what needed to be done."

Grigory found a chair and sat down heavily. He put a hand to his head, and looked at the doctor as if in a daze. His large forehead broke out in a sweat.

"Tell me again what has happened to Ilya." Grigory's voice was monotone.

"He needs surgery to repair his torn ACL. That means he's out for the rest of the games. I need your approval for hospitalization and treatment."

Nik's words were cold and emotionless. She had no sympathy for Grigory's predicament at this point.

Grigory nodded, "Go ahead and treat him. Is there any other choice?"

"No, there isn't. The sooner we get on this, the better Ilya's chances are for recovery. I'll get him set up with the surgeon."

Grigory heaved himself up from the chair and walked slowly out the training room door. He glanced back at her one time, and he looked devastated. It surprised Nik when she realized that she actually felt some small amount of sympathy for him.

Peter walked beside Ilya's wheelchair as they came slowly back to the training room. Tom walked behind, silently pushing the chair, his face set in a deep frown. Ilya was beginning to have pain and swelling in his injured knee.

Although Ilya said very little, Peter could see by the set of his shoulders, and the way he bit his lower lip, that he was having pain. Peter noticed, too, that the knee was visibly more swollen than it had been when they left the training room. It didn't look like something that Dr. Kellman could fix easily.

Peter knew that he would not be skating with Ilya today, or even in the near future, and he felt a sense of sadness and loss. They were not only teammates, they were friends, and had shared many victories, and a few defeats. When they were on the ice, each seemed to sense the other's moves. Peter knew that, if *he* felt sick about Ilya's injury, Ilya must be heartbroken.

Nik had put in a page for Ken Brockman, and was on the telephone requesting a hospital transport for Ilya. She had already set up his admission to Indiana University Hospital when Peter, Ilya, and Tom returned to the training room. She had not had any success contacting the orthopedic surgeon, Dr. Reynolds, but had given his answering service the message that he had a new patient coming to I.U. Med Center.

"We're back, Doc." Tom was very subdued.

"Pete, Tom, the training table is serving, and Coach Grigory wants the team to get an early lunch, so you'd better get down there. I'll stay here with Ilya. We've got some things to discuss."

Peter shook his head. "I'd rather stay here with Ilya, doctor." He wasn't asking her permission.

"Yes, doctor, it would help me if Peter could be with me for this. I am a little nervous about what is happening, and having my friend with me will be very helpful to me." He looked up at Peter as he spoke.

Nik sighed audibly, and replied in Russian, "All right, I guess I understand what you're telling me. Ilya, you're lucky to have a friend like Peter."

"I know doctor. I've never had a better friend." Ilya bowed his head so that Nik wouldn't see the tears filling his eyes.

"Doc? I'm going down for lunch. Should I bring something back for the three of you?" Tom pointed with his index finger and made an arc indicating Peter, Ilya, and the doctor.

"No, Tom. Right now, I think I'd better see that Ilya is taken care of…but thanks for offering."

"I'll be back in about twenty minutes, Doc." Tom walked toward the door.

"That sounds fine. See you then."

Nik turned back to Ilya and continued in Russian, "You are going to need surgery, Ilya. I just talked with the Radiologist, and he confirmed what Tom and I thought when we first examined your knee. You have a ruptured ACL. It's the anterior cruciate ligament, and it stabilizes your knee."

"It is very serious, then?" Ilya had become pale; much more than he had been a moment ago.

"Yes, it's serious enough to require surgery. The hospital transport will be here soon. That's why you're going to have to wait for your lunch."

Peter was watching the doctor as she told Ilya the bad news. He could see that she was upset. She's kind, and compassionate, too, he thought. We've been nothing but trouble for her since we arrived, but here she is again, trying to fix what is broken.

"Pete, I need to get Ilya to the ambulance bay. Can you grab his coat for me?"

Peter took Ilya's coat from his locker and brought it over to her, "I can put it on for him, doctor."

Ilya put first one arm, then the other into his coat sleeves, and they were ready to roll, literally. Peter pushed the wheelchair, with the doctor at his side.

When they got to the ambulance bay, the transport team had arrived and parked inside the building. There were two of them, a man and a woman, and they looked at Ilya's chart and spoke at length to the doctor. Although Peter stood next to her and heard everything that was said, he hadn't understood much of it. Medicine didn't interest him, but he wished now that he had at least studied some of the aspects of sports injuries. His ignorance, and not knowing what lay ahead for Ilya, caused him to be even more concerned for his friend.

Nik prepared Ilya for transport by wrapping him in blankets from the blanket warmer, all the while trying to give him some assurance that he was going to be all right. He was quickly put in the ambulance and secured by the EMT's, and Peter climbed in beside him.

Nik leaned on the transport door and talked to Peter, "I'll follow in a couple of minutes so that I can get Ilya admitted and also talk with the surgeon. Pete, I'm going to have to bring you back with me for the game."

Peter nodded his understanding and looked at Ilya as he answered, "I just want to help Ilya right now, doctor. He needs to know that someone will be there for him."

"Okay, Pete, but you may have to leave him before he goes to surgery. Just so you know…"

"I know, doctor. But for now, I want to help him as much as I can."

The EMT's closed the transport doors and jumped into their seats, slamming those doors as well. Nik pounded on the back door to let the transport team know that they were all clear and good to go. As the transport pulled out of the building, Nik could see that Pete was looking out the back door at her. She waved at him, and he waved back, and then the ambulance turned the corner and was gone.

Nik hurried down to the dining room to find Mickey and Tom. Should I call for extra help? I can't be in two places at once, but Ilya needs someone to be with him for his surgery and afterward. She was running down the steps two at a time, heart pounding. What am I going to do?

Nik burst through the swinging door entrance to the dining room. As luck would have it, her team had the table nearest that entrance, and Mickey and Tom were still there.

"Tom, Mickey, we're going to have to put a plan together for this afternoon. I just sent Ilya to I.U. for surgery. You both know that our game is just three hours from now. Someone's going to have to stay with Ilya at the hospital during his surgery and recovery. Do I have a volunteer?"

Tom and Mickey looked at each other for a moment, eyebrows raised, shoulders shrugged. Nik knew that neither of them wanted to be away from the team during a game, but she didn't have many options. Ilya needed someone that he would recognize when he came out of surgery. He deserved no less.

"Uh, Doc? I guess that I could miss this game for Ilya's sake." Tom's face had softened as he volunteered.

"Well, Tom's stronger than I am, Doc, and he might be able to give you more help during the pre-game wrapping and stuff." Mickey was more pragmatic than Tom, and he was resigned to the fact that Tom's physical strength was greater than his own.

"Decide between the two of you which one will get the short straw. My car is in the doctor's parking area. It's the silver Cougar, and I'll be leaving in ten minutes."

Nik looked around the room for Grigory. When she didn't see him or Vladimir, she turned back to Mickey and Tom.

"Where's Grigory? I've got to let him know about Ilya. Have either of you seen him?"

Mickey shook his head, "He didn't come down for lunch, Doc, and I don't know where he could've gone to."

"I'm going to get my coat and head down to the parking lot. I'll see one of you in a few minutes. The other one needs to find Grigory to let him know that I'll be back in plenty of time to get the team ready for the game."

"Okay, Doc. Everything will be ready when you get back." Tom practically stood at attention when he stood up and answered her.

Nik needed to call Ron to let him know that she was going to need help for the game this afternoon. When she got to the training room, she tried to reach him, but his answering machine was on, so she left a message. She put in a page for him, too. Well, she decided, I can call him from the hospital if all else fails. Nothing was going right for her today. Nik half expected or half hoped that Grigory, Vladimir, or both, would be in the training room, but they were nowhere to be found.

Mickey was waiting beside her car when Nik arrived. He didn't look glum, but she was certain that he wasn't happy with the arrangement.

"Short straw, huh?" She smiled at him, and tugged at his coat sleeve.

Mickey nodded. "Yeah, but Ilya deserves to be treated right. He's a good guy."

"It's open." Nik indicated the passenger door.

"Don't you lock your car, Doc?" Mickey was surprised.

"Sometimes..." Nik smiled at him again.

Nik's pager went off as she pulled into the doctor's parking lot at the hospital. She and Mickey made their way into the hospital as quickly as they could, considering the amount of snow on the pavement and traffic in the area. And the snow continued to fall.

As soon as she and Mickey got inside the building, Nik searched right and left for a telephone, and found one just inside the security office.

"Mind if I use this, Richie? I just got a page." Nik had grabbed the telephone and held it in one hand.

The beefy, warmly dressed security guard grinned at Nik. "Knock yourself out, Doc."

He knew Dr. Kellman from having seen her often coming into, and going out of, the hospital during her training and residency at Indiana University Hospital. She had always been friendly, and had never pulled rank on him or behaved in a superior way to him with the, I'm-more-important-than-you-are, act.

Nik dialed the number showing on her pager, and tapped her fingers on the desk as she waited for an answer. He'd better answer, damn it, he couldn't have just paged me and then walked away from the phone, could he?

On the fourth ring, she heard the familiar, "Yes?"

Without preamble, Nik started to tell Ron what she would need, "I'm going to have to have some help this afternoon, Ron. One of the athletes has been injured, and he's going to surgery in a few minutes. I'm here at University Hospital already."

"Hold it, hold it, Nik. Who, what, where, and when…? Slow down and tell me what's going on."

"I don't have a lot of time to explain everything now, Ron, but it would really help me if you could send another athletic trainer to get the team ready for the game."

He paused, "Okay, but how long will you need another trainer, and do you need another doctor, too? Garibaldi will want to know the details."

Nik exhaled a long, frustrated sigh at the mention of Dr. Garibaldi. "I may have to keep the trainer for another game. One of my trainers will be staying here in the hospital with the injured athlete for his immediate post-operative recovery, and perhaps beyond. Right now, I don't need another doctor, so Garibaldi shouldn't have a shit hemorrhage over this."

At that point, Richie and Mickey exchanged a look that said, "uh-oh."

"Nik…" it was Ron's turn to exhale a sigh of frustration.

"If you can send someone, fine, if not, we'll do the best that we can. I've got to go now." Nik hung up the telephone before Ron could respond.

"Thanks Richie, I owe you."

"You're welcome, Doc."

"Mickey, let's go."

They hurried to admissions to find Ilya and Peter, and had to dodge around a multitude of people in the hallways of the hospital, in various stages of dress and undress, with or without I.V. poles, on foot or in wheelchairs.

Nik's pager went off three times while she and Mickey looked for Ilya and Peter. Each time she checked the pager and placed it back on her belt.

She didn't want to talk to Ron again, at least not yet. *Finally*, they found Peter in the hallway beside an inpatient admitting room. He was restlessly pacing back and forth, and when he saw them, he was visibly relieved.

"The surgeon is with Ilya, Dr. Kellman. He said to send you in when you arrived."

Nik could see that Pete was rattled by the prospect of Ilya having to undergo surgery, and that he would be out for the rest of the games. She knew that the stress and tension that Pete had had to endure since he had come for the games were taking their toll. He looked tired, and he also looked as if he would rather be *anywhere else* than this hospital.

Nik touched his arm lightly and said, "Thanks Pete, now it's time for you to settle down. I know how difficult this is for you, but you have to step back and take a deep breath."

Mickey nodded his head in agreement, "Yeah, Pete, you're gon'na lose it if you don't."

Chapter 15

Tuesday Afternoon

Peter got into the car beside the doctor. He was quiet and contemplative, and hadn't said a word since he had said goodbye to Ilya. He was glad that Mickey was going to stay with Ilya until after his surgery. He knew Mickey to be kind and competent, too, as Peter himself had experienced those qualities first-hand with Mickey when he had first arrived. But having to leave his friend before he went to surgery was difficult for him to do. *Where do my loyalties lie?*

Peter glanced at the doctor's profile briefly as she looked straight ahead, concentrating on her driving. As it had almost from the moment he had first seen her, his heart had let him know that he thought of her as much more than just his doctor. But, as he had realized before, he knew that in a few more days he would leave and never see her again. He felt a painful stab of impending loss at the thought, but he was fully aware that, no matter how he felt about her, or about leaving her and never seeing her again, it probably didn't make a difference to her at all. *She is only doing her job, and she does take it seriously. That's why she has fought to help and protect the team,* he decided. *Otherwise, what could the explanation be?* She had certainly shown some internal fire when she had lost her temper with Yakov and Grigory. Her strength had surprised him. She had been fearless in protecting him from Yakov. More than that, she had saved his life. If nothing else, he owed her a debt of gratitude, but his feelings ran much deeper than that.

He bore the burden of shame, too, for having caused her harm. How could he have done so? The thought of what he had done caused a deep anguish inside him. But she had forgiven him, had acted as though it had been an accident, and that he had not intentionally hurt her.

Nik wasn't concentrating on her driving as much as she appeared to be. She wanted to speak to Pete, to reassure him, to help him somehow, but she knew that there was little that she could say or do to change his feelings of apprehension about his friend. Pete's actions on Ilya's behalf had made her look at him differently than she had in the beginning. It had added another dimension to this young man that she had not expected. More than just an exceptional athlete, he had continued to surprise here with the depth of his character, and his courage, since she had first looked into his eyes. Those strange, expressive eyes of yours, Pete, they're really something. Your heart and soul shine through those eyes.

Nik forced herself to think ahead to the game. She realized that she did not have the luxury of time to spend wondering about Pete right now. I'd better get my mind working on how to get everything done before this game. For a moment, she wondered where Grigory and Vladimir had gone. Surely they'd be back before game time. She wasn't sure, either, that Ron was going to help her. Nik was sorry that she had hung up on him. Her temper always seemed to get the best of her. There were times when she just couldn't rein it in, and they usually happened when she was dealing with Ron.

When she and Peter reached the arena, Nik parked in her space, and they hurried into the building. Neither said anything, but they exchanged a look briefly that said, "Here we go again." The wind had picked up, and blowing snow was adding to the already serious weather-related problems on the roads. It was only one-fifteen, but it seemed much later. The sky was dark and heavy with rolling clouds.

Nik felt overwhelmed with all that she must accomplish with the athletes before the game. The training room was lit up, and Tom was busy with the athletes. He looked up to see her come in, and waved a happy greeting in her direction.

"We've got another athletic trainer, Doc." Tom pointed toward a young woman who was busily taping an ankle for Arkady.

Nik nodded and turned to Pete, "Have a seat over there, table three will do, and I'll get you ready for the pre-game action."

"Doctor...I want to thank you for the way you took care of Ilya. He's in good hands because of you." Peter touched her shoulder briefly as he spoke to her.

Nik's eyes held Peter's for a moment. Such beautiful eyes, she thought, "You're welcome, Pete."

Grigory's voice interrupted, "Where have you been for so long, Dr. Kellman? I was worried that you wouldn't be here in time to get the team ready."

Nik gave Pete a rueful look, and then turned to address Grigory. "The question is; where have *you* been? Ilya is in the hospital having surgery right now, and I couldn't find you before he left."

Peter took this opportunity to walk away from Grigory without having to speak to him. He hoped that if the doctor couldn't do his wrap, that maybe Tom would do it for him. As he walked over to Tom, he wondered briefly if he would even get the chance to play, given the way Grigory had treated him during practice.

Grigory watched Peter for a moment as he walked away, and then answered the doctor's question. "Your Indianapolis police came to ask me some questions regarding Yakov's passing. They wouldn't take no for an answer, and so I cooperated, and gave them what little information I had to give. Vladimir is with them now."

Nik wanted to reply, I'll *bet* you cooperated, but she simply said, "Okay, so now are we back on track for the game this afternoon?"

"Da, *yes*, but please tell me about Ilya. He is having surgery now?"

"He should be out of surgery before the game starts. I left Mickey with him, and the surgeon will page me with Ilya's outcome. After the game, I'll go back to the hospital to check on him. Do you want to go with me?"

Grigory was still not himself. Ordinarily he would have been booming instructions and strutting back and forth while talking with Nik. Instead, he sat down and behaved as if he were very tired.

"I will go with Vladimir after your open house tonight. Ilya will probably not be fully awake until then, anyway. He should rest, and then we will see him."

The open house, Nik thought. I almost forgot about my mother's party! Nik inwardly congratulated herself on having made some preliminary transport arrangements for the team the day before. Thank heaven I was thinking clearly yesterday! She slapped her forehead with her hand.

Grigory looked at her in puzzlement, "Is something the matter, doctor?"

"No…no, I just remembered that I haven't told the team how they're going to get to the party. After the game, a large van will be available outside the hotel entrance. The van will have the Westin logo on the side. The driver will be there at about six, and he's going to wait until six-thirty or so for the team before starting out for Geist. I'll announce it to the athletes after the game, so that they'll know when they need to be ready to go."

"What is Geist?" Grigory didn't understand Nik's instructions.

"Oh, that's the reservoir that my parents live on. It's their address, their location." Nik could see that Grigory was processing information slowly.

Vladimir came into the training room and walked directly over to Grigory. Surprisingly, he had something to say this time.

"We must talk, Grigory. I have some information that you may not like."

Nik watched Grigory's reaction, and was concerned when the big man reddened and held his head with his hand. I wonder what his blood pressure is, she thought. He's a good candidate for a stroke.

"Grigory, are you feeling unwell? Maybe I should take your blood pressure and listen to your heart and lungs."

"Nyet. I am doing fine."

Grigory got out of the chair slowly, and walked toward the training room entrance, with Vladimir directly behind him in lock step, as usual.

Nik was curious about what Vladimir was going to tell Grigory, but she didn't have time to dwell on it. She looked at the clock and calculated that, if everything went well with the athletes' preparations, they would be ready to go to the ice at two-thirty.

She looked around for Peter and saw that the new athletic trainer was doing his wrap. Nik walked over to them so that she could introduce herself. It concerned Nik that the trainer hadn't spoken with her first to get her order for Pete's wrap. Maybe Tom instructed her. I should give her the benefit of the doubt.

When Nik was a few feet away, walking toward Pete and the trainer from the side, she noticed that the trainer, a very pretty red-haired young woman, was looking up at Pete in what might be called an unprofessional, almost flirtatious, way.

"Hello, I'm Dr. Kellman. You must be the athletic trainer that Dr. Michael sent over to help us." Nik smiled and put out her hand to shake the new trainer's hand in greeting.

"Oh, hi Dr. Kellman, I'm Rebecca Autry."

The young woman, upon seeing the doctor, jumped up and bounced lightly for a moment on her feet, almost like a cheerleader, before taking Nik's hand. For some reason, this irritated Nik greatly.

Peter had been submitting to the new trainer's ministrations, but he realized very quickly that she wasn't as practiced as Mickey, Tom, and especially, Dr. Kellman. He was in a quandary about what to do, because he knew that if there was even an outside chance that he might get to skate, this wrap was not going to be supportive enough. He was very relieved to see the doctor, and began to speak to her in Russian.

"Pomasch, *help*, I'm glad that you are here." He paused, trying not to laugh. "As you can see I need some help. Otherwise, I won't be able to skate like this."

Nik put her hand to her mouth for a moment. Her reply was in Russian. "Hmmm…I see your predicament. How can we be diplomatic and still get you ready for the game?"

Peter shrugged, "All I can say is *please* help me."

Turning to Rebecca, Nik said, "Thanks for helping Pete. I have another assignment for you now. Could you please check with Tom and help him prepare the water bottles and sports drinks for the athletes? It's time to get them ready."

Rebecca gave the doctor an odd look, and then said, "Okay. Is there anything else that you want help with?"

"Tom will show you what needs to be done. Thanks for coming over to help us."

Rebecca looked up at Peter and said, "'Bye," after which she gave him a big smile.

Peter smiled back at her and repeated, "'Bye."

Continuing in Russian, Nik told Pete, "We're going to have to let her save face. It would hurt her feelings if I re-wrapped you here, so go over to the rubdown room, and I'll come down there to do your wrap."

"How long will she be staying with the team, doctor?" Peter was watching Rebecca walk away.

"Well, I think she's going to be with us for a couple of games, or so. Why do you ask?"

Peter was shaking his head, then turned, and with a wry look said, "It could prove to be very interesting, doctor."

Nik laughed a short laugh, and pointed toward the rubdown room. "Troublemaker."

Peter actually laughed, too, and then quickly headed in the direction of the rubdown room. Nik watched him until he went out the door of the training room.

After grabbing some under wrap, tape, and a few pads to place at pressure areas, Nik held the supplies in one arm, and pushed through the training room door into the corridor with the other. She thought of Ilya for a moment, hoping that he was doing okay. I've got to call and check on him, she thought.

When she reached the rubdown room, Peter had prepared for the wrap by shedding his warm-up clothes down to his shorts.

"This is going to be quick, Pete."

Nik set the supplies down on the table and began Pete's wrap. After doing the under wrap, she placed the tape anchor pieces around his waist and mid-thigh, and then proceeded to do his hip wrap. Using the anchors as the beginning and ending points for the serpentine pieces, Nik placed a strong but light supportive wrap over Pete's hernia. Beneath the tape, Nik put an inverted cup-shaped piece of soft plastic directly over the hernia for the purpose of splinting the weakened area.

Peter watched the doctor as she set up and started his wrap. He admired her, and her skills were as good as any that he had experienced in Russia, or in his travels with the team. Besides, he had never had such a beautiful doctor or trainer before.

"How does that feel? Bend and stretch a little to check it out." Nik felt pressured to get back to the training room to make sure that all the athletes were ready for the ice.

Peter reached down to help the doctor to a standing position, and then moved about the room. "It's very good, doctor. Thank you once again for helping me."

As Nik stood in the doorway, she turned to look at him, "Good luck, Pete."

He returned her gaze for a moment, and then she walked through the door and into the corridor.

"Spaseeba," *Thank you* Peter said quietly to the empty room.

The players that needed to be were wrapped and, in some cases, held together with tape. In spite of this, they were ready to head out to the ice. Grigory, still low-key and dispirited, gave the team a lukewarm pep talk about vanquishing the American team. However, the energy that Nik had seen before in pre-game preparations wasn't there for the coaching staff or the players this time.

Nik looked at Pete to see if he was going to have something to say to the team, but he was silent. Briefly they exchanged a glance, and then Pete looked away. His glance had been non-committal, and Nik's heart dropped. What are we in for now?

Grigory, with Vladimir stuck to him, started out the training room door toward the arena. Slowly, the team began to follow them out into the corridor. Tom walked beside Rebecca, towering over her as she bounced along. Good grief, thought Nik, someone's going to have to show that girl how to walk without jiggling and bouncing. And then Nik thought, oh no, I *am becoming my mother* after all!

The telephone rang, and Nik went over to her desk to answer it. Mickey gave Nik the good news that Ilya had come through his surgery successfully, and was now in recovery. He also told her that the surgeon would be in touch with her shortly, so that he could answer any medical questions she might have.

"Oh Mickey, that's wonderful news. Ask the surgeon to have me paged when he's ready to talk, and I'll call him right back. Please tell Ilya when he wakes up enough to talk to you, that Peter and I will stop by to see him after the game."

"Did Dr. Michael send you any help?" Mickey hoped that he had.

"Well, yes, but she's a little green. She seems very nice, though. I had to re-wrap Pete because he didn't feel confident in her abilities, but that's common when athletes get attached to someone and don't want anyone else working with them."

"Yeah, I know how hard it was for me when I started, too. I hope Tom's treating her well."

"Of course he is. I wouldn't expect anything less." Nik was sort of tongue in cheek.

Mickey laughed, "Yeah, he's an old smoothie."

"I called the Nursing Registry, and a Registered Nurse should be there within a half-hour to relieve you. Thanks for helping. I don't know what I'd have done without you. Well, Mickey, I have to go. The team's already headed for the ice. Page me if you need me."

"Okay Doc, I'll page you when Ilya gets his room assignment. I'll just put the room number into the pager."

"Good. Are you coming over to the game when the nurse gets there?"

"I'm going to get a bite to eat, and then I'll head back to the arena, Doc."

"Thanks again, Mickey."

Nik hurried after the team, and she could hear the noise of the crowd increase in decibels as she approached the entrance to the arena. When she actually got into the arena, the noise level was almost painful. She spotted Sheldon Levin and his friend Marty Pelham near the Russian box. They were standing and talking with Ron. The three spotted her at about the same time, and waved her over.

As Nik approached, Ron was looking at her with frustration written all over him, "Nik..." he began.

Nik held up her hand, "Truce. I don't have time now to argue with you."

Sheldon and Marty looked at one another questioningly. Then, as though they had rehearsed it that way, they said together, "Hi Doc."

"Hello gentlemen. It's nice to see you. Have a seat there behind the team." Nik pointed over to her area.

"Thanks Doc. Do you think your team is going to win this one?" Marty smiled hugely at Nik.

"Hockey's a rough game, and I've heard that the American team is pretty tough, so your guess is as good as mine." Nik was all business.

"Yeah," said Sheldon, "but the Americans don't have Peter Genchenko."

"That's true enough. Look, fellas, I've got to get to work here."

Sheldon and Marty nodded, and headed over to the bench.

Ron had been waiting patiently for Nik to turn her attention to him. He was angry, but he was trying not to let his anger show. He realized what Nik had been up against from the beginning with this Russian team, and he knew that it was his fault for having gotten her into the games in the first place. Ron knew, too, that he, himself, had been stretched very thin trying to please Garibaldi, and also trying to keep everything running smoothly regarding the medical component of the games. It hadn't been easy, and he was tired and frustrated. And now Nik was angry with him. He hadn't been able to please anyone in the whole damned mess, even though he had struggled mightily to make it all work. For some reason, too, he felt that Nik was becoming more distant with him. What am I going to do if I lose Nik? He fully realized that if that happened, it would be his own fault.

"Ron…I just can't take another discussion right now. I really can't. Please, let's not argue here. I can see that you're upset with me, and I deserve it because I hung up on you, but I can't really deal with it now."

Nik was standing close to Ron as she told him this, because the noise of the crowd was increasing moment by moment. He could see a look of near-desperation in her eyes, and it wrenched his heart. He put a hand on each of her shoulders and gently pulled her closer to him.

"Okay, Nik, but can I stick around here with you? I won't bother you, I promise. But I'd just like to be here in case you need my help. Is that all right with you?"

"Yes, I'm glad that you want to be here." Nik patted his arm, and tried to smile, but her eyes filled with tears.

"I'm sorry Nik, so sorry that I got you into all this mess." He pulled her even closer, and hugged her tightly for a moment.

Peter, sitting on the bench next to Boris, was watching the doctor with her fiancé. It caused a spreading ache of cold and sadness inside him when he saw them share an intimate moment. Fool, he thought, I am a fool for feeling like this, and looked away.

Grigory tapped the starting players, and Peter did not receive a tap. Vanya would be skating Peter's left wing position. Peter's heart was pounding as the starting players took the ice. He held his stick and moved it back and forth almost imperceptibly as he watched the play on the ice. Even though he was sitting the bench, he was on the ice with his team.

Arkady had two saves initially, but the American team was relentless. After less than five minutes of the start of play, they had scored a goal. They were a physical, scrappy group of misfits who, nonetheless, came together as a team when they saw the need.

Nik could not sit still. She kept pacing back and forth, like an animal in a cage. Ron had followed her pacing for a few moments, and then sat down with Marty and Sheldon. He watched her as she paced, and wondered why this was so difficult for her? Why did she care so much about this team? At first, she had professed a dislike for the Neanderthals, as she called them, so why be so upset now? Ron knew that Nik was an excellent physician, and he had marveled many times when she came up with some obscure diagnosis that was proven to be correct. How could someone so obviously gifted take *this crap* so seriously? It was beyond him.

It was painful for Nik to watch Pete sit there on the bench. Nik saw that every few minutes or so, Rebecca would approach to offer him some water or sports drink. Rebecca was kneeling down in front of Pete at the moment, and Nik could see that he was trying to be polite, while still staying in the game. Finally, he stood up to watch a play that he couldn't have seen with Rebecca in the way. It didn't faze her. She looked up at him and continued to give him a wide smile as he watched the game.

"Hey, Doc? Is Genchenko injured? The coach isn't putting him in, and the Americans are slaughtering your team." Marty Pelham had a puzzled look on his face as he cupped his hand and spoke into Nik's ear.

The score was now 3-zip, in favor of the Americans. The crowd was calling for, "SEVENTEEN, SEVENTEEN"! Marty obviously wasn't the only spectator who was puzzled over the reason that number seventeen was sitting the bench.

Nik shrugged and said, "I guess it's a sort of strategy on Coach Grigory's part."

Marty was frowning, "Some strategy!"

The Russian team struggled mightily in the absence of Peter and Ilya. By the middle of the second period, Arkady had five saves, and Vanya had even made a goal against the American team, but there was no spark, no fire, on the part of the Russian team. Vanya and Mikhail had been given penalties at different times for one minute each for roughing. That left Boris and Dimitri with the burden of defending against attacks on goal. Boris, more often than not, sat the bench, and was not a starting player. Today, however, he had been pressed into play because of Ilya's injury. The Russian bench was not deep. Slava was the only player sitting the bench with Peter.

Late in the second period, Grigory pointed a finger at Peter, and he nearly knocked Rebecca, who was kneeling next to him, over in his haste to get out on the ice.

Vanya came off the ice looking relieved and happy to be out of the brawl. The Americans had a policeman on the ice, and he had dogged Vanya up and down the ice, wearing him down.

Peter had gotten cold on the bench, and he moved swiftly around the ice, turning and stopping, then starting out as if he were in a race, trying to warm up. The policeman immediately tried to attach himself to Peter, and found that he was no match for Peter's moves. Peter was much faster, and could stop and turn, deke, so quickly that the policeman found himself out skated at every turn and lagging behind.

Peter went directly after the puck that was being brought down the ice toward the Russian goal by the skillful American center. With the policeman attempting to chase him, Peter poke-checked the puck away from the American center with the blade of his stick. Peter then deked toward the American goal. Mikhail was with him and they passed the puck back and forth, while blocking each American attempt to take it away. Peter took a flip pass from Mikhail, over the policeman's stick, and then rushed at top speed toward the attacking zone.

"*SCORE*! Genchenko's scored!" The sportscaster's voice was hoarse and emotion-filled as it boomed over the loudspeakers. The noise from the crowd was ear splitting.

Nik, who was near Sheldon and Marty when Pete scored the goal, heard them shouting at the top of their lungs and saw them hugging one another.

"Did you see that, did you *see that? He was out there less than thirty seconds and he scored!"* Sheldon was elated as he pointed toward the ice and Peter. "*Pete on ice,* he shouted, "*Pete on ice!"*

Nik saw that even the predominantly American spectators cheered Peter's skill in setting up the play and scoring the goal. How could they not? It was absolutely beautiful, thought Nik.

Ron stood behind Nik as she clapped her hands and shouted for her team. The guy *is* good, he decided. He placed his hands on Nik's shoulders and gently squeezed them. When Nik turned around to look at him, he was very happy to see that she was smiling.

"I think we can win this game!" Nik's face was glowing.

Nik had gone from near-despair to elation in a matter of moments. When she looked over at Grigory and Vladimir, she saw that they were also out of their seats and cheering, arms raised above their heads.

Mickey arrived in the arena for the last five minutes of the game. He was happy to be back in his own element. Hospitals were not his favorite place to be, and he had been very relieved when the private duty nurse came in. Ilya was awake, intermittently, and Mickey had assured him that everything had gone well, and that Peter, the Doc, and his coaches would come to see him this evening.

Mickey spoke to the doctor. "I didn't need to page you with Ilya's room number when I saw that I'd have time to get over here before the game was over. Ilya's doin' okay and he's in 5337."

"Thanks, Mickey, for being the one to stay with Ilya. It took a load off of me, and I know that it helped Pete, too."

Tom came over to tell Mickey how bad everything had been until Peter was put into the game. "The guy scored a goal in less than a minute after Coach put him in!"

Tom slapped Mickey on the back when Peter scored a second goal almost single-handedly, and Mickey thought for a moment that he might cough up some blood. Mickey returned the favor with an elbow to Tom's ribs, because that was about as high as he could reach, and the two laughed hysterically.

The Americans were held to the three goals that they had scored before Peter got into the game. Even though the Americans had those three goals, Peter scored a third goal for a hat trick in the last minute of the game, and with Vanya's earlier goal, the Russians won 4 to 3.

Grigory took Peter in his arms and squeezed him in a bear hug when he came off the ice. To Peter's absolute astonishment, Vladimir followed suit. And then Grigory, with Vladimir again behind him, led the team out of the arena amidst the uproar of the crowd. Peter was near the back of the group, and Rebecca, who was empty-handed, chose to walk next to him. Mickey and Tom, arms loaded with equipment, towels, and water bottles, followed the team. Ron had an arm around Nik's waist as they came slowly down the corridor toward the training room.

"Peter, let me help you out of your wrap. Come over here and sit on this table and I'll help you." Rebecca patted the table with the palm of her hand and inclined her head.

Peter wondered how he could gracefully get away from Rebecca without hurting her feelings. Why has she attached herself to me? Peter wasn't flattered. He just wanted to get out of his gear and wrap, take a shower, and put on some dry clothing.

When Nik and Ron came into the training room, it was noisy, but it was well organized. Mickey and Tom were working in tandem to get the athletes taken care of. Nik noted that Rebecca had cornered Peter, so she walked over to them in order to assist him. Ron came with her.

In Russian, she asked, "Do I hear pomasch, *help,* here?"

"Da, Vratch, *Yes, doctor.*" Peter's relief was palpable.

Ron tried to follow the rapid patter, but didn't have a good enough grasp of the Russian language to really understand all that was being said. For some reason, he felt a rising tide of resentment at the apparent ease with one another that his fiancée and the hockey player seemed to share.

"Rebecca, I'm going to have to change the steri-strips on Pete's head wound, so I'll just help him out of his wrap, too. Ask Tom or Mickey where you might best help them."

Rebecca's disappointment was obvious, "All right Dr. Kellman." She turned on her heel and quickly walked away.

Ron congratulated Peter on his outstanding game as he offered his hand and said, "The Russians weren't in the game until you came out."

Peter took Ron's hand, enveloping it in his own large hand, and shook it firmly, "If it hadn't been for Arkady's saves at goal, Mikhail's defense, and Vanya's goal we could not have won. It was a team effort."

There was no false modesty in Peter's words. Ron wondered, is this guy for real? He's a bruiser on the ice and a gentleman when he's off. It was the first time that the two men had spoken, and each was taking the measure of the other. Peter, almost a head taller than Ron, held Ron's gaze and didn't flinch or look away. It was disconcerting for Ron, because he knew that Peter was probably only in his early twenties, but here the guy was, acting like a *mensch.* Ron could feel, for lack of better words, the presence and strength of this young man. Was there a challenge in those eyes?

"Nik, I could help out by working with Peter. That way you could do your rounds and make sure that your other athletes are in good shape." Ron wanted to be alone with Peter for a few minutes in order to talk more with him and get a feel for the kind of person that he might be.

"That would be great, Ron, but aren't you committed to help one of the teams during the next game?" Nik wanted to make sure that Ron didn't renege on his promise to help. Heaven forbid that Ron might disobey Garibaldi!

"Oh *damn*, I'd better get over to their training room. You're right, they probably could use some help." Ron was less than enthusiastic about having to leave Nik.

"Do you know what time you're going to get to the open house? Mother said she'd delay the start of the main buffet until you get there."

Ron shook his head, "Nik, I don't really know what to tell you, except that I'll get there as soon as I can. Tell your mom not to hold anything up for me, but she *could* set some of the good stuff aside."

Nik smiled at Ron's request, "You know that she will put a huge plateful in the warming oven for you, Ron."

Peter was watching the two of them as they talked, and he was envious of Ron's possessiveness with the doctor. Ron touched her, hugged her, and it was clear that he considered her to be his own. She was wearing his engagement ring, and the familiarity and warmth of their conversation made Peter ache inside for something that he was sure he would never have. Too, it hurt him even more, because of his own attachment to her. He turned away when he couldn't watch them anymore.

Nik and Ron said their goodbyes. Ron kissed her on the forehead and told her, "I'll see you at about seven or so, Nik. If you need me between now and then, just page me."

"Pete..." Nik spoke quietly to him. "Pete, I can help you now." She touched his shoulder gently.

When Peter turned to look at her, Nik could see sadness in his eyes again. It surprised her, and she didn't know what to do for a moment. He should be happy about the game, but he's obviously hurt or sad about something.

"Let me change those steri-strips, Pete. Then I'll get you out of that wrap." Nik put her hand on the side of Peter's head gently. "You've had quite a day, haven't you?"

"Da. *Yes.*" Peter, who had been the stoic throughout most of his life, felt emotion well up inside him. He felt ashamed of his emotion, and he didn't want the doctor to see his vulnerability.

"You should have heard Marty and Sheldon cheering you on when you got out on the ice. I think that they're going to start a fan club for you."

Nik looked into Peter's eyes and smiled. She gently removed the steri-strips from Peter's head wound. As she did so, she continued to talk to him about the game, and how much she had enjoyed seeing him play.

Nik told Peter about Ilya, too, "Mickey said Ilya came through the surgery very well, and that he was talking when Mickey came over to the arena."

"I'd like to go to see him before the party, if that could be arranged."

"I'll take you with me when I go to check on him. Grigory told me that he and Vladimir weren't going to see him until after the open house."

"Thank you, doctor. I appreciate your kindness." Inexplicably, he again felt the chill and ache of emotion in his chest, and his throat constricted, making it difficult for him to speak.

Chapter 16

When Nik finished with Peter, she sought Grigory out to tell him about the travel arrangements she had made for the open house. "Could you remind everyone that the van for the party at my folks' place will be at the main entrance of the hotel between five-thirty and six-thirty? I'm going over to the hospital to check on Ilya, so I'll see you at the open house."

"Yes, doctor, I think a party is just what everyone needs right now. Please tell Ilya that I'll see him tonight." Although Grigory was still low-key he managed a smile for Nik.

As Grigory was making the announcement to the team, Nik checked with the athletes to make sure that everything was in good shape for each of them. She was thinking about Ilya, and hoping that he was doing well. Mickey told her that Ilya was given a private room and the private duty nurse assigned to him had the doctor's pager number in case anything happened. So far, Nik's pager had been silent.

Peter hung around the entrance to the training room until the doctor saw him. He didn't want Rebecca to spot him, and perhaps attach herself to him again, so he looked inside the room occasionally until he got a signal from the doctor.

Nik gave Peter a nod of her head across the room, grabbed her coat and bag, and ran to the door. "Let's go see Ilya."

On the way over to the hospital, Nik explained to Peter the type of surgery that Ilya had undergone. He listened intently, and enjoyed the brightness of the doctor's eyes as she told him what to expect when he saw Ilya. He felt warmed, illuminated by the attention. The cold ache in his chest and constriction in his throat melted away in her presence.

Peter wanted to learn from the doctor, to see things from her perspective. Of course, he understood very little of the medical terminology that she used, but each time he didn't understand something, he would ask for an explanation, and she helped him to understand.

"You love your profession, don't you Dr. Kellman?" Peter was half-turned toward her in the car seat, wanting to see her reaction to his question.

Nik slowly nodded, then replied, "Yes, I do love what I do, but there was a time that I wouldn't have dreamed of being a doctor. Actually, I'm living someone else's dream."

Her answer greatly surprised Peter, and he didn't know how to respond at first. Finally, he asked, "Whose dream is it then; your parent's, your fiancé's?"

As Nik pulled into the parking garage of the hospital, she spoke to him in a very quiet, sober voice, "It's a long and painful story, Pete, and I'll share it with you sometime…"

Once inside the hospital, they hurried to the elevators and caught one to the fifth floor. Nik looked up at Peter and said, "I think Mickey said room 5337."

They walked down a long corridor into a post-surgical care unit with a large nurses' station. Peter could see a great deal of activity on the part of the hospital staff in and out of the nurses' station. He had never been in such a facility before today, and it was almost overwhelming.

When they reached room 5337, Nik said, "Yup, there he is." She stepped aside and pushed Peter through the door to Ilya's room first.

Ilya saw Peter, and his face lit up, "Petrosha, this has been a most unusual day."

"In more ways than one, my friend. Have you heard that we beat the American team?"

"Without my help, you won? How can that be?" Ilya smiled widely at Peter, and then saw the doctor behind him.

"How are you feeling, Ilya?" Nik took his hand in hers and squeezed it gently.

"I am in no pain at all, doctor, thanks to this wonderful nurse who speaks my language." He pointed to the nurse who had been sitting in a chair beside him, and had stood up when Peter and the doctor came into the room.

Nik offered her hand, and, speaking in Russian said, "Hello, I'm Nik Kellman, and this is Peter Genchenko, Ilya's teammate. Ilya looks like he's in good shape."

Nik saw that the nurse was petite, and she was very attractive. Lucky Ilya, she thought.

The nurse nodded to Nik and Peter as she replied in Russian, "It's nice to meet you, doctor, Mr. Genchenko. I'm Susan Anderson, and I'm going to be staying with Ilya for the next forty-eight hours. And, yes, Ilya has been doing very well."

Peter was surprised that the nurse could speak Russian and would be staying in the room with Ilya. Well, she will be immediately available for Ilya whenever he needs her. How different this environment is from Russia's, he thought. This would be a luxury afforded to only a few very important people in Russia.

"Pete, if it's okay with you, you can stay here and visit with Ilya while I check his chart. I still haven't heard from the surgeon, but Ilya looks very good. Ms. Anderson, would you like to join me and fill me in on Ilya's immediate postoperative period?"

Illya's nurse replied, "I'll be right there as soon as I adjust the positioning pillows for him. And you don't need to call me 'Ms. Anderson'. I prefer 'Susan'."

At the nurses' station, Nik checked the chart thoroughly, and was pleased by what she found. The surgeon's postoperative note was detailed, and well written. Ilya's surgical course had been straightforward and uneventful according to the surgeon's notes. The anesthesiologist's records and post- anesthesia note also looked very good.

Susan's notes were excellent, and her assessments were also well written. The same was true of the perioperative notes written by Ilya's surgical and recovery nurses. This is a thorough picture of Ilya's condition, Nik decided. She was very much relieved to see that Ilya was getting the best of care.

When Susan came to the nurses' station, Nik talked with her a few minutes, and determined that all was well with her patient. His vitals had returned to baseline very quickly, and he had surprised the recovery nurses with his near-perfect Aldrete Score within twenty minutes postoperatively, indicating that he was alert, awake, with stable vital signs, and moving all extremities, much more quickly than the average patient.

Nik told Susan, "It's amazing to see his Aldrete Score at ten so quickly. Well, he's an athlete, and a very good one at that."

Susan replied, "I like taking care of athletes. They're in good shape to begin with, and they are *very* motivated to recover quickly."

When Nik and Susan returned to Ilya's room, Peter had pulled a chair close to Ilya's bed and they were laughing and talking; enjoying themselves.

"Doctor, Ilya has told me that he will be playing hockey again the day after tomorrow." Peter was still laughing as he spoke to her.

"Yeah, *right*. Pete, his biggest challenge is going to be getting out of bed and standing first. I think his story about getting out on the ice with you tomorrow will change drastically at about that time."

It was wonderful to hear Pete's rich laughter. It started deep in his chest and bubbled upward in mellow notes.

Ilya joined in the laughter, too, "Well, perhaps next week, then?"

"It's going to be a bit longer than that, Ilya." Nik knew that Ilya fully understood how long his recovery would be.

Nik looked at her watch, "It's almost six, Peter, and we need to get to my parents' for the open house. The drive time from here is nearly twenty-five minutes. And that's in good weather.

"Ilya, I'm very pleased with your progress. I'll be back tonight when Coach Grigory and Vladimir come to visit you. It wouldn't surprise me a bit if Peter comes along then, too."

Peter grabbed Ilya's hand and shook it, "I will come back with the doctor. In the meantime, you need to get some rest. Being on the ice isn't the same without you there."

"Susan, I know that Ilya is in good hands now, and we all appreciate what you're doing to help him." Nik approved of the private duty nurse who was assigned to Ilya.

Peter and Nik left and headed quickly to the parking garage. Much to her chagrin, Nik realized that they'd be in the tail end of the rush hour. Poor planning, but she couldn't have done anything differently. She wouldn't have hurried Pete's visit with Ilya for any reason.

In the car Nik said, "I was hoping to get a chance to get cleaned up for the party, but I guess that it's going to be a come as you are party."

Peter wanted to tell her that she looked beautiful just the way she was, but he didn't think that such a comment would be appropriate. He looked down at his own dark blue, well-worn slacks and sweater, his threadbare coat unbuttoned, and decided that a come as you are party was a very good thing.

Nik saw him looking down at his own clothing, "Pete, you'd look good in a gunny sack."

"What is…?" he started to ask.

"A gunny sack," Nik completed his sentence, "is a burlap bag, or a cloth sack. The cloth is very scratchy, thin, and the color is an ugly beige-gray. If someone could look good in such a garment, then that person would more than likely look good in just about anything."

Peter laughed and replied, "So…the weather is much too cold here to wear such a thing?"

"Right!" And her laughter sounded wonderful to Peter.

Chapter 17

Tuesday Evening

When Peter and Nik arrived at the Kellmans' home, the festivities had already begun. The van that had transported the team was parked out front, and one other car, as well.

Peter was overwhelmed by the appearance of the home of the doctor's parents. It looked more like a very fashionable small hotel to him. The large, oak double doors had a Christmas wreath on each door, the lamps adjacent to the doors held huge red ribbons, and there were two fully trimmed Christmas trees; one on either side of the double doors. The flash of brass and glass on stone said 'money' to Peter.

Nik pulled into the driveway and asked, "Pete, I'm hungry, how about you?"

"Yes, very." Peter, however, wasn't thinking about his hunger. He wondered what the inside of the house was going to look like.

Peter got out of the car, went around to the driver's side and held the door for Nik. He then walked her up to the doors, opened one and held it for her. He is a gentleman, thought Nik, who was not used to such treatment when Ron was her escort. Ron usually was preoccupied, or talking with someone, and didn't think about the niceties, the pampering, that any, *every*, woman appreciates.

Once inside, Peter helped the doctor with her coat. He knew that his actions were just a pretense on his part, but he didn't care. It felt wonderful to be with her, as though she were his, if only for this brief little charade.

"Thank you, Pete." Nik looked up at him and smiled, her eyes shining.

"*Niki*! You're finally here." Marina gracefully came from the dining room into the large foyer wearing a beautiful velvet coatdress in a lovely shade of mauve. Duchess accompanied her wearing a matching bow on her collar.

Marina hugged her daughter, and then looked up at the man who was holding her daughter's coat, "And who is this young man?"

"Mother, this is Peter Ivanovich Genchenko. Pete, this is my mother, Marina Kellman."

Peter gently took Marina's small hand in his very large one, "It is very nice to make your acquaintance." He spoke to her in Russian.

"Jintlmyen, *gentleman*, you have a gentleman here, Niki." Peter had charmed Marina.

"It would seem so." And how refreshing, thought Nik.

Duchess, who felt that she was being ignored, put her paw on Peter's foot and growled. It startled Peter, and he stepped back from her.

"Duchess, you are being impolite. You shouldn't growl at a guest." It surprised Nik that Duchess had misbehaved.

Peter got down on one knee next to Duchess, and the dog lifted a paw and placed it on his knee. Again she growled, but Peter understood that she was talking to him.

"Hello Duchess, my name is Peter. I am glad to make your acquaintance." He took her paw in his hand and shook it.

Duchess licked Peter's hand and growled again. This time, Peter laughed out loud.

"I think she likes me," he said.

"I have never seen her behave this way before, but Duchess is a strange girl, Pete. Let's put our coats in the master bedroom. Is that a good place, mother?"

"Oh yes, that's the best place for now. Niki, are you staying the night?"

"I'm not sure. I have an athlete in the hospital. He had surgery this afternoon, and I'll need to check on him this evening."

"Is that where Myron is right now?" It was an innocent question on Marina's part, but Nik didn't take it that way.

Nik looked at her mother and colored a little. "No, I said that *I* have an athlete in the hospital. *Ron* had to stay for part of another game because of Dr.Garibaldi, but he said he'd try to be here by seven. He said to tell you to save something for him from the buffet table."

"Oh, Dr. Garibaldi's here for the open house. He surprised me by being the first to arrive."

Nik was caught off guard. *Great, that's just great.*

"I didn't know that he had been invited, mother." I'll bet the old womanizing idiot has already snooped throughout the whole house by now, thought Nik.

"Well…Myron mentioned that Dr. Garibaldi was actually heading up the team of doctors for the games, so I thought that I probably should invite him, too."

Peter, with Duchess looking up at him, was standing just inside the entrance to the foyer, holding the doctor's coat and gloves, watching the mother and daughter interacting. The doctor had told him at the beginning of their acquaintance that she had an interesting family. The dynamics here, he decided, were quite interesting, indeed.

Nik looked at her mother with one eyebrow raised, and then turned away. She took Peter by the arm, and led him down a long hall to the master bedroom. Duchess trotted after them.

"Sometimes I have to count to ten when I talk with my mother." The doctor seemed to be on the verge of gritting her teeth.

The doctor's comment puzzled Peter, because he wasn't aware of anything that her mother had said or done that could have upset her. In fact, his first impression of Marina was that of a very pleasant and charming woman.

Peter stopped at the doorway to the master bedroom as the doctor went in. He looked around the room and could see that it was well appointed and decorated in quiet, muted tones of white and beige. The overall effect was one of soothing comfort and luxury. There was a thick velvet duvet cover on the bed, and multiple pillows were stacked decoratively against the headboard of the bed in a seeming random, yet attractive, way. The furniture was substantial, heavy, and of a dark wood; hickory or cherry perhaps?

Peter liked the room because it reminded him of the décor in his parents' Moscow apartment and the dacha on the lake in Tver. He and his sister had been surrounded with luxury, but he hadn't really thought for a while about how prosperous his family once had been, until this room brought the memories flooding back.

"Pete...Pete? Hello, is anyone at home?" The doctor was waving her hand in front of his face.

"Oh, I'm sorry, Dr. Kellman, I didn't realize that you were talking to me." Peter, as if coming back from a distance, walked to the bed and put the doctor's coat and gloves with the others already there.

"You seemed to be miles away, Pete." Nik saw that the sadness had returned to his eyes.

"I was several thousands of miles away, actually," and many years, too, he thought.

Nik wondered about Pete's reply, but didn't pursue it any further. She realized that he was probably speaking about his life in Russia, and that was not a topic about which he readily volunteered information.

"You must be starved after the game. Let's see what my mother is serving on her buffet." Nik walked back down the hallway, and Peter followed. Duchess had been patiently waiting for them, and again followed behind.

On the way to the dining room, they walked past what Peter thought might be a drawing room, where there were shelves full of books, tables with what appeared to be antique games, and an exquisitely beautiful, shining black concert grand piano. The room, unlike the master bedroom, was decorated in many shades of red. He liked the use of the color red, because it was vibrant and energizing; just the way a room should be if it was to be used for gatherings and guests for daytime or early evening pursuits. His curiosity was piqued by the grand piano. He decided that he would come back to this room if he got the opportunity.

Once past the drawing room, Nik took Pete through what she called the great room. There was a huge stone fireplace with a roaring fire in the center of one wall. Several of Peter's teammates, Boris, Slava, Mikhail, Dmitri, and Arkady, were warming themselves in front of the fire, and spoke to him and the doctor as they passed by. Duchess decided to stop and make their acquaintance.

Peter saw that the stone chimney of the fireplace rose from its broad mantel to the full height of the vaulted ceiling. Was it twenty or thirty feet? Peter couldn't gauge the height of the ceiling. The overstuffed furniture, occupied by Tom, Grigory, Vladimir, Mickey, and Vanya, was arranged in such a way as to be able to view a large television, in a cabinet with doors, and the fireplace as well. Peter saw a staircase that turned in a relaxed arc from the great room, as it ascended to what he thought might be a balcony. He then saw six doors that opened onto the balcony, and wondered if they might be bedrooms.

When they reached the dining room, Nik saw that her father was talking with Garibaldi and his wife near one of the bay windows in the room. She could see that her father was being polite to the man, and she also knew that her father was astute enough to see through Garibaldi's facade to the man underneath.

Peter decided that he liked this room the best of those he had already seen in the house. A huge oil painting of a scene in turn-of-the-century St. Petersburg, Russia was hung above the large buffet cabinet. He wondered whether it was an original oil painting. It was lighted to its best advantage, which gave the painting a lovely light golden hue and added the illusion of depth. An ornate crystal and brass chandelier hung from the center of the ceiling, ten feet above his head.

And then Peter looked at the table. It was set with fine linen, crystal, silver platters, bowls, and serving dishes filled with enticing and wonderfully aromatic foods. There were zakus'ki *appetizers* of ikra *caviar,* and seld *herring.* There were several kinds of salat *salad,* mya'so *meats,* gulyash *goulash,* blini *pancakes with fillings,* piroshki, *small hot pastries with fillings,* khleb *bread,* ovoschi *vegetables,* sup *soup,* frukti *fruit, and* sladkoye *desserts.* It was overwhelming to his senses. This room, this feast, more than all the other rooms combined, evoked the deepest feelings of Peter's former life within him.

Upon seeing his daughter come into the dining room with a young man he didn't recognize, Klaus excused himself from Garibaldi and his wife, Mary, and went to her side.

Klaus put an arm around his daughter's shoulders and said, "Niki, is this the athlete that won the game for the Russians today?"

Nik looked up at her father, and then looked at Peter. The two men were roughly the same height, but her father had several pounds on Peter.

"Hi, dad, this is Peter Genchenko. Pete, this is my father, Klaus Kellman."

The two men looked at one another for a moment, and then shook hands. Klaus liked what he saw in this young athlete's eyes. They were direct and intelligent, Klaus decided. He glanced down at his daughter and saw that she was looking up at Peter Genchenko and smiling. He had never seen her look that way at any man before; not even her fiancé, Ron. It surprised him very much, and he didn't know what to make of his daughter's obvious admiration for this young man.

Before Klaus could strike up a conversation with Peter, Dr. and Mrs. Garibaldi joined them, much to Nik's dismay. *Oh no, what am I going to have to do to get away from these people?*

Garibaldi was rubbing his hands together as if he were washing them, and he had an ingratiating grin on his pudgy, round, bejowled face. He stared directly at Nik with his round eyes and raised his eyebrows so high that it almost appeared as though he had hair. Mrs. Garibaldi, upon seeing her husband's obvious interest in Nik, looked at her with eyebrows raised at the corners, nostrils flared, and mouth tightened into a false smile.

Nodding his head toward Nik, he said, "Hello, Dr. Kellman, have you met my wife, Mary? Please introduce us to your star athlete. This young man is Peter Genchenko, am I not correct?"

Nik was terse, "Yes. Peter Genchenko, this is Dr. and Mrs. Joseph Garibaldi. He is the Dean of the Sports Medicine Residency Program for Indiana University."

Garibaldi grabbed Peter's hand and pumped it up and down, "Genchenko, I have watched you skate this week, and you're one of the best amateur hockey players that I have ever seen. I was born and raised in Minnesota, so I know whereof I speak."

Peter had not had an opportunity to get into the conversation up to this point. In perfect English he replied, "Thank you for the compliment, Dr. Garibaldi. Mr. Kellman, I appreciate what you said about winning the game against the American team this afternoon, but it was a team effort for the Russians, and I'm glad that we were able to win."

Klaus liked Peter's response. There was nothing falsely humble about what he said, and Klaus could see that Peter was sincere in his reply.

Mrs. Garibaldi had never before seen such a young man so tall, handsome, and well mannered; and *oh, that wonderful accent.* The Garibaldis were very similar in that they were always on the prowl for new blood.

Tom, Slava, Mickey, Vanya, Boris, Grigory, Mikhail, Dmitri, Arkady and Vladimir came into the dining room and began filling their plates from the many delicious choices on the table. Soon, all the athletes were around the table, and this gave Nik the out that she needed in order to extricate herself from the Garibaldis. She moved to join the others at the table.

Grigory spoke to Peter in Russian about the food, "Genchenko, this food is like no other training table that you will ever see. The doctor's mother has been very kind in preparing for us a wonderful Russian feast. Dusha, the Russian spirit is alive and well here."

Peter smiled at Grigory's effort at polite chatter and replied, "Da, *yes*, and I intend to eat my fill."

Marina stood in the kitchen entrance to the dining room, beaming, and enjoying the obvious success of her buffet. It was always interesting, too, to see her guests interacting.

To the group in general, she said, "Please let me know if there is anything else that you need. There is much more in the kitchen. The beverages, chai, kofe, and vino are on the buffet."

Peter excused himself from Klaus and the Garibaldis, and got in line behind the doctor. He saw many dishes that he had not seen, or smelled, since he was a child. When he had filled his plate almost to overflowing, he followed the doctor into the great room, where she hesitated for a moment, and then headed for the drawing room. Duchess, who had been shadowing Peter's every move, padded quietly after him.

They found a table to their liking, cleared it of a jade chess set, which they carefully placed on a book shelf, and sat down to enjoy their food. The room was quiet, except for the crackling fire in a small and quite ornate alabaster fireplace that Peter had not seen from the doorway before. A wide bay window with open draperies looked out on the frozen Geist Reservoir, and the snow had begun to fall again.

"This is wonderful. I love this room. It reminds me of my childhood in so many ways." Peter was smiling as he looked around the room.

"Is that where you were earlier when you said that you were "thousands of miles away"?"

Peter hesitated for a moment, and then told her, "I know that it's hard for you to believe that someone like me lived like this at one time, but as I told you before, my family was wealthy until my father was cast out of the Communist Party."

Nik tilted her head to one side and asked him, "Why would you think that, Pete? It isn't hard for me to see you in this setting. Everything about you says that you were to the manor born."

Peter smiled tentatively, and his eyes were soft as he said, "Do you actually think that?"

"Yes, I do. You have something called charisma. You have *presence.* When you walk into a room, everyone pays attention to your arrival. Remember what I said about the gunnysack? You know, I said you'd look good even in a gunnysack? Well, very few people could pull that one off, and you're one of the few."

Peter didn't know how to respond to what the doctor was telling him. In fact, he was embarrassed, and became quiet as he concentrated on the food on his plate.

Nik saw that she had probably said too much. I've made him uncomfortable, she thought, and then wondered what she might say or do to make him comfortable again. Nik picked at her food for a few moments, trying to think of something to say to him.

Peter, for his part, wanted to resume their easy conversation, too. But he felt awkward and didn't know how.

Finally, he said, "Niki…your mother calls you Niki, and so does your father. I have heard others call you Nik at times, as well. Which do you prefer?"

Nik was quiet and thoughtful, "Well, when I was a child, my parents and brothers called me Niki. I was the baby of the family. As I got older, I didn't really want to be called what I considered by then to be a childish name. But, as you have heard, my parents can't help themselves; I will forever be Niki to them."

Peter again said, "Niki." It sounded like *Neehkeeh.*

"When you say it, it doesn't sound childish." Peter's very Russian pronunciation of her name brought a smile to her face.

Soft music began filtering into the room from speakers concealed in the bookcases. It wasn't intrusive. In fact, it added to the fairytale atmosphere. When "Pachelbel's Canon" began to play, Peter excused himself and got up from the table where he was sitting with the doctor. He walked over to the grand piano, and stood in front of it for a few moments, savoring the beautiful lines of the instrument.

"May I…?" He looked at her questioningly.

Nik's eyes widened in surprise, and then she smiled and said, "Of course."

Peter opened the piano almost reverently, sat down and began to play a variation on "Pachelbel's Canon" in perfect time with the music floating from the speakers. It was a variation that Nik had not heard before.

Fascinated, she came over and stood behind Peter as he played. He looked up at her and smiled a sad smile that intrigued her. Nik sat down next to him and began to play her own variation that swirled around, note for note, point and counterpoint, and perfectly complemented Peter's version of the music.

Marina and Klaus looked at one another across the great room when they heard the piano music. As if drawn by the Pied Piper, they went to the entrance of the library, the room that Peter had called a drawing room, and peeked around the door. What they saw brought tears to their eyes. Niki, sitting with Peter Genchenko at the piano, was playing a duet with him.

Other guests also came slowly to the door to watch and listen to the piano duet. Peter's teammates were quietly talking back and forth about being unaware that he could play the piano. Grigory was transfixed. He could not believe that he had not known about this aspect of Peter Genchenko.

Garibaldi rubbed his hands together and kept saying, "Well…well, well."

Mrs. Garibaldi glared even harder at Nik's back than she had to her face earlier. Mary Garibaldi had no musical skill, and even if she had, she probably would not have worked hard enough to play the way Nik and Peter were playing. Joy spilled over from their music as it filled the room. But it was lost on Mary Garibaldi after the thirty years she had spent with her philandering husband.

Finally, Peter and Nik stopped playing, and then realized that they had an audience when they heard the applause for their presentation. They looked at each other and laughed, then began playing again.

This time, Nik started, and Peter followed in a duet of "Fuhr Elise." When they finished, they stood, and then bowed, in acknowledgment of the applause from their small audience.

Klaus and Marina came forward and hugged their daughter, and then shook Peter's hand as if he had just created a miracle. Peter's teammates came into the room to congratulate him on his previously unknown talent. Slowly, Grigory entered, Vladimir by his side, and when they reached Peter, Grigory put a hand on his shoulder.

Grigory shook his head for a moment. "You have surprised me again, Genchenko. How is it that you have such a command over this beautiful instrument?"

"My mother taught my sister and me to play the piano from the time that we could crawl up on the piano bench with her. I think that she wanted us to have exposure to what she considered to be culture."

"From what I heard just now, your mother was successful, indeed. And doctor, you too have the same wonderful gift of music." Grigory was nodding his head, and Vladimir kept perfect time with him as he, too, nodded.

Nik smiled at Grigory, graciously accepting the compliment. "There was a time when I thought that the piano would be my career."

"Well, it must have been a difficult choice for you; the piano or medicine."

"Not really. I think I made the wisest choice in medicine." Nik was polite but non-committal.

"Genchenko? What about you? Is this another career for you to pursue?"

"I think not. My mother sold her beautiful piano several years ago so that we could continue to stay in our apartment in Lyubertsy. I haven't had much of an opportunity to play since then." Peter was matter-of-fact.

Peter's comment filled Nik with dismay. How sad to have to part with something so valuable that meant so much to Peter and his mother, and probably his sister, too. His story is filled with so many hardships, Nik realized, and her heart went out to him.

Marina Kellman came over to Peter again and thanked him for playing such beautiful music with her Niki. Klaus, who had been standing behind her, again took Peter's hand and shook it firmly. He didn't say anything to Peter, and Peter was puzzled by the look on his face. It was as though Klaus Kellman had been crying.

The door chimes rang, and Marina hurried away to answer the door. Much to her surprise, it was Myron, with a young lady beside him.

"We couldn't get in, Marina. Someone must have locked the door." Ron's cheeks were red from the cold.

"Oh, I'm so sorry. Come in, come in." Marina continued to look at the young woman with curiosity.

"Marina, this is Rebecca Autry. She's helping Nik's Russian athletes. Marina is Dr. Kellman's mother."

Rebecca politely said, "It's very, very nice to meet you. Dr. Kellman does a great job with the athletes."

Nik came around the corner at that moment, with Peter behind her. Marina observed that the young lady, Rebecca, brightened considerably when she set eyes on Peter. She also saw that Myron had the same reaction when he saw Niki.

When Peter saw Rebecca, he backed up a few steps. It didn't matter. She immediately latched onto him. Marina saw the discomfiture on his face, and it was almost comical. Poor girl, she thought, she doesn't know that she is supposed to be aloof, nonchalant, hard to get. *That's* the way to get him interested, my dear.

Then Marina saw the dynamics between her daughter and Myron, too. But their interaction caused her some concern. While Myron only had eyes for Niki, she was looking at Peter and Rebecca.

Tom and Mickey came over to join Peter and Rebecca, much to Peter's relief. With the return of the doctor's fiancé, Peter didn't want to stay at the party any longer. He just wanted to go back to his hotel after making another visit to see Ilya. He watched as Ron put his arms around the doctor and kissed her on the cheek. It caused an actual physical ache inside his chest. The cold began to close in on him again.

Nik was angry with Ron for having brought Rebecca with him to the open house. She knew, however, that it wouldn't help anything if she told him how she felt.

Once Rebecca and Ron had the opportunity to sample from the buffet table, Nik told Ron that the athletes were going to have to get back to their hotel because they needed to rest up for their game tomorrow. She and Ron had been sitting in the great room before the fire, and then the Garibaldis joined them, monopolizing the conversation, each interjecting opinions into every topic of conversation that Ron introduced. Nik, having lost interest in the conversation, was keeping tabs on Pete's attempts at extricating himself from Rebecca, but she could see that the girl was relentless. She saw that he had finally given up, and was sitting with her across the room.

Luckily for Peter, Mickey, Tom, and Vanya had joined them. It took some of the pressure off Peter, but he was still uncomfortable with the unsolicited attentions of Rebecca.

Finally, Grigory began to say his farewells, telling everyone that he needed to go to the hospital to check on Ilya. Standing by his side, Vladimir nodded with each third or fourth word that Grigory uttered.

The athletes began to gather their coats, and Marina and Klaus stood by the door for the farewells that were soon to be made. Marina loved to entertain; Klaus did not. He had endured the evening with equanimity and good manners. Now, however, he was anxious to have his wife and his home to himself again.

Klaus wanted to talk to Marina about the remarkable event of seeing and hearing their daughter at the piano again. What had caused her to sit down to play the piano with Peter Genchenko? Although Niki hadn't played seriously since her brother Josef's death, she had been trained as a concert pianist. She had started playing at the age of four, when she clambered up onto the piano bench and told him in her sweet way and soft voice that she was going to be a pianist just like him. Thinking about those times made Klaus wonder if his family could ever be truly happy again. They would talk, he and Niki, he promised himself, when things were quiet again.

"Ron, are you going to be able to drop Rebecca off at the arena to pick up her car? I want the athletes to get back to their hotel without too many distractions. If you've been watching her this evening, she likes the athletes and one in particular, too much."

Ron looked at Nik as she spoke, and then he replied, "Hon' I haven't seen anything from Rebecca that would indicate that she's a problem."

"Okay, Ron, but I'd like to have you take her back to get her car. That way, the van driver won't have to detour to the arena. Does that meet with your approval?"

"Hey, don't get upset. I hear you, and I'll take Rebecca back to the arena." Ron was tired, and more than a little defensive.

When Garibaldi and his wife came over to them, Ron didn't seem too happy to see them again. Nik thought that Ron's ears probably hurt, because both Garibaldis had been bending them ever since Ron arrived. The thought made her giggle briefly, and the three of them looked at her as though she might have a mental problem.

"Sorry, I just thought about something that struck me as funny." Nik looked at Ron.

"Well, I have to get going, Nik." Ron hugged her to him and kissed the top of her head.

Ron briefly shook Garibaldi's hand, bid Mrs.Garibaldi goodnight, and then followed Nik's finger, pointing in the direction of Rebecca. Ron, with a look of resignation, went over to her. On his way out the door, Ron shook Klaus' hand, and hugged Marina, then gave a final wave at Nik, and bounded down the steps with Rebecca.

"Well, Dr. Kellman, your parents have certainly entertained us well this evening. And you...how extraordinary it was to hear you playing the piano with Genchenko." Garibaldi started to intrude upon Nik's personal space, and she stepped back away from him.

Nik was creative when she replied, "I'm sorry to have to excuse myself, Dr., Mrs. Garibaldi, but I have to head back to the hospital to check on an athlete." With that, she turned on her heel and walked away from them toward the stairway.

Garibaldi frowned as Nik quickly walked away. He disliked her because she had seen through him, had deflated his ego, but of course, he couldn't allow himself to consciously acknowledge this. Because he was the kind of man that he was, he would find some way to get even with her. Mrs. Garibaldi, however, was delighted that Dr. Kellman had snubbed her husband.

Peter stood at the door with Marina and Klaus. He had the doctor's coat on his arm, and had put his own on. He wanted nothing more than to go back to his room to sleep, but then he also wanted to make sure that Ilya was doing well. The doctor had been kind in offering to take him back to the hospital with her.

Nik came quickly down the stairway from the second floor, an overnight bag in her hand. She looked as though she had been relieved of some burden, because there seemed to be a little spring in her step.

"Mom, dad, I'm not going to be able to stay tonight. It would mean that I'd have to come all the way back after I check on Ilya in the hospital, and I'm pretty much worn out."

"That's okay, Niki." Klaus patted his daughter's shoulder.

He didn't want her to feel badly. Klaus knew that she had some heavy responsibilities with the Russians.

"Alice is going to come over at ten tonight, and we're going to clean up the buffet, Niki, so go ahead and get your own work done." Marina leaned against her husband's shoulder as she spoke to her daughter.

Nik's parents hugged her from both sides, making her the center of their family hug. Nik laughed. She hadn't had such a hug for a very long time.

Peter stood waiting for her, and it warmed and saddened his heart at the same time to see such a display of family love. What would it have been like to be raised by a loving father? It was something that he would never know.

On the way back to his hotel, Peter and the doctor visited Ilya, and found him to be in good spirits. Grigory and Vladimir arrived soon after, and the group was in a celebratory mood. When the doctor and Peter were saying their goodbyes, Ilya challenged Peter to win tomorrow's game against Finland. Peter promised him that he would do his best, but that he would need the help of the rest of their team.

"Da, Peter," said Ilya, "Da."

In the doctor's car, Peter told her that he had enjoyed her parents' open house more than anything that he could think of in recent memory. He told her that the food, and especially the desserts, *sladkoye*, had been wonderful.

The doctor replied with a "thank you" on behalf of her parents, "Mother loves to do things like this, Pete, and my father goes along with her. Believe me, they are probably planning the next soiree even as we speak." She gave a little giggle that made him laugh, too.

"What is…?"

"Soiree?" She giggled again. "I've probably mispronounced the word. It's French. It means a fancy party. Being Russian, you should have a fairly good grasp of French. After all, it was spoken exclusively in the Russian Court, when there was one, that is."

Peter nodded, "Yes, when there *was* a Russian Court, French was spoken preferentially. Actually, I thought that you were using American slang, and I wasn't sure of your meaning." To Peter's ears, the doctor's pronunciation had sounded like swah-hray, and he had almost laughed when he had realized what she had said.

"In the *south*, especially in Louisiana, there are a great many words that are taken from the French and incorporated into the American vernacular." The doctor was amused.

"Tell me about the beautiful grand piano in your parents' study. Which of your parents plays the piano?"

The doctor was quiet for a moment, and then said, "Both my parents play. You should hear my father play sometime. He's wonderful, but he isn't in your league. Your skills are much more refined."

Peter hesitated, and then replied, "My mother, as I told you, was a trained concert pianist in Poland. She wanted my sister, and me as well, to at least learn the rudiments of her craft. I found that I loved the instrument, and thought that, for a while, I might want to seriously study the piano."

"And?" She glanced over at him with a question in her eyes.

"My father's arrest brought everything, the music, skating, and our education, to a halt." Peter shrugged, as if that fact spoke for itself.

"I'm sorry, Pete. I'm sorry that things have been so difficult for you."

"There is no reason for you to feel that way. I don't worry about "what if" this or that might have been different if my father had not gone to prison. There was no choice; it was fate."

So many things in life depend on fate, thought Nik…just the luck of the draw.

"Now, tell me about the piano. Is it yours?" Peter was curious.

The doctor was silent for a long while. Finally, she gathered herself and answered him. "Yes. I trained for many years on that piano. I loved my music more than anything…*anything*!"

Peter was surprised at the doctor's passion when she spoke about her music. Her skill on the instrument earlier in the evening showed that her training had been thorough.

"And you stopped playing to study medicine?"

"No, although it might seem that way, I stopped playing…"

She didn't, or couldn't, continue. When she looked over at him, Peter could see tears shining in her eyes.

"I'm sorry, doctor, I shouldn't have asked you such a personal question." Peter was upset that he had blundered into hurting her feelings.

She pulled her dark, silken hair back from her face and behind one ear. Peter had seen her make this graceful, and somehow elegant, gesture many times, but especially so when she was nervous or upset.

"Please don't apologize, Pete, and don't feel badly for me. I guess I'm just a little weary after everything that's happened today."

Later in the evening, after the doctor had dropped Peter off at his hotel room, he got ready for bed, but found that he couldn't sleep. He turned from side to side restlessly, trying to get comfortable in the huge bed. Why did he always seem to do something that caused hurt to the doctor? He was angry with himself for having done so. Gradually, out of sheer exhaustion, he drifted off to sleep after kicking his blankets aside.

Peter was standing on line in the cold rain, waiting his turn to buy beets for his mother's borscht. Lyubertsy on a warm summer's day was ugly, but it was even more so when the weather began to turn cold. His nostrils and eyes stung from the acrid pall of smoke spewing from numerous factory chimneys all over the city.

Everything was colored in various shades of gray: the buildings, the streets, and the people. Out of the corner of his eye, Peter caught a glimpse of something white amidst the gray. When he turned his gaze in that direction, he saw that a young woman, without a coat, clad in a white cotton smock and light-colored slacks, was walking quickly past him. Her head was erect, and her dark, shoulder-length hair moved in the breeze. Her shoulders were square, and her stride was purposeful, as though she might be late for an appointment. Puzzled, he stepped out of line to see her more clearly, and realized that it was the doctor. Yes, it was Dr. Kellman. He was sure of it.

Peter hurried after her, wanting to stop her, if only for a few brief moments, so that he could talk to her. He tried to call her name, but could make no sound. He began to run after her, but still she seemed to be increasing the distance between them. Finally, his throat aching and parched from his effort, he called her name aloud.

"Niki," he cried. "Wait, please!"

She turned toward him, smiled and waved her hand, then turned the corner onto another street. When he got to the corner, he frantically tried to find her in a teeming and noisy throng standing on line for some commodity. She was nowhere to be seen, and he knew in his heart that she was lost to him. He would never see her again.

When Peter awakened, he was very cold and distantly aware that he had been dreaming. His heart was pounding, and he knew that his dream had been about Dr. Kellman. Shaking, Peter pulled the covers around him.

"Niki he whispered, "Niki."

Chapter 18

Wednesday Morning

Nik made a special effort to get to the arena early. It was six forty-five, and she had been happy that the streets were almost empty as she drove to the arena from her downtown condominium. Most of the snow had been cleared away from the pavement, and it made the short trip uneventful.

The hospital visit of the night before had gone well. There had been laughter that raised the spirits, and true concern for Ilya's recovery on the part of his coach. Nik couldn't figure Grigory out. He ran hot and cold, and just when she thought she had him pegged, he did something that changed her opinion of him for the better.

Afterward, she and Pete sat talking in her car for a few moments about the events of the day and evening, and then Nik had dropped Pete off at his hotel. Bleary-eyed and tired, she had headed to her downtown condominium and her own comfortable bed.

When she got to the training room, Nik flipped on the lights, and started a tape with some of her music favorites. She was energized by the music and it gave her a jumpstart on her day. Listening to Dire Straits, Huey Lewis and the News, Lovin' Spoonful, Jim Croce, and Aretha Franklin always raised her spirits.

Peter arrived at seven fifteen, and found the doctor singing accompaniment to "It's a Beautiful Mornin'." She moved and turned gracefully, with little dance steps thrown in, between each treatment bay as she stocked supplies for the start of the day.

Peter watched her from the doorway, delighted with the spirit and beauty of this extraordinary young woman as she worked. When the music came to an end, and before the next selection began, Nik made her final turn, which put her in a direct visual line with the door, and she saw Peter standing there.

Nik began to laugh, and said to Peter, "Well, Pete, you caught me off guard."

Aretha Franklin's "Chain of Fools" began with thumping bass chords, and it was Peter's turn to laugh.

"Aretha," he said, and it sounded like, *Ah-rheee-thah*, his deep voice resonating with each syllable.

"You like Aretha Franklin?" Nik was surprised.

"Well…in Russia we don't just sit around whistling "Moscow Nights" or singing "Volga Boatmen" all the time. There is the black market, and most western goods, including music tapes and players, clothing, and other things western that are worth having, can be bought if you have the dollars. Not rubles, mind you, but dollars. Besides, I like the music."

As Aretha sang soulfully, Peter took the doctor's hand and led her through some dance steps. His lead was gentle, yet persuasive. Nik was caught up in the excitement of the moment and felt the music as if it were inside, rather than outside, her body. When the music ended, Peter twirled her around three times, and caught her at the waist. They were startled to hear applause from the doorway.

"Great show. When's the next show? We got here at the end of this one." A rotund, dark-haired man in a suit and topcoat, with boots partially zipped and flapped open, flanked by a uniformed police officer, stood just inside the training room door.

Nik turned off the tape player and struggled to regain her composure. "May I help you?"

The man in the suit nodded. His thick, dark eyebrows seemed to be stuck in a look of apprehension or surprise.

"We were told yesterday that we should probably talk to a Dr. Kellman, and also Peter Genchenko, about the death of the Russian hockey team interpreter, Yakov Popov."

Nik froze for a moment, and then asked, "Who told you this?"

"We've questioned several people about what happened to Popov, and one of them told us that Dr. Kellman and Peter Genchenko might be helpful in our investigation." The man's eyes stared, unblinking, into Nik's.

"You haven't shown us any identification. Who do you represent?" Peter spoke quietly, but with the sound of authority.

"Smart man. Always make 'em identify themselves, I say." He reached into a pocket and flipped open a badge.

"I'm Walt Myers, *Detective* Walt Myers, and this is Patrolman Shelly. So, do you know the two people I just mentioned?"

"I'm Peter Genchenko, and this is Dr. Kellman." Peter was matter-of-fact, and had taken the lead in dealing with the detective.

Detective Myers smiled, "I hit the jackpot right off, didn't I? Say, you speak English pretty good."

Peter didn't like the man's flippancy, and he also didn't like the way the detective squinted at him. However, Peter was more concerned for the doctor. Why did they want to speak to her?

"Tell you what...I'll just have Genchenko here come down with us to the police station to talk. That way, we can get his official statement there, and he won't have to come back at a later time."

The patrolman moved a step closer to Peter. Internally, Peter was sick with anger and fear, but his outer demeanor didn't change from that of a calm and in-control man.

"Why can't you question me here?" Peter didn't want to go anywhere with the police, known as *militia* in Russia, if he didn't have to.

"I explained why, Mr. Genchenko. The choice is yours to make, but you'd better do it quick. I've got a lot to do today."

"Now wait just a minute here, what gives you the right to take Peter *anywhere* for questioning? Is he under arrest?" Nik was immediately angry with the detective.

"Not yet, but the day's just started. We can do this the easy way, or the hard way. It's up to you." Detective Myers had a sly smile on his face and he crooked a finger, a beckon call, at Peter.

Grigory, Vladimir and Vanya came into the training room at that moment, and then stopped in their tracks at the sight of the patrolman and detective. Grigory knew who they were because Myers had questioned him yesterday, while the patrolman looked on.

Vladimir leaned over to whisper something into Grigory's ear, "Yesterday, I *told you* that this detective wanted to talk to Genchenko."

Detective Myers focused on the new group, "Hello, Coach Serov. I took the advice of your Assistant Coach here about questioning Genchenko. We're going downtown. Want to come along?"

"Myers, what could Vladimir have said that would make you want to take Genchenko to your police station for questioning?" Grigory, first glaring at Vladimir, turned to the detective for an answer.

Detective Myers smirked at Grigory and said, "I don't really have to tell you *why*, but in the interest of international harmony, I guess I can bend the rules a little. He told me that Genchenko, who, he says, has a very bad temper, was angry with the deceased over some kind of hockey fight. He said Genchenko even attacked the guy in front of your entire team and had to be pulled off of him. Could be a motive in there somewhere, don't you think?"

For a moment, Grigory looked as if he might grab Vladimir by the throat. Grigory's hands actually came up and made semicircles as he glared at him. Vladimir slunk backward and stood behind Vanya, who was rooted to the spot that he had occupied since coming into the room, trying to follow what was happening.

Peter watched the action until, at a certain point he decided that it might be better for him to go downtown with the Detective. He was sure that it would be better for the doctor if he did so, and she was really his only concern. He wanted to lead the Detective away from her. After all, the Detective had not asked her to accompany them on the trip downtown. Peter's anger and fear had diminished, and his only thought was what would be best for the doctor.

"I'll go with you. Just let me get my coat." Peter's voice was flat.

He was in command of his emotions, and his stoic face was in place. Peter didn't dare, however, to look at the doctor. He was afraid of his emotions where she was concerned, and it wouldn't do to get upset here. Besides, the Detective might try to make something out of any communication that Peter might have with her.

"*No, wait.* Peter, let me go with you. You shouldn't have to go alone." Nik had gone from exhilaration when she was dancing with Peter, to anguish at the thought that he would now be taken into police custody.

Grigory came forward, "I'll go with him, doctor. You and Vladimir can handle everything here with the athletes, and Peter and I will return as soon as possible."

"Peter, I'm going to call my dad. He has an attorney who can represent you." Nik's voice had a note of desperation in it.

Peter, Grigory, Detective Myers, and Patrolman Shelly left the training room. Nik felt a terrible wrench when Peter turned to look at her as he went out of the door.

Tom, and then Mickey, arrived immediately afterward, and Mickey asked the Doc, "Was that Peter and Grigory leaving with the police?"

"Yes." That was all that Nik could manage to say.

Vanya finally moved away from the door and went over to one of the training tables to sit down. He spoke to Vladimir in Russian, asking him about what had just happened.

Nik saw Vladimir shrug, and she wanted to slap him. Lying bastard! Nik walked over to her desk to call her father. When he answered, she had a difficult time explaining what had happened, but he told her that he would contact his attorney, Les Barnes, and then he'd be down to help as soon as he could get away from his office. It helped Nik to hear her father's voice, but she was frantically worried about Peter. What would happen to him if he were charged with Yakov's death? Dear God, help him please.

The athletes began coming into the training room singly and in pairs after breakfast. Though Nik's heart was burdened, she struggled to perform her duties. Mickey and Tom were helpful and kind, as always. However, the kinder that they were to her, the more she felt like crying. Finally, the athletes were all set, and she had a moment to herself. She had to leave the training room because her tears were so near the surface.

Nik found a quiet place in the rubdown room and sat down to cry. She knew in her heart that Peter, for all his anger and temper, could not have harmed Yakov, yet she was frightened that he might be caught up in a situation that would ensnare him. She was startled when Tom came into the room.

"Doc, there's a Dr. Reynolds on the 'phone, and he wants to give you a report on Ilya. Should I tell him you'll call him back?"

Nik hesitated a moment, "Tell him I'll page him in a few minutes. Okay, Tom?"

"Sure, Doc, I'll let him know. Oh, and Doc? Your dad's here."

"Please tell him where I am, will you, Tom?"

"I'll bring him down here for you." Tom, feeling helpless, and not knowing what to do to help the Doc any further, left the room.

When Klaus saw his daughter, it surprised him to see how upset she was. Nik wasn't crying anymore, but she hadn't recovered completely from her earlier tears.

"Niki, what's going on?" He sat down beside her and put an arm around her shoulders.

"It's a very long story, dad, and I don't really know where to begin. A very mean spirited little man named Yakov Popov, the so-called team interpreter for the Russian team, died in the hotel fire that you probably read about in the Star. Except, he didn't die in the fire; he had a broken neck, so now the police are questioning some of the team about their involvement with him."

"But Niki, I still don't see why you are so upset. If there was wrongdoing on the part of one of the athletes, then the police should be able to question whomever they wish."

"It isn't that, dad, it's just that Yakov Popov was a wretched human being. I'm not saying that he deserved to be murdered, but I know that Peter Genchenko didn't harm him, no matter what others might say to the contrary."

"Okay, Niki. I called Les Barnes, and he's going to go down to the police station and make sure that Genchenko gets fair treatment." Klaus had some serious misgivings about his daughter's seeming inability to be rational about this situation.

Peter looked out the car window as he rode to the police station. There were so many things to see in this big city. Wouldn't it be wonderful to be able to visit this place under better circumstances? Grigory had not said a word to him since getting into the police car. Peter, for his part, was glad of that. He didn't want to have to waste his energy on small talk. The detective and patrolman were silent, as well, and Peter was grateful for that, too.

They pulled up to a parking place in front of a building with a limestone facade. Peter had a sinking feeling as he got out of the car. He had nowhere to go. No friendly face to look into. He thought of his mother and sister. What would happen to them if he were put in jail in this country?

Grigory saw that Peter had become pale, and he knew that it was probably from a mixture of fear and dread of what was about to happen. Grigory came around the vehicle and put his hand on Peter's shoulder. The gesture was meant to convey, "I'm here for you." Grigory was ashamed and sorry for the way that he had treated Peter yesterday during practice and the game. If Peter hadn't been the extraordinary athlete that he was, Grigory's team would have lost because of his own hardheadedness.

"C'mon Genchenko, get a move on. I haven't got all day." Detective Myers was in a hurry and he grabbed Peter's arm roughly.

"Perhaps it would be wise for you to treat your witness with dignity and respect." Grigory stood head and shoulders above Detective Myers, and he moved close to him as he spoke.

Detective Myers looked a little taken aback by Grigory's words and actions, but he wasn't going to let some big Russian intimidate him.

"Serov, we can grill you again, too. So don't be a smart ass, because I can make your life pretty miserable if I want to." The detective was full of himself.

Grigory chuckled, "You shouldn't make idle threats, Detective Myers. Sometimes, it pays to know your adversary, and his connections. I can put *you* in an uncomfortable situation with just one telephone call, so perhaps you should go easy on Genchenko."

Peter watched as the two men sparred. He was very surprised at Grigory's behavior toward the detective, and hoped that Grigory knew that this would only make the detective more dangerous. It worried Peter, too, that Grigory still looked as though he might be ill. His face and throat were flushed and red.

The detective put his hands in the air, "Who gives a shit, anyway? You and I both know that Genchenko did the deed."

These words startled Peter. His throat was dry as he asked, "What do you mean by that, Detective Myers?"

"I mean that you had motive and opportunity, and according to Vladimir, you have a real bad temper. He said you attacked Popov in front of everyone, and they had to pull you off of him."

Inside the building, Patrolman Shelly separated from the group and Detective Myers led Peter and Grigory into the interrogation wing, where he found an empty room. He hadn't intended to escalate the word game so quickly. He didn't like to tip his hand, but he could tell by looking at Peter Genchenko that the kid was "spooked." You got to scare the hell out of them, he thought. Soften them up.

Peter's head was swimming. He thinks I'm guilty before he ever asks me any questions. Is this how the famous justice system of the United States works? I'd be better off in the Soviet Union.

Myers had just closed the door, but before anyone had the chance to sit down, someone was knocking on it. The look on the detective's face betrayed the short fuse that was his Achilles heel.

A uniformed officer opened the door a few inches, and beckoned to Myers. Peter and Grigory watched as the officer spoke quietly into the detective's ear. When the detective turned back to them, his face was a mask of fury.

"Who the *hell* called an attorney for Genchenko?" Myers glared at Peter, and then turned to glower at Grigory.

Another knock at the door caused the detective to look almost apoplectic. He grabbed the doorknob and pulled on the door forcefully; so forcefully, in fact, that the door got away from him and slammed against the wall.

The man standing in the doorway stepped back quickly, as the door rebounded, and then walked into the room. His face and body were youthful, but he had a head full of thick, silver-gray hair. His eyes were remarkable, a bright and penetrating shade of blue.

"Peter Genchenko? I'm Les Barnes. I have been told that you want me to be your attorney. Is that correct?" He put his hand out to shake Peter's hand.

Dumbfounded, Peter could only nod his head as he took the hand that Les Barnes offered.

"Barnes, what the devil are you doing here?" Detective Myers knew of the formidable reputation of this attorney, but he had never had to face him like this before.

"Why...I'm here to represent Peter Genchenko's interests. You saw him agree that I am his attorney, didn't you?"

Detective Myers was almost at the point of grinding his teeth, "Who called you?"

Ignoring the question, Les Barnes turned to look at Peter as he asked his own questions, "Has this man been charged with anything? Has he been arrested?"

"No! He's just here for questioning." Myers' easy case was unraveling.

"Have any other witnesses been brought down here for questioning? It seems to me that you've singled Peter out for unfair and unjust treatment. In fact, he may want to bring charges against *you*."

"Now wait a minute! I just wanted to question him here where there wouldn't be any distractions."

Gregory found his voice, "That isn't what you said to Genchenko as we were walking in from your police car, detective. You said that you believed that he was guilty of Yakov's death because of something that Vladimir said to you."

Les Barnes smiled a wide smile, "Well, that's very interesting, Myers."

"He's misinterpreted what I said." The veins at the detective's temples were beginning to stand out and he broke into a sweat across his forehead.

"Be that as it may, you might want to look at this." Les handed Detective Myers a court paper that was an order for Peter's release.

"How the hell did you get something like this so quickly?" Myers now looked almost stricken.

"Judge Farnham and I go back a long, long way and he gave me the courtesy of hearing me out regarding Peter Genchenko. When he heard what you were doing, especially when it concerned a Russian national, he immediately gave me the release order."

Myers raised both hands, turned upward, to shoulder height. "But he hasn't even been arrested yet."

"It's a just-in-case kind of thing, Myers. You understand, don't you?" The smile on Les' face was cherubic.

"Mr. Barnes, does this mean that I can leave this place?" Peter's face was a study in renewed hope.

"Yes, that's exactly what it means, Peter. Coach Serov, I can take you both back to the arena. Myers, you might want to consider the need to start looking for another type of employment. You just might get busted down to sidewalk patrol over this mess." Les Barnes pointed at the detective for emphasis as he spoke.

Detective Myers was left open-mouthed and speechless, an "oh shit" look plainly on his face, as the trio filed past him to the door.

When they went out into the crisp, cold air, Peter took deep gulping breaths, savoring the smell and taste of freedom. His eyes were moist with tears, but he hoped that Grigory and Barnes would think that it was because of the cold. It really doesn't matter, though, he thought. At least I am free.

Les Barnes unlocked his BMW with the small remote on his key ring. "Get in and we can talk while I take you back to the arena."

Peter and Grigory got into the car. It smelled of new leather and the dashboard looked like the cockpit of an airplane. Grigory sat up front with Les, and Peter got into the back seat.

Although Peter didn't have much experience with automobiles, he instinctively knew that this one was something special. He sat back in the seat and found it to be more comfortable than any armchair he had ever sat in. When Les started up the engine, it purred quietly. Classical music played softly from hidden speakers.

What would it be like to live like this? Peter wasn't envious, but he wished that he could provide this kind of life for his family. He wondered, too, what it would be like to provide this lifestyle for the doctor. Briefly, he visualized her sitting next to him in the front seat, smiling and talking. She deserved no less than this way of life. He was sure, however, that no matter what he might do, he could never provide it for her, and that, even if he could, she would never consider him as a suitor.

When they were all settled in the car and Les had started the motor, he asked Peter and Grigory, "Is it okay with you two if I interview you and record it for my records? It will save us a great deal of time later, if there is a later."

Peter nodded immediately, but Grigory didn't agree for several moments. After mulling over the pros and cons in his mind he also agreed to the interview and taping. What harm could there be? His team would be leaving the United States very soon, within three days.

"Peter," Les began, "I want to know everything that you know about what happened to Yakov Popov."

There was no hesitation in Peter's reply, "I think that I must tell you, first, that he was my father's enemy. When my father died, Yakov transferred his need for vengeance to me."

"What was the nature of the animosity between them?" This might prove to be an interesting case, and Les was curious as to the history between the two men.

Peter sighed deeply, and then began to explain about his father and Yakov, "My father is, was, Ivan Genchenko. He was a dissident, and was thrown out of the Communist Party and imprisoned because of his views. He wrote several books on democracy and freedom while he was in prison, and they were published in the west. One of his early interrogators at Lefortovo Prison was Yakov Popov. Yakov couldn't break my father, couldn't get any information from him, and was demoted from his position with the KGB as a result. When my father died, Yakov transferred his hatred of my father to me. He arranged to have an assignment with the hockey team that I play on, mostly, I think, to cause me harm."

Les gave a low whistle, "What happened to bring this situation to a head?"

Grigory answered before Peter had the chance to respond, "Yakov enlisted two of my athletes to attempt to take Genchenko's life in such a way as to make it look like an accident. Thanks to Dr. Kellman, Yakov's plan backfired. One of the athletes was injured, and the other was taken into custody for the attack on Genchenko. He is still in police custody, and will be deported soon. The injured athlete will be released from the hospital in two days, and will be deported as well."

"Well," said Les, "there's more intrigue here than a spy novel."

Grigory smiled toothsomely, "Yes, you could say that."

"Did you attempt to harm Yakov?" Les looked at Peter in the rearview mirror as he asked the question.

"Yes." Peter didn't hesitate before he answered.

"Tell me about it, Peter." Les glanced again at the mirror to see Peter's reaction.

"I wasn't rational after Nikita and Josef attacked me, and I realized that Yakov was behind it. I was angrier with Yakov than I have ever been with anyone. Even before the attempt on my life, Yakov tormented me whenever he got the opportunity. It was his peculiar way of getting even with my father. Yakov was a KGB operative assigned to our team to keep us under control."

"Grigory?" Les turned momentarily to see his immediate response.

Grigory was silent for several moments, and then began to reply in a voice filled with bitterness. "Yakov was the most vindictive, hateful man I have ever known. He enjoyed toying with those that he hated. His threat to me was that he would make certain that I could not support my family. He insinuated that he could harm me at any time if I did not cooperate with him. He was very controlling, and even tried to tell me what to do as a coach."

"What about the way that he treated Peter?" Les wondered what the compelling circumstances were there.

Grigory gave a derisive snort, "He often spoke of his intent to get Peter sent back to the Soviet Union, and from there he would make sure that Peter would end up fighting in the war we are waging in

Afghanistan...a terrible and almost certain death sentence, as you might guess."

Les was shocked, "How could he do that? What kind of power did this man have?"

"Peter just told you, but you must not have heard. Yakov was KGB. Why would our team need an interpreter? I speak English, and many of the athletes at least *understand* spoken English. Even Vladimir understands and speaks English. Of course, you are also well aware that Peter speaks English, too. What need did we have for an interpreter? Yakov reported our every move to another operative in Moscow. That was his job."

"Well," said Les. "Well, this is the most interesting case I have had in recent memory."

"Will the militia, I mean the police, come after me again?" Peter didn't want to live under the shadow of the police.

"The only way that they can do that is if they decide to charge you with the crime. Of course, they can question you, or at least attempt to, again, but I'll be with you if, and when, that happens." Les was confident that he could help this young athlete.

"Mr. Barnes, what will your services cost?" Peter knew that he couldn't afford this attorney.

Les glanced in the rearview mirror at Peter before he replied, "I'm working pro bono here. That means that I'm not going to charge you anything for my services."

"But how can that be? This is how you earn your living, and I can't ask you to do this."

"Don't worry about it, Peter. My good friend, Klaus Kellman, asked me to help you, and he's a man who rarely asks a favor of anyone."

Peter didn't know how to reply. The doctor. *Of course,* she had helped him once more. Surely it was more than coincidence that her father had asked Mr. Barnes to help him. Then Peter remembered that she had told him before he left the training room with Detective Myers that her father would send an attorney to help him. Peter had been so upset when he left with the police, that he had forgotten what she had said to him.

Grigory was listening intently to the conversation between Peter and the attorney. Well, he thought, this is an odd turn of events. Who would ever think that an attorney would not charge for his services? In Moscow, if you don't have money, they take their fees out in blood. Either way, you rot in jail.

At the arena, Les parked his car close to the athlete's entrance, "I'll go in with you, Peter. Klaus is going to be there with Niki, and I am sure that they will both want to hear the status of this situation."

The team was still in the training room, getting ready for practice. Everyone looked up when Peter, Grigory, and the attorney walked into the room.

Klaus, sitting near the doorway, stood up quickly and went over to the group. He called out to his daughter to let her know that the coach and athlete were back and in the company of her favorite "uncle" Les Barnes. Actually, Les was a dear friend of the family, but Nik thought of him as an uncle.

Nik came over to them, smiling tentatively. She looked into the eyes of Les, Grigory, and then Peter, in order to try to read what their experience had been with the police. She was very relieved that Detective Myers had not returned with them.

Nik's demeanor puzzled Les. He thought of her as one of his own children. Over the years he had watched her grow into the beautiful young woman standing before him. But, for the life of him, in spite of all the years he had known her, he couldn't understand her reaction to this situation. She seemed to be actively engaged in whatever was happening here, but he didn't know why.

When Nik spoke, she looked at Grigory, "Will Peter practice with the team this afternoon?"

Grigory smiled, spread his arms wide and said, "Da, *Yes*!"

Nik's eyes came to rest on Peter, "Well, what are you waiting for? Get over there and get ready for practice." She smiled a wan smile as she delivered this command.

Finally, Peter found a reason to smile, too. He nodded his assent, and headed toward Tom, who was cleaning up after his last athlete's wrap.

Grigory put a hand on Les' shoulder and thanked him, "You have given me back my best player, and I thank you."

"Glad to be of help to both of you." Les put out his hand and shook Grigory's huge paw.

Nik came over to Les and hugged him tightly, "Thanks, thanks so much Uncle Les."

She then turned and hugged her father, "Thanks, dad. I appreciate what you've done for Pete."

Nik turned away from them and walked over to where Peter was sitting, waiting for Tom to get to him. Peter's eyes were on her from the time that she turned away from her father. As she approached, their eyes met and held. She stopped about three or four feet from him. Professional distance...she had to maintain professional distance.

A feeling of deep gratitude welled up within Peter. He started to thank the doctor, but she stopped him.

"That isn't necessary, Pete. I'm just glad that you're back, and that you're going to play tonight."

Klaus and Les stood watching the two from a distance. They couldn't see Niki's face, but they saw the look of longing on Peter's face, and the sadness, too. Both men had some idea of what the other was thinking, but neither wanted to say anything.

Damn, thought Les, *the poor bastard.* He's got it bad. Les remembered that look, because he had seen it before, and it had been his own face in the mirror, a time or two, also.

Les broke the silence, "How's Niki's fiancé doing?"

Klaus realized that Les really *was* thinking the same thing that he was about Niki and Peter, but he was being diplomatic about it. "Ron was at the game yesterday afternoon and the open house last night. Marina put on the finest Russian buffet that you have ever seen or tasted."

"Oh yes," Les replied, "Marina is one fine cook, Klaus."

Klaus looked at Les, "Back to business," he said. "Is everything settled, or will Peter Genchenko have to talk to the police again, Les?"

"Right now, Detective Myers is licking his wounds, but he's the kind of man who is ruthless in his pursuit of closing a case, no matter whether he has the right person, or not. We haven't heard the last of him yet, I'm afraid." His face was grim as he spoke.

Les continued, "If Myers comes near Genchenko, call me, and I'll handle it. The Detective isn't above stretching the truth, or pressuring the person he thinks can close the case for him. He's a dangerous little son-of-a-bitch, so don't let him get his hooks too far into Genchenko again before calling me."

Klaus looked down at the floor before answering Les, and then looked up at him, "My friend, I thank you. And, I'll heed your advice. Right now, I'm not really sure of what is happening, but I can tell you that I don't like the way that Niki has become entangled in this mess."

"Do you want me to talk to her?" Les felt exactly the same way as Klaus.

"I'm not sure that it would be helpful right now, but maybe in a little while. I'll call you day after tomorrow."

"Good," Les turned to leave.

Grigory came back to Les and offered him two tickets for the evening game, "Come and see us play, Mr. Barnes, I think you will be impressed with the team."

Les accepted the tickets, thanked Grigory and told him, "I'll come if I can get away."

Peter had been sitting on the training table, watching the interactions between Les Barnes, Klaus, and Grigory, still waiting for Tom to get to him. He felt lightheaded and giddy after his release by the police. When the doctor had come over to talk to him, he had wanted to take her in his arms and hug her for having rescued him once again. The thought had stirred him and made him sad all at the same time.

Tom began working on Peter, "I'll bet you're glad to be back, aren't you?"

In fact, Peter felt an overwhelming sense of relief that the morning's activities had ended with his return to the arena, "Yes, I am very glad to be back."

"Sometimes the cops, uh, the police, can be pretty tough to deal with. The thing is you just never know how they're going to react in any situation." Tom was looking intently at Peter.

Peter realized that Tom was trying to be his friend. It seemed odd to him, given their earlier animosity, but he appreciated Tom's effort.

"It was a very unpleasant experience, but I did learn something. Your police tend to give up a lot more quickly when challenged by someone in the practice of the law. In Russia, once the militia…uh, police, have someone, it is very difficult to obtain a release until they are ready to let the unlucky person go."

"It helps if you know the right people here. The Doc called in a "big gun" for you. Mr. Barnes is a pretty big fish here in Indy."

Peter almost laughed at Tom's analogy. He didn't see any resemblance between Mr. Barnes and a "big fish." English is a strange language, he thought.

Nik, who was standing across the room, saw that Pete seemed to have found something funny that Tom had said. It pleased her to see Pete's face relaxed instead of stress filled.

Klaus came up to his daughter to say goodbye, "I have to get back to the plant, Niki. I think most of the danger to Genchenko is past, but I'm not really sure that Detective Myers won't try something new to get at him."

Nik hugged her father. She was so grateful to him for his quick intervention on Pete's behalf.

"Thanks, dad, I don't know what would have happened to Pete without you."

Klaus looked down into his daughter's face and said, "Take care, Niki; please take care. Peter Genchenko will be returning to Russia, soon. You shouldn't get so wrapped up in his difficulties."

His words puzzled Nik, "Why do you say that, dad? He hasn't got anyone to help him. Besides, he didn't choose Yakov for his enemy. Yakov chose him."

"Okay, Niki, I understand what you're saying, but I have to go now."

Klaus kissed his daughter on the top of her head, as he always did, and hugged her tightly. He wished to God that she were out of this bad situation.

Chapter 19

Wednesday Evening

The Americans won their afternoon game. They were two games behind the Russians, who had won every game they had played up to this point. The Russians were the team to beat because they were now in first place, with the Norwegians right behind them. Nik was proud of her team. When she thought back, was it really just a few days ago? She remembered how reluctant she had been to take on the Neanderthals. Now, unbelievably, she was very attached to them all, but especially so to Peter Genchenko.

Nik had talked with Ilya's surgeon in the early afternoon, and was very pleased with his progress. The surgeon told her that he would be discharging Ilya sometime on Friday. It was amazing how knee surgeries of the complexity that Ilya had undergone were now commonplace, and the athletes were recovering so much more quickly.

Briefly, Nik thought of Josef, one of Peter's attackers. She knew that he was still in the hospital. In fact, he was in the same hospital that Ilya was in, but she couldn't bring herself to visit him, not after what he tried to do to Pete. The surgeon who removed the broken hockey stick from Josef's thigh kept her updated on his condition, and beyond that, she hadn't wanted to see him at all. Grigory told her that the athlete would be sent home as soon as he was discharged from the hospital. No charges had been filed against Josef or Nikita for their attacks on Pete because he had refused to do so, much to Nik's surprise.

Nikita was still in the Marion County lockup because he had assaulted a police officer with his hockey stick during his capture. Otherwise, he too, would have been sent home by this time. Grigory had kept the doctor apprised of the status of Nikita, but Grigory absolutely did not want the athlete to return to the team. They had trouble enough with everything else. Grigory didn't want to add to the team's difficulties if he could help it.

Because practice had gone well during the afternoon, Nik felt that tonight's game might be less stressful than the last two had been. Preparation for the game in the training room was uneventful. Nik checked every athlete's wrap, and the readiness of each team member, and even had the opportunity to do Pete's wrap. Rebecca had botched it again, and both Tom and Mickey didn't want to hurt her feelings by doing a re-wrap. They beseeched the Doc to do the 're-do', and she took pity on them.

"Tell him to head over to the rub-down room." Nik couldn't suppress a smile, and it surprised her that she felt a little flutter of excitement at the prospect of doing Pete's wrap.

A very relieved Peter Genchenko was waiting there when the doctor arrived. When Rebecca had wrapped him, she had talked non-stop about how she loved to watch him play hockey. Her inattention to detail left Peter with a lop-sided and very loose wrap. He knew that it wouldn't take him through the first period of play, and was desperate to get it done right.

Nik stopped in the doorway to the rubdown room and put her hands on her hips, "Is there someone in here who needs to have his wrap checked?"

Sheepishly, Peter raised his hand and he implored her, "Please, doctor, I can't play like *this*." He unraveled a length of wrap and held it up, "This isn't going to work, doctor."

Nik nearly doubled over with laughter, and struggled to regain her composure, "Okay, Pete. Let's get you put together right."

They talked as Nik did his wrap. The rubdown room was quiet and afforded them some privacy so that they could talk about the stressful day they had endured thus far.

"Are you recovered from what happened this morning?" Nik looked up into Pete's face as she spoke to him.

Peter nodded his head and slowly replied, "Yes, I think so," he hesitated, and then continued, "but I was very frightened at first. Detective Myers told me he thought that I was guilty of killing Yakov, even before he had a chance to question me. Then Mr. Barnes arrived, and I began to have some hope. I thank you for my freedom."

Nik closed her eyes for a moment, "If our roles were reversed, you'd do the same for me, wouldn't you?"

"I would, yes, I would." He also wanted to add that he would do anything for her, but left it with the briefest of answers.

As he had before, Peter was acutely aware of the doctor's nearness, her wonderful light scent of flowers and musk, and the radiant warmth of her body. For these few moments, as he had earlier in the day when he danced with her, he was happy just to be close to her.

For Peter, the doctor's ministrations ended much too soon. He had closed his eyes as she worked, savoring her warmth, the touch of her hands, and the scent of her. And then she was finished. He opened his eyes and looked down, offering his hand to help her up. She took his hand, and Peter was thrilled by her touch. Years from now he might have some regrets at not having told her of his feelings, but for now, holding her hand for just a moment, made him feel happy inside.

Peter donned his jersey, hockey gear and pads, laced up his skates, covered the blades, and stood. For some reason, the doctor had waited for him, and her presence comforted him. Together, as before, they walked back to the training room quietly, without speaking.

When game time drew near, the Russians were ready for Finland. The Finns, although they had lost two games, were still known as a very rough team that wouldn't be beaten easily.

Grigory, with Vladimir, the disgraced and separated Siamese twin at some distance from him, asked his team to forget all the problems that they might be harboring, and to concentrate on winning. He thanked them all for their efforts up to this point and told them to give their best for the next two games.

"Who knows?" he said, "Maybe we might walk away with a championship here. It could happen."

Mickey, Tom, and Rebecca were heavily laden with fluids and equipment, and it surprised Nik to see that Rebecca was actually helping the guys. She hadn't once looked in Peter's direction. Well, well, maybe I've misjudged her.

Grigory started out the door, and the trainers followed with Vladimir behind them. Then the players fell into step after the others, moving in ungainly strides on their covered skate blades out the door. No one spoke. The only sound was the clump, clump of covered blades as the team moved toward the arena. Peter was the last player in line, and Nik walked next to him. They didn't speak, but Nik lightly touched his hand, as if to say, "good luck."

Peter appreciated the touch. It warmed his entire hand. My good luck talisman, he thought, and silently dedicated his efforts to her.

Marty and Sheldon were waiting expectantly when the team came into the arena, "Hey, Peter, Doc, are we gon'na win this one tonight?" Marty cupped his hands and called out to them.

Nik looked up at Pete, "Well, what's the word?"

Peter mustered a smile and gave a "Babe Ruth" gesture, pointing toward the starting goal for the Finnish team. "Could be good," he said, "it could be very good."

Marty put his hand out to shake Peter's, "Good luck, Pete, you were a miracle worker during the last game, so maybe you can do the same for this one. I honestly have never seen anyone play hockey like that before."

Peter's smile was gradual in coming, "Thank you, Marty."

The two men shook hands, and then Sheldon stuck his hand out for Peter to shake, too, "You can skate circles around the Finns, Pete."

Peter didn't answer Sheldon. He *hoped* that he would be able to skate better than the Finns. As always, he had doubts before he took the ice. But when he actually got out onto the ice, he forgot his doubts, and another part of him took over. On the ice nothing else mattered but the game, and winning. Time and again, his sadness, and the cold aching place inside him, disappeared when he was on the ice.

The crowd, growing rapidly in number, was raising the noise to a higher decibel level more quickly than before, in other games, if that was possible. Nik realized that this game would decide which of two teams would move to the championship game.

The announcer was calling the starting lineup for the Finns and the noise in the arena reached a fever pitch. He then began announcing the Russian lineup: Goalie, Arkady Kuryakin; Center, Dimitri Prelov; Defenseman, Mikhail Teretsky; Right Wing, Vanya Milachev; Left Wing, Peter Genchenko; Defenseman; Boris Slonim. Grigory had tapped each on the shoulder as their name was called, and they shot out onto the ice. The applause was deafening.

Nik stood statue-still amid the uproar around her. She was thinking of Pete, and only of Pete. She hoped that this contest would go his way. Please, please let him play well. And *please* don't let him get hurt!

As team captain, Peter could choose who would stand for face-off, and he chose Mikhail. The Finn who skated up to the face-off circle looked the size of a polar bear in hockey gear. As it turned out, the Finn wasn't there to take possession of the puck. He was there to maul the unlucky Russian player who faced him. His coach had been sure that it would be Peter Genchenko. They were wrong, however, and so it was that Mikhail was taken out of the game at the very beginning.

The Finn received a lengthy penalty for intentional roughing, to be served when play resumed. The referee and linesmen conferred over whether or not to assess a monetary fine from him for so obviously and intentionally trying to harm his opponent.

Tom and Mickey rushed out onto the ice, assessed Mikhail, stabilized and immobilized him, and brought him back to the bench treatment area for the Doc to examine. Nik's examination revealed that Mikhail had had his "bell rung" and probably had a mild concussion.

My God, we're going to run out of players! Nik was almost frantic when she realized what losing Mikhail meant to the team. Even if it might be for only one game, it was devastating.

The spectators that were pro-Russian shouted their outrage at what the Finnish player had done, while the pro-Finland crowd hissed and booed at the length of penalty box time given their player.

Peter cursed himself inwardly for not having been in the face-off circle with the Finnish marauder. He had every reason to believe that Mikhail, an exceptionally quick player, could handle himself during the face-off, but Peter knew that Mikhail had not anticipated a full frontal assault, given with the intention of putting him out of the game.

Anger began to churn inside Peter. He tried at all times to be the best hockey player that he could be, but he would never intentionally injure another player in order to gain an advantage. He took great pleasure in out skating and outwitting his opponents, and was not above "boarding" another player when necessary, but he was not a predator. It wasn't in his nature. Instead of retaliation with bodily harm, he would hit the Finns where it would hurt them most, in the goal.

Play resumed with the Finnish player in the penalty box for five minutes. Peter returned Mikhail's injury to the Finns by scoring two quickly successive goals while they were short a player.

Two Finnish players shadowed Peter's every move. They were intent on keeping Peter from scoring another goal. One of the Finns, known as a chippy because of his excessive roughness, attempted to charge Peter from behind. Peter deked to the right and the chippy ended up charging his own teammate from behind, knocking him flying into the boards. The crowd erupted, *SEVENTEEN, SEVENTEEN*! They shouted their approval of Peter's skill.

Grigory, without Vladimir to mirror his every move, actually jumped in the air. Nik witnessed his excitement, and was amazed at his agility, given his size. For her part, Nik was excited, too, by Pete's skill. Ordinarily, Pete was quiet, aloof, withdrawn, but on the ice, he came alive.

The Finns called a time out in order to re-group. Their coach was animated, arms moving and waving. He looked as though he might be exhorting his team to dig deeper for the plays that surely would come their way if they would only try harder.

Grigory had a hand on the shoulders of Arkady and Vanya, who were standing closest to him during the time out. He was taking advantage of the Finns' time out call, and wanted to tell his players to run one of their special plays. Mickey, Tom, and Rebecca tossed water bottles to each athlete, and they drank thirstily, holding the bottles away from their mouths and squirting the water in. Towels were also quickly thrown to the athletes for a much-needed wipe down.

Grigory wanted the team to run his "dvoynoy vosim" *double eight*, play, so named because the right and left wings would actually be skating a wide, looping, figure eight as they protected their center, who was in possession of the puck, thus keeping him within the overlapping top loop of their figure eights. And then the center would pass the puck to the player in the forward position, enabling him to do a breakaway from defenders and move quickly to the goal with the puck. This play had worked well for them many times, and, unbelievably, their opponents were usually unprepared and surprised by it.

Nik watched the team as she continued to tend to Mikhail, who was recovering nicely from the mauling he had received at the hands of the Finn chippy. Pete turned to look in her direction, and smiled at her. He held one fist in the air briefly. *We're going to win.*

The Russian team took the ice after the time out, and they were ready for whatever the Finns wanted to hand out. The few moments' rest had energized Peter. His resolve to win had hardened, and he was anxious to get on with the game.

Mikhail was sitting up, and his dizziness had subsided. He tried to convince the doctor that he could go back into the game. Nik, however, was having none of it. She didn't want to release Mikhail for play because he might have a serious concussion. She had ordered a transport for X-Ray. In the meantime, she told him to "sit tight." While she was focused on Mikhail, Nik heard a roar of disapproval from the crowd, and she returned her attention to the action on the ice.

Peter was checked from behind by one of the Finns, and had gone flying into the boards. Nik stifled a scream of dismay. He lay against the boards for several seconds, and then rolled over to his back. Slowly, he pulled himself up into a sitting position. Nik could see that he had a dazed look on his face. The linesmen and referee stopped the play so that the injured player could be assisted.

Tom went out onto the ice to help Peter, and easily hefted him into a standing position after performing a quick assessment. Together, they slowly headed to the Russian bench where the doctor was waiting at the gate. Peter's left shoulder ached from hitting the boards, but that wasn't his biggest concern. His head had snapped back when the Finn had hit him from behind, and he had seen stars. Now, the muscles in his neck felt as if they were being pulled into a knot where his neck met his left shoulder. His vision had blurred briefly, but was now back to normal.

He was glad for Tom's strong arms helping to support him. The spectators applauded thunderously when Tom helped him to stand up. He appreciated both Tom's assistance, and the support of the crowd. Peter lifted his head and saw that the doctor, a frightened look on her face, was standing at the gate. Mickey joined her there, and the three of them, doctor, Tom, and Mickey, put their hands upon him, and helped him to the examination area. He was vaguely aware that Sheldon and Marty were hovering on the periphery somewhere, and that Grigory, his big face set in a worried scowl, was standing by. Peter was helped onto an examination table in the doctor's alcove, and even though his neck and shoulder were painful, he immediately felt comforted to have her standing there in front of him.

Nik checked Peter's pupils for size and reactivity first. When she was satisfied with what she found, she began talking to him in Russian.

"Did you lose consciousness, Pete?"

"Nyet, but I was a little dazed for a moment, and my vision was blurred."

"Are you sick to your stomach?"

"Nyet."

"Tell me exactly what happened when you hit the boards." Nik swallowed her fear in order to let the doctor side of her take over.

"I was blind-sided by the chippy Finn when he hit me from the back. The next thing I knew, I was in the boards. I didn't lose consciousness, but my vision blurred for a few moments. It hurt so much when I hit, that I just lay still for a moment. Now, my neck and shoulder on the impact side are sore, and they're drawing up."

Nik tried not to wince when Pete told her about the pain he was experiencing. Somehow, incredibly, she felt the pain, too.

Nik turned to Mickey, "Start Pete on a warm pack on the left side of his neck and shoulder, then gently stretch his arm, and have him rotate his head to the right. It's going to hurt in the beginning, but Pete's a good patient. I'll be right back."

To Pete, Nik said, "When Mickey finishes with you, try to sit and rest for a bit. I have to check Mikhail again, and I'll come right back." Nik lightly touched his cheek as she stood.

Mickey carried out the doctor's orders, and Peter cooperated, even though the treatment was very painful at first. Peter was glad to rest when Mickey finished. He knew it would give him more time to recover from hitting the boards, and he leaned his head back and closed his eyes. When the doctor had touched his cheek, he had wanted to reach up and hold her hand against his face. Sadness replaced his physical pain, as he fully realized that he could never do that.

Grigory hovered near Peter until the doctor came back, "Is Genchenko going to be able to play for the rest of the game?"

"Yes, I think so. He had a muscle spasm in his neck after he hit the boards. I'll do another assessment, and I'll give you a definitive answer." Nik was trying to be upbeat and non-committal at the same time.

"Your head wound opened when you hit the boards, Pete, but it isn't bleeding very much. I'm going to clean it up and put some steri-strips on it, and then I'll run another neuro check on you." Nik looked directly into his eyes when she spoke to him, searching for some indication that he was going to be all right.

Peter saw concern in her eyes, and perhaps fear, too, even though she was doing her best to be professional. If he could only assure her that he wasn't hurt, he could change the expression in the doctor's beautiful eyes.

She quickly cleansed the re-opened wound, steri-stripped and dressed it, and ran a neuro check on Pete. She found that her patient was within normal limits. "Thank you, Lord," she whispered, "*thank you.*"

"Doctor?" Peter began.

"I know, Pete, I know. You want to get back out on the ice. But are you okay now? Be honest with me, because I'd never forgive myself if I let you play when you shouldn't."

At first, Peter didn't know how to reply to the doctor's question, but then he said, "Please don't worry about me. I can go back in now, and I'll be fine."

Nik saw that Pete's "game face" was back. His gaze was intense when he wanted to play hockey.

Play had resumed after the Russian time out, and Grigory had sent Slava in to skate Peter's position, "How is Peter doing, doctor?" Grigory very much wanted Peter out on the ice.

Nik looked at Pete as she replied, "If he feels up to it, he's good to go, Grigory."

Sheldon and Marty were standing a few feet away, and gave a thumb's up when they heard the doctor's opinion. They didn't want their superman to be taken out of the game.

Grigory sent Peter into the game; a "change on the fly" and Slava came quickly back to the bench. There was a minute and a half left on the clock in the second period.

The Finn who had put Peter into the boards immediately came after him again. Peter, still feeling soreness in his shoulder and neck, nonetheless grinned a wicked grin at the offending player. "I'm going to get you," the grin was meant to convey. It was the look in Peter's eyes, however, that startled the Finn. He had never seen such anger and intensity, and a pronounced ferocity, directed at him before.

The Finn lunged at Peter, but Peter deked at the last moment, before the Finn collided with another Finnish player, who was in possession of the puck. Peter skated away with the puck, heading directly toward the Finnish goal in a breakaway. Not one of the Finnish defenders could catch him, and he scored, without an assist by anyone on his team. Nothing the Finn goalie tried to do to save the puck had worked.

Pandemonium broke loose in the arena. The crowd stood to applaud, and began chanting, "SEVENTEEN, SEVENTEEN!"

Les Barnes was amazed with Peter Genchenko's abilities on the ice, even in the face of injury. He was glad that he had decided to take Grigory up on his invitation. Otherwise, he might not have witnessed this kid's astounding ability to play hockey.

He had brought his wife, Helen, to watch the game with him, and to his surprise, she was enjoying herself. It made Les chuckle, because Helen ordinarily was a very shy and quiet person. Here, however, she had shed her inhibitions and had shouted and hollered with the noisiest of the crowd.

The third period began with a Finn rush on Arkady at goal for the Russians. Arkady had an amazing six saves during the game, but the score was nonetheless tied at three to three. The Finn center charged directly at Arkady as the Finn right wing brought the puck in for an attempt on goal. Out of the corner of his eye, Arkady saw a patch of red hurtling toward the Finn center.

Peter and Slava had teamed up to protect their goalie from the Finn assault. Dimitri followed and put his stick out so that the Finn right wing couldn't get a clear shot on goal. Peter saw the opportunity, and stole the puck away from the Finn. He, Slava, and Dimitri, with Vanya, turned and headed quickly toward the Finn goal.

Like angry bees, the Finns swarmed down the ice in pursuit of the flying Russians. But they didn't catch them in time to prevent a Russian goal.

Vanya took over the puck with a pass from Peter, and then Dimitri headed directly at the goal, awaiting a pass from Vanya. Peter also headed toward the goal, and the Finn goalie wasn't sure who had the puck. He swung back and forth in an arc in front of his goal, looking like a giant insect in his mask and gear, unsure from where the actual assault might come.

Peter took the puck on a pass from Vanya and looked as though he might shoot at the goal, and the Finn defenders started after him. Dimitri, however, came into the perfect position out of sight of the goalie, and Peter sent the puck flying in a pass to him. Dimitri hammered in the goal and the arena shook with the crowd's roar of approval.

Grigory was so elated that he grabbed Vladimir and hugged him. Nik jumped up and down, screaming with the rest of the spectators. Marty and Sheldon took turns pounding on each other's backs.

Ron, who had just arrived to check on Nik, stood watching the spectacle, "What the hell?" he said aloud, but no one heard him over the uproar.

Mikhail stood up, but Nik made him sit down again. As she checked on him, she looked up to see Ron.

The puzzled look on his face made Nik break out in laughter. When she could speak, she said, "Yes, I know we look a little crazy, but if you had just seen what we saw, you'd be cheering, too!"

"So, the Neanderthals are doing well, are they?" Ron was still shaking his head in wonder.

"Yep...they're mopping up on the Finns." Nik's eyes were bright.

Ron stepped over to her, "Come here."

He put his arm around her and hugged her to him. "It looks like you're doing okay, right?"

"This whole sports thing has its ups and downs. Mikhail," Nik nodded toward him, "got boarded and had his "bell rung." That's why he's sitting the bench."

"X-Ray?"

"I'll order it if I think he needs it. He's doing okay during my neuro assessments. I'm just being conservative with him."

"How's Genchenko doing? I saw him get boarded a few minutes ago when I was on the other side of the arena."

"He's back out on the ice, and you just saw one of his plays. I think he's doing fine."

"Last game's tomorrow, Nik. What do you say to an invitation to visit my folks in Chicago over the weekend?"

Nik smiled at this, "I thought I had to clean up my act before I got to meet them. What if I swear or sneer, or sneeze, or something?"

The crowd roared again, and Nik quickly turned her attention to the ice in time to see that Pete had made a fourth goal for his team. The Russians now led the Finns by one point. She looked up at the clock. There were three and a half minutes left in the third period.

"Nik..." Ron moved closer so that she could hear him over the din of the spectators. He touched her shoulder, "I'm serious about Chicago. What do you think? My brother and his wife will be there with my folks for Hanukkah, and it would be a perfect time for you to meet everyone. And...we might have some time alone, too." He smiled a hopeful smile at her.

"It sounds wonderful, Ron. The games here will be over, and we can finally get back to normal."

Nik, however, felt a tug at her heart when she thought of the games being finished. In just two days, everything would go back to the way that it was before Peter Genchenko came into her life. The thought caused a feeling of sadness within her. She realized with a start that Ron was talking to her.

"...I just wondered why you looked so sad for a minute there. Are you okay Nik?" Ron had a concerned look on his face.

Nik nodded, and closed her eyes for a moment. Suddenly, inexplicably, she felt very close to tears. Ron put his arms around her and pulled her close.

"Hey, now, it's almost over, Nik. Just a couple more days, and they'll be gone. I've told you this before, but if I had known how hard this would be for you, I wouldn't have asked you to do it. I'm sorry, Nik, really sorry."

Nik regained control quickly and stepped back. "I'm just tired, Ron. I plan to take the longest sleep of my life when this is over; no alarm clocks, no assignments, no appointments, just sleep, sleep, sleep." She gave him a small smile.

"You've earned it Nik. Who would have thought that you'd have encountered so many problems with this team?"

"Neanderthals, after all."

"Yeah, Neanderthals," Ron's smile was rueful.

Sheldon shouted, "Doc, *Doc*, look at the ice!"

Nik turned in time to see her Russian team ganging up on the Finn goalie again. The result was a goal made by Vanya with an assist from Pete. And then the final buzzer sounded. The Russian team had won. They were going to the final game!

Ron lifted Nik off her feet, "Okay, babe, *okay*! You're going to the championship game."

Grigory's joy knew no bounds. He backslapped his way over to Nik, but then gave her a kiss on the cheek instead of a slap on the back. Nik said a silent prayer of thanks.

Sheldon congratulated Grigory and Nik on the Russian team's win, "They're great, just great! You both should be very proud of them."

Grigory thanked him and replied in his heavily accented English, "The team created what amounts to a miracle. They've been a great team, but we've had some injuries and other things, so this is all the sweeter for having suffered through the bad things."

The Russians came off the ice, excitement in their every movement. When Peter passed by the doctor, he smiled, nodded, and touched her shoulder. He mouthed, "Spaseeba, *Thank you,*" to her.

Rebecca latched onto him almost immediately, Nik saw. The look on his face changed from one of elation to an "oh no" kind of look.

Marty handed the doctor his card and said, "Doc, your team, and Peter Genchenko, have given me one of the best week's entertainment that I've had in a very long time. I've got to go back to the east coast tomorrow, so I'm going to miss the championship game. But I want you to know that if, *at any time*, Peter Genchenko is available to play hockey in the U.S., I want you to call me, and I'll find a spot for him on a professional team. My pager and home telephone numbers are on the back of my card, and I don't usually give those out."

Nik nodded, "Thanks, Marty, I'll tell him, but I don't think that it will make a difference. He has a mother and sister in Russia, and he would never leave them over there by themselves."

Ron was standing next to Nik when Marty offered his card to her. It surprised him that Marty was so interested in Genchenko, although Ron could see that the guy could really play hockey. For some reason, though, it made Ron uncomfortable that Marty thought Nik would or should have anything to do with Genchenko after the games were over.

Nik looked at Ron, "One more game to go. I can't believe it."

"One more game, then the awards thing, and you're in the clear hon'."

"Yup, in the clear. Well…tonight I still have to check Mikhail's CT scan, and it wouldn't hurt to check on Pete, too. They both were hit very hard."

"Need some help?" Ron had several other duties to complete this evening, but he would forego them if Nik needed help.

"No, I can see by the look on your face that you are up to your eyeballs in other commitments. You do your thing and I'll do mine."

"Tomorrow, the final game is at one-thirty, isn't it?" Ron was frowning, trying to keep all his responsibilities straight.

"One-thirty is the start time. My team will be on the ice for practice/warm-up about ten, and we will be out on the ice for the game at about one-ten."

"Did you hear who's going to be playing against the Russians?" Ron had to grin over this one.

"*Your team, right?* The Norwegians. You should be an actor, Ron. For a moment, I almost bought your "forgetful professor" line about the start time for tomorrow's game." It was Nik's turn to smile.

"What about Chicago, Nik?"

"We have lots of time to plan that one, Ron. If you want, call me tonight. Otherwise, we can talk after the game tomorrow. We don't have any responsibilities for the awards ceremonies, so tomorrow night is it! No more responsibilities, duties, or whatever."

"Okay, see you, hon'." Ron hurried away, turning and blowing a kiss at her as he climbed the stairs two at a time.

Nik wasn't the only one counting the days until the end of the games. Peter knew that after tomorrow night, and the awards banquet the following evening, he would be on an airplane back to Moscow with his team. He sat on a training table, awaiting Tom's, Mickey's, or Rebecca's help in taking off his wrap. He didn't care now, who unwrapped him. He was as dejected and unhappy as he could be at the prospect of returning to Russia.

Of course he wanted to see his family. He missed them terribly. But he knew that upon his arrival in Moscow there might possibly be endless hours of questions in regard to Yakov's demise. That, however, was not weighing so heavily upon him. His dejection stemmed from his imminent separation from Niki. He no longer thought of her as just "the doctor." The object of his affection, his devotion, was Nikola Kellman, who would forever be on his mind and in his heart, his Niki. She would never know of his feelings for her, and even though she probably did not feel the same as he did, Peter felt a deep sadness that they would be parting.

"Hey Genchenko, are you all right?" Tom's voice and eyes expressed concern.

Peter looked up at the big man in front of him, "What did you say?"

"I asked you several times if you were ready to get your wrap removed and go to the showers, but you didn't respond. I was afraid that you had some residual problems from the game."

Peter shook his head, "No, nothing like that…it's just…" He couldn't finish.

Tom looked at him keenly. "I'm gon'na do a neuro check on you just to be sure that you're okay."

Nik came alone into the training room and looked around at the athletes. Everyone that needed it seemed to be getting some attention, including Pete. She was mildly surprised that it was Tom, not Rebecca, taking care of him. With everything under control, she decided that she'd look in on Mikhail to see about his CT, but she heard Tom calling her, and looked to see what he wanted.

"Hey Doc, I think you need to check on Genchenko here." Tom pointed down at Peter as he spoke.

Nik walked over to them, "What's up?"

Tom said, "He's acting kinda' funny, Doc. I'm not sure what's goin' on. I was just about to do a neuro check, but you're lots better at that than I am."

"Okay, Tom. Why don't you go over to check on Mikhail for me? His CT report is due back. Bring it over to me if the Radiologist's written report says that there are abnormalities."

"Genchenko, if you've got a problem, you'd better tell the Doc here right now. She's been awful good to you." Tom turned and hurried away toward Mikhail.

Nik and Peter looked at each other for a long moment. Neither had any idea that what was actually wrong with both of them was the rapidly approaching end of their time together.

Peter spoke first, "Doctor, there's nothing wrong with me. I don't know why Tom is concerned. I just wasn't paying attention to him, that's all."

Nik saw more than sadness in his eyes. Was it anguish? "There's something wrong, Pete. I can see it in your eyes. Are you in pain?"

"*Nyet!* I am not in pain. Please, doctor, just take off my wrap and I'll go to the showers. I don't want to cause you any problems. I just want to go back to the hotel." Peter looked down at the floor as he spoke.

Reality is what is wrong with me, he knew. My foolish imagination has led me into a dangerous lapse in my ability to understand my place in life. She is kind to me, and has been more than kind all along. She enabled me to play hockey when I was sure that I could not. And then she saved my life, literally. She even saved me from the police. Is it any wonder that I am so pitifully grateful to her? Pathetic, I am a pathetic wretch who has deluded himself into believing that such a woman could care for, or about, me.

"Pete," Nik said softly, "please don't be upset, but I know you. In these few days that we have been…" she hesitated, "since we have been working together so closely, I have come to know you very well in some ways. We have shared stories of our families, of our lives, and now I just want to help you. Your eyes are telling me that you are somehow in trouble."

Peter let go of his anger and hurt. It was not the fault of this lovely woman that he had allowed himself to become attached to her. It was no one's fault, really.

"It isn't anything that you can help me with, doctor. I have my own peculiar problems. Sometimes reality hits me squarely between the eyes, and it is painful. Anyway, I will be going home soon, and I will no longer be *your* problem."

Peter's words hurt Nik. But she realized that he was trying to withdraw from his dependence upon her.

"All right, Pete. Fair enough. But can't I at least help you out of your wrap? And I'd like to do a neuro check on you just to make sure that you're okay. You were hit very hard this afternoon, and I wouldn't be doing my job if I didn't check you out."

Peter used the doctor's words, "Fair enough."

"First, let's get you out of that wrap." Nik was the professional again.

Her touch was gentle, yet firm. Nik quickly removed Pete's wrap, and then asked him to lie down on the table. He had shed his pads and uniform, and lay in his quilted under wrap. Nik covered him with a blanket from the warmer, and he was thankful for her thoughtfulness.

"I'm going to check your head wound first, and then your neck and shoulder, Pete, and then I'll do a complete neurological check on you, including reflexes."

Nik took the dressing from Pete's healing head wound and found that the wound edges were still approximated. That's good. She lightly manipulated Peter's neck and shoulder on the side where he had hit the boards. There was a knot in his sternocleidomastoid muscle near the base of his neck. When she touched the area, she could see that Peter was guarding it. The same was true of his shoulder.

"It's sore, isn't it, Pete?" Nik gently massaged the areas with her fingertips.

Peter closed his eyes tightly. "Da."

"I'll ask Mickey to give you an ultrasonic treatment on your neck and shoulder. There is no bruising in the area, so I'm not worried that you'll have a bleed. The warmth and pulsation of the ultrasonic treatment should take the kinks out of those muscles, and help to relieve the spasms." Nik continued to massage the painful areas gently with her fingertips until she felt Pete relax.

"Now it's time for the neuro check."

Nik checked his eyes, cranial nerves I through XII, all his reflexes, and included pinpricks to his neck, shoulders, back, arms, trunk, hips, legs, and feet. Everything was within normal limits. Pete did not report numbness, or needles and pins sensations anywhere on his body.

Nik stood above Peter as she pronounced him "good to go." Her heart ached as she saw that Pete's eyes still held pain. Was the pain organic or psychic in origin? She truly did not know. Briefly, she placed her hand, palm down, over his heart.

"You're going to be all right, Pete. You will get through whatever the source of your pain might be. You are one of the strongest persons that I have ever met, physically and mentally, and I will never, ever forget you and this big heart."

For the few moments that her hand lay over his heart, Peter felt warm there; a sensation that he had never before experienced. It felt as if her hand was a magnet, pulling the heartache and sadness out of him, and melting the ice that dwelled inside. He could not speak. He could not move. She took his breath away.

Tom came back to see how Peter was doing, "How is he, Doc? Is he okay?"

"Mickey is going to do an ultrasonic treatment on Pete's neck and shoulder, and then he's ready for the showers." She looked at Pete and smiled as she spoke to Tom.

Chapter 20

Thursday Morning

Nik dragged herself from bed after the third hit on her alarm snooze button. She had slept fitfully, and it seemed that she had looked at the bedside clock every hour, on the hour, all night long. She sat on the edge of the bed and rubbed her eyes briefly. Will grogginess go away if I rub my eyes? Probably not, she decided, and laughed aloud.

One more day, she thought, and this will all be over. My life will go back to normal. With that thought in mind, she wondered what her "normal" life would be like without Peter Genchenko? It hit her very hard when she thought of the finality of their parting. How will I be able to say goodbye to him?

Nik rushed through her shower, dried her hair quickly, threw on her usual blue shirt, khaki trousers, and white lab coat, and grabbed a yogurt and apple from the refrigerator. They would have to do for breakfast. Briefly, she looked out her kitchen window to check on the weather, and groaned. More snow...great, that's just what we don't need.

For some reason, Nik was chilled, so she grabbed her heaviest coat, wrapped a scarf around her neck, pulled on her warmest gloves, and took the elevator down from her condo. Her small garage was cramped, but it kept the snow from her car, and it was much better than parking the car on the street. Her condominium furnished tiny garages with each unit, and today she was very thankful that she had this small luxury.

Nik climbed into the cold interior of her little Cougar. For some reason, which the mechanics at the dealership had never diagnosed in a dozen visits, her radio and clock wouldn't work until the heater warmed the inside of the car. Shivering, she started the car, grasped the wheel and backed out of the garage. The snow under her tires was just wet enough to be very slippery. Oh great, it's one of those, one step ahead of reverse, days.

By her reckoning, Nik was only a few minutes late in her arrival in the training room, but when she checked her wrist, she realized that she had forgotten her watch. What a grand start to the day.

Traffic had been lighter than she had ever seen it at this hour, but the weather probably had something to do with it. She expected that many of the athletes would already be here, waiting for treatment, or wraps, or whatever. But there was no one there at all when she opened the door. When she passed the security desk, she was surprised to see that no one manned the desk. Briefly, she wondered where Terry, or one of his men, might be, but it hadn't worried her.

Nik slipped out of her coat, scarf and gloves and placed them on her desk. She glanced at the clock, and then did a double take. It was *five, not seven o'clock*. How…? It puzzled her for a moment, and then she decided that she had somehow set her alarm clock wrong last night. She remembered being very, very sleepy as she had tried to set her alarm. Well, the joke's on me.

Still very sleepy, Nik kicked off her shoes, curled up on a training table and covered herself with her coat. Maybe I can grab another forty winks before the athletes arrive, she thought. In a matter of moments, she was fast asleep.

Peter's wake-up call came at five forty-five, but he had been awake for quite some time staring up at the light patterns on the ceiling of his hotel room. He had left the draperies open when he had gotten into bed, and the outside city lights, even this early, were quite bright.

Peter knew that it would be important for his team to become the champions of these games, but he was past the "gung ho" stage. Now, he just wanted to go home. Perhaps the distance would be the final thing that would break his attachment to Niki. But of course, the actual break will be painful, he knew. Sometimes pain was the only thing that could cut through the numbing cold inside him.

It didn't take Peter long to ready himself for his day. When he looked outside at the snowfall, he decided to wear two pairs of socks with his thin-soled shoes. The boots that he had worn on loan from the arena security police the day that he had lunched with Niki…yes, Niki, he smiled at the thought of her, would have been wonderful to have this morning for his trek to the arena.

Peter made a pass by the registration desk in the hotel lobby and grabbed two apples from the large basket there. This will have to be my breakfast today, he thought. He would have preferred to have a warm breakfast of cereal, eggs, and bacon, an American style meal, but the apples were readily available, so he chose them.

As Peter entered the arena, he had noted that Niki's car was already parked in her spot, and had been there long enough for the snow to cover the top, windshield, and side windows of the car.

Peter checked the time on the clock above the information desk as he passed it. It was just six thirty-five, and all was still quiet. Apparently, it was too early for someone to be at the security desk.

Peter's plan, before he saw Niki's car outside in the parking lot, was to get some ice time when no one else was around to observe him. He made directly for the training room so that he could take his figure skates out of his locker there. He would not mind if she wanted to watch him skate for a few moments. In fact, he rather enjoyed the thought.

The training room door was ajar, and he fully expected to see or hear Niki somewhere inside the room. There was no music playing, but he went into the room still expecting to see her. She was nowhere to be found at first, and then he saw her curled up on a training table, a pillow fashioned with towels, her coat a blanket. It surprised him to see her sleeping there. What could have happened to cause her to fall asleep here? Has she been here all night, he wondered?

It tugged at his heart, seeing her there, sleeping so peacefully, and quiet as a kitten. He walked over to her, just to be sure that she was all right. Yes, she is just sleeping. In repose, he thought, she is even more beautiful, if that was possible. Her soft hair lay across her face like strands of dark silk, and her thick, dark lashes fanned her cheeks.

As he stood watching her, she moved and stretched her arms above her head. She sighed deeply, and then opened her eyes.

"Doctor, are you all right?" Peter spoke quietly so that he wouldn't startle her.

Nik's eyes widened, and she sat up quickly. "Oh…no. I fell asleep, didn't I?"

Peter smiled at her, "I think so. Have you been here overnight?"

"No…I…was just so sleepy when I got here. I must have set my alarm clock wrong, or something, and I got here at five o'clock, thinking it was seven. Then I saw the actual time, and I decided to take a little nap." Nik's smile was sheepish as she looked up at Pete.

"I didn't mean to awaken you, doctor, but I didn't want someone else from the team to come in and startle or frighten you."

She thanked him for his kindness and then said, "Well, you caught me sleeping on the job. But how come you're here so early?"

Her question caused Peter to laugh, "I wanted to get some ice time to do my own skate routine, so I came over early. When I found you sleeping, you looked so comfortable that I hated to awaken you."

"What time is it now?" Nik started to slip down from the training table, but Peter gently stopped her by touching her shoulder.

"Wait, doctor, the floor is cold. I'll help you with your shoes." He got down on one knee.

Nik's shoes were penny loafers, and Peter gently held each slender ankle as he easily slipped one, and then the other, onto her feet.

"You have rather small feet, doctor." Peter looked up at her, and then stood to help her down from the table.

Peter's gaze caused Nik some discomfiture. "No, not really…I wear a six and a half, and that's about average, I think."

"In answer to your question about the time, it's ten minutes until seven, doctor." Peter noticed that her face still held the rosy glow of sleep, and he found it to be rather endearing.

Vanya, Dimitri, Boris, and Arkady came into the training room followed by Vladimir. They were noisily discussing the championship game to be played that afternoon. Nik breathed a sigh of relief that Pete had awakened her so that she wouldn't be embarrassed in front of the other athletes.

"Hi, Doc." Mickey came in full of energy.

"You're early today, Mickey." Nik was glad to see him.

"Where do I start?"

"I, uh…I'm not sure just yet, but maybe you could stock the tables." Nik was still not completely awake.

Peter stood at some distance and watched her appreciatively. He wasn't sure that he could do as well as she immediately upon awakening.

Nik walked over to him to ask him how he was feeling this morning. "Are you having any soreness or stiffness in your neck and shoulder, Pete?"

Peter shook his head, "Not very much, doctor. Actually, I am doing well."

"Well, if you think a massage or a whirlpool treatment might help, Mickey's here, and Tom should be here shortly so either one can help you. And spaseeba, *thank you*, again for heading off what might have been a very embarrassing situation for me."

"You're welcome, doctor." Peter again pictured Niki asleep on the training table, and he had to chuckle at how vulnerable she had looked.

Tom came through the training room door and ducked as he always did. His bulky coat, hat and gloves made him look even larger than usual.

He called, "Hi, Doc, what do you want me to do?"

Nik waved him over to her, "Let's do what we have done for the past couple of games, but you can switch with Mickey. He needs some time with the more difficult treatments."

"Okay, Doc. What do you want Rebecca to do when she gets here?"

Nik thought for a moment, and then replied, "Ask her to monitor the athletes' whirlpool treatments. That way, she can work more closely to coordinate with you and Mickey."

Turning to Pete, Nik said, "Are you going to do a whirlpool treatment, or are you going to skate for awhile?"

"I'm going to do some routines on the ice, doctor. No one else will be out there for at least another hour, so that's probably my best choice." Peter was sure that he had made the right decision since Rebecca would be in charge of the whirlpool treatments.

"If I get the opportunity, I'll come out and watch you for a little while. I love to see you skate that way."

When Grigory came into the training room, everyone, the athletes, the trainers, and the doctor were busily working on something or someone. This is the way that it should be, he thought. There had been too much drama, apart from the games, in almost everything else. Although Detective Myers had contacted him this morning, he was not going to communicate that fact to anyone. Grigory did not want anything to hurt the team's chances for winning the championship by bringing such a sore subject to their attention.

Grigory wanted to tell the doctor that the surgeon had left a message for him that said that Ilya would be discharged from the hospital at noon today. It was one more problem to be taken care of today.

The doctor was at her desk using the telephone when Grigory approached her. Dr. Reynolds had called to tell her that Ilya would be discharged today around twelve or so. He told her that Ilya's prognosis was good, and that he could possibly resume his hockey play within six months if the athlete worked hard.

"Good morning Grigory. What can I do for you?" Nik was finally beginning to feel awake.

"Doctor, I received a message from Ilya's surgeon. He said that Ilya would be discharged mid-day from the hospital."

"I just talked with Dr. Reynolds, and he told me about how long Ilya's rehabilitation is going to take, and when he will be discharged, too."

"What kind of arrangements can we make to transfer him here?" Grigory knew that Ilya would need special care after discharge.

"I'm going to ask Tom if he will do the transfer for us. He's big and strong, and will be able to lift Ilya if he needs to be lifted or moved. Also, Mickey has volunteered to stay with Ilya overnight at the hotel to make sure that he does okay." Nik watched Grigory's expression for any sign of dissent.

"It will be very good to have Ilya in attendance at the game, doctor. I think that his presence will boost morale."

Nik thought, I know one athlete in particular who will be "morale boosted" to see Ilya at the game. Then she remembered that Pete was out on the ice, at this very moment, and she wanted Grigory to see him skate.

"Grigory, there is something that I want you to see. Follow me, please." As she passed Tom, she asked him to take charge of the training room for a short time, and walked out the door with Grigory.

Grigory was puzzled, but nonetheless followed the doctor out to the arena. This woman is a strange one, he thought. Most women are reticent, but give some hint as to their thinking. This one I can't read at all.

"There, look on the ice at your star athlete. What do you think?" Nik was curious as to what his opinion might be of Pete's abilities.

For several moments, Grigory did not speak. Nik could see by the expression on his face that he had not known that Pete was a figure skater.

Together, Nik and Grigory watched as Peter skated. Neither spoke; they were captivated, just as Nik had been upon first seeing him skate his figure routine.

"I didn't know this about Peter. First the piano, and now this figure skating." Grigory spoke almost in a whisper.

"I was very surprised the first time that I saw him skate like this, too. He is remarkable, isn't he?"

"Da" said Grigory, rubbing his chin, "Da, but he will have to go back to his life in Lyubertsy. He has no other choice as long as those in power remember that he is Ivan Genchenko's son."

"Is there a chance, because of his abilities, that his talent might override his family drawbacks?"

Grigory almost snorted, "*Never!* They will never forgive him for being Ivan's son. Perhaps if Ivan's books hadn't been so successful, at least outside the Soviet Union, then, maybe Peter might have had a chance. If raw talent, and plenty of it, at that, isn't enough, then I think that Peter will finish his days in a Lyubertsy factory."

With that pronouncement, Grigory turned to leave after he shot her a sharp glance. Nik watched as he walked out of the arena. His words had stung, but she knew that he was only being honest.

Peter waved at her from the ice. Even at this distance, his smile was something to behold. He spun, did a jump, and skated over to her.

"I was surprised to see Grigory with you, but why didn't he stay?" Peter was breathing hard, but still smiling.

"You've been full of surprises this week, Pete. I think that you have truly astounded Grigory, although I'm not sure why he couldn't see that your skating style is very different from all of his other hockey players'."

Peter shrugged, "I'm just happy to be able to skate like this, and also to play hockey."

"Have you had any dizziness while you were on the ice? Any nausea, or anything like that, Pete?" Nik wanted to make sure that he didn't have any residual injury from the boarding he took yesterday.

"No, nothing like that, doctor. Don't worry about me, I am fine." This time, his smile was lopsided, and he shook his head at her.

He wanted to ask her if she might still be sleepy, but he had second thoughts about sounding impertinent. Peter came in the gate, sat down, and unlaced his skates. He quickly slipped into his shoes, and slung his figure skates over one shoulder as he stood up.

"What are the plans for today, doctor?" He looked down at her, a small smile still on his face.

Nik looked up at the scoreboard clock, "It's five after eight, and I think everyone has been to the training table for breakfast except you."

"I grabbed some apples for breakfast because I wanted to come over to the arena to get some ice time. Of course, you got here before I did." Petr's smile widened.

"*Oh* yes. Don't remind me, Pete. I still can't believe that I fell asleep on a training table."

He laughed, and Nik joined in. It was their secret, something they shared that no one else knew. Nik felt comfortable in Pete's presence. There was no pretense, no attempts to impress her. And, they could laugh so easily about a shared secret. Nik wondered again what her life was going to be like without Pete.

As they stood together, the primary light banks came on in the arena by quadrants. When the quadrant where they were standing lit up, they stepped out of the light and started walking back to the training room.

"Pete, I'd like to do a neuro check on you again this morning, because I want to be sure that you're in good shape and ready for the game this afternoon."

He nodded his assent, "That will be fine doctor, and I appreciate your interest in my health."

Back in the training room, Nik did a quick, but thorough, neuro assessment on Peter. He passed easily, although he still had some residual pain at the base of his neck on the right side.

Nik told him, "Everything's normal Pete. You shouldn't have any problems during the game. By the way, are you coming to the awards dinner and dance tomorrow evening?"

"Is it a come as you are party like your parents' open house?" He gave her a rueful look. "If not, I will be seriously challenged to come up with something formal to wear."

Nik laughed, "Oh, it isn't *that* formal. In fact, I'm going to wear something exceptionally comfortable, rather than something I'd have to be tied into."

"I can see some merit in that." Peter couldn't help but smile at her descriptive words.

"Seriously, though, you *are* going to come, aren't you?"

"I wouldn't miss it for anything." It will be the last time that I see you, he thought.

The morning went quickly for Nik. She, Mickey, and Rebecca finished up the treatments for the athletes. The high point was when Tom brought Ilya into the training room amid cheers from the athletes.

For once, Pete ate lunch with the team at the training table. He sat next to Ilya, and Nik could see that they were enjoying themselves. Mikhail, mostly recovered, sat on the other side of Peter, and the three of them held court with their teammates. Grigory, and even Vladimir, joined in the festivities.

This was the way Nik wanted to remember her Neanderthals. Whether they win this afternoon, or not, I can see that they're together now. It's wonderful to see them like this. At that moment, Pete caught her eye and smiled a broad smile. Her heart leapt in her chest, and she felt happier, bathed in the warmth of his smile, than she had in a very long time. She couldn't help but smile back at him.

Game time was upon them. All Nik's athletes were taped, wrapped, stitched, or otherwise held together by whatever means, in readiness for the approaching battle on the ice. All they need now is war paint, she thought.

Grigory's pre-game pep talk was simple. "We have come this far," he said, "and now it's all up to you. My coaching won't make any difference at this point. You know what to do, so get out there and do it."

Ilya, pushed in his wheelchair by Peter, led the team out to the arena, with Mickey, Tom, and Rebecca falling in behind them. Grigory and Vladimir, reconciled, walked with Nik at the very back of the group.

Russian red swiftly took the ice, and the spectators erupted in a tremendously loud welcome. The Norwegians, already on the ice, slowed their maneuvers to watch, and take the measure of, their opponents.

Sheldon came over to Nik and put his arm around her, "I really wish Marty could be here to see this."

"I do too, Sheldon, I do too."

Peter left nothing to chance as he stood in readiness at the face-off circle. He had decided to do the face-off himself after what had happened to Mikhail in the last game. The Norwegian player across the fifteen foot circle from him tried to look menacing with lowered brows and a scowl twisting his lips. Peter gave him a boyish smile and a wink in return. This broke the Norwegian's train of thought, the puck went down, and Peter hammered it to Vanya.

The Norwegian player knocked the linesman, who had thrown the puck down, into the air in his haste to go after Vanya and the puck. Whistles blew, play stopped, and trainers from the Russian and Norwegian teams came to assist the immobile linesman. He was out cold and didn't move for several seconds.

Peter, Vanya, Boris, Mikhail and Dimitri hurried to their bench for a quick discussion with Grigory about setting up a special play. When the whistle blew to resume play, the Russians had possession of the puck.

The offending Norwegian was given a two-minute penalty for steam-rolling the linesman. He sat in the penalty box with his head down, holding onto his stick.

After what had happened to Peter during the last game, Nik was on edge, afraid that he might get hurt again. She hadn't known just how rough and demanding hockey could be until she was assigned to the Neanderthals and saw their battles on the ice up close.

With the Norwegian player in the penalty box, the Russians wanted to use the opportunity of their man advantage. Dimitri had control of the puck, and he and Boris planned an attack on goal. The Norwegian goalie, sensing that the Russians were coming for him, got ready for the onslaught. His elongated, shiny headgear, painted with the blue and gray of the Norwegian team colors, made him appear as a grotesque insect with slits for eyes.

Dimitri made a backhand pass to Peter, who streaked forward, suddenly deked, circled back and passed the puck to Boris, who moved it forward quickly.

Peter, with Boris ahead of him, Dimitri to the right side of him, and Vanya coming up the middle with Slava, headed for the Norwegian goal. The Norwegian left and right wings crossed over in front of the Russians, and Boris went down on the ice. Peter, taking the puck, stopped and, using his downed teammate as a screen from the Norwegian goalie, hit a tremendously powerful slap shot at goal. The red light went on behind the Norwegian goal.

"SCORE! The Russians have scored the first goal." the announcer called over the shouts and cheers of the spectators.

Seventeen reigns! Seventeen reigns! The crowd stomped and clapped their approval of Peter's skill.

In the midst of the din, Mikhail had been pestering both the doctor and Coach Grigory to let him skate.

"I'm fine, just fine," he told Grigory in Russian.

"*Da*, but I defer to the doctor. It is her decision as to whether you are able to play or not."

Nik hesitated a moment, and then said, "Okay, Mikhail, you can get into the game. But be honest with me. If you have any blurred vision, or dizziness, or head pain, *tell me*. Is that clear?"

Mikhail nodded, "I am well, doctor, and I know that I can go back into the game."

"Very well, Misha, I'll put you in at the first opportunity." Grigory was chewing his bottom lip and holding his head at an angle as he looked intensely at Mikhail.

Nik went over to the Doc's Box to sit with Ilya and Sheldon. They both nodded at her as she sat down, but were immediately back into the game.

The Russian man advantage evaporated when the Norwegian player's penalty was satisfied. He came over the boards as if something was chasing him from behind. He tried to latch onto Peter, but Peter's moves were too quick for him, so he went after Vanya.

Peter saw what was happening, and swung back behind the Norwegian, taking his mind off of Vanya. Having decoyed him, Peter sped away from the Norwegian and swiftly assumed his left wing position. He saw Mikhail come in on the fly, and Slava sped out for a rest.

The Norwegian center had possession of the puck, and was being flanked by his right and left wings. Their forward line came into the slot, and the right wing was given a flip pass from his center. Peter saw the play that the Norwegians were putting together, and with Vanya, Mikhail, Boris, and Dimitri, spread across the ice in a Russian defensive line. Peter chased down the Norwegian center and began to shadow him closely. When the Norwegian center attempted a rush at goal, Peter easily poke checked and took the puck from him, moving the puck away from the Russian goal to clear it by moving it into a position of safety. Arkady, at goal for the Russians, let out a tremendous sigh of relief.

At the end of the second period, the Russians still led one goal to nothing. The Norwegians had played hard and had stayed with the Russians, defending their own goal, and attacking the Russian goal, with the ferocity of Vikings, but they had not been able to score.

Grigory was speaking rapidly to his athletes. "You have another twenty minutes to win or lose this game. Although the Norwegians have not scored up to this point, they are going to be frantic to get on the scoreboard. Because our bench is not deep, this is my strategy: Slava, Vanya, Boris, Mikhail, and Dimitri will go in at the buzzer. I am going to send Peter in on the fly in the first two minutes, and Boris will come out. In the next two minutes, Mikhail will come out, and Boris will go in on the fly, then Dimitri, and so on. I am going to continue to do this rotation to give everyone a rest, because we need Peter and Mikhail to play the last eight or ten minutes, when the Norwegians are going to throw whatever they can at us. You see that Norwegian player over there? The one who looks like Goliath? He's their policeman, and he's going to try to put one or two of you out of the game. It doesn't matter if he gets a penalty, because he's slow and can't hit the goal anyway. But you can be sure that he will be out there trying to injure one of you. Don't let him near you if you can help it."

The Russians had all been watered and toweled, as Nik watched from a distance. Rebecca was standing next to Peter, looking up at him and talking, but Peter was quickly looking around, and then his eyes came to rest on the doctor. He nodded his head and mouthed, "*I am fine,*" and then headed toward the bench, ignoring Rebecca, but not intentionally. He was just intent on the game. The buzzer sounded, and play resumed.

Grigory's assessment of the third period was completely accurate. His tactics regarding rotation of his players seemed to be working, because the Norwegians were rattled. His biggest concern, however, was that Arkady was showing signs of tiring, and with Josef gone, Grigory had no one else to replace his goalie. Grigory decided on a bold move; something that the Norwegians would not anticipate. He would pull the goalie. Although this strategy was usually employed at the end of a game in order to gain an advantage for scoring to tie a game, Grigory knew that this was the only way that he could give Arkady a rest from the relentless Norwegians. The Russians had possession of the puck when he called time out.

"We have eleven minutes on the clock. I am pulling Arkady for a three-minute rest, and sending Dimitri in to gain our man advantage. The Norwegians will think that we are crazy to do this, but I know that Arkady needs some rest in order to finish the game. Peter, I want you to protect the goal if the Norwegians get that far. Questions?"

They looked at one another, eyebrows raised. And then, each one shook his head. No, there were no questions, but they all hoped that this rather unorthodox strategy would work.

The buzzer sounded for the resumption of play. When the Russian goalie did not come out to cover his goal, the crowd became strangely quiet. Nik could see that the Norwegians were looking back at their coach, shoulders shrugged, hands upraised in the universal non-verbal, "*what's this all about?*" language.

Play resumed with the Russians in possession of the puck. The Norwegian's Goliath went after Peter, but soon realized that he would never be able to catch him. He turned his attention to Slava, who eyed the giant warily, and gave him a wide berth.

Dimitri brought the puck into the attacking zone, while Peter came swiftly up the left side to join Slava coming up the right. Dimitri passed the puck to Peter, who did a breakaway from the Norwegian defenders and headed straight for the goal. The Norwegian center, in a desperate move to stop him, caught and held Peter with the crook of his stick low on the abdomen. Whistles blew, and an illegal play, hooking, was called against the Norwegian. The Norwegian center was sent to the penalty box for one minute.

Nik watched as Grigory threw his arms in the air in exultation. This could work in the Russians' favor. Sheldon, sitting just behind her, did likewise. But Nik's biggest concern was whether Pete had been hurt when the Norwegian hooked him with his stick.

Peter knew that the doctor would be worried about him, so he gritted his teeth briefly against the pain in his right groin, and then turned, took off his glove, and gave her a thumbs up to tell her that he was unhurt.

Play resumed again, and the Russian team still had possession of the puck. Eleven minutes had evaporated into eight, and both teams began to feel the *need,* the desperation, to score.

Grigory knew that the Norwegians had one hell of a goalie. His goals against average statistic that indicated the average number of goals made on him each game, was low. He was good at catching the puck in midair, and he was deadly with his blocking glove, used to block or deflect the puck during attempts on goal. His saves were legendary. Grigory wished that he had some strategy to make the Norwegian goalie less effective, but there was really nothing to be done.

Boris, who had come in on the fly to take Mikhail's place, took a pass from Dimitri, and made an attempt on goal with a slapshot. The Norwegian goaltender caught the puck, and held it aloft for a second before returning it to the ice in front of one of his teammates, who swung around behind the goal.

Three players, one Russian and two Norwegians, were mucking for the puck in the corners behind the goal. Peter, coming in to join them, saw an opportunity, and poke checked the puck away from one of his opponents. Peter then came just to the edge of the goal, and flipped the puck inside while the goalie was still concentrating on the other players at the opposite corner. Again, the red light came on.

"*SCORE! Genchenko scored when no one was looking!*" The announcer was excited, but could barely be heard above the noisy celebration going on in the arena.

Sheldon saw pure poetry on the ice. This Genchenko guy's really something. *Damn*, I wish Marty were here to see this. He's gon'na get a call tonight.

This time, the Norwegians called time out. Peter glanced over at their bench, and he knew that he didn't want to be in their skates right now. The Norwegian coach looked as if he had lost it. He was flailing his arms and then tearing at his hair. Although he looked funny, Peter could relate to the frustration the coach must be feeling. Hockey is a strange game, thought Peter. Even though you love it, there are times when you can really hate it, too.

Arkady was rested, and Grigory told him to go back in when play resumed. There wasn't much for Grigory to say to his team during this time out, except that he told them that he was proud of what they had done during these games. Towels and water bottles flew back and forth, and then the Russians were ready to go back out on the ice. Ilya, who had been wheeled by Mikhail over to where the team stood at their bench, told them that he knew they were going to win. Mikhail agreed, and the team included them in their team hug.

Nik's eyes followed each of her Neanderthals, and then came to rest on Pete. He had taken his helmet off, and his thick, dark blond hair was unruly and damp. She watched as he drank deeply from his water bottle and poured some of the water over his head. Rebecca threw him a towel, and he wiped his face and rubbed his head, then quickly put his helmet back on. As he had since the first game, Pete looked over at the doctor before he went back out on the ice.

Arkady took his place at goal, to the loud applause of the crowd. His teammates skated around and in front of him briefly before settling down to do the face-off. Vanya took the honors this time for the Russians, and Goliath stood for the Norwegians.

The puck went down, and both teams swarmed around the face-off circle. Vanya was quicker than Goliath, but a Norwegian player took the pass. Slava finally managed to take the puck by intercepting the Norwegian's attempt to pass to another player. Slava passed to Boris, who passed to Peter. Peter was skating backward when he took possession of the puck, but immediately deked, leapt in the air, turned, and began skating toward the Norwegian goal.

Nik, who was watching the play closely, thought for a moment that Pete was going to start his figure skating routine with the leap and turn. It made her smile and laugh a little.

"What's he up to doctor?" Sheldon had also seen Peter's moves, and was curious as to what he might be doing.

Nik laughed in earnest, "With Pete, your guess is as good as mine."

Ilya had his own comment, "He's going for goal, doctor, and he's not going to stop until he gets another one."

Mikhail had been sent in on the fly for Slava, and he and Peter brought the puck down the ice toward the Norwegian goal without ever being in jeopardy of losing it. None of the Norwegians could catch them. The Norwegian goalie, still stinging with humiliation from Peter's last goal, readied himself for this rush on goal.

Dimitri was being followed by Goliath, but was staying ahead of the slower, heavier Norwegian. The clock unbelievably had less than a minute of play left in the third period. Peter and his teammates began ragging the puck to use time while they kept the puck out of the hands of the Norwegians.

The spectators began to count down when the clock reached ten seconds, and Sheldon came unglued.

"They've kept the Norwegians *scoreless!*" He shouted.

The buzzer sounded the end of the game, but it also signaled a noisy and jubilant celebration on the part of the crowd. The organ was thundering and people were stomping and screaming.

Grigory and Vladimir had locked arms and were dancing. Ilya rejoiced with Mickey and Tom, while Rebecca stood at the gate waiting for Peter to leave the ice.

Nik stood quietly in the midst of the commotion and celebration of the crowd. My Neanderthals *did* it, they really *did it; they won the tournament!*

Peter searched the Russian bench from the ice, looking for the doctor. He didn't see her at first. Finally, he spotted her standing quietly in the midst of the uproar with an expression on her face that he had not seen before. She had a half-smile on her face, but he could see that she was not focused on anyone in particular. Had she felt his eyes on her? She had then looked directly at him, smiled and waved, and raised her arms above her head in a victory sign just for him. He returned the gesture, holding his hockey stick high above his head.

The awards ceremony started almost immediately. A riser with three levels was pushed out onto the ice, and the games committee chairperson, with Governor Robert Orr and Dr. Garibaldi at his side, came out onto the ice via a slip-proof carpet. A sound system had been set up with microphones for both the committee chairperson and Dr. Garibaldi. The captains of each of the competing hockey teams came forward onto the ice and stood in a single line, side by side in full gear. Three young women came out onto the ice, each with a bouquet of roses; one red, one pink, and one white. Media cameramen from the major local stations, Channel 6, Channel 8, and Channel 13, began filming the proceedings, while their reporters stood quietly, waiting to interview the athletes after the awards ceremony.

The committee chairperson, a smallish red-haired man named Patterson, began, "We are gathered here to award the top three hockey teams in the International Winter Games hosted by the great city of Indianapolis. We have seen some excellent play in all sports, not just by athletes in hockey. Tomorrow evening, the winners in all sports will be honored during the dinner dance celebration. In addition, two athletes, a male and female, will be chosen for their spirit and exceptional contributions to these games. Will the hockey team captains please come forward at this time?"

The line of team captains came forward to stand in front of the risers. Peter's heart was pounding as he stood waiting for the committee chairperson to continue.

"And now, we wish to recognize the winner in the hockey category of the International Winter Games: The Soviet Union. Team captain, Peter Genchenko, please come forward to stand on the top riser."

As Peter moved forward, he was handed a trophy and a bouquet of red roses. He took his place at the top of the risers. The spectators loudly proclaimed their approval of his team's first place standing.

"Second place goes to the Norwegian team. Team captain, Sven Andersen, please come forward to stand on the second riser."

The Norwegian team captain skated up to the committee chairman to receive his team's award, and was handed his trophy and yellow roses. He took his place on the second riser. Again, the crowd applauded mightily.

"Third place goes to the American team. Team captain, William Strube, please come forward to stand on the riser."

The American team captain came forward to receive his trophy and white roses. He then took his place with the Russian and Norwegian team captains on the risers amid cheers from the crowd.

The Russian national anthem played as the three team captains stood upon the risers, their trophies raised for all to see.

"And now the committee chairman announced, "The Governor of the State of Indiana, the Honorable Robert D. Orr, will speak to the athletes."

The Governor was a distinguished-looking gentleman as he stood at the podium. He spoke of the importance of the International Winter Games in regard to global understanding and working together. He complimented the hockey teams for their outstanding abilities, stating that he knew how hard each team had worked before and during the games in order to compete here in the great state of Indiana.

The Governor ended his speech by telling the athletes, "You have honored your countries by your sportsmanship and strong spirit of competition. I congratulate each one of you for your participation in these games."

Again, the spectators applauded loud and long with whistling, hand clapping, and foot stomping thrown in. When they began to quiet down, the committee chairman came forward to the microphone again.

"I wish now to introduce the physician responsible for the group of physicians who served each team during these games, Dr. Joseph Garibaldi."

Dr. Garibaldi came to the microphone. He was obviously uncomfortable as he shuffled the small cards that he would use to make his comments. His balding pate shone under the bright lights of the arena.

After the third clearing of his throat, he began, "My doctors have been dedicated to excellence in their work with the athletes. Tonight, I am speaking to those doctors who worked with the hockey teams. Without exception, each of them has provided skill, knowledge, and expertise in their care of, and interactions with, the athletes. One doctor, Myron David Michael, has had the responsibility of coordinating the efforts of the other doctors assigned to care for the hockey teams. It is my great pleasure to present an award to Dr. Michael for service above and beyond that which was required. Dr. Michael, please step forward to receive your award."

Ron was caught off guard by Dr. Garibaldi's remarks. He had not been notified of the award prior to this moment, and he hesitated before going out onto the ice. His eyes searched for Nik, and he found her standing at the Russian gate. He saw that she had a huge smile on her face, and he grinned back at her as he came down onto the ice.

Dr. Garibaldi presented Ron with a certificate of commendation. "Thank you, Dr. Michael, for your contributions to these games."

Ron, red-faced, accepted the certificate, shook hands with Dr. Garibaldi, and headed toward the Russian gate to show Nik his award.

The committee chairman again took the microphone. "Thank you again to all of the participants of this segment of the International Winter Games. These ceremonies are now ended."

Peter was relieved to be able to step down from the risers. He had seen the non-verbal communication between Dr. Kellman and Dr. Michael. Although he knew that they were engaged, and would, therefore, be very likely to be happy when one of them received an award, it nonetheless hurt Peter to see them as a couple.

Tom and Mickey, with Rebecca close behind, came out onto the ice to celebrate with their team. Rebecca had reached Peter and thrown her arms around him while he was looking up at the doctor. When Rebecca threw her arms around Peter, the doctor had turned and walked away, and for some reason, Peter believed that there was a sense of finality in this act.

The media swarmed around Peter, vying for an opportunity to interview him. Cameras flashed, and he was jostled and pushed back and forth before he put his hand up and said, "One at a time, please. Let's be polite."

Grigory and Vladimir came out to be interviewed, too, and Peter was relieved to see them. Grigory was an old hand at this sort of thing, and took over.

"Each of you will get one minute, and one minute only, to interview Genchenko. When I say we are finished, I expect all of you to honor my wishes."

Grigory began to feed interviewers; The Indianapolis Star, Channel 13, Channel 8, and Channel 6 were the only media members that he allowed to interview Peter. When they finished with Peter, they began to mob the American and Norwegian team captains.

"Thank you, Grigory. I am very thankful that you are here to organize this mob." Peter wiped his face on his sleeve.

Grigory chuckled. "Blood suckers, they are blood suckers. You must be firm with them, or they will suck you dry. It doesn't matter what country you are in. They are all alike."

Peter hurried to the training room. He hoped that he had not missed the doctor, because he wanted very much to talk to her.

Peter saw her from a distance when he reached the training room, but she had been all business, and he had ended up allowing Rebecca to unwrap him. He was anxious to talk to the doctor, to share his joy at winning the game, but he saw her walking out of the training room with Mickey who was pushing Ilya in his wheelchair. When she didn't return, he felt sorely disappointed that he couldn't share this victory with her.

He had waited for her to return, and when she did not, he went with the team to a celebratory dinner at their hotel. In addition to the rest of the team, Ilya was there with Mickey, Tom, and Rebecca. Grigory was in high spirits, toasting the team over and over again for their championship. He had even allowed Vladimir to sit next to him again.

"Not a point, not even one little point did you give up to the Norwegians! Every one of you, after all that you have endured, should be very proud of this accomplishment. We are the only team to have won every game that we played during this tournament."

The doctor had not come to celebrate with the team. Peter couldn't understand why she hadn't at least come to congratulate them on their amazing feat.

When the dinner was finished, and the team was getting ready to leave, the doctor came in with her fiancé, Dr. Michael, to tell them all that she was very proud of their accomplishments, and that she looked forward to seeing them tomorrow evening at the awards ceremony. She had glanced at Peter, had smiled, and then looked away.

Afterward, in his hotel room, Peter's hurt feelings had made it almost impossible for him to sleep. He tossed and turned, but couldn't get comfortable. His heart ached, because he didn't know why the doctor's behavior toward him had changed so drastically. What had he done to deserve such dismissive treatment? And, to add to his discomfort, his right side had begun to be painful. Without the doctor, there was no one he could tell about it. There was no one to help him now. He didn't know what he was going to do, and he was miserable.

Chapter 21

When Peter got out of bed, he decided that he had better pack his clothing because he knew that his team would leave the first thing next morning to fly back to Moscow. His heart ached at the prospect of leaving without getting to say a proper goodbye to the doctor. He couldn't continue to think of her as Niki. He had no right to do so.

Peter avoided the training room altogether this morning. If the doctor were distant or unfriendly, it would hurt him even more. He didn't want to have a training table breakfast with his team, either, so he splurged on a real American breakfast in the hotel.

He loved scrambled eggs, and ordered a breakfast of bacon, eggs, toast, and fruit. No one, as far as he was concerned, could scramble eggs the way the Americans did.

As Peter ate his breakfast, a plan came, unbidden, into his thoughts, and it surprised him. The doctor said that she was going to attend the dinner dance and awards ceremony tonight. Will she dance with me again? He wanted to be close to her, with his arms around her, one last time. Dancing with her tonight would be one more memory that he would have of her.

After breakfast, Peter thought that, if this was to be his last day in this city, he should at least explore the downtown area. The wind had picked up when he left the Westin. Snow swirled around him as he began his exploration of Indianapolis.

He walked a few blocks east on Washington Street and found a huge excavation site at the Illinois and Washington Street intersection. Peter looked around a bit to see how deep the excavation might be. He had always had a keen interest in civil engineering, and had read as many books as he could find on the subject. This project looked like a huge challenge to any civil engineer. Although he couldn't tell with any certainty because of the depth of the snow, it appeared that this excavation was one of long-standing. He couldn't determine how much erosion and collapse had occurred at the site because of the snowfall. It piqued his curiosity, however, because he knew that a project of this size could be very costly when delayed.

Peter continued his exploration of the downtown area, and found both restaurants where he had dined with Dr. Kellman. A bittersweet feeling came over him as he thought of sitting across from her, close enough to touch her, talking and laughing. In the few short days that he had known her, she had made more of an impression upon him than that of any woman he had known before her.

As Peter roamed the streets of downtown Indianapolis, he came upon some unusual places. St. Elmo's Steakhouse was one of them. A curious name for a restaurant, he thought. He walked on for a while, and saw an old restaurant called Acapulco Joe's. Peter enjoyed the heat of Mexican food. He loved the taste of chiles, cilantro and cumin. If not for his hockey travel, he might never have discovered how much he liked Mexican food.

Peter walked around Monument Circle and admired the unique sculptures there. He wished that he could be with someone…Niki would be his choice, who might explain some of the things that he was seeing. There were times when loneliness engulfed him on his short trek through the downtown, and the cold ache inside him became almost unbearable.

Peter felt out of place in this strange city. He admitted to himself, however, that he would feel the same in Moscow or Lyubertsy. It was a state of mind, not location.

The city was decorated for the Christmas season, and even though it was now fully daylight, the lights glowed in a myriad of colors. Storefronts displayed brightly colored clothing, with holiday decorations that should have lifted Peter's mood. They did not.

The state buildings had lighting that seemed to add more definition to the gothic beauty of the buildings. What would it be like to live here in this city in the middle of the land of plenty?

Heart sore, and tired of his tour, Peter decided that he would try one more time to use the arena ice for some figure skating exercises. Skating that way always lifted his spirits. He had to pack up his belongings in his locker, anyway, so he would do both things, skate and pack. He wasn't sure whether he wanted to see the doctor or not. If she were distant or indifferent to him, he didn't know if he could bear it.

The training room door was ajar when he arrived. A part of Peter hoped against hope that she would be there, but another part of him didn't want to face the pain of rejection if she were there but didn't want to see him. Peter held his breath for a moment, trying to slow his pounding heart, and then went into the training room.

All of the overhead lights were burning, but the training room was empty. He walked around looking in each cubicle, in the hydro-treatment area, and the showers, but no one was there. In a way, he felt a sense of relief. It freed him to clean out his locker, and to go out into the arena to skate one last time on this ice.

As Peter approached the ice, he saw the security officer, Terry, coming toward him. Terry smiled widely at Peter.

"I want to tell you that you have made a hockey fan of me, Genchenko." Terry put out his hand to shake Peter's.

The two men shook hands, and Terry continued. "Detective Myers came by this morning. He said he wanted to talk to you again. I directed him to Dr. Kellman, or your Coach, but he said he only wanted to see you. He left his card with me, and asked me to give it to you. He wants you to call him."

Peter nodded his head, looked down at the floor for a moment, and then replied noncommittally, "Thank you."

He put the card in his pocket, and asked Terry, "Would it be all right if I skated awhile? I'd like to get on the ice just one more time."

"Sure, sure you can. No problem. The lights in there are on low, though. I hope that's not a problem."

"No, actually, it's easier to skate with the lights lowered a bit. And, thank you for letting me skate."

Terry patted Peter on the shoulder. "Have at it, then, Genchenko. You're quite a skater."

Peter wondered briefly what to do about Detective Myers's card, but decided that he was not going to call him, and so put on his skates and took the ice. He didn't notice the figure way up in the semi-darkness of the higher seating.

Nik had been sitting high up in the arena, trying to sort out her thoughts and feelings. This was the only place where she could get away from everyone and everything. There were no telephones to answer, and she had left her radio-pager in the training room. She didn't want to talk to anyone right now.

Ron had convinced her last evening that she hadn't needed to attend the celebratory dinner for her Neanderthals' winning the championship. But she had had second thoughts, and could see when she and Ron went to congratulate the team, that her absence had hurt Pete and his teammates. She couldn't face the look of hurt in Pete's eyes, and had averted her own. She was ashamed of her behavior, and she should have followed her own instincts by attending the dinner with the team, no matter what Ron said.

It startled her when Pete came into the arena, laced up his skates, and went out on the ice. As he started his warm-up routine, Nik's eyes filled with tears. Life isn't fair, she thought, it isn't fair at all. How can a man so talented be destined to work in a factory the rest of his life?

One of Peter's favorite skate routines was set to the music of Tchaikovsky; the Nutcracker Suite. He and his sister, nine years old at the time, had skated their routine in Victorian costumes, and had won an international children's figure skating competition. Peter's family, including his father, had been allowed to go to West Germany for the competition. The four of them had done things together; sightseeing, dinners, and even a night at the theatre. It had been the happiest time in his life. They were a *family*, if only for a short time. Pravda had published a story on the trip, competition, and the championship. There were even pictures of the happy Genchenko family along with the story in the newspaper.

Peter could hear the opening strains of the music in his head, and started to move to its rapid beat. He threw his heart and soul into his skating, moving from one end of the ice to the other. In his mind, he skated with his sister, and bowed when the routine required it. He held his arms as if Katya was there to hold onto.

Beautiful, Nik thought, from high above, he's so beautiful. I will never forget this moment.

The routine lasted only seven minutes, but when he finished, Peter was out of breath. It was as if he had tried to skate the perfect routine, as he might in competition.

When he stopped, he looked around the arena, committing it to memory. He was certain that he would never have the opportunity to return to the ice here. He caught a slight movement in the upper seating area, and concentrated on the spot. The small figure stood and waved to him.

Peter was delighted to see that Doctor Kellman…yes, it was Niki, and she was high above in the arena! He waved back at her with both arms.

"Doctor, please come down and talk to me." Peter cupped his hands as he called to her.

Nik started down the first set of stairs, and was surprised to see Pete coming up to meet her with his skates on. He bolted up the steps two and three at a time.

Finally, they stood facing one another. They started speaking at the same time, and then laughed.

"You go first," Nik said, smiling at Pete's obvious delight at seeing her.

"I…I just wondered if you might be upset with me. You seemed so distant yesterday, and I didn't know what I had done…" Peter's voice trailed off.

"Oh Pete, I'm so sorry that you thought that. No, of course I wasn't upset with you. I allowed myself to be talked out of attending the team dinner, that's all. And then I was very embarrassed that I hadn't joined you sooner when I finally put my foot down and insisted on offering my congratulations in person."

Peter's relief was immediate and visible. His countenance changed to one of hope. He didn't want to embarrass her by asking who had convinced her not to come to the team celebration. It doesn't matter, he thought. She's here in front of me now.

He reached out and took her hand, "It doesn't matter at all. I'm just glad to know that you're not angry or upset with me."

They walked down the steps together, and Nik sat next to Pete as he took off his skates and put on his shoes.

Peter gathered his gear and bag, and looked at the beautiful Niki, "We are okay then, doctor?"

"Yes, we are okay, and I'm going to miss you, Pete." Nik looked out over the ice, and then back at him.

"Genchenko!" Detective Myers shouted across the arena. "I want to talk to you."

"Oh my God, Pete, it's that idiot detective." Nik's heart sank.

Peter turned and shouted back, "What do you want with me?"

"I'm going to call Les Barnes, Pete. Come with me." Nik's heart was now in her throat.

"Hey, *hey, Genchenko!* You'd better not run out on me." Myers shouted hoarsely.

They went into the corridor and hurried to the nearest training room. Nik knew that Myers probably had someone waiting in the Russian training room, so she decided not to go there. She needed to use a telephone quickly.

"Hey, Nik, how does it feel to be the team doctor for the winning hockey team?" Dr. Curtis Aeschliman smiled at her, his fair skin blushing beneath his even fairer, white-blond hair.

"It's great, Curt, just great. Uh…I'm in a hurry right now. Could I use your telephone?" Nik was beginning to feel frantic.

Dr. Aeschliman's pale blue eyes glanced at Peter, and then turned back to Nik. "Of course, Nik, it's over there." He pointed as he spoke to her.

Nik hurried over to the telephone. With shaking hands, she dialed Les Barnes' number. After four rings, a soft, feminine voice answered, "Barnes, Clabaugh, and Barnes, may I help you?"

Nik swallowed hard, "Yes, I would like to speak with Mr. Barnes, Sr., please. Tell him that Nikola Kellman wants to talk to him."

There was a pause, and the polished voice said, "I'm sorry, but Mr. Barnes, Sr. will be leaving for court in five minutes, and he is not to be disturbed. I can take a message for him, and he will return your call at his earliest convenience."

"*No,* I need to speak to him *now*. My father is Klaus Kellman, and I know that you would put him through to Mr. Barnes immediately. This is an emergency, and I *must* speak to him now."

Dr. Aeschliman had struck up a conversation with Peter, who was struggling to listen to what the doctor was saying to someone at the other end of the telephone line.

"You're the Russian hockey team captain, aren't you? Genchenko, right?"

"Yes, that is correct." Peter turned to look at Dr. Kellman again.

"Your team was great, Genchenko. You won *every* game, didn't you?" Dr. Aeschliman grinned at him.

"That's right…" he turned to hear her speaking into the telephone again, and tried to listen.

"Uncle Les, thank God! I'm sorry to interrupt your court preparations, but Detective Myers is back here at the arena trying to get at Peter Genchenko."

Les let out a low whistle, "I thought Myers was smarter than that."

"What should I do, Uncle Les? I'm afraid of what he might try to do to Peter."

"I'll send Sarah Williams over right away. You haven't tried to elude the Detective, have you?"

"Well, not exactly, but I wanted to call you before Myers grabbed Peter, that's all."

Les laughed and wondered what dear little Niki had gotten herself into this time? "Where are you right now?"

"We're in the Canadian training room, but it's only a matter of time before Myers finds us."

"Hold on just a minute, Niki." Les spoke to someone in the background.

Peter came over to the doctor. "What is happening?"

"Les can't come because he's due in court right now, but he's sending someone in his place." Nik held up her hand when Les came back to the phone.

"Sarah is a junior partner, and she is on her way, Niki. Just sit tight, okay? I'll finish up in court about 3 o'clock, and then I'll be in touch with you and Peter."

"Thanks so much Uncle Les. I owe you!"

"I have to get going, Niki, but Sarah will be there soon. Bye, hon'."

"Goodbye." Nik held onto the receiver for a moment, and then hung up.

Peter was standing next to her as she hung up the telephone. Nik turned to him and smiled tentatively.

"Uncle Les has to be in court in a few minutes, so he's sending one of his associates. Her name is Sarah Williams, and she's on her way over here Pete. It's going to be all right."

Detective Myers was furious. Where had Genchenko gone? That Russian bastard wasn't going to get away from him this time. Oh no, this time he was going to nail him.

Two uniformed officers were with him. Each had taken one side of the hallway, and they were opening every door to check inside.

It's only a matter of time, Genchenko, Myers thought...only a matter of time.

Sarah Williams stood a full six feet two inches in her winter high-heeled boots. She was an imposing, and very attractive young woman. A native Tennessean, and a graduate of the University of Tennessee, she had played the center position on the women's basketball team. She was a dynamo for the Lady Vols during her college years.

The energy that Ms. Williams had expended in basketball play was now focused on her very successful career as a Junior Partner with Barnes, Clabaugh, and Barnes, one of the most successful and influential legal teams in Indianapolis. She made her way quickly into the arena, long legs striding. As she entered, she spotted Detective Myers and his uniformed officers canvassing the building door to door.

"Oh shit." Myers couldn't help himself as he saw Ms. Williams striding toward him.

When she reached his side, she looked down upon his balding pate, and gave him a spectacular smile.

"Detective Myers?" Ms. Williams spoke in her soft Tennessee lilt, "are you up to something that you shouldn't be?"

She tapped a folded sheet of paper against the palm of one hand. "Cease and desist," she drawled. "You must cease and desist." It sounded like three syllables; *dee-see-ust.*

With another brilliant smile, Ms. Williams handed the paper to Detective Myers. "I am standing in for Mr. Barnes, Sr. in representing Peter Genchenko. If you wish to speak with Mr. Genchenko, I will be there to represent him. If you, somehow, have gotten a warrant, the paper that I have just handed you states that Peter Genchenko is a Russian national, and that you have no jurisdiction over him. It's signed by a judge."

Myers lost his temper and stomped his foot, "Son-of-a-*bitch*!"

"My, my, Detective, I think that you are upset." Sarah Williams' eyes danced with impish glee.

Myers mopped his brow with one hand. "Look, Ms. Williams, I only want to talk to Genchenko. I told his coach to have him get in touch with me, but he hasn't called. I wouldn't be doing my job if I didn't question him to find out what he knows about what happened to Yakov Popov. Two people have come forward after reading about Popov's death in the newspapers. They swear that they heard and saw Popov and Genchenko arguing in an elevator at the Westin the day before Popov was killed."

"Well, Detective Myers, this is your second attempt to railroad Genchenko, and you can't have him this time, either. The paper in your hand says so. By the way, where is the Russian training room?"

Detective Myers was speechless and filled with impotent fury. He turned on his heel and called to his two uniformed officers, "C'mon, let's get out of here!"

Peter and Nik, after waiting fifteen minutes with Dr. Aeschliman and trying to make small talk, started out for the Russian training room. Nik took Peter a different route, rather than walking in the main corridor in order to avoid a chance meeting with Detective Myers. When she looked up at Peter, he was pale and very quiet.

"Pete, don't worry, Uncle Les has sent someone who can make Detective Myers go away."

"Perhaps, but why is Myers doing this to me? Why? I didn't kill Yakov."

Nik stopped walking and tugged at Peter's sleeve, "I know you didn't, Pete. I remember how hurt you were when you thought that I believed you had."

"There was fear in your eyes, doctor. I could see it, and I thought that you were afraid of me." Peter's voice was oddly restricted, almost choked, as he told her this. He could not, or would not, look at her.

"Look at me, Pete, *please,* look at me." Nik again tugged at his sleeve.

Nik saw Pete's jaw tightening, and he swallowed hard, trying to regain control as he continued to look away from her.

Nik's voice was soft as she told him, "Okay, Pete, okay. I know that this whole thing is terrible for you, and I'm sorry, really sorry, that you thought I could ever believe that you would harm anyone, even someone as despicable as Yakov."

She let out a sigh and squared her shoulders, "Let's go see Ms. Williams, Pete."

This time, Nik put her right arm through Peter's left, and they walked on. Holding the doctor's arm so close to his heart warmed him, and some of the pain and sadness began to leave him as they walked together.

Sarah Williams was sitting on the edge of a training table when Peter and Nik arrived in the Russian training room. She observed that they were arm in arm, and wondered, briefly, why that was so?

"Hello, I'm Sarah Williams. My clients and friends call me Sarah." She put out her hand to shake Peter Genchenko's hand.

Peter took her hand, and Sarah was surprised that his hand was so much larger than her own. That was usually not the case. She could palm a basketball as well as any professional player.

She turned and offered her hand to Dr. Kellman, "It's nice to finally get to meet you, Dr. Kellman. Mr. Barnes, Sr. loves to talk about how proud he is of you. He says he couldn't be more proud of you if you were his own daughter."

Sarah could see the strain on the faces of these two very handsome people. Are they a couple, she wondered? If that was the way things were, would this issue complicate, or ease, the problems that Peter Genchenko was experiencing? If she was going to help him, she needed to find this out.

"I just handed Detective Myers an order that essentially states that he must cease and desist in his attempts to bother Peter, who is a Russian National."

Sarah watched as the doctor and Peter exchanged a look of relief and renewed hope. Again, she wondered just what was going on here? Her mind had always had an analytic bent, and her colleagues told her that she had good instincts when it came to judging the actions of others.

"Beyond what I have just done, is there anything else that I can help you with, Peter? Is there anything that you want to discuss with me?"

Again, Sarah watched, and then listened to, both Peter and Dr. Kellman as they spoke to one another before answering her questions.

Peter looked at Nik and leaned toward her, "I know nothing about your laws here, doctor. What do you think I should do, now? I leave with the team tomorrow morning…" He looked down at the floor and didn't, or couldn't, finish what he was saying.

Nik replied, "There isn't anything more that you have to do, Pete. Detective Myers can't harm you now. Isn't that right, Sarah?"

"Yes, that's right, but Mr. Barnes, Sr. said that Myers is kind of sneaky, so we have to be on the lookout for more shenanigans."

"But for now, Pete's safe, isn't he?" Dr. Kellman's eyes were almost pleading with Sarah to tell her that this was so.

"It's simple, really, Dr. Kellman: Myers comes back, you call, and we will come. He's not going to get anywhere on this one, and he knows it." Sarah was matter-of-fact.

"Pete, do you feel safe going back to your hotel?" Nik was worried that Detective Myers might be waiting there for him.

"I hadn't really thought about that." Peter shrugged his shoulders.

"Peter, why don't you go back to your hotel with me? I'll check to make sure that Myers isn't there. I don't mind if it's okay with you." Sarah hefted her briefcase to her shoulder and buttoned her coat.

"That's a wonderful idea, Pete. You could rest and take it easy until this evening. You're still coming to the dinner dance and awards ceremony, aren't you?"

Peter nodded his head and answered her in Russian. "Da, *Yes*, I will be there."

During the ride to his hotel, Sarah attempted to draw Peter out to see what might be going on in his life. In particular, she wanted to know what he thought about Dr. Kellman, and she tried several different tacks to try to get at the same information.

For his part, Peter was very noncommittal. He felt that this attorney had no business asking him such pointed questions about Dr. Kellman.

"It sounds as if Dr. Kellman has been very helpful to you, Peter, am I right?" Sarah looked over at Peter and smiled.

Slowly Peter turned to her, "Yes, she has been. When I first arrived, I was ill, and probably wouldn't have been able to skate, but the doctor helped me, and I have played in all of the games. Then, when Yakov put two of my teammates up to injuring me, she stitched me up, and I was able to play hockey that day, too. When Detective Myers came after me the first time, Dr. Kellman sent Mr. Barnes to help me. And now, she has helped me again, by calling you to take care of Detective Myers."

"Dr. Kellman thinks a great deal of you, doesn't she?" Sarah smiled as she asked this question.

When Peter looked at Sarah, the only adjective that she could think of to describe the look in his eyes was "fierce." She could see that he was angry.

Quietly, and with emphasis on each of his words, Peter answered, "She has been very professional in her assistance to me."

Wow, thought Sarah, this guy is pretty forceful in his defense of Dr. Kellman. I wonder what Mr. Barnes is going to say when I give him my impressions of this situation?

There was a great deal more to this athlete than she had at first thought when she was introduced to him. Her first impression had been that he was very dependent upon Dr. Kellman. Although she was sure that he was very young, maybe twenty or twenty-one years of age, he came across as much more adult. He had a direct gaze, and she realized that, as much as she was appraising him, he was taking her measure, too. So much for first impressions, she decided.

Even though he didn't seem to realize the impact that he had on people, Peter Genchenko nonetheless took charge of a situation, anyway. Of this, Sarah was quite sure.

"Well, Peter, here's your hotel. I'm going to park out front here, and we can go in together and check out the lobby and your room, okay?"

Peter nodded in acquiescence, giving Sarah an enigmatic look. Man, oh man, she thought, Peter Genchenko, you are very intriguing.

As luck would have it, Peter and Sarah shared an elevator with the bellhop that had helped Peter check in when the doctor was with him. The bellhop eyed Sarah the whole time that they were in the elevator together. Peter kept his gaze on the doors, but a small smile took shape on his lips.

When they reached the concierge level, Sarah was impressed that Peter had been put on this floor. Where do these people get the money to do this, she wondered?

Peter opened the door to his suite, and Sarah went in as he held the door.

"Would you care for something to drink, Ms. Williams?" Peter was the good host.

"Umm…no thank you. I just wanted to make sure that Detective Myers wasn't going to try to pull something on you. Have you been in this suite for the entire week?"

"Yes, the doctor checked me into this room because Yakov had turned what would have been my room back to the hotel on the day that I arrived. This suite was all they had left, so Dr. Kellman authorized my staying in this room."

"Why would Yakov Popov have done that? Didn't he know that you were going to arrive that day?"

"He was aware of my schedule, but he released my room anyway. The doctor arranged to put me here because there was nothing else available."

Sarah was nodding, "He wanted to make your life as difficult as possible. Is that it?"

"Yakov was creatively single-minded when it came to causing me as much trouble as he possibly could."

Sarah handed him a business card and started toward the door, "Well, Peter, everything looks okay here to me. However, if you have any further problems with Detective Myers, call me."

"Ms. Williams?" Peter, who was taller than she, looked down at her as she stood before him and said, "Dr. Kellman is the kindest, most honest person that I have ever met. I am the better for having known her, and she may have, in fact, saved my life. For that, I will always be grateful to her. I don't know what you were trying to get me to say to you about Dr. Kellman while we were in your car, but I wanted you to know how *I* feel about *her*."

Peter's eyes held hers for several moments, and Sarah could see that he was sincere. The anger that she had seen earlier had left his eyes.

Sarah felt chastised, but gently so. She realized that Peter Genchenko was the type of man who would stand up for what, or who, he believed in. She respected that.

Chapter 22

As soon as Sarah Williams departed, Peter called Ilya's room to see if he could come to visit him. Mickey answered the telephone and told Peter that Ilya would really enjoy seeing him.

Peter, Ilya, and Mickey sat and talked, with Peter doing some translation, as needed. Then the three watched old hockey videos on television.

Peter gave Ilya a play by play of their team's last, championship, game from his vantage point on the ice. When it was his turn to talk about his part in the games, Mickey told both Ilya and Peter what it was like for an athletic trainer.

"I didn't really understand, until I worked with your team, what it meant to be an athletic trainer. You guys have been a huge challenge." Mickey told them.

Ilya ran his thin fingers through his unruly red hair and replied with a chuckle, "What a surprise, Mickey. What do you say to that, Peter?"

Peter tilted his head to the side and replied in a serious vein, "We have not always been easy, but this week has been one of the worst we have ever had, I think, from the perspective that many things, some very bad things, have happened. For instance, your knee, Ilya, and the hotel fire, and Yakov's death; I think that we *have been* a huge challenge, as Mickey just said." He didn't mention the attack on himself as one of the bad things.

Peter wanted to change the subject, and asked them if they were getting hungry. It was decided that they would order some room service for lunch. When the food arrived, the three of them made short work of the sandwiches, fries, and salads that they had ordered.

"How are your workouts coming along, Ilya? Are you going to be able to travel tomorrow?" Peter hoped that Ilya was recovering well, and that he could go home with the team.

"I am surprising even myself, Petrosha. Mickey is strict with me, and works my poor knee very hard." Ilya looked at Mickey as he spoke, and then laughed.

"Yeah, I think that Ilya's goin' home with all of you tomorrow. Coach Grigory watched his workout this morning in the weight room here in the hotel. Dr. Kellman has been watching him, too, and she's happy with the way Ilya's been progressing."

Ilya stretched, and adjusted himself in his wheelchair. "The only thing that I really don't like very well is sitting in this chair. I've been walking a little but it's slow and very painful still."

"Nonetheless, Ilya, you have been well cared for here. Especially so, since you might have had to wait a very long time for your surgery at home." Peter was happy that Ilya had received such good care.

"Da, da, I know that I am very fortunate. I won't forget the doctor's kindness, either. She has made sure that I have gotten the best of care, and I am grateful to her for that." Ilya's eyes misted for a moment.

"Mickey, will you be with Ilya this evening for the awards celebration?" Peter wanted to make sure that Ilya would have some help getting there.

What would it be like to have a car, and to do whatever one pleased, wondered Peter? If he had a car, *he* could take his friend to the celebration tonight. Well, perhaps that wasn't so. He'd have to learn how to drive a car, first, wouldn't he?

"Oh, sure, the Doc's already arranged a van for us. She said that Ilya needed good transportation and help when he got there, so the van's got a paramedic driver. What do you think of that?"

"I think it's wonderful, Mickey. She thought of everything, didn't she?" Peter thought of how much effort the doctor had invested in helping him, too.

"Yeah. Well, at first I didn't understand her, but I think that I do now. Most doctors are perfectionists in some way or another and the Doc's no exception. She kept on me when I first started working with her. I thought that she just wanted things her own way, but I finally realized that she was really looking out for the athletes."

Peter could see that Ilya was tiring, "You need to rest, my friend. Otherwise, you won't be able to keep up with me tonight."

At that, Ilya and Mickey both laughed. They realized that they probably could not do so even if both were at their healthiest.

"I'm getting used to an afternoon nap, Petrosha. What will I do when I have to go home?"

"Grigory will install a cot for you near our bench at the practice arena, what else?" Peter shrugged.

Ilya couldn't contain himself. He laughed long and hard at the ridiculous picture that Peter's words had painted.

"C'mon Ilya, I'll tuck you into bed. It's time for your medicine, anyway." Mickey was shaking his head at the two friends' sense of humor.

Peter got up and walked toward the door. "Tonight, then…we will celebrate our good fortune."

It was only four o'clock, but the skies were already darkening as Peter looked outside through a hallway window. He took the stairs, rather than the elevator to get back to his room. He had enjoyed his visit with Ilya. The earlier loneliness and sadness that he had felt while he explored downtown Indianapolis had been dispelled, if only for a short time.

The telephone rang, and Nik picked it up. She had been busy straightening up her condo, because she had neglected it while she had been the Neanderthals' doctor. It had gotten to the point where she couldn't stand it anymore.

"Hello." Nik wasn't happy with the interruption.

"Hi, hon', it's me," Ron said.

Uh-oh, thought Nik, he doesn't sound too chipper, "What's up, Ron?"

"What time do we have to leave for the dinner dance?"

"It starts at six thirty, Ron, and we should probably leave my place at a quarter after. Is there a problem?"

"Well, no, there isn't, but I might not get to your place until about six thirty. I didn't pick up my shirts at the cleaners, and I'm going to have to go out there to pick them up."

"That sounds like a problem to me, Ron." Nik gave a short laugh.

"We shouldn't be too late, Nik. It's about ten after four now, and I'm clearing out my messages and telephone calls. I'll go to the cleaners at about five, okay?"

Again Nik chuckled a little, "I don't have any choice, do I?"

Ron hesitated, "I could meet you there, but I'd rather go together if we could, Nik."

"That's okay, Ron. I'll be ready and waiting when you get here."

Ron was relieved that she wasn't taking exception to his little problem. "Great, that's great, hon'. I should be there to pick you up at six thirty. We won't miss much, either. These things never start on time. Oh, and I wanted to tell you something funny about how nepotism works, because you'll see it, well, I should say, hear it, tonight."

Nik was puzzled, "Nepotism? What's that got to do with this evening?"

"Garibaldi, your favorite headache, has a nephew who started a big band, and does music for wedding receptions, bar mitzvah's, proms, and the like."

Nik's heart sank, "So the nephew is our entertainment tonight? Great...I can just hear these young athletes when they get an earful of this big band. Doesn't Garibaldi know what the younger generation likes?"

"Even if he does, he probably doesn't care, and tonight might be a big thing for the nephew. It'll give him a boost, if not a good paycheck. Garibaldi once used a cousin to teach one of the anatomy and physiology classes at the med school, cadaver lab no less, and it was a disaster. The guy was definitely not professor material, even though he had M.D. behind his name. The students said he was actually afraid of dead bodies."

"You're just full of information, Ron. See you at six-thirty."

As Nik hung up the telephone, she was shaking her head. Well, she could take earplugs to prevent ear damage from the big band.

When the time came to get ready for the celebration, Peter dressed in his only presentable clothing; a black sweater and slacks that had just come back from the one hour cleaning service in the hotel. He had taken the time to shave his face smooth, and had combed his hair into a passably manageable mane.

Lacking even the fundamental articles for his toilette, he had no lotion for his face after he shaved, Peter used the lotion provided in his bathroom. It didn't have a sweet fragrance, and it made his scraped face feel better. At least he hadn't cut himself shaving.

Peter studied the healing wound above his eye, and removed the steri-strips. Gently, he scrubbed around the wound to remove the tape residue. Luckily, it didn't re-open, but the healing scar was darker than the surrounding skin. He shrugged. Another battle scar, he decided.

More than ever before, Peter felt the need to be presentable tonight. A cautious excitement was building within him. He would dance with her. Even if it were just one more time, he would dance with her.

Grigory told Peter that the team would go to the party in a van. However, Peter didn't want to wait for the van, he wanted to go on ahead to look over the accommodations. He threw on his coat, wrapped a threadbare scarf around his neck, pulled on his well-worn gloves, and started out for the downtown Shrine Auditorium.

The wind had picked up and had caused the top layer of snow to swirl around Peter's feet as he walked and jogged toward the Shrine. It was now very dark, about five forty-five, and all the Christmas lights were lit in the downtown area. The circle was beautiful, with lights sparkling from the monument to the ground.

The Shrine Auditorium was colorfully lighted as Peter approached. He saw that the building was several stories tall, and was of an interesting architecture, although he couldn't exactly say what it might be; Ottoman perhaps?

Peter bounded up the steps and presented his athlete's identification tag at the door. The nicely dressed older woman standing guard at the door smiled up at Peter.

"You're a little early, aren't you?"

Peter agreed, "Yes, I am. Is that going to be a problem?"

"No, everything's ready for the athletes and the rest of the dignitaries for the International Winter Games. You can go right in. The Russian tables are to the left in the ballroom and toward the front of the room."

Peter found the coatroom, checked his coat and scarf, and then began to explore the building. He located the Russian athletes' table first, and then walked around the ballroom. He wanted to find a place where he could watch for Dr. Kellman's arrival.

As he searched for his vantage point, strolling, hands in pockets, he saw that the stage was set up for a large band. He smiled at the thought of dancing with the doctor to the sounds of a Forties-era big band. The ballroom was beautiful. The walls were ornate, but tastefully so. He could see an Ottoman influence inside the building as he had outside. The colors were those found in precious stones, and the trim was done in gold. He didn't, however, see anything that had a gaudy appearance. On the stage, the heavy curtains appeared to be of a velvet material that changed colors with the lights illuminating them. The overall effect was one of sumptuous luxury.

The ceiling had a myriad of small points of light; stars, he thought, that twinkled above the dance floor. Again, he smiled. I will dance with her under the stars.

Peter found what he was looking for near the coatroom adjacent to the foyer. There was a stairway that circled up to a mezzanine, and he could stand by the railing and see everyone who came into the building.

As guests began arriving, Peter saw that most of them were dressed formally. He wished that he could be better dressed, but there was nothing to be done about it. Anyway, he believed that the doctor would not judge him by his clothing.

Peter saw his teammates coming into the foyer with Grigory, Vladimir, Mickey, Tom, and Rebecca. He could see that they were in a celebratory mood, laughing and talking. He had also told Mickey that he wouldn't be riding to the dinner dance with the team so that they wouldn't wait for him.

The arrivals eventually slowed and were down to a trickle of two or three people every few minutes. But the doctor had yet to appear. The band began playing and Peter recognized the music. It was pure big band: "In the Mood." He could see a clock in the foyer. It was now six forty-five. She is late, he thought. Why is she so late? And then he felt a cold stab of dismay. What if she isn't coming at all?

At five minutes to seven Peter started down the mezzanine stairway, disappointment slowing his steps. He was halfway down the stairs when he heard her voice in the entryway near the coat check. He stopped, wanting to make sure that he wasn't just hearing things. Yes, it was the doctor's voice, and she sounded upset, but he couldn't make out her words.

The doctor, with her fiancé at her side, came into Peter's line of vision, and he again felt dismayed. What had he been thinking? Of course she would be with her fiancé tonight. They stopped in front of the coat check counter, and Dr. Michael took his own coat off and laid it down on the countertop. The doctor stood waiting for him to help her with her coat, but he was looking toward the tables in the ballroom.

Nik started to take her own coat off, and had one arm partially out of a sleeve, when Ron turned to her with an animated look on his face. What now, she wondered?

"Oh, Nik, Sully's over there," Ron nodded his head toward the ballroom, "and I've got to talk to him for a minute. It'll just take a minute."

To Nik's surprise and chagrin, Ron hurried into the ballroom, leaving her with one arm in, and one arm out of her coat. If she had been upset with him before, she was now fully angry.

A familiar voice, rich and deep in its resonance, asked in Russian, "May I help you with your coat?"

Startled, Nik turned to see Peter standing behind her. Her face lit up and she smiled when she saw him. Peter's spirit lifted with the brightness of her smile.

"*Yes*, I'd really like some help with my coat."

She was wearing a white coat of soft wool, belted at the waist. Her shining dark hair was pulled up on one side and held with a pearl-studded comb, showing a delicately shaped ear. The other side flowed like silk to her shoulder. Her fragrance combined with the cold that she had just come out of, producing a wonderfully fresh scent.

Peter placed his hands on the doctor's shoulders, and helped her out of her coat. He took the red leather gloves that she was holding and placed them in the pocket of her coat. He then handed it to the coat check lady who eyed him from head to toe in admiration before taking the coat and putting it on a hanger. She returned with a tag, and Peter gave her a tip as he took the tag from her.

He handed the tag to the doctor, "You will need this when you leave tonight."

Nik nodded but her throat was dry with emotion, and she could say nothing.

She was wearing red. She wore a soft cashmere knit dress that skimmed her slender, yet shapely, figure and fell to calf length, with a slit to the knee on one side. At her throat she wore a single strand of pearls that matched the pearls at her ears. Her feet were wrapped in red, strappy heels that looked too delicate to walk in, and he noticed that she had painted her toenails red.

"You look beautiful tonight, Dr. Kellman." Peter said quietly, for her ears only.

Nik stammered, "Thank you…so do you. And Pete, please call me Niki. You don't have to call me 'doctor' anymore."

They both laughed awkwardly for a moment. For some reason, Nik felt as shy as a young girl at her first prom.

Peter said one word, "Dance." It wasn't a question or an invitation, but a statement of fact. They would dance.

He held her hand as they walked out onto the crowded dance floor. The bandleader was announcing that the band would play a set of three romantic songs from the Big Band Era, beginning with "Moonlight Serenade."

Peter took Niki in his arms and put one hand at the small of her back. With the other, he gently caressed her hand, holding it against his chest. The soft cashmere material under his hand at her back moved sensuously against the satin of her undergarment. Peter's heart turned over.

They began to dance, moving slowly to the beat of the music. At first, she maintained a small distance from Peter as they swayed to the music, but then, as his hand gently pressed at her back, pulling her toward him, she yielded and moved against him. She was his, if only for this small moment in time, and Peter's heart soared.

By the end of the first song, Niki's head rested on Peter's shoulder. The band swung into "Stairway to the Stars" deftly, without missing a beat.

Niki opened her eyes and looked up into Pete's face. He smiled at her and then looked up at the ceiling. Her eyes followed his, and she was delighted to see the multitude of stars there, artificial though they may be.

"We are dancing under the stars, you and I, Niki, and I will never forget this night or this feeling." He pulled her gently even closer to him, and she again yielded, resting her head on his shoulder.

The last song included a vocalist with three backup singers for "Blue Moon." The words struck a chord with Peter; "...now I'm no longer alone..." He held Niki, both arms now around her, dancing to the hypnotic beat, as the band played.

The dance floor was crowded, and they moved in a small circle on the floor. But it was as if there was no one but the two of them, Pete and Niki, dancing close together, melting into one another.

When the last note of the music died away, the lights came up on the dance floor. Peter continued to hold Niki for a moment, and she did not move away from him until the other dancers began to move off the floor.

"There you are. Good God, Nik, I've been looking for you everywhere!"

Peter looked at Ron, and Nik saw that the old saying, "If looks could kill" was an apt statement.

Ron nodded in greeting to Peter, using only his last name, "Genchenko."

Peter did not return the favor. He continued to stare at Ron.

Turning to Nik, Ron said, "They're about to start serving dinner, and we need to go to our table now."

Nik responded slowly, "What table? I thought that I was going to sit with my team. I'd really rather sit with them."

Nik put a hand to her forehead. She was having difficulty thinking straight. Her heart was beating rapidly, and she actually felt unsteady on her feet, unaccustomed as she was to her footwear. Peter placed his hand under her elbow to steady her.

"Garibaldi has a table reserved for all of the physicians who have worked with the athletes during the games. We are all supposed to sit there. I thought you knew about the seating arrangements, Nik."

Nik shook her head. "No…no, I didn't realize…"

"Niki, are you all right?" Peter spoke to her in Russian.

Turning slowly toward him she replied, "Da, Petrosha."

"*Nik, we have to go to our table.*" Ron was becoming exasperated with Nik's behavior, and he reached for her hand as if to pull her away.

"Just one moment, Dr. Michael, I think that Dr. Kellman might not be feeling well." Peter put his large hand on Ron's outstretched arm briefly; long enough so that Ron was aware that he shouldn't continue to insist that Nik leave with him just now.

Nik looked from one to the other. She knew that her behavior must be odd to both men, and she wondered how she could avoid a scene.

After a few moments, Nik made a decision and spoke to Pete in Russian, "Petrosha, I am fine, so don't worry about me. I should go with Ron to sit with the other doctors. *I don't want to*, but it's the right thing to do."

Peter nodded his head, and replied in Russian. "I understand, and I really wasn't going to cause any trouble for you; I just wanted to make sure that you were all right."

Nik looked up at him, and her eyes held a certain sadness that he understood only too well. She then turned and walked away with Dr. Michael, who shot a glare back at Peter.

Peter stood rooted to the spot, looking after them as they walked away from him. He thought of his mother's words again, "Can you see her soul in her eyes, Peter?" His answer now would be, "Yes, oh yes I can, and it is as beautiful as she is."

Heavy-hearted, Peter went to sit with his teammates. As luck would have it, Rebecca had saved a seat for him next to herself. Dinner service was well underway, but Peter had no appetite for it. He watched Niki and Dr. Michael at their not-too-distant table. Niki was directly in his line of vision, and he couldn't stop looking at her even though Rebecca talked to him incessantly.

Grigory was in good spirits, "Genchenko, you and Dr. Kellman made a handsome couple out there on the dance floor. At first, I didn't recognize her. How beautiful she looks in red! I noticed, too, that she has slender ankles. Who knew when all she wore to work with us were those baggy, dull trousers?"

Vladimir added his observations, "You must have been practicing your footwork with the doctor, Peter; she stayed with you, not missing a beat, for the entire medley."

Ilya grinned at Peter and leaned toward him as he spoke, "Don't worry about what those two say to you, Petrosha, they are more jealous than you know. After all, you got to dance with the most beautiful woman here tonight, and they will not."

Ilya's comments made Peter smile. He had briefly allowed his anger with Dr. Michael to cloud the wonderful feeling that he had experienced dancing with Niki, but Ilya helped him to understand his good fortune.

"Thank you for reminding me, my friend."

Peter closed his eyes for a moment as he thought of how he had felt with his hand at the small of her back, sliding sensuously over her soft knit dress and the satin undergarment beneath as they danced.

The dinner service was winding down, the lights were lowered, and the band began to play again. When the band started a Beatles medley, Rebecca grabbed Peter's hand.

"Dance with me, Peter." Her grin was infectious.

Reluctantly, Peter got up from his chair and followed her to the dance floor. When he passed Niki's table, he looked over at her and smiled. Her face, however, was solemn as she watched him walk by with Rebecca.

To Peter's surprise, Rebecca was a good dance partner. Of course, she talked non-stop as they danced, but she seemed to anticipate his moves, and he found himself enjoying the dance. Occasionally, he glanced in the direction of Niki's table, but he didn't see her again. Then he realized that she was on the dance floor with Dr. Michael.

Nik watched over Ron's shoulder as Peter danced with Rebecca. She was uncomfortable watching them. Could she be feeling envy, jealousy? All she knew was that *she* wanted to be the one dancing with him, and that she didn't want him to dance with Rebecca, or anyone else.

Nik was relieved when the music ended. Without a word to Ron, she turned and walked back to their table to sit down.

Peter also felt relief when the music stopped. Rebecca held onto his arm, insisting that they dance another dance, but he declined as kindly as he could, and headed for his team's table with Rebecca in tow.

The band played for another half hour, and then the lights came up. The committee members for the International Winter Games filed up onto the stage and the portly, balding committee chairman took the microphone.

"Good evening, ladies and gentlemen. Tonight we celebrate the completion of the International Winter Games. In each sports category: women's and men's basketball, women's and men's volleyball, women's and men's gymnastics, and men's hockey, we have awarded first, second, and third places.

"This evening, we are going to give awards to the most valuable player in each of the aforementioned sports categories. As we call the names of those receiving awards, please come forward to the stage: Beth Byrde; Women's Basketball, Steven Lynn; Men's Basketball, Alysse Fedorova; Women's Volleyball, Christopher Aaron; Men's Volleyball, Sarah Tyler; Women's Gymnastics, Sergei Orlovski; Men's Gymnastics, Peter Genchenko; Men's Hockey."

When Peter heard his name called, it surprised him enough that he didn't move for several moments. Rebecca came out of her chair and began jumping up and down and clapping her hands. Nik watched as Peter finally got up and made his way to the stage.

Applause filled the room as the recipients began coming forward. As they filed up onto the stage, the applause increased.

Grigory spoke to his athletes, "This is wonderful; Genchenko deserves this honor, and it brings honor to all of us as Russians!" He looked around the table acknowledging each of them, even Vladimir.

Nik was very happy for Pete. He had overcome tremendous odds, had worked hard, played hard, and carried his team to victory. She was certain of that. Without Peter, his tenacity and skill, the Russian team would probably not have won the championship.

As she watched, each athlete was given the opportunity to say a few words as the awards were presented. Pete was last, and as he took the podium, Nik's heart almost stopped.

Shoulders straight, and head erect, Peter paused a moment before speaking. In the spotlight, his hair was shining gold. He looked directly at Nik as he began to speak.

In his deep and mellow voice, Peter told the gathering that he felt very fortunate to have been able to compete against some of the best men's hockey teams in the world. He told them that he was accepting the award on behalf of his teammates, his coaches, and Dr. Nikola Kellman.

"All of them, and especially Dr. Kellman, played a large part in placing me here on this stage tonight, and I thank them from the bottom of my heart."

Chapter 23

Saturday, Early Morning

Peter lay in bed, trying to get comfortable. The clock on his bedside table showed two-thirty. When he had returned to his hotel, he had lost what little he had eaten of the meal at the Awards Dinner, but it had not relieved the pain in his abdomen. In the beginning, the pain had radiated throughout his abdomen from his pubis to his rib cage. When he had lightly pressed his abdomen with his fingertips, and released the pressure, it hurt with a deep and burning pain. Too, his abdomen was rigid. So rigid in fact, that he could not even lie on either side. Lying on his back was painful, too, but that was the only position that he could tolerate. The pain eventually localized in the right side of his abdomen, and then he was sure that it was his hernia.

He had experienced pain and discomfort from his right-sided hernia many times before, but this pain was different. It was unrelenting, and didn't go away with his previously successful measures such as standing on his head, reversing the tension, until the pain and pressure went away.

Grigory had told the team to be packed, dressed, and ready to board the airport shuttle no later than six-thirty in the morning. Peter was packed and had laid out his clothing for travel, but now he was beginning to realize that he couldn't travel in his condition.

He wanted to call Niki. In spite of his pain, he kept thinking of how she had looked when she left the Awards Banquet. She had turned to him, offered her hand in congratulation for his most valuable player award, and had placed her other hand on top of his when he had shaken her hand. She had repeated to him the words he had spoken to her when they were dancing, about "never forgetting this night", had smiled a melancholy smile and walked away on the arm of her fiancé, turning once to look back at him.

Peter broke out in a sweat, but then he began shivering too. Nausea washed over him in waves, and he made a supreme effort to get out of bed, barely making it into the bathroom. He lay on the cool tiles of the floor for several minutes and then made a decision. He had to call someone for help. He knew that Mickey was still staying with Ilya in the hotel, and Peter was now desperate.

Bent forward, because the pain in his abdomen made it unbearable to stand erect, Peter made his way back into the bedroom area. For a moment, he puzzled over Ilya's room number. He was having difficulty keeping his thoughts together. Finally, he dialed what he thought was the number.

On the fifth ring, Mickey answered in a sleep-dulled voice, "Yeah?"

"Mickey, it's Peter. I'm...having a problem, and I'm not sure what to do. Can you help me?"

Mickey asked nervously, "What's the problem, Peter? Is it serious? Should I call Dr. Kellman? Or...I could come down and check you out and call an ambulance. It's your call."

Peter wiped the sweat from his face with a forearm, "Please call Dr. Kellman, Mickey. I know that she can help me. I'll wait for her to get here before I do anything else."

"Okay Peter. I'll call her right now, and then I'll come on up to your room."

"You will have to get a special key from the registration desk, Mickey. I'm on the concierge level."

Ilya awoke in the next room and called out to Mickey, "Is there a problem? Is something wrong?"

Mickey went to his door, "Yeah, Peter's not feeling too good, and he asked me to call the Doc."

"Is there anything I can do?" Ilya was now awake.

"Not right now, Ilya, I think that I'd better get hold of the Doc. She can help him better than anybody."

Mickey fumbled with his billfold, trying to extract the card that the Doc had given him with emergency numbers where he could reach her after hours if Ilya had a problem. He sorted through his cards twice before he found the card, and then he had trouble dialing the telephone.

Finally, the Doc's telephone was ringing. Please, please be there, Doc. If she wasn't there, he didn't know what he would do.

Nik's telephone was at her bedside, and she answered in a sleepy voice on the second ring, "Hello?"

"Doc, it's Mickey. There's a problem…"

"Is something wrong with Ilya?" Nik was immediately awake.

"No, Doc, it isn't Ilya. I just got a 'phone call from Peter, and he sounds real sick. I told him that I'd call you and then come up to his room."

Nik felt her stomach tighten, "I'll get dressed, and come right over. If you think that he should go to the hospital before I get there, send him, and don't worry, I'll find you."

"Okay, Doc, I'm on my way to his room right now."

Nik jumped out of bed, shed her nightgown, and ran to her closet where she grabbed jeans, a sweatshirt and a pair of boots. As she passed her dresser, she pulled open a drawer and grabbed underwear and socks. She dressed hopping from foot to foot, almost toppling at one point. When she was dressed, more or less, she grabbed her coat and purse and ran out the door, locking it behind her.

Nik didn't know how long it took her to get to the Westin from her downtown condo, because she was intent on staying on the road. The temperature had dipped below ten degrees, and there was ice on everything, making it very difficult to drive.

At the Westin, she left her car at the entrance, flashed her physician's badge from the International Winter Games to the bellman there, and headed for the elevator, where she found that she couldn't activate it without the special concierge level key. Nik dashed over to the registration desk, again flashed her badge, and quickly told the person there what was happening. After she got the key, she asked that an ambulance be called.

Nik's heart was pounding wildly as she ran back to the elevators. Once inside, she was frustrated at the slowness of her ascent. Come on...come *on*!

The doors opened with a "ding" and Nik ran to Peter's door. It was open, and she saw that Mickey was waiting for her.

"I'm glad to see you, Doc." Mickey looked relieved.

Nik approached Peter who was lying on his left side on the bed. His eyes followed her as she came into the room. She could see that they were dulled with pain.

"Pete, what's wrong?" There was anguish in her voice.

Peter touched his abdomen on the right side and uttered one word, "Bol, *Pain*."

She took his hand, and it was hot to the touch. When she put her hand on his forehead, he was wet with perspiration, and he was hot. She saw that Pete's lips were dry, but Nik knew that she shouldn't try to give him anything to drink.

"Pete, I'm going to check your abdomen. I'll try not to hurt you, but I have to see exactly what's going on."

Nik spoke to Mickey, "I've already called an ambulance. Do you think that you could keep an eye on the elevator to show them where to go?"

"Sure, Doc, I can do that. Is there anything I can help you with here for Peter?"

"No, there isn't anything to be done until we get him to the hospital, Mickey." Nik's eyes felt hot with unshed tears.

Mickey stepped outside the door, and Nik pulled the covers down to Peter's abdomen. To her surprise, he wasn't wearing pajamas, and she worried that he would become chilled. She quickly tested him for rebound tenderness, McBurney's pain, or herniation, and noted that his abdomen was rigid and board-like. There was no sign of herniation or incarceration of the bowel, but his other signs were positive. She then pulled the covers back up to his chin.

Peter began to gag, and Nik grabbed a towel for him, as there was no basin. He brought very little up, but she saw that it was probably bile, from the yellow-green color. Nik moistened a washcloth with warm water in the bathroom and gently wiped his face.

"Spaseeba, *thank you*...I'm sorry, so sorry," he said weakly.

"It's all right, Pete, it's all right. You can't help it if you're sick. The ambulance will be here soon." Nik wanted to hold him, to comfort him, and her throat tightened with emotion. She gently laid a hand on his cheek, and he looked at her for a long moment before closing his eyes.

She went into the bathroom, and found a bathrobe hanging on the door. She brought it to Peter, and asked if he might be able to put it on before the ambulance crew arrived.

"Da, I think so." His voice had a hoarse quality.

The look on his face, however, made her wonder if he could. His brows were knit, and his mouth was pulled down into a grimace.

Nik pulled the covers away from his shoulders and put one and then the other arm into the sleeves of the bathrobe.

"Okay, Pete, here's the hard part. I've got to slide this down under your hips. Do you think that you can lift them high enough to do that?"

He smiled a fleeting smile at her. "I don't know, but I'll try."

They were successful, and Nik loosely tied the sash of the bathrobe as the ambulance crew came into the room.

"Hi, I'm Jack Terhune. You must be Dr. Kellman." One of the ambulance crewmembers came over to Nik and offered his hand.

"Yes, and this is Peter Genchenko. He's in a lot of pain, and I checked him for McBurney's Point pain, rebound tenderness, rigidity, and potential incarceration. He has a right inguinal or femoral hernia. He was positive for the first three, but I couldn't determine whether he has herniation or incarceration. I'm going to admit him for a surgical work-up. Let's get him ready to go, and then I'll contact the surgeon on call."

Jack bent down and took Peter's blood pressure, asking him questions as he did so in regard to Peter's history and the duration of symptoms, or any possible mitigating factors. After listening with a stethoscope to Peter's heart, lungs, and abdomen, and taking pulse, respirations, and temperature, he wrote down his findings quickly.

"Okay, Missy, he's ready for transport." Jack spoke to his partner, who was getting ready to assist Peter in moving to the gurney.

Turning to Nik, Jack said, "His temp's 103 and heart rate and respirations are up, too. I didn't want to repeat your exam, so I'll write down your findings, and you can sign, if you would, please."

Nik nodded and watched as Jack deftly stepped over to help Peter in his transfer to the gurney.

Mickey looked in the door and asked Nik, "Should I go on back and stay with Ilya, now?"

"I think that's best, Mickey. I'll go with Peter to the hospital, and I'll let you know what's happening. Could you get in touch with Coach Grigory for me? He needs to know about Peter."

"Sure Doc. Ilya's pretty worked up about this. Is there anything that I can tell him to make him feel better?"

Nik's reply surprised Mickey, "Tell Ilya that Peter's in good hands, and that he is being taken care of by those who care about him."

"Doctor? We're okay to go." Jack was at the doorway, ready to push Peter, on the gurney, into the hall. Nik sat next to Peter on the way to the hospital. When he reached out and took her hand, she was happy to hold his.

Inside the ambulance, the doctor took the patient's hand and held it. Missy, the EMT in the back of the ambulance with them, saw what the doctor had done. Well, they must be good friends, she thought. Most doctors didn't hold their patients' hands anymore.

Peter was admitted to the surgical services unit. His surgeon was pacing in the hall outside Peter's room, awaiting final word on the tests that he had ordered.

When Nik conferred with Peter's surgeon, Dr. Ralph Edward, it was decided that he should be listed on the schedule as an emergency exploratory laparotomy.

"Genchenko's labs just got here and they could mean that he has a hot appendix, an incarceration, or some other nasty condition that we don't see right now. Anyway, his tests warrant surgical intervention, so he's going in as an emergency laparotomy." Dr. Edward spoke rapidly to Nik.

Continuing, he said, "His labs show that he's a bit anemic, and his total protein and albumin are a little low, too. He's an athlete, isn't he? Don't they eat better than that?"

Nik bit her lip, "Yes, when they can afford to, I guess. You don't know the whole story here."

"Well, *enlighten me.* I need to know everything I can about this patient before we go into surgery."

Nik thought, *Edward, you are an ass,* but she also realized that she had gotten the best surgeon for Peter.

"He's Russian, he works for a living when he's not playing hockey, and he can't afford to eat three squares the way we do here. He eats when he's playing hockey for the Russians, but he's on his own most of the time. If you look at his various injuries, you will see that, among his scars are bullet holes and marks of past beatings. Anything else you want to know?"

Dr. Edward replied, "Oh, shit, he's one of those challenging cases, isn't he?"

A scrub nurse from surgery came in to tell Dr. Edward that she had opened his room and they would be setting up the back table and mayo stand when he was ready.

"You're in OR 3, Dr. Edward, and we are ready for whatever you want to bring our way."

"Okay, Lucy, and thanks. We'll be in when Matt Jackson gets here."

Nik asked, "Is he doing anesthesia?"

Dr. Edward smiled, "You don't think that I'd use anyone but the best, do you? I've got Matt Jackson lined up. In fact, I think he's here right now to do his pre-anesthesia work-up."

Dr. Jackson came shuffling in wearing his green scrubs and humming, "Tell Me Something Good." He and Dr. Edward 'high-fived' each other and said almost in unison how they *really liked* being gotten out of bed to do surgery in the wee hours of the morning.

"Well, let's see what we've got here…" Dr. Jackson read the surgeon's handwritten history and physical, and then whistled.

"This guy's Peter Genchenko, the Russian hockey player? Ralph, did you catch this guy in any of the games they just played? He's a regular dynamo on the ice. I took my son, who's in a junior hockey league, to two of the games. Even when he's injured, this guy could skate rings around the other athletes, no kidding."

Dr. Edward nodded, "Well, he's not going to be skating anytime soon, Matt, so get in there and check him out so we can go to surgery."

Nik left while the doctors were talking to each other and went back into Peter's room. His eyes were closed and he was lying on his back, his knees flexed to take the pressure off of his abdomen. His hair was wet with perspiration, and his breathing was rapid and shallow.

Nik dampened a washcloth in warm water, wrung it out, and came over to him, calling his name softly.

"Pete, I'm going to wipe your face with a washcloth."

Peter, his eyes still closed, nodded to her in assent. As she gently cleansed his face, he opened his eyes, and they were filled with pain. Please, God, help him, she prayed. He doesn't deserve to suffer like this. Nik held his hand and told him that he would be going to surgery very soon. At that moment, Dr. Matthew Jackson came into the room to do a pre-anesthesia examination on Peter.

Peter was so thirsty that he could hardly speak because his tongue nearly stuck to the roof of his mouth. The pain came in waves, and when he gagged now, nothing came up. Niki was holding his hand, and he was very grateful to have her there.

Dr. Jackson pulled up a chair next to Peter, explained why he was there, and told Peter that if he couldn't answer some of his questions, he would see if Dr. Kellman could help out. Dr. Jackson's face was kind, and he told Peter that he would keep the history short.

"Nik, maybe you could help me here. I want to check his vitals for baseline readings."

In Russian, Nik told Peter, "I'm going to help Dr. Jackson take your blood pressure and temperature, Pete."

True to his word, Dr. Jackson's examination was quick. Lucy, the pre-op nurse lightly medicated Peter before the orderly came to take him to surgery.

Nik touched his face and told him, "I'll be here when you wake up, Pete."

Peter looked up at her, "Thank you, Niki, for staying with me."

Nik held his hand and walked alongside the cart until they came to the restricted surgical area, and then she stood outside watching his cart go down the hall until the automatic doors closed completely. Tears of helplessness welled up in her eyes, but she didn't wipe them away.

"How is Genchenko doing?"

Nik looked behind her and saw Grigory standing there. The tears spilled down her cheeks.

"He's just gone into surgery."

Nik looked down at the floor as her tears began to fall. Her shoulders shook with silent sobs.

Grigory said nothing, but took her in his arms to comfort her. Doctor, doctor, he thought, what is *this* all about?

Nik struggled to get control of herself and then stood back, wiping the tears away with her fingertips, "I'm sorry, Grigory, really sorry. It's just that..."

He studied her face and said, "Genchenko's lucky to have someone like you in his corner, looking out for him. With the exceptions of his mother and sister, I doubt that he has been so fortunate before."

Nik didn't know how to reply to Grigory at first, but then she spoke quietly, "I think that you like Pete much more than you let on. He deserves to have people that care about him. He's as good a human being as I have ever met."

Grigory slowly folded his big frame into a chair, bowed his head, and nodded in agreement, "Yes, he is a decent man who tries to do the right thing. If I could have had a son, I would have wanted him to be like Peter.

"Let me tell you a story. Peter's secondary school hockey coach told me much of his history. The coach wanted to help Peter, because he could see how talented he was. Even so, that coach knew that Peter was going nowhere because of his father. Peter could not go to university, and no one would touch him in regard to his sport. That's why the coach asked me to put Peter on my team. Peter used a friend's name because he wouldn't have been considered, otherwise, with the name Genchenko. Ivan's son started winning games for us before the Party knew who he was. He was good enough to earn a place on the team in *spite of* his name. Peter hasn't had an easy life."

"I think I know why you were so angry with Pete when you found out that he had a physical problem that he didn't tell you about. He disappointed you, didn't he? He kept the truth from you. Do you think that you could have been reacting the way you might have if he were your son?"

Grigory looked at her from beneath his dark, craggy brows, cleared his throat and replied, "Perhaps..."

Nik smiled and nodded at him, "You aren't nearly as gruff as you pretend to be."

Grigory shrugged, "Do you know why I went with Peter when that stupid detective decided to take him for questioning at the militia...the police station?"

It was Nik's turn to shrug, "I don't know; expedience, maybe?"

He cleared his throat before answering, "No, I actually wanted to see what Detective Myers was up to. I wanted to know what *he knew*, and I didn't want Peter to catch the worst of what might happen."

"You wanted to protect Pete if you could. He told me how grateful he was for your presence."

Grigory rubbed a stubbled jaw, "Yes, Peter thanked me for that. But Detective Myers hasn't given up yet. He called me yesterday morning and said that he still wanted to talk to Peter. I did my best to convince him to let Peter alone, but he insisted. I found out later that Myers came looking for him at the arena."

"Pete was skating, the way he was when I took you down to see him. He had just finished his routine when Detective Myers shouted at him across the ice about wanting to talk to him again. I called Les Barnes and we hid in Dr. Aeschliman's training room until Les sent one of his junior attorneys over to browbeat the detective."

"Now that would have been worth seeing!" Grigory laughed very hard, wheezing and coughing as he did so.

Nik and Grigory were quiet for a long while. Each had thoughts about what was happening to Peter, and each said silent prayers for a good outcome.

Grigory stirred in his chair, "Dr. Kellman, my team must be on an airplane in three hours, or forfeit the fares. We can't afford to do that, and so I am about to ask a huge favor of you. Peter's condition is unknown to us right now, but we do know that he will not be able to travel after his surgery for at least two to three weeks, if then. He will need to have someone who can take care of him while he recuperates. You have your medical residency responsibilities, but do you think that your mother and father might let him stay with them until he can travel back to Russia? I will personally pay for a private duty nurse for him, and any other expenses that might be incurred."

Grigory's proposal took Nik by surprise; she hadn't thought that far ahead. She had panicked when she found that Pete was so ill, and she hadn't thought of anything beyond getting good surgical treatment for him.

"That's a wonderful idea, Grigory. I'm sure that my parents would be happy to have him." I'll have to do a little convincing, Nik thought, but they'll help him, I know they will.

"I don't know how your health care system works, but Peter will need a great deal of care while he recovers from his surgery. I do know that." Grigory pointed at Nik as he spoke.

Nik looked at her watch. It was four-forty five. Her mother was usually up and making coffee by five or five-thirty.

"I think that your idea is truly wonderful, Grigory. I'll call my mother in a little bit, about five, and I'll be very persuasive. Pete deserves no less, and I can keep an eye on him, too, while he's there. Thanks, Grigory."

"No, I must thank *you*, doctor. If it hadn't been for you, getting Peter in shape to play hockey, we wouldn't have won the championship. Do you know how critically important it is to the Soviets when their teams win championships?"

"I didn't understand that, or many other things for that matter, when I first started working with your team, but I can definitely tell you that now I understand a great deal more."

Grigory stood up from the very uncomfortable, too small, chair in which he had been sitting. "Do you like coffee, doctor?"

"I'd love a cup of coffee, Grigory." Nik reached for her purse.

Grigory started walking toward the door and waved his arm at her, "I'll get it. Don't worry about it Dr. Kellman."

Nik called her mother from the telephone in the waiting area. "Hi, mom, sorry to call you so early, but I've had a bit of a rough night...No, no, not me, but one of my athletes...Peter Genchenko; you met him at your open house...He's had to have surgery, mom, and he won't be able to leave with his team this morning...His surgery's being done right now at I.U. Med Center, and Coach Grigory and I are waiting to see how he's doing...Uh, the main reason that I called is that Peter's going to need a place to stay until he's able to travel...Yes, he's going to be pretty weak for awhile...You mean it? He can stay with you and dad? That's wonderful, mom...I'll stay, too, so that I can keep an eye on him...Thanks, mom, thanks so much. Later this morning I'll call you when I know something more...Yes, I love you, too. Bye."

Nik's spirits lifted briefly after her conversation with her mother, until she saw Dr. Edward come into the waiting area.

"It was a hot appendix, Nik. He ruptured, so we've had to put drains in all over the place. We irrigated the hell out of his gut, dusted in some antibiotics, and looked around inside a little. He had a femoral hernia, too, and we repaired that as well. Actually, he's in pretty good shape right now. Any questions?" It took him less than thirty seconds to deliver the information to Nik.

Nik was insulted that Dr. Edward had so easily "depersonalized" Peter Genchenko, and in an icy voice asked, "When do you think he might be discharged, Dr. Edward?"

"Well, ordinarily we keep these kinds of cases in the hospital for about four days or so, but Peter is going to need intravenous antibiotics. You know as well as I do what a ruptured appendix can do."

Nik's heart sank with Dr. Edward's pronouncement, "He's going to have a tough recovery?"

"Well, he's an athlete, and he's in pretty good shape overall. We're going to give him intravenous antibiotics, as I said, and nutrition supplementation to get his hemoglobin, hematocrit, total protein and albumin levels up where they belong. I didn't see the need to transfuse him, but that may be something we might consider if we can't get his hemoglobin and hematocrit where they need to be. He's a classic hypochromic anemia. He doesn't eat well."

Grigory returned with the coffee and set the cups on a table, "Ah, doctor, how is Genchenko doing?"

Nik made the introductions, "Dr. Edward, this is Peter's Coach, Grigory Serov."

Dr. Edward had to look up at Grigory as he offered his hand. The two men shook hands vigorously.

"He's doing well, Coach Serov. I just told Nik that he not only had a hot appendix, he had a hernia that we repaired, too."

Nik then told Grigory that Pete's appendix had burst, and that his recovery might be extended because of it.

Grigory shook his head."Peter doesn't deserve to have another bad break." he handed Nik her coffee.

"No, he doesn't, but it won't make any difference to me how long it takes to get him healthy again. He's going home from the hospital to my parents' house, and I'll be there to help him recover."

Grigory looked at her and beamed, "You have already asked them?"

"I didn't have to ask. When I called my mother, she offered to take him before I had the chance to ask her."

Dr. Edward told them, "That's good, because he's going to need some TLC when he's discharged. If you have any other questions, don't hesitate to call me. Oh, and you can go see him in the recovery room now."

Grigory looked at his watch. "It's getting close to my team's departure time, but I want to go in and see him. I'd like to say goodbye."

Grigory and Nik set their coffee cups down quickly, and headed to the recovery area.

Nik's legs felt weak as she walked through the doors to the recovery area. Grigory filled the doorway, and he ducked out of habit, even though the doorframe was taller than he was. For a moment, they stood inside the doors, and then one of the nurses came over to them.

"Hi, Dr. Kellman, Dr. Edward said that you and Coach Serov would be coming in to see Peter Genchenko. He's in bay 10." The nurse pointed toward a nearby curtained cubicle.

Nik and Grigory approached the cubicle and Grigory pulled the curtain aside gently. Peter, looking very pale, lay on his back covered with white blankets. Nik quickly saw that he had two intravenous lines running, a nasal cannula set at two liters of oxygen per minute, and a urinary catheter bag hanging from the lower bed frame.

Before Nik or Grigory could get closer to Peter, a nurse came into the cubicle and began to pull Peter's covers down to the level of his abdomen. Nik realized that the nurse was checking Peter's dressings and drains. Dismayed, Nik observed the heavy dressings and drains across his abdomen. How will he recover from all of this? She felt overwhelmed by what she saw.

As the nurse began recording Peter's vital signs from the monitor, he opened his eyes and lifted his hand. When he saw Nik and Grigory standing there, he smiled. In spite of all that he had been through, he smiled. Nik's heart melted.

She called his name barely above a whisper, "Pete," she said.

Nik went to the bedside and Peter reached for her hand. She took his hand and reflexively brought it up to her lips.

When Grigory saw her kiss Peter's hand, he was surprised, but then thought, Genchenko, you are one very fortunate man. Perhaps your life has just made a turn for the better. It was clear to Grigory that there was more than just a doctor/patient relationship between Peter and his doctor. After all, he had seen them on the dance floor together last night.

"How are you, Pete?" Nik was still holding his hand.

In a hoarse voice, barely above a whisper, and with a weak smile, Peter replied, "I'm not sure right now, but I'm thankful that I'm still here."

"Genchenko," Grigory patted Peter on the shoulder, "you have been through quite a lot."

"Da, but I am happy now to see both of you." No sooner had he said those words, than Peter closed his eyes.

"Doctor, I am going to have to leave for the airport soon." Grigory whispered and checked his watch.

Nik nodded and said, "Pete, Grigory has to leave for the airport now. He's going home with the team."

Peter opened his eyes slowly, as if coming out of a deep sleep. "I can't go with him right now."

This pronouncement brought an unaccustomed smile to Grigory's otherwise solemn face, "Rest well, Peter. I will see you in Moscow."

Grigory momentarily put his hand on Peter's forehead, and then turned to leave. Somehow, he seemed diminished, less imposing, as he walked, head bowed, out of the cubicle. He did not look back.

He had ten minutes to spare when Grigory hit the boarding area. His athletes, and Vladimir, swarmed around him, talking at once, trying to find out what had happened to Peter. Airline personnel were attempting to get the team on the airplane. Tempers were starting to rise on both sides.

Finally, Grigory put his hands in the air and shouted, TEEKHEE! *QUIET!*

Everyone in the vicinity, which included four boarding areas, stopped talking and looked at Grigory.

"Peter had surgery and he came through it well. He is resting and recuperating at this time, and he will finish his convalescence with Dr. Kellman's parents. Peter is in very good hands, and now, I want all of my athletes, and Coach Vladimir, to get on the airplane immediately. Otherwise, we will be left behind, and each of you will have to buy another ticket out of your own pocket."

Grigory took out his airline ticket, handed it to the boarding agent, and began to walk up the jetway to the airplane. His team, and Vladimir, followed him without a word.

Chapter 24

When Peter was being wheeled into the surgical suite, he was frightened and in pain. If it had not been for Niki, he would have been completely alone. She had held his hand and talked to him, helped him not to be afraid. He clung to the thought of their dance. He had held her close to him, his senses filled with her scent, her warmth, and her touch.

Inside the surgical suite, a nurse in a mask and green-colored clothing and hair covering, at least he assumed she was a nurse, came over to him and took his hand. "Hi, I'm Tessa. Can you tell me who you are?"

"I'm…Peter Genchenko." His senses were heightened with apprehension as he watched her turn his wrist over to check the plastic bracelet there.

"That's what your ID bracelet says, too. Do you know what kind of surgery you are going to have?" Her lovely eyes were kind, and, although he couldn't see her mouth, it seemed as though she might be smiling.

"My zhivat…*stomach* is painful, and I have a hernia on the right side…but the doctor told me that he was going to 'explore' to find out what is wrong."

Tessa nodded her head, "That's just what Dr. Edward is going to do."

The cold temperature and bright lights in the room assaulted Peter's senses, and he began to shiver. He turned his head and saw that three other people were there. One of them, wrapped in a long green gown, tied in back, was working at a table toward the back of the room. Peter recognized Dr. Jackson, the doctor who had talked to him in the other area where he had been waiting with Niki.

Dr. Jackson beckoned to the nurse, "Let's put him on the table, Tessa. Hello again, Peter. Don't worry; you're in good hands here. When Ralph called me and said that Nik Kellman wanted only the best for you, I was flattered and came right over."

A second circulating nurse appeared on the other side of Peter. "Hello, Peter, my name is Ashley. Tessa and I are going to take good care of you while you're here with us. That's Mary, at the back table. She's your scrub nurse, and she will take good care of you, too."

Ashley was also masked and in green-colored clothing and hair covering. All that Peter could see of her were her beautiful and expressive blue-green eyes.

The nurses pushed his cart up against a table that he watched as it moved automatically up to the level of the cart. Dr. Jackson got on one side of the cart, and the nurses, Ashley and Tessa, both on the other side of the table, lifted him with the draw sheet beneath him onto the operating table.

Peter's immediate feeling was one of cold on his back, bare buttocks, and legs, as he lay down on the table. Even though he realized that there was a pad on the table, it nonetheless felt very hard to him. Peter was visibly shivering now. As he looked up toward the ceiling, he saw that a huge light, as yet unlit, was directly above him.

Ashley brought a soft and warm blanket to cover him with, and wrapped it around him and tucked it under his feet. "Is that better?"

"Yes…Thank you," he croaked.

Tessa was placing some kind of belt or strap across his legs. "This is to help you stay on the table, Peter."

He had to admit that he was beginning to feel as though he should jump from the table and run out of the room, so the safety strap was probably a good thing, at least from the nurse's perspective. Peter thought that everyone, at least those on the verge of surgery, needed something to keep them on the table.

Dr. Jackson, at the top of the table, behind Peter's head, was busily manipulating intravenous lines, and checking his anesthesia gas machine. "We'll be ready here in a minute, Peter."

Again, Peter shivered uncontrollably as he lay on the operating table awaiting his fate. If only Niki could have come in with me for just a few minutes. Only a few minutes, he thought, and I might have been able to withstand all of this like a man. Instead, he thought, I am lying here on this cold, hard table, shivering in fear like a coward.

Dr. Edward opened the door and looked into the room. "How's everything going in here? I'm going to scrub now, and then we can get started."

Tessa answered, "We are ready when you are, Dr. Edward."

Dr. Jackson, with an assist from Ashley, put an arm board out to Peter's left, non-operative, side and gently placed his arm on it. Deftly, he cleansed an area on Peter's arm at the bend of his elbow and inserted a needle. Peter hardly felt the stick, and was surprised to see that the doctor had an intravenous line established so quickly. Almost immediately, Peter felt drowsy.

"Goodnight, Peter, you're going to take a little nap now," said Dr. Jackson.

The anesthesiologist placed a mask over Peter's nose and mouth, and for several moments, gulping and swallowing as the strange-smelling gas filled his airway, he was afraid that he might suffocate. Peter's vision went from white, to gray, and then there was nothing.

The first thing that Peter saw when he awakened was that Niki was standing there, and she was calling his name softly. He felt as if he was returning after a long journey, and he was very happy to see her. He reached for her hand, and she took his hand and kissed it. When he realized what she had done, a burst of joy swelled inside him.

Try as he might, Peter could not stay awake, but he knew that Grigory was there with Niki. He also knew that Grigory had touched him on the shoulder and forehead, and had told him that the team would be leaving for home in a short while.

Tom and Mickey, who had accompanied the Russian team to the airport, were now going east on I-465 toward the I-70 junction, heading into downtown Indianapolis to the Indiana University Medical Center to see Peter. They were talking and laughing about Grigory's "little talk" with the team when he arrived, very late, in the international flight boarding area.

"Man, did you see the look on their faces? Boris almost fell over backward, 'cause he was directly in front of Grigory when he shouted for them to be quiet. I looked at the other boarding areas, and everyone, I mean *everyone*, stopped to listen to Grigory." Tom was laughing at the memory.

"This whole International Winter Games experience has been a blast. But right now, I'm wondering what's gon'na happen to Peter? Dr. Kellman called me when she found out that he was going to surgery. She sounded real sad, too. But who wouldn't be?" Mickey raised his eyebrows questioningly.

Tom was thoughtful for a moment, and then told Mickey, "At first, I didn't like Genchenko very much, in fact, I thought he was a 'showboat' and a pain in the ass. When he got hurt and then knocked the Doc down onto the ice so hard, I thought she might have broken her arm. I wanted to smack him the side of the head. But then I realized that the Doc's explanation of his behavior was pretty much on target. We've been trained not to startle or surprise someone who's been injured for the very reason that the Doc got hurt. She said it was really her fault, and I guess it was."

"Yeah, that's probably right, because Peter could have hurt her pretty bad if that was his intention."

Tom smiled at Mickey's opinion, "Well, he's pretty strong for someone who's underweight by twenty or thirty pounds, but it's his speed that keeps him from getting his ass kicked on the ice."

Chapter 25

Saturday. Late Morning

When Tom and Mickey came into Peter's room, they saw that Dr. Kellman was sleeping, curled up in a chair, her head cradled on a pillow, her coat over her shoulders. Peter was lying in bed, awake, and saw them as they entered the room. He raised a forefinger to his lips, and then beckoned to them.

Mickey stood on one side of Peter's bed, and Tom stood on the other. Both smiled as they glanced at the Doc and back at Peter.

"Please let her sleep," he whispered to them, "she has been awake for many hours."

Tom leaned down to Peter and whispered back, "Okay, Peter, but how are you doing?"

Peter replied, "Good, I am very good, Tom, and very lucky, too."

"Yeah," said Mickey, "you didn't look too good the last time I saw you."

As Peter and his two guests talked quietly, there was a rather loud conversation in the corridor outside. Several people in white lab coats stood near Peter's door, and seemed to be carrying on a conversation about approaches to treatment for a patient.

Mickey hurried over to close the door, but it was too late. Nik moved, stretched, and sat up in the chair. At that moment, there was a tap on the door. Mickey, standing at the door, saw that it was Dr. Michael.

"Hello, Mickey, is Dr. Kellman in here?"

Mickey turned to look at the Doc, "Uh, yeah, she's here, Dr. Michael."

"Nik?" Ron came through the door into the room.

Ron saw Nik, and then glanced over at Peter. He nodded at Peter, and then returned his attention to Nik, walked over to her in the chair and crouched down in front of her.

"Hon', I've been trying to get in touch with you, and if it hadn't been for your mother, I would have been frantic. Why didn't you call me about Genchenko's surgery? I could have been here with you."

Nik was quiet for several moments, and then answered him, "I should have called you, but everything happened so quickly, Ron, and then when they brought Peter to his room, I only meant to close my eyes for a few minutes until Dr. Edward came in to check on him…and then I was going to go home. I would have called you when I got home."

"You called your mother this morning around five, and if I hadn't called her when you didn't answer at your condo, I don't know what I would have done. I was getting pretty upset. Do you know that it's almost eight-thirty now?" Ron's face was filled with emotion.

It upset Peter to listen to Dr. Michael talking to Niki in a chiding way, as if he might be talking to a child. Peter fervently wished that the intravenous and oxygen tubing were not attached to him. He wanted very much to be able to stand and defend her, if only from what he considered to be a demeaning verbal assault.

Mickey and Tom were embarrassed, and felt as though they were eavesdropping on a private conversation. Too, they were fond of the Doc, and didn't think that she should be treated the way that Dr. Michael was treating her.

Dr. Edward joined the fray, medical record in hand, "Well, Peter, how are you doing? Is your pain pretty well controlled?"

Peter nodded noncommittally, and replied, "I am doing as well as can be expected, given the circumstances."

Dr. Edward looked around at the assembled group, and spoke to Dr. Michael and Nik. "Hello, Ron, Nik, it looks like Peter's got a 'full house' here."

He turned back to Peter, "We're going to have to keep you for about five days, until your IV antibiotics have finished, and then we will start you on an oral dosage. We are also going to keep a close watch on you with cultures of your drainage, and we'll monitor your temps closely, too. I've called in our epidemiologist to do a consult on you, just in case there's a problem from your appendix rupture. We will also start pulling some, maybe most, of your penrose drains within three to four days. You should be much more comfortable after that."

Nik paid close attention to what Dr. Edward was saying to Peter, and then spoke, "Pete has arrangements after he's discharged. He will have a private duty nurse too, so that we can keep tabs on his progress, and make sure that his meds and treatments are okay."

"That's excellent, Nik. Peter will need one on one care while he's recovering. When the time comes, I'll write an order for home care, so that you can get reimbursed for your time, trouble, and money."

Nik looked over at Peter for his reaction to Dr. Edward's words, and quickly replied, "He's not a charity case, Dr. Edward, he's private pay. So don't worry, his expenses are not a problem."

Dr. Edward shrugged, "Okay, that's good to know, Nik. Peter, I'll be back to check on you later today. In the meantime, I want you to get some rest, so all of these folks," he said, making a circuit of the room with his hand, "are going to have to leave."

Mickey and Tom headed for the door immediately, waving as they went.

"'Bye, Peter, we'll come back tomorrow to check on you." Tom looked at Peter and gave him a "thumbs up" gesture before going out the door.

"Nik, you've been up most of the night, so why don't you go get some sleep? Keep your pager on, and I'll page you if there's anything that you need to know about, okay? Ron, take her home and make her get some rest."

Dr. Edward sensed that there was some tension in the room, and was puzzled by it. His first obligation was to his patient. So clearing the room seemed to be the right thing to do. He was aware that Peter's monitor showed that his pulse, respirations, and blood pressure were above baseline, and it troubled the surgeon.

Ron answered, "We're gone. Take good care of your patient, Ralph."

Nik went to Peter's bedside, "I'll be back this afternoon, Pete." Her eyes were brimming as she spoke.

"Thank you for your help, Dr. Kellman." Peter spoke formally to her, and took her hand briefly, squeezing it gently. He didn't want to precipitate more embarrassing remarks from her fiancé.

"Nik…" Standing at the door, Ron held his hand out to her, as if to a child.

To her credit, and to Peter's gratification, Nik did not take Ron's hand, but instead walked past him and out into the corridor. She didn't stop or wait for Ron to catch up to her. She was as angry with Ron as she had ever been in their short courtship and engagement, and her rapid footsteps were meant to carry her away from him quickly.

Dr. Edward followed Ron out of the room. He watched as Ron hurried after Nik, thinking, now *there's a story, I'll bet."*

Peter lay in his bed looking up at the ceiling. He closed his eyes tightly against the anger churning within. The pain in his abdomen was nearly as bad as it was before his surgery, and he felt as helpless as he had been when he was shot.

"Hi, Mr. Genchenko, I'm Beth Leonard, and I'm going to be your nurse this shift." A petite brunette with expressive dark eyes smiled at him as she came into Peter's room.

Peter nodded his head and tried to smile, but couldn't bring it off. "I'm not, I'm not…" He couldn't finish.

"You look like your pain meds aren't working too well for you." She walked over and checked his intravenous line.

"Dr. Edward wrote a PRN pain med for you, too, so I'll give you that. I'll be right back." She quickly left the room.

Peter closed his eyes. He knew that he had to relax, to sleep, in order to recuperate, but the pain that he was feeling, not only in his abdomen, but now in his right groin, was going to keep him awake and in near agony if something wasn't done about it.

Beth was back quickly, "This is an IV med for pain, Mr. Genchenko, and I think that it's going to help you rest."

She busied herself with Peter's IV line, and then began checking his abdominal dressings and drains, and his Foley catheter. When she finished with those things, she turned his pillow over and straightened out his bedclothes.

Peter was surprised that something as inconsequential as turning his pillow could help him to feel better. The coolness of the turned pillowcase was refreshing to him.

"I'm going to show you how to splint your abdomen and groin so that you can cough and deep breathe. It's the best way to keep your lungs clear after surgery." Beth handed him a pillow to place over his abdomen, and showed him what to do with it.

Peter couldn't believe that one small cough could be so excruciating. God in heaven, help me.

"Okay, that's good. Now, you need to do this at least every couple of hours. I'm going to be in and out of your room throughout my shift, too, and I'll help you with this. In about a half-hour, I'll bring some ice chips for you so that you can moisten your mouth a little."

Peter was grateful to Beth Leonard. "Thank you…" His voice trailed off.

She closed the door as she left the room. Poor guy, she thought, he's in for a little bit of misery before he starts feeling better.

Beth came back in to check her patient, and brought ice chips for him to melt in his mouth. She documented his vital signs, pulse, temperature, heart rate, blood pressure, and respirations. She also checked his IV lines, drains, and his dressing to make sure that he had no active bleeding. Peter was lucky that he got Beth as his nurse. She prided herself on being thorough, and considered nursing as a vocation, rather than a job.

When Nik had left Peter's room, she hurried down the corridor in the hospital, away from Ron, but he caught up to her and put a hand on her shoulder.

She shrugged his hand away. "Please let me alone. I just want to go home."

"Wait a minute, Nik, I don't know what I've done *this time* to make you mad, but I want you to know that I have good reason for being upset, too." Ron stopped, hands on hips.

Nik turned toward him, and replied, "This isn't the time or the place to talk about anything, Ron. I just want to go home. Last night was a very bad night, and I'm worn out, that's all. And I really didn't appreciate the way that you talked to me in front of everyone. It was condescending, demeaning. I'm not your property yet."

Her words stung him, "Why are you involved with this guy now, anyway? The games are over, and you don't owe him anything. So, he gets sick. You could've called an ambulance and sent him on his way, but you didn't. You should have called me at least to let me know where you were, but you didn't. My question is, why not? I was only concerned for your safety, Nik."

"Okay, I should have called you, but everything happened so quickly that I wasn't thinking straight. Grigory came to see Peter before he and the team had to leave, and I called my mother, and the morning just *went*; I don't know what else I can tell you. When Peter was given a room after recovery, I went to check on him and I fell asleep waiting for Ralph Edward to come in to see him.

"*Wait a minute*, you told me that you were going to Fort Wayne this morning, and I wasn't expecting to be able to talk to you until tonight, anyway. So I didn't just forget about you, Ron. How can you try to make me feel guilty when I didn't know that you would be here instead of Fort Wayne?"

Ron bowed his head and then shook it back and forth, "You should have been a lawyer, Nik. You really should have been a lawyer. Now it's all *my* fault, isn't it?"

Nik turned and started walking again, but Ron kept pace with her. He decided not to say anything more, because he didn't want to make things worse between them.

When they reached Nik's car, Ron put his hand on her shoulder lightly, and said gently, "I'm sorry Nik. I shouldn't have embarrassed you in front of everyone. And yes, I was going to Fort Wayne this morning, but there was a change of plans at the last minute, so I tried to call you at your condo to let you know. That's when I started to get worried about you, because I didn't know where you were. Finally, I called your mother."

Nik stood leaning against the unopened door of her car, her head resting on a mittened hand. "I'm sorry, too, Ron. I realize that you were just worried about me. But sometimes I wonder..." Her voice trailed off.

"Yeah, we're oil and water, aren't we? When you said that you weren't my property yet, it hurt me a lot. Is that what you really think our marriage is going to be like?" He gently rubbed her back as he spoke. When Nik turned to speak to him, Ron put his arms around her, "I don't want to lose you, Nik."

They stood there for several moments, while passersby glanced their way, no doubt curious about this public display of affection.

Nik's heart was in turmoil, and she ached for Ron, because she realized that their engagement was in trouble, perhaps near an end. It's my fault, she thought. But she didn't know how to fix it.

"Come on, Nik, get in the car, you need to go home. You've got to be exhausted."

Ron looked into her sad eyes, and he immediately felt deep pangs of remorse because he thought that he was the one responsible for that sadness. He opened Nik's car door for her, and she climbed inside. He wanted to insist that he drive her home, but he knew that now was not the time to insist on anything with Nik.

"I'll call you." Ron stopped for a moment, "Is it all right if I call you tonight?"

Nik, looking like a waif, her eyes wide, said, "Yes."

Ron leaned in the window and kissed her on the cheek. "I love you."

As Nik drove away, Ron stood watching and felt his own sadness. Normally buoyant and gregarious, Ron was not used to feeling like this. When he couldn't see Nik's car anymore, he started walking slowly toward his own.

As soon as Nik got home, she quickly stripped, took a hot shower, and put on her warmest flannel nightgown. She felt numb inside as she crawled into bed and pulled up the covers. Within minutes, she was sound asleep.

Peter looked at the wall clock. It was now six o'clock in the evening, and he had been awake, and in pain again, since four. His nurse, Beth, had gone off duty at three, and assured him that the evening nurse would be in soon to check on him. He had, however, seen no one after she left.

Peter had looked about the bed for the call light, but he couldn't see it. He couldn't sit up high enough to look over the side of the bed, either. He thought about calling out for assistance, but he wasn't quite desperate; at least not yet.

Nik arrived at the hospital at six-thirty, refreshed by a good sleep. When she awakened, she had dressed quickly and had put together a care package for Peter, consisting of books, a tape player and some tapes that might help him when he got bored with being in bed. She resisted the temptation to include snacks because she knew that he wouldn't be eating anything solid for a while.

"Hi, Pete." Nik came into Peter's room and stopped dead still when she saw his condition.

"Niki…" Peter tried to smile when he saw her.

He was soaked with sweat, his hair damp and hanging in his face. His bedclothes were tangled around him. Nik noticed that his catheter bag was nearly overflowing, and that his IV was about to alarm.

"My God, Pete, what's happened here? Where's the nurse?"

He shook his head. "I don't know. I fell asleep, but I woke up around three when my first nurse left for the day. No one has been in since then."

"You're in pain, aren't you?" Nik felt sick at the thought.

"Da, I am in pain." His brow was furrowed in apprehension.

"I'll be right back Pete." Nik went quickly out the door.

When she reached the nurses' station, Nik asked for the charge nurse. Everyone seemed to be busy, and the first person that she spoke to glanced at her and then looked away as someone else in the nurses' station got her attention. Nik then tried to talk to another person, but everyone seemed to be involved in current tasks. It was difficult to determine who was who, because they all wore scrubs and their identification tags were impossible to read at a distance.

"Hey! *Listen up*! I want to speak to the charge nurse, *now*!" Nik was through being polite or waiting any longer.

All activity stopped within earshot of Nik's command. Nik didn't care; Peter was in pain.

"What's the problem?" A young woman came over to speak to Nik.

"I am Dr. Nik Kellman, and my patient is Peter Genchenko in 5537. He's less than twenty-four hours post-op, and he hasn't seen a nurse, or anyone else for that matter, since the first shift nurse left at three. It is now six-thirty. He is in pain, his catheter bag is ready to run over, and his IV will be alarming very soon. Now, I am asking you, *what's the problem*?"

Nik's in-your-face approach worked. The young woman's facial expression and attitude changed drastically as she realized that she was addressing a doctor.

"Give me his chart. I want to see what documentation has been made since the first shift. Also, I want to see your nursing duty roster and assignments, *now*." Nik was beyond anger.

Without a word, the charge nurse handed Nik the medical record. Nik flipped it open to the nurses' notes, and pointed out to the charge nurse that there had been no documentation, thus far, on the second shift. She then looked at the medication administration record, and found that Peter's scheduled pain medication had not been given. Nik placed the chart on the counter top and also pointed this out to the charge nurse.

"And the nursing duty roster and assignment sheet?" Nik held out her hand.

The charge nurse reached for a notebook on the desk and handed it to Nik. After turning to the current date, Nik saw that Peter had a nurse assigned to him for the day shift, but that the nurse's name assigned to him for the evening shift had been crossed out.

"What's this? It looks like no one's assigned to Peter for the evening shift."

The charge nurse looked at the duty roster and said, "Oh my gosh. Shelly called in sick, and then one of her patients, the one in room 5537, didn't get re-assigned!"

"I want the following verbal orders carried out *STAT!* First, give Peter his pain medication as ordered, check his IV, check and reinforce his abdominal dressing as needed, check his penrose drains for drainage and take cultures, check his intake and output, empty his Foley catheter bag, give him a bag bath and change his linens. In a word, I want him taken care of immediately!" Nik's freight train look was in place as she delivered the orders to the charge nurse.

Nik hurried back to Pete, "Help is on the way."

Relief flooded his face. "Niki…thank you."

A wide-eyed nurse came into the room with a syringe. After checking Peter's armband, she asked, "Mr. Genchenko, I have some pain medication for you. Could you please tell me what your level of pain is right now on a scale of one to ten? One is the lowest, and ten is the highest."

Peter replied, "It is about an eight or nine, I think."

Two more nurses came in, Katie Roberts and Cynthia Kennedy. Both started to work on Peter after introducing themselves and explaining what they were about to do. Katie emptied his catheter bag, and Cynthia began checking Peter's abdominal and inguinal dressings. After she finished his dressings, she started the cultures of Peter's penrose drains. Then Katie explained that she was going to start his bath.

Peter blanched and looked over at Nik, "I'd rather wait on that, if I could, I have a visitor, and she is a very busy person."

"It's okay, Peter, don't worry about my schedule. I'm going to be here for as long as you need me." And then she realized why he might not want to start his bath. He was probably embarrassed, and probably still in pain, too, in spite of his pain medication.

"Pete, is your pain med working? Are you feeling better?"

"It's working, and yes, I'm starting to get some relief." He attempted a smile, but it didn't reach his pain-filled eyes.

Nik thought for a moment, and then asked Katie, who would be giving the bag bath, to leave the supplies in the room and come back later.

"What about the linen change doctor? He will be a lot more comfortable if his linens are fresh." Katie wanted to help.

"Good idea. I'll help you." Nik's answer startled the nurse.

Together, Nik and Katie quickly changed Peter's bed linens with as little physical disturbance to him as possible. When they finished, Peter smiled wanly at both of them.

"How's the pain now, Pete?"

"It is much better." Peter passed a hand across his face.

"Do you feel up to your bath now? I know that we've sort of done the reverse of what we should have when we changed your bed, but I think that you'll feel even better after your bath."

"Yes, a bath would be...helpful, I think." Peter still wasn't convinced.

Katie smiled a beautiful smile and said, "A bag bath is very different from the old basin and washcloth baths we used to do. The cloths stay warm, and you don't have water running down your arms to make you uncomfortable. And, it's a lot quicker, too."

"Okay, so what do I need to do to help you, Katie?" Nik wanted to make sure that the bath went quickly for Peter.

Again, the nurse was surprised that a doctor would be helping her, but she began to put out the bag bath supplies, "They're still warm from the microwave, Dr. Kellman, so here's what we can do."

They opened the packs of moistened warm cloths and began Peter's first bag bath. Nik wiped his face and neck, and then proceeded to his chest. Katie washed his arms, legs and feet. It took both of them to wash his back. When the bath was completed, Katie put a clean gown on Peter and pulled up his covers. Nik combed his hair away from his face and then stood back to check the result.

Katie giggled, "I'd say medicine, rather than hair styling, is your strong point, Dr. Kellman."

Peter managed a real smile this time, "How bad is it?"

"Better than it was, mister, much better." Nik laughed, too.

Katie told Peter that she was now his second shift nurse, and that she would be checking on him throughout her shift. "Your call light is now attached to the bedrail, so use it whenever you need to. I'm not sure why it wasn't there when you needed it before, but you're my responsibility now, so call if you need me."

"Thank you, I feel so much better now; clean and medicated. It's amazing how a bath can make such a difference." Peter closed his eyes.

"Get some rest now." Katie walked toward the door, put a finger to her lips as she looked at the doctor, and went out into the corridor, closing the door behind her.

Peter stirred and started to speak, "Niki..."

Nik stood beside him, "Hush. You need to rest, Pete."

Eyes closed, he smiled and asked, "What is 'hush'?"

Nik placed her fingertips on his lips, "Quiet, it means, 'be quiet'."

Peter raised his hand to hers and held her fingers to his lips for a moment, only a moment, before he fell asleep.

Nik sat down in a chair that she had moved close to Pete's bed and pulled some of the books that she had brought for Pete out of the bag. Thumbing through a couple of them, she found that she couldn't concentrate on reading, because her gaze was drawn back to Pete again and again.

She brought the fingers that Peter had kissed to her own lips. Nik fully understood that, no matter how she felt about this wonderful man, he would have to go home when he recovered. She closed her eyes then too, and put her head against the back of the chair. Ron deserves a better person than I am, she thought, and her heart ached for both of the men that she loved.

Only one light in Peter's room was lit when Dr. Edward came into the room at eight-thirty that evening. The door was closed, but he had pushed it open without knocking. Dr. Edward made a quick scan of the room, and saw that Peter was sleeping. Nik Kellman was sitting in a chair, reading. She smiled at him, stood up, and beckoned for him to follow her back out into the hallway.

"Did you hear what happened to Peter today?" Nik's gaze was direct.

Ralph shook his head, "No, I just flipped through his chart to see what his labs were, and then I was going to look at the nurses' notes for his progress today."

"Things were very good for the first shift, but they went to hell for a while during the evening shift. Peter wasn't assigned to a second shift nurse until I got here at six-thirty. The nurse that was assigned to him after I complained did a great job, but he didn't see anyone from three until six-thirty."

"No one called me about it. You mean he didn't get pain meds or anything?" Ralph frowned and bit his lip.

"He got nothing. When I arrived, I raised holy hell with the second shift charge nurse, and things improved drastically after that. He's been sleeping since about seven."

"What was the reason for not having a nurse for Peter? Who was responsible?"

"Don't worry about that, Ralph, I took care of it. Apparently, the nurse who would have had Peter called in sick, and Peter wasn't added to someone else's assignment."

Ralph flipped through Peter's chart to the medication administration record and whistled. "He didn't get anything for pain until six-forty-five? Damn it, what's the matter with these people? They wouldn't treat a dog like this."

"Ralph, it was an oversight, and when it was brought to the attention of the charge nurse, Peter's room was swarming with nurses. The nurse that he's assigned to now is excellent. She's been in and out of Peter's room several times to check on him while I've been here."

He let out a long sigh of frustration, "This is the first time, to my knowledge, that this has ever happened to one of my patients. The nurses on this unit usually do a great job."

"It was just a fluke, Ralph, and although Peter had a bad time of it with his pain, he's okay now, so don't be upset with the staff. When they knew about their mistake, they overcompensated."

Ralph nodded, "Okay, well, let's go back in and check on our patient. By the way, did you get any sleep today?"

"Yes, Ron made sure that I went right home after we left."

"Good, you were pretty wiped out."

Peter was awake when they returned to his room, "Hello doctors."

Ralph began immediately with his apology, "I heard about what happened today, and I want to apologize to you. That never should have happened, and I told Nik that it's never happened to one of my patients before."

Looking at Nik, Peter replied, "Dr. Kellman saved me once again. She has been very good to me."

Nik noted that the timbre was back in Peter's voice, and his coloring was not so pale. He's coming back, she thought, he's bouncing back.

"So I've heard. Well, let's see here. You know that you've had an appendectomy, and a femoral hernia repair, right?"

Peter nodded, "Yes, but tell me again about all these little plastic things."

"Your appendix ruptured, so the drains are for carrying any drainage out of the abdomen so that you'll heal more quickly. I saw in your chart here that Nik has ordered the initial cultures from the drainage, so we'll have to wait forty-eight to seventy-two hours to see if anything grows."

Peter arched his eyebrows, "...And?"

Ralph completed Peter's sentence, "You're already on an antibiotic intravenously, so that should take care of any potential infection."

"Earlier, you told me that I'd be in the hospital for about five days. Will I be able to fly back to Moscow after I am discharged?"

"Oh no, not for some time. I want to see you after you're discharged to be sure that there are no complications, Peter. A ruptured appendix is a serious thing, and I want to monitor you to make sure that there's no abscess formation or something like that."

Nik spoke up, "My parents want you to stay with them while you recuperate and get back your strength. I'll be there, too, to keep a watchful eye on you. We are considering a private duty nurse, too, at least for the first three days or so."

Peter's surprise was evident, "But that's an imposition on you and your family. I don't want to impose upon you."

Nik was emphatic, "It's all set, and my mother is looking forward to having you as a houseguest. Besides, Duchess can't wait."

With this, Nik and Peter both laughed, remembering how Duchess had literally dogged his footsteps when he had been there for the open house.

Ralph laughed, too, "I didn't know that you had royalty in your family, Nik."

"You know very well, Ralph, that Duchess is my father's Weimaraner."

"Yeah, I've heard that she's quite a character."

"Let's say she fits right in with my family."

"Well, okay, back to business. Do you have any questions, Peter?" Ralph was beginning to feel better about the prospects of this young Russian.

Peter thought about that for a moment. He certainly had concerns, and even fears about his recuperation and return to playing hockey.

"Will I still be able to play hockey? I mean, is the hernia completely gone?"

"Oh yes. Your hernia has been repaired and reinforced with Marlex Mesh. You shouldn't have any problems there, Peter. Anything else?"

"No, that was the most important thing. I need to be able to play hockey." Peter was relieved beyond measure to know that he could continue to play hockey.

Chapter 26

Thursday December 25, 1986

Nik wheeled Peter through the Kellman's garage into their home, and he was surprised to see the group of people waiting there. The Kellmans, along with Ron, Tom and Mickey, and a new male face he didn't recognize, were there to greet him.

In unison, they said, "Merry Christmas, Pete."

Marina added, "Welcome home, too," and smiled warmly at him.

As Nik wheeled him into the great room, Peter caught sight of a huge and beautifully decorated tree, all in white. It soared almost to the rafters in the room. Beneath the tree, there was only one gift, a large box wrapped in vibrant red. Christmas music played in the background, and there was a fire in the fireplace. Duchess came bounding over to him and put her chin in his lap. This made Peter smile, and he patted her on the head.

The "welcoming committee" followed Peter into the great room, where the unknown guest came to him and offered his hand.

"I'm Nik's big brother, Mike," he said, shaking Peter's hand.

Peter saw that Mike had Niki's coloring and his father's size. "It is nice to meet you, Mike."

Mike went to Nik and gave her a hug and a kiss, "You look beautiful, Niki."

Nik beamed and kissed him on the cheek, "Thanks, Mikey."

She had chosen an ice blue sweater and slacks to wear for the day's festivities, and had pulled her hair back into a ponytail. The only adornment that she wore was a pair of small silver hoops at her ears. Peter had said the same words that her brother had spoken to her just now, at the hospital earlier when she had come to pick him up.

Marina, noting that Peter appeared to be overwhelmed, called, "Let's allow Peter to get settled, shall we? We can sit by the fire with some eggnog while Niki takes him into his room. Duchess, that means you, too."

Ron followed as Nik pushed Peter to his room, where a hospital bed had been set up for him. It was the beautiful drawing room decorated in red with the alabaster fireplace and view of the lake that he had so admired as a guest at the Kellmans' open house.

Ron asked him, "How are you doing, Peter? Nik says that you had a bit of a rocky road to recovery, but you look very good now."

Peter stood slowly from the wheelchair and offered his hand to Ron, "I think the worst is over now, and I feel better today than I have for a long time."

Nik reached up and pulled Peter's coat from his shoulders, then hung it on a coat tree that her mother had placed near the door to the room.

"Spaseeba *thank you,*" he said.

Ron could see that Pete had lost weight during his convalescence that he didn't need to lose, and that his well-worn dark slacks and sweater hung on him. His illness though, had not extinguished the brightness of his eyes, and, Ron noted with more than a little envy, the guy was as handsome as ever.

Up to this point, Nik had been quiet, but now she spoke to Peter, "Pete, do you think that you want to rest a little while in bed, or do you want to join the others in the great room now?"

Nik folded the wheelchair and put it in a corner. She then busied herself in turning down the bedclothes on Peter's hospital bed.

Before Peter could reply, Ron said to Nik, "Hon' there's a private duty nurse who's coming in about an hour; she can do that sort of thing for Peter."

Looking from Nik to Ron, Peter said, "He's right, you know, that's not something that you have to do. Let's join the party. I haven't been to a Christmas Party in a very long time."

Nik pointed at the wheelchair, but Peter shook his head, "I think that I need to exercise the way that I did in the hospital. Surely I can walk as far as the great room without falling over."

Because they couldn't walk three abreast in the hallway, they walked single file; Nik in the lead, Peter second, with Ron walking behind.

"We have a nice, comfortable chair for you, Peter, right here near the fireplace." Marina was solicitous.

"Spaseeba, *thank you.*" Peter sat down gingerly.

Marina smiled at the Russian thank you from Peter. "We are glad to have you as our guest, Peter."

It was Peter's turn to smile. There was so much activity in the room. People talking, moving, Duchess winding around through the people, and then his eyes found Niki. She lit up the room wherever she went. He wished that he could be more mobile. He'd follow her all over the room.

"Would you like some eggnog Peter? How about the rest of you?" Klaus was holding a tray with cups and napkins.

They all accepted Klaus' offer, and he dispensed the eggnog with the ease and graciousness of a good host.

"The Christmas table is set, everyone, so we should sit down to dinner in about fifteen minutes." Marina's eyes danced as she made this pronouncement

She was in her element, entertaining. For her Christmas Dinner party costume, Marina had carefully chosen a tailored emerald green tea length dress and wore emerald earrings. She had thoughtfully placed a matching bow on Duchess' collar.

Duchess gravitated toward Peter, as if to show off her holiday finery, and Nik smiled at him as the dog flopped down beside his chair. Tom, and then Mickey also came over to sit with Peter.

Tom shook Peter's hand and told him, "You look great, Peter, but you had us worried for a little while there."

"Yeah, I'll say. But you seem to be doing okay now." Mickey was glad to see Peter up and about.

"Well, I think I am, but I still have a long way to go." He reflected a moment and then added, "It feels odd, not being with my team." Peter's answer was quiet and lacked the force of his usual speech.

"I wonder how they're doing right now; I mean, they're playing hockey without you, aren't they?" Tom was sure that the team couldn't do well without Peter.

Peter inclined his head, "Yes, they are playing hockey in Sweden. I was only one member of the team, and everything we did was a team effort. Even someone like your Larry Bird needs a full team to play and win at basketball, doesn't he?"

Tom laughed, "Okay, you got me, Peter, but you have to admit that it helped when you were on the ice."

Mickey wanted his say, "Look, Tom, you're never going to get Peter to admit that he's anything else but one of the team."

Ron was sitting with Nik and Mike on one of the sofas, and they were making small talk, but Nik was watchful that Peter was doing well and not tiring too much.

The tinkling of a bell signaled that the feast was about to begin. Marina stood in the doorway between the great room and the dining room, holding a crystal bell in her hand and smiling.

The group moved to the dining room and Peter found that he had been placed between Mickey and Tom in the seating arrangements. He saw that the Kellman men were seated at the head and bottom of the table, with Nik, Ron, and Marina on the other side of the table.

Peter felt lightheaded briefly, but he was determined to enjoy this Christmas Dinner with Niki and her family and his friends Tom and Mickey. He was certain that he would never have another such opportunity, so this would be a special time for him, a special memory.

Marina had announced that she was serving a traditional American feast, and Peter was curious about how the turkey would taste. It certainly looked grand in the center of the table, golden brown and surrounded with roasted vegetables.

The elder Kellman asked his son to say grace, and Mike bowed his head. Everyone at the table did the same, and Mike intoned a brief prayer, asking that all those around the table be blessed and that God would keep them all safe from harm.

Peter could not remember a time that he had sat at a table where a prayer was spoken. So this is what having a loving family is really like? But then he decided that his own family only lacked a loving father. His mother, sister, and he were a loving family. When he thought of them, he felt guilty that he was here in the midst of plenty, and that they were undoubtedly not so fortunate.

He looked in Niki's direction, and he was surprised when he saw that she was looking at him, too. When Nik's eyes met Peter's, he smiled a gentle smile, and his eyes were soft.

Mike, who had been talking to Ron, saw the look that his sister shared with Peter, and it made him curious. *What's this?*

As the food was passed, Peter, his appetite returned, sampled some of everything and wasn't disappointed. Tom and Mickey heaped their plates and dug in with gusto, which made Marina very happy. It was a wonderful meal, and Marina was delighted that everything had gone so well. She served mincemeat pie with whipping cream for dessert, accompanied with a special amaretto flavored coffee. Mincemeat pie was another new taste for Peter, and he relished each bite. He even drank coffee with it; something that he might not ordinarily have done, and it was the perfect beverage with the pie.

The men in the party retired to the great room for continued conversation, and to rest their overfilled stomachs. Klaus made Peter comfortable in his own recliner chair, raising the leg support, with Duchess snuggled in by his side.

The Kellman women quickly picked up the remnants of the Christmas Dinner, and had the kitchen sparkling within a half-hour. They joined the men in the great room afterward, where politics were the topic under discussion.

Ron addressed Peter, "What's it like in the Soviet Union? You don't have elections there, do you?"

Peter was quiet for a moment and then answered, "Of course you know that the freedoms that you have here, the freedoms that you probably take for granted, do not exist in my country."

"But what is it really like there? How do you make a living, buy a house, whatever?" Ron was insistent.

Mike decided to get into the conversation, "Hey Ron, what's the question, really? You read the papers, don't you?"

"Have you read anything written by Ivan Genchenko, Ron?" Nik looked at Peter as she asked the question.

"Genchenko?" Ron said, pointing at Peter.

"Yes, *that* Genchenko family," Nik smiled.

Marina could no longer contain herself, "Three books he wrote, Ivan Genchenko, while he was imprisoned in Lefortovo; three books on freedom, democracy, and capitalism."

"Ivan's books were never published in the Soviet Union, for very obvious reasons," Peter said flatly.

"And Ivan is…?" Ron asked

"Ivan was my father," Peter replied.

Mickey told the room at large that he had seen a television documentary on the smuggling of the Genchenko books out of Russia. "It was neat how they did it. They brought several chapters out at a time, and then assembled the books in this country. That way, they were less likely to get caught coming out of the Soviet Union."

Peter looked at Mickey with interest, "That is something that I didn't know. Were the identities of the smugglers revealed?"

"No, I think that there was probably a good reason why they didn't tell who they were." Mickey shrugged his shoulders elaborately.

Klaus and Tom had added nothing to the conversation. Instead, they were talking to each other about a shared interest, football.

Tom laughed out loud. "I can't believe that the Colts left Baltimore in the middle of the night for Indianapolis. Irsay must have been out of his mind."

The room became quiet, and Mike and Nik exchanged glances before looking at their mother.

Marina's face was pale when she got up and walked from the room. Peter saw that Niki soon followed her mother, and he wondered what had happened.

Within a few minutes, Marina and Nik came back into the room and sat down next to each other on the sofa, arm in arm, in front of the fire.

Mike went over to them and sat down, too, and they began to talk quietly together.

Peter had put his head against the back of the chair and closed his eyes momentarily, and hadn't seen Niki and her mother come back into the room. Duchess caused him to open them rather suddenly when she attempted to change her position in the chair and put her head in his lap. He gently moved her head away from the still-tender surgical wound in his right groin, thus averting disaster.

He looked around the room and saw Niki, her mother, and Mike sitting together. He also saw that Ron had joined Klaus, Tom and Mickey. Peter was curious about the dynamics at work in the room. When Niki looked in his direction, Peter saw that something seemed to be wrong. The look on her face was one of sadness.

The doorbell rang, and Klaus got up to answer it. Everyone looked expectantly toward the entrance. Even Duchess lifted her head, but didn't leave Peter's side

Klaus returned with a young woman at his side and introduced her to the group, "This is Lauren Kaye. She is going to be helping Peter recuperate."

Marina stood from the sofa. Always the hostess, she asked, "Have you had your Christmas Dinner, Lauren?"

Lauren nodded, "Yes, my family just finished, and that's why I'm a little late. I apologize for the delay."

Nik came over to Lauren, "I'm Pete's doctor, and you can call me Nik. Let me introduce you to Pete. He's been a good patient, and I know that you will like him very much."

As Nik brought Lauren close to Pete, Duchess growled briefly, "Oh be quiet, Duchess, you're such a jealous girl."

Peter stood slowly and put his hand out to take Lauren's, "Hello, I'm glad that you are here."

Lauren blushed as she took Peter's hand, "Thanks…uh, I guess that you and I should sit down and talk about how you're doing, and maybe Nik could be there so that I know exactly what we're going to do."

Tom and Mickey came over to Peter to say goodbye, and stood waiting while he and Lauren talked.

Nik talked to her "men" as she called them, "I'm so glad that you two could come today. I'm sure Peter loved it. Did either of you talk with your folks yet?"

"I called my mom and dad earlier today. They said it's snowing in Pawtucket, and they wished that I could have come home." Tom smiled a wistful smile.

Mickey said, "I haven't called my folks, yet. They're in Lisbon…North Dakota, that is. But I'll call them tonight. We've got a big family, so one less won't be noticed right away. Thanks, Doc, for inviting me to your Christmas Dinner, It was great."

"Yeah, Doc, it was fantastic." Tom patted his rounded abdomen.

"Tell that to my mother, and she will love you forever." Nik gave Mickey a quick hug, and then did the same to Tom.

Peter turned his attention to Mickey and Tom, "This has been a wonderful day with my friends. I wish you a Merry Christmas."

Nik watched while the three of them shook hands and slapped backs, although, it must be said that the back slapping that Peter received was gentle. It made her smile, and when she realized that Lauren was watching, she laughed and made a thumbs-up gesture at her. Lauren returned the favor, and laughed too.

I think that I'm going to like this young lady, thought Nik. She seems good natured and sweet.

Nik walked Tom and Mickey to the front door. "Come back to visit anytime, guys, Peter's going to be lonesome, and I know that he's going to get 'antsy' for something to do."

Peter was beginning to tire so he walked slowly back to where Lauren was sitting. He saw that Klaus, Ron, and Mike stood by the fireplace, and they seemed to be talking about a serious subject. As he sat down next to Lauren, he saw Marina go quietly down the hall to another part of the house, with Duchess behind her. Again he wondered what had, or was, happening. It puzzled him, because he couldn't recall any specific event that might have changed the tone of the day.

Lauren was busy with the supplies that she had brought with her for Peter's care when he sat down next to her. She looked up at him and smiled a shy smile.

"Your accent is very unusual and interesting Peter. Where are you from?" Lauren wanted to build a rapport with her new patient.

"Russia. Am I the first Russian that you have ever met?" Peter put his head against the back of the sofa to rest.

"As a matter of fact, yes, you are. Perhaps, as we work together, you can teach me some Russian words; I'd really like that."

"You would?" He was curious as to her reason for wanting to learn about his language, "Do you have command over other languages besides English?"

Lauren nodded, "I studied Spanish in high school, and got to stay a whole summer with a family in Madrid. We spoke only Spanish the entire three months that I was there."

Immersion, he thought. Many times his mother had told him that immersion in a culture, a language, was one of the best ways to really learn to speak, and to think, in a language.

Lauren continued. "In college I studied French, but I really didn't become very proficient with the language. French is a very difficult language as far as I'm concerned."

"Yes it is. But did you know that French was the language of the Russian Court, when the Czars ruled Russia?"

Lauren shook her head, "No, I didn't know that. Do you speak French, Peter?"

"I studied French, among other languages, in school, but I haven't used it for many years."

Peter thought about the time that he had traveled with his hockey team to Quebec to compete in a hockey tournament. It had been very interesting to listen to, and understand, what the opposing team was saying, and he chuckled at the memory.

Lauren's large gray, thickly lashed eyes, her pale skin, with freckles sprinkled across her nose, combined to give her an Irish beauty, with her dark red hair, that Peter found attractive. Her best attribute, however, was her sweetness, he decided. He liked talking to her.

"Pete, I think that you need to get some rest." Nik stood behind him.

Peter smiled, eyes closed, "Yes, I know that it's only six o'clock, but I would welcome the chance to get ready for bed."

Nik came around to kneel in front of him, "You've had a big day, and it's time for you to get comfortable, take your medication, and get some rest."

Peter sat forward on the sofa, nodded, and stood up. He felt a little dizzy and swayed briefly.

"Whoa, maybe I should go get the wheelchair." Nik stood quickly and reached for his hand and took it to steady him.

"No, I'm just tired, but I can walk to my room." He enjoyed holding her hand.

Lauren was efficient and quick. Peter was bathed, and in his pajamas, his wound dressings changed, and in bed within twenty minutes. He was still on an antibiotic, so he took his evening dose and drank a 12-ounce glass of water with it, Doctor's orders. Lauren finished by pulling up his covers.

"How's that, Peter? Are you comfortable, and do you need anything else?" Lauren stood back to check her efforts.

"I am fine, and thank you for getting me ready for a good night's rest. Spaseeba, *thank you*." Peter could hardly keep his eyes open, and he ran his fingers through his hair.

"Okay, goodnight, Peter. I'll see you in the morning." Lauren came out of Peter's room and went to Nik to let her know that Peter was set for the night.

"Thanks Lauren, I'll keep an eye on Pete throughout the night. He's had several good nights since his surgery, so I don't see that we'll have a problem."

They walked to the front entrance and talked for a while at the door. Ron was watching from a distance, and came over to Nik just as she was closing the door.

"Why is the nurse leaving so quickly? I thought that she would be here for a whole shift." Ron put an arm around Nik's shoulders.

"Nope, she was here just to help with the "ADL" stuff." Nik looked up at Ron and grinned a wicked grin.

"Okay, hon', what is an 'ADL'?" He gave her a sidelong glance.

"Activities of daily living are the things that we do every day; wash, eat, dress, work, and so on. When you've been sick or had surgery, it's hard to do those things, so someone like Lauren, a nurse, helps you with them."

"Yeah, yeah, yeah…so? Lauren's not staying the night."

"Nope."

"What happens if there's a problem?"

"It won't, don't worry. Mom and I can handle anything, and we can call dad, too, if we have to."

"Nik? Are you still mad at me the way you were at the hospital?" Ron's face became serious.

"I was overwhelmed, and tired, and I was more upset with myself than you could imagine. I let Peter down. I let him play with an injury, a problem, and I shouldn't have, and I thought that I was responsible for his having to undergo surgery."

Ron put his hand on her shoulder. "*That's* what was wrong? You mean that it wasn't just me?"

"It was everything that night, that morning. I had had it, that's all." Nik was shaking her head as she remembered how angry she had been.

"Good. Well then, let's enjoy the rest of the Christmas party; it's my first, you know." Ron's face had relaxed, and he now had a genuine smile on his face.

They walked together into the great room, to join Nik's family. As they approached them, Nik realized that they were talking about Josef.

Ron pulled Nik down onto a loveseat set at a right angle to the sofa in front of the fireplace. Nik could see the sadness in her mother's face, and knew that this could be a difficult evening.

"Klaus, Mikhail, Nikola, let's not talk about what happened to our beloved Josef; not on this Christmas Day. We can remember him, of course, we can tell our wonderful stories, too, but let's not re-live what happened to him." Marina's face was pale and drawn.

"It's okay, mom, we aren't going to go through what happened to Joey again, but you have to understand, too, that dad and Tom were only talking about football, and their comments had nothing to do with Joey." Mike's face was earnest as he spoke to her.

"I know that Mike, I really do, but you know how hard holidays can be. It doesn't get any easier." Marina was wringing her hands.

Klaus had been silent for some time, but now he spoke to his family. "We cannot undo what has happened to our Josef. I believe that he is here with us, that he knows how much we loved and continue to love him. Tom meant no harm, and I should have steered our conversation away from," he hesitated, "what we were talking about, but I didn't want to be impolite."

Nik got up from the loveseat and went over to her father to give him a hug. She then walked to her mother, and hugged her as well.

Ron didn't like what he called the "emotional stuff" and stood up to tell everyone that he needed to get going because he had some written work to do. He was uncomfortable with the level of emotion in Nik's family on this night, and he thought that they could talk more freely if he left. When he said his goodbyes, he took Nik by the hand and walked to the foyer with her.

"It was a little tense in there, wasn't it? I feel bad for you and your family, Nik. There are some things that you never get over."

Nik nodded, but said nothing.

"We missed our beautiful weekend in Chicago, didn't we?" Ron's smile was almost wistful.

"Life intervened, Ron, or should I say, interfered." Nik stood looking up at him, arms folded.

"My mother was very disappointed when I told her, Nik, she really wanted to meet you…finally," again the wistful smile.

Ron hugged Nik to him almost spasmodically, and kissed her briefly on the lips. "I have to go, Nik."

As Ron was leaving, the fire in the fireplace was only dying embers. It had begun to snow again, and Nik told Ron to drive carefully. They made plans to get together the next day.

Nik went to check on Pete and found him sleeping soundly. She stepped inside the room and watched him for several moments to make sure that he was breathing. Isn't that what mothers do for their children thought Nik? But she knew in her heart that her concern for this man was far different than that of a mother for her child.

Peter was turned on his side facing the window. Moonlight lit his face, and it formed a halo of silver and gold around his hair. Nik felt a catch in her throat as she stood watching him.

Duchess found Nik as she approached the great room. She bowed down in front of Nik and wagged the stump of a tail on her elevated rump.

Nik had partially closed the door to the room where Pete slept, "Hush, Duchess, you're going to waken Pete."

Duchess followed Nik into the great room. "Mikey, we've got to let our precious little Duchess out to frolic in the snow."

Her brother laughed at her, "Okay, come on, we'll put her out together."

Mike waved Duchess toward the kitchen, "Let's go, girl, it's time for your nightly run."

Nik opened the French doors off the kitchen and Duchess went airborne onto the deck. With two reindeer leaps, she was off the deck and into the deep snow, barking and dancing, throwing clouds of snow around her.

"Lady Gray used to do that, too." Mike's face was a study in solemnity.

"It doesn't seem that long ago, either, but it has been years." Nik was pensive, too.

"Yeah, the years do go by, don't they? Let's see, I'm going to be thirty-two next month, so that means that *you* are approaching twenty-seven, right?"

Nik giggled, and then laughed out loud. "I just had my twenty-eighth birthday two weeks ago!"

Mike slapped his forehead, "Damn, I missed it, didn't I?"

She rubbed her brother's back, "I know that you're a busy entrepreneur out there in San Francisco, but you really ought to try to keep in touch with your Hoosier relatives."

Mike nodded and gave her his version of an ornery brother's grin, "How's the doctoring business?"

"I have learned more about medicine in the last two weeks than I did the whole time that I was an intern."

"How so?" Mike was curious about her meaning.

"Ron dragged me into the International Winter Games; well actually, he asked if I'd help out, and I agreed to take a team. I was thinking women's volleyball, and he was thinking men's hockey. You know, we always think alike," she said wryly. "Well, anyway, I got the Russian hockey team, and I called them my Neanderthals."

Mike nodded his head toward the front of the house. "Is that how Peter Genchenko got here?"

"Sort of, I guess. He has a very unusual story. I wish that you could have seen him play hockey. Of course, I'm no judge of skill there, but a scout for professional hockey spent most of the games week watching the Russians play hockey. Peter was a standout, and he received the MVP for men's hockey."

"Ron said that there were some strange things that happened during the week of the games. He said that Peter was at the center of all the crazy stuff." Mike leaned on the doorframe, hands in pockets, as he talked to his little sister.

"I don't know how long you'll be home this time, but it's a long story. I want you to know, though, that none of what happened was Peter's fault."

Nik didn't like it that Ron had said something about the events of the games week to Mike, and that he had off-handedly put the blame on Pete. At that awkwrd moment, Duchess bounded up on the deck and put her feet up on the glass of the door.

"I think she wants in, Mike, what do you think?"

"Could be. Where's the towel?" Mike looked around the floor.

Nik tossed him the dog towel from the laundry room. "I think it's your turn to wipe feet and tummy."

When Mike opened the door, Duchess skidded inside, her beautiful Christmas bow askew. She immediately rolled over on her back so that Mike could dry her belly, and then offered one, and then another paw until she was satisfied that she was dry enough.

"Hold it, hold it Duchess. Let me have that bow. I think the color's going to run now that it's wet." Nik quickly untied the bow and put it in a wastebasket. Duchess scrambled to her feet and ran quickly into the great room.

Mike and Nik heard their father speak to the dog as if she were a child, "Settle down Duchess, you can't run around in here."

The Kellman family members said goodnight to one another, hugged and kissed, and went to their bedrooms. Mike and Nik walked together up the stairs to their rooms arm in arm.

When they reached the top, the siblings stood at the railing looking down upon the great room, the way that they had when they were children. Only one lamp in the great room was lit on low, and the Christmas tree was unplugged. Nonetheless, the room, because of its height and breadth, was spectacular with its vaulted ceiling and huge fireplace, with a view directly into the foyer.

"Goodnight Niki, I'll see you in the morning." Mike turned and rubbed the top of his sister's head affectionately.

"Thanks for the way you handled the football thing, Mikey. I hate to see our parents so sad. But it's something that will always be there." She kissed Mike on the cheek.

Nik got ready for bed in record time. She was so sleepy that she could barely keep her eyes open. A glance at her little bathroom clock showed that it was only nine-thirty, but it seemed much later.

The past week was difficult for her, but, if it had been difficult for her, it had been terrible for Pete. She had seen it in his eyes. He had never complained, not once, but he had endured pain and indignities that she knew had wounded his very private spirit.

When she crawled into bed, she said a prayer for Pete's complete recovery, as she had every night since he had become sick. Please, Lord, help him. He's a good man, and he deserves good health and happiness. Her bed was soft and warm, and she fell asleep almost immediately.

Nik was awake and looking at her bedside clock. It was only twelve-thirty, but she felt rested. How strange, she thought, and wondered what might have awakened her. Then she thought of Pete, and decided that she should go to check on him.

Her robe and slippers felt warm and comforting as she walked down the stairs. The house temperature automatically dropped to sixty-five degrees after eleven o'clock at night, but it seemed colder than that to her.

As Nik walked through the great room she could see a small light reflected in the hallway near the room that Peter was in. When she reached his door, she saw that he was sitting on the side of the bed, and Duchess was sitting at attention in front of him.

Peter smiled when he saw Nik. He looked as if he had just awakened; his hair was tousled, and his pajamas rumpled. His bare feet were flat on the floor, even though the hospital bed was higher than most beds.

"Did Duchess awaken you, Pete?" Nik shook a finger at the dog.

Again he smiled, "No, I've been awake for about an hour. Duchess came in when I turned on the light."

Duchess turned to look up at Nik as if to say, "see, I'm not bothering him." Nik giggled and rubbed her dog's head.

"Okay girl, you're off the hook."

Peter hesitated, and then spoke to Nik, "I…am not sure where the bathroom is."

"Oh, my gosh, oh, I'm sorry Pete! I didn't even think about that when we settled you in here." Nik put her hand to her forehead.

"If you would show me now, I'd be very grateful." Even though he was physically uncomfortable, Peter was laughing quietly at Nik's discomfiture.

Nik took his hand, "It's right across the hall. That's why mom and I put you in this room. Well, that, and the fact that you really liked the room when you were here for the open house."

After putting Pete's slippers on his feet, Nik took him across the hall, opened the door and flipped on the light. "I'll be in your room with Duchess; call me if you need me."

Duchess rolled over on her back, begging for a tummy rub, and Nik complied. Poor Pete, he must have been miserable. Just thinking about it made her feel miserable, too.

Peter came out of the bathroom still smiling as if he had made some private joke. "I am very hungry. Even though I ate more today than I have in a long time, I am hungry again. Maybe it's a good sign?"

"Yes, it definitely is! Come on, let's raid the refrigerator." Nik put her arm through Peter's and they began the trek through the great room.

He looked down at her, with her hair mussed, and her outlandish pink robe and slippers, and he knew that he could never love another human being as much as he loved this woman at this moment.

They enjoyed a veritable feast of cold turkey, cranberry sauce, salad, hot tea, and sliced bread with butter. Duchess had her share, too, so that she would be quiet and not wake Nik's mom, dad, and brother.

When they finished with the main course, Nik poured tall glasses of milk for both of them, and sliced two pieces of mincemeat pie. She rummaged around in the refrigerator until she found the leftover whipped cream, which was not nearly as fluffy as it had been for the Christmas Dinner. It would do, however, for their midnight supper, and she plopped a large spoonful on each piece of pie.

When they finished their pie, Nik said, "I've got something for you, Pete."

She went into the great room and came back with the red-wrapped box that had been under the Christmas tree when Peter arrived.

"This is for you. My family always opens gifts on Christmas Eve, and I was hoping that you'd be home by then, but now is a good time, too."

Peter was so surprised that he didn't know what to say. He had never received such a beautifully wrapped gift, and certainly had never received a Christmas gift, so he wasn't sure how he should act.

Slowly, carefully, Peter opened the gift. Inside he found a heavy coat, gloves, and hat. There were beautifully wrapped gifts inside the box, too. One was for Eda, the other for Katya.

"You can take those to your mother and sister, Pete, when you go home. I got them leather gloves and silk scarves. I hope you like your Christmas gifts."

Peter was speechless. Finally, he said, "I like them very much, and I thank you."

Duchess, head down, hips up, ready to pounce, growled, and Nik got up from her chair to put her outside to play. Peter laughed at Duchess' leap through the doorway out into the snow.

"Good form," he said, laughing. "She's like an Olympic athlete performing snow acrobatics!"

Peter walked slowly to the doorway to watch Duchess' antics in the snow. "She should have been a reindeer."

"Well, she may be part reindeer, the way she jumps and leaps around, and loves the snow."

Duchess didn't stay outside very long. The temperature had dropped five degrees since ten o'clock, and a light snow filtered down, dusting the trees with more white. Nik toweled the snow from Duchess, and Peter commented that he had never seen a dog before that actually cooperated during grooming.

"Duchess is quite a girl, but I wish that you could have met her mother, Lady Gray. She had a very long pedigree, and she thought that she was an aristocrat, very dignified. I think that Duchess must take after her father."

They laughed, talked, and were serious at times as they relived the three short weeks that had brought them to this point in time. Peter even alluded in an oblique way to their dance at the Awards Banquet. Nik had closed her eyes for a moment, only a moment, remembering the way that she had felt with his arms around her. When she opened her eyes, Peter was smiling a tender smile at her. As they continued to talk easily, comfortably, Nik could remember no happier time in her mother's kitchen than this, with this wonderful, witty, intelligent man.

Chapter 27

Friday December 26, 1986

"Hey Nik," Mike called up the stairs. "I've got to get going if I'm going to catch my plane. Are you coming with us, or not?"

Nik stuck her head out of her bedroom door. "I'll be down in five minutes. Is Lauren here yet?"

"Yeah, she got here about twenty minutes ago, and she's got Peter all fixed up for the day; Duchess, too."

Mike looked over at Peter, sitting in his father's recliner chair with Duchess at his side, and nodded at him.

Peter nodded back and smiled.

Nik came tearing out of her room, putting an earring in one ear. "Okay! I'm ready."

As she came down the stairs, Peter's heart skipped a beat. Niki looked beautiful in a soft beige suit and high-heeled boots. She looked in his direction and smiled at him, and his heart skipped another beat.

"Were you hungry this morning, Pete?" Nik looked at him with one eyebrow raised.

"Surprisingly, yes, I was." Peter nodded his head, "Lauren has been so kind as to help me with my breakfast."

Peter and Nik had left no signs of their midnight raid on the refrigerator, because they had washed the dishes together and put them away. It was another secret that they shared.

"Hello, Lauren. How is our patient this morning?"

"He's A-okay, doctor, and he's getting around very well. His temp's normal, stomach soft, wounds well-healed, and his blood pressure, pulse and respirations would put all of us in this room to shame."

Mike added his opinion, "Yeah? Well, do you want to check mine?"

Lauren blushed. "If you think it would be helpful, I will."

"Don't worry about Mikey. He's ornery and loves to tease pretty girls." Nik gave her big brother a stern look.

The door to the garage opened, and Klaus leaned in to ask, "Are we going to the airport, or not? It's time to leave."

Nik and Mike looked at each other and laughed silently, hands over their mouths. Peter and Lauren shook their heads at them.

Mike already had his coat on and opened the closet door for Nik, "Pick one."

Nik grabbed her camel's hair coat, threw a scarf around her neck, pulled on her gloves and said, "Go!"

As she ran to the door, she waved at Peter and Lauren, and then she was gone. Peter wished fervently that he could go with her; that he could freely get up, walk around, and be the captain of his own ship.

"It was nice meeting you, Peter. Be kind to my sister," Mike said, looking into Peter's eyes as he shook Peter's hand briefly.

"Come *on*, Mike, now you're the one who's making us late," Nik called from the garage.

There was much laughter in the Kellman's Lincoln on the way to the airport. Nik and Mike laughingly called their parents' car a gas-guzzling, "obscene barge." They were all talking at once, but managing to communicate anyway. Nik and Mike sat in the back, just as they had when they were children. Nik reached over and put her hand in his. It was a small gesture, but Mike looked at her and squeezed her hand gently, big brother style.

"I love you, too," Mike said. "You know that you can call me anytime, anywhere, if you need me."

Puzzled, Nik replied, "I'm a big girl now, Mike, and I'm okay, so don't worry about me."

"Yeah, I know, but sometimes I worry about you because you have such a big heart."

The airport was crowded, but there were few delays in departures despite the weather, and Mike's plane was ready to take off with only a few minutes' delay. Mike hugged Nik and then his father. Marina's eyes filled with tears when Mike kissed her on the cheek and stepped up to the boarding agent. He disappeared up the jet way with a parting wave.

My tall, dark and handsome brother; he's out of sight too quickly, thought Nik, feeling an ache in her heart. Klaus was quiet, and Nik held onto her father's arm tightly, while Marina held the other. Saying goodbye was always hard because Mike only came home twice a year, Christmas and Easter.

His parents and sister visited him in California every year in July, when they all stayed at the beautiful old white clapboard, red-roofed Del, the Del Coronado Hotel near San Diego. It was a weeklong 'retreat' of sorts, when the Kellman family came together to spend quality time dining, beach walking, and swimming. Nik loved San Diego, too. It was one of her all-time favorite places to visit.

As they were riding to the airport, Mike had told Nik that he had invited Ron to come to the family gathering at the Del next year. She told him that it was a wonderful idea. After all, Ron was almost part of the family, thought Nik.

But, she and Ron hadn't had the opportunity to set a date for their wedding. Nik was sure the reason was that she had not had the required meeting with his parents. She felt that she would be on display, and would be scrutinized, and get a thumbs-up, or thumbs-down. She wondered about the Michael family. Ron seemed to revere his mother and father, but he also kept some distance between himself and his parents. His brother, also, lived a good distance from them. And then Nik thought about Mike, living in San Francisco, where her family never visited, and she wondered why he had gone so far away to establish his independence?

The ride home was much quieter than the ride to the airport. Nik realized that it was very difficult for her parents to say goodbye to their son, knowing that they wouldn't see him again for several months.

Klaus was talking about the weather as he carefully drove his wife and daughter home on a very slushy I-465. He pointed out how dark the sky was in the west.

"There's another storm front coming. Can you believe it? We're probably going to get more snow," said Klaus.

Chapter 28

While Lauren was making his bed, Peter walked up and down the hall and around the great room. He had to get his strength back. He knew that it was too soon after his surgery to risk anything but the lightest exercise, but he could walk. Each day since his surgery, he felt stronger.

Thinking about the midnight raid of the Kellmans' refrigerator last night made him smile. Well, we were hungry, he rationalized, and the raid had satisfied that hunger, for the most part.

Duchess was Peter's constant companion on his walk. He liked her, and wished that he could have a dog of his own. Of course, he realized the impossibility of his wish. His mother, sister, and he could barely make enough money for food and shelter. No, a dog would be a luxury that they couldn't afford.

At the foot of the stairs, Peter looked up and then asked Duchess if she thought that they could make it to the top. Duchess declined to answer, but sat down in front of the first stair, blocking his way.

"Hmmm..." Peter mused, "I think you may be right. Maybe we can try tomorrow."

Peter heard the garage door open, and he was immediately happy. Like Pavlov's dog, he almost salivated. Niki is home. He started walking to the garage entry door to the great room, with Duchess at his side.

He was halfway across the room when Niki came into view. "Hello," he said, smiling at her.

Nik was pleasantly surprised to see that Peter was dressed and up and about. She quickly walked to him. "Pete, you're beginning to look like your old self."

"And I am beginning to feel like my old self, too." He was standing erect, without guarding of his abdomen.

Nik pulled her hair behind one ear, "Mike's plane took off almost on time. We couldn't believe it. We were hoping for a few extra minutes with him, but no such luck."

"I like your brother. He's a lot like you, only taller." Peter smiled as he saw the effect that his comment had on Niki.

Nik beamed, "All through school, everyone said that they could tell who the three Kellman kids were. We all had the same coloring, straight dark hair, and dark eyes. But my dad always said that I was prettier than my brothers."

"You have more than one brother?" Peter wondered why Niki hadn't spoken before about her other brother.

At that moment, Marina and Klaus walked into the great room. Klaus began taking off his coat, and then he helped his wife with hers. Neither seemed to have heard Peter's question to Nik, and she breathed a sigh of relief.

Nik placed her hand on Peter's arm and looked up at him, "Come with me. I need to tell you something."

They walked to Peter's room where Lauren, her hair pulled back from her face, was busily straightening up after getting Peter ready for the day.

"Hi doctor, uh, Nik," Lauren's face reddened with her faux pas.

Peter found a chair and sat down to rest after his brief bout of exercise. He watched passively as Nik and Lauren discussed his progress. He felt as if he was eavesdropping on gossip about a stranger. Am I ever going to get my strength back? He worried about his mother and sister, and knew that they would be frightened when he didn't make it home with his team. There was no way to contact them, they had no telephone, but he had asked Grigory to tell them in person. He hoped that Grigory would be able to do so.

Nik asked Lauren how Pete's breakfast and exercise had been for the morning. She was hopeful that he was improving.

"He's doing very well. In fact, he's one of the best patients that I've ever had. His vitals are great, his wounds are healing beautifully, and he's motivated to exercise. I watched him make about ten circuits of your great room without stopping." One of Lauren's hands was on her hip, as she pointed toward the great room with the other.

"I'll look at Pete's wounds tonight when you change his dressings. It's great that his temp is holding at normal. He's far enough past his surgery that we can breathe easier about infection."

Lauren nodded, "Pete's very lucky," she said.

"Looks like you're wrapping up for the day. I've got to warn you that the traffic is horrible."

"It always is the day after Christmas. I have some things that need to be exchanged, so I'll probably be joining the traffic jam."

Glancing over at Peter, Nik said, "Our patient is going to be in good hands today until you come back tonight."

Lauren put her coat and hat on quickly, grabbed her purse and gloves, "'Bye Pete, Nik, I'll see you at six this evening."

"Thank you Lauren, you've been very kind and helpful." Peter was truly grateful to her.

Marina was just in time to say goodbye to her, "See you tonight, dear," and turned to Nik, "I'm planning to serve lunch in about an hour. Do you have any special requests?" Marina looked at her daughter and Peter expectantly.

"Oh...*lunch.*I'm supposed to have lunch with Ron." Nik frowned for a moment.

Peter felt a stab of disappointment when Niki remembered her lunch date with Ron. He had hoped that he would get to spend some time with her today.

"Maybe Myron could come to lunch with us here at home. I could fix a very nice meal in just a few minutes." Marina looked hopefully at her daughter.

Before Nik could answer, the telephone rang. The Kellmans had put telephones in every room for convenience because of the size of their house, and Marina walked to a nearby table to pick up the telephone.

She answered, "Hello?"

"Marina, is Nik there?" There was an edge of irritation in Ron's voice.

"Yes, Myron, she's right here. Niki, it's for you." Marina handed the telephone to her daughter.

"Hi, Ron, where are you?" Nik's tone was bland.

"I'm at a pay phone in the Greenwood Mall. I was out here trying to take advantage of a couple of bargains, and got into a three vehicle accident."

"Are you okay? Was anyone hurt?" Nik was immediately concerned.

"No one was hurt, but it's going to be a while until I can get away from here."

"I can come out to get you," Nik offered.

"No, no, that's okay, I can still drive my car, but I'm going to have to get to a garage. Anyway, lunch is off, at least for today. Sorry, hon'."

"That's all right, Ron. Will you call me when you get everything settled?"

"Sure, but I don't know how long this is going to take, Nik." He let out a long sigh of frustration.

"I've got plenty to do here, so don't worry about it. I'll talk to you later." Nik was inexplicably filled with a sense of relief, of liberation.

"What's wrong, Niki? Has something happened to Myron?" Marina's face showed concern.

"He's all right, mom, but he was involved in a three-way fender bender near the Greenwood Mall."

Marina put her hand to her face, "Oh no, are you sure he isn't hurt?"

"Mom, he said he's okay, so don't get upset." Nik put her arm around her mother's shoulders.

Nik looked over at Peter as she hugged her mother, and saw that he was looking out of the window toward the lake. Duchess was practically in his lap, and was gazing up at him adoringly as he absently rubbed her neck.

"Well, I guess that I'll be home for lunch. Would you like to have some help in the kitchen?" Nik smiled at Marina as she made her offer.

"Pete? Would you like to come with us, too?"

Peter stood slowly from the chair, "Yes, but you'll have to tell me what I can do to help you."

"Why don't you two just sit and visit? I have a casserole in the oven, and it will only take a few minutes to put a fresh green salad together. Does that sound good to both of you?"

"Are you sure that I can't help, mom?"

"Your father has already volunteered to set the table. We're going to eat in the breakfast nook instead of the dining room. It's more cozy," she smiled, "and it's easier to clean up."

When Marina left the room, Nik turned to Peter, who was still standing, and said, "I want to show you something, Pete."

She then went over to the bookcases and seemed to be looking for something on the shelves. After a short time, she pulled what appeared to be a book from a shelf.

"When we were in the great room, do you remember that I told you I wanted to talk to you?"

Peter looked at her intently, his brows furrowed, trying to read her face, trying to understand what this was about. "Yes, but I wasn't sure why."

He moved closer to her, close enough to catch the scent of her soft fragrance. When he looked into her eyes, he could see sadness, but also a certain resolve.

"My brother, Josef," Nik began, "was my idol. Of course we disagreed, argued, whatever, but we loved each other. He was everything that I was not; popular, outgoing, happy-go-lucky, athletic."

Nik was quiet for a moment. She was overcome with emotion, and had to gather herself to continue.

"I am the baby of the family. Joey was six years, and Mikey four years older than I."

Nik opened the book that she had taken from the bookshelf, and Peter saw that it was a photograph album. He noticed that Niki's hands were shaking as she opened the album.

Nik paged through the album until she came to a photograph that Peter might recognize as one of her, and of her brothers. She told Peter that the photograph was taken when Nik was twelve, Mikey was sixteen, and Joey eighteen. They were standing in front of a car.

Peter saw that Marina was off to the side in the photograph, and probably had been unaware that she was in camera range. She was proudly smiling at her handsome children.

"This was taken about sixteen years ago. Joey is the tallest brother in the picture, and he is, was, my oldest brother. This was taken two months before Joey died on a football field as the result of being tackled at the same time by two players from the opposing team."

Peter studied the smiling, handsome young man in the picture. Joey and Mikey looked very much alike, and anyone could tell that they were brothers. Their little sister, Niki, stood between the two brothers, and they each had an arm around her shoulders.

She looked up at Peter with anguish in her eyes. "He could have survived if he'd gotten the right kind of care immediately, but they did everything wrong. Dad and mom, especially mom, have never gotten over it. That's why football is a sore subject in this house. I think that my mom has feelings of guilt because she talked my dad into letting Joey play football. Dad had reservations, he said that football was a dangerous sport, and he didn't want his sons to play. Mom gave in to Joey's pleading, and pressured dad to let him play.

"Joey was in pre-med when he died. I picked up his dream of a medical career, because I wanted to make sure that what happened to him wouldn't happen to someone else."

Peter didn't know what to say. His heart ached for Niki and her family, but what could be said, what could *he* say, that would even begin to convey the sorrow he felt for what had happened to Niki's brother?

Klaus stood in the doorway, "Your mother has lunch on the table."

Nik turned her head and answered him, "We'll be right out, dad."

Klaus had a smile on his face as he left the room, "Okay, Niki, you know that your mother likes punctuality."

"Pete, I just wanted you to understand what happened yesterday when my mom was upset. Holidays are especially difficult for her, and just hearing the word football, caused her to react the way that she did."

Finally, Peter found his voice, "Niki, I am so very sorry that your family had to experience the pain of this tragedy." He put a hand on her shoulder as he spoke.

Nik placed her hand on top of his and patted it. "Thanks, Pete. Sometimes, no matter how well fixed a family might seem to be, and no matter the outward appearance of the perfect life, terrible losses do occur."

She took his arm, "Let's go have a nice lunch, and smile and talk, and be a happy family. That's the only way that my mom can cope."

"All right, Niki, I will do whatever it is that helps you and your family. I can never repay what you and your parents have done, are doing, for me."

Nik looked up at him and said, "Hush," and they walked down the hall to the great room and into the kitchen, with Duchess trotting behind.

Marina served a turkey vegetable casserole, a green salad, and freshly baked wheat bread. "If you clean your plates, I'll serve some mincemeat pie with hot spiced tea."

Luncheon conversation centered on two topics, mostly; Mike's departure, and Peter's convalescence. The mood was light and happy for the most part. Marina wanted to know if she could make Peter's stay more comfortable.

"Oh, I'm completely comfortable. Please don't go to any more bother on my behalf. I'm doing quite well."

"Mom, you've had a good influence on Pete's eating habits. He must like your cooking."

At this pronouncement, they all laughed. Nik thought that she detected a little blush spreading over Pete's face, and reached over to pat his hand.

He looked down at his plate, and then looked up with a smile on his face, "I can honestly say that I haven't eaten this well for a very long time."

"What about the athletes' training table, Peter? Surely they fed you well to keep you at your peak performance, didn't they?" Klaus was interested in Peter's experiences as an athlete.

Nik looked over at Peter with a wry smile, "Pete didn't always eat with his teammates, dad. Especially not when…" She stopped short of naming Yakov Popov as the reason why Peter didn't go to the training table for his meals.

The doorbell chimed, and Klaus got up to answer it. Duchess followed him out of curiosity.

Nik could hear a muffled conversation, and she thought that she heard the voice of Detective Myers. Oh no, she thought, it can't be. Why on earth would he bother Pete now?

After a few moments, Klaus came into the breakfast room and told Peter that Detective Myers wanted to talk to him. "I'll call Les, and tell him that the Detective is here to see you, Peter."

Peter's face was a study in aloofness, but Nik knew that he must be very upset at the prospect of talking to the Detective again. "I'll go with you Pete."

"If you wish, Niki, but you don't need to." Peter's answer was noncommittal.

Peter got up from the table, and slowly walked toward the great room. Nik followed, and Duchess interposed herself between them. Klaus and Marina looked at each other with raised eyebrows.

"I've got to call Les, Marina. I don't know what this visit is all about, but I am thinking that it's not good." Klaus put his arm around her shoulders and pulled her close to him.

"I feel sorry for Peter. He isn't up to this while he's recuperating." Marina looked up at Klaus, and her face showed apprehension.

Nik was ready for battle as she, Pete, and Duchess approached Detective Myers, who was sitting on the sofa in front of the fireplace. He turned as he heard them come into the room.

Nik began, "Detective Myers…"

Peter gently placed a hand on her arm, "It's okay, Niki, I will talk to the Detective."

Nik saw the expression on Pete's face, and realized that he was in control of himself, and the situation. She sat down on a loveseat opposite the Detective, and Peter sat down beside her. Duchess flopped languidly in front of the fireplace, her eyes unwaveringly trained on Detective Myers, and she seemed to be alert for sudden movement or signs of aggression.

Peter started the conversation, "What can I do for you Detective Myers?"

Nik saw that the Detective was not his usual ebullient self. He had a frown on his face instead of the flippant, gum-chewing, persona that he usually affected.

"I'm here to tie up some loose ends, Genchenko, and to apologize to you for yanking you downtown the other day."

Peter hesitated for a moment before he replied, "Apology accepted. What can I do for you now?"

"I received a letter yesterday, and I've taken it to my captain, and to a judge to look at. I'm hoping that maybe this will close the Popov case. I want you to read it, too." Without saying anything more, Myers got up from the sofa and handed Peter an opened envelope.

Peter looked at the address on the envelope, and it was in Grigory's handwriting. Inside, there was only one sheet of paper. Peter took it out of the envelope with care and began to read what Grigory had written.

20 December, 1986

Detective Myers,

You have targeted Peter Genchenko unfairly in the death of Yakov Popov. Peter had nothing to do with his death. Yakov was KGB, and was placed with our team in order to watch us and report our actions to his superiors in Moscow. I write of this at my own peril, because I have now broken the oath of silence in this matter.

Peter's father was an old enemy of Yakov's, and Yakov was hateful to Peter. I tried my best to be a buffer between the two, but Yakov was relentless. When he tried to have Peter injured, or worse, killed, and when he threatened to harm my own family, I decided that I had to intervene.

I went to Yakov's room to talk to him, to try to reason with him, the night that he died. I was angry, and I had been drinking. It was never my intent to physically harm Yakov, but my temper got the best of me. I grabbed him and realized that I had broken his neck.

His death was immediate. However, I did not set a fire in Yakov's room, and I do not know how the fire got started.

You may wish to attempt extradition to bring me back to the United States, but you probably know it is difficult, if not impossible, to extradite a Russian citizen for prosecution of an alleged crime in your country.

Please do not continue to hound Peter Genchenko. Although he, too, was very angry with Yakov, and rightly so because of the attack that he suffered at the hands of Yakov, Peter did not harm him.

Grigory Mikhailovich Serov

Peter handed the letter to Niki because he wanted her to know of its contents. His heart had pounded as he read Grigory's words, and he couldn't understand how Grigory could have done the thing to which he had confessed in his letter. It just wasn't like him to do such a thing.

Detective Myers cleared his throat. "We never told anyone that Yakov Popov's neck was broken, and that it was the cause of death. It wasn't published in the media at all, but Grigory knew how Yakov died. Also, the Fire Marshall investigated the cause of the fire, and found that it had started from a lit cigarette, and probably wasn't set intentionally. Everyone that I've talked to so far, and have shown the letter, agrees that it's probably authentic."

"What will happen now?" Peter was concerned for Grigory.

Detective Myers rubbed his forehead and brushed his bushy eyebrows upward. "From here on? Well, nothing, I guess. We can't extradite him. Of course there will be a problem if he tries to return to the United States, but I think he's much too smart to do that. Anyway, I just wanted you to know about the letter. When you go home, will you be seeing Grigory?"

Peter looked at Niki before he answered, "Yes, I will see him when I reach Moscow. I'll have to report in with the authorities and be checked for fitness to play. Grigory will certainly have something to do with that."

"Give him a message for me, will you? Tell him that I got his letter, and that I believe him. Will you do that for me?"

Peter nodded, "Yes, but I'm not sure what else to say to him. I've known Grigory for many years, and I would never have believed that he could actually harm anyone, no matter how threatening he may appear to be."

Detective Myers stood and buttoned his overcoat. "We probably will never know. Well, how are you doing now, Genchenko? I checked several times with the hospital to see how you were getting along. Will you go back to playing hockey?"

"I am beginning to feel my strength return, thanks in large part," he looked at Niki, "to my doctor and her parents. They have been very kind to me. I'll return to the ice as soon as I can."

"Great, that's great. Well, good luck to you, Genchenko. You're one hell of a hockey player. I watched you play a couple of times, and I was there for the awards dinner, too, just keeping an eye on you." He looked directly at Nik as he spoke to Peter.

Peter walked him to the front door, and the two men shook hands. When Peter came back to the sofa, he pulled Niki to a standing position and hugged her.

"It's over, Niki, *it's over!*" He felt almost weightless, as though the detective had removed an albatross from around his neck.

The doorbell rang again, and Klaus came from the kitchen. "That should be Les Barnes."

"You called Uncle Les?" Nik was amused.

"Of course Niki, how was I to know that Detective Myers' visit was just that; a visit?"

Les had pulled up in his car just as Detective Myers was driving away. Well, he didn't stay long, did he? Les wondered what mischief Myers was up to now.

As he stood waiting for the door to be answered, Les thought about the conversation that he had had with Sarah Williams, and he was worried about Niki. Sarah seemed to believe that Peter was a "straight up good guy" but Les had seen that look on Peter's face in the training room, and he knew that Peter cared for Niki. What he did not know, however, was how Niki felt about Peter. There's no way that this is going to be a happy ending, he thought.

"Les, come in, come in." Klaus was happy to see his friend.

"I just saw Myers leaving. How did it go?"

Klaus shrugged, "He showed Peter a letter, they talked a little while, and then he left. Peter and Niki will tell you what they talked about."

"Hi Uncle Les." Nik kissed him on the cheek.

"How are you, sweetie?"

"I'm fine, just fine." Nik smiled at him.

Peter stood to shake his hand, "Thank you for coming, Mr. Barnes."

"What did the erstwhile detective have to say?" Les raised his brows in anticipation of an answer.

Peter told him that the detective had brought a letter that he had received, and that he wanted Peter to read it.

"Niki and I both read the letter, and I believe that it was authentic. I recognized Grigory's handwriting."

"What did he say in the letter?" Les was now very interested in that letter.

"Grigory told the detective that he was angry and had been drinking when he went to see Yakov on the night that Yakov died. He told the detective that he didn't mean to kill Yakov, that it was an accident." Peter's face was sad as he told Les what Grigory had written in his letter.

"Well, that sounds like that's the end of their interest in you, Peter." Les was happy for him.

"Hello Les, it's good to see you. Did your family have a Merry Christmas?" Marina came into the great room and gave Les a hug.

He held her at arm's length, "You're as pretty as ever, Marina. Yes, we had a great Christmas."

Klaus cleared his throat, "Mike was here until this morning, but he had to fly back for business. I wish that you could have seen him, Les."

"I do too, Klaus. I haven't seen Mike since..." he thought for a moment, "a year ago last Thanksgiving."

"His business is doing very well. They're even talking about going public with their stock." Klaus was the proud father.

Les beamed. "Well, that's our boy. He always had a good head on his shoulders."

They made small talk for a while, and Les had a cup of Marina's excellent coffee. Peter and Nik sat by the fireplace, enjoying the warmth of the fire, and chatting quietly. Duchess had moved from the fireplace rug to Peter's side, the side *between* Nik and Peter.

Les watched Peter and Nik for a few moments as he sipped his coffee and then said to the group, "Well, folks, I've got to get going. I've got some briefs to put together. Come to think of it, I'm not sure why they call them briefs...they take a long time to do."

This comment made Klaus laugh, "You do have a way with words, Les."

After Les departed, Marina and Klaus sat down in the great room to read their newspapers. Peter and Nik stayed by the fireplace for a short while and then decided to play the piano.

Marina and Klaus loved hearing their daughter play again, and they agreed that both Nik and Peter were talented on the instrument. Klaus closed his eyes and put his head against the back of his chair.

They played Bach, Beethoven, and Buxtehude, with a little Mozart thrown in for balance. When they tired of the piano, Nik took more photo albums from the bookshelves, and had Peter laughing over the way that she and her brothers had looked from babyhood on. They sat on the floor in front of the alabaster fireplace, stoked with a small but warm fire. Nik placed large pillows near the hearth, and they sat next to each other, poring over the albums.

"You were such a lively, beautiful little thing, Niki." Peter's deep voice was soft, borne of the tender feelings that he had for her.

"Mom loves to tell everyone that I weighed only five pounds when I was born, but the doctor didn't put me in an incubator because he said I was very strong. She said that I latched onto the breast with such force that she could hardly stand it, and that I was worse than her boys." Nik was laughing when she told Pete this story.

"You are amazing, Niki, and I'm not surprised at your mother's story. There is much strength in your small person. Remember, I have seen you in the midst of battle."

Nik nodded, and became quiet. For a few brief moments, she relived the horror of seeing Peter attacked by his teammates at the instigation of Yakov, and she shivered at the memory of his blood on the ice.

Peter put his hand on her forearm, and was surprised to feel gooseflesh there, "I'm sorry Niki, I shouldn't have brought that up. Let's talk about something else. Tell me about your music."

"I've told you that there was a time when I wanted to be a concert pianist. My parents bought this beautiful piano," Nik pointed to the baby grand, "and I had lessons and practiced, and practiced. It sort of took over my life. I was very shy, so it was easy to become completely absorbed with my music. I went to competitions, and I even won some of them. But when Joey died, everything changed."

"You had promise, judging by the way that you play now," Peter said gently.

Before she could thank him, the telephone rang. One of Nik's parents must have picked it up because it only rang twice.

Marina called from the end of the hall, "Niki, Myron's on the telephone for you."

Nik closed her eyes briefly, and then got up from her pillow, "I'll be back in a minute, Pete."

She took the telephone in her parents' bedroom. "Hi Ron, did you get your car fixed?"

"I'm driving a rental, Nik. My block was cracked, and the mechanic said that I shouldn't have driven my car after the accident. He was right. Now I'm either going to have to get a new engine or a new car. What a day!"

"I'm sorry, Ron. What bad luck," Nik felt badly about Ron's situation.

"Well, I guess it could be worse. My car wasn't any prize, and I've needed to get a new one, so maybe this isn't as bad as it could be.

"Nik, I'm going to have to go see my parents this weekend. I've been promising them for the past month that I'd come for a visit and bring my pretty little fiancée with me."

"Ron," Nik said hesitantly, "I'd like to know when we could have made the trip; especially in the last two weeks?"

"Hey Nik, I know how it's been, so don't get upset with me. Also, I know that you now have an obligation to take care of Peter, so I'm going to drive this nice little red rental car up to Chicago by myself."

"Your parents are going to think that I'm a nut. I hope that they won't be insulted if I can't come with you."

"No, Nik, they won't think you're a nut. Probably won't until they actually meet you. *Then* they might decide you're a little weird." Ron laughed a nervous laugh.

"Ohhhkay…" Nik laughed too, "So how are you going to get your foot out of your mouth this time?"

"Uh, let's see…how about dinner tonight? We could go to St. Elmo's for a steak. What do you think?"

Nik wanted to stay at home, but she knew that Ron wanted to see her, "We could go early, if that's all right with you. Do you want me to drive?"

"Timing is everything, hon', so early is fine. I'll pick you up in my fancy red rental car."

Ron hesitated for a moment, and then asked, "Do you want to do anything after dinner?"

"I'd better not Ron. Peter's nurse will probably leave about eight-thirty or nine o'clock, so I should be back at least by ten. I don't want my parents to do Peter's care if they don't have to."

"Yeah, I guess you're right. Well, I'll pick you up about six, is that okay?"

"Six is fine. See you then. 'Bye." Nik looked at her watch. It was nearly three-thirty already.

When she returned to Pete's room, she found him sleeping on his back on the bed. One arm was above his head, and Duchess was curled up in the crook of his other arm. Nik took a knitted blanket from the sofa and gently placed it over them. Duchess growled at her as if to say, "don't bother us." It made Nik smile. Her dog was very jealous of anyone who came near Pete. How strange, she thought. But she did know that Duchess was a good judge of people, just as her mother, Lady Gray, had been. Well Duchess, Nik thought, you've picked a good one this time.

I should have known that Pete needed to rest. He's only seven days post-op, and I was boring him with family pictures and stories. Nik left the room quietly, looking back at the sleeping two, and saw Duchess put her head back against Pete's chest. For a moment, only a moment, Nik wished that she could change places with Duchess, and then realized how silly this thought was.

In the great room, Klaus had raised the footrest on his chair, and was napping, his newspaper covering half of his face. Marina raised a finger to her lips, and smiled at Nik as she entered the room.

Nik whispered, "It looks like we're the only two left awake in the house. Duchess is grabbing forty winks with Pete, and I covered them up with a blanket so they wouldn't get chilled."

"Niki," Marina said in a serious tone, "I want to apologize for the way I acted on Christmas. I can't seem to put the sadness behind me...especially on Christmas. I try, I really do try."

Nik came over to Marina and put an arm around her shoulders, "I know mom, it's hard to let go, and I'm not sure that it's humanly possible to put the memories of Joey behind us. We all mourn his loss, and we have to learn to live with it as best we can."

Marina nodded, but she didn't look up, "I will always feel that it was my fault. If I hadn't begged Klaus to let Josef play football, he would still be here with us."

"Mom, have you forgotten how persistent Joey was? He really wanted to play football, and when he really wanted something, he found a way to get it. I loved my brother, but I have always thought that he used you to convince dad to let him play."

When Marina finally looked at Nik, there was surprise on her face, "You don't blame me? I thought you blamed me. You were so angry at everyone for such a long time...but especially me."

"I was only twelve years old, mom, and I didn't really know what to do with what I was feeling. That was sixteen years ago. I'm an adult now, and I have come to realize that Joey was the one person who was mostly at fault. He wanted to play football. What happened to him while he was playing was an accident and it was no one's fault."

"You stopped playing the piano…I thought it was your way of punishing me about Joey."

"No," Nik shook her head, "I stopped playing because I didn't have time. I traded my dream for Joey's, and it was very *hard* to make the kind of grades that I needed to eventually get into medical school. I told you as much when I stopped taking piano lessons. Something had to give."

It was Marina's turn to shake her head. "I thought that you were just making excuses when you said you had to stop playing the piano. You were very good, Niki, very good on the piano."

Nik had a distant look in her eyes, and then replied, "You're my mother. You're supposed to think that about your child's talent."

Klaus, who had awakened a few moments before, said, "You *were* very talented, Niki. Did you know that I had contacted Julliard to see if you had a chance there?"

Nik was surprised by her father's words, "No, I didn't know that."

"I sent them home movies of your performances, and also sent recordings. They were interested in you."

"The two of you were my best cheerleaders." Nik was grateful to her parents.

She kissed them both on the cheek, "I'm going up to my room and get ready to go out to dinner with Ron. We're going to St. Elmo's tonight."

"Niki, I could fix a nice supper if you want to eat at home."

Klaus laughed out loud, "*Marina*, I think they want to be alone."

"Oh…of course they do." Marina laughed, too.

Nik turned as she went up the stairs, "Will you keep an eye on Pete for me? I'll be down in a little while."

Klaus got up from his chair, "I'll go check on him now, Niki."

Chapter 29

In her room, Nik lay across her bed, face down, for a few moments. No matter how hard we try to pretend that our lives are okay, they're never going to be. Not ever again. Not without Joey. She closed her eyes.

"Niki, Niki…Myron's here. Aren't you going to dinner?" Marina gently shook her daughter's shoulder.

"What? What time is it?" Nik was disoriented for a moment.

"It's about six-thirty, Niki, and Myron's been waiting for you."

Nik rubbed her face, "I fell asleep, didn't I? Uh…tell Ron I'll be down in ten minutes. Is Pete doing all right?"

"Yes, Peter is fine. His nurse has been here since six, and we all had dinner together. I'll go tell Myron that you will be down shortly." Marina caressed her daughter's cheek with her hand briefly and then went to the door.

Nik quickly washed her face, and put some powder on it to hide the shine. A little mascara, a slight daub of perfume on her throat, a quick brushing of her hair, a fresh outfit, and she was ready to go. She looked in the mirror and decided that she wasn't at her best. I'm not being fair to Ron, she thought. What's the matter with me?

Peter was sitting in the great room with Ron, Klaus and Marina. Lauren had gone back to his room to straighten things up, and put clean sheets on his bed. Duchess lay on the floor next to his chair.

Peter was quiet, and had added little to the conversation in the room. When he heard Niki's bedroom door open, he looked up at the balcony and saw her walking toward the stairway. He smiled as he saw her walk quickly down the stairs. She was dressed all in black, and she looked beautiful. When she joined the group, Peter could see that she still had the blush of sleep on her cheeks. Again he smiled, and she looked at him and returned his smile.

"Did you and Duchess have a good nap?"

Peter nodded his head. "We did, and you?"

She laughed, "I had a good nap, too, I guess."

"Nik, it's about time." Ron put a possessive arm around her shoulders and grinned at her.

She looked up at him and apologized, "I'm sorry, Ron. I can't believe that I fell asleep. I don't even remember that I was tired."

Ron laughed and said, "It's okay, Nik. Our reservation is for seven, so we'd better head on out."

"We'll be home around ten or so, won't we?" Nik again looked up at Ron.

"If we get seated and served right away, I think that we can make it back by then. So…let's go."

Nik went to the coat closet and pulled out a black coat. The perfect color for my mood, she thought. Ron didn't offer to help her into her coat, he was talking to Klaus, and so she put it on herself. She turned and saw that Peter, who had been watching her, now turned away.

Peter had seen the interaction between Niki and Ron, and it caused him to ache and feel cold inside. He wished that he could be the one taking her to dinner. As he had before, he wondered what such a life would be like?

Ron took Nik by the arm and started toward the door. Klaus and Marina followed them, wishing them a good time, patting their shoulders.

Without saying goodbye, Peter got up from his chair and began walking toward his room. He wanted to be by himself. He knew that Lauren would be leaving soon, and he could be alone. Duchess trotted behind him.

Nik looked past Ron's shoulder and saw Peter walking away. She felt sadness, because she knew that, for some reason, her behavior had hurt his feelings.

When Peter walked into his room, Lauren, who was finishing his bed, smiled up at him. She finished turning down his bed.

"You're walking faster, Pete. Does that mean that you're feeling stronger?"

Peter had given no thought to his gait, "Well, yes, I guess it does."

He didn't want to say that anger had made him forget his aches and pains, and had propelled him to his room. Was it anger? He didn't think so, but he had wanted to get away from the scene that had caused him sadness and pain. It wasn't Niki's fault. No, it was just the return of the cold ache in the middle of his chest.

"I noticed, too, that you're standing a lot straighter. That's a good sign. You aren't guarding your abdomen any more. It means that you are healing very well inside." Lauren's smile was engaging.

"That means that I'll be able to go home, soon, doesn't it?" The thought filled him with both longing and sadness…longing to see his mother and sister, and sadness at having to leave Niki.

"As soon as I finish your bed, I'd like to change your dressings. Dr. Kellman said that she'd like to look at your incisions with me this evening. She could probably tell you how soon you'll get to go home."

"She's gone out for the evening, Lauren, and probably won't be back until after ten o'clock."

Lauren hesitated for a moment, "Well, maybe tomorrow she can give us an idea of how you're doing."

Peter nodded, "Tomorrow."

"I'm ready to change your dressings, Peter. This shouldn't take too long this time. You're down to only two four by fours for dressings. Tell Duchess to stay back, too, will you?"

"Duchess, did you hear Lauren? You have to stay where you are until she's finished with me."

When Peter began speaking to her, Duchess cocked her head to the side, as if she actually understood what he was saying.

Peter lay across the bed and Lauren slipped his pajama bottoms down to expose both dressings. Gently, she pulled the paper tape and gauze from his wounds, and then cleansed them with peroxide.

"These look very well-healed, Peter. All of the staples and sutures are out, there's no drainage, and the redness of the wound approximations has nearly all gone away. The drain wounds look good, too."

As he had from his first dressing change, Peter felt exposed lying there on his back, looking up at the ceiling. He wondered if all nurses had cold hands? Perhaps it was a prerequisite for training to be a nurse, and he thought of asking Lauren if this were true, but then thought better of it.

"Okay, we're done, Peter." Lauren slipped his pajama bottoms back up to his waist.

Peter was unaccustomed to having to roll to his side to sit up, and did so rather clumsily. He resolved to work hard to get his strength and vigor back. He couldn't continue to sit still, waiting to heal. He felt anxious, and wanted to speed his recovery.

Lauren sensed that something was going on with Peter. He was quiet, and almost withdrawn, and she worried that she had said or done something to cause him to be sad.

"Peter…is something wrong? You seem to be concerned about something."

After adjusting his pajamas and standing, Peter answered, "I'm not used to having everything done for me. I need to begin to get back in shape. I'm an athlete, and I'm worried that maybe I won't be able to get back into playing form, that's all."

Lauren nodded in understanding. "Most of the athletes that I have worked with go through what you have just described. Athletes want to see results, and that doesn't happen very quickly after the kind of surgery that you have had, Peter.

"But there are things that you can do, just you, to help yourself greatly. You've got to drink at least two quarts of water a day. That seems like a lot of water, but it isn't. When you've had an injury, and surgery is a controlled injury to the body, then your body needs to be able to repair itself, and carry away the injured tissue.

"You need to start an exercise program. Not something that's going to strain your abdominal muscles, but something that will strengthen your heart and lungs. For right now, you need to walk as much as you can.

"The last thing is that you need good nutrition. I think that you're eating well, right now, but you could benefit from vitamins. Do you take them?"

Peter didn't answer right away. He was amazed at what this seemingly very young woman had just told him. Her wisdom seemed beyond her years.

"You look surprised, Peter, but what I've just told you is the best way for you to get back to where you need to be. And you'll be able to go home a lot sooner."

"You're right about everything, Lauren. I just haven't been able to put it all together, I've been waiting for a miracle, I guess. But now, I see that I can use what you just told me, and I'll recover more quickly." Peter was smiling now.

"Of course, your doctor should have some input on your recovery, too."

"Yes, and she's insisted that I eat properly and drink plenty of fluids, but I don't think that I was ready to listen when she told me. She was there in the hospital with me every day, making sure that I was doing the right things so that I'd recover. Maybe I had to get through the worst of everything before I got to this point."

"That may be part of it. Well, I'm going to have to leave shortly. I'm sorry that I missed Nik, but I'll catch her in the morning. In the meantime, you can get started on your new strategy."

"Thank you for everything, Lauren."

"Goodnight…see you in the morning." Lauren put on her coat, hat, and gloves, and waved at him as she left his room.

Chapter 30

It was very dark outside, and had been since five o'clock. The sky had been overcast and threatening for most of the day. Peter pulled an upholstered rocking chair up to the fireplace where the fire still burned brightly, turned off all the lamps in the room, and sat down to think through his situation. Duchess, who had dutifully waited for his dressing change to be completed as he had told her, joined him near the fireplace. He gently stroked her neck and ears as he rocked and thought about what to do.

Peter felt as if he was being pulled apart by his own wants, needs, and thoughts. His situation now was almost intolerable, and his hurt ran deep. He could see Niki every day, and be tantalizingly close to her, could even touch her at times, but it would never become anything more than friendship on her part. Or worse, if the only feelings she had for him were those of sympathy, if she just felt sorry for him…? It took some time, but he finally settled down enough to reach some answers.

Hope had kept him from completely giving up before now, but he had reached some of these conclusions before. It was time to look dispassionately at where he now found himself. I'm jealous of Niki's relationship with Ron, and their engagement. But I have no right to be jealous. She has no idea how I feel about her, and it really wouldn't matter if she did. My feelings for her will not cause her to change her life. She has been more than kind to me, but I am not her fiancé. She knows that I will soon be gone. I'll be going home. There is no reason for her to include me in her life beyond her commitment to see that I recover from my surgery. The hurt that he felt every time he saw how possessive Ron was with Niki was something that he could not control. But he had to try.

Marina looked in on Peter to ask him if he needed anything, "I promised Niki that I'd take good care of you while she's with Ron."

Her words stabbed Peter, but he responded kindly, "Spaseeba, *thank you*, Marina. I'm doing well."

"Duchess, you need to go outside now. Come with me." Marina gave Duchess a beckon call.

Peter looked down at Duchess, "You must be obedient to your mistress, Duchess."

Marina tried coaxing her again, to no avail. "*Duchess*, it's time for you to go outdoors."

Peter stood and told Marina, "I need some exercise, and I'd be happy to take her outside."

"Oh Peter, I couldn't ask you to do that. Niki would never forgive me." Marina had one hand to her mouth.

Peter chuckled, "I will make sure that she knows that I volunteered. Come along Duchess."

Marina, Peter and Duchess walked through the great room, and Klaus looked up in surprise. "I'm seeing a parade here. Where are you going?"

"Duchess was disobedient. She didn't want to go outside unless Peter brought her out." Marina was shaking her head at her dog.

Klaus found this funny, "She has a mind of her own, Peter. And it seems that she has attached herself to you."

"I have never had a dog of my own. Duchess has shown me how nice it would be to have a pet."

"Yes and no. A dog is a great commitment. It's like having a three-year-old child that never grows up to become independent."

This comment made Peter smile. "I look forward to having a child, children, someday, although I haven't had any experience with them. So, a three year old child is sometimes difficult to deal with?"

Marina and Klaus nodded at the same time, and then laughed.

"Yes, very," said Marina, "but I am looking forward to grandchildren. Some of my friends have grandchildren, and they love it."

Peter continued out to the kitchen where he opened the French door so that Duchess could do her reindeer act. He closed the door and watched as she leapt for joy. As he tired, he put his forearm against the door and leaned his head on it, but Duchess didn't show any signs of tiring.

"Hi, Pete." Nik had walked into the kitchen in stocking feet, unnoticed by Peter.

Peter continued to lean against the door for a moment, and then turned around to smile at her. "How was your dinner?"

Even though he smiled at her, there was a distance, an aloofness that she hadn't seen before. She hesitated and then answered him.

"It…was very nice, Pete."

Peter looked past her into the great room to see if Ron was there but he didn't see or hear him. Nik turned to see what he was looking at, and then realized that he was probably trying to see if Ron had come back with her.

At that moment, Duchess jumped up onto the door with both front paws and barked. Peter opened the door to let her in and she plopped down on the rug, and one of his feet. Nik ducked into the laundry room and came out with a towel for Duchess.

"Would you like to dry her off?"

Without answering, Peter got down on one knee, which caused him a little "stretch" pain, and looked up at her with his hand out for the towel. Their eyes held for a moment, and then Peter looked down at Duchess.

"Belly first, then feet," he said to Duchess, who seemed to be very happy that he was doing the toweling this time.

When he finished, Duchess went running into the great room where Klaus again had to tell her to settle down. This made Peter laugh when he thought of the earlier discussion about three-year-old children and pets.

Nik knew that it hadn't been easy for Pete to get down on one knee to dry Duchess off. He got up slowly and took a deep breath.

"You're getting stronger, Pete."

"I've got to get back in shape so that I can go home to my family. And I shouldn't be imposing on yours any longer than I have to."

"Pete?" There was hurt in her eyes.

He couldn't stand to see that hurt, and he turned away to look out of the door toward the frozen lake. When he turned back, she was gone.

Nik went up the stairs after saying goodnight to her parents. Klaus and Marina watched her climb the stairs and then saw Peter come through the great room quietly. Duchess left Klaus' chair to follow him. Peter bid Marina and Klaus goodnight and continued to his room. His heart was heavy, and he didn't know how he was ever going to forget the look of hurt in Niki's eyes.

Marina turned off the lamp next to her chair, and Klaus followed suit. He started down the hall toward their bedroom while Marina checked the door locks and turned off the kitchen lights.

Klaus was in his pajamas and brushing his teeth when Marina came into the bedroom. She turned down the bed and put on her nightgown, and then went into the bathroom to talk with her husband.

"I'm not sure what happened between Niki and Peter, but there seems to be an estrangement there."

Klaus nodded, his mouth full of toothpaste, and then he shrugged. When he had rinsed his mouth he answered her. "Les and I noticed a week or so ago that Peter seemed to be attached to Niki. It's understandable. Just look at her. She's as pretty as her mother." With this pronouncement, Klaus smiled.

Chapter 31

December 27, 1986

Peter could not sleep. He would lie down for a while, and then get up to look out of the window. He was angry with himself for his behavior toward Niki. How could he have treated her so coldly? She is only living the life that she had before she met me. There is no fault on her part, yet I have behaved like a spurned lover.

The sky held no stars, and a heavy snow had started just before midnight. He looked at the mantel clock for what seemed to be the hundredth time, and it was now twelve-thirty.

The only occupant of Peter's bed, Duchess, jumped down to the floor, shook herself, and trotted over to Peter. She put her paw on his leg and whined a low whine.

He looked at her with raised eyebrows, "I think that you want to go outside, Duchess. Is that what you want?"

Duchess whined again, and headed for the door. Peter followed her as she led him through the great room. To Peter's surprise, there was a dim light coming from the kitchen.

Duchess preceded him into the kitchen, and he heard her give a low whine of recognition to someone before Peter came into the room. Niki was sitting at the kitchen bar with a cup in front of her, holding it with both hands. Only the light over the range was lit.

For a moment, they looked at each other, and then started speaking at the same time. They fell silent, and then Nik spoke.

Softly, she said, "Pete, I'm not sure what I've done to hurt you, but I know that you're upset with me."

Peter found his voice, "You haven't done anything to hurt me Niki. I'm just getting anxious to go home."

"No, there's something the matter, and I want to put it right. Please tell me." Her voice was husky, as if she had been crying.

Peter didn't answer as he walked over to the French doors and let Duchess out to run. He saw that she almost disappeared in the deep snow, and it was still coming down. He stood there, arms folded, watching Duchess as she performed her acrobatics in the snow. He didn't know what to say to Niki, he only knew that his heart ached and he could do nothing to turn off his feelings for her.

Nik watched Peter for a few moments, and then came over to where he was standing at the door. She stood next to him, looking out at Duchess and the snow. For a few seconds, the moon broke through the overcast sky, and shone brilliantly, making each snowflake sparkle.

"Beautiful, how beautiful…" Nik murmured.

Peter looked down at her, "Yes, beautiful…"

He gently put his fingertips under her chin, tilted her head toward him, and bent to kiss her. Her eyes were wide, looking up into his, and then she closed them as he kissed her.

"Oh no, I can't do this, I just can't." Nik turned and ran from the room.

"Wait, Niki, please, I'm sorry, I shouldn't have…" Peter started after her.

When he got to the kitchen entrance, he saw that she was running up the stairs, and he wanted to call out to her again, but thought better of it. Peter didn't want to awaken Klaus and Marina.

Peter stood watching as Niki ran across the balcony to her room and closed the door. He hung his head. What have I done, he thought, what have I done now?

His heart was in his throat as he went back into the kitchen. He brought Duchess inside, wiped her off and turned out the kitchen light.

As he walked through the great room, he kept his eyes on the door to Niki's bedroom, hoping that she would come out so that he could apologize to her. He had been hurt and sad before, but now his emotions bordered on anguish.

Peter paced up and down in his room, while Duchess sprawled in his bed with an expectant look in his direction. He had committed the unforgivable. He had acted on impulse when he kissed Niki, and all because he had been on the outside looking in. That's all that it really was. For him, it had always been so. His own jealousy had gotten the better of him, because it had hurt so much when he saw Niki with Ron.

Nik lay in her bed, her hands holding the covers pulled up to her chin, her heart pounding, and her mind in a quandary. Why did I run? Now I've hurt and insulted him, and I don't know what to do about it. My fault…it's my fault, really. I can't have it both ways, and I haven't been fair to Peter or to Ron. I have to tell Peter what's happened to me, what I shouldn't have allowed to happen.

Peter stood leaning against the window frame of his room, again staring out at the frozen lake. He had let his guard down, had let Niki thaw the cold place within him. And with the thaw had come pain.

Nik stood in the doorway. "Pete," she said softly, "please, I want to explain to you…"

He quickly turned away from the window, and, forgetting himself, spoke to her in Russian, "Niki, I apologize; I owe you an apology for what I did. I had no right to do such a thing."

"Let me explain, I've got to tell you what has happened, and it's all my fault." Nik's knees were shaking, and her legs were becoming weak.

Peter moved away from the window and sat down on the edge of his bed, "Niki…"

She held her hand up, and in a small voice said, "Pete, just let me explain. This is all my fault and I should have been the one to behave professionally."

Nik's emotions were running high, her legs trembling, and she sank to her knees, "I just wanted to tell you…that I tried very hard, from the very beginning, to maintain a professional distance, but I couldn't. From the very first, I tried not to love you, but I didn't succeed."

She placed her hands, childlike, over her face and began to cry softly.

"*Nyet,*" Peter groaned aloud.

He reached down and lifted her to him as he stood. With his arms wrapped around her, he gently rocked back and forth in an attempt to comfort her as she wept, her face buried against his chest.

Finally, her sobs gave way to deep sighs, and she looked up at him with a tear-stained face, "I'm so sorry, Pete, so very sorry, because I've hurt you, and I know it every time that I look into your eyes."

Peter cupped her face in his hands and whispered, "I love you, too, Niki."

"I never meant for this to happen, Pete. I tried to remain professional, to do my job. But from the very first, something inside me knew, even when I denied it to myself. I knew that I was falling in love with you."

His hands still cupping her face, Peter showered her with hungry kisses. He kissed her forehead, he kissed her cheeks, he kissed her throat, and then he kissed her mouth...deeply. His happiness knew no bounds.

They stood holding one another until Niki gently pulled away, took Peter's hand in hers and asked him to come with her. Hand in hand, they walked through the great room toward the stairway, with Duchess trailing behind.

Marina, who had awakened when she thought that she had heard someone crying, walked down the hallway from her bedroom in time to see her daughter and Peter going up the stairs. Her hand to her mouth, and holding her breath, Marina's heart sank.

She and Klaus had talked about what Klaus considered to be an infatuation for Niki on the part of Peter Genchenko, but *this*, the two of them walking up the stairway together, meant that her daughter felt the same toward him. What had happened tonight to bring this about? Niki had dinner with Myron only a few hours ago. Everything seemed perfect between them then.

Should I intervene? This liaison will surely bring hurt to Niki and Myron, and Peter, too. As she watched, Niki and Peter reached the top of the stairs, where Marina saw Peter pull her into his arms. Marina felt as if she were a voyeur, and turned away. Has Niki thought this through? She has always been the proper daughter, and has not caused us a moment's worry about her behavior.

What will happen now, thought Marina? She went back to her bedroom as quietly as she possibly could. For some time, she sat in a chair, too upset to get back into bed. Tears filled her eyes, and she felt helpless to do anything for her Niki. Marina liked Peter, and admired him, too. He was a handsome, and seemingly kind and honest young man, but he would be returning to Russia soon. What would happen to Niki then? With a sense of defeat in her heart, Marina got back into bed, trying not to disturb Klaus as she pulled the covers up.

Peter kissed Niki at the top of the stairs, and then whispered to her, "Niki, is this really what you want?"

Her eyes were luminous as she looked up at him, "Yes, Pete, with all my heart."

When they reached Niki's bedroom door, she bent down and told Duchess to lie down on the hall carpet. She went inside her room and brought out a knit blanket to cover her with.

"You've got to be quiet, Duchess. Be a good girl." Peter patted her head.

He took Niki's hand and walked her into the bedroom, closing the door behind them. She went to her dresser, and he saw that she was taking the engagement ring from her finger. When she turned back to him, she loosened the sash of her robe and shrugged it from her shoulders, exposing the soft blue, nearly transparent nightgown beneath.

She came to him, and put her arms around him. His heart turned over, and then he was kissing her, tentatively, gently at first, and then more deeply. Her surrender was complete, and she answered his kisses eagerly.

With shaking hands, Niki unbuttoned Peter's pajama top and pulled it from his shoulders, letting it fall to the floor. She lightly moved her hands over his chest, ruffling the soft red-gold hair as she looked up into his eyes.

Peter's fingers were clumsy as he tried, unsuccessfully, to unbutton the small buttons of her nightgown, but she helped him, and soon her nightgown lay next to his pajama top on the floor. He pulled the comforter and blanket aside on her bed, lifted her, and placed her gently in the middle of the bed.

Niki admonished him, "Pete, you shouldn't lift me. I don't want you to hurt yourself."

"In all my life I have never felt so strong," he whispered as he got in beside her and kissed her again, a deep and lingering kiss.

He lay next to her and lightly stroked her skin, his heart racing with excitement. She was as soft and smooth as velvet. He traced her face with his fingertips, and slowly brushed them past her lips to her throat and then to her breasts. Her firm breasts were surprisingly generous. He kissed each one gently and continued to travel with his hand down the course of her slightly rounded abdomen that quivered under his touch.

"Sweet, beautiful Niki," he whispered hoarsely, his throat constricted with passion.

She tugged at the waist of his pajama bottoms, "Please…now…please."

Peter slid his pajama bottoms off and tossed them to the floor. It was now Niki's turn to explore his naked body.

She caressed his face with both hands and kissed him, and then tenderly placed her palms on his chest, moving slowly down to his abdomen. She lingered gently on his newly healed wounds, but he felt no pain. Instead, her touch filled him with fire. All his senses were acutely, exquisitely, aroused.

Their first union was deeply satisfying. They were wonderful, splendid, together, their bodies a perfect fit, their spirits soaring to an intense and complete fulfillment. Afterward, they lay, his arms around her, her head on his chest, an arm around his waist, his manhood resting on her abdomen, their legs intertwined.

Niki had fallen asleep almost immediately, but Peter lay awake, marveling at the new feeling coursing through him. And so this is what joy feels like?

He pulled her closer for a moment, and whispered her name, "Niki."

Chapter 32

The telephone beside Niki's bed rang only once, but it awakened Peter. He looked at the clock radio on the bedside table and saw that it was nearly four o'clock in the morning. The wind outside buffeted and pushed against the house, causing it to creak and moan.

Peter still held Niki in his arms, and he saw that the telephone had not disturbed her sleep. He settled down to sleep again, pulling her close. It was a light sleep, and he was awakened again by sounds of activity within the house.

Klaus had the telephone on his side of the bed, in case anything went wrong in the processing area, and he was needed at the plant. The telephone hadn't rung during the night very often of late, but when it did, he always managed to pick it up on the first or second ring so that it wouldn't awaken Marina.

"Hello, Klaus? This is Irina. Something has happened to Karl. The doctor is working on him now in the coronary care unit, but I'm afraid that something terrible is going to happen."

"Wait, Irina, slow down. Karl has had a heart attack?"

"I'm afraid that is what the doctor has decided has happened, Klaus." Irina sounded as if she were close to tears.

"What is it, Klaus?" Marina was awake.

Klaus held up his hand, "We will be on our way as soon as we can, Irina. Where can we reach you?"

When he hung up the telephone, he looked at Marina and said, "Karl is ill, a heart attack. We must go to be with him."

"Oh Klaus, this is awful. How bad is it?"

Klaus shook his head as if in a daze, "I don't know, Irina was upset, and I'm not sure that she really understands what's happening to Karl. She's all alone, and we've got to help her."

They quickly packed their clothes and discussed what to do about Peter, Duchess, and whether or not to awaken Niki to let her know what was happening.

Marina didn't want Klaus anywhere near Niki's room, "Klaus, I'm going to leave a note for Niki. We should just let her sleep. Anyway, she can't go with us because of Peter. And I think that we should take Duchess along with us."

Klaus turned to look at her in amazement, "What are we going to do with Duchess on a trip like this?"

"There are kennels in Pennsylvania, too, Klaus, and having Duchess with us will make it easier for Niki."

He shook his head, "Sometimes, Marina, I don't understand your logic."

"Will you pack Duchess' leash, food, and bowls, please, Klaus? Oh, and she will need her coat, too."

His answer was a curt, "Yes."

Marina climbed the stairway, and when she was halfway up, Duchess came happily down to meet her, dragging a blanket across her back.

Marina was relieved that she didn't have to go to Niki's door. It's none of my business. But this is my house, she thought. How can she do something like this in my house? Again, Marina felt heartache because of what she was certain was happening under her roof.

In the kitchen, Marina wrote her daughter a note to tell her about Uncle Karl. She included information about Duchess, too, and said that she would call as soon as they knew something. When she finished her note, Marina put Duchess outside in preparation for her journey. The weather was cold and the skies were dark. The wind had been picking up, and was now lifting the snow into drifts. Marina shivered as she waited for Duchess, who, buffeted by the wind and cold, did not tarry.

Peter heard the garage door open, and one of the cars was started up and backed out, and then he heard the door close. The house was again quiet, but he continued to listen for several minutes. He wondered why Niki's parents were leaving at this hour to travel somewhere in the cold and snow? He hadn't heard them say that they were going anywhere. In fact, Marina had asked him what she should fix for his breakfast. How strange, he thought, and wondered if there was something wrong? When he hadn't heard any sounds for some time, he pulled Niki closer to him, and soon fell asleep again.

Peter was in his own room. He knew that it was so because the familiar cold was there, the winter cold of Lyubertsy. There was no sound in the apartment. He could not hear his mother or his sister in the adjacent rooms. Where were they? He struggled to awaken, but he couldn't open his eyes. I've got to wake up! He started to take his covers off, and then he heard someone call his name.

"Pete? Pete, what is it? Are you all right?" Niki was shaking his shoulder.

He sat up in bed and looked at Niki. The room was very cold. When he spoke, he could see his breath.

"I was dreaming, and my mother and sister were gone." Peter was bewildered for a moment.

"Get back under the covers, Pete." Niki held the comforter open for him.

"It's cold in here, isn't it? Something has happened." Peter looked around the room.

He lay back and Niki covered him and put her arms around him. She shivered and Peter pulled her to him.

"I can see my breath, Pete. That's never happened in this house before."

The wind, moaning before, was now howling and slamming against the house. The eaves creaked and shuddered like an old wooden ship caught in a tempest.

"We need to get up and find out what's going on, Niki."

"But it's so cold Pete." Nik scooted up against him under the covers.

"If we don't check it out, Niki, the pipes could freeze and break."

"I wonder if my mom and dad know that there's something wrong?"

Peter shook his head, "I don't think so, because I heard them leave a little after four this morning."

Nik raised her head to look at him, "They left?"

"I think that they did, but we should go look to see if I'm right."

Peter got out of bed, and even though the light was dim in the room, Nik's heart beat quickly, seeing him standing there, magnificently nude. She climbed out of bed, too, and, shivering, grabbed her nightgown, bathrobe and slippers.

Peter gave her an appreciative grin. "You're quick when you need to be."

Nik opened the bathroom door and walked over into her brother's room, "Come in here, Pete, I've got to get something warm for you to wear."

She pulled a pair of sweats, and some socks from one of the bureau drawers, and then got into the closet and found a thick bathrobe for him to wear.

"Let's get something on your feet, too."

Nik looked again in the closet and brought out a pair of her brother Mike's slippers for Peter's feet. She smiled when he put them on and they fit as though they were made for him.

When he was warmly dressed, they went downstairs. Nik tried several lights, and found that they didn't work. She went over to the thermostat in the great room and was surprised to see that it read thirty-eight degrees.

Nik's face was filled with concern, "Where are my parents?"

She took Peter's hand and walked across the great room to the hallway leading to her parents' bedroom. The door was open, and when they looked inside, they saw that the bed was made. Marina and Klaus weren't in the room.

Nik looked up at Peter, "Something's happened, Peter. Duchess is gone, too."

The kitchen was cold and dark. As she looked desolately around the room, she saw a sheet of paper on the table.

"What's this?" She grabbed the paper and saw that it was a note from her mother.

Nik put a hand to her mouth, "Oh! Something's happened to Uncle Karl! Dad and mom have gone to Pennsylvania to help Aunt Irina."

Peter held her close and she clung to him, "Perhaps we should try to call them, Niki."

"Yes, that's a good idea. We can call them," she looked at her mother's note again.

When she picked up the telephone, there was no dial tone, "The phone's dead, Pete. What in the world is going on here?"

Peter opened the draperies in the great room, and the snow was far enough up on the windows that they could not see out. They stood looking at the blank windows, and then looked at each other, eyes wide. The view was the same from the kitchen, where there was another wall of snow against the French doors. Nik felt helpless and didn't know what they were going to do.

"A generator," Peter said, "does your father have a generator?"

For a moment, Nik frowned, and then her eyes lit up, "Yes, I think so. He bought one after we had a blizzard seven or eight years ago. It's probably somewhere out in the garage."

They went into the colder atmosphere of the garage, where Nik saw that her parents' four wheel drive Chevy van was gone. She looked at Peter with frightened eyes, shivering.

Peter reached for her, "Come here and let me hold you. I'll keep you warm."

He stood behind Niki, his arms around her, and thought about what they should do next. He knew that the fireplace in the great room burned real wood, so they could make a fire, but how much wood was available? He glanced around the garage, and his eyes came to rest on a nicely stacked pile of wood; more than three cords. Maybe enough to last for three or four days, he calculated. Niki continued to shiver in his arms, and he knew that he would have to find some way to keep her warm.

Peter had survived many bad winters, when the radiators would get cold in the Lyubertsy apartment. At times, his mother, sister, and he had huddled near the small hot oven in the tiny kitchen of their apartment, blankets wrapped around their shoulders, sipping hot tea to keep warm. He wanted to spare Niki the hardship of being cold, if he could.

He rested his chin on the top of her head and asked quietly, "Where is the generator, Niki? If we can get some electricity going, maybe we can start the furnace again. I don't want you to be cold, my dear, sweet Niki."

She turned in his arms, stood on tiptoe, and kissed him. In spite of the cold, he felt warm inside.

"Niki…the generator?"

"It's over there in that cabinet, Pete."

Nik hurried over to a wooden cabinet that was as tall as she was, and perhaps four feet wide. There was a padlock on the double doors of the cabinet, and it stopped Nik in her tracks.

"Oh no, it's locked. What are we going to do?" Nik was shivering.

Peter looked around for a moment, and then picked up a wrench setting on a nearby workbench. He held the lock in one hand and hit it forcefully with the wrench, causing it to break.

"Well, Pete, it looks like you've had some experience with breaking and entering." Nik was laughing as she spoke.

His face, however, was serious, "You could say that. But it was a survival tactic."

Peter opened the cabinet and saw the generator across the back. He ducked inside and tugged on its frame. He was trying to be careful, because he knew that he could open his wounds or injure himself if he pulled too hard.

"Let me help, Pete. That thing is heavy, and you really shouldn't be straining yourself."

Nik got in beside him and grabbed the other side of the generator. They dragged it over to a window, where Peter set it up and held the exhaust hose in one hand.

"We're going to have to put the exhaust out this window, Niki, and we also need a heavy duty extension cord and some gasoline." Peter opened the window and looked at the snow obliterating the opening.

"That's easy. The yellow cabinet over there has the lawn mower gas cans in it." She pointed to a wall with hanging tools, "and there's an extension cord over there."

"Good. Now let's see if this thing has any oil in it." Peter pulled out the dipstick and found that it registered to the full mark.

Peter used a broom to force an opening in the snow at the window, and was very surprised to see how deep the snow was. He actually had to put the entire length of his arm with the broom to reach clear of the snow. The wind was still making a tremendous noise, slamming into the house and then roaring past, the sound decreasing in pitch as it moved away. Each time it hit, the house shuddered with the impact of the wind.

In order for the generator to power the house, Peter had to locate the bypass system for the main electrical service. He didn't have to worry. Klaus, true to his German heritage, had been thorough in his emergency generator set-up, and the bypass was labeled clearly. Peter smiled at the thought of Klaus' organization.

They filled the generator with gasoline, and Peter calculated that they'd have to refill it every six to seven hours. Klaus had even put an alarm on the generator so that he'd know when to put more fuel in the tank. Peter noted with relief that Klaus' generator had a battery and was electric start. Again he smiled as he primed the engine and pressed the start button. It roared into life. Thank you, Klaus. Peter wasn't sure that he'd have been able to pull hard enough on a recoil rope starter to start the engine otherwise.

He looked up at Niki, and she was still shivering. He reached for her hand, and clasped it in his. "Let's take some wood inside, and then we can wrap up in blankets near the fireplace after I've started a fire."

"Okay, Pete." Her teeth chattering, she lifted his hand to her lips and kissed it.

The sound of the furnace starting up was music to their ears. Peter stood up and hugged Niki, and then kissed her, their breath commingling visibly.

In the great room, Nik turned on the television, but found that the cable was out. She turned on the radio and searched for a station that was on the air. She listened to a newscaster whose voice she didn't recognize. The city was paralyzed, he reported. A snow emergency had been called, and no vehicles of any kind were allowed to travel on the roads. All schools, factories, and businesses were closed due to the weather. The snow and high winds had caused a countywide loss of power and communications. He said that the unofficial snowfall was fifteen inches, and the wind had caused drifting and closure of all roads, even the interstate highways into, and out of, Indianapolis.

"Well, that doesn't answer all of your questions, Niki, but it does explain what has happened to the telephone and the electricity."

"I guess so, but I wish that I knew what's happened to my mom and dad."

Nik was concerned for her parents, but thoughts of Ron came unbidden to her as well. She hoped that he had been able to get to Chicago safely. When he had taken her to dinner last evening, he had his luggage with him, and had left for Chicago after dropping her off at home.

I should feel guilty about what's happened, Nik thought. In truth, however, she did not, and she was glad that Ron was in Chicago with his parents, and that she was here alone with Pete.

Chapter 33

Peter built a fire, while Niki gathered blankets and pillows, piling them in front of the fireplace. They searched the pantry and refrigerator together, and brought milk, cookies, crackers and cheese in little glass jars to eat while they huddled under the blankets. Soon the fire was blazing, warming them.

"Pete, I'm so worried about my parents. I don't know how to get in touch with them, and this weather is frightening and dangerous."

He hesitated for a moment, and then slowly nodded, "Yes, I know how you feel. I've been worrying about my mother and sister since I left Russia. The weather there is probably about the same as it is here."

He reached for her and held her close. "We can't even tell how bad the weather really is, but it must be bad, I think, to have cut the power and communications, too."

"I feel so helpless, Pete. I remember the stories my parents told about the blizzard of '78, and they were very frightening. I'm especially worried about what might happen to them if they get stranded on the road. Even with the four wheel drive, they could get stuck."

"They must have left a little after four this morning, Niki, and I didn't hear the wind really begin to pick up until some time after that. They may have been ahead of the storm until they reached their destination."

"Oh Pete, I hope so, I fervently hope so."

Peter wished that he could give her more assurance that her parents were safe, but he could not. If this weather caught up to them on their journey east, he didn't want to think of what might happen to them.

The house was warming nicely, and soon, Nik and Peter decided that they could get up from in front of the fireplace and move about. Peter went out into the garage and checked on the generator. Everything looked good, and he returned to the house.

Nik smiled at him and took his hand when he came back inside. "It's warm enough to shower now, and I should check your incisions to make sure that they're healing okay and that you haven't injured yourself with all of your activity."

Peter's eyes twinkled with mirth, "Yes, activity…but do you think that the water heater has had time to recover?"

"Well let's go and find out." She put her arm through his and they went up the stairs together.

Niki's bathroom had an electric wall heater, and she turned it on to warm the room. She reached into the shower and started the hot water, tempering it with cold. There were thick towels in a closet and she pulled four out, placing them on the towel rack on the shower door.

"Shower's ready." She slipped out of her robe and nightgown, and stepped inside the shower, beckoning to him.

She literally took his breath away, and for a moment, he stood looking at her through the glass door of the shower. He paused for only a moment, and then Peter pulled his sweats and underwear off and quickly joined her, his heart pounding, his excitement quite evident.

They washed each other's hair and bodies. Niki had to stand on the ledge inside the shower stall to wash Peter's hair. When it was his turn to wash her hair, he was gentle, but thorough.

"Your hair is wonderful, Niki. Soft, it's so soft, like silk." He squeezed the water from her hair, and reached for the body soap.

Peter lathered her body from shoulders to toes. His massage was slow and sensuous as he progressed downward. They stood together under the spray when he had finished bathing her until they were both rinsed clean.

He bent to kiss her and she answered his kiss passionately. When he lifted her onto him, she did not protest at all about his condition, but encircled him with her arms and legs. They balanced against the shower wall, murmuring, whispering their love for each other, as they moved together on their lovers' journey.

The water began to run cold, finally, and they quickly exited the shower. Each toweled the other off, delighted in the sensation and physicality of the act.

Wrapped heads and bodies in towels, they went seeking fresh clothing. Niki searched through her brother's things and found warm corduroy pants, a forest green sweater, and some heavy socks for Peter. In her room, she let him pick out something for her to wear. He chose a pink sweat outfit that she told him she had worn during her high school days.

"You are beautiful in pink, Niki, almost as beautiful as you were in red." He held her hands in his and pulled her to him.

Back in the bathroom, Peter combed Niki's hair out, and she combed his. She sat him down on a stool and used a hair dryer to dry his hair, telling him that she didn't want him to get a chill. Peter realized that he loved to have his hair brushed and dried. Or was it just because Niki was the one doing it? It was a sensation that he had never before experienced.

"There," she said, "How do you like it?"

Peter stood and ran one hand over his hair as he looked into the mirror. "You have tamed it. And it's never looked better."

Taking the hair dryer, he asked, "May I?"

Niki smiled and nodded, "Of course." and handed him the hairbrush.

Peter had brushed his sister's hair when they were children, and he had enjoyed brushing her thick and wavy dark blond hair. Niki's hair, in comparison, was thick, but silky and very straight. It was smooth, and moved softly when she turned her head. When he finished drying it, he put his face against her hair, breathing in her soft, clean scent.

They cleaned the bathroom and made Niki's bed together. Peter had never had the opportunity for such domesticity, and he liked working with her. It gave him a sense of normalcy, of belonging.

"Pete, are you getting hungry again?"

"Yes. We have expended many calories, I think." He gave her a crooked smile.

She laughed, "*Oh yes.*"

In the kitchen, Niki looked in the freezer to see what was there. She found pork chops, steaks, hamburger, chicken, and even some lamb. She pulled out a package of chicken, deciding that she and Pete could find a recipe and experiment with cooking it together later.

"Pete? What are you hungry for?" Niki stood in front of the open refrigerator, rummaging inside to see what their options might be.

"An American breakfast," he replied.

She looked up at him, "Tell me what that is, my dear."

He raised his eyebrows, "Why, it's bacon and eggs and potatoes, and…"

Niki started laughing, "You're serious, aren't you?"

"*Da,*" he said, "let me help you."

They worked together very well, each anticipating the other's needs. Peter cooked the bacon, and Niki prepared the eggs. Together, they made biscuits. Peter was fascinated by the canned dough, and popped the can open without peeling the wrapper. When it popped, Nik jumped and squealed. She recovered her composure, put the biscuits on a cookie sheet and put them into the hot oven.

"How many times have you fixed bacon before, Pete?" Niki watched as he deftly turned the bacon in the frying pan.

"It is safe to say that I have never cooked bacon before." How hard can it be, he wondered?

"Never? Well, maybe your mother…"

"No, my mother would never cook or eat bacon, Niki. Do you remember why?" Peter was now laughing.

"Ohhhh…yes, you must think I'm an idiot." Nik put a fist to her forehead.

Peter left his cook's station for a moment and gave his Niki a kiss on her forehead where she had placed her fist. "There. Now you shouldn't feel so bad. Actually, I don't know very much about my mother's religion because she didn't practice it overtly. My father you see…well, let's just leave it at that. Anyway, I *love* your American breakfasts. Are the eggs ready yet?"

They quickly set the table and dished up their brunch. The biscuits, although from a can, were light and buttery. Nik poured large glasses of milk and sat down. She delighted in watching Peter eat. It made her happy to know that she was helping him to regain his health.

"How are you feeling today, Pete?"

He looked at her across the table, his eyes soft, "Happy, so very happy. And you are the reason, Niki."

When they finished their meal, Peter washed and Niki dried the dishes and silverware. They could have put everything in the dishwasher, but they decided that it was more fun to do the dishes together.

Niki tried the telephone in the kitchen. It was still dead. When they went out into the great room, she turned on the television long enough to see that the cable wasn't working yet. She tried the radio, and found that the station she had gotten earlier was still broadcasting. The radio announcer, the same one that had been on earlier in the day, sounded tired as he repeated information that there was a snow emergency. He had an additional message this time. Anyone who was caught out on the road attempting to go somewhere in any type of vehicle would be arrested.

"Seriously folks, you don't want to be out there. The wind is so bad that there are whiteout conditions everywhere, and we are going to get more snow as the day goes on, so stay indoors. Don't risk your lives by going outside. The wind chill factor is minus ten degrees Fahrenheit."

Peter pulled Niki down beside him on the sofa and kissed her on the back of the neck. She put her head on his shoulder and they sat quietly together. There was no need to speak. He took her hand and kissed it, and then held it against his heart.

The alarm on the generator buzzed, startling both of them. They laughed as they headed for the garage.

"Wow, this should get our circulation going." Nik was shaking her head.

"Da," Peter shut off the generator, filled the gas tank, and restarted it while Nik watched.

Out of curiosity, she pushed the garage door opener, and watched as the door lifted, exposing a solid wall of snow all the way up.

Peter said one word, "Siberia."

"Oh...my...God, *yes*!" Nik's eyes were wide as she pushed the button to close the door.

"Let's bring some more wood inside, Niki. We will need it sooner or later." They both brought armfuls of wood from the garage and put them next to the fireplace in the large basket there.

Peter put a few more logs on the embers in the fireplace and stoked the coals to get the new wood burning. He was thoughtful and quiet as he bent down, tongs in hand, to get the fire to flare up again.

"I have never known this house to be drafty, but it feels cold, even though the furnace is running." Nik went to the sofa, sat down, and wrapped a knit blanket around her.

"Judging by the strength of the wind gusts hitting the house, I think the wind may be upwards of thirty to forty miles per hour. Sometimes it gets like this in Lyubertsy, and no one goes anywhere until the storm is over. Several people freeze to death in Lyubertsy every winter. Sometimes, too, they aren't found until the spring thaw."

He got up and came over to her, "This morning, when you were teasing me about breaking and entering and I told you that it was a survival technique, I was serious."

Nik was sitting cross-legged on the sofa, and he sat down facing her, also crossing his legs. Nik pulled another knit blanket from the back of the sofa and put it around his shoulders, then held his hands in hers as he continued.

"When my family was forced to move to Lyubertsy, we struggled to survive, literally. My mother made just enough rubles teaching to pay the rent on our apartment, and for a little food besides. My sister and I were only twelve when we moved there; too young to get jobs, so we couldn't help. We were slowly starving. I could see it in my mother's and sister's faces. Finally, in desperation, I began to burglarize stores. The ones that cheated everyone were my targets, and I didn't take very much from any one store. Usually I took just enough to feed us for two or three days, and then I'd have to find another source of food or rubles. I told my mother that I was working, earning money for odd jobs, and she didn't question me. At least we had something to eat.

"As I got a little older, I decided that it wasn't fair to steal from the store owners, even the ones who cheated everyone. No, I decided that it would be better if I took from the Party Apparatchiks. By the time that we were into our second winter in Lyubertsy, I was going out to the brothels and bars in the middle of the night, waiting for drunken party members to come out…"

Chapter 34

Peter shivered in the cold. His too-small coat tight across his shoulders, and barely covering his hips, he wondered if this would be the night that he would freeze to death. He had wrapped an old black scarf of his mother's around his cap and then tied it under his chin. He wore his sister's gloves under his own for more insulation from the cold. The only parts of his body that he couldn't insulate well enough from the cold were his feet. They were cramped inside outgrown shoes, but he had stuffed newspaper as insulation against the cold anyway, further cramping them. He was too young to know that the tightness of his shoes could cause problems with his circulation, and thus make his feet cold more quickly.

At thirteen, Peter was almost as large as an average-sized man, although he was underweight. Peter used his size to his advantage when dealing with the reeling drunks that he caught unaware, stumbling from brothels or bars. He never harmed them physically, except to push the tottering drunks into the snow in order to retrieve a wallet, or even at times, a money belt. He'd help them up then, and push them back inside the bar or brothel so that they wouldn't freeze to death.

Peter never went to the same place twice. He knew that the militia was looking for him because there had been drawings of the robber posted at kiosks throughout the city. The drawings had made Peter laugh because they depicted a large and ferocious-looking older man with facial hair. Peter wondered about that for some time until he decided that the black scarf of his mother's that he wore to hold his hat in place and protect his throat looked like a beard to an inebriated man. Too, it would have been embarrassing for those who had been robbed to admit that a beardless youth had taken their money. So, the story of the large, ferocious, bearded man who was feared by those who frequented haunts in the seamier side of the city was begun.

On this night, Peter had been waiting in the cold so long that he wondered if he would be able to move if he saw a likely prospect. He stood in the doorway of an abandoned building, out of the lamplight, and out of the cold wind. It always helped if he could stay out of the wind. He heard a disturbance at the entrance to a brothel three doors down from where he stood.

"Nyet, nyet! Get away from me you little bastard. I'm going inside, so don't try to stop me." The man was in uniform, and was weaving unsteadily as he shouted at the little man standing next to a car.

"But Colonel, my commander told me to stay with you. I can't just leave, now, can I?"

"This car will stick out like a sore thumb, you idiot. I don't want everyone to know that I am here. Go for a drive, I don't care what the hell you do, but leave me here for at least an hour!"

The smaller man threw up his hands in disgust, "It is twelve forty-five, Colonel, and I will return at one forty-five. Please understand that we both have to report to our posts tomorrow morning at seven o'clock."

The smaller man got into the car, raced the engine, put it in gear, and left the unsteady Colonel to his own devices. The Colonel made his way toward the door of the brothel, but slipped and fell down. He struggled to get up, but didn't seem to be able to do so. Peter watched him for about five minutes and decided on a bold move. He would help the Colonel inside the brothel, while hopefully relieving him of his wallet.

Peter stepped out onto the sidewalk, his heart in his throat. There was no one in sight on the street, only the struggling Colonel, who now seemed to be weakening.

"Sir…sir, can I help you?" Peter had a hard time getting the Colonel's attention because the man was grunting and puffing loudly with his efforts to get up.

The Colonel looked like a walrus stranded in the snow, "What?" He craned his neck to see who was talking to him.

"Here, let me help you, sir." Peter reached under the Colonel's arm with one hand while checking the inside pocket of his coat with the other.

"Da, help me inside. Here, right here." he pointed to the door of the brothel.

Peter looked up, and there was no one at the door or windows. He had the fat wallet of the fat Colonel in his own pocket now. He lifted and pushed the man to a sitting position.

"Sir, can you stand now if I hold onto your hand?" Peter was the model of a helpful youth.

The walrus…Colonel, got one knee under him, held onto Peter, and pulled himself up hand over hand on Peter until he was standing. Peter reached over to open the door for him, and half-walked, half-shoved the Colonel inside and closed the door.

Peter saw a car turning the corner about two blocks away, and ducked into the shadows of the building. When he saw that the car was not going to stop, and the street was clear, he made his way to the street behind the brothel, and turned onto his own street. He only had one more kilometer to go, just one more, and then he would be home.

Peter came up the three flights of stairs to his apartment as quietly as he could, given that they were old, and creaked loudly with any weight. He had his key in the lock when he heard movement on the other side of the door. His mother pulled the door open and grabbed him by his coat collar.

Her face was white with anger, "Where have you been? I've been crazy with worry. You could have frozen to death in the snow and not be found until spring!"

Peter held out the wallet to her. He didn't know what else to do, and he was close to tears.

"What is this? Where did you get this, Peter?"

"We are slowly starving to death, mother, and I took this wallet from a fat, drunk Colonel who can spare it and get more money when he wants to."

Eda's jaw dropped, "My son is a thief? Peter, you have been stealing?" Tears filled her eyes.

"Yes, I have been stealing so that we could survive. Look at Katya, mother, she is so thin. Aren't you worried about her? And look at you. I have seen you put food on our plates when you should be eating, too. I couldn't stand it anymore, and so I have become a thief. But I only take a small amount, and I haven't hurt anyone, either."

"Petrosha…my God, what have I done to you?" Eda hugged him to her.

"You thought that I was earning some money from errands and cleaning, but there were no jobs to be had, mother. I tried, I really tried to find something that would help us. Finally, this was all I could think of to do." Peter was heartbroken that his mother had called him a thief, and he was near tears.

"I'm sorry, Petrosha, this is my fault. I can't earn enough to feed and shelter us, too. I've sold everything that I could think of, except the piano. It's going to have to go."

"No, please, mother, I will find a way to help us. I will."

"Promise me, Peter that you will never do this again." She held the wallet in front of him.

Chastised, he looked down at the floor, "Never, I will never again take what is not mine."

Eda sat in a kitchen chair long after Peter had fallen asleep, looking at the wallet that he had stolen. Finally, she opened it. What she saw brought her to tears. There were more rubles packed into the wallet than she had seen for a long time, higher denominations, crammed into the wallet, and dollars, too, American dollars. This would help them to survive for a long time, a very long time. She was an honest woman, but she knew that without Peter's bounty, they would not be able to survive much longer, and there was no one to help them.

Peter and his mother never again spoke of the fat Colonel or the fat wallet that Peter had stolen. The only things that he knew were different were that they had milk three days a week and honey for their tea, and bread almost every day. He delighted in seeing the color return to Katya's cheeks, and the furrows in his mother's brow relax.

Chapter 35

"I have never taken anything that doesn't belong to me since then, Niki, and I wish that I could make restitution for what I did."

Peter looked into her eyes as he spoke, hoping that he would not see condemnation there. Instead, he saw a stricken look.

"Oh Pete, it must have been terrible for you and your family," and she choked back tears.

He opened his arms, "Come here," he said softly.

They lay, cuddled together on the sofa, arms around each other, not saying a word. Both were filled with heartache. Hers was for him, and what he had suffered. His was for her because he had caused her more sadness.

Niki broke the silence, "Pete," she whispered, "I am so sorry for the things that have happened to you. I wish that I could change them, but I can't. The only thing that I can say to you is that I love you. I love you more than I can even express in words."

He stroked her hair, brushing it away from her face, "Last night, when we first made love, I realized that you had not…had never…"

She turned to face him and nodded, "That's a long story, Pete."

"But you are," he stopped for a moment, "were, engaged. I don't understand."

Nik took a deep breath, "Sometimes I eavesdropped on my brothers' conversations about girls. I was ten or eleven, and I was beginning to be curious about the boy/girl thing. They talked about how their friends bragged about being with some girls, and I understood what they meant. My brother Joey was especially angry one time when one of his friends ruined the reputation of a girl that Joey liked. He told Mikey that it didn't matter if she was guilty or not. Everyone would think the worst of her. Joey ended up taking her to the senior prom, anyway. He was that kind of guy.

"Having brothers helped me to decide what my own behavior would be when I got older and wanted to start dating boys. I was called the 'Frigid One' behind my back and even to my face. It didn't matter, because I wouldn't let peer pressure change my behavior. It helped to have two rather large older brothers, too. The boys pretty much left me alone. I didn't even attend my junior or senior proms…dances."

"And your engagement?" Peter's voice was soft as he looked into her eyes.

"Ron and I became engaged two weeks before the International Winter Games began. We were rarely alone, and we had so much to do completing our medical residencies, and then the Games, that we never had the opportunity to do what most new couples do. And I guess that it was mostly my fault. I always found an excuse, or something to fill all of my time. I still have not met Ron's family. In fact, that's where he is right now. He's in Chicago, and I was supposed to go with him until you got sick."

"Last night…"

"It was my decision. I promised myself a long time ago that I would wait until I really loved a man enough to spend the rest of my life with him."

Her words didn't register at first, but the truth of what she said finally began to come clear to him. Niki loved him as much as he loved her. With that realization, he felt warmth begin to spread inside him that melted the cold place, the place where he had always felt the constant cold ache of loneliness.

His eyes filled with wonderment, and in a soft voice he asked, "Niki, are you saying that it was me that you were waiting for?"

"Yes, I didn't know it at first, but I was waiting for you, Pete."

Nik slowly got up from the sofa and went to the stereo where she put in a tape. She beckoned to Peter to come and dance with her. The tape was soft mood music set in orchestral arrangements.

Without a word they danced to the end of the tape, their bodies as close as they could get, and their arms around each other. When it ended, they held onto each other, not wanting to let go.

Finally, Nik stood back, smiled up at Peter and said, "Lovers enjoy doing things together, and I have an idea. Let's experiment with something in the kitchen."

He bowed with a flourish, "I am at your service, my beautiful Niki."

In the kitchen Niki began by pulling her mother's recipe box down from a shelf above the desk. She and Peter sifted through several recipes until they found one that looked enticing, Smothered Chicken.

"Now comes the hard part, Pete. We'll have to find all the ingredients in my mother's kitchen. I took a chicken from the freezer to start thawing, but we need some spices."

Peter read the recipe and began searching through Marina's spice collection for the spices that were listed. He wondered briefly why anyone would want to smother a chicken. Nik put the chicken in the microwave to thaw the rest of the way. While they waited they talked and laughed, as if this were their normal, everyday, life.

Together, they assembled the chicken recipe, prepared it in a pan, put the whole chicken in with the sauce, and added the spices and cheese. When the recipe was ready, they put it in the oven, and set the timer for an hour.

Peter asked her if she wanted to play the piano. Nik was delighted with his suggestion, and they went to Peter's drawing room/bedroom hand in hand. The windows in this room, too, were covered with snow, and they turned on the lamp above the piano for light.

"Who is your favorite composer, Niki?"

"Tchaikovsky, Liszt, Mozart, Lennon, McCartney...I love them all."

Peter looked up at the ceiling and chuckled, "Ahh, a Beatles fan. And your favorite Beatles composition would be...?"

"Penny Lane of course," and she began playing and singing it for him.

Her singing voice, a lilting soprano, surprised and pleased him very much. His Niki was full of surprises. When she finished he applauded, as she blushed and laughed.

"And your favorite is…?" She looked at him with one eyebrow raised.

Peter started playing "And I Love Her" and sang the words to Niki. At the end of the song, he told her that he now knew the feeling that Lennon and McCartney were trying to convey in their song.

It was Nik's turn to applaud Peter's efforts, and she loved his deep-voiced rendition of the song. She put her arms around his neck, hugged him from behind, and kissed the top of his head.

"Pete, what would you like to do with the rest of your life? I mean, after your hockey career, what do you want to do?"

Peter smiled a wistful smile before replying, "If I could go to university, I'd study civil engineering. I have always read as much as I could about civil engineering; it fascinates me. Hockey isn't something that will last. I know that, and I've seen what happens when a player gets 'too old', or injured too many times. An athlete's time to play a sport is very short, really, and if I had the choice, I'd study engineering, but that will never happen, Niki."

"But it could, Pete, it could. If you decided to stay here, I know that my father would help you to get into the Purdue Engineering program. It's one of the best Engineering Schools in the country, if not the world."

Peter turned on the piano bench to face her, "Niki," he said as gently as he could, "I can't stay. My mother and sister have nothing, and no one but me. If I don't go back to help and protect them, I don't know what might happen."

Nik knelt down on the floor in front of Peter, looking up into his face. The realization of what he was saying hit her very hard, and her eyes filled with tears.

"Niki," he wiped away the tears that spilled onto her cheeks, "I love you. Completely and without reservation, I love you. For the rest of my life, you will be with me, in my thoughts, in my heart, no matter where I go or what I do. If there is ever a time that I can return to you, I will."

She bowed her head as he spoke, and even though she understood what he was saying, and why, it hurt terribly to hear him say it. But she knew in her heart that he was right.

Peter hurt, too; she could see that, and so she moved next to him on the piano bench and took his hand. For several moments, they sat together quietly, hand in hand, each wishing that the other did not feel the pain of their precarious and finite relationship.

"Let's make some beautiful music together, and let's not talk about anything but the here and now. We have that, Pete, the here and now."

Nik went to the bookcase and pulled a large, ornately decorated brocade box tied in red ribbons from a shelf. "Many of my favorite piano arrangements are in this box. Some are even from competitions that I entered."

They sat on the floor and rummaged through the contents of the box. Nik told Peter of her experiences in competition. In the beginning, she told him, her shyness made it difficult for her to get up on a stage to play in front of an audience. After she had gotten through a few of them, she said it got easier, and her parents were always there in the audience, their faces shining with pride.

"My first win was Gershwin's "Rhapsody In Blue." I practiced and practiced, until my brothers threatened to leave the family. My father intervened and worked out a schedule of practice that incorporated my brothers' absences for their own activities into the equation. It worked, too." Nik laughed in remembrance.

Peter was beaming at her, "Will you play it for me?"

"Ohhh...gosh, Pete, this arrangement's a difficult one. I'm not sure that my fingers and brain will be able to work well enough together."

He whispered, "Please, I really love this music," and he kissed her on the forehead.

Nik smoothed the sheet music over her legs with her hands, "Okay, Pete, but don't hold me to a perfect performance."

She went to the piano and placed the music on the harp. For several moments, she ran the keys up and down from treble to bass and back, working on intricate scales, trying to get her courage up to play for Pete. When she stopped, she took a deep breath, and began to play the introduction of the piece with the force that it required.

Peter sat, rapt, watching her, his beautiful Niki, as she played the powerful music. His throat tightened with emotion, because he knew that these moments would never be repeated. These few hours, and perhaps, if they were lucky, days, were theirs only at the whim of the weather, and the continued absence of others. Their time together was truly an accident of nature. But he was grateful for what they had, and he would never forget this wonderful woman.

Nik played the last note and sat very still on the bench, her head lowered. Then, she sat up straight and turned to smile at Peter. The here and now, she thought, I'll concentrate on the here and now.

"It was so *beautiful,* Niki, and so very powerful. Thank you for granting my wish. Now I will carry this moment with me always." Peter put his hand over his heart.

Nik didn't know how to respond to his words, but finally said, "Thank you," in a hushed voice.

She took his hand, "Let's go check on dinner, Pete," and they started toward the kitchen, just like any young couple, testing their togetherness.

Peter decided that he liked "smothered chicken." The combination of herbs, sour cream, cheese, and rice brought out the flavor of the chicken very nicely. He helped to set the table in the kitchen, and again poured tall glasses of cold milk to drink. Nik peeled tangerines from a Christmas fruit basket as edible garnish for their chicken, making the meal even more appetizing as well as delicious. They enjoyed their dinner, especially so because they had prepared it together. They were so comfortable in each other's company, that it seemed that they had been together as a couple for a very long time.

While they ate, Nik looked at Peter's complexion with a physician's eye toward his health. He was beginning to look healthy again, and she was very pleased to see his improvement. She briefly worried about their earlier combined athletics in the shower, but decided that she'd check him thoroughly before bedtime. At this thought she chuckled aloud.

"What…?" Peter stopped, fork in midair, and looked ruefully at her.

"Tonight I'm going to check your incisions before bedtime. I'm going to check you over very thoroughly." Nik returned his rueful look.

"A good idea, I think. One can never be too careful in matters of health," he replied with a wry smile.

Chapter 36

They cleaned the kitchen and talked about Nik's piano solo. Peter was curious about her training, and she explained that her formal training had started when she was five years old. Nik's mother had an ancient spinet that Nik played from the time that she was three. She told him that she had loved her lessons, and pestered her parents incessantly about getting a concert grand piano.

"I used to tell them that I found ads in the newspaper about pianos for sale. That's how they found out that I had learned to read."

Five-year-old Niki called out to her mother, "I found it mom, there's even a *picture* so we can see what it looks like."

Marina took the newspaper from her daughter to look at the picture of the piano Niki wanted. "Well, it looks very nice, but it's best if we go see it and actually listen to its tone, its sound."

"Can we?" Niki closed her eyes tightly. She could *feel* the keys, the blacks, the whites, under her fingers.

"I think it's time to look at pianos Niki. Let's see what your father has to say." Marina put an arm around her daughter as she spoke.

Klaus took his daughter seriously in regard to her interest in the piano. He had been her best fan from the very first. He found it hard to believe that one so young, his daughter, had the beginnings of what might be a great talent. He immediately agreed to go with Niki to see about the piano she had found for sale in the newspaper.

He talked to Marina to get her thoughts on the piano that Niki had found. "What do you think, Marina? She's very serious about this, isn't she?"

"Oh yes, Klaus, she is determined to have a good piano to play."

As it turned out, the entire family went to see Niki's piano. They made a day of it, including a nice lunch, because the owner of the piano lived more than thirty miles from Indianapolis.

It was a beautiful, clear spring day. The air was warm and fragrant with daffodils and crocuses. The sun shone brightly on her parents' big Lincoln. Of course, Niki didn't care what the name of the car was, but she liked its roominess, and thought that it was wonderful that she didn't have to sit so near to her brothers, who would tease her mercilessly if they got the chance.

They arrived in the small town of Elwood, and Klaus easily found the home where the piano was waiting. The elderly lady who answered the door was very pleasant, and she asked them to come in. The first thing that Niki saw in the large formal living room was the concert grand piano. It dominated the room, setting adjacent to a red brick fireplace. It called to her, but Niki waited politely until the lady asked if she would like to sit on the bench with her as she demonstrated the piano. Niki's heart soared.

"Oh *yes, I'd love to.*" Niki glanced at her mother to see if it was permissible.

Marina nodded at her, "Go ahead, dear."

The lady's name was Mrs. Fielding, and she certainly could play the piano. When she finished her demonstration, she asked if Niki would like to play something, and Niki's face was immediately wreathed in a huge smile.

"Yes, I'd like to play something," Niki said in her most grown-up voice.

Niki played "Fuhr Elise" flawlessly, and Mrs. Fielding complimented her.

"Is this piano going to be yours?"

Again, Niki's face glowed as she answered, "Yes, and I'm going to be a concert pianist, too."

Mikey and Joey applauded and asked their little sister to take a bow. Niki looked askance at them and shook her head. Mrs. Fielding nodded her head in agreement with Niki's opinion, but nonetheless smiled.

The beautiful black concert grand piano was delivered two weeks later, and was placed in the library of the Kellman home, where Niki practiced throughout her elementary school years. She prepared diligently for concerts and competitions on her concert grand, and played and practiced every day until, in the first semester of seventh grade, her heart was broken.

Peter was listening intently to Niki's story, and saw her face change to sadness when she talked about being heartbroken.

"What happened, Niki?"

"It was because of my brother Joey," and she continued her story.

Niki loved October. She loved the fall of the year when the air became clear and crisp, and the sky was the bluest blue possible. On this gorgeous October day, brightly lit with a sun that shone in the azure blue heaven, her family, mom, dad, and Mikey, were going to see Joey play football for the first time in college. Joey's football career was hotly contested in discussions between his parents, but he had finally won out, and was now a starter in the running back position for Purdue.

Purdue's opponent on this perfect day was Ohio State. Ross Ade Stadium was going to be packed because Purdue was 3 and 0. A perfect start to what might be a perfect year for the football team; maybe a shot at one of the premier bowl games.

Niki and Mikey watched their parents' interaction from their back seat vantage point. Klaus was still not convinced that Joey should be playing football, but Marina's excitement was catching, and he was in a good mood.

West Lafayette was jammed with traffic coming into the city for the game. Horns were honking, engines throbbing, and racing. Exuberant fans were sticking their heads, among other body parts, out of car windows, and shouting and howling.

Inside the stadium the spectators swarmed as if they were bees in a beehive. Except...the beehive was separated in an unusual way, by color.

There was the black and gold of Purdue, and the red and white of Ohio State, both concentrated in distinctive cells of the beehive, each cell moving, undulating with color.

By the time the Kellman family got into the stadium, the kickoff was made, and play had begun. While they looked for their seats in the bleachers, they also looked for number 20 in Purdue colors, and found that Joey was on the field playing in his running back position. Purdue had possession of the football and the quarterback was looking for a receiver as he was being rushed by some burly Ohioans. He snapped a pass in Joey's direction, and the crowd roared as Joey picked the football from the air and began to run.

Niki was standing next to her father when she heard a collective groan swell up from the spectators, and then everyone around her on the Purdue side was on their feet. An eerie silence followed for several moments, and then the sounds of dismay began to swell until they filled the stadium.

Someone nearby said, "Did you see that hit? My God, he was tackled from both sides!"

Niki couldn't see over the heads of those around her, and she looked up at her father, who had turned ghostly pale.

"What is it, Klaus, what's happening?" Marina had a scared look on her face.

Mikey, standing next to his mother, was almost as tall as his father, and could see what had happened on the field. "Joey, Joey," he shouted, and turned with a stricken look toward his father.

Klaus forgot himself, "Mein Gott in himmel!" He placed a hand on his forehead in disbelief.

Niki pushed past the people crowding around her, until she reached the railing. Her hands froze there when she saw that Purdue's number 20 was lying face down and motionless on the field. Several people from his team hurried out to him, and as she watched, they turned him over onto his back. They turned him and his body followed in rag doll fashion, flopping as he reached his back. Joey moved his arms and legs as they got down on their knees to administer to him. Then Niki saw his arms and his legs go slack.

Niki screamed, "Joey!" But in her heart she knew that he was gone.

In a quavering voice, Nik told Pete, "It was then that I decided to go into medicine. I didn't want what happened to my brother to happen to anyone else if I could prevent it. That's when my music became secondary in my life."

She fell silent and Pete sat quietly, wanting to comfort her, but not knowing what to say. From the outside, Niki seemed to have led a perfect life, without strife or sadness, but he now saw the pain and sadness in her eyes and on her face. Because of the way he felt about her, Peter took on her burden, too.

He stood up and took her hand, "Let's go sit by the fire for a little while."

She nodded, "That's a good idea." Her voice was subdued, almost flat.

Hand in hand, they went back into the great room. Peter stoked the fire, placing two more large pieces of wood on top of the embers. As he hunched down in front of the fire, using the poker to vent the largest of the embers to release some flame to start the new wood, Peter was trying to understand the story that Niki had just shared with him. The enormity of her loss, the heartbreak of losing her brother, was hard for him to fathom.

Peter pulled the cushions and blankets back in front of the fireplace. "Help me choose some music, Niki, and then let's rest here."

They looked through the music tapes on the bookshelves next to the fireplace and each pulled out a tape. Both chose soothing mood music. His was from Nat King Cole's repertoire, and hers was from Johnny Mathis' greatest hits. Slowly, Nik loaded them in the tape player built into the bookshelves.

Peter rolled back the blankets, lay down, and pulled her down next to him. When she was in his arms, they pulled the covers up and held each other, not needing to speak. The soothing music played, and soon they were both asleep.

From a distance, Peter heard an annoying noise. He wasn't quite sure what the noise might be, but it wouldn't go away. Finally, he opened his eyes and realized that what he was hearing was the alarm on the generator. The room was now almost dark because they had not left any lamps burning.

"Niki…Niki, I have to refill the generator," he whispered.

She stirred in his arms, "Okay, Pete, I'm awake."

Peter threw the covers back. The fire in the grate had burned low again, too. Nik crawled out from under the covers and followed him to the garage. She rubbed her eyes with her long fingers balled into fists, and yawned widely. Peter chuckled at his beautiful Niki. For the most part, she came across as a very self-contained woman, but there were times when she seemed vulnerable and disarmingly childlike. He kissed her lightly on the lips and she put her arms around his neck. They stood holding each other until the generator alarmed again and made both of them jump.

Peter got a flashlight from Klaus' workbench for light when he shut off the generator to refill the gas tank. He hit the battery-fed starter, but it didn't fire. He tried a second time; it still didn't start. Peter looked up at Niki and shrugged. She had a look of consternation on her face.

"What if it doesn't start?" Niki's eyes were wide.

Peter took the cover off of the motor and checked to make sure that the battery cables were tight. When he tried to tighten the first one, it seemed to be fine. The second one, however, had loosened, probably from vibration of the engine, so he tightened the fitting, and shut the motor cover. This time when he hit the starter, the generator roared into life, much to his relief.

He went over to the window and checked the exhaust hose to make sure that it was still venting to the outside. Some of the snow had melted around the hose and had made a puddle just inside the window. But everything seemed to be working properly, and he was thankful that their source of electricity was still functional.

"It looks like we've dodged a bullet, Pete."

He smiled, "For now, at least."

They listened to the radio to find out what was going on in the outside world, and were surprised to find that weather conditions had improved very little, and that more snow and high winds were on the way. As night fell, they sat on the pillows in front of the fire reading poetry to one another.

Peter recited from memory Pushkin's, "The Fountain of Bakhchisary" to Niki, about a Tartar king who kidnapped and fell in love with the beautiful Mary, who, when killed by the king's favorite concubine in a fit of jealous rage, weeps voluminous tears, and her forgiving soul becomes the fountain of tears. When Mary dies, the king realizes that there is nothing more important in this world than true love.

Nik read Percy Bysshe Shelley's "The Skylark" to Peter, and he closed his eyes, the better to concentrate on her voice, and the words of the poet. She read the poetry expressively, beautifully, and he felt gooseflesh arise, born of his exquisite enjoyment, as she read to him.

Between readings, they talked of their previous lives. Peter told Nik of his childhood, and how he and Katya depended upon each other for companionship and safety. He told her that when they were together and quiet, their father left them alone mostly. They learned at a young age not to make noise or to cry. If they stayed out of his way, Ivan would not bother with them.

"You may think that my childhood was very unhappy, but it wasn't, really. My mother always kept Katya and me busy with interesting activities so that we wouldn't feel the absence of our father. That's why we skated and played the piano, visited the Pushkin Museum of Fine Arts, saw the Bolshoi perform, and studied foreign languages. She took us to the symphony and to the theatre, too. My mother wanted us to become cultured, and she made sure that we were exposed to the finest that Moscow had to offer."

Peter told her that he and Katya went with their parents to their dacha near Tver in summer every year when Moscow became unbearably hot. They played and swam in the cool waters of the lake.

"It was beautiful there, Niki. We swam and went boating with our friends. In many ways, the first twelve years of my life were those of a child of privileged Party members."

"To the manor born," Nik chuckled, "Remember?"

Peter nodded, lowered his eyes and smiled. "Da, I remember, Niki."

Nik shared stories of her own childhood. She told him how her brothers always teased her, but that she knew that they loved her, too.

"Both of my brothers were very protective of me. They looked out for me and wouldn't let anyone hurt me."

"I understand why your brothers protected you. I feel the same about Katya. She is so kind and gentle, and I don't want anyone to take advantage of her."

"Pete, tell me about Katya and your mother. What are they like, and who do you look like?"

Peter laughed, "Niki, where should I begin?"

"At the beginning of course; you've already told me that your father didn't want to have children…"

Peter had a distant look in his eyes when he began his story, "We never knew what to expect from Ivan. I think that he used vodka as a tranquilizer to get him through his manic periods. When he was drinking, he was very unpredictable. There were times when he must have thought that he could conquer the world. He behaved like that at some of the dacha gatherings when he was among his friends. And…he must have been very charismatic. Not to his family, but, everyone else hung on his every word. My mother said that he could persuade anyone to do anything he wanted. She succumbed to his persuasion that way at first, she said, but then, when they married, he changed. He became very controlling."

Chapter 37

Eda dressed in her best suit for her dinner date with the very handsome newcomer to her university class in English. He was tall, taller than she, and had unruly dark blond hair that he kept sweeping back from his forehead in an absent-minded way. He had a beautiful smile, but it was his eyes that were his best feature. When he looked at her, she felt that he could hypnotize her with those dark eyes.

Her parents were aghast that she was actually going to go out in public with the Russian. What would their families; their friends and neighbors think when he came to call for her?

"Mama, he is witty and interesting; more interesting than anyone that I have ever known. He makes me laugh, and he tells me that I am beautiful. He brings me flowers. No one else has ever brought me flowers."

"Eda, you are young and naive. When I look at this man, I see a wolf with long teeth, a Russian wolf. He will hurt you, if not physically, then he will most surely break your heart. He will return to Russia, you know."

Eda's heart was pounding and she blushed. "Mama, please don't say these things to me. Ivan has made the effort to speak our language, and he speaks it well. He wants to know all about me. When we are together, he looks at me alone, and not the pretty girls who pass by and stare at him."

Sophie shook her head and closed her eyes. My only daughter, she thought, and this *Russian*, this charming, disarming man, is going to take her far away from my protection.

"Your father," Sophie began, "is very upset over this man, Ivan Genchenko. Apparently, he could go to university anywhere, his family is wealthy, but why did he come to Warsaw? Your father thinks that he is in exile for some reason. He is hiding here in the heart of Poland. Why?"

Tears filled Eda's beautiful green-gold eyes, "He makes me happy, mama, and none of the men that you and papa have tried to force on me these last three years have ever made me feel this way. I have been forced to dine with the Rabbi's son, the goldsmith's son, and, worst of all, the banker's son. I have been pleasant and kind and ladylike, even when they were insulting me about my height. Is it my fault that they were all shorter than I am?"

"I will not greet him when he comes for you, Eda. I do not want to talk to him, or even attempt to be civil. You have always been headstrong, but in this instance, it will be your downfall. Mark my words; he will make you wish that you had never met him."

Over the summer, Eda and Ivan spent a great deal of time together. They took long walks in the city, dined at fashionable restaurants, and enjoyed their mutual friends who told them that they were a "lovely couple." The early sixties in post-war Poland were anything but quiet, but university students are the same the world around. They all thought that they knew what was best for the world. They discussed politics until the early hours of the morning, smoking their cigarettes and sipping tea. Of course, the Soviet Union, and its ever-present Communist Party, frowned on the students as potential fomenters of unrest.

Ivan Genchenko was the "chosen one" who reported to the Polish Communist Party Headquarters at regular intervals to assure them that the students whom he had befriended were unimportant, innocuous, and not a danger to the Soviet Union. In doing so, he more than likely saved several of the male students from being arrested, roughed up, and interrogated.

Ivan had his father to thank for this arrangement. Although Sergei was very angry with his son over his adulterous liaison with one of Sergei's friend's wives, he did not want any harm to come to Ivan. He wanted only to teach him a lesson in humility. Banishment to Warsaw, Poland would certainly instill some humility in Ivan.

It had not been a conscious plan in the beginning of Ivan's exile in Poland. But lately, Ivan had begun thinking that the best slap to his father's face, the best way to get even with Sergei, would be to marry a Polish Jewess. Yes, he'd come home to Moscow with a beautiful Jewish bride. His mother would cry, his father would fume, and he would thumb his nose at them. He savored the thought.

One thing that never crossed his mind was the effect that his family's outrage would have on Eda, his intended Polish Jewess bride. It never occurred to him that she would be terribly hurt by their lack of acceptance of her. In fact, if he had thought about it at all, he would have realized that his sister, Tatiana, would be especially cruel to Eda because of Eda's beauty, first of all, and then because she was a Jew.

Ivan kept company with Eda for two years before he heard from his mother that he could return home. During that time, he had not heard one word from his father, and in truth, he had had very little communication from his mother. The letter arrived in early March 1964. Ivan read the letter again and again, feeling a sense of growing excitement and jubilation. His exile would soon be over! He would have packed his luggage that very day and not have given a second thought to leaving Eda, but for one thing: she was part of his plan for revenge.

The day after Ivan received his mother's letter to return home, he proposed to Eda. In the two years that he had known her, he had never pressed her for intimacy beyond holding hands and an occasional kiss. He had always treated her with respect and kindness, no matter that his behavior was contrary to his true feelings. When Ivan needed sex, he knew where to find it in Warsaw. It was a matter of convenience for him, nothing more.

Eda was swept off her feet by Ivan's proposal. He had been the perfect suitor, kind, generous, courtly. He had never once taken advantage of her, although at a certain point, she would have welcomed his advances. Eda was in love with the man whom she thought Ivan was.

Ivan went with Eda to announce their engagement to her parents. He wanted to see the look on their faces when Eda told them that she was going to marry the *Russian.* As Eda said the words, Sophie's eyes teared up, but Wadislaw, his mouth set tightly in a straight line, said nothing.

Eda went to her room and packed her belongings in a single valise. She came down the narrow staircase of her home for the last time. She went to kiss her mother, and her father in turn. Neither parent raised an arm to return her hugs. Instead, they stood silently together, watching their beautiful daughter leave what once had been their happy home.

Ivan closed the front door, and looked up to see the lace curtain pulled aside at the window next to the door. Eda's parents stood, unmoving, witnesses to their daughter's defection.

Ivan and Eda were married that same day in the Communist Party Administration Building in the center of Warsaw. The Magistrate was a sad-faced man with tremendous jowls that quivered when he spoke or moved his head, and his eyes were mere slits in his puffball face. The single ceiling light in the room shone on his hairless pate. His robe had dark, greasy stains down the front, and his fingernails needed trimming and cleaning. In spite of his appearance, Eda was so very happy on this, her wedding day. Ivan had bought flowers for her for the occasion, and had greased the wheels of the bureaucracy by gifting the Magistrate with a tidy sum, assuring that they would have no waiting at his office door. Ivan had thought of everything.

The newlyweds spent the night in a fashionable Warsaw hotel and had a delicious meal with champagne. To Ivan's surprise later in the evening, he discovered that his new bride was a virgin. He was gentle with her, and found that making love to her was a gratifying experience, and so much different than the prostitutes that he was used to. In every way she pleased him; her beauty, her shyness, and the gift of her virginity made him as happy as he had ever been in his life. He hadn't been prepared for this experience, this change of heart, but there it was. The next morning, Mr. and Mrs. Ivan Sergeiovich Genchenko boarded a train that would take them eventually to Moscow.

March could be as bitterly cold as any January in the countryside they traveled by rail from Warsaw to Moscow. There were delays while snow was shoveled from narrow passes, but Ivan and Eda spent the majority of their time in their own compartment, and didn't notice much of what was going on around them.

He made love to her every night, and sometimes during the afternoon, not to mention the blissful awakenings of morning. Eda, unstudied in the skills that most brides were aware of for preventing pregnancy, joyously participated in this wonderful new experience with her beloved Ivan. By the time that they reached the Byelorussia Rail Station outside Moscow, conception had occurred. Eda was pregnant when she stepped onto Russian soil.

Ivan found a taxi outside the rail station, and told the cabbie to head directly to 433 Arbat Boulevard. Before they knew it, they were on the Garden Ring Road. Although it had been snowing, the cabbie sped along the ring road, and traffic was fairly heavy at five-thirty in the afternoon. Ivan had planned to surprise his parents at the dinner hour. Usually, they had guests on Sunday evening, and he wanted the greatest amount of exposure, therefore the greatest amount of embarrassment to his parents, for his wedding announcement.

Ivan glanced over at Eda, and had a moment's misgivings over what he was about to do. He knew that this beautiful and vulnerable woman loved him. He had no doubt whatsoever about that. Their time together on the train had shown him how wonderful it was to be with her. And yet, because of who, no, *what* she was, there was a part of him that considered her to be far beneath him. He had, however, already decided to stay married to her; the better to rub salt into his parents' wounds that this marriage would inflict upon them.

When they reached the Arbat, the cabbie slowed and began looking for the address. Eda looked at the beautiful homes, mansions actually, and began to feel a bit uneasy about the imminent meeting with Ivan's family. Ivan reached for her hand and she smiled at him, while reciting an inward prayer that everything would go well.

They pulled into a driveway that had an iron-gated entrance, and the property was surrounded by ornate ironwork fencing that extended back as far as Eda could see. The cabbie stopped under a portico that was brightly lit, and came around to assist his fares from the cab. At just that moment, the large double doors to the house opened, and a man dressed in formal attire came out on the steps to greet them. Judging from the look on the man's face, Eda saw that he immediately recognized Ivan.

The man gave a stiff bow, and then asked Ivan whether he could be of help in carrying the luggage. Ivan laughed aloud and said, "Of course," he and his new bride would require assistance. Eda realized that the man was a servant, and that he was struggling to remain composed. How strange, she thought.

Inside the house, judging by the hum of conversation and clinking of crystal, china and silverware, dinner had already commenced. Ivan turned to the butler and told him to take his and his wife's luggage to the east-facing bedroom. Then, taking Eda's arm in his, he strode directly to the dining room. As they entered, Ivan's smile was genuine, as he counted no less than fifteen people seated at his father's table. Conversation stopped, and knives and forks were set on plates. Ivan let the tension mount for a moment and then bade everyone a good evening.

"My wife and I have just arrived, and we apologize that we are late to dinner, but we must freshen up before joining you." He nodded toward the head of the table and smiled again, "Father," and then looked toward the foot of the table, "Mother."

Eda was somewhat dismayed by the looks that she received from Ivan's parents and their guests. Of course, she thought, my clothes, aren't Moscow-styled. Actually, they weren't even Warsaw- styled because she had designed and made them from others' discarded clothing.

"Is something the matter, Ivan? I don't think that I have seen a more surprised group of people in my life."

Ivan laughed a short, dry laugh, "You will get used to them, Eda. Most of them are frauds, pretentious, or pretentious frauds, so don't worry about what their opinions might be. They have never seen the likes of you before, my dear; tall, patrician, and absolutely beautiful without adornment of any kind. Of course they were surprised."

The butler awaited them in their bedroom. He had unpacked their clothing and personal items, and had taken care to hang them in the closet, or fold them into the chest of drawers. Eda looked around the room and was astounded by the luxury that she saw there. Brocades in red and gray, dark wood, a huge bed full of brightly colored pillows, layers of silver-gray draperies that hung from ceiling to floor at three tall windows, and the most exquisitely woven floral wool carpet she had ever seen were some of the things that she took in as she turned in wonder.

Ivan patted the butler on the shoulder and thanked him for his help. The butler bowed stiffly and left the room.

"Ivan, this is the most beautiful bedroom that I have ever seen. Are we really going to stay in this room?"

He turned to her, "Does it meet with your approval, dear wife? If not, there are ten others decorated differently that might be more to your taste. This one, the eastern room, is so-called because it faces east and is therefore cool in the evening during the summer."

Ivan opened the closet and looked through his wife's small wardrobe. He chose a simple black dress that dipped low in the back, and then he bent down to retrieve a pair of elegant black shoes that she had brought with her. From his pocket he took a small ribbon-wrapped package.

"Will you do me the honor of wearing what I have chosen for you this evening?"

He handed her the small package and she opened it with shaking hands. Inside, she found a ring with a large pear-shaped diamond surrounded by pearls, and a pair of diamond earrings.

"These pieces of jewelry have been in my family for many generations, and they are now yours. My grandmother gave them to me when I was fifteen. She passed them directly to me without telling my parents. My grandmother and I were close, but she didn't like her son-in-law, my father."

Tears rolled down Eda's cheeks as she looked from him to the diamonds, and back to him, "For me?"

Ivan smiled and said, "Yes, for my beautiful Eda, my wife."

He took the ring from the box and placed it on her third finger, left hand. "It's a little large, so we'll have to wrap something around it so that it will fit."

Next he placed the earrings in her ears. "Perfect," he said, "perfect."

Eda swept her thick dark hair up into an elegant chignon, and pinned it in place. Then she and Ivan quickly changed clothes, and hurried downstairs. When they returned to the party, it was as if they had not left the dining room. Everyone was still seated, and as the newlyweds entered the room, quiet reigned.

Sergei got up from his seat and escorted Eda to a chair at the table as Ivan followed. After being seated, they were immediately served their meal and wine was poured for everyone. While the amenities were being observed, the room remained rather quiet. Eda could not help but notice that all eyes were riveted on her, but she maintained her composure and ate daintily from her plate. Ivan was very solicitous of her, and bent to whisper encouragement in her ear several times, which was noted by all seated at the table.

The appropriate amount of time having passed for the latecomers to finish their meals, Sergei tapped his wine glass for attention, and then asked Ivan to introduce his wife to the group. "Please, Ivan, present your lovely wife to our friends."

Ivan stood, enjoying the moment, the agony of his parents, before he introduced his wife. "As all of you know, I have been studying abroad. While I was in Warsaw at university, I met the most beautiful young woman that I have ever seen. It took me two years to convince her to be my wife, and I was surprised when she said yes. Ladies and gentlemen, I present my wife, Eda Wadislawa Genchenkova."

Ivan took her hand and she stood beside him as the group raised their glasses in a toast to the young couple.

Eda and Ivan, lying on satin sheets with the brocade comforter pulled up for warmth, talked into the early hours of the morning before finally falling asleep. Ivan relished the evening's victory; he had thumbed his nose at his mother and father in the presence of their friends.

The couple arose late the next morning, and dressed for travel before going down to breakfast. As he descended the staircase with his wife, Ivan beckoned to the butler.

"Please pack our things for travel Yevgeny. We will be departing after breakfast." Ivan pressed a wad of rubles into his palm.

"Yes sir, I'll see to it immediately."

The dining room was still set for breakfast, and the buffet had all the serving pieces in place. Ivan wondered how long the food had been simmering, but when he picked up the ornate sterling silver covers, he found that fresh foods had been added. When he and Eda were seated, a maid came out to pour tea, and asked what they would like to have for breakfast.

They were nearly finished eating when Ivan's parents came in to join them. The maid, who had come in when the master of the house had entered the dining room, again left the room to prepare a tea service. Sergei took this opportunity to ask Ivan pointedly about when his marriage had taken place. Ivan's mother kept staring at the ring on Eda's left ring finger. Ivan knew that his mother recognized the ring, it had been her mother's, and her mother had worn it often.

"Eda and I were married in a civil ceremony at Party Headquarters in Warsaw. We could have been married by the Rabbi, but we didn't want to delay anymore than we had to, so we were married by the Magistrate."

At the mention of a Rabbi, Ivan's mother gasped. His sister, Tatiana, came into the dining room at that moment. Her face was pale, and her eyes seemed pale, too, a dull gray. Her hair was of a nondescript, fair color, worn long and straggling, and her light-colored clothing hung on her frail body.

"What is this I hear about you, Ivan?" She shot an angry look at the beautiful woman sitting next to her brother, "Is this your new bride?"

Instead of answering his sister, he turned to Eda and told her, "Darling, this is my older sister, Tatiana. Sometimes she is out of sorts, or just plain impolite, so don't feel that you are being singled out."

Eda saw the drama at work in Ivan's family, and couldn't help wondering what her role might be in the present circumstances. She was uncomfortable, but she remained quiet and composed.

"I think that we should go upstairs and prepare to depart, Eda." Ivan took her arm gently and smiled at her.

Without another word, the young couple left the dining room and went to their bedroom. The butler had finished packing their things and their luggage awaited them. Ivan locked the bedroom door and leaned on it for a moment. Eda looked at him expectantly.

Ivan told Eda that he had a surprise for her, "Stand right there, I won't be a moment."

He took out his keys, sorted through them, and picked out an elongated, old-fashioned key that he held up to the light from the window. Ivan then went quickly to the walk-in closet and opened the double doors with a flourish. The closet was antiquated according to current construction, but nonetheless quite roomy. Eda saw that Ivan moved one of the clothes poles from its mount at the back of the closet, revealing a keyhole. With his key he opened the false back of the closet where several pieces of luggage were stored inside. There was also a full-length sable fur coat hanging on a clothes rack. It was covered with cheesecloth to prevent dust from settling in the fur.

Ivan brought out the luggage and Eda saw that it matched his own. There were four pieces of differing sizes, in addition to Ivan's two that set near the door to the bedroom. The new additions seemed to be heavy, judging by the level of Ivan's effort as he carried them out of the closet. He went back into the closet, removed the cheesecloth from the sable and took it from the rack. He held it from the shoulders and asked Eda to put it on.

"Perfect," he told her, "yes, it is perfect on you. The color of the coat matches your hair, Eda."

Eda was speechless for several moments. The coat was lined in satin and it was luxuriously warm. She had never in her life experienced such a coat.

Ivan said, "Look in this full-length mirror, Eda, the coat looks as if it were made for you."

"Ivan…I can't believe that this coat, this beautiful coat, is now mine…you really want me to have it?"

"My grandmother gave it to me. She told me that one day I would have a beautiful wife, and she wanted my wife to have this sable coat. She said that her health would prevent her from seeing me married, but she wanted to join in the celebration, and so she gave me her favorite coat for my wife.

"This house belonged to my grandmother. She came to it as a bride, and she knew all of its secrets. Grandmother showed me her closet when I was twelve, and made me promise that I wouldn't tell my mother or father about it. This room was her bedroom and that's why I asked for it last night. No one, as far as I know, has dared sleep in this room since my grandmother died. She never shared the secret of the hidden closet with anyone else."

Eda wrapped herself in the sable coat, hugging it to her throat with both hands, and gave Ivan a brilliant smile. "This is the most wonderful coat that any woman could ever have, Ivan."

On impulse, he went to her, lifted her off her feet, and hugged and kissed her. At times, his spirits were so high that he thought he might burst. He had waited patiently for this day, and now that it was here, he felt that he could move mountains if he had to.

Ivan used his antique key to close the back panel of the closet. When it was secure, he put the clothes pole back into place. He had taken all of the precious contents from the secret chamber, his grandmother's gifts to him to start his adult life as a wealthy man. He didn't think that he would ever set foot in this house again. Not after today.

He wasn't quite finished with his parents, but he would be soon. Ivan used the bell pull to call the butler. When he came into the room, the butler looked surprised to see the extra luggage. Ivan pulled more rubles from his pocket for the butler and politely asked him to call a cab and see to it that the luggage was taken downstairs.

Ivan, hand in hand with his beautiful wife in her gorgeous sable coat, went slowly down the staircase. Judging from the dumbfounded expressions on his parents' and sister's faces, Ivan's exit with his wife was quite spectacular. When they reached the bottom of the stairs, Ivan smiled at his family and bid them adieu.

He walked past them and then turned, "Before we go, I must tell you, father, that your friend's wife, the one for whom I was exiled to Poland, seduced me when I was fifteen. She used her extensive library as a trap. Father, do you remember how much I loved books? Well, Svetlana used her books as a lure to get me to come to her home. Our relationship lasted for five years, and wouldn't have been discovered, except that I told her that I no longer wanted to see her. That was when she chose to tell her husband about us. I thought that you should know this, since you blamed me entirely for the affair."

Without another word, Ivan again took Eda's hand, and led her toward the door. Outside, Ivan thanked the butler, who was holding the door of the cab, and assisted Eda into the cab. He smiled and waved at his parents and sister who stood in the doorway, watching their departure.

Eda was in turmoil over what Ivan had just said to his parents. There was something about his words that had caused the hair on the back of her neck to rise. For some reason, she remembered her mother's admonition; "Mark my words; he will make you wish that you had never met him." Early in Eda's marriage, the seeds of doubt were sown.

Chapter 38

Peter took a deep breath, "My grandmother was right, and my mother told Katya and me about what our grandmother had said to her all those years ago as we were moving from our very nice apartment in Moscow to Lyubertsy after Ivan was imprisoned."

"When did your mother realize that she was pregnant?"

Peter shrugged, "Mother didn't tell us everything, but she did say that Ivan had a fit of temper when she finally told him that she was pregnant. And when the doctor told my parents that they were going to have twins, my father was absolutely furious."

"But didn't he relent when he saw his babies? Wasn't he overjoyed that he had produced two beautiful children?"

"Honestly, I don't think that he did, Niki. He didn't have the capacity to really love anyone, my mother, and his children, included."

"I'm just amazed that he couldn't feel something for you and your sister. Surely there were times when he must have realized how special you are."

He shook his head, "No, I don't think that he ever did. He would often tell us just how worthless he thought that we were."

Nik moved next to Peter on the pillows, put her arms around him, and kissed him on the cheek. "You *are* special, Peter, very special to me."

"Sometimes," he said, "I think that I must be dreaming that you feel that way about me."

"Well, let's dream together. Are you getting sleepy, Pete?" Nik's voice was soft.

He nodded, "Let's sleep here in front of the fire, Niki, it's closer to the generator. I wouldn't have to come all the way downstairs when it needs attention, although I'm doing much better than I ever thought I would since my surgery."

"That reminds me, Pete, I've got to check your incisions."

He smiled a slow smile at her, "I was expecting this."

They went upstairs to get ready for bed, washing their faces and brushing their teeth together. They looked at each other in the mirror for a long moment, and then Peter asked if he could brush out her hair. Nik agreed with a girlish giggle. He was gentle as he pulled the brush through her dark hair, the texture of satin, and Nik loved it. She closed her eyes, the better to experience his touch.

Peter whispered in her ear, "Have I put you to sleep, Niki?"

She opened her eyes, looked up at him, and with an emotion-filled voice said, "No, Pete, it's just that I have never in my life felt so much…" She struggled for words, and then whispered, "so much love."

"I know. It's overwhelming, isn't it?" He lifted her to him, put his arms around her and kissed her deeply.

They helped each other into their night clothing. But before Peter pulled his pajama bottoms on, Nik pushed him back onto the bed.

"Let's check your tummy, Pete."

Nik rubbed her hands together to warm them before she lifted his pajama top to expose his abdomen. Her hands were gentle as she palpated methodically from the upper abdomen to the inguinal area. His surgical wounds were healing nicely. The stab wounds used for openings for the drains were completely closed. Nik pressed lightly against each wound to check for fluid beneath the skin, but found nothing unusual. Peter's skin was cool to the touch, a good sign, and there was no redness except for the actual wound edges. When she checked the inguinal wound, Peter's arousal was becoming apparent.

Nik was still all business, "When I press down on your incisions, Pete, can you describe for me what it feels like?"

Peter looked up at the ceiling and frowned in concentration, "It feels like a deep bruise, but not too painful. I've had deep bruises before, playing hockey, among other things, and that's what it feels like."

"Good, that's good, Pete. Your incisions are healing beautifully." She reached for his pajama bottom and dangled it above him.

Peter grabbed the pajama bottom from her and tossed it across the room. Nik was startled, and then she began to laugh.

He stood for a moment, threw back the bedclothes and said, "Come here," holding his arms open wide for her.

They stayed the night in the bedroom instead of going downstairs in front of the fireplace. Nik's nightgown covered Peter's pajamas on the floor. Their lovemaking was unhurried and deeply satisfying, each freely giving pleasure to the other. It was as if they had been together always. Afterward, they lay as before, their bodies closely aligned, their limbs intertwined.

Peter heard the alarm on the generator around three-thirty in the morning and quickly put on his pajamas and slippers and went downstairs. He and Niki had left the lights on in the great room, and the pillows and blankets near the fireplace were rumpled. This made him smile. They were rumpling bedclothes in different parts of the house on this night.

In the garage, Peter could hear the wind outside, and it had picked up considerably, impacting the sides of the house and then howling past. After re-fueling the generator, Peter was relieved to find that it started without any problem.

He checked the temperature on the thermostat in the great room and saw that it was sixty-five degrees. They had decided not to make the furnace run too much, for fear of overtaxing the generator, but sixty-five degrees was comfortable when they were wearing warm clothing. He picked up the telephone and it was still dead. Peter turned on the radio to listen to the latest news, and found that the storm had stalled over central Indiana, and the worst might not be over yet. He then straightened the blankets and pillows in front of the fireplace. He knew that Niki would be happy about it in the morning. When he started up the steps, he looked up and saw that she was standing at the balcony railing. She had put her nightgown back on.

"I missed you," she said, and gave him a sleepy smile.

Peter slowly climbed the rest of the stairs, and at the top, put his arms around her. "Let's go back to bed my beautiful Niki."

She leaned on him a moment, her head on his shoulder, and then took his hand and led him back to bed. They lay awake, cuddling each other for warmth, and talking quietly.

"I think the weather has turned bad again, Niki, the wind has picked up. I could hear it very plainly while I was in the garage. I checked the telephone, too, after I started the generator, and there was still no dial tone. The radio had news that the storm is stalled over central Indiana."

She shivered briefly in his arms, "If the weather doesn't clear soon, we're going to be in trouble, aren't we? The gasoline for the generator is going to run out tomorrow, isn't it?"

"That's possible, but I checked the gas tanks on the two cars in the garage, and both are nearly full. I can siphon gas from them if I need to."

"Of course…why didn't I think of that?" She kissed him on the cheek and snuggled closer to him.

"I'm sure that you'd have thought of it when you needed to."

"Maybe not, Pete…" Nik didn't complete the sentence as she fell asleep.

Peter marveled at her ability to fall asleep so quickly. In the short time since they had become intimate, she had fallen asleep two or three times in mid-sentence when she was talking to him in bed. He pulled her closer to him as he felt a rush of tenderness and emotion for this woman, his love, his Niki.

The emotion still running high inside him, Peter began to think about his responsibilities. His mother, his sister, needed him and he had no choice but to return to them. His emotion now was one of sadness. He knew that he would have to leave Niki, and soon. Although the weather had intervened, and had allowed them to be together, to discover the depth of their feelings for one another, he realized that when the weather cleared, Niki's parents would return. With their return, the intimacy that he shared with Niki could not continue. He told himself that he needed to think only in the present moment. If he fretted and worried, it could spoil the small amount of time that they had left. He vowed not to do that. Peter rolled over and put his arm around Niki, and quickly fell into a sound sleep.

Chapter 39

Sunday December 28, 1986

Nik awoke first. She sat cross-legged facing Peter, who was still sleeping. She hadn't been aware of any noise that might have awakened her. The bedside clock showed eight- fifteen. Peter lay next to her on his side. His breathing was regular and quiet. There was light, yes, *light* coming in the window, and it shone on his face, giving it a sort of Greek God golden look. She saw a kind of nobility there, too. No matter the suffering, this man is strong and he isn't going to give up.

My love, she thought, my only love. How will I be able to let you go when the time comes? Just thinking about it made her heart ache. She slipped back under the covers and lay facing him. I'll hold him while I can. That's all that I can do. She began to cry quietly, put her arms around him, and soon fell asleep again.

"Niki," Peter whispered, "we've slept until after ten o'clock."

He lightly brushed her arm with his hand. He loved touching her; the smoothness of her skin was wonderful beneath his fingertips. Peter watched as she moved and then stretched. When she opened her eyes, he smiled down at her.

"Good morning," he bent to kiss her cheek.

Nik returned his smile. "Have we overslept?"

Peter shrugged, "Only if you think we have, Niki. Are you hungry?"

Nik stretched again, catlike, "Very," she said.

They had an oatmeal breakfast with juice and toast and tea. Nik poured honey on Peter's buttered, whole wheat toast, and he put honey in her tea. They pretended that everything was normal, that they weren't facing an end to their time together. It was Peter's turn to wash the dishes and Nik's turn to dry. They worked well as a team and quickly cleaned up after their breakfast before going into the great room.

Peter had attended to the generator earlier in the morning while he was waiting for Niki to awaken, "You were sleeping when the generator alarm went off, Niki, and you didn't move a muscle."

"I didn't? It's a good thing it wasn't an earthquake." Nik put a hand to her face and laughed.

He nodded, "I think you probably could sleep through an earthquake. Did you know that you fall asleep so quickly that you sometimes stop talking in mid-sentence?"

Nik laughed again, "How on earth would I know that? You are the only person that I've ever slept with."

They listened to the radio for news of the weather and learned that the storm had finally passed eastward. Nothing had, however, returned to normal, not the roads, or airport, or communications, or electric power. Everything was still "down" and would be for an unknown amount of time, possibly days, in some of the outlying areas.

Nik checked the telephone, and there was no dial tone. She held it up and shrugged her shoulders. Next she tried the television. The cable was still out.

"I guess you're going to be stuck with me a while longer." The smile that she gave him was sweet but sad.

"I sincerely hope so, Niki." He stood looking down at her, his hands on her shoulders.

"Let's get our shower and get dressed, Pete. Then…it's your turn to play the piano for me."

"*Yes!*" He took her hand and moved toward the stairway.

They spent more than a half hour in the shower, until the water started to run cold, and then they jumped out and toweled off quickly. They had followed the pattern of their first shower together; there was something sensuous about the warm water as it fell on their coupled bodies. Nik realized that Peter was getting his strength back, but she nonetheless was concerned that he had lifted and supported her weight again.

"We probably shouldn't be showering together, Pete. You shouldn't be lifting weights." Nik, wrapped in a large lavender towel, looked at him with a wicked grin.

"I disagree. I think showering together is wonderful." Peter, wrapped in his own large towel, returned her wicked grin.

Peter helped Niki raid Mike's closet again, "Your brother has good taste in clothes, Niki."

"Well, you look great in them, sweetie. Besides, he probably doesn't even remember they're here." Nik held up a navy sweat outfit for Peter to wear, "Is this okay?"

When Peter put on the sweats, Nik stood back, "Oh, *yeah.*"

In Nik's room, Peter watched as she pulled out a pair of red IU sweats, complete with logo, from her dresser. Standing there in her bra and panties, she was somewhat embarrassed, and she blushed.

Peter laughed, "Niki, are you embarrassed that I am watching you get dressed? Surely you're not…?"

"I've never…before you…I haven't dressed or undressed in front of a man."

It was a wonderful day. Peter played a Rachmaninoff concerto for his Niki, and she gave him a standing ovation. They went into the great room where he built a roaring fire in the fireplace and they played Dire Straits, Huey Lewis and the News, the Beatles, and Sting on tapes. They danced until Nik realized that Peter was beginning to tire, so she led him to the pillows by the fireplace and switched their activity to Monopoly.

After carefully questioning Nik about the rules of the game, Peter began to buy up and monopolize the properties on the game board. When Nik was forced to relinquish some of her properties to the new tycoon, and her available cash dwindled to fifty dollars, she gave Peter a glum look.

"How was I to know that you could roll the dice so well?"

His heart melted, "Niki, I did it all for you. After all, I can't ask for your hand if I have nothing to offer, now can I?"

Yes, thought Nik, you could ask for my hand, darling Pete, and I would be yours forever. Aloud, she told him, "You won fair and square, Pete. I've been playing this game all my life, and you play it for a half hour and you're an expert."

"Perhaps I should be working on your Wall Street." Peter couldn't hide his ornery grin.

Nik pounced on him, pushing him back into the pillows, "Okay, mister, that's enough."

In one quick movement, he took her by the shoulders and spun her beneath him. Nik was startled by his quickness and physical strength. Her eyes were wide and she laughed breathlessly. Peter smiled, bent to kiss her and slipped his arms under and around her.

"I love you," he whispered, and then rolled over to lie next to her.

Nik turned to look at him, "and I love you." She took his big hand in hers and held it tightly.

They lay together, talking about their present circumstances and their aspirations. Peter reminded Nik that he had hoped to go to university to study engineering. Now, he said, it was probably too late for this dream.

"I'm twenty-two, and I don't believe that I will ever be able to attend a university. It's strange to think that, at my age, the rest of my life is already determined. It's almost absurd when you think about it, but there it is."

"Well, you know that I thought that I'd have a career as a concert pianist, but look at what I'm doing now. I'm living my brother Joey's dream."

"You are a good doctor, Niki, a very good doctor. Perhaps medicine wasn't your first choice, but it fits you well. And you just may have saved my life when I first arrived to play hockey."

"Thanks for saying so, Pete, but I wasn't really very sure of myself when Yakov brought you in that day. You looked so startled when you saw me, and then you just keeled over."

"I was surprised when I first saw you, Niki. It was your face. You have a very Russian face. It's perfectly oval, your eyes are slightly tilted upward at the corners, and, you are very beautiful. I truly was surprised to see a Russian face looking up at me when I was so far away from home."

Nik rolled over and put her head on his shoulder, and an arm across his chest. "When did you know, Pete...that you loved me?"

"I must be thick-headed, Niki. It took me awhile to realize, and to admit to myself, that I was in love with you. But then, your fiancé kept appearing, and I was unsure of myself. Of course, he had every right to be there with you, but I resented his presence. When he touched you, I felt such terrible jealousy.

"Anyway, it was at the awards program dance when I finally accepted my own feelings because I knew that I just had to dance with you, hold you, if only for a few moments. You didn't know that I had been watching and waiting for you to arrive, and you were late. I had almost given up hope when I heard your voice in the foyer."

Nik's eyes held his, "Oh Pete, I had no idea...I thought that I was just losing my mind. Yes, I felt the same way," she replied. "I melted inside when we danced and you put your arms around me and pulled me close. I didn't want the music to end. I felt hypnotized. But even then, I wouldn't, I couldn't admit to myself that my feelings for you were as strong as they were."

Peter gently laughed, "We were both in denial, Niki. But it's a miracle, really, the string of events that put us here together like this, my illness, your parents leaving, the storm, and being alone with you. In my entire life, I have never been so fortunate, or so happy."

Peter told her that in a perfect life, they would marry, and they would find an old house on a body of water somewhere. He would fix up and repair and she would decorate the house. His study, his library, would have bookshelves full of books from floor to ceiling, and would be decorated in shades of red, his favorite color. Niki could use her favorite colors in the rest of the house, but he loved the color red, and wanted one room done in that color.

Most of all, he said, he wanted a family; three, four, five children? That wouldn't be too many. He and Katya had always talked of having families when they grew up and found the right mate. They wanted to see if kindness and love would make a difference in the lives of their children; so different from the way that they were raised.

Nik closed her eyes and visualized Peter's "perfect life" and wanted nothing more than to share it with him. She would give anything if she could share his life. The loud buzz of the generator alarm brought her back to reality.

"Well, so much for dreams, Niki. I'd better go answer the call of the generator."

"Are you getting hungry, Pete?"

He turned and smiled at her as he got up from the pillows. "As a matter of fact, I am."

When Peter came back from the garage, Nik had lunch preparations well underway, and was setting the table.

She looked up from what she was doing and told him, "We're having cheese toasties and tomato soup. It's one of my favorite lunches from when I was a little girl. Cheese toasties are best with dill pickles. Do you like dill pickles, Pete?"

"Yes, I love them. Sometimes that's all Katya and I had to eat for a whole day."

"Oh…Pete, I'm so sorry," Nik's face became sad.

He came over to her and put his arms around her, "You shouldn't take what I tell you so hard, Niki. Well, I really shouldn't have told you. Sometimes I say too much, don't I?"

Nik's arms were around Peter's waist, and she held him tightly, "It's just that I wish that you hadn't had such a bad time, that's all, Pete."

Peter liked the tomato soup and cheese toastie lunch. He pictured Niki as a child, sitting up to the table, eating her favorite lunch, and it made him smile.

"Niki, could we look at some more of your family photo albums after lunch? I'd like to see what you looked like from babyhood on. I wish that there were more pictures taken in my family before everything fell apart. My mother has some pictures of our family at the dacha at Tver, but I haven't seen them for a long time. Sometimes I think that I was born an adult, and never had a childhood. I always had to be on guard. I had to be wary for Katya and myself. But the photographs from our summer holidays at Tver on the lake remind me that I really was a child at one time."

Nik reached for his hand and held it. They sat quietly, not talking, but just holding hands, comfortable in each other's company. Nik looked into the great room from the kitchen table. The fire was dying back again. These days, she thought, these few short days with Peter, will always be with me. Whenever it snows, I'll think of our time together, here in the house where I grew up.

They had their routine well in hand; they cleared the table, washed the dishes, and dried them, and then went into the great room and sat on the pillows next to the fireplace.

"I need to rebuild the fire, Niki. Most of the wood is gone, but we have enough for a few more roaring fires." He got up to go to the garage for wood, and Nik followed him.

"Let me help, Pete, you really shouldn't be lifting and carrying so much weight." And then she bent over with laughter, remembering his feats of weightlifting in the shower.

Peter shook his head and laughed, too, and then asked, "When we come back, let's go get those photo albums, Niki."

In the garage, each took an armful of wood and started toward the door into the house. When the telephone rang, they nearly dropped what they were carrying. Nik put the wood down near the fireplace and caught the telephone on the fourth ring, "Hello…"

"Niki? Niki? It's mother. Oh, I'm *so glad* that the telephone is finally working! Your father and I have been so worried about you."

"We're okay, mom. Pete and I have done very well, actually. But, please tell me about Uncle Karl, how is he doing?"

"He is recovering, but it will be slow. He had a very serious heart attack. For a while we thought we might lose him."

"Oh my gosh mom, I wish that you had told me…" But then, Nik remembered where she was when her parents left for Pennsylvania.

"What is the weather like, there, Niki? Is the snow deep?"

"It's deeper than I can ever remember it. We can't see out of any of the windows or doors, except upstairs. Peter has been the one to get the generator going, and to keep it working. Actually, we've been quite comfortable."

"Is Peter doing well, Niki? Is he ready to return home?"

Nik hesitated a moment, recognizing the implication in her mother's questions, "Yes, he's doing well."

"Have you heard from Myron, dear?"

"No, but you remember that he went to see his mother and father in Chicago. The telephone has been out since the morning that you left for Uncle Karl's, and you're the first telephone call that we've gotten. Is Aunt Irina doing all right? I know she's got to be worried about Uncle Karl."

"She has been so grateful that your father and I could come to be with her and Karl. You know the storm that was so bad in Indiana caused just as many problems coming through Ohio and into Pennsylvania."

"We've been listening to the radio, mom. The cable is out on the television, so we have been getting our news on the radio. It's been a very damaging storm. You and dad must have left just before the storm hit."

"Yes, we did, and we were lucky to outrun it into Pennsylvania. The State Police here won't let anyone travel, as yet, because even the Turnpike is a mess, but we hope to start for home tomorrow or the day after."

"How is Duchess? I couldn't believe it when I read your note and you said that you were taking her with you."

"Duchess is fine. She's had to be in a kennel for a day or two, but she is okay. We took her with us because we didn't think that it would be fair to you to have to take care of her in addition to Peter."

Peter was sitting in front of the fireplace listening to Niki's half of the conversation. He had hated the sound of the telephone when it rang, signaling the end of his and Niki's time alone. He was sure that the next time it rang it would more than likely be Ron, wanting to talk to Niki. He didn't want her to talk to Ron. Peter was jealous *before*, not *after* the fact.

"When did you say that you'd be starting for home, mom? Oh, tomorrow or the day after? Well, we haven't heard any snowplows out this way, and the electricity is still off, so I wouldn't be in any hurry if I were you."

"This little corner of Pennsylvania wasn't hit as hard as some other areas, but we can't get out on the secondary roads, just yet. I'll call you when we start for home, dear."

"Okay, mom, I love you. Tell dad that I love him, too, and give my best to Uncle Karl and Aunt Irina. See you soon. 'Bye."

Nik was almost afraid to look at Peter, "Things will be getting back to normal pretty soon, I guess."

When she turned to face him, there was sadness and hurt in his eyes. "Pete…"

He reached for her, put his arms around her, and rested his chin on top of her head, "Hush," he said.

They both knew what was coming. The telephone was going to continue to interrupt their time together, and neither of them was ready to let go. Not yet, not now.

"Let's look at those photos, Niki." Peter's voice was quiet and subdued as he reached for her hand.

Nik considered unplugging the telephone, but she'd have to unplug the six or seven other telephones throughout the house, and she knew that it would only delay, not prevent, the inevitable. It suddenly occurred to her that they now had a fairly good idea of how much time they had left to be alone. Her heart filled with resolve. She would make this precious time perfect, at least for today and tonight. They would have candles, and firelight, and the most romantic afternoon and evening that she could create.

"Pete, you've got to help me…we are going to unplug the telephones all through the house. The rest of today and tonight will be ours, alone."

He looked at her in wonderment, and then slowly began to smile, until he was smiling broadly, "Niki, that's a fantastic idea!"

"Come on, hurry, we won't let them ring again until tomorrow or even the day after!" She unplugged the telephone in her hand and started for the kitchen.

They covered the downstairs and then headed quickly toward the stairs when the telephone began to ring again. Nik had a stricken, startled look on her face.

"We are not going to answer it, Pete. We're not!" There were tears in her eyes.

Peter counted the rings; five, six, seven, eight…the answering machine was turned off, and the telephone stopped ringing on the tenth ring. Nik ran frantically up the stairs and turned into the first bedroom at the top, Joey's room. Peter was still climbing the stairs as she dashed out of that bedroom and into the next. He heard her run through the bathroom between her room and Mikey's.

"Done!" Her voice was triumphant as she came out of her bedroom.

The ache inside Peter's chest that had begun to grow with the ringing of the telephone started to subside as he realized that Niki was doing this for the two of them. She wasn't ready to relinquish the remaining time they had together to anyone. He opened his arms and she hurried into them.

Downstairs, Niki fixed the blankets and pillows, arranging them for an afternoon in front of the fireplace. Next, she lit several candles and placed them on the hearth where they added a soft glow and light fragrance. After turning off the two lamps that were lit, she took Peter's hand and they went into the kitchen. She opened a cabinet at the front of the breakfast bar and Peter saw that there was what appeared to be a refrigerator with a fully glassed-in door. He could see wine bottles stacked on forward-tilted shelves inside.

"Let's pick a good one, Pete." Nik got down on her knees in front of the wine cellar.

They looked at several wines, a chardonnay, a white zinfandel, a cabernet, and a merlot. There were several champagnes, even some imported French wines.

"Oh!" said Nik, "Here's a Pinot Grigio, an Italian wine. Would you like to try it?"

"Yes," Peter nodded, and Nik saw delight in his eyes.

She rummaged through an "everything" drawer in the kitchen and found a corkscrew. She held it out to Peter, "Will you do the honors while I get some fruit, cheese, and crackers put together?"

Peter was uncertain of the process, but nonetheless opened the bottle of wine with aplomb, "Wine glasses?"

"Up there," Nik pointed to a cabinet above the refrigerator.

Peter easily reached into the cabinet and brought out two glasses. He opened several drawers in the kitchen until he found the towel drawer, and pulled one out, placing it, folded, across his forearm.

"We should let the wine breathe, Niki, before pouring it. I remember that much from my privileged past."

This brought a giggle from her, and a, "Yes, darling."

Nik assembled everything on a tray and Peter carried it into the great room. He put it down on the cocktail table that they had pulled close to their fireplace "nest." Nik loaded two tapes into the tape deck and pressed play. Henry Mancini's soft, romantic orchestral music began to fill the room.

"You asked for more photos from yesteryear, Pete? Have I got photos for you! True to my father's German heritage he has meticulously cataloged and placed in photo albums all of the Kellman family film history. We've already looked at some of them, but are you ready for this?"

"More than ready," was his reply.

They went to the library and each took four albums from a bookcase shelf that was filled with photo albums. Nik explained that they were in chronological order, beginning with her parents' wedding. In fact, she told him, her brother Joey was in the wedding pictures, too, but somewhat hidden by the voluminous folds of Marina's wedding gown. Peter raised his eyebrows questioningly, and Nik nodded. *Yes.*

"We have already looked at some of these albums before, but it helps if we can see everything from the beginning."

Peter poured the wine and they nestled together into the pillows and blankets near the hearth, their backs to the warmth of the fire. Since it was daylight, there was natural light coming in through the tops of the windows in spite of the snow, and there was also the candlelight that Nik had artfully arranged along the hearth.

"Was your father the primary photographer, Niki?"

"In the beginning, yes, but my mom did some of the later photography, too."

"These are wonderful pictures," he looked at her and smiled, his eyes soft and filled with love.

"Thank you, Pete. We weren't quite Gerber's Babies, but my parents thought that we were."

Nik's wine glass was empty and she held it up for a refill. Peter obliged, and filled his own glass again, as well.

"What is…?"

"A Gerber's Baby…? Gerber is a brand of baby food that features very photogenic infants on its labels. If you can make Gerber's Baby status, then you're a plump, smiling and happy, perfect example of babyhood."

Peter inclined his head, "Ah, I understand. But from what I am seeing in these pictures, you certainly met the criteria."

Having finished the first eight photo albums, they trekked back to the library and retrieved eight more. Nik laughed as she told him that these eight represented her childhood beginning with her fourth year, Joey's tenth, and Mikey's sixth.

"Do the albums go all the way up to the present?" Peter was curious.

"No, Pete, my parents stopped our family's recorded history at the time that Joey died. Well, I shouldn't say stopped altogether, but they haven't done much photography since then, except for special occasions like holidays and vacations."

They were on their third glass of wine when they finished albums twelve through sixteen. Nik asked Peter if he might be getting bored, and he laughed and told her no, he loved her photographic family history. In fact, they were both finding much to laugh about.

Peter wanted to know how many more albums there were for viewing, and Nik tried to answer seriously, but she had a difficult time saying 'seventeen and eighteen', so she just held up two fingers and giggled.

"I think things are beginning to get out of hand." Peter rubbed his eyes with the backs of his hands.

"One can only hope!" Nik was seized by a fit of giggling.

"Let's take a short nap, Niki. Can we just close our eyes for a little while?"

For some reason, Nik found Peter's request hilarious, and giggled even more. Peter reached for her, pulled two pillows into position on the blankets, lay down and cuddled her from behind, his arms around her. In a very short time, she was asleep.

Peter lay there holding her against his chest, and wondered, irrationally, if a person's heart really could burst when filled to overflowing with love for someone? That was the way he felt about his beautiful Niki, his love. He embraced her still closer and pulled a blanket over both of them. In a few moments he followed her into slumber.

The little boy looked up at Peter and smiled. He was a handsome child, with thick dark hair cut short and dark brows above expressive deep brown eyes. The child was speaking to him, but Peter couldn't seem to understand what he was saying. Something about the child tugged at his heart and he bent down on one knee, the better to hear what the child was trying to tell him. It surprised Peter when the child put his arms around his neck and laid his head on Peter's shoulder.

Peter was suddenly awake. He had been dreaming. It was only a dream. His heart was pounding, but he didn't know why. Niki stirred next to him, and then turned to face him. He pulled her to him, and when she opened her eyes to look at him, he could see the child's eyes, the child from his dream, in her eyes.

Nik caressed Peter's face with her fingertips and stretched up to kiss him. It became a long, deep kiss, and it touched him to his very soul.

"Pete," she whispered, "you know that, no matter what happens to us, no matter how far away we are from each other, you will be a part of me always."

"Da, Niki, I know. And you will always be with me."

They had napped through dinnertime, it was now nine-thirty, and so they decided to have peanut butter sandwiches with raisins, pickles, and celery sticks. Nik suggested chocolate milk as their beverage and Peter eagerly agreed.

Peter turned on the radio while they ate, and they heard that the main roads in the city were being cleared, and that the highway department had been working around the clock. The announcer also said that some telephone service and electricity were restored in "spotty" areas.

"I wish that the electricity, and not the telephone, was restored for us," Nik said glumly.

Peter smiled at her, "Da, I'd have to agree on that one."

Peter gassed the generator again at eleven. There were now less than ten gallons of gasoline left in the cans, and he was greatly concerned that he would have to begin siphoning gasoline from one of the cars inside the garage.

Nik was cleaning up after their late-night snack while Peter tended the generator. And then they went slowly upstairs together, arms around each other's waists. Nik turned to look up at Peter, and she smiled at him.

Peter raised his eyebrows at her, "What is it Niki?"

"I was just thinking that we need to shower before we get into bed..."

Chapter 40

Peter got up only one time during the night to feed the generator, and went back to bed, thanking God that Niki provided so much warmth as she slept. He cuddled up behind her and fell asleep again very quickly.

Unbelievably, they slept in until nine-thirty in the morning. Nik awakened first and snuggled up against Pete, who began to stir when she pulled the covers up to keep him warm.

"Good morning," she whispered in his ear.

"Awakening next to you is more than just a good morning; it's a *wonderful* morning." Peter kissed her lightly on the mouth.

"I'm going to fix you a young chicken sandwich for breakfast. How does that sound?" Nik had an impish grin on her face.

Peter shook his head, "I don't know. You're full of surprises, Niki, so tell me, what is this young chicken sandwich?"

She lay with her cheek against the pillow, looking into his eyes, her hair fanned out above and behind her. Peter saw that her face was still flushed with sleep, and he reached out and gently brushed his fingertips against her brow.

"Well, it's an experiment, Pete, but I'm not sure how well the fried eggs are going to turn out. It's been a long time since I have fried an egg. That's what a young chicken sandwich is; a fried egg sandwich."

Peter lay on his side, half-sitting, with an arm supporting his head, "Let's do it. I can fry an egg as well as most men, I think."

Their breakfast was delicious. Peter fried the eggs while Nik made orange juice. During breakfast, the generator sounded again. It was hungry, too.

After filling the generator, Peter came back into the kitchen where Nik was washing the pan and few dishes that they had used. He put his arms around her waist from behind as she stood at the sink. He was now an old hand at domesticity, and grabbed a dishtowel to dry what Nik washed. He surprised her when he was able to put everything back where it belonged.

"You're getting pretty good at this kitchen stuff, Pete." Nik dried her hands on his towel and put her arms around his neck.

"I have a good teacher," he replied, "a very good teacher."

They had listened to the radio while they cleaned the kitchen, and the news was beginning to sound more positive. Most major roads were passable, and now the city and county crews were concentrating on the outlying areas. But Peter and Nik didn't consider it to be good news. They would have been happy if it didn't thaw until spring, and both started to say the same thing at the same time. It was a moment of mirth, and it broke the gloom of the news that they had just heard.

When they went into the great room Nik tried the television. Much to her surprise, the cable was back on. Channel 13 was showing scenes of snowbound businesses, homes, roads, abandoned cars and trucks, and broken telephone and light poles.

"Pete, look at how deep the snow is. It's bad *everywhere.* Just look at the downtown area. The circle looks unreal with all that snow piled around the monument!"

"It looks like a mid-winter street scene in Moscow. But at least here, you have machinery and equipment to clear your roads." Peter was shaking his head.

Nik looked at him, "Today's the day, Pete. We're going to have to reconnect the phone lines sometime this afternoon. I hate the thought…"

"Da, and so do I." Peter had a wistful look on his face.

"What would you like to do with the rest of our morning, Pete?"

"Let's listen to music, Niki. We could sit by the fireplace and just listen to music."

Peter built a fire in the fireplace while Nik looked for music tapes. She asked Peter what he liked to hear, and called off different artists so that he could make some choices. They ended up reading poetry to each other and listening to Franz Liszt's Hungarian Rhapsodies. They were particular favorites of Peter's, and Nik loved them, too.

The early afternoon sun shone brightly through the tops of the windows in the house, and Peter was now helping Niki reconnect the telephones. No sooner had they connected the first two, than the telephone began to ring. It gave Peter a sinking feeling, and, when Niki turned to look at him, he could see that she felt the same way.

She waited until the sixth ring, and then picked up the receiver, "Hello?"

"Oh, Dr. Kellman, I'm so glad that I finally got through. This is Lauren, Peter's nurse. The phones have been out in Greenwood, and everywhere else, I guess, and I haven't been able to call you."

"Lauren, that's all right, Pete has been fine. We're snowed in, anyway, and I don't think the rest of the county is any better."

"They've started to clear the main roads down here, but the State Police still say that only emergency vehicles can be out on the road. I'm awfully sorry, Dr. Kellman, I have never neglected an assignment like this before."

"Please don't worry about it Lauren, our patient is doing very well."

"I'm so glad to hear that, Dr. Kellman. Do you think that you will need me anymore this week? That is, if I can ever get out of the house."

Nik turned to look at Peter and then smiled, "No, I don't think so, Lauren, Pete is pretty independent now."

"Okay, but if you need some help, don't hesitate to call me."

Nik said goodbye to Peter's nurse, and then turned to him, "That was Lauren, Pete, and she just now got her telephone service back."

Peter hoped that the relief that he felt was not reflected in his face, "This has been quite a storm, Niki."

Nik understood Peter's look. He was concerned that Ron was going to call. Sooner or later, Ron was going to call.

After a few moments, Nik took Peter's hand, brought it up to her lips, and then told him, "I know why you're worried about the telephone, Pete. We both know that Ron will probably call now that the telephone is working again."

"Da, Niki, and I don't know if I can bear it." Peter's face showed his inner turmoil.

Nik whispered, "Pete, I took off Ron's engagement ring, remember? I took it off for you, because I love you."

"I know it in my head, but it hurts in my heart when I think about what's going to happen when I have to leave, Niki, and I *will* have to leave."

Nik closed her eyes for a moment and took a deep breath, "I know that, Pete, but I want *you* to know that I won't be putting Ron's ring on again, whether you're here or not. You have my heart, and nothing will ever change that."

He put his arms around her tightly, "And you have mine, Niki. Always, you will have my heart."

They stood there holding one another for a very long time. Finally, Peter held Niki at arms length and told her that they needed to see about the generator.

Peter asked her to come out to the garage with him to check on the generator, "The next time I have to fill it, I think I'm going to have to siphon some gas out of one of the cars."

He was getting proficient at fueling and restarting the generator, and was surprised to see that there was still enough gas in one of the gas cans to keep the generator going for another ten hours or so. At least he wouldn't have to siphon gas…yet.

Together they went through the house, straightening up, plumping pillows, folding blankets, and putting the few pieces of furniture that they had moved back into place. Nik vacuumed as Peter dusted surfaces. All the while, Nik admonished Peter not to lift or do too much. It made him smile, and every now and then he would kiss the nape of her neck, or tug her ponytail.

They took time out to dance after Nik found a tape with the same "golden oldies" that they had danced to at the awards ceremony. Bodies touching, their eyes gazing into one another's', they moved and swayed in time to the music. It was as if they were trying to commit to memory the touch, the feel, and the exhilaration of dancing, of being together. Nik again experienced the sound of Peter's beating heart as she danced with him, her head resting on his chest, and she knew that she would never forget it.

When the tape ended, they went back to housework, changing bed sheets and making up the beds in the upstairs bedrooms. Their domestic activities gave them a sense of permanence, albeit ephemeral, a sense of belonging together. Nik wouldn't let Peter push the vacuum on the carpet in the bedrooms, so he continued dusting.

Their cleaning chores completed, they had a discussion on what to do next. Peter suggested cooking school, because they had worked through lunch, and Nik happily acquiesced.

In the kitchen they busied themselves making an elegant dinner. Nik broiled steaks and fixed rice pilaf. Peter created a colorful salad with various greens and vegetables from the refrigerator crisper, dousing the whole with Russian salad dressing. For dessert, they had to be creative because their staples were dwindling, and so they made a trifle of mixed fruit, heavy cream, and vanilla wafers, tossed together and refrigerated.

Together they chose Mozart on tape for background music during dinner. They put linens on the dining room table and set it with china and silver. Peter lit a pair of candles. They sat at the table in candle light and enjoyed what they thought might be their last meal by themselves.

After dinner, Nik brewed some tea and they took cups of hot tea with them to sit in the great room by the fire that Peter had rekindled in the fireplace. Nik lit the candles along the mantle and they didn't turn on any lamps in the room. As the day progressed to night, the room became semi-dark, lit only by the fire in the grate that Peter kept feeding. Peter and Nik talked quietly about their lives before they met, and about how they now felt since coming together.

"My mom kept telling me that I lost something, my personality changed, after Joey died."

"And did you feel differently, Niki? Something so terrible would certainly have changed the way you looked at the world."

"It did. I became more serious about my schoolwork. And I guess that also could be translated into a different attitude toward just about everything else."

"I had that kind of change, too, Niki, when my father was imprisoned, and my family was stripped of everything. But that is nothing in comparison to what happened to you when you lost your brother."

The candles burned down to almost nothing, and the fire in the grate was becoming embers. The house was now almost dark, yet still they talked, as if they had to compress a lifetime of communication into this one remaining evening that they had together.

At about eleven-thirty Nik stretched and yawned, "Let's get ready for bed, Pete."

She shut the fireplace screen and folded the blankets in preparation for bedtime. Peter put his arm around her shoulders and they walked slowly up the stairs, like a long-married, loving couple.

They chose Nik's bedroom for the night and turned down the bed together. As they did so, her eyes filled with tears. When she looked up at Peter, the tears spilled down her cheeks.

"I'm sorry, so sorry, Pete, but I just can't help it. I don't know what I'm going to do without you."

Peter's heart ached, too, and he took Nik into his arms, "I feel the same, Niki, and if I had a choice, if I were free to choose, I would be by your side for the rest of my life."

Their lovemaking was tender, with a sense of poignancy, each giving the other bittersweet pleasure. Afterward, Peter gently ran his hands over Niki's body. He wanted a tactile memory of her. They talked quietly into the early hours of the morning, each trying to tell the other all the things that needed to be said. Although there was no one to overhear them, they whispered their words of love and of hope to one another.

"Pete, I know that we won't always be apart. I can't conceive of a life without you. Somehow, some way, we will find each other again. There is something inside me, is it hope? I don't know, but we *will* be together again." Leaning over him from behind, she lightly massaged his back as she whispered into his ear, her long, silken hair brushing against his cheek.

Peter rolled onto his back and turned his face toward her, "I feel the same, but it doesn't take this terrible, cold ache inside away, Niki, not here in our present circumstances. I have nothing to give to you, nothing at all, except a promise that I will *always* keep you here." He placed his hand over his heart.

"Once more," she whispered, "please, just once more."

Even in the dimness of the room, he could see that her eyes were bright with tears, 'Da, *yes*!" he replied.

Chapter 41

December 29, 1986

Peter heard the sound of heavy machinery. It had awakened him, and he lay listening, trying to determine what he was hearing. He glanced over at Niki, and eased himself from the bed to look out of the window. To his surprise, he saw a large yellow truck with a blade on the front pushing the snow aside from the road. He knew that the loving and quiet time that he had shared with his Niki was nearly over.

He looked down at her as she slept. She was on her side, an arm flung over Peter's pillow, the blankets pulled up to her chin, her face rosy with sleep. Unfair, he thought, it is so unfair, to have to leave the woman that I love so much.

Quietly, he pulled on his sweats from the day before, and put on the slippers that Niki had given him. It was time to feed the generator again.

As he serviced the generator, Peter got the idea that it would be great to have breakfast in bed with Niki. After he finished gassing and restarting the generator, he went into the kitchen to see what he might be able to put together in the way of breakfast.

Peter scrambled eggs, made toast and hot tea, and quickly put them on a tray he found on a kitchen countertop. Halfway up the stairs, he heard Niki calling sleepily to him.

"Pete? Pete, where are you?" Her voice was soft and muffled with the remnants of sleep.

When he entered the bedroom, her face was wreathed in smiles, "What have you been up to, Sir Galahad?"

"Breakfast, m'Lady, I've prepared a feast for you."

Nik sat up in bed, plumped a pillow behind her, and said, "You are absolutely fantastic, Pete!"

Side by side in bed, supported by pillows, they enjoyed their breakfast, each taking turns feeding the other. Nik told him that he was spoiling her, and he said that he wouldn't have it any other way. When they finished, Peter put the empty china and tray on the floor next to the bed.

"Did you hear the snow-moving equipment earlier this morning, Niki? I think the street in front of the house is probably clear by now."

Her eyes were sad as she replied, "I heard it, but I put my pillow over my ears. I was hoping that I was just hearing things, but no such luck, huh?"

"No such luck," he echoed.

"Well, I'll have to shovel the front entrance and the driveway now, so that my parents can get into the garage when they come home."

"That's very heavy work Niki, and you shouldn't have to do it by yourself. I'll help."

"Oh, no you won't, Pete, you aren't going to be out shoveling snow with me. My dad has a snow blower, and you can help me get it started, but you're not going to do anything else."

Peter shook his head, "You can't do it all by yourself, Niki. I just can't let you do that."

"Chauvinist," Nik said, laughing, "I'm not going to be able to shovel ten feet of snow out of the driveway, but the snow blower might work. Besides, Pete, I'll probably just do the front sidewalk."

"That sounds more reasonable. Uh, I was just thinking. What do you say to a shower, m'Lady?" His smile was mischievous.

"Privaskhodny! *Wonderful!*"

The pattern for their showers was set. Peter's strength was returning, and he felt no ill effects from his weight lifting and acrobatics in the shower with Niki. When they finished bathing, they stood together, soapy from head to toe, embracing before rinsing off.

Peter loved brushing and drying Niki's long hair. "I *have* missed my calling he said, "I really should have started a career in hair dressing."

Nik laughed, "Nope...you're the best hockey player that Sheldon and Marty, and I, have ever seen. Maybe my opinion doesn't count, but Sheldon's and Marty's opinions sure do. Grigory told me that you absolutely should be playing professional hockey, Pete."

Peter was sober for a moment at the mention of Grigory's name, and then said, "Where are the recruiters? I don't see any recruiters."

"Marty gave me his card, Sheldon did, too. They both said to call them if you wanted to play."

He nodded, "They told me the same thing, Niki, but it doesn't matter because I can't accept their offers."

"Yes, I know you're right, Pete." Nik's eyes were downcast

"It's my turn, Niki." Peter sat down in front of the mirror.

He closed his eyes while Niki dried his hair and brushed it out. Her touch was gentle and loving as she worked with his thick, dark blond hair. When she finished, he stood and kissed the top of her head.

They raided Mike's closet yet again, and found something presentable and comfortable for Peter. He was wearing Indiana University sweats, and Nik decided that red was also *his* color.

In her bedroom, Nik quickly dressed in sweatshirt and jeans and then dug in the closet until she pulled out an old snowmobile suit.

"I wonder if I can still wear this thing, Pete. It's been *years* since I've put it on. My brothers and I used to snowmobile all over Geist Reservoir, but I haven't done that since I started college."

"Snowmobile? Is that a sport?" Nik had piqued Peter's curiosity.

The telephone rang, interrupting her answer. They were both startled, and gave each other an "oh no" look. This time, Nik decided to answer it.

"Hello," she said in an unsteady voice.

"We should be home by ten o'clock tonight, Niki," Klaus said without preamble.

"Dad? How is Uncle Karl doing now?"

"Very good, he's very good, Niki. Everything's calmed down now, and Irina thinks that she can manage his care by herself with a little help from a home health service."

"I'm glad that he's doing well. What a relief! Oh, by the way, the county plowed the road out front this morning, and I'm going out to clear the driveway and front walk. Hopefully, you and mom won't have any problem getting up to the house."

"Oh, Niki, don't do that. You shouldn't be trying to clear this snow. It's too heavy. I'll call right now after I finish talking to you to see if I can get Bertram's son to clean the driveway. Please don't get out there and hurt yourself." There was concern in his voice.

"All right, but I think that I could put a dent in the snow."

"Don't let Peter do any snow shoveling, either, Niki. He really shouldn't do that, you know."

Nik laughed, "I'm the doctor, remember? Pete's actually doing very well, but he's not going to be shoveling snow, and that's that." Nik gave Peter a stern look.

She had just hung up the telephone when it rang again. For some reason, she sensed that this call was probably from Ron. Reluctantly, but with resolve, Nik picked up the telephone again. She was afraid to look at Peter, but she did, anyway, because she wanted to reassure him. She saw him swallow hard and then look away.

"Hello," Nik had a lump in her throat, too.

"Nik, *finally*, you won't believe how hard I've tried to get in touch with you. I've been so worried!" Ron's voice held exasperation and relief, at the same time.

"Where are you, Ron?" Nik didn't want him on the front door step any time soon. Selfishly, she wanted to spend these last few hours that she had with Peter alone.

"I'm still in Chicago, Nik. After the State Police re-opened I–65 yesterday, there was a thirty-car pile-up near the southbound Crown Point exit. The road's been closed ever since."

"We didn't get that news here, Ron. Mostly, we've only heard weather-related stuff, and warnings to stay off of the roads."

"Everything here in Chicago has been closed; airports, roads, railroads; everything. My parents' condo was without heat, lights, or other important things like telephone and water utilities, for two days. We didn't have a workable telephone until twenty minutes ago, because the circuits were jammed with calls. All I got was a busy signal, but I kept dialing, hon'."

"Were you caught in the wind and snow on your way into Chicago?" Nik was trying to keep her end of the conversation neutral.

"Oh *hell* yes. I didn't think I was going to survive the last twenty miles, but I kept on going. Actually, from Rensselaer on it was horrible. It's good that I didn't have you along."

Nik used a white lie to end the conversation, "Ron, I'm expecting a call from my parents. They had to go to Pennsylvania because my Uncle Karl had a heart attack, and they're supposed to be home sometime this evening."

"That's terrible, Nik."

"Yes, but he's out of the ICU now."

There was a moment of silence before Ron asked, "Who's been helping you with Peter? Was the nurse able to make it to your folks' house during this weather?"

Nik hesitated, "Indianapolis, well, actually Marion County, and all the counties in the northern half of the state have been in a snow emergency, so no one, nothing, has been moving on the roads. Our telephone and electric service were out, too."

"So you've been without heat and lights, too?" There was concern in Ron's voice.

"No, Peter hooked up dad's generator, and it took care of the furnace, well pump, and a few lights."

"So your Uncle Karl is doing okay now, Nik?"

"Yes, mom told me that he had a bad time, but that he was doing well when she called yesterday."

"Well, I'd better let you go, Nik. I should be back in Indy by sometime tomorrow, or the next day. I'll call you then."

"Okay, Ron. Be careful on the trip back. It's still bad out there."

Nik reactivated the answering machine. If the telephone rang again, she was going to let the machine pick up the call. She didn't want to speak to anyone else. Not now, not with her precious time with Peter getting so short.

Peter had gone into the kitchen because he didn't want to hear Niki's conversation with Ron. He sat on a stool at the breakfast bar, leaning forward, with his head in his hands. The cold ache inside him had returned with a vengeance.

Quietly, Nik came into the kitchen, stood behind Peter, leaned into him, and encircled him with her arms. They didn't speak, and didn't move for several minutes.

Nik broke the silence, "We knew it was coming, Pete. It was just a matter of time."

Still leaning against the bar, head in hands, Peter answered, "I know, but it's almost more than I can stand, Niki."

She put her cheek against Peter's broad back, "Pete, listen to me. I love you. There is nothing in this world, nothing, that will ever change the way I feel about you."

Peter turned to face her, "Niki, you are human, I am human. At some point, these few days that we have had together will begin to fade from our memories. *That's* why I hurt right now. The reality of our situation is that I will leave, and your life will go on as if nothing ever happened between us. It's as simple as that, Niki."

She put her fingertips against his mouth, "Hush, Pete, that's not going to happen." She took his big hand and placed it over her heart, "not ever, Pete."

They went into the great room and rekindled a fire in the fireplace. As it took hold, Nik fetched the last two family photo albums that they hadn't seen before.

"Would you like some hot chocolate while we look at the albums, Pete?"

A smile flickered briefly across his face and Peter replied, "Da, Niki, let me help you."

Nik reached for his hand as he came to her, and they went into the kitchen. They made hot chocolate the old-fashioned way with dried cocoa boiled in milk and sugar on the range top. Peter stirred the mixture while Nik searched in the refrigerator for a can of whipping cream to top off their steaming cups of hot chocolate.

They sat with their backs to the warm fireplace, leaning on pillows, while they sipped their cocoa and paged through the heavy, thick photo albums. Nik described the settings in the photos and identified the people in them in a running narrative. Peter asked questions about relationships, and Nik explained them. Peter studied the photographs of Niki's brothers. He admired them for their strong good looks, and their apparent ease in front of a camera. They smiled from the photos, as if nothing could ever touch them to cause them harm. Peter was aware that it was hard for Niki to talk about her brothers, especially Joey. When she fell silent, he turned to look at her.

Peter cupped her chin in one hand and lifted her face to him, "Niki," he said softly, "are you all right?"

Her eyes were large and luminous, "Yes, but it's so hard to look at some of these photos, especially those where my brothers look so healthy and happy. Even now, I can't really accept what happened to Joey."

How can one accept the unacceptable? Peter knew that there was nothing that would change the fact that Joey had died tragically and worse yet, needlessly.

It was now past one o'clock and Nik felt the passage of time keenly. Her parents would be home around ten this evening, that's what her dad had said when he called. With each passing hour, her heart grew heavier. I can't let Pete see how I feel, she thought. It will only make him feel worse than he does now.

"Are you hungry, Pete?" Nik stood up and stretched.

Peter looked up at her, enjoying the beauty of her body as she stretched. Then he closed his eyes, put his head back and said, "I don't know, Niki, maybe just a little."

In the kitchen, they checked the pantry, freezer, and refrigerator. Sadness clung to them and hung in the air around them, slowing their progress. They stayed close to one another, touching hands, brushing shoulders, as reassurance that they were still together.

"Comfort food, that's what we need, Pete. What do you think about macaroni and cheese with a vegetable on the side and hot buttered toast?"

"It sounds good, Niki. Is there a special recipe for this dish?"

"No, it's a, 'by gosh and by golly' kind of thing, Pete. The basic recipe is easy, and then you add things that you like."

"I should ask you what is 'by gosh and by golly' but it must mean eclectic, or chef's choice, am I correct?"

Even though Nik was sad, she laughed at Peter's definitions, "That's pretty good, Pete. In fact, that's *very* good. You've caught on quite nicely."

They combined their chosen ingredients, which included mushrooms and green peppers, prepared them, and combined everything in a casserole, put buttered bread crumbs on top, and put it in the oven to bake.

In a half hour, the macaroni and cheese was nicely bubbling and lightly browned on top. Nik heated frozen corn on the cob and lightly buttered it before she put it on their plates. She dished up generous portions of the casserole, and finished with hot buttered toast. For a moment, she wondered how many calories the butter added to their meal, but she wanted Pete to continue to regain the weight he had lost since his surgery. Nik knew that he wouldn't be able to do so when he returned home. With that thought, her heart dropped in her chest, but she tried to keep her feelings to herself.

At the table, Peter reached for Niki's hand. They didn't need words now; their feelings could be expressed by touch just as easily. Nik was happy to see that Pete was eating well. He told her how much he enjoyed their 'by gosh and by golly' macaroni and cheese, and that the corn on the cob was delicious.

When the meal was over, they cleaned up the kitchen. Nik had not realized, before falling in love with Peter, that such a mundane task could be accomplished with so much love. When she bent over the sink, Peter brushed her hair aside and kissed her lightly on the back of her neck as his body rested against hers from behind. Nik turned toward him, and in spite of her wet and soapy hands, hugged him tightly before standing on tiptoe to kiss him.

When the doorbell rang, they both jumped. Nik hurried to answer the door, and found Aaron Bertram, rosy cheeked from the cold, face enwreathed in exhaled breath, standing there.

"Hi, Niki, my dad told me that your dad called and wanted me to do the snow shoveling for you so that you could get out of the house and garage. I finally got it finished for you with some help from Tyler and Alysse." He pointed to his helpers, who waved from the street.

"Come in, Aaron, it's cold out there." Nik stood away from the door to let him in.

"Oh, no, Niki, that's okay. I have another job down the street to start. I'm going to be rich by the time I get done in our addition!" Aaron grinned at her, and gestured with a gloved hand toward another house.

"How much do I owe you, Aaron?"

"Your dad said he'd take care of that when he gets home, so don't worry about it. See you…" Aaron ran down the steps and waved at her as he headed to the street.

Before Nik closed the door, she saw a Federal Express truck turn the corner onto the street in front of the house. It surprised her when the truck turned into the driveway. The driver, dressed in bulky winter clothing, jumped from the cab with a thick envelope in his hand and approached the door.

"Hi, I've got a package for…" the driver hesitated as he looked at the name on the envelope, "Peter Genchenko."

"Oh, just a minute." Nik turned and called to Peter, "there's a Fed Ex package for you, Pete."

Peter came slowly to the door, "You've got a package for me?"

"Yeah," said the driver, "sign right here." He tapped a blank line on his clipboard, and handed a pen to Peter for his signature.

"I have to apologize for the delay in delivery. The airport was closed for two days, and it took another day to get some of the roads cleared so that our trucks could make their deliveries."

"Yes, it's been some of the worst weather that I have seen in a long time," Peter replied, thinking of the Russian winters he had experienced.

Nik closed the door, and then she and Peter stood looking at one another for a moment. Neither thought that the Fed Ex package was good news. No, it more than likely carried some very bad news for both of them. Peter tore open the end of the package and pulled out an envelope. It was addressed to him in Cyrillic.

"It's from Grigory." Peter stared at the envelope.

They walked back into the great room and sat down together on the sofa in front of the fireplace. Peter turned the envelope over and over in his hands before he opened it.

"It's an airline ticket, Niki, and it's dated for tomorrow. There is also some money for expenses. Grigory leaves nothing to chance." His look was that of surprise and consternation.

"For tomorrow, Pete, he sent it for tomorrow?"

All Peter could do was nod in answer to Niki's question. He felt numb inside. Nik put her face against his shoulder and began to cry quietly. Peter pulled her onto his lap, put both arms around her, and lightly rested his chin on top of her head. No, no, no, he thought, this can't be happening so soon. I'm not ready to leave her; not yet, please God. But in truth, he knew that he would never be ready to leave her.

The telephone began to ring, but Nik ignored it as she clung to Peter. After the sixth ring, the answering machine picked up, and Marina's voice came on, telling Nik that there was a delay because of the road conditions, so they would have to stay the night near Springfield, Ohio, just off of Interstate 70.

"The winds have started up again, and there are white-out conditions, so I'm not going to estimate when we will get home, but we should be there sometime tomorrow. Duchess is not traveling well. I think that she is homesick. I hope that you two aren't outside shoveling snow!"

Peter lifted Niki and carried her upstairs to her bedroom. She didn't protest or scold him for doing so. In the bedroom they wordlessly undressed and crawled into bed, pulling up the covers around them. Gently, he pulled her close, and they made bittersweet love. And then they held each other until they fell asleep.

Chapter 42

December 30, 1986

Peter awakened by degrees. First, he opened his eyes, glanced over at Niki, who was sleeping quietly as a kitten next to him, and then he looked at the clock radio. It read 5 o'clock, but he wasn't certain whether it was morning or evening. What time had he carried Niki to bed? He couldn't remember, but he knew that it hadn't been very late in the evening. Then his thinking cleared completely, and he remembered the airline ticket that Grigory had sent to him. Peter got a sick feeling in the pit of his stomach, and ice formed in his chest.

He rolled up into a sitting position, trying not to disturb Niki, and got up from the bed. The generator, he thought, he hadn't heard the generator alarm. How many hours had it been since he had checked it? It's got to be out of gas, he decided. Picking up the clothing that he had discarded onto the floor last evening, he dressed quickly and went downstairs. The house seemed warm enough, so maybe the generator hadn't been off too long.

Peter went into the garage, but didn't hear the comforting chug, chug, chug, of the generator. Without thinking, he turned on the garage light, and to his surprise, it lit. He realized that the electricity had been restored, and he was glad for Niki's sake. We won't have to worry about the generator anymore, he thought. But then, he realized that there would no longer be a "we" because he was going to have to leave her.

Back in the great room, he found the envelope from Grigory that contained the airline ticket setting on the coffee table. His flight was scheduled for three-thirty this afternoon. Again, his stomach tightened, and he felt sick. There was now a band of ice cinching his chest.

Peter didn't want to awaken Niki this early, so he decided to check his belongings, and pack them in readiness for travel. Head down, he wiped tears from his eyes, and then went to the drawing room to gather his things.

Nik turned over in bed, and Pete was not beside her. The bedside clock radio indicated eight-thirty. How long have I been asleep? She quickly jumped out of bed and put on her bathrobe. Where is Pete? Her heart beat rapidly and her throat was dry.

She ran across the balcony and hurried down the stairs calling to him, "Pete…Pete? Where are you?"

Although he was in the drawing room, Peter heard the fear in her voice as she called to him, and came out into the great room, "Niki, what's wrong?"

"*Pete*!" She ran to him and threw her arms around him, "I thought that you had left already, and I didn't get a chance to say goodbye!"

Peter could feel her trembling as he held her, and he tried to comfort her, "Niki, it's all right, please don't be frightened, I'm here, I'm still here."

Try as she might, Nik couldn't control herself, and she blurted out, "Please take me with you, Pete. Please, I can't stand losing you…I just can't!"

He kissed her to calm her. He didn't know what else to do. When she began to relax in his arms, he kissed her again, and then began talking quietly to her.

"Niki, please help me. I'm going to need your help to get through this day. I have no choice but to be on the airplane this afternoon to return to Russia. *No choice, Niki!*"

She began to tremble again but remained in control, "I know, Pete, but it hurts so much…"

"Yes, I know. It hurts here." He put one hand over his heart, the other over hers, and closed his eyes for a moment.

When he opened his eyes, Nik could see the anguish there. It tore into her heart and emotion gripped her throat. She was unable to speak as tears spilled down her cheeks.

Peter whispered, "Help me, Niki. I can't do this alone." Gently, he wiped the tears from her face with the tips of his fingers.

Nik found her voice, "All right…I'll help you, Pete. Let's go get your packing done."

Some of Peter's things needed washing, and Nik started that process before she fixed breakfast. They sat quietly, neither of them hungry because of the sadness welling up inside.

"Drink your juice, Pete, and you'd better finish that cereal. It will stick with you for awhile, and I don't want you to get hungry," her voice broke, "on the way home."

Peter put his big hand over hers and squeezed it gently. His eyes met and held hers. Such beautiful eyes, he thought, and such a beautiful soul.

With breakfast out of the way, Nik finished drying Peter's clothing and completed packing his duffel bag. Nik threw in extra socks and underwear of Mike's because she knew that Pete needed them. Anyone watching her fold and pack these things would have been struck by the loving way in which she performed the task, smoothing out wrinkles gently and folding them perfectly. She didn't tell him that she had added them, because she was afraid that he would be embarrassed.

Nik also put the gifts that she had gotten for his mother and sister in his duffel bag. From her purse, she took an envelope that contained the rest of her Christmas money, nearly seven hundred dollars, and placed it inside one of the pockets in the bag. Nik wrote a note to Pete and put it inside the envelope with the money. When she finished, it was difficult to zip the bag shut, but she persevered until she had everything zipped in.

And then it was time to shower and dress for the trip to the airport. But before they showered, Nik checked Peter's surgical incisions to make sure that there was no problem or infection. Peter was aroused by her gentle touch and probing during the examination. Their last shower together was tinged with sadness, and their lovemaking was an expression of their love and feelings of loss at Peter's impending departure. Their tears intermingled as each tried to give voice to the love so deeply felt for the other.

Nik had a sense of strangeness as she dressed in regular clothing. She grabbed a soft green sweater and slacks from the closet, her warmest winter outfit, for the trip to the airport. It was odd to wear something other than the comfortable sweats that she and Pete had been wearing during their time alone.

"You look beautiful, Niki. Every time that I see you in a different color, I think that it's the perfect color for you." Peter attempted to smile.

He was in his traveling clothes, black pants and sweater, and he wore the coat, gloves and hat that Niki had given him for Christmas. Nik thought that he was the most handsome man that she had ever seen.

"And you look beautiful, too, Pete."

Peter's duffel bag was already in Nik's car. He had carried it out after he finished dressing. The bag seemed heavier than it had before, but he knew that he still hadn't completely recovered his strength. The weather was still bitingly cold, and the snow was deep, so their heavy outerwear was much needed.

Now they were ready to leave. They stood facing one another, Niki looking up into Peter's face, and then she was in his arms, the layers of clothing a minor impediment to their embrace.

"We have to go now, Niki," he whispered.

"Yes, I know…" and Nik pressed the garage door opener.

Peter opened Nik's driver's side door and she slipped into the seat. She started the car as he got in beside her. She began to back out of the garage when a horn sounded loudly behind her.

"What in the name of heaven?" she was already overwhelmed and this intrusion exasperated her even more.

She looked in her rearview mirror to see Ron getting out of his car and walking toward her. Nik's hands froze on the steering wheel. Oh my God, oh my God, oh my God, she repeated to herself.

"What's wrong, Niki?" Peter turned to look out the rear window of the car.

"Nik! Where are you going?" Ron's face showed concern and aggravation at the same time.

She pushed a button and the window slid down, and, as calmly as she could, she told him, "We're going to the airport, Ron, Pete's plane leaves at three this afternoon."

Ron nodded hello to Peter and said, "Wait a minute, I'll back my car up, and I'll go with you."

When he came back, Ron signaled to Peter that he needed to slide his seat forward so Ron could get into the back seat. Peter got out of the car and Ron climbed into the back seat.

"Okay, I guess we're ready to go." He reached forward and patted Nik on the shoulder.

The three of them rode to the airport in silence. When Nik couldn't stand it any longer, she turned on the radio for "white noise" to drown out her chaotic thoughts.

Peter's ticket was on American Airlines routed through Pittsburgh and on to Kennedy for connections with British Airways. He stared down at the ticket, wishing fervently that he could just tear it up. If he could tear it up, he would be able to stay with his Niki. But then, what would happen to his mother and sister? He couldn't leave them alone in their present situation.

As they got closer to the airport, the heavier the traffic became, until they were almost at a standstill on the Airport exit off of I-465. Nik realized that this was due to the terrible weather and the tail end of the holidays. Today was December 30th, and tomorrow was New Years Eve. At the point at which Nik thought that she was beginning to lose her mind, the traffic crept forward.

"Peter," Ron began, "are you feeling up to traveling today? How have you been since your surgery?"

Ron's voice was like a small explosion inside the car, startling the occupants of the front seat. For what seemed several moments, Peter didn't answer.

"Yes, I am recovered enough to travel. Grigory sent my airline tickets by Federal Express, but they were delayed because of the weather. They were delivered yesterday when the roads were finally opened as far as Geist Reservoir," he responded.

"How long does it take to get back to Moscow by air?" Ron winced as he realized that his question was rather inane.

Peter turned and looked briefly at Ron, "Not nearly as long as it does by sea," he replied.

Ron looked up and shut his eyes tightly, "Okay, I deserved that. What I meant to say is…what will your flight time be?"

"Well, there will be a tail wind going east, so the journey will be about an hour and a half less going east than it was coming here flying west into the wind. I estimate flying time will be twenty or more hours, even if I make all of my connections on time."

There was snow piled everywhere around and near the airport as Nik drove into the area. Some snow piles were as high as three story buildings. Nik could see that there was going to be competition for parking space because the lots couldn't be thoroughly cleaned. There was just too much snow.

Nik started to speak, stopped to clear her parched throat, and started again, "I'm going to try to get into the short term parking area, but I'm not sure that I'll succeed. If I don't find something there, I'll drop you off at the boarding area, and then I'll catch up to you."

"What's the problem, Nik?" Ron looked around and realized for the first time just how bad the traffic was.

"Nothing, it's nothing, Ron…" Nik didn't finish her sentence.

They were fortunate enough to find a spot when someone pulled out of a parking space in close proximity to the terminal. Nik quickly pulled into the space, and then briefly put her forehead against the steering wheel. Peter saw her, and reached his hand out and touched her cheek. She turned toward him and he could see the misery in her eyes. It cut him to his very soul

What in the hell is going on here? Ron wondered. He didn't like the familiarity of Peter's touch on Nik's face, but said nothing.

Inside the terminal, they went to the American Airlines counter, and again, there was only silence among them. Ron didn't offer to put his arm around Nik, or to hold her hand, and that was just as well. Peter picked up his boarding pass rather quickly in spite of the crowd waiting at the ticket counter. He looked up at the clock near the counter, and saw that he only had fifteen minutes until boarding started. Peter had a sinking feeling in his chest. Fifteen minutes, and if that weren't bad enough, Ron was watching his every move with Niki. Peter turned to look for her, and saw that she and Ron were standing together outside the gate. The two might as well be strangers, for all the contact they had.

In the boarding area, passengers were already lining up, and the ticket agent opened the gate. When the line was down to just one passenger, Peter, he turned to hold Niki just one more time, and to tell her goodbye.

Nik's knees became weak when Peter put his arms around her because she knew that this would be the last time she would feel those strong arms around her. She began to weep silent, helpless tears.

The agent at the gate came to Peter's side and touched him on the shoulder, "It's time; you have to get on the plane or stay here."

Ron looked at Peter and Nik with incredulity, and although he had never truly hated anyone before, he hated this man. He now knew for a certainty that he had lost Nik to Peter Genchenko.

Peter looked at Ron, his eyes pleading, and said, "Help her, please, help her. I cannot stay."

Ron put his arms around Nik from behind, and turned her toward him so that he could hold her. Peter, head down and shoulders hunched, walked into the jet way and disappeared.

Chapter 43

Long afterward, when Nik finally talked with her friend Stephanie about what happened on the day that Peter left, she told her that she remembered nothing of her ride home from the airport with Ron. She could not remember whether she, or Ron, had driven her car back to her parents' home.

Nik's parents were unpacking their vehicle, with Duchess prancing around them in the snow, when Ron and Nik pulled into the driveway. Nik got out of her car and ran into the house without greeting them. Inside she continued up the stairs and ran into her bedroom. In a frenzy of activity, Nik threw her things into her suitcase, wiped her face with tissue, and went downstairs to face her mother and father, and Ron.

They stood near the front door and turned to stare at her as she came down the stairs. The looks on their faces showed the shock and dismay that they felt at Nik's behavior.

Marina took one look at her daughter's face, however, and started toward her because she recognized the terrible state that her daughter was in, "Niki, Niki, what has happened? Let me help, Niki, please."

"Niki," Klaus, too, reached for his daughter when he saw her face.

Without a word, Nik ran past them, leaving Ron and her parents gaping at her as she got into her car and drove away.

Klaus spoke to Ron, "She is angry with you Ron? What is happening here?"

Ron's reply was tinged with anger, "I don't really know, Klaus, but I *do know* that Nik's and my engagement is off."

Marina put a hand to her mouth when she heard Myron's words, "Was it because of Peter? Is that why your engagement has ended?"

His loss was beginning to sink in with Ron, and he could only reply, "Yes," before he turned on his heel and walked quickly to his car.

Nik's hands gripped the steering wheel tightly as she drove as fast as she could safely go toward her midtown condo. I'm a coward, she thought. I didn't even have the courage to tell Ron or mom and dad what has happened to me. But they wouldn't understand about Pete and me.

When she thought of Pete leaving her, flying away to some place unknown to her, beyond her reach, somewhere that she could never go, hysteria rose inside her. She was almost rigid with the effort to hold herself in, just a few more miles, and then I'll be home where no one can corner me or question me, or...but Pete's gone, *he's gone.* His loss caused a physical pain inside her so deep that she began to wail.

She was stopped at a traffic light when the crying began. It was as if something had taken control of her, and she couldn't hold it off any longer. She heard a loud horn behind her, and looked up, her eyes swimming in tears, to see that the light was green. Then someone was tapping on her window, and she saw that it was a man in uniform.

"Could you roll your window down, miss?" He had a kind face, and he made a gesture for her to roll down her window.

Nik realized that there were red and blue lights flashing next to her. She hit a button, and the window slid down smoothly and quietly.

"Officer, I'm, I'm just upset. I'm sorry if I've caused any problems. I'm just trying to go home."

"How far are you from home, miss? You look awfully upset, and I'm worried that something might happen to you. You don't look like you're able to go very far."

Nik wiped the tears from her face with both hands, "I've just had a very bad...day," she replied, and a sob broke loose from her throat, in spite of her efforts to stifle it.

"Have you been drinking?" A flashlight appeared in his hand, and he shined it into her car.

"No, I haven't been drinking. I've just lost someone; I'll never see him again, and I don't know what to do. I've just got to get home, please, officer, I've got to get home."

"Is there someone that I can call for you? Let me see some identification, and we can go from there."

Nik fumbled in her purse and handed him her billfold. Her hands were shaking too much for her to be able to pull out her license, "It's in there, officer, in my billfold."

He shone the light on her open billfold and then briefly put the light on her face, to compare it with the photograph on her driver's license. "Dr. Nikola Kellman?"

Nik nodded, "Yes." She was calmer now.

The officer took off his hat and scratched his head for a moment, and then spoke to her, "Look, let's do this; I'll follow you home and see that you get inside and that you're all right. Is that okay with you?"

Another sob broke loose as she nodded and said, "Yes, and thank you, officer."

City Police Officer Rob Franklin scratched his head again as he got into his cruiser. This poor woman was almost hysterical, and he wondered what had happened to her to set her off like this?

Nik drove slowly, with the police officer directly behind her, his lights flashing. She had never had a police escort before, but in her present state, it really didn't matter. All that mattered was that Pete was gone, and she began to cry again.

She managed to park in her condo garage without hitting either side of the door, and sat for a moment in the car before turning off the engine. Nik got out of the car, and the police officer came to her side to assist her.

Well, he thought, she doesn't smell like booze. That's good to know. Maybe I made the right decision on this one.

Nik pulled her suitcase from the back seat of the car, and the officer took it from her. The garage was narrow, and they backed out single file.

"Which one is yours, Dr. Kellman?" He looked up at the highrise condos and whistled. "These are nice, aren't they?"

"Yes, I like it here," she almost whispered, her voice husky from crying.

Carefully, Nik walked, stepping one foot at a time, feeling disoriented and unreal. Here I am with a cop chaperoning me to my condo. But she had to admit that his kindness was above and beyond what he was probably required to do.

Nik keyed the elevator, and the door opened almost immediately. When she and the officer were inside, she keyed the eighth floor and the elevator made a swift and smooth ascent. They stepped off the elevator into Nik's living room. The décor was a tasteful rendition of English Country, with muted colors, and tone on tone accessories.

The officer seemed surprised to see that the entire eighth floor of the condominium building was her condo, "I didn't know that this was how these condos were laid out. I guess that I thought it would be more like apartments or a hotel."

Nik was trembling with the effort to control herself. She couldn't be the proper hostess. Otherwise, she would have offered the officer refreshments, or at the least tried to make small talk, but she could not.

He put her suitcase down, took his hat off, and asked, "Are you going to be all right when I leave? I mean, I could call someone for you. Maybe you could use a doctor yourself, Dr. Kellman."

For a moment, his kindness made Nik's throat close, and she struggled to answer. Besides, he was just about Pete's height, and his coloring was similar, except for his eyes. He didn't have the strikingly beautiful eye color that Pete had.

Finally, she said, "Thank you, Officer…?"

"Tyler, I'm Chris Tyler."

"Thanks for not arresting me. I must have looked like a wild woman to you."

He smiled, "Well, you were blocking traffic. Did you know that you sat through three lights at the intersection of Martin Luther King and New

York? You were in the left lane and I was in the far right lane and couldn't get to you until I put my lights on and did a U-turn. I knew that you were in trouble, that's for sure."

"I feel a lot calmer, now. But…in my entire life, I have only had one other day that was worse than today has been. In both instances, I lost someone that I loved very much."

Officer Tyler looked down at the floor for a moment, at a loss for words. When he looked up, he told her, "I don't know what happened, but I'm sorry for your loss."

Again, Nik felt the tightness in her throat, and when she spoke, it was in a husky whisper, "Thank you."

When Officer Tyler left, Nik leaned her head against the door, unable to move. The telephone rang, and she jumped as if she had been struck.

The answering machine beeped, and then her mother's voice said, "Niki? It's mother. Please, if you're home, pick up the phone. I'm so worried about you, and I'm worried about Myron, too. He looked heartbroken when he left. Please, Niki, your father and I are so worried. Please call us when you get this message."

Nik went to the telephone and bent down to unplug the connection. She went into her bedroom and did the same. When she looked out into the living room, her suitcase was setting in the middle of the room where the police officer left it. She didn't care. Nothing mattered, really.

Nik took off her clothing, letting it fall in a pile on the floor next to her bed, and went into the bathroom. There was a night light in the bathroom, and Nik didn't bother turning on any other light. She turned on the shower, let it warm up, and stepped in, closing the glass door behind her.

Nik began to wail again. Peter was not there with her. He was never going to be there with her in the shower, not ever again. Her legs gave out, and she sat down, knees up, arms around her knees, with her face resting on them while the water continued to spray and swirl over and around her, making her tears seem like a torrent as they flowed out of her. She didn't move until the water ran cold.

She had no sense of time. Was it daylight? Nik did not know how long she had been in bed. The draperies in her bedroom darkened the room for sleeping. She had insisted on them when she worked different shifts during her residency. Irrelevant. That seemed so irrelevant now. She turned over and pulled the comforter up to her chin. I should get up, she thought, but she knew that she didn't have the strength to do so. She wanted her mind to become blank. She wanted to think of nothing, of no one. If I could just go back to sleep…

The next conscious thought that she had, found her sitting on the edge of the bed. Had she been to the bathroom, or was she just getting up to go? It seemed like hours ago that she had heard someone ringing her doorbell. It meant nothing to her. She had no energy, or desire, to see who it was. Go away, just go away; she didn't want to see anyone.

Nik laid back down in the bed and began to cry again, only, this time, her sobs were dry. There were no tears left in her, but her heart required that she cry. Otherwise, she was sure that it would break into tiny pieces that would never fit back together again.

Klaus made a frantic call to Les Barnes. Niki hadn't called them for three days now, and they were unable to leave messages for her. He and Marina had gone to Niki's condo and had rung the doorbell for half an hour, but she hadn't answered. Klaus had looked inside her garage door window, and had seen her car, so he was sure that she was there.

"Les, something has happened to Niki. No, no, she isn't hurt, well as far as we know she isn't, but this is such a mess, I don't know where to begin. Peter returned to Russia, and Niki broke off her engagement with Ron, and then Niki got hysterical and left our house, and I'm sure that she's at her condo, but she won't answer the telephone or the door."

"Calm down, Klaus, this is going to make you sick if you don't calm down." Les' voice was quiet.

"But Marina's been crying, and she's so worried about Niki, and Ron, too. I just don't know what to do."

"The first thing that we need to do is contact the condominium management to see if they might help us check on Niki. I think that I can approach them by telling them that they don't want any bad publicity, and then ask if they can let us into Niki's condo to check on her. That might work."

"Anything, Les, anything. This is unbearable for Marina, and for me, too."

Klaus was waiting for Les in the garage with the doors up when he arrived. He wanted to tell Les in more detail what had happened when Niki left three days ago, and what he thought the cause might be without getting Marina more upset.

Klaus spoke quietly to Les, "I honestly thought that Niki had more sense than to get involved with someone like Peter Genchenko. That's what Marina seems to think has happened. We don't know all the details, but we have speculated that Ron was out of the picture for several days when he went to Chicago and the weather turned bad. And at about the same time, Marina and I left to see about my brother when he had his heart attack. That left Niki here alone to take care of Peter. Who knows? He may have seduced her, or something! Anyway, we have been frantic to talk to Niki. We want to help if we can. I know that if she can talk things out with Ron, everything will be all right again."

Les mulled over what Klaus was saying to him. What really has happened here, he wondered? Of one thing, he was certain; if Niki came to feel about Peter the way that Peter obviously felt about her, then there was nothing to be done to patch things up between Niki and Ron.

"Right now, Klaus, the most important thing that we need to do is to find out if Niki's okay. She's an adult, and no matter what has happened, whether or not she's involved with Peter and broken her engagement with Ron, that's really none of our business."

"But it happened under my roof, Les. Marina and I took Peter in when he had nowhere to go and he was recovering from his surgery. Marina feels that she's been betrayed."

Les shrugged, "I don't understand why Marina would feel that way Klaus. Don't you remember how you and I speculated about Peter's feelings for Niki when we were in the training room that day? What if Niki felt the same way about him?"

"I hope not, Les, I can't imagine that Niki would do something like that. Well, let's go in and talk to Marina."

When Les saw Marina, he understood Klaus' feelings of concern. She looked like a ghost, pale, with dark circles under her eyes.

Marina attempted a smile, "Les, I'm so glad that you're here. Can you believe what's happened? All that we want to do is talk to Niki, and we can't get in touch with her. We even went to her condo, but she wouldn't answer the door."

After some discussion, it was decided that Klaus and Les would go to see about Niki. When Marina protested that she should go too, both men knew that two tearful women would be much harder to handle than just one.

Les said, "Just let us go first, Marina. If we can persuade her, we'll bring Niki here. How does that sound to you?"

Marina acquiesced, "My first instinct is that I should go, but you, the good lawyer, have made your point. I will stay behind and wait for you to bring her to me."

The condominium manager cooperated nicely, and assisted Klaus and Les in their entry into Niki's condo. He stayed in the elevator when the door opened into Niki's living room, saying that he would "wait downstairs."

The room was dimly lit with light coming in the windows around the draperies as the two men looked around for signs that Niki was there. There was a piece of luggage setting in the middle of the living room. Les went over to the telephone, and pulled up the line to show Klaus that it was unplugged.

Klaus called, "Niki, Niki, are you here?"

There was no response, just the silence of what appeared to be an empty condominium. Then they heard a toilet flush. Their hopes rose; she's here. They heard the sound of water running and then what sounded like the movement of a latch on a door inside the bedroom followed by rustlings and other sounds of movement, and then there was silence. No, not silence; there were muffled sounds that were the sounds of a woman crying. Niki was crying.

Les put his hands up, palms out in front of him, and shrugged. He shook his head and pointed toward the elevator. Klaus nodded in agreement, and started, as quietly as he knew how, for the elevator. Les followed him. Thank God the elevator could be actuated by a push button from the condo. They both winced as the elevator doors made a faint metallic click as they closed.

On the way back to Geist, Klaus asked, "What do we tell Marina about this?"

Les took a deep breath, "Well, we can tell her that Niki's resting in bed. I wouldn't mention the crying, and if she doesn't press you, I wouldn't say anything that might lead Marina to want to go to the condo on her own."

"If I told her that Niki needs time, do you think that would be helpful?" Klaus was not good at subterfuge.

"That's the truth, Klaus, and nothing is better than the truth in a situation like this."

Chapter 44

December 31, 1986

The young man had been very restless in the last hour. Enough so, that the stewardess noticed his restlessness, in spite of her boredom and fatigue. The flight had just passed the point of no return, and soon they would be flying into "tomorrow." A "freakin" time machine this is, she thought.

The stewardess decided to check on the restless young man to see if she could make him more comfortable. After all, that was her job, wasn't it?

"Sir? Is there something that I can get for you to make you more comfortable?" She lightly touched his shoulder as she spoke. It was a broad shoulder, and it stuck out into the aisle.

Peter turned to look at her, and was surprised when she stepped back from him, "No, there is nothing you can do," he replied.

The stewardess, who had looked into many faces over the years that she had served aboard British Airways, and thought that she had seen it all, had never before seen such anguish in such a young face.

She crouched down in the aisle near him and whispered, "Are you ill, or in pain? I think we have two physicians on this flight. Perhaps they could help you."

Peter shook his head, "They can't help me…no one can help me."

The stewardess realized that this young man had experienced something very painful. A lover left on a distant shore? A broken heart, perhaps?

She racked her brain for something to do to help this suffering soul, "Are you allergic to alcohol? May I bring you a hot toddy?"

Peter had been unable to eat anything since he boarded the first flight in Indianapolis. He had tried to drink fluids because he didn't want to become dehydrated again, but he could eat nothing.

"I'm not allergic to alcohol, but…I've never had a hot toddy before, so I'm not sure…" He didn't finish the sentence.

"I'll be right back," and the stewardess hurried off.

She prepared a magnificent hot toddy for the young man. She mixed Jack Daniels whiskey, sugar, fresh lemon juice, and hot water together; the elixir of the angels.

"Here you are." She handed the drink to Peter, "drink it all, and you'll feel better, I assure you."

In a few minutes, the stewardess made it a point to check on him, and she was glad to see that he was sleeping. She threw two of the cabin blankets across his body so that he would be warm. "Goodnight," she whispered, and thought, I hope you can sleep a little now. Reality will come again soon enough.

Peter dreamed of Niki. They were laughing together, sliding down mounds of snow. They had just come from a restaurant, and they had fallen in the snow. No, they were inside the arena, and she was out on the ice with him. She skated with him, turning around and around…but, no, it was the dance floor that they were on, and they were dancing to a very old song. He could hear it, just barely. It was muffled, as if the musicians had put something inside their brass instruments to mute them.

Peter managed to get some sleep on the British Airways flight, and then on Aeroflot, as well. He was no longer tense because of the flying. No, he was numb inside. The chill that he had always carried inside him before he met Niki had now encircled his heart. His emotions were again blunted and shutting down. It was an unconscious protective mechanism, and his survival depended upon it.

Of one thing, and one thing only, he was certain. No matter the cost, and even if it took the rest of his life, he would find his way back to Niki. He would return to her, if not in this life, then in the next.

"Niki he whispered, "Niki."